Friedrich Christian Diez, T. C. Donkin

An Etymological Dictionary of the Romance Languages

Chiefly from the German of Friedrich Diez, T. C. Donkin

Friedrich Christian Diez, T. C. Donkin

An Etymological Dictionary of the Romance Languages
Chiefly from the German of Friedrich Diez, T. C. Donkin

ISBN/EAN: 9783337351069

Printed in Europe, USA, Canada, Australia, Japan

Cover: Foto ©Andreas Hilbeck / pixelio.de

More available books at **www.hansebooks.com**

AN

ETYMOLOGICAL DICTIONARY

OF THE

ROMANCE LANGUAGES;

CHIEFLY FROM THE GERMAN

OF

FRIEDRICH DIEZ.

BY

T. C. DONKIN, B. A.

WILLIAMS AND NORGATE,

14, HENRIETTA STREET, COVENT GARDEN, LONDON;
AND
20, SOUTH FREDERICK STREET, EDINBURGH.

· 1864.

LIST OF ABBREVIATIONS.

A. S.	— Anglo-Saxon.	Lorr.	— Lotharingian(Lorraine).
Alban.	— Albanian.	M. Du.	— Middle Dutch.
Andal.	— Andalusian.	M. H. G.	— Middle High German.
Arag.	— Aragonese.	Mil.	— Milanese.
B.	— Basque.	Moden.	— Modenese.
Bearn.	— Bearnese.	Neap.	— Neapolitan.
Berr.	— Berrichon.	Norm.	— Norman.
Bret.	— Breton.	O. E.	— Old English.
Burg.	— Burgundian.	O. H. G.	— Old High German.
Cat.	— Catalonian.	O. N.	— Old Norse.
Champ.	— Champenois (Champagne).	O. S.	— Old Saxon.
		Occ.	— Languedocian.
Com.	— Comasque.	Parm.	— Parmesan.
Cremon.	— Cremonese.	Pg.	— Portuguese.
Dauph.	— Dauphinese.	Pic.	— Picardian.
Du.	— Dutch.	Piedm.	— Piedmontese.
E.	— English.	Pr.	— Provençal.
Flor.	— Florentine.	Rh.	— Rhæto-Romance (Grison).
Fr.	— French.		
Fris.	— Frisian.	Romagn.	— Romagnol (Romagna).
Galic.	— Galician.	Ron.	— Ronchi.
Gasc.	— Gascon.	Sard.	— Sardinian.
Gen.	— Genoese.	Sic.	··· Sicilian.
Genev.	— Genevese.	Sp.	— Spanish.
Goth.	— Gothic.	Sw.	— Swiss.
H. G.	— High German.	Swed.	— Swedish.
Ir.	— Irish.	Val.	— Valentian.
It.	— Italian.	Ven.	— Venetian.
L.	— Latin.	Ver.	— Veronese.
Lim.	— Limousin.	Wal.	— Walachian.
L. G.	— Low German.	Wald.	— Waldensian.
L. L.	— Low Latin.	Wall.	— Wallon.
Lomb.	— Lombardian.		

PREFACE.

The present work is based on the "Etymological Dictionary of the Romance Languages" by Friedrich Diez (2nd edition, Bonn 1861). The Author has, however, availed himself of the labours of other eminent writers on the same subject, amongst whom he would specially mention Wedgwood (Dictionary of English Etymology), Littré (Histoire de la Langue française) and Mahn (Untersuchungen auf dem Gebiete der Romanischen Sprachen). He is also indebted to various papers in English and Foreign Periodicals, reference to which is made, where due.

As to the plan of the work, the very inconvenient arrangement adopted by Diez has been abandoned, and the whole Dictionary reduced to one Alphabet, a Vocabulary being added of such English words as are connected with any of the Romance words treated of.

To prevent excessive bulk, words are excluded:

(1) where the etymology is unknown, and

(2) where it is so obvious and familiar as to require no explanation.

For the general principles of Romance etymology, Diez's Introduction to the Grammar of the Romance Languages (translated by C. B. Cayley B. A.) may be consulted.

A.

A ad It., Sp. Pg. *á*, Pr. *a az*, Fr. *à*, Wal. *a* from the Lat. *ad*,
sometimes an abbreviation of *apud*, Rom. Gr. 3, 145. From
de ad is formed the It. *da*, Rh. *dad*, which correspond to the
O. H. G. *fona*, N. H. G. *von* from *af ana* (Grimm 4, 782). The
Pr. *daus* (in meaning = Fr. *dès*) is prob. from *de ab* with an
epenthetic *s*, O. Wald. *dos*.

Ab — *appo*.

Aba — *alabe*.

Ababa ababol Sp., Pg. *papoula* a red poppy, corn-rose: a corruption of *papaver*, v. *parol*.

Abait, abah Pr. in Gir. de Rossillon, a henchman; from *ambactus* or *andbahts*, v. *ambascia*.

Abalcar — *balicare*.

Abandonner — *bando*.

Abarca Sp. Pg. a coarse shoe of untanned hide worn by the
Spanish peasants, used as a nickname of Sancho one of the
kings of Navarre: from the Basque *abarquia* which is made
up of *abarra* twigs (of which these shoes would originally be
made) and *quia* things: so = things made of twigs.

Abarcar — *barcar*.

Abbaco It. arithmetic, Pr. *abac;* from *abacus*.

Abbagliare — *bagliore*.

Abbandono — *bando*.

Abbedul — *betula*.

Abbeille — *ape*.

Abbentare — *avventare*.

Abbozzare — *bozzo*.

Abbrivo — *brio*.

Abeja — *ape*.

Abellucar — *bellugue*.

Abéquer — *becco*.

Abés — *avieso*.

Abisso It., Pr. *abis abisme*, Fr. *abime* or *abyme*, Sp. Pg. *abismo*,
Sard. *abismu*, an *abyss;* It. *abissare* and *sobbissare*, Pr. *abissar*,
Sp. *abismar*, Fr. *abimer* or *abymer* to precipitate; from *abyssus*
(ἄβυσσος). *Abisme abismo* is a substantival superlative like

the L. *oculissimus*, L. L. *dominissimus*, It. *casissimo* &c. cf.
Rom. (ir. 2, 48. 3, 14. The It. *nabisso* arose from the frequent
combination *in abisso* like *ninferno* from *in inferno;* hence the
G. *nobis.*

Able Fr. ɴ whiting, L. L. *abula;* from *albulus* euphon. for *alble*
(cf. *foible* for *floible*), Swiss *albele*, Austr. *albel*, Triers *alf*, follows in meaning the L. *alburnus* (Ausonius), Sp. *albur.*

Abonner Fr., *s'abonner* to subscribe; from *bonus* good, well-
secured, cf. Sp. *abonar* to bail, secure, E. *bonus.*

Abois — *aboyer.*

Abomé aboemé O. Fr. dejected; from *abominatus* one who feels
abhorrence or aversion (past passive becoming present active)
R. (ir. 3, 253.

Aboyer to bark, O. Fr. *abayer, abboyer;* from *adbaubari* (*baubari* Lucr.). Hence a sbst. *abois*, *être aux abois* to be in the
last extremity, properly of a stag "at bay". — The Eng. *bay*
(and perhaps the form *abayer*) is from *bada, badare* q. v.

Abra Sp. Pg. a bay, cove, defile, fissure. The Fr. *barre* differs
from it both in gender and in sense. Its primary notion is
that of an "opening", so that like some few other nouns from
verbs of the fourth conjugation (*mulla* from *mollire, tupa* from
tupir) it may come from *abrir*, Lat. *aperire.*

Abrego Sp. the South-West wind; from *africus*, It. *affrico.*

Abricot v. *albercocco.*

Abrigo Sp. Pg., Pr. *abric*, Fr. *abri* shelter; *abrigar, abricar,
abriter* (for *abrier* with euphonic *t* as in *cafetier, cailloteux,
juteux* from *jus* &c.) to shelter, cover. In the Jura *arriller* is
used for *abriter* of which it is a diminutive. The Bernese has
aprigá with the tenuis. Mahn (Etym. Untersuch.) and Littré
(Journal d. Savans) support the old derivation from *apricus.*
The original and principal meaning of the Rom. word is a
place of shelter from cold, rain, and bad weather generally.
This notion would be involved in the Lat. *locus apricus*, which
meant sunny in contradistinction to *opacus* shady. In Wallon
ése à l'abri de l' pluire == être exposé à la pluie, which perhaps
points to the fact that *abri* once bore the meaning of "*expo-
sure*" and after, by association of contrast, that of "*shelter*".
Diez, without noticing this, argues against the Lat. etymology.
Besides the difference in meaning the Lat. deriv. is, he says,
rendered suspicious by the fact that the Rom. word is not
found in the It. dialects, except in the Sard. which borrowed
many words from the Span. (*Aprico* is indeed found in some
of the poets in its Lat. sense.) It seems to have taken root
espec. in Spanish, which has numerous compounds and derivatives: *desabrigo desabrigar* to strip, *abrigada, abrigaña, abri-
gamiento, abrigador* (Pg.). Diez derives it from the O. H. G.

rihan to cover, whence *birihan* A.S. *berrîhan*, *a* being prefixed as in numerous Sp. words. It is noticeable that the meaning *"to cover"* is found in O. Fr.: *la tres precieuse corone que Jhesu Crist ot en sa teste, si com li Juis l'en abrierent.* He also suggests the O. G. *bergan (bergen)* to protect, hide. The abst. *bere gebere* asylum would be nearer *abric* in meaning than *apricum*.

Abrojo — *broglio.*

Abrojo Sp., Pg. *abrolho* a thistle, caltrop; a compound from *abre (el) ojo* open the eye i. e. beware.

Abrostino It. a sort of wild grape; from *labruscum*, Sp. *lambrusca; sc* becomes *st* as in *mistio* for *mischio, l* being rejected as though it were the article.

Abrunho — *brugna.*

Abubilla — *upupa.*

Abutre — *avoltore.*

Abuzzago — *buse.*

Acá — *quà.*

Acabar Sp. Pg. Pr., Fr. *achever*, to bring to a head, finish, *achieve;* from *caput* which in Rom. meant the end as well as the beginning of a thing: *far capo* = to commence, *venire a capo* to accomplish.

Acaecer Sp. Pg. (O. Pg. also *aquecer* to be distinguished from *aguecer* to warm v. *calentar*) to happen; from *accudere* (for *accidere*) *accadescere.*

Acamar — *cama* (1).

Acarar — *cara.*

Acariâtre — *cara.*

Acatar — *catar.*

Accabler — *caable.*

Accattare It., O. Sp. *acabdar*, O. Pg. *achatar* S. Ros. to earn, gain, O. Fr. *acater* to procure, Fr. *acheter* to buy, Neap. *accattare;* It. *accatto*, Pr. *acapta acapte*, Fr. *achat;* from *adcaptare* (L. L. *accapitare*) to take to oneself, to buy, a meaning first developed in Fr., and supported by the passage in Festus: *emere, quod nunc est mercari, antiqui accipiebant pro sumere.* On *emo* (orig. = to take up, cf. eximo, dirimo, promo, demo, sumo, como) cf. Donald. Varronianus. Hence the compound It. *raccattare*, Pg. *regatar*, Fr. *racheter* to redeem = Sp. *rescatar*, Pg. *resgatar*, from *re-ex-captare*, subst. *rescate*, *resgate.*

Acceggia It., Sp. *arcea*, Prov. Fr. *acée* a snipe, L. L. *accia, acceia;* from *acies* or *ἀκή* a point, so = bird with the *pointed* bill. The word has very ancient authority, for in the Erfurd Glossaries p. 250ᵇ we find *accega hollana* or *acega hollana* = A. S. *holt-hana* a woodcock, snipe.

Accertello It. a bird of prey: dimin. from *accipiter*.

Acchines — *haca*.

Accia assa It., Sp. *hacha*, Pg. *facha acha*, Pr. *apcha* for *acha*,
Fr. *hache* (*h* asp.), E. *adze*. Whence M. H. G. *hätsche* and
hätsche, a hatchet, axe; It. *acciare*, Fr. *hacher* to hash, cut in
small pieces. The form of the Rom. words is against their
deriv. from the Lat. *ascia*, but the Fr. agrees with the N. H. G.
and Du. *hacke* a mattock, hoe, a word not found in the O. H. G.
but supported by the masc. form *hacco* (a hook) and the A. S.
haccan to hack. The German *k* is preserved in the Picard. vb.
héyuer to hew wood = Fr. *hacher*. The other Rom. forms are
all derived from the Fr., the Pg. *f* representing the aspirate,
v. sub *arpa*. The It. *ascia*, Pr. *aissa*, is a different word coming from the Lat. *ascia*; the Sp. *aza* or *axa* is not found, but
there is a derivative from it in O. Sp. *axada*, Sp. *azada*, Pg.
enxada mattock, hoe; also a Sp. form *azuela* an adze.

Acciacco — *achaque*.

Acciajo It., Sp. *acero*, O. Pg. *aceiro*, N. Pg. *aço*, Pr. Fr. *acier*,
Wal. *otzêl*, Hung. *atzél*, L. L. *aciare aciarium* steel; from
acies &c. *ferri*. *Acies ferri* is used by Pliny for steel. Hence
also It. *acciale*, Ven. *azzale* &c., O. H. G. *ecchil*, M. H. G.
eckel.

Accidia It., Sp. *acidia*, Pr. *accidia*, O. Fr. *accide* laziness, sloth.
Chaucer uses *accidie* = lukewarmness in religion to be cured
by fortitude, in Fr. theology *acédie*; cf. the *accidiosi* in Dante's
Inferno. The word comes from the Gr. ἀχηδία through the
L. L. *accidia acedia*.

Accismare — *esmar*.

Acciuga It., Sp. *anchoa anchova*, Pg. *anchova* and *enchova*, Fr.
anchois, *anchory*; from *aphya*, *apua* (used by Plin. = small
fry of any fish), ἀφύη, with the suffix *uga* might be formed
in Italian *acciuga* = *apj-uga*, the other words being corruptions of this. The Piedm. and Sicil. form is *anciova*, Veron.
ancioa, Gen. *anciua*, Ven. *anchioa*. But Mahn (Etym. Untersuch.)
refers the word to the Basque *antzua* to dry so = the dried
or salted fish. A dialectical form of *antzua* is *anchua* in Biscay *anchuba* (pronounced *anchuva*). Both these are represented
in the Span. *Tz* and *ch* are frequently interchanged in Basque,
thus: *baltza*, *beltza*, *balcha* black, *aitza acha* a rock, *itzuli*
and *ichuli* to turn, alter, *ortza* and *orcha* a tooth. *Anchua* in
Basque also means a weaned lamb, doubtless from the same
root. In the It. *acciuga* there is, probably, a reference to *asciugare* to dry, the truer form being preserved in the dialects.

Accointer — *cunta*.

Accordo It., Sp. *acuerdo*, Pg. *acordo*, Pr. *accort*, Fr. *accord*
agreement, *accordare*, *accorder* &c. to agree: formed in ana-

logy to the Lat. *concordare*, *discordare* from *cor*, not from *chorda*. The Swiss *cordere cordre* = Wall. *keure* opp.: *mes-keure* to grudge.

Accorgere — *corgere*.

Accoutrer — *cucire*.

Acebo Sp., holly-tree; abbreviated from *aquifolium* with the accent thrown back as in *trebol* from *trifolium*. An old form *acereto* is found. Hence also Pg. *azerinho*. The Cat. *grévol* is from acrifolium.

Acechar Sp., Pg. *asseitar* to lie in wait for, spy; from *assectari*.

Aceite Sp. Pg. oil; from the Arab. *al-zait (azzait)*, Heb. *zait* Freyt. 2, 269.

Acelga Sp., Pg. also *selga* beet; from Arab. *selg* (Freyt. 2, 344), which prob. came from the Gr. σιχελός Sicilian, whence the Gr. τεύτλον or σεύτλον, M. Gr. σεύχλον, σέσχλον N. Gr. σεύχλον, whence it has passed into many of the Sclavonic languages.

Acero It., Pg. *acer*, O. Sp. *asre*, Sp. *arce*, Cat. *ars* maple; from *acer*. The Fr. has *érable* (Greuoble *izerablo*) = *érarbre es-rarbre* = *acer arbor*.

Acesmer — *esmar*.

Acetre — *secchia*.

Acezar O. Sp. to pant, *acezo* breath; from Basq. *hatsa* breath with the same suffix as *bostezar* to yawn.

Acha — *ascla*.

Achaque Sp. Pg. illness, disorder, pretext, excuse, whence It. *acciacco*; from the Arab. *al-schakd aschschakd* sickness. The It. *cagione* also unites the meanings "illness" and "excuse". O. Pg. *achaque* = accusation.

Achar Sp. Pg. to find. A word as obscure as its synonymous *trorare*. The oldest form found is *aftar* (A. D. 1166 S. Rosa), *ch* = *fl* as in *enchar* from *inflare* (but Mahn derives *enchar* from *inchoare*). In the Rh. we find *aftar*, Wal. *aflà*, Neap. *asciare* (*sci* for *fl* as in *sciume* from *flumen*), also *acchiare* (Sic. *asciari*). It prob. comes from the Lat. *afflare* to blow upon, then to touch, meet with. *Conflare* besides the sense of "blowing together" has that of "bringing together", "joining". From the notion of *blowing* we easily get that of *striking* cf. the Eng. *blow* and the Germ. *puffen* (the Pg. *ache* = a hurt), and the German *treffen* means both to *hit*, and to *hit upon*, to *find* (cf. the Lat. offendere). In old glosses we find *adflavit* = *adtegit (attigit)*: *adfulavit* (for *afflavit*) *leviter tetigit*; *afflata pifundan (befunden)*: Papias has *afflare* = *aspirare*, *aspergere*, *attingere*. In It. we have *inaffiare* = to besprinkle. V. s. *hallar*.

Acharner Fr. to set on, incite; from *caro* flesh, prop. of dogs to urge on by offering flesh: part. *acharné* provoked, exasperated; It. *accarnare* to penetrate into the flesh, cf. the Pg. *encarniçar* to provoke, exasperate.

Achat acheter — *accattare.*

Ache Fr. a sort of parsley; from *apium*, It. *appio*, Sp. *aipo.*

Achever — *acabar.*

Achier — *ape.*

Aoiago — *auce.*

Acibar Sp., Cat. *cever* aloe-tree; from Arab. *al-çabir aççabir.*

Acicalar Sp., Pg. *acicalar açacalar* to polish; from Arab. *çagala* Freyt. 2, 509.

Acicate Sp. Pg. a spur with a single prick instead of a rowel; according to some from the Arab. *al-scharkah aschschavkah* a goad; Larramendi derives it from the Basq. *cicatea* in same sense.

Acier — *acciajo.*

Acipado Sp. well-milled, compact (of cloth); from the Lat. *stipatus.*

Aconchar — *conciare.*

Acontecor — *contir.*

Acotar — *cotejar.*

Aootar — *quota.*

Acre Fr. a square measure, acre; from G. *acker*, E. *acre.*

Acucia Cucia O. Sp. agility, dexterity, *acuciar* to hasten, Sp. *accioso* diligent; from the Lat. *acutus* v. Ducange s. v. *acutia.*

Acudir — *cudir.*

Adaga — *daga.*

Adala — *dala.*

Adalid Sp., O. Sp. *adalid*, *adalir*, Pg. *adail* a commander, general; from Ar. *ad-dalil* guide, vb. *dalla* to lead.

Adarga — *targa.*

Adarve Sp. a rampart with battlements; from Ar. *al-darb* a narrow way, Freyt. 2, 19.

Adastiare — *astio.*

Addobbare It., O. Sp. *adobar*, O. Pg. *adubar*, Pr. *adobar*, O. Fr. *adouber* to fit out, equip, N. Sp. Pg. to prepare, pickle, tan. From the A. S. *dubban*, O. Norse *dubba* to strike (Fr. *dauber* to beat), and first used of the accolade or blow with the sword given in the ceremony of knighting: A. S. *dubban to riddere* to dub a knight, Fr. *addubber à chevalier*; it was next used of any solemn preparation or equipment, cf. Ducange s. v. *adobare:* Raoul l'adoube qui estoit ses amis: premiers li chausse ses esperons massis e puis li a le branc au costel mis, en col le fiert si con il ot apris: hence *adouber richement* to equip magnificently, *se douber* to arm oneself, this simple form being rare. Wedgwood (s. v. *dub*) considers that the notion

of preparation, equipment &c. is the primary one and traces
the word to a Sclavonic root, Bohem. *dub* an oak, oak-bark,
tan, *dubiti* to tan. From dressing leather the term got to be
used of any kind of dressing or preparation, the *dubbing* of a
knight consisting in investing him with the habiliments of
his order. In Eng. to *dub* cloth is to dress it with teasles; to
dub a cock to prepare it for fighting by cutting off the comb
and wattles; *dubbing* a mixture of tallow for dressing leather,
also a dressing used by weavers.

Adelenc Pr. of noble birth (only in Girard de Roussillon), O. Fr.
elin; from the O. H. G. *adaline ediling*, A. S. *ädheling*, Eng.
Atheling (prop. name), L. L. *adalingus*.

Ademan Sp. Pg. motion, look, bearing; from the Basque *adie-
man (aditzera eman)* to give to understand, from *adi aditu* to
understand and *eman* to give; *desman* = *des-ademan*.

Aderedor — *redor*.

Ades — *esso*.

Adeser adaiser O. Fr., Pr. *adesar* to stick to, touch, lay hold
of: a frequent. from *adhærere adhæsus* v. s. *aerdre*.

Adesso — *esso*.

Adissare — *izza*.

Admonéter — *amonestar*.

Adonare It. to subject, subdue, Dante Inf. 6, 34: *l'ombre ch'
adona la greve pioggia.* The Pr. has *adonar* to give in, Sp. *ado-
narse*, Fr. *s'adonner* to suit oneself to, from *donare;* hence the
notion of subduing, cf. Sp. *rendir* from *reddere.*

Adouber — *addobbare*.

Adrede Sp. Pg. purposely; prob. from the Prov. *adreit* rightly,
exactly, cf. Cat. *adretas* (1) rightly (2) purposely.

Aduana — *dogana*.

Adur aduras O. Sp. = Lat. vix; from *durus*.

Adurer O. Fr. Wall., Pr. *abdurar* to harden, also to endure,
like Fr. *endurer*. *Aduré adurat* enduring was a frequent epithet of warriors; from *obdurare* with change of prefix, cf.
entamer.

Aerdre aderdre O. Fr. Pr. to hang, attach to: from *adhærere*
(pronounced *adhérere aderre*) with a *d* inserted, It. *aderire*.

Afa — *affanno*.

Afagar — *halagar*.

Afeitar Sp. Pg. to trim, curl the hair; from *affectare*, the Sp.
coming through the Pg. The Pg. *enfeitar* is from *infectare
inficere*.

Afeurer — *foro*.

Affaler Fr. a nautical word = to let down; from Du. *afhalen*
'to *haul* down.

Affanno It., Sp. Pg. Pr. *afan*, O. Sp. *afaño* anxiety, fatigue,

Fr. *ahau* hard labour; *affannare* to grieve a person, Sp. *afa-
nar*, Fr. *ahaner* to labour, toil, frequently of field-labour in
L. L. and O. Fr. *terram ahanare*, whence *ahans* cultivated
fields, also *ahanables*, Rouchi *ahan* culture, Wall. *ahans* (re-
sults of it) = légumes encore en terre. The oldest meaning
we can arrive at is that of *"bodily pain"*, which, under the
forms *afan*, *ahan*, *aan*, it bears in some of the earliest extant
poems; in other early passages it signifies grief, torture, and
bodily toil, fatigue. Carpentier notes also an O. Fr. vb. *haner*
to work, whence *enhaner* e. g. *un cortil* to work a garden.
The word is of French origin, being found neither in Latin
nor in German. From *ahan* to *afan* the transition is easy, v.
Rom. Gram. 1, 311, and for the Fr. *affanner* v. Pougens arch.
franç. 1, 11. The derivation from the It. *afa* anguish is not
to be thought of, since no suffix *ann* is known to the Rom.
languages: it would rather appear that *afa* is shortened from
affanno. Ducange and others derive it from an interjection
han, which expresses the want of breath caused by a stress
of bodily exertion. This is preserved in the Berrichon *ahau-
ner* to be out of breath (which meaning it bore in O. Fr. up
to the 16th century), and also in the Rouchi *e-han-cer* to be
out of breath, cf. Ven. *afanà* to pant, gasp. The Celtic languages present no roots identical with these Rom., the Gael.
fann W. *gwan* weary being certainly not so, for the *f* = *gu*
gives in Rom. not *f* but *v*. As to W. *afan* dispute, tumult,
which owen quotes from Taliesin, it only remains to consider
whether their form, confined to one of the Celtic dialects, and
based on no native root, be still indigenous, or whether it be
merely adopted from the Rom. The root *han* is doubtless one
of those onomatopœia for which the language is indebted to
itself alone.

Affare It. (m.), Pr. *afar afaire* (m.), Fr. *affaire* (f., probably because *chose* is f., in O. Fr. m.), O. Sp. *afer*, *affair*; from *a fare*
in such phrases as *avere a fare con uno*; in the Romagna *dafè*
i. e. da fare. Cf. It. *avvenire*, Fr. *avenir* the future = *il tempo
a venire*.

Afficher — *ficcare*.

Affrontare It., Sp. *afrontar afrentar*, Pr. *afrontar*, Fr. *affronter*
to *affront*, to contradict or insult one to his face (ad frontem).
Hence the It. *affronto*, Fr. *affront*, Sp. *afrenta*, *affront*. The
Fr. *effronté*, Pr. *esfrontat*, It. *sfrontato* shameless (Eng. *ef-
frontery*) is from *effrons* (Vopiscus Num. 13. consilium *effrons*).

Affubler to mask, muffle; for *affibler*, L. L. *se affibulare* to wrap
oneself up, prop. to fasten the mantle with the *fibula*, Pr.
fievela, It. *affibbiare*, Rom. *afiubé*.

Affût — *fusta.*

Afouto — *holo.*

Afre O. Fr. (Fr. plur. *affres*, Burg. *afre*) fright, dismay, Fr. *af-freux* frightful, from the O. H. G. abst. *eiver eipar.* The It. *afro* sour may be referred to the same origin.

Afrenta — *affrontare.*

Afro — *afre.*

Agace — *gazza.*

Agalla — *gale.*

Agasajar — *gasalha.*

Agastar — *agazzare.*

Agazzare It., Fr. *agacer* (Pg. *agastar*) to irritate, entice, set on edge (teeth); from O. H. G. *hazjan* G. *hetzen* to bait, the Rom. *a* being prefixed to help the pronunciation of the *h* which becomes strengthened into a *g.*

Age Fr., O. Fr. *edage aage* eage; from *ætaticum* (*ætas*): so *hommage = hominaticum*, Pr. *antigatge = antiquaticum.* For *æ = a* cf. O. Fr. *ae = ætatem.* The *ed*, which in the Lat. was no part of the root (*ætas = æritas*), has vanished.

Agencer — *gente.*

Ageno Sp., Pg. *alheio* strange, foreign; from *alienus*, It. *alieno*, O. Fr. *aliene.* Sard. *allenu* is used for It. *altrui*, like the Sp.

Agenus Sp. fennel, flower; from Ar. *asch-schenuz*, v. Engelmann.

Aggecchire — *gecchire.*

Aggueffare It. to add, Dante Inf. 23, 16: *se l' ira sovra il mal voler s' agguessa;* prop. = "to weave on" from O. H. G. *wi-fan* to weave, cf. *adtexere.* Of the same origin is the Lomb. *wiffa, guiffa* a mark of possession attached to a property, vb. *guiffare* to attach such a mark to a thing. Hence Fr. *giffer* to mark a house with chalk, confiscate it; v. Genin.

Aghirone It. Pr. *aigron*, Cat. *agro*, Sp. *airon*, O. Fr. *hairon*, Fr. *héron* (*h* asp.), Berrichon *égron*, a *heron*; Fr. dim. *aigrette*, E. *egret*, and *héronceau, heronshaw;* from the O. H. G. *heigir heigro.*

Agina gina swiftness, strength; *a grande aina* Dante de Vulg. Eloq. 1, 11, O. Sp. *agina* and *ahina*, O. Pg. *aginha* swift. In a L. L. glossary we find *agina* i. q. *festinancia et inde agino festinare.* It cannot be the same as the word in Festus *agina* = the opening in the upper part of a balance in which the tongue plays: it comes from *ago* as *ruina* from *ruo* and in meaning approaches *agitatio, agilitas.*

Agio It. (rarely *asio*), Pr. *ais aise*, Fr. *aise* (m.), Pg. *azo*, ease; Pr. *ais*, Fr. *aise, easy;* It. *ad agio*, Pr. *ad ais*, O. Fr. *à aise*, Fr. *à l'aise* comfortably, conveniently, whence It. *adagio*, O. Fr. *aaise*, O. Pg. *aaso* convenience &c.; *agiare adagiare*, Pr. *aisar*, O. Fr. *aisier, aaisier* to take care of, *agiato, aisé* comfortable,

well-off. In Pr. there are still more derivatives: *aisir* to house,
harbour, *aisi* lodging, dwelling, *aisina* facility, opportunity,
aizinar to arrange &c.; so that the word probably spread from
this source. Its derivation is uncertain. Ménage refers it to
otium, Ferrari to *adaptare*, Frisch to the German *behagen* to
please. We require a form *ais* or *asi*. According to Perion
Ling. Gall. p. 45, it comes from the Gk. αἴσιος luck-fore-
boding, necessary, proper, convenient, pleasant. Others, as
Junius, Schilter, Castiglione, recognise in it a Gothic root
found in the adj. *azets* easy, pleasant, *azéti* comfort. J. Grimm
inclines to this etymology, v. Wiener Jahrb. 46, 188, and his
Hist. of the Germ. language p. 352, where the Goth. word is
referred to the A. S. *eadhe*, N. H. G. *odi*. The Pr. *viure ad
ais* = Goth. *vizon in azetjam* to live in ease and luxury. To
hold this derivation we must suppose a substantive *azi* which
is very doubtful. The Basque *aisia* rest, *aisina* leasure are
rather from the Prov. than vice versâ, such double forms (m.
and f.) as *aisi aisina* being common in the latter: cf. *plevi ple-
vina*, *trahi trahina*: *aisina* would be from the Pr. *aise* (pl. in
older form *aisi*) as the adj. *aisa* agrees with the Pr. *ais*. Among
the compounds from *agio* are It. *agevole*, *disagio*, *malagiato*,
Fr. *malaise* hardship. The It. *aggio* agio, rate of exchange &c.,
is from *agio* with a different spelling for distinction. The
Piedm. *agio* combines the meanings of both words.

Aglan Pr., Cat. *aglà*, O. Fr. *agland* which is still preserved in
Berry, in Lorrain *aiguiand* an acorn; from the Lat. *glans* influenced by the Greek ἄχυλος or rather by the Goth. *akran*
(*acorn*), the prosthetic *a* being unusual in Pr.

Aglayo — *ghiado*.

Agognare It. to desire anxiously, Gr. ἀγωνιᾷν.

Agora — *ora* (2).

Agraffer — *graffio*.

Agréable agréer — *grado*.

Agrès Fr. (m. pl.) rigging; vb. *agréer* to rig; O. Fr. *agrei* = preparation, *agreier* to prepare, fit out; from Du. *gereide gerei*
apparatus (with prefix *a*), vb. *gereeden parare* = Goth. *ga-
raidjan*, M. H. G. *gereiten* to make *ready*, v. *redo*.

Agrosto It., Sp. *agraz*, Pg. *agraço*, Pr. *agras*, O. Fr. *aigret*,
Dauph. *aigrat*, Wal. *agrisi* unripe grapes, juice thereof, verjuice; from *acer*, O. Sp. *agre*, Fr. *aigre* with the suffix *as*,
corrupted in It. into *est*. *Agraz* corresponds closely to *pira-
cinm* perry (Jerome).

Agrotto grotto It. a pelican; from *onocrotalus*.

Aguet — *guadare*.

Aguglia It., Sp. *aguja*, Pg. Pr. *ugulha*, Fr. *aiguille* a needle.
Not from *aculeus*: the It. *agocchia* requires a L. *acucula* (cf.

colucula, conucula, conocchia, quenouille), which was thus altered from *acicula* whilst the *c* was still pronounced as a guttural, cf. *genuculum* for *geniculum* &c., v. Rom. Gr. 2, 265. Among the derivatives are Sp. *aguijar*, Pg. *aguilhar* to goad, Fr. dim. *aiguillette* tag for drawing a lace through an eyelet hole, English *aglet*.

Aguijar — *aguglia*.

Aguilen — *aiglen*.

Agussino — *alguacil*.

Ahan — *affanno*.

Ahi — *ivi*.

Ahora — *ora* (2).

Aib aip Pr. quality, disposition, manners, character, *aibit* gifted. Diez derives it from a very doubtful Goth. word *aibr* = gift, which occurs only once in Ulfilas S. Matt. 5, 24. Mahn (Etym. Untersuch.) points out the true derivation from the Basque *aipua* report, reputation, which is from *aipatu, aippatcea* to speak of, mention. The Pr. argued from effect to cause so *aib aip* meant *character*, espec. *good character*. *Aipatu* bears a striking resemblance to the Gr. εἰπεῖν (*§εx.*), Lat. *vocare*, Sansk. *vach*, v. Pott, Et. Forsch. 1, 180, 234.

Aide — *ajuto*.

Aie Fr. an interjection of pain; an old imperative of *aider: aie nos Mahum!* Ch. d. Rol. p. 74.

Aieul Fr. a grandfather; dimin. from *avus*, It. *avolo*, Sp. *abuelo*, Pg. *avô*. For a similar use of diminutives in O. G. cf. Grimm 3, 677.

Aiglent O. Fr., Pr. *aguilen* thorn; hence Pr. *aguilancier, aiglentina*, Fr. *églantier églantine, eglantine;* from *aiguille aguilha* with the suffix *ent*, as if from a Lat. *acuculentus* prickly.

Aigrette — *aghirone*.

Aigu Fr. sharp; from *acutus*. Hence E. *ague*.

Aiguille — *aguglia*.

Ailleurs Fr., Pr. *alhors* otherwise; from *aliorsum* which became obsolete after the time of Cato and the Comic writers, and was revived in L. L., v. Müller's Festus.

Aimant — *diamante*.

Aim O. Fr. a fish-hook; from *hamus*, It. *amo*.

Ainçois ains — *anzi*.

Ainda — *inda*.

Aine — *Aine, inguine*.

Ainé Fr. elder; from *ains-né (ante-natus);* cf. *aлуado*.

Ains — *anche*.

Ainsi — *cosi*.

Air — *aria*.

Airain — *rame*.

Aire — *aria.*

Airon — *aghirone.*

Ais Fr. a plank; from *axis assis*, It. *asse;* dimin. *aisseau* a shingle, from *axicellus assicellus*, It. *assicella.*

Ais — *asco.*

Ais alsina — *agio.*

Aisil aissil O. Fr. vinegar; a corruption of *acetum*, It. *aceto*, Wal. *otzet*, Rh. *as-chaid, ischeu.* The same word is the E. *eisil, esil*, O. E. *aisyl*, A. S. *aisil, eisele.* The common Rom. term is *vinum acre, vinaigre* &c.

Aisne O. Fr. grape; from *acinus*, It. *acino.*

Aisso — *ciò.*

Aja It. a threshing-floor; from *area*, Fr. *aire*, Pg. *eira.*

Ajar to maltreat; identical with the Pg. *achar*, Obs. Sp. *ajar* to find = *hallar;* cf. the Lat. *offendere* to hurt and to hit upon, find, Pg. *ache* = hurt.

Ajo — *ayo.*

Ajouter — *giusta.*

Ajuto It. help; from *adjutus -us* (Macr. Sat. 7, 7); fem. Sp. *ayuda*, Pg. Pr. *ajuda*, O. Fr. *aüe*, Pic. *aïude;* It. *ajutare*, Sp. *ayudar*, Pg. Pr. *ajutar* from *adjutare.* By the side of this we have a shortened form It. *aita*, Pr. *ahia*, O. Fr. *aïde aïe*, Fr. *aide*, Eng. *aid*, It. *aitare*, Pr. *aidar*, Fr. *aider;* the last two = *ajtare*, which, however, does not suit the accented *i* of It. *aito* (*aitare*).

Al O. Sp., O. Pg., Pr. *al als*, O. Fr. *al el* a neuter pronoun sometimes joined with a abst. *(al ren, ren al)*, from *aliud*, or, better, from *alid* (Lucil., Catull., Lucret.), neut. of *alis*, v. Ritschl de declinatione quadam latinâ reconditiore.

Ala — *enola.*

Alabar Sp. Pg. to praise; from *allaudare* (Plaut.), Pr. *alauzar.* The *d* being dropped the *u* takes a consonantal form as in *Paolo* = *Paulus.* In *loar* from *laudare* the vowel is kept (o = au).

Alabarda labarda It., Sp. Pg. *alabarda*, Fr. *hallebarde* (*h* asp.), a *halbert;* from the M. H. G. *helmbarte* (G. *hellebarte*); the purest form is found in the Rh. *halumbard.*

Alabe Sp. a branch, espec. one drooping to the ground, an olive branch, the ladle of a wheel, the eaves of a house; from the Basque *alabea* "that which bends or droops" v. Larramendi. Hence Pg. *aba* a projecting surface, eaves, cf. *paço* from *palaço.*

Alacha — *laccia.*

Alacran Sp., Pg. *alacrão* scorpion; from Arab. *al-áqrab.*

Alafé alahé alaé an interjection of cheering, rousing up &c., prop. of protestation from *fe* = *fides.*

Alaga Sp. spelt; from *alica* a sort of wheat.

Alambic — *lambicco*.

Alamo Sp., Pg. *alamo alemo* a poplar-tree; the Sp. philologers derive it from *ulmus* comparing the N. *almr alm*, Eng. *elm*; but ph. better from *alnus*. The alder is called *alamo negro*, the poplar *alamo blanco*. The Sp. avoids the conjunction of the consonants *ln* (*ana* = *alna*, *julde* = *julne*), so *almo alamo* from *alno*.

Alano It. Sp., Pg. *alão*, O. Fr. *alan* a mastiff; Ménage shows that *Alano* was used for *Albano*, and so *Alano* would be a dog of *Albania* (Epirus); cf. the Lat. *Molossus*, also from Epirus.

Alarbe Sp., Pg. *alarve* a clown, rustic, prop. = an Arab; from Ar. *al-arab*.

Alarde Sp. Pg. a review of soldiers; from Ar. *al-ár'd*.

Alare — *lar*.

Alarido Sp. Pg. a confused battle-cry, outcry; from Ar. *al-arir* a song of victory, din, clatter Freyt. 1, 24. In the O. Fr. Chans. d'Antioche the Saracens cry *aride! aride!*

Alazan Sp., Pg. *alazão* reddish-yellow, sorel (of a horse); from the Arab. *al-'has-an* beautiful, Pihan Gloss., Freyt. 1, 381, or, according to Sousa, from *al-'haçan* a strong fine horse. Hence Fr. *alesan*.

Alba It., Sp. Pr. Pg. Rh. *alva*, Fr. *aube* dawn; from *albus* light, clear, bright, as in *alba stella* (II.), cf. *lux albescit, coelum albet (Albunea*, according to Pott = *Matuta)*, Dante *"il sol imbianca i fioretti"*. Ariosto gives the dawn more colours: *poi che l'altro mattin la bella Aurora l'aer seren fe' bianco e rosso e giallo* 23, 52.

Alban Pr., also *albanel*, It. *albanello*, Fr. *aubrier* a bird of prey. The corresponding Pg. form *alvão* signifies another kind of bird. Trévoux explains *aubrier* by *aubere* = white and dappled, from *albus*.

Albañal albañar a sewer, gutter; from *alveus*.

Albarda — *barda*.

Albaro albero the black poplar, Fr.(Berrichon) *aubrelle*, O.H.G. *albari*, G. *alber*. In Cat. the poplar (of any kind) is called *alba*, Pr. *aubra (aoubre)* = the white-poplar, Piedm. *albra arbra* = the black poplar, *albron arbron* = the white, Mil. *albera* (It. *alberella*) = the aspen. From *albus*, so prop. = the white poplar, afterwards used generally. The dialectical forms disprove Blanc's derivation from *albero* (arbor), as being the commonest tree.

Albasano — *baio*.

Albedrio Sp. free-will; from *arbitrium*, Pr. *albire*.

Albedro Sp., Pg. *errado* from *arbutus*; Cat. *arbosser* from *arbuteus*, Sp. (dialect.) *alborzo*, Fr. *arbousier*.

Alberare It., Sp. *arbolar*, *enarbolar*, Fr. *arborer* to raise, rear

(e. g. a mast); from arbor, It. *albero*, O. It. *albore* &c. For
similar formations, cf. *vitulari* to skip like a calf, It. *piombare*
to fall like lead, *brillare* to shine like beryl, *braccare* &c.

Albercocco albicocco It., Roman *bericuocolajo bricoccolajo*, Ven.
baricocolo, Sien. *bacoco*, Sp. *albaricoque albarcoque albercoque
alvarcoque*, Pg. *albricoque albercoque alboquorque*, Fr. *abricot*,
N. Pr. *ambricot*, *aubricot auricol*, M. Gr. βερύκοκον βερί-
κοκον, M. Gr. πραικόκκιον, βερικουκία, βερικοκκία, βερι-
κοκκίον, βερίκοκκον, O. Eng. *apricock*, an *apricot*. Diez
derives it from the Lat. *praecoquus*, apricots ripening earlier
than other fruits of the same kind. (Martial has *praecoqua*
= apricots: Vilia maternis fueramus *Praecoqua* ramis Nunc in
adoptivis *Persica* cara sumus.) He adds that the Latin word
finds its truest expression in the M. Gr. πραικόκκιον, the
Rom. forms having been influenced by the Arabic *al-berqûq*.
This account is not quite right. The Rom. words, doubtless,
came direct from the Arabic through the Span. The Ara-
bians, probably, got the word from Dioscorides, who has
(1, 165): τὰ μῆλα ἀρμηνιακά, Ῥωμαϊστὶ δὲ πραικόκια, and
whose works were early translated into Arabic. The Arabic
has no *p* and therefore represents the Latin *p* by a *b*. V.
Mahn Etym. Untersuchungen.

Albergo It., O. Sp., Sp. Pg. *albergue*, Pr. *alberc*, and O. Fr. *her-
berc* (*helberc* Ch. d'Alexis st. 51, 65), fem. Pr. *alberga*, O. Fr.
herberge Ch. d'Alexis 116 &c. &c., N. Fr. *auberge* an inn, O.
Eng. *herberwe*; It. *albergare*, Sp. *albergar*, Pr. *albergar ar-
bergar*, Fr. *héberger*, O. Fr. *herbergier*; from the O. H. G.
heriberga (f.) (*heer* army and *bergen* to shelter = station of an
army on its march through the provinces), O. N. *herbergi* (n.),
O. H. G. verb *heribergôn*. The O. Fr. kept the original meaning "army-station". Brut. 2, 160 *ses herberges et ses faillies*
the tents and huts of the army. Through the Fr. come the
Eng. forms *herberwe*, *herber*, *harbour*, *arbour*, *herbergage*,
herbergeour, *harbinger* (one who looks out for a harbour or
lodging for another): in Wiclif we find "I was *herbarweles*
and ye *herboriden* me". S. Matt. Hence E. *harbinger* for *herbergeour*, the *n* being inserted as in *messenger*, *scavenger* &c.

Albornos Sp. Pg. a woollen mantle, Fr. *bournous*; from the Ar.
al-bornoz a cloak with a cape to it, Freyt. 1, 115.

Alboroto Sp., Pg. *alroroto* outcry, riot; from Arab. *al-foro't*
"what is beyond measure" Freyt. 3, 336. Hence *alborozo* joy.

Albran — *halbran*.

Albricia Sp., O. Sp. *alvistra*, Pg. *alríçara* (generally in plur.
only) reward for good tidings; from the Ar. *al-baschârah*
good tidings, vb. *baschara* Freyt. 1, 124. In the Sp. the *r* is
transposed not inserted, though *alvicia* is found in Berceo.

Alcabála duty on goods sold; according to Sousa from Ar. *al-gabalah* (which, however, has a different sense, Freyt. 3, 394) which is from the verb *gabala* to take, to receive a price. Engelmann refers it to the Ar. *al-gabalah* a tax.

Alcachofa — *articiocco*.

Alcahuote Sp., Pg. *alcayote*, Pr. *alcaot alcavot* a pander; Ar. *al-qauvâd*.

Alcaide Sp. Pg. an alcaid, chief magistrate; from Ar. *al-qâid* Freyt. 3, 513.

Alcalde Sp. a justice of the peace; from Ar. *al-qâ'di* judge Freyt. 3, 461.

Alcali It. Sp. &c. *alkali*, from Ar. *al-qali* salt of ashes Freyt. 3, 494.

Alcanço Sp. Pg. pursuit, capture, grasp, reach, means, *alcauzar* to pursue, capture; from Ar. *al-qanaç* prey, booty (of hunters), vb. *qanaça* to hunt, Freyt. 3, 501. The Pg. *alcauços* is of the same origin.

Alcandara Sp. a falcon's roost; from Ar. *al-kandarah*.

Alcaparra — *cappero*.

Alcaravoa — *carvi*.

Alcarraza Sp. an earthen pitcher; from Ar. *al-korraz*.

Alcatras alcartas Sp., Pg. *cartaz* bill, account; from *chartaceus* with the Ar. article.

Alcavala — *gabbella*.

Alcázar a fort, also a quarter-deck; from Ar. *qaçr* (Freyt. 3, 452), pl. = castle. Hence It. *cassero*.

Alchimia It., Sp. Pg. *alquimia*, Pr. *alkimia*, Fr. *alchimie*, M. Gr. ἀρχημία *alchemy*, It. Sp. Pg. *chimica*, Fr. *chemie*, *chemistry*. There are three derivations given (1) from Gr. χυμός (χέω, χύω) = juice, sap, espec. the liquor obtained by infusion and decoction of herbs. (2) from the Arab. *al-kimia* which, however (as Diez, who holds this etymology, remarks), has no native root. (3) from chemia, χημία, Egypt, so called, acc. to Plutarch, from its *dark* soil (the Coptic *kame kami* = black). So the word would orig. mean the Egyptian science. This last derivation is the one now generally maintained (amongst others by Humboldt Kosmos 2, 451): it is, however, rejected by Mahn (Etym. Unters.) who successfully asserts the Greek origin of the word. The word χημεία (v. l. χυμεία) is first used by Suidas (c. A. D. 1100). *Alchemia* (or *chemia*) is first found in J. Maternus Firmicus (c. A. D. 340), where it means the art of gold-making. Up to the middle of the *fourth* century χυμεία was used by the Greek physicians to mean the art of extracting juices from plants for medicinal purposes. From then up to the middle of the 16th century it meant the art of gold-making, transmuting the baser metals into gold, which was supposed, in its liquid form (aurum potabile), to

lengthen life, renew youth, and cure diseases, such as gout,
leprosy &c. The art of gold-making was much practised by
the Egyptians and Alexandrian Greeks. Hence it was that
χυμεία in becoming χημεία was influenced by χημία which
was the native name for Egypt. From the Alexandrians the
word passed to the Arabs, who devoted themselves to the
study of chemistry and alchemy about the middle of the 8th
century. The Arabic word was introduced into Spain and
thence into the other Romance languages.

Alcohol from the Arabic *al-kohl* the impalpable powder of an-
timony used in the East for darkening the eyebrows. From
the extreme fineness of this powder the word got to be used
of any pure fine substance, and espec. of refined spirit, pure
spirits of wine. cf. Pihan, Glossaire des mots français tirés
de l'Arabe.

Alcor Sp. a rugged hill; from Ar. *al-qûrah*, pl. *alqûr*.

Alcornoque Sp. Pg. (m.) cork-tree, whence It. *alcornoch;* from
quern-oco spungeous oak? *oco* = *hueco* q. v.

Alcorque Sp. Pg. (m.) a shoe with cork sole = Sp. *corche,*
whence our *cork.* From the Lat. *cortex,* so = *alcorgue,* cf.
codigo from *codex, peja* from *pix, pulga* from *pulex.*

Alcova It., Sp. *alcoba,* Fr. *alcove* (f.), Pr. *alcuba,* O. Fr. *aucube,*
an *alcove,* recess in a room &c. Introduced from Spain and,
therefore, most likely of Arabic origin: *al-gobbah* in Arab.
means a vault or tent (Freyt. 3, 388ª). It occurs, under the
form *Alcoba,* as the name of a Portuguese village, v. Sousa.

Alcuno It., Sp. *alguno,* Pg. *algum,* Pr. *alcun,* Fr. *aucun;* from
aliquis unus. In the O. Fr. (Burgundian) we find the forms
alquen auquen alcon (m.) (f. *aucune*), which seem to point to
aliquis homo alc'uen, alc'on, though the word is also used as
an adjective. The Norman dialect has an analogous form
cascons for *quisque, chescon;* also *ascons (aliquis homo?), ascun.*

Alcuño Sp. a surname; from the Ar. *kunje* = a christian or surname. The O. Sp. fem. *alcuña,* Pg. *alcunha* sex, seems rather
to be connected with the Goth. *kuni* genus, *athala-kuni* = O.
H. G. *adal-kunni* nobile genus. But Engelmann gives Ar. *al-
konjah* "renombre de linage".

Aldea Sp. Pg. Cat. a hamlet; from Ar. *al-'dai'ah* an estate
Freyt. 3, 34, like Sp. *almea* from Ar. *almai'ah.*

Aleoe — *laccia.*

Aledaño Sp. a boundary, adj. = contiguous; from *limitaneus;*
so = *alendaño.*

Alenare It., Pr. Cat. *alenar* to breathe, Fr. *haléner* to scent; It.
alena lena, Pr. *alena,* Fr. *haleine* (h mut.) breath. From *anhelare* (1) to pant, (2) in later writers to breathe; It. *anelare,*
Sp. *anhelar,* Fr. *anheler;* the subst. comes from the vb. the

termination *ena* being too rare and doubtful to allow the derivation from *halare*.

Aléne — *lesina*.

Aleroe Sp. the larch; from *larix*, It. *larice*, with Arab. article, perhaps influenced by Ar. *al-arzah* cedar = Pers. *arz* pinus.

Alerte, alerto — *erto*.

Alesna - - *lesina*.

Aleve Sp. faithless, O. Sp. sbst. *alere*, Pg. *aleive* perfidy; not from *allevure* (which verb is not found in Sp.), but, perhaps, from the Goth. *lêvjan* to betray, A. S. *læva* a traitor.

Alesan — *alazan*.

Alfaoe Pg. lettuce; Ar. *al-khass*.

Alfadia Sp. a bribe; Ar. *al-hadiyyah*.

Alfalfa Sp. lucerne; Ar. *al'halfah*.

Alfana Sp. a strong spirited horse; hence O. Fr. *destrier aufaine*.

Alfange Sp. Pg. a sabre; from Ar. *al-khangar* a dagger, Freyt. 1, 530.

Alfaras Sp. Pg. a light Moorish cavalry horse; from Ar. *al-faras*.

Alfarda — *furdo*.

Alfarma alharma Sp. wild rue; Ar. *al-'harmal*.

Alferez Sp. Pg., O. Sp. *alferece alferce* an ensign, in earlier times = a high dignity: *alferez del rei* comes stabuli, constable; from the Ar. *al-fâres* a knight; It. *alfiere*.

Alfido alfiere It., Sp. *alfil arfil*, Pg. *alfil alfir*, O. Fr. *aufin* a bishop at chess; from the Pers. *fil elephant*, with the Ar. article, v. Duc. s. *alphinus*; cf., however, Pott in Lassen's Zeitschr. 4, 12.

Alfiere — *alferez*.

Alfil — *alfido*.

Alfiler alfilel Sp., Pg. *alfinete* pin, pl. Sp. *alfileres* pin-money; from Ar. *al-khildl* a skewer.

Alfooigo alfostigo alfonsigo Sp., Pg. *alfostigo* pistachio tree; from Ar. *al-fostoq*.

Alfombra Sp., Pg. *alfambar* a small carpet; from Ar. *al-khomrah* a prayer-carpet.

Alforga Sp., Pg. *alforge* a wallet; from Ar. *al-khorg*, Freyt. 1, 472.

Alfos Sp. Pg. district; from Ar. *al-hauz*.

Algalia Sp. Pg. civet-cat; from Ar. *al-guliyah*.

Algar Sp. Pg. a grotto; from Ar. *al-gâr*, Freyt. 3, 301.

Algara Sp. Pg. a marauding party (like It. *gualdana*); from Ar. *al-gârah*, Freyt. 3, 301, whence, too, *algurear* to shout hurrah!

Algarrobo — *carrobo*.

Algebra It., Sp. *algebra*, Fr. *algèbre*, *algebra*; from the Ar. *al-gabr* a resetting of anything broken (e. g. limbs), a meaning it still bears in Sp.; hence a combination into one whole, a representation of several operations by means of a few symbols. v. Golius p. 462, Freytag 1, 293[b]. Contrary to the usual rule in Arabic words, the accent is on the article.

Algez Sp. *gypsum*, whence it is derived, Sp. also *geso*, It. *gesso*.

Algier *algeir* a spear, Ch. d. Rol.; from O. H. G. *azger*, A. S. *ätgär*, O. N. *atgeirr*.

Algo Sp. Pg., Pr. *alque alques*, O. Fr. *auques* (in Lorrain *éque*, in Champ. *gauque*); from *aliquod*, *aliquid*; cf. Sp. *alguien*, Pg. *algwu*, from *aliquem*.

Algodon — *cottone*.

Alguacil *alvacil* Sp., Pg. *alguazil alvacil alvacir* a magistrate, bailiff &c., Pg. *guazil* a governor; from Ar. *vazir*, *al-vazir* the manager of a state, a *vizier*, which from *razara* to bear, Freyt. 4, 461. From *alguacil* = an overseer comes the Fr. *argousin*, It. *aguzzino* an overseer of slaves.

Alguien — *quien*.

Algures Pg. = Lat. *usquam*, O. Pg. *algur alluur*, for *algubre* from alicubi, like *alubre* from *aliubi*. Cf. *neuhures*.

Alholba Sp. a plant, foenum Graecum; from Ar. *'holbah*, Freyt. 1, 415; Basque *allorbea*.

Alhondiga — *fondaco*.

Alhondre — = *aliunde*.

Alice — *laccia*.

Aliento Sp., Pg. *alento* breath, vb. *alentar*; from *anhelare*, *n* and *l* being transposed; cf. *peligro* from *periclum*.

Aliso Sp. an alder-tree; cf. the G. form *else*. *Aliso* from *alysson*.

Alise Fr. service-berry, service-tree; from G. *else* (-beere). O. Fr. *alie*, *alier*.

Aljaba Sp., Pg. *aljaba* quiver; from the Ar. *al-gabah*, Freyt. 1, 281.

Aljofar Sp. Pg. a small pearl; from Ar. *al-gauhar* a pearl, a word of Persian origin, Freyt. 1, 327.

Aljuba — *giubba*.

Allá — *là*.

Allarme It. (m.), Sp. Pr. *alarma*, Fr. *alarme*, Wal. *larmë*, alarm; *attarmare* &c.; from the cry *all' arme!* to arms! Hence *alarum*, and occ. *alarmo* an interjection expressing wonder, It. *arm'arme!*

Allazzare It. to tire; from Goth. *latjan*, O. H. G. *lezjan* to let, hinder, Goth. *lats*, O. H. G. *laz*, *lazy*.

Allóger — *lieve*.

Alleggiare — *lieve*.

Allegro It., Sp. Pg. *alegre*, Fr. *alégre* sprightly, merry, with several derivatives; from *alacer alacrem* with the accent on the penult. From the change of *a* into *e*, the word would seem to have been orig. Fr.; we find an O. Fr. *halaigre* preserved in the proper name *Aligre*. The Basque *alaguera* is nearest the original.

Allende O. Sp., Pg. *alem* on the other side; from *alli ende*.

Allor — *andare*.

Alleu — *allodio*.

Allovare It., Pr. *alevar*, Fr. *élever* to rear, bring up *(tollere puerum)*. Partly, perhaps, from the carrying the child at baptism. In O. Sp. *alero* a baptized person, It. *aliero*, Fr. *élève* pupil.

Allí — *lì*.

Alligator — *lacerta*.

Allodio It., Sp. *alodio*, Pr. *alodi aloe alo*, Fr. *alleu*, an *allodium*, *allodial* lands &c., held in absolute independence without acknowledgment of any lord paramount, opp. to *fief*. The Lat. *allodium* suits all the Rom. forms; for the Pr. *aloe*, cf. *fastic* = *fastidium*, Fr. *aleu* = *aloe*, as *feu* = *foc*, *lieu* = *loc*. *Alodis* (Lex Salic.) *alaudis* are older forms of *allodium*. Grimm (Rechtsalt. p. 493, 950) gives a conjectural derivation from a Germ. compound *al-ôd* "all one's own". But Wedgwood, with more probability, connects it with the Icel. *ôdal* in same sense, Dan. Sw. *odel* a patrimonial estate. The landed proprietors of the Shetland Isles are still called *udallers* according to Sir W. Scott. Ihre (s. v. od) derives it from the Gothic *"alldha odhol"* an ancient inheritance, like *allda-vinr* an ancient friend, *allda-hæfd* an ancient possession. The L. L. form *alaudis* was, probably, influenced by *laus* in L. L. = a grant made by a feudal lord, who was said *"allaudare"* to make a grant, whence *"allow, allowance"*, v. *allouer*.

Allodola lodola It., Sicil. *lodlana*, O. Sp. *alueta* (*aluda* Canc. de Baena), Sp. *alondra*, Pr. *alauza alauzeta*, O. Fr. *aloe* (whence O. N. *lôa*, Grimm Reineke Fuchs p. 370), *aloue*, *aloëte*, Fr. *alouette*, L. L. *laudila* a lark. This is one of the few words which we may certainly refer to a Celtic origin. It was known to Cæsar who raised a "legio *Alauda*" in Gaul. This Suet. says was the Celtic for *galerita* or lark. Pliny and Gregory of Tours also refer it to the Celtic. Various derivations have been given of the Celtic word: (1) from W. *al* excellent and *aud* song, so = excellent songstress; (2) Villemarqué and others refer it to the Breton *alchoueder échoueder chouéder*, W. *alaw-adar* = bird of harmony; (3) from *alaw-hedez alauhed* (*hedeg* to fly); (4) Bullet derives it from *al* qui s'élève *chicedl* chant: *alchweder* qui s'élève en chantant. The W. for lark is *uchedydd ehedydd hedydd* (*hedegu* to fly, *uchedu* to soar) = prop. the soaring bird; the Cornish form is *eridil* for *echidil*, whence the Breton *echouedez chouedez*, *echoueder chouweder*, *alchouedez alchouweder*. The Lat. *alauda* dropped the guttural.

2*

It is noticeable that other names of birds of the same genus came from the Celtic, e. g. *finch*, It. *pincione*, Sp. *pinzon*, Fr. *pinçon*, from the W. *pinc*; Pg. *catoria*, Sp. *totoria*, Fr. *cocheris* tufted lark from the Bret. *kodioch*. V. Mahn (Etym. Untersuch.) p. 23. V. also Dief. Or. Eur. p. 219.

Allouer It., E. *allow* to praise, approve, permit; from *laudare*, Pr. *lauzar alauzar*, O. Fr. *loer louer allouer*. *Allouer*, *allow* in the sense of granting (an *allowance*) is, however, from *louer* == *locare*, It. *allogare* to assign, hence also *alloué* an attorney, substitute *(allocatus)*. As *laudare* and *locare* coalesced in *louer* the confusion was carried back to the L. L., where *allocare* == to approve, *laus* == a feudal grant.

Allosa Sp. green almond, *allozo* almond, tree; from Ar- *al-lanzah* almond-tree.

Alma — *anima*.

Almacen — *magazzino*.

Almaden Sp. mine, ore; from Ar. *al-ma'den*.

Almadraque — *materasso*.

Almagre Sp. Pg. red ochre; from Ar. *al-magrah* red earth.

Almanacco It., Sp. *almanaque*, Fr. *almanac*, Eng. *almanack*. Perhaps from the Ar. *al-mana'h* a present, vb. *mana'ha* to give as a present. The Ar. expression is *taquim* (v. Pihan p. 33). See Engelmann, p. 50.

Almea — *aldea*.

Almear — *meta*.

Almece Pg. whey; from Ar. *maçl*.

Almena Sp. a battlement; from the Lat. *mina* (only in plur.), with the Ar. article prefixed.

Almendra — *mandorla*.

Almete — *elmo*.

Almez Sp. nettle-tree, celtis australis; from Ar. *al-mais*.

Almidon — *amido*.

Almirante It. Sp. Pg., It. *almiraglio ammiraglio*, Pr. *amiran amirahl amiratz*, O. Fr. *amirant amiral amiras*, Fr. *amiral*, L. Gr. ἀμηράλης ἀμηράλιος an admiral, L. L. *admiraldus admirabilis*, in which, of course, there is a reference to *admirari*. The Fr. *amiral* and the Pr. *amirahl* present the most correct form, coming, as they do, from the Ar. *amir al bahr* chief at sea. The last syllable was dropped, when the word was introduced into the Rom. during the Crusades. So Mahn. But Diez considers the forms without the final *l* as older, and derives from *amir* simply, the various terminations being used to give the word a Rom. appearance. *Almirante* on the analogy of *imperante*, *comandante*. The orig. meaning, too, was "chief" not "chief at sea".

Almizcle — *musco*.

Almofalla O. Sp. O. Pg. an army; from Ar. *alma'hallah* a camp.

Almofar almofre Sp., Pg. *almafre* a cap of mail; from Ar. *al-migfar*.

Almogarave — *mugarero*.

Almohada Sp., Pg. *ulmofada* a bolster; from Ar. *al-mekhaddah*.

Almohaza Sp., Pg. *almofaça* a curry-comb; from Ar. *al-me'hassah*.

Almoneda Sp. an auction, Pg. *almoeda:* from Ar. *al-monddiya* auction, from *nada* to cry.

Almoradux - *majorana*.

Almorranas Sp. (plur.), Pg. *almorreimas*, Cat. *morenas* == *hæmorrhoides*, of which it is a corruption.

Almoxarife Sp. Pg. custom-house officer; from Ar. *al-moshrif* overseer.

Almud Sp., Pg. *almude* a ½ bushel-measure; from Ar. *almudd*.

Almuerzo Sp., Pg. *almorço almoço* breakfast; vb. *almorzar* (Cat. *esmorzar*); from *admorsus* (Symmachus), *l* for *d* as in *Alfonso* = *Adfonsus* (Hadufnus), cf. M. H. G. *anbiz*.

Almussa Pr., Fr. *aumusse*, O. Fr. *aumuce* (whence Du. *almutse amutse*), Sp. *almucio* (Seckendorf), Pg. *mursa;* dim. Pr. *almuceta*, O. Pg. *almucella almocella*, Sp. *almoceta* (*almucella almoçata* Ducange), O. Fr. *aumucette*, Sp. *muceta*, It. *mozzetta*. These words signify a headgear falling down to the shoulders, worn chiefly by ecclesiastics, in the dim. form a short mantle. They do not belong to the Arab., though like many others, they have assumed the Ar. article, but are evidently the same as the G. *mütze*, cap, bonnet, Du. *mutse*, usually derived from the vb. *mutzen* to crop. v. sub *mozzo*.

Alna auna alla It., O. Sp. O. Pg. Pr. *alna*, Sp. *ana*, Fr. *aune* an ell. Probably from the Goth. *aleina*, O. H. G. *elina* which is of the same gender. This, Grimm (3, 559) says, comes from *ulnus*. So Diez. But there is no word *ulnus* in Class. Lat.; *ulna* == elbow == Gk. ὠλένη, G. *ellen*-bogen.

Alnado andado Sp., Pg. *entendo* a stepson, from *antenatus*, Sp. also *antenado*, Isid. Gloss. *antenatus* privignus; Gr. πρόγονος.

Alocco — *locco*.

Aloi — *lega* (2).

Alora — *ora* (2).

Aloser — *lusingar*.

Alosna — *aluine*.

Alouette — *allodola*.

Alquile Sp. Pg. hire, *alquilar* to take on hire; from Ar. *al-kirâ* wages.

Alquitran — *catrame*.

Alrededor — *redor*.

Alrotar — *arlotto*.

Altaleno It. a swipe, *altalena* a see-saw, swing; from *tolleno* and *altus*.

Altresi It., Sp. *otrosi*, Pg. *outrosim*, Pr. *attresi atresi*, O. Fr. *autresi*; from *alterum sic*, as *aussi* from *aliud sic*.

Altrettale It., Sp. *otro tal*, Pg. *outro tal*, Pr. *attretal atretal*, O. Fr. *autretel*, from *alter talis*. So *altrettanto* &c., from *alter tantus*: Pr. *atrestal*, *atrestan* from *alter-sic-talis*, *alter sic tantus*.

Alubia Sp. a French bean; from the Ar., Gk. λόβος.

Alubre O. Sp. (and in Berceo *a iubre*); from *aliubi*.

Aluine Fr. wormwood; from *aloe* with suffix *ine* (as in *amarantine*, *argentine*, *arcttine*, *balsamine*, *églantine*), *ui* for *oi* as in *muid* from *modius* &c. Another form with weak *n* is found, O. Fr. *alogne*, Sp. Pg. *alosna*, *losna*.

Aluir Pg. to rock, swing, knock at or against, to hollow (of water); from *alludere* or, perhaps, *alluere*.

Alumelle — *lama* (2).

Alvaoil — *alguacil*.

Alverja — *erro*.

Alvicara — *albricia*.

Alzare It., Sp. *alzar*, Pr. *alsar ausar*, Fr. *hausser* (*h* asp., cf. *haut* II. c), O. E. *haiese* (whence *haieser*), Wal. *in-altzà* to raise; from *altus (altiare)*. The Fr. *exhausser* (Pr. *eissausar*, Sp. *ensalzar*) deserves consideration from its assuming a distinct form *exaucer* with the meaning to hear (a petition) thus: Dieu a *exaucé* mes prières = has heard (prop. has exalted, favoured) my prayers.

Ama Sp. Pg. housewife, mistress, hence *amo* master of the house; Isidorus uses *amma*: hæc avis (strix) vulgo "*amma*" dicitur ab amando parvulos, unde et lac præbere fertur nascentibus. The word is prob. the same as the Gael *am*, W. *mam*, Basq. *ama* mother, Occ. *ama* grandmother, Ar. *amm*, Sansk. *ambá*, O. G. *amma*, G. *amme* a nurse.

Amaca It., Sp. *hamaca*, by transpos. *amahaca*, Pg. *maca*, Fr. *hamac* (*h* asp.), Eng. *hammock* from the Du. *hangmak*, G. *hangematte* (lit. = suspended bed), or, more probably, a native American word, the Du. being adapted to a false etymology.

Amadouer Fr. to allure, caress, hence sbst. *amadou* tinder, also a lure, cf. *esca*; hence *ramadouer*. The O. N. vb. *mata*, Dan. *made*, meant to feed young birds (Goth. *matjan* to eat), Eng. *meat*, hence with *ou* (= o cf. *évanouir*) *a-mad-ourr* to give meat to, entice with meat, It. *ad-escare*. The Goth. *t* becomes *d* as in *guider* from *ritan*, *hadir hair* from *hatan*.

Amagar — *amago*.

Amago Pg. the core, innermost part of a thing, vb. Cat. Pr. *amagar* to conceal. The Sp. *amago*, Cat. *amay amad* denotes a peculiar taste of honey. Sp. *amago* also = disgust, aversion. The connexion has not been made out.

Amalgamare It. &c. to *amalgamate*, to form a mixture *(amalgam)* of mercury and some other metal; from the Gk. μάλαγμα.

Amande — *mandorla*.

Amanevir — *manevir*.

Amapóla Sp. a poppy; from the Basque *ematopa* "that sends to sleep", from *ema eman* to give and *lopa lopea* to sleep. Cf. the Sp. *adormidera*.

Amargo — *amaricare*.

Amaricare It., also *amareggiare*, Sp. Pg. Pr. *amargar* to embitter; from *amarus* v. Ducange. Adj. Sp. Pg. *amargo*, Cat. *amary*, sbst. *amargor*. Hence It. *rammaricarsi* to lament, *rammarico* lamentation, adj. *amaro* grieved (Sic. *amaru*), Wal. *amar* an interjection of grief: so in O. Pg. *amaro de mi!* Gil. Vic. 2, 465.

Amarillo Sp., Pg. *amarello* yellow, amber-coloured; for *amarillo* from *ambar amber* which is of Arab. origin *anbar* being prop. a fish supposed to yield *ambergris*. The word was introduced into Europe by the Phœnicians, v. Mahn (Etym. Unters. p. 62).

Amarrar Sp. Pg., Fr. *amarrer* to moor a vessel, Fr. *démarrer* to unmoor; *amarra amarre* a mooring-cable; from the Du. *marren* to moor, also to delay, retain = O. H. G. *marrjan* to stop (v. s. *marrire*): the form *merren* has also both meanings = A. S. *merran* to hinder *(mar)*.

Amatita matita red chalk, Fr. *hématite*; from *hæmatites*.

Ambasciata It., Sp. *embaxada*, Pr. *ambaissada*, and m. *ambaissat*, Fr. *ambassade embassy*; It. *ambasciadore* &c., *ambassador*; from the L. L. *ambaxia ambactia* commission, charge, business. This *ambaxia* is seemingly connected with the word *ambactus* used by Cæsar (B. G. 6, 15) for servant, vassal: "equites circum se *ambactos* clientesque habent". From *ambactus* comes *ambactia*, afterwards pronounced in France *ambacsia (ambaxia)* and by transposition *ambascia*, cf. *Brescia* for *Brixia*. The verb *ambasciare* to convey a message, serve on an embassy, from which the Rom. derivatives immediately come, was also known in L. L. The Pr. masc. = *ambasciatum*. Festus says the word is Gallic "*ambactus* apud Ennium linguâ Gallicâ servus appellatur". Hence Zeuss 1, 89, 179 refers it to a Celtic origin, viz. the W. *amaet* husbandman, workman, for *ambaeth* (tho *b* being dropped, as often happens after *m*, cf. *amarillo*). J. Grimm derives the word from the Gothic *andbahts* a servant, O. H. G. *ambaht* (Goth. *andbahti* service, M. G. *amt* office, charge). *Andbahts* he resolves into *and* and *bak (back)* whence the meaning *back-holder*, supporter, servant (cf. *henchman* = *haunchman*). Pott and Bopp, however, connect *and-bah-ts* with the Sanskrit *bhaj* colere, venerari, partic. *bhakta* (= -*bactus*) deditus, devotus. In favour of Grimm's etymology it may be urged that the Rom. *ambactia* (which does not occur in Latin) is not so easily obtained from *ambuctus* (the suffix *ia* being unusual) as from the Goth. *andbahti* whence it would be regularly formed, like the Pr. *fanha* = *fania* from the Goth. *fani*. The notion of manual labour, which appears in the W. word, is preserved in the Du. *ambagt* a handicraft; *ambagts-mann* an artizan. Icel. *ambatt* a female slave. The It. uses *ambascia ambascio* to mean shortness of breath, distress, anxiety; *ambasciare trambasciare* to be out of breath, be in distress &c., prop. = to be oppressed with work; for a similar connexion of meanings cf. s. *affanno*. Diefenbach (Goth. Dict. 1, 255) has a learned discussion on *andbahts* and *ambactus*.

Ambiare It., Sp. Pg. Pr. *amblar*, Fr. *ambler*, to *amble*; from *ambulare* not used in Class. Lat. in this sense, which was first introduced some time after the 9th century. The Wal. *émblá* still keeps the Classical meaning.

Ambidos amidos O. Sp. unwillingly; from *inritus*, It. *invito*, O. Fr. *enris*.

Ambone It., Fr. *ambon*, an *ambo*, a kind of pulpit in the choir from which the lessons were read; from the Gk. ἄμβων any rising as a hill, a stage &c. (*umbo*).

Ambra It. (f.), Sp. Pg. *ambar alambar alambre* (m.), Fr. *ambre* (m.), *amber*, M. H. G. *amber dmer*, G. *ambra*; from the Arab. *'anbar* a sweet-scented resin (Freyt. 3, 227), orig. the name of a fish from which *ambergris* was supposed to come. The word was probably introduced into Europe by the Phœnicians who used it to express the yellow amber found on the shores of the Baltic and called by the ancient Germans *glas* or *gles* (Tacit. *glæsum*), v. Mahn (Etym. Unters.)

Ame — *anima*.

Amenass — *minaccia*.

Amender Fr., *amende, amendement*, E. *amend*, used by Boethius (c. 1150) who writes both *emendament* and *amendament*; from *emendare*.

Amido It., Pg. *amido amidão*, Sp. *almidon*, Fr. *amidon* starch; from Lat. *amylum* (ἄμυλον). The only instance, says Diez, of *l* becoming *d* in Rom.; but we have Pg. *escuda* = *scala*. In Latin the interchange was not uncommon: *calamitas, cadamitas, scando scala* &c.

Amiraglio ammiraglio, amiral — *almirante*.

Amito Sp., O. Fr. *amit amice*; from *amictus*.

Ammainare Sp. Pg. *amainar*, Fr. *amener* (les voiles) to lower sails. From *ad manus* cf. *demener* from *de manus*, L. L. *minare* to lead drive, which is better der. from *manus* than; with Diez, from *minari*. For *a = e*, cf. *menottes* handcuffs.

Ammañare — *maña*.

Ammazzare — *mazzo*.

Ammiccare It. to wink; from *admicare*.

Ammutinare — *meute*.

Amo — *ama*.

Amojar Pg. to milk; from Ar. *mascha'a?*

Amonestar Sp. Pr., Pg. *amoestar*, O. Fr. *amonester*, Fr. *admonéter*, to *admonish*, Pr. also *monestar*, O. Fr. sbst. *monneste;* from *monitare* (used by Venantius Fortunatus, A. D. 600), with *s* inserted to distinguish it from *montar* which would come from *monitare* as *rontar* from *ranitare*. But v. Littré p. 34, who derives it from *monestus* a partic. of *monére*, cf. *semondre*.

Amortiguar — *santiguar*.

Amparar — *parare*.

Amusco — *musco*.

Amuser — *muser*.

Ananas It. Fr., Sp. *anana* pine-apple, Pg. *ananaz* (tree), *ananazeiro* (fruit); a South American word.

Anappo nappo It., Pr. *enap*, O. Fr. *hanap henap* (*h* asp.); from O. H. G. *hnapf hnap*, G. *napf* a bowl. Hence L.L. *hanaperium* a cup-basket, E. *hamper*.

Anc — *anche*.

Anca It. Sp. Pg. Pr., Fr. *hanche* (*h* asp.), *hanxch (henchman)*, Sp. Pg. plur. *ancas* the croup of a horse &c. Hence It. *sciancato*, Fr. *éhanché* hip-shot. From (1) Gk. ἄγκη a bend, or (2) from G. *anke*, O. H. G. *ancha* nape of neck, neck, prop. a curve. The Rom. languages have made use of the Greek word in another instance (v. *anco*), and Festus even mentions a Lat. *ancus* = "qui aduncum brachium habet ut exporrigi non possit". But the German word, particularly in its chief meaning (a *joint*) lies nearer the Rom. than the Gk. or the obsolete Latin. From the O. H. G. *ancha* = tibia, crus, is derived the Fr. *anche* a pipe or tube (of an instrument &c.), from which *hanche* was distinguished by the aspirate (cf. the Friesl. *hancke henke* Kil.).

Anceis — *esso*.

Ancêtres Fr., O. Fr. *ancestres*, acc. *ancessors, ancestors;* from *antecessores*.

Anche anco It., Rh. *aunc aunca*, also, still (etiam), Pr. *anc*, O. Fr. *ainc* (= unquam), Wal. *incë* (= adhuc). From *adhuc*, whence *adunc aunc* (cf. O. Fr. *ainsinc = æque sic*), Sp. *aun* (Pg. *ainda*) cf. Sp. *nin = nec*, Pg. *assim = sic*, *allin = illic*. In It. a *d* between two vowels is seldom lost, so the process

would be: *adunc, ad'nc, anc, anche*. The derivation from *haue*
(sc. *horam*, cf. It. *issa* sc. *hora*) suits the form but not the sense;
moreover, we should have a supply *ad* as well as *horam*. For
the O. Fr. *aine* we sometimes have *ains* e. g. Alex. 66, 3,
which must be distinguished from *ains* = Sp. *antes*. *Anc* (euphon. *anca*, cf. Rh. *aunca*) is, probably, the first syllable of
the compounds Pr. *ancui*, O. Fr. *encui*, It. *ancoi* to-day, Pr.
ancanuech, O. Fr. *enquenuit* to-night.

Anche — *anca*.

Ancho Sp. Pg. broad; from *amplus* (It. *ampio* &c.), like *henchir*
from *implere*; *ensanchar* to widen = *examplare*.

Anchoa anchois — *acciuga*.

Anciano ancion — *anzi*.

Ancidere It. (poet.) to kill; from *incidere*, cf. *anaffiare, aucude,
anquinaglia* for *inaffiare* &c.

Ancino It., Sp. *anzuelo*, Pg. *anzol*, Fr. *hameçon* a fish-hook;
from *hamus*.

Anco Pg. an elbow, a bending; from the Gk. ἄγκος a bend, a
valley; Sp. *ancon* (m.) a bay, a road, from ἀγκών = elbow,
recess. In Breton *auk* = a corner *(angulus)*. v. Ducange, s.
ancus.

Ancolie Fr. columbine (a plant), G. *aglei*; from L. *aquileja* (unclass.), It. *aquilegia*: for the insertion of *n* cf. s. anche, andare.

Ancona anconeta Bresc. a small image; from εἰκών, whence
also Wal. *icoane*.

Ancora — *ora*.

Anose — *se*.

Andado — *aluado*.

Andamio — *andama*.

Andana Com. Piedm. (1) gait, manner of life; (2) the sweep
that the mower takes at each stride, swath = Fr. *andain* (f.),
Norm. *andain* (m.) step, Berrichon *audain* a layer of mown
grass &c., a swath, Sp. *andana*, Pg. *andaina* a row, rank;
from *andare*. The first meaning would be "stride", then the
length or extent of a stride, and, lastly, layer, row; so the
G. *schwaden*, Eng. *swath* = both the sweep of the scythe in
mowing and the row or layer of mown corn. Hence, with unusual suffix, the O.Sp. *andamio* gait, L.L. *andamius* a passage,
= O. Pg. *andamo* (cf. Rouchi *andame* = Fr. *ondain*); hence,
too, the Sp. *andamio*, Pg. *andaimo andaime* a passage, gang-
way, also a scaffold in which sense some refer it to the Arab.

Andare It., Sp. Pg. *andar*, Cat. Pr. *anar*, Wald. *anar*, Lomb.
anà to go. The Fr. has another word *aller*; the Rh. and Wal.
have neither of these forms, the former making up a verb
from *ire*, *vadere* and *meare*, the latter using *mearye* (from
emergere), which in conjugation *(mearsi, mers)* betrays its

Latin origin. The verb is complete in Sp. and Pg. and was once so in It. (as it is still in some of the dialects, e. g. the Sard.). It is now mixed up in conjugation with *vadere* which, in Latin wanting the perfect and tenses thence derived, had to supply them from elsewhere; *iri* would have been too short, so *andare* was coined. This had the accent on the syllable of flexion (whilst *vadere* is marked on the root-syllable), and was, therefore, used in those parts of the conjugation which bear that accent: *ro, rai, va: andiamo, andate, vanno; andara; andai* &c., cf. *esca (exire), esci, esce: usciamo (ostium). uscite, escono. Andare* and *stare* in Rom. were two parallel auxiliaries: what wonder then if they tended to adopt similar forms in their conjugation? Such analogous formations are not uncommon. Thus the Sp. *andure* corresponds to *esture, andido* to *estido, andudo* to *estudo;* O. It. *andetti* to *stetti, andiedi* to *stiedi.* In Sp. other verbs of the 1st conj. had similar forms: *entrido* from *entrar, catido* from *catar* (v. s. *fegato*), *demandudo* from *demandar.* It is usually derived from the G. *wenden wandern* as *aller* from *wollen;* but the G. *w* does not disappear thus in Rom. (the Sp. *andalucia* came through the Arab., which avoided the harsh *gu* (= *w*) of the Rom. *Guandalucia:* so *impla* for *guimpla*). *Wenden,* Goth. *vandjan* would be in Rom. *guandir, wollen* in Fr. would be *gauler.* A Celtic verb W. *athu,* Ir. *eath* to go, would deserve more consideration were not the derivation from the Lat. *aditare,* quite regular and complete. Ennius uses the word once: *ad eum aditavere;* its meaning, "to enter often", "to go in and out", occurs in the various Rom. derivatives: thus, Sp. *andante caballero* = a knight-errant, *andorro* a rambler = Sard. *andaredda.* The *n* was inserted to give the word more force as in *rendere* from *reddere,* cf. s. *anche, ancolie,* and cf. *andido* = *aditus,* L. L. c. 800 *cum viis et aquis et anditis suis* v. Muratori and Ducange. For the termination cf. O. It. O. Sp. *renda* for *reddita.* The Fr. *aller* is for O. Fr. *aler (allar* occurs in the Pass. de J. C. str. 114), which was for *aner* (cf. Chron. de Benoît 1, p. 92, *si qu'en exil nos en anium,* Choix 6, 300, *que vos anez por moi fors terre*), the two forms being current at the same time, like *venin* and *velin, orphenin* and *orphelin.* From *aditato* by syncope of the *d* may come the Com. *oitée* = *andato;* similarly, from *adita* the Ven. *aida* = *vanne* (imperat.). The Wal. defective verb *aide aidatzi* = δεῦρο δεῦτε, Goth. *hiri hirjith,* perhaps = *adita aditate,* unless it be of the same origin as the Servian *ajde ajdate.* From *adire* comes the Burg. *ai (air)* = *aller.* From *aller* comes the abst. *allée* an *alley* which Ducange refers to *laie* (q. v.); cf. It. *andata.* But v. Littré, Hist. de la langue franç., vol. I, p. 40.

Andario Sp. a water-wagtail; from *andar* to go and *rio* a river.

Andas Sp., Pg. *andes* (only in plur.) a sedan, litter, bier; from *amites; amites hasternarum* = the poles of the sedans (Palladius). Cf. *hante,* and for the change of *mt* into *nd* in Spain cf. *conde, duendo, lindar, senda* &c.

Andorinha — *roudine.*

Andouille Fr. a sausage, black-pudding, Rh. *anduchiel,* Basque *andoilla.* For *endouille* from *inductilis,* by which word the O.G. *scubiling* (a sort of sausage) is translated in old Glossaries, v. Graff, 6, 409, Schmeller 3, 313. This latter is from O. H. G. *scioban,* G. *schieben, shove,* both being named from forcing the meat into the skin *(inducere);* for *in* = *an* cf. *ancidere.*

Andromina Sp. a fib, a tale told to deceive, trick, artifice; from the Basque *andraminue* women's sickness (as being often alleged as a pretext), which is compounded of *andrea* a woman and *mina* pain.

Anegare — *negar.*

Angar hangar (*h* asp. and unasp.) a carriage-shed. It is difficult to see the connexion between this and the Lat. *angaria* service, soccage. It meant orig. a covering, and is especially used in the Wall. *(angar).* It occurs also in Celtic, at least in the Gaelic.

Angarde engarde O. Fr., Pr. *angarda* vanguard, also = a watch-tower; from *ante* and *garde,* like *avant-garde (vanguard).*

Angarier angariser Fr. to compel a vessel, even though neutral, to do service for the government (hence generally to compel); such compulsion was called *augarie.* In Eng. we have *angarisation* = compulsion; from the Gk. ἄγγαρος, ἀγγαρεύω.

Angaro Sp. a signal-light; from the Basque *garra* flame, *an garra* = yonder flame, v. Larramendi. The word is remarkably like the Gk. ἄγγαρος, Aesch. Ag. ἀπ᾽ ἀγγάρου πυρός, from the beacon-fire.

Anglar Pr. stone, rock; prop. something *angular,* from *angularis.*

Angoscia It., O. Sp. *angoxa,* Pr. *engoissa,* Fr. *angoisse, anguish; angosciare, angoisser* to vex; from *angustia.* The Sp. (Pg. and Cat.) is *congoxa,* in which the supposed prefix *an* is changed into *con,* whilst in Pr. it became *en.* The idea of pressure easily yields that of vexation, torment, cf. oppress, Fr. *grever.* The original meaning of *anger* was oppression, trouble, torment (*angor*). *Ang* as a root meaning pressure is widely spread: Sansk. *an-hu* = ἐγγύς, ἄγχι (cf. *presso*), G. *eng* compressed *enge* distress, *angere, angina,* ἄγχω, ἀγχόνη, Sansk. *an-hura* distressed.

Angra Sp. Pg. a bay, a cove: in a L.L. Glossary we have *ancra* ἄγκεα, αὐλῶνες, cf. ἀγκών, ἄγκος a valley, ἄγκυλος curved, *angulus,* ἀγκύλη &c.

Anguinaglia — *inguine*.

Angurria Sp. a water-melon; according to Larramendi, a Basque word.

Anima It., Pr. *anma* Boeth., O. Fr. *anime anme*, Fr. *âme*, in It. (poet.) Sp. Pg. *alma*, Rh. *olma*, also Pr. *arma*, O. Fr. *arme airme*, soul, Wal. *inimë* soul, and heart; from *anima* breath, life. The Lat. *animus* is not found in Fr. and Pr., one of its meanings being supplied by *courage, coratge*.

Annegare — *negar*.

Anqui — *qui*.

Ansare — *asma*.

Ansi — *cosi*.

Antaño Sp., O. Pg. *antanho*, Pr. *antan*, O. Fr. *antan entan* = "last year" (opp. *hogaño*, v. *uguanno*), once: from *ante annum*. Hence O. Fr. *antenois*.

Antes — *anzi*.

Antienne Fr. an *anthem*; from *antiphona* (cf. *Étienne* from *Stephanus*), A. S. *antefn*, En. *anthem*, as from A. S. *stefn*, En. *stem*.

Antif O. Fr. old; from *antiquus*, as O. Fr. *eve* from *aqua*. *Antif* in the sense of "high" must be for *altif* = Pr. *altiu*, Sp. *altivo* (haughty).

Antojo Sp., whence Pg. *antojo* for *antolho* whim, freak; from *ante oculum*. In the plur. Sp. *anteojos*, Pg. *antolhos* spectacles.

Antoroba — *torciare*.

Antuviar — *tuviar*.

Anzi It., Sp. Pg. *antes*, Pr. *ans*, O. Fr. *ans ains* a preposition and adverb from the Lat. *ante* with the adverbial suffix *s* so that the It. form is for *ansi*. From *antea* would have come in It. not *anzi* but *anza*, cf. *poscia*. A longer form of *antes* is found in the Pr. *anceis*, O. Fr. *ainçois*, from *ante ipsum*. Hence the It. *anziano*, Sp. *anciano*, Pr. *oncian*, Fr. *ancien*, ancient: It. *avanti*, Pr. *abans avant*, Fr. *avant*, from *ab ante*; It. *avanzare*, Sp. Pr. *avanzar*, Fr. *avancer* to *advance* (where the *d* has been inserted from a false notion of the etymology); It. *vantaggio* for *avantaggio*, Pr. *avantatge*, Fr. *avantage*, Sp. *ventaja*, Pg. *ventagem, vantage, advantage*; also It. *davanti*, Pr. *davans*, O. Sp. Fr. *devant*, from *de ab ante*; Pr. *davancir*, Fr. *devancer*; It. *innanzi innante*, O. Sp. *enante*, Pr. *enan(s)*; Pr. *enantar enantir*; It. *dinanzi*, Sp. *denante delante*, Pg. *diante*, Pr. *denan*; It. *dianzi* &c.

Anzuela — *ancino*.

Añadir Sp. to add, exaggerate; from *inaddere*, O. Sp. *enadir*, O. Pg. *emader*, Wal. *innédi*.

Añafil Sp., Pg. *anafil* a pipe or trumpet; from the Ar. *ol-nafir annafir* a brazen trumpet. The Ar. is derived from the Persian (Freyt. 4, 312ª). Pr. has *amafil* "parva tuba cum voce altā".

Añagaza ñagaza Sp., *negaça* Pg., a bird-call, lure. Larramendi derives it from the Basque *aña gaza* a sweet nurse! Ferreira (Lus. 1, 86) from Lat. *illex*, whence *euagaza* (cf. *encina* from *ilex*), *añagaza* as *añadir* from *enadir*. This etym. suits the meaning well, though an easier change would be that from *eugañaza* (*engañar* to deceive).

Añil añir Sp., Pg. *anil* indigo-plant; from Ar. *an-nilah* "indigofera tinctoria", which is from Pers. *ail* (Sansk. *nila* black, dark-blue).

Añusgar Sp. to be choked, stifled; from the Basque *añusca* the throat.

Apaciguar — *santiguar*.

Apañar — *pan*.

Ape It., O. Fr. Pic. *es* for *eps* a bee, from *apis;* It. *pecchia*, Sp. *abeja*, Pg. Pr. *abelha*, Fr. *abeille*, from *apicula*, Norm. dim. *avette*. Hence too It. *apiario*, Pr. *apiari*, Fr. *achier*, a beehive, L. *apiarium* (Gellius), v. Rom. Gr. 1, 7. In Wal. the bee is called *albiaĕ*, from *alvus* a hive.

Apoar Sp. Pg. to alight, remove; from *pes* Sp. *pié*.

Apenas — *appena*.

Apero Sp., Pg. *apeiro* implements, farm-implements, sheep-fold; *aprisco* sheep-fold, cf. Com. *aper* a partition between a stall and a hayrick; from *apparare*, whence a sbst. *apparium* might be formed.

Apesgar — *peso*.

Apitar — *pito*.

Aposentar Sp. Pg. to lodge a person, *aposento* a lodging, room; a participial verb from *pasar* (L. *pausare*). It should have been *aposantar*, but was spelt as if connected with *sentar* to fit, set up.

Apostille — *postille*.

Appanor O. Fr., Pr. *apanar* to provide for, maintain, whence Fr. *apanage* a provision for a child, jointure, Eng. *appanage;* from *panis*.

Appareil — *parecchio*.

Appât — *pasta*.

Appeau Fr. lure, bird-call, Wall. *apell;* from *appellare*.

Appena It., Sp. Pg. *apenas*, Fr. à *peine* = vix; from *peua* prop. painfully, so = with difficulty, hardly, scarcely, cf. L. *ægre*, O. H. G. *kúmo*. *Ple* is found in Sp. *apes*, q. v.

Applicare — *pegar*.

Appo It., from *apud*. Hence Pr. *ab amb aoi emb*, Bern. *dap*, Cat. *ab*, Wald. *au*, O. It. *aoi*, O. Fr. *ab*, *a*, *ob*, *o*. In the oldest L. L.

apud was used = *cum* (cf. Rom. Gr. 3, 157), but its orig.
meaning was more usual: e. g. *encusar ab alcun* to accuse to
a person, Leodegar str. 13; *aprendre ab alcun* Parn. Occ. 142;
fud ensereliz od ses ancestres Liv. d. rois p. 304. v. s. *avec.*

Approcciare approcher — *proche.*

Appui — *poggio.*

Après — *presso.*

Aprisco — *opero.*

Aquecer — *calentar.*

Aquende O. Sp., Pg. *aquem* = Lat. citra; from *aqui inde* (Lat.
eccu inde) = It. *quindi.*

Aquese Sp., O. Pg. *aquesse*, demonstr. pron.; from *eccu ipse.*

Aqueste — *questo.*

Aqui — *qui.*

Ara — *ora.*

Aragan haragan Sp. lazy, inactive: probably from the O. H. G.
arag arg worthless, lazy, G. *arg* bad, Icel. *argr* lazy, cowardly
(Eng. *arch* = mischievous), hence as a term of abuse; its use
was forbidden by the Lombard law: *si quis alium argam per
furorem clamaverit*, Paul. Diac. 6, 24: *memento quod me ...
vulgari verbo arga vocaveris.* In the district of Como, the ancient abode of the Lombards, the word is preserved *(argan)*
= poltrone. The Sp. word could hardly come from the Gk.
ἀργός.

Araldo It., Sp. *haraldo heraldo*, O. Sp. *harante*, Pg. *arauto*, Fr.
héraut for *hérault* (*h* asp.), Sp. Pg. *faraute* a herald; from the
L. L. *haraldus heraldus.* This would be in O. H. G. *hariwalt*
(G. *heer* army, *walten* to rule) an army-officer; a proper name
Charioraldus occurs, in O. Sax. *Hariolt*, Eng. *Harold*, O. N.
Haroldr.

Aramir arramir O. Fr., Pr. *aramir*, O. Cat. *aremir* (Ducange) to
assure judicially, to assure, promise, appoint &c. e. g. *aramir un soirement* to promise the performance of an oath, *aramir ou jurer* to promise or swear, *aramir bataille* to proclaim
a combat (notify i. e. the time and place), *aramie* a combat so
proclaimed, in M. Norm. = arrangement. So in L. L. *arra-
mire sacramentum*, *bellum.* In old MSS. various forms of the
word are found: *adrhamire*, *adehramire*, *aderamire*, *agramire*,
adframire. These point to a German word beginning with *hr*,
with the Lat. *ad* prefixed. Grimm refers it to the Goth. *hram-
jan* to fasten on the cross, fasten, fix, appoint, akin to the
O. H. G. *ramen* to aim at, strive for. According to Müllen-
hoff L. Sal. p. 277, *adhramire* = *adripere*, rapture. Cf. Dief.
Goth. Lex. 2, 589.

Arancel Sp. Pg. a fixed price of things, a rate; perhaps from
the Ar. *al-risála*, or -*risálla* a letter.

Arancio It., Milan. *naranz*, Ven. *naranza*, Sp. *naranja*, Pg. *laranja* (Basq. *larania*), Cat. *taronja* (sic), Wal. *nëranzë*, L. Gr. νεράντζιον, N. Gr. νεράντζι, Fr. *orange*, an *orange*. Not as Salmasius says from *aurantia* = *aurata (aurea mala)*, which would give not *orange* but *orance*. The word came from the Persian *nârang* through the Ar. *nârang* (Golius 2346). The Fr. had, undoubtedly, a reference to *aurum*; but *arangia* is the L. L. form (end of the 13th century). From *arancio* comes the It. adj. *rancio* orange (of colour).

Arañar Sp. to scratch, scrape, sbst. *araño*, also *aruñar aruñu* (pop.). The former word is derived from the latter, with a reference to *radere*. Is *aruñar* from *arare*, as *rasguñar* from *rasgar*, or from the Sp. *roña* (Pr. *runha*, v. *rogna*) itch?

Arátro arátolo It., Sp. Pg. *arado*, Cat. *arada* (f.), Pr. *araire*, O. Fr. *arére*, Wal. *aratru arutu* plough. The Fr. has substituted *charrue* from *carruca*, Pg. *charrua* a kind of plough, a ship. The G. *pflug*, E. *plough* is also found in Rom., L. L. *plous*, Lomb. *piö*, Tyrol. *plof* = L. L. *plouus* or *plovus*. Piedm. *sloira*, Lomb. *sciloira* = an O. Fr. *silleoire*, *silloire* from *siller* to furrow the sea. Piedm. *arn* is a corruption of *aratrum*.

Arazzo razzo It., tapestry, *arras*; from *Arras (Atrebates)*, in the Pas-de-Calais, where it was manufactured.

Arbaléte Fr., Pr. *arbalista* an *arbalist*; from *arcuballista* (Veget.).

Arban O. Fr. feudal service; for *harban* from O. H. G. *heriban* summons to military service; v. Ducange *heribannum*.

Arbolar — *alberare*.

Arborer — *alberare*.

Arbousier — *albedro*.

Arcame — *carcasso*.

Arcasse Fr. stern-frame (in a ship); it is the same word as the It. *arcaccia*, Sp. *arcaza* a chest, from *arca*.

Arce Sp., Cat. *ars* a maple; from *acer*, It. *acero*, O. Sp. *asre*, Pg. *acer*.

Arcea — *acceggia*.

Archal — *oricalco*.

Arcigaye — *zagaia*.

Arcigno — *réche*.

Arcilla Sp. clay; from *argilla*. A similar change of the medial into the tenuis is found in *arcen (agger)*, *encia (gingiva)*, *ercer (erigere)*, *uncir (jungere)*. In the Vocab. S. Gall. we find *arcilla laimo (loam)*, and the Wall. has *arzëie* = Fr. *argile*.

Arcione It., Sp. *arzon*, Pg. *arção*, Pr. *arson*, Fr. *arçon* saddle-bow, saddle. Not from *arctio*, but from *arcus* with the termination *ion* (like *clerçon* from *clericus*, *oison* from *auca*, *écusson* from *scutum*) = "something bowed or bent", cf. G. *bugen*, *sattelbugen*, Eng. *bow*.

Arcobugio archibuso It., Sp. *arcabuz*, Fr. *arquebuse*, Eng. *arquebuss;* from the Du. *haak-bus*, *haeck-buyse*, *haeck-busse*, G. *hakenbüchse* = a gun fired from a rest (*haak haeck haken* a hook or forked rest, *buss busse büchse* a fire-arm); this in O. Fr. became *harquebuse*, Wall. *harkibuse* (*h* asp.). The Italians altered the word so as to convey a meaning to themselves, *arco bugio* or *buso* meaning a hollow or perforated bow; for similar false popular etymologies cf. *palafreno, battifredo, baccalaureus, malvagio, mainbour.*

Arçon — *arcione.*

Arda ardilla Sp., Pg. *harda* a squirrel. Larramendi derives it from the Basque *"ari da"* "he is ever moving", but the B. name is different. Perhaps from the Lat. *nitella* by prosthesis *anedilla*, whence *aredilla ardilla arda.*

Ardid ardil — *ardire.*

Ardiglione It., Fr. *ardillon*, Pr. *ardalhó* the tongue of a buckle. The derivation is uncertain. An old glossary has *ardelio acutus* (Class. Auct. 6, 509ᵃ), but here we should read *glutus.* Against Casaubon's der. from ἀρδίς an arrowhead is to be urged the rare use of this word. Ménage gets it from *dard* thus: *dardillon* (which still exists in Mod. Prov.), *lardillon, l'ardillon, ardillon.* The Sp. for *ardillon* is *rejo.*

Ardire It. to venture, dare, Pr. *ardir en-ardir*, Fr. *enhardir* to embolden. The Fr. *hardir* (*h* asp.) evidently comes from the O. H. G. *hartjan* to harden. The adj. *ardito ardit hardi* (Eng. *hardy*) must be a participle of this verb since there were few Rom. adjectives in *it*, like the L. *auritus, pellitus.* The participle of *ardere (ars)* to burn is quite different in form. In Sp., however, they gradually came to refer *ardito* to *arder* and used it as = "inflamed, incensed"; but the O. Sp. *fardido* bold, corresponds to the Fr. *hardi* (Rom. Gr. 1, 311). It is curious that in Pic. *hardiment* is used just like O. G. H. *harto: hardiment dur = harto herti.* Hence come the Pr. *ardit* and O.Sp. *ardil* boldness: but the Sp. *ardid* crafty, Sp. Pg. *ardid* craft, cunning, seem to come from *artitus*, v. *artigiano*, the *t* being assimilated *(ardid* for *artid).*

Ardite Sp., an ancient Spanish coin, Limous. *ordi:* from the Basque *ardita* which from *ardia* a sheep (cf. *pecunia* from *pecus*, and cf. Léchuse, Basque gram.).

Ardoise Fr. O. Fr. *erdoice*, L. L. *ardesia, ardosia, ardesius lapis*, It. *ardesia* (and *lavagna*), Pg. *ardoisa* (and *picarra*) slate. Adelung says it is Celtic, but without any evidence. The Celtic words are connected with the English: W. *llech*, Gaelic *sgleat leac*, Ir. *leac.* Vergy derives it from *Ardes* in Ireland, a place not to be found in the maps. The slate used in France probably came from the *Ardennes* where the hills are composed of slate; hence the name: *Arduenna, Ardenna, Ardennensis, Ardenois, pierre Ardenoise, pierre Ardoise, lapis Ardesius* (cf. *Burdigala, Burdigalensis,* O. Fr. *Bordelois, Carthago, Carthaginiensis, Carthaginois*).

Arenga — *aringo.*

Aresta — *arista.*

Arête — *arista.*

Arezzo — *rezzo.*

Argano It., Sp. *argano argana argüe* a windlass, crane, Cat. *arga,* Pg. *argão* a crane; Fr. *argue* a wire-drawing machine; It. dim. *arganello,* Sp. *arganel,* Fr. *arganeau* a ring, anchorring; according to Ménage, for *organo* from *organum,* ὄργανον a tool. Vitruvius uses *ergata* = a windlass, which comes from the same root, so, perhaps, from ἐργάτης, which was altered so as to present a more familiar form.

Argine It. (m.) a dam; from *agger,* cf. *cecino* from *cicer* and the Ven. form *arzare* which preserves the *r*. *Ar* in Lat. = *ad* as in *arcessere* &c.; so *argine* points to a Lat. *urger = agger (adgerere)*. *Argine* = Sp. *arcen* an edge, border (cf. *arcilla* for *argilla*). Cf. the Ven. *arfiare = adflare* and v. Pott (Aufrecht and Kuhn's Zeitschr. 1, 326) who quotes *armessarius* from the L. Sal. and Wal. *armësariu = admissarius.*

Argolla Sp., Pg. *argola* an iron ring, iron collar, pillory: from *aro* hoop and *gola* throat, the Sp. *l* being liquefied as in *gollete.*

Argot Fr. slang, thieves' talk: the etymology, according to Diez, is unknown. Was *argot* a term of reproach from G. *arg* bad, mischievous, with a termination formed on the analogy of *bigot, cagot?* Some write it *ergot* from *ergo* a word usual in scholastic disputes, *ergoter* to dispute, wrangle. *Arcage* is found = dialect, perhaps formed of the analogy of *lang-age.*

Argot ergot Fr., Champ. *artot* the end of a dead twig, the spur of a cock &c. Der. unknown.

Argousin — *alguacil.*

Arguer Fr., according to Diez, to embroider, from O. H. G. *arahòn,* Grimm 2, 311, but *arguer* is to wire-draw gold with an *argue* a machine for drawing it = Sp. *argüe* for which v. *argano.*

Aria It. (poet. *aere*), Sic. *ariu* (m.), Sp. *aire,* Pg. *ar,* Pr. *air aire,* Fr. *air, air* all masc.; from *aer,* the It. fem. coming either from the L. L. plur. *aera (aira aria),* or from an adj. *aerea.* The same word means also "outward appearance", "disposition", and the Pr. *aire* means "family", "race", whence *de bon aire, de mal aire, de gentil aire* &c. This is the L. L. *arum* = *ager,* farm, house, family. The Fr. *aire* (f.),

E. *aery* is the same word: *un faucon de bonne aire* of good nest = of good family.

Aringa It., Sp. *arenque* (m.), Pr. *arenc*, Fr. *hareng* (h asp.), Wal. *hêring*, a *herring;* from the O. H. G. *harinc*, A. S. *hœring*, G. *hering*. Called in Du. *nêring* = G. *nährung* nourishment, food.

Aringo It., a pulpit, rostrum, place of combat, course, ring, Sp. Pg. *arenga*, Pr. *arengua*, Fr. *harangue* (h asp.) an *harangue;* It. *aringare*, Sp. *arengar*, Fr. *haranguer* to *harangue*. The Fr. asp. shows that the word comes from the O. H. G. *hring*, G. *ring* a ring, circle, stage, place of combat &c. Hence the Rom. word = a speech delivered before an assembly, cf. *homily* (ὁμιλία).

Arisco Sp. Pg. wild, untractable, shy; according to Constancio, who derives it from *arena*, = also *dry*, e. g. *terra arisca*. Not from *rigidus (riisco risco)*, the prosthesis of the *a* in adjectives being supported by no analogy, but from *arriscado* bold, free, rugged &c.

Arista It., the chine of a pig, Sp. *aresta* coarse tow, sack-cloth, thorn, fish-bone, Fr. *arête* fish-bone, Sp. *arista*, Fr. *areste arête*, Eng. *arris* edge of a stone, It. *resta* an ear of corn; from *arista* an ear of corn, a fish-bone.

Arlecchino It., Sp. *arlequin*, Fr. *arlequin* (formerly *harlequin*), a *harlequin*, a comic personage on the Italian stage, a buffoon &c., Sp. *arnequin* = a mannikin: of unknown, and perhaps quite fortuitous, origin. For the various etymologies v. Flögel, Gesch. des Grotesken p. 35. Genin gets it from *arlecamps (= Elycamps = Champs Elysées)* a churchyard at Arles, next = a ghost-chorus, the chief of which, Hellequin, was afterwards ludicrously represented in masquerades. This wants corroboration, though we may concede a connexion between *harlequin* and *hellequin* (g. v.). The word occurs so early in Fr. (Ren. 4, p. 146: *à sa siele et à ses lorains oc cinc cent cloketes au mains* [moins], *ki demenoient tel tintin con li maisnie hierlikin*) that its der. from the It. seems doubtful. It has a Du. appearance.

Arlotto It., Sp. *arlote*, Pr. *arlot*, O. Fr. Pic. *arlot harlot (herlot* Trist. 1, 173) a glutton, idler, O. Eng. *harlot herlote* a rascal; a word, says Trench, which though for the most part implying slight and contempt (but cf. Chauc. Prol.: he was a gentil *harlot* and a kind), implied nothing of that special form of sin to which the modern *harlot* refers: cf. for a similar process of meaning "lewd": it was formerly used of both sexes but now, like so many other words (bawd, courtesan, hoyden, shrew, termagant &c.), is confined to females. From the W. *her-*

3*

lawd, herlod a youth, lad, *herlodes* a damsel. Cf. L. *adulter*
orig. : - a young man.

Arma — *anima.*

Armadillo Sp., whence E. *armadillo;* from *armado,* so = the
armed beast.

Armellino ermellino It., Sp. *armiño,* Pr. *ermini ermin,* O. Fr.
erme ermine, Fr. *hermine ermine;* from *armenius* because found
in Armenia (O. Fr. *Ermenie*), by the Romans *"Mus ponticus"*
(Pontus). Others derive it from the G.; O. H. G. *harmo,* dim.
harmelin, M. H. G. *hermelin, harmo* = Lith. *szarmu.*

Armet — *elmo.*

Armoire Fr. a cupboard, for *arméoire* which would correspond
to an It. *armatoja,* prop. = a chest in which arms are kept,
armarium, whence O. Fr. *armaire,* = It. *armario,* Sp. *armario*
almario, W. *armari,* Bret. *armel,* G. *almer,* L. L. *armaria al-*
maria a bookcase, *armarius* a librarian, Eng. *ambry almery*
aumbry aumber. The *ambry* in churches is the niche by the
side of the altar to hold the sacred utensils.

Arna Pr. Cat. Sard. a moth (also *arda*), N. Pr. *darna, arnar* to
gnaw. Der. unknown. The Rh. has *tarna,* which corresponds,
however, to the It. *tarma.*

Arnese It., Sp. Pg. Pr. *arnes,* Fr. *harnois harnais* (h asp.), *har-*
ness; O. Fr. *harnas* for *harnase,* Fr. *harnacher,* Pr. *arnescar*
arnassar to *harness;* hence M. H. G. *harnasch,* N. *hardneskja.*
Not from the O. N. *idrn jdrn* (iron), which would have given
another form in the Rom., cf. *joli* from *jol,* but from the W.
haiarn, O. Bret. *hoiarn,* Ir. *iaran (iron)* = G. *isdrn.* It is not
usual for a language to form a derivative from a foreign root
which it has not itself adopted. We must, therefore, hold
that from the W. *haiarnaez,* iron-tools, was formed the Eng.
harness and from this the Rom. words. v. Villemarqué *(homar-*
nach), Schmeller 2, 238, Diefenb. Goth. Wb. 1, 15, Orig. Europ. p. 367.

Arnia It., Sp. Cat. *arna* bee-hive; from Gael. *arcan* cork? cf.
Sp. *corcha,* Pg. *curtiço* (1) cork, (2) bee-hive.

Aro Sp. Pg. a hoop, ring &c., O. Pg. circuit of a town; from
ἅλως?

Arpa It. Sp. Pg. Pr., Fr. *harpe* = (1) a *harp,* (2) Sp. Pr. Neap.
claw, hook; Pr. *arpar,* O. Fr. *harper,* It. *arpeggiare* to play
the harp; Sp. Pg. Pr. *arpar,* Fr. *harper* to seize, hook, tear;
It. *arpicare incrpicare* to clamber; Fr. *harpin* a hook, whence
se harpigner and *se harpailler* to grapple together, scuffle; It.
arpignone a large hook, *arpione* a hinge; Sp. *arpon,* Pg. *ar-*
pão, Fr. *harpon,* a harpoon, Fr. *harpeau* a grappling-iron. For
Sp. *arpa* a hook the Pg. has *farpa* (f == aspirate), so also
farpar farpão, whence ph. the It. *frappa* a lappet, *frappare*

snip out, slash, and the Pg. *farapo*, Sp. *harapo* a shred, tatter. All these forms have their origin in the G. *harfe*, O. H. G. *harpha*, O. N. *harpa*, A. S. *hcarpe*; Venant. Fort. who first uses *harpa*, calls it a barbarous, i. e. a Teutonic instrument. *(Romanusque lyrâ, plaudat tibi barbarus harpâ).* The *hooked* shape of the harp gave rise to the second meaning. The Gk. ἅρπη would scarcely have had an aspirate in Fr., nor can *harpon* come from *harpago* for then we should have had an O. Fr. *harpaon harpeon*. The Sp. Pg. *farpa* = shaft or point of a banner seems to be connected with the Arab. *'harbah* a short spear, Freyt. 1, 361ᵇ, whence, perhaps, It. *frappa, frappare,* cf. Pg. *farapo*, Sp. *harapo*.

Arpent Fr., Pr. *arpen*, O. Sp. *arapende* = Lat. *arepennis* Colum. 5, 1, 6: Galli semijngerum *arepennem* vocant. The Lat., however, is probably from the Celtic.

Arquebuse — *arcobugio*.

Arrabalde arrabal Sp. Pg. a suburb; from the Ar. *al-raba'd,* Freyt. 2, 111.

Arracher Fr., Pr. *araigar eradicar esraigar* to pull out, extract; from *eradicare exradicare* (Plaut., Ter., Varro), It. *eradicare sradicare.* With *arracher araigar* cf. *pencher,* Pr. *pengar* from *pendicare*.

Arraffare — *raffare*.

Arraial — *real* (2).

Arrappare — *rappare*.

Arrate Sp., Pg. *arratel* a pound of 16 ounces; from Ar. *ratl* 12 oz. Freyt. 2, 160.

Arrebol Sp. Pg. red appearance of the sky at sunrise or sunset; from the Ar. *rabâh* (with the article prefixed) nubes alba aut quæ modo alba modo nigra apparet, ph. contracted from *arrebabol* the final *l* as in *admiral* being the article which belonged to some fuller expression, v. Mahn. But Diez derives it with more probability from *rubor* with the Ar. article, *l* for *r* as in *marmol, arbol, bergel, e* for *u* (or *o*) as in *arredondar* from *arrodondar*. The verb *arrebolar* would = It. *arrovellare (rubellus)* and the subst. may come from the verb the *ar* = Lat. *ad*.

Arrecife Sp., Pg. *arrecife recife,* Fr. *récif ressif,* Eng. *reef*; from the Ar. *al-racif arracif* a row of stepping-stones across water, O. Pg. *arracef*.

Arrecisse — *recio*.

Arredio — *radio*.

Arredo — *redo*.

Arrel arrelde Sp. a 4 lb. weight; from the Basque *erraldea* a 10 lb. weight.

Arreo — *redo.*

Arresto It. O. Sp., Pg. *aresto* from the Fr. *arrêt* the decree of a supreme court of justice from which there is no appeal; properly = the conclusion of a law-transaction from *arrestare*, *arrêter* to stop, L. *ad-restare*, cf. G. *beschluss.*

Arriba Sp. Pg. = supra; from *ripa* cf. *derribar.*

Arriar — *arriser.*

Arrière — *retro.*

Arrière-ban — *bando.*

Arriero Sp., Pg. *arrieiro* a mule driver; from their shouting *arre* (N. Pr. It. *arri*) to urge on their mules: the word is prob. Arabic.

Arriffare — *riffa.*

Arrimar, arrimer — *rima.*

Arripiar Pg. to shudder; from *horripilare?*

Arriser Fr., Sp. *arriar* to let fall, let down, lower sails = prendre les ris, replier les voiles par moyen des ris et des garcettes; from the O. H. G. *arrisan* to fall down. Is *ris* from *arriser?*

Arrivare It., Sp. Pg. *arribar*, Pr. *aribar*, Fr. *arriver* to arrive; from *ripa*, L. L. *adripare*, It. *arripare* to come to shore. The introduction of this verb caused *advenire* to assume a special meaning, v. *avventura.*

Arroba Sp. Pg. a 25 lb. weight; from Ar. *alrob'a arrob'a* a 4th part (sc. of a cwt.) Freyt. 2, 113.

Arroche Fr. a plant, *arrach*, Wall. *aripp* (f.); from *atriplex* (n.), It. *atrepice.*

Arrogere arrosi arroso It. (antiquated) to add; from *arrogare*; for the change of conjugation cf. Rom. Gr. 2, 118.

Arrojar Sp., Pg. *arrojar* to fling, dart, sprout, *arrojo* intrepidity, fearlessness; possibly from *ruar*, as the Fr. *ruer* tr kick from *ruere* with *j* inserted to prevent the hiatus *rujar rojar arrojar*; v. *trage.*

Arroser — *ros* (1).

Arrostire — *rostire.*

Arroyo Sp., Pg. *arroio* a rivulet, brook, *arroyar* to overflow, O. Sp. *arrogio*, L. L. *arrogium*; ph. connected with the Lomb. *rogia* a stream for watering meadows, L. L. *rogium* (9th cent.), which Murat. (It. Antiq. 2, 1105) refers to ῥοή ῥέω. Cf. also the Wal. *crugé*, Ilung. *urók.*

Arros — *riso.*

Arrufar — *ruffa.*

Arrumar — *rombo.*

Arrumer — *rombo.*

Ars O. Fr. plur. the fore-quarters of a horse; from *armus*, *m* vanishing between *r* and a dental, cf. *dors*, *dort*, *ferté* from dorms, dormt, firm'tas, Fr. saigner un cheval des quatre ars fore and hind-quarters.

Arsenale arsanà It., Sp. Fr. E. arsenal, L. Gr. ἀρσενάλης; It. darsena, Sic. tirzanà the part of a harbour which is chained off, a wet-dock = Fr. darse darsine, Sp. atarazana, atarazanal covered shed, Pg. taracena tercena; from the Ar. dâr aççind'a house of industry, Freyt. 2, 69, 526.

Artalejo — artoun.

Artesa — artoun.

Articiocco It., Fr. artichaut an artichoke; perhaps corrupted from It. carcioffo, Sp. alcachofa, Pg. alcachofra which is from the Ar. al-'harshaf or al-harshof.

Artiga Sp. Cat., Pr. artigua land newly broken up for culture; Adelung refers it to the W. aru to plough. The Lat. arare would be nearer. The Basque has artica artiga, and to this language the word probably belongs.

Artigiano It., Fr. artisan, Sp. artesano, Pg. artezão an artisan; prob. = artitianus from artitus = bonis instructus artibus Fest. Then the Sp. must be for artezano. Cf. partigiano from partitus.

Artiglio It. a claw, talon, Sp. artijo, Pg. artelho a limb, joint, Pr. O. Fr. arteil (which form is still found in some of the dialects), Fr. orteil the toe; from articulus.

Artilha Pr. a fortification, entrenchment (?); O. Fr. artillier to fortify; Pr. artilharia, O. Fr. artillerie, O. Pg. artelharia catapults &c. or wagons for transporting them, Fr. artillerie, It. artiglieria heavy guns, artillery. From ars artis, cf. engin from ingenium, machine from μηχανή. O. Fr. artilleux = crafty, cunning.

Artisan — artigiano.

Artoun N. Pr. bread, It. artone (Veneroni); Sp. artalejo artalete a tart, artesa, Pg. arteça a kneading trough. Not from ἄρτος but prob. from the Basque artoa maize-bread, which Humboldt says meant orig. acorn-bread, from artea a sort of oak.

Aruñar — arañar.

Arveja — ervo.

Arzon — arcione.

As — asso.

Asca Lomb. a preposition = præter; from absque?

Ascella It., Pr. aissela, Cat. axella shoulder; from axilla, whence, accord. to Cicero, ala a wing, shoulder. Axilla became ascilla as early as Isidorus.

Ascia — accia.

Asciolvere It. to breakfast, Rh. ansolver = solvere jejunia.

Asciugare asciutto — suco.

Ascla Pr. Cat. a splinter, asclar to split; from astula (MSS. for assula), astla, ascla. Hence, too, the Sp. astil handle of an

axe, *astilla* a chip, splinter, O. Fr. *astele*, *astillar* to splinter,
astillero a spear-stand, Fr. *attelle (= atelle)* a splint (in surgery)
also = *hames* (v. *atteler* = to yoke), Pr. *astela*. In Occ.
fend-asclat = fendu.

Asco Sp. Pg., Sard. *ascu*, Pr. *ais* loathing, disgust, *ascoso asco-*
roso asqueroso loathsome. Some derive from the Gk. αἰσχος
αἰσχρός, but the Goth. *aiviski*, A. S. *arise*, adj. Du. *aisk*
aisch, of the same signification, would be nearer: cf. the G.
interj. of disgust *aiks!* Larramendi and Diefenbach refer the
word to the Basque *ascó (asqui)* much, too much; but the B.
word for *asco* is *nasca* which from the Sp. would have had no
reason for altering. Cf. also the Rh. *ascher* impure, *aschria*
impurity. The Sp. has also *usgo* for *asco*.

Ascoltare **scoltare** It., O. Sp. *ascnchar*, Sp. *escuchar*, Pg. *escu-*
tar, Pr. *escoutar*, Fr. *écouter* to listen; from *auscultare* which,
however, would not have given *asciltare*, so that this latter
form must have existed in the Latin. Hence It. *ascolta scolta*,
Sp. *escucha* a scutry, *scout*.

Ascua Sp. Pg. red-hot coal; prob. from the O. H. G. *ascá*, Goth.
azgó, G. *asche*, E. *ash*, *ascua* from *asca* as *eslingua* from *slinga*.
Cf. the Lat. *favilla* = ashes and spark. The Basq. *auscua* is
ph. of the same origin.

Ascar Sp., Pg. *asseiar* to adorn; from *assidere* to suit, become?
Asermar **asesmar** — *esmar*.
Asestar — *sesta*.
Asi — *cosi*.
Asiento — *sentare*.
Asinha Pg. adv. for L. *statim*; from *agina*, or from *ad signum?*
Asir Sp. Pg., O. Sp. *azir* to grasp, seize; from the Lat. *apisci*,
whence *apiscire* (cf. *sequi sequire*), *apsir*, *asir*, Pres. *apiscor*
apsco asgo.
Asma asima ansima It., *asthma;* from *asthma* (ἄσθμα). Hence
ansimare (1) to pant, (2) to desire eagerly, cf. Sp. *anhelar*. For
ansimare are used also *ansiare ansare*, from *anxius* (Sp. *ansiar*
= to covet). *Ansimare ansima* are formed as if connected with
anxius.
Asolare — *scialare*.
Asomar — *sommo*.
Aspettare to wait for, Wal. *asteptà*. If from *adspectare (aspetto*
look. = *adspectus)* the O. H. G. *warten* = aspicere and expectare may be compared; if from *expectare*, cf. *asciutto* from
exsuctus.
Aspo naspo It., Sp. *aspa*, O. Fr. *hasple*, Pic. *haple* a reel; from
O. H. G. *haspa haspel*. The gender in It. has conformed to
that of *naspo* from *inaspare*.

Assai It., O. Sp. *asaz*, Pg. *assaz*, Pr. *assatz*, Fr. *assez*; from *ad satis*.

Assassino It., Sp. *asesino*, Pr. *assassin*, Fr. *assassin*, an *assassin*. From the Ar. *'hashishin* the members of an Eastern sect, who, intoxicated by a drink (*'hashish* Golius p. 613) prepared from the hemp-plant, took an oath to the Sheik or Old Man of the Mountain (*Shaikh al-ĝabal*) that they would do murder in his service if required. The word was unknown in Europe before the 12th century.

Assembler — *sembrare*.

Assentare — *sentare*.

Assettare It., to arrange, set in order, put on table (Pr. *assetar*); hence It. *rassettare* to mend, It. *assetto* ornament, Pr. *assieta* an arrangement, Fr. *assiette* a place at table (v. Casenenve) whence = a *plate*. The It. *assettare* also means "to cut off", "castrate", in which sense it must come from *secare sectus*. This sense may have given rise that of "ordering, arranging" just as O. H. G. *skeran* to shear is connected with *skerjan* to portion off, arrange. It. *assetto* a little board, is from *assis*.

Asses — *assai*.

Assiette — *assettare*.

Assisa — *assises*.

Assises Fr. (plur.), E. *assizes*, an extraordinary session of a court of justice, a session on a certain day named beforehand. O. Fr. also sing. *assise*, Pr. *asiza*, which meant, besides, a decree passed at such a session, a decree for taxing, a tax, hence L. L. *levare assisiam* to raise a tax, It. *assisa* tribute, excise, Neap. *assisa* an impost on provisions. It is a participle from the O. Fr. Pr. *assire* to place, place oneself, Lat. *assidere*, and so meant anything placed or laid in position, Fr. *assise* = a layer of stones, Pr. := place, position (also *cizias* plur.). Thus it would prop. mean not the session itself but the day appointed for it or the decree passed in it. A variant form of *assise* is found in the Fr. *accise* (formed as if from *accidere*) == E. *excise*.

Asso It., Sp. Pr. Fr. *as*, Pg. *az* an *ace*; from the Lat. *as* which denoted a unit. Muratori, misled by the expression *lasciare uno in asso* to leave one in the lurch, derived it from L. L. *absus* = *ager incultus*. But this phrase, like the corresponding G. *einen im stiche lassen (stich* = *ace)* is, probably, borrowed from card-playing.

Assoager assouagier Fr., Pr. *assuaviar* to *assuage*; from *suavis* cf. *levi-are, molli-are* &c.

Assommer — *salma*.

Assouvir Fr. to satiate. Perhaps from the Goth. *ga-sôthjan* (χορ-

τἁζειν) *v = th* as in *pouvoir* = O. Fr. *podoir*, Pr. *poder*. The deriv. from *adsatire*, *adsair*, *assa-ou-ir* (cf. *évanouir*), *assouir*, *assouvir*, is inadmissible. We should expect *assavouir*. Gachet instances an O. Fr. *asouffr*, which points to *sufficere*, a more satisfactory etymon than *ga-sôthjan*, which is too remote.

Assoviar — *soffiare*.

Astilla — *ascla*.

Astio aschio envy, rancour, *adastiare* to envy, grudge; from the Goth. *haifsi-s* discord, *haifst-j-an* = *ast-i-are*.

Astiou — *hâte*.

Astore It., O. Sp. *aztor*, Sp. Pg. *azor* (whence the name of the islands *Azores*), Pr. *austor*, O. Fr. *ostor*, Fr. *autour* a goshawk. Usually derived from *astur* (= the bird of *Asturia*), Maternus Firmicus A. D. 400; but this would have given *astre*. The grammarian Caper mentions a word *acceptor* as vulgarly used for *accipiter; azor* would = *acceptorem* just as *rezar = recitare*. The Pr. *austor* is, probably, an irregular form of *astor*, like *austronomia* = *astronomia*. The N. Pr. is *astou*. From *azor* may come the Sp. verb *azorar* to frighten, bewilder, orig. of birds chased by the hawk, *perdiz azorada; cf.* Sp. *amilanar* to frighten, from *milano* a kite, Cat. *esparverar* from *esparver* a sparrow-hawk.

Astre aistre O. Fr., Fr. *âtre* hearth, L. L. *astrum;* hence Lomb. *astrac*, Sic. *astracu*, L. L. *astricus plastar* (pavement), Vocab. S. Galli, O. H. G. *astrih*, G. *estrich*. Diefenbach derives it from the Lat. *asser*. The addition of the article gives the It. *lastra* a slab, *lastrico* pavement, Sp. *lastre lastra*, Pg. *lastro* a stone-slab, ballast.

Astreindre — *étreindre.*

Astro It. Sp. Pg., Pr. Fr. *astre*, a constellation, also = fate, luck. Hence Sp. Pg. *astroso* unlucky (Isidor. *astrosus quasi malo sidere natus);* O. Sp. *astrugo*, Pr. *astruc* lucky. Hence Pr. *benastre*, *benastruc*, O. Sp. *malastrugo*, Pr. *malastre*, *malastruc*, O. Fr. *malostru* for *malastru*, Fr. *malotru* (= ineptus); It. *disastro*, Sp. *desastro*, Fr. *désastre*, E. *disaster.*

Astuccio It., Sp. *estuche* (*estui* in Berceo), Pg. *estojo*, Pr. *estug estui*, Fr. *étui* a case, box, repository; Pg. *estojar*, Pr. *estuiar estoiar*, O. Fr. *estuier* to preserve, store up. *Estug étui* come from the M. H. G. *stuche stauche* a case for arms (v. Adelung); the form *astuccio* (Veron. *stuccio*) must be referred to an O. H. G. *stûchjo*, cf. *guancia* from *wankja.*

Asurarse Sp. to be burnt (of meat); for *arsurarse*, cf. It. Pr. *arsura*, Sard. *assura* (and Lat. *assus = arsus*).

Ataballo taballo It., Sp. *atabal*, Pg. *atabale* a Moorish kettle-drum, It. *timballo*, Sp. *timbal (timbrel);* from Ar. *al-'tabl, a't-'tabl.*

Atal — *cotale.*

Atalaya Sp. a watch-tower; from Ar. *'tal'aah* a view, Freyt. 3, 65.

Atambor — *tamburo.*

Atancar — *stancare.*

Atanto — *cotanto.*

Atar Sp. Pg. Cat. to tie, lace; from *aptare* (cf. ἁρμόζειν).

Atarazana — *arsenale.*

Atarfe Sp. tamarisk; from Ar. *a't-'tarfá.*

Atargea — *targa.*

Ataud Sp. Pg., Pr. *tauc*, O. Fr. *taüt taüc*, Neap. *tavuto* a box, coffin; from Ar. *al-tábút, at-tábút.*

Ataviar Sp. Pg. to adorn, *atavío* embellishment; from the Goth. *ga-tevjan* to set in order, *téva* order, or better from Goth. *taujan* (pret. *tavida*), A. S. *tavian*, E. *taw*, Du. *touwen*, O. H. G. *zawjan* to prepare, dress, cf. Sp. *parar* to prepare, adorn. The *a* = Lat. *ad.*

Ate O. Fr. hot, rash, Charlem. v. 613 (not *atés*), also *aate, aatir* to incite, *aatie, atine* deadly enmity. From the Norse *at* incitement to fight, *att* incited (hence *ate*), *etia* to incite. The form *austie* is not connected with the It. *astio.*

Até — *te.*

Atear — *tea.*

Atelier Fr. a workshop = Pr. *astelier*, Sp. *astillero* (from *hasta* but v. *ascla*) a lance-stand, stand for tools, workshop. The N. Pr. *astelier astier* = an andiron (place for laying logs).

Aterecer — *intero.*

Atisbar Sp. to search, inquire into; from Basque *atisbeatu* which is compounded of *ateis* closed doors, and *beatu* to spy.

Atizar — *tizzo.*

Atoar — *touer.*

Atobar Sp. to astonish; from *tuba*, cf. *attonare* from *tonus.*

Atorar — *tuero.*

Atracar Sp. a nautical word = to come alongside a ship; from *attrahicare* or better from Du. *trekken, aantrekken.*

Atravesar — *travieso.*

Âtre — *astre.*

Atreverse Sp. to be too forward, to venture, O. Sp. *treverse.* From *sibi attribuere, sibi tribuere* == to presume, be arrogant. The existence of the verb *atribuir tribuir* does not affect this etymology. The Sp. keeps the Lat. accent *atrévo* = *attribuo.*

Atril Sp. a reading-desk, lectern; ph. corrupted from *latril letril* as if from *lectorile*, O. Fr. *letrin, el atril* being a mistake for *el latril.* The form *letril* occurs.

Atropellar — *tropa.*

Attacher, attaquer — *tacco.*

Atteler — *teler*.

Attelle — *ascla*.

Attiffer — *tiffer*.

Attillare It., Sp. *atildar*, Pg. *atilar*, Pr. *atilhar* to deck, trim; from a L. *attitulare* to below the utmost care on dress &c., prop. to forget not a *jot* or tittle, from It. *titolo* = dot over a letter, Sp. *tilde*, Pg. *til*. L. L. *attitulare* = to mark (adorn): *crucis signaculo frontem ejus attitulans.*

Attimo It. a moment; from ἄτομος. Papias has: *hora habet atomos XXII milia.*

Attiser — *tizzo*.

Attizzare — *tizzo*.

Atturare It. to stop, Sp. Pg. *aturar* to hold out, persevere, endure (ph. for *aturarse*), Cat. Pr. *aturar* to stop, shut up, keep back, *s'aturar* to hold up, exert oneself, persevere, *atur* exertion; from *obturare* (with change of prep.) to stop up, hence = to stop, hold out, persevere (cf. G. use of *aufhalten*). The Sp. occurs in the Lat. sense. Shortened from *atturare* is the It. *turare* (hence *tura* a dam), Sp. *turar*, not from a Lat. primitive.

Attutare — *tutare*.

Atufar — *tufo*.

Aturdir — *stordire*.

Aubain Fr. a foreigner, L. L. *albanus;* from *alibi* with the suffix *anus* which is frequently added to adverbs, cf. *proche prochain, loin lointain, ante ancien.*

Aube — *alba*.

Auberge — *albergo*.

Aubier Fr., Pr. *albar* sap, the white soft wood next the bark; from *albus (albarius)* whence, too, L. *alburnum*, O. Fr. *aubour*, Lim. *oouboun*.

Aubour — *aubier*.

Auce abce O. Sp. (f.) fate, lot, *con dios e con la vuestra auce* Poem. d. Cid v. 2376; *buen auce* v. 2379; the etymology is doubtful. Apul. Met. 9 has: *bona et satis secunda aucilla* which may come from *auce* (v. s. bubbone), but it is better, perhaps, to refer it to *auspicium* which might follow the gender of *suerte*. With *auce abce* is connected the Sp. *aciago*, Pg. *aziago* unlucky through the O. Val. form *abziach;* the *i* of the Sp. supports the derivation from *auspicium*, though the suffix *ago* for *aco* is unusual. Diez thinks that the etymology remains to be discovered. May not *auce abce* come from *avis avica*, *aucilla* = *avicella*? If so the words *abce mala*ᵒ(Alex. 545) would correspond to the Lat. *mala avis.*

Aucun — *'alcuno*.

Auferrant — *ferrant*.

Aufin — *alfido.*

Auge It., Sp., Pg. the highest point (of glory &c.); from the
Ar. *auġ* an astronomical word borrowed from the Persian
auk, Freyt. 1, 69.

Auge Fr. (f.) a trough; from *alveus*, It. *alveo.*

Augurio It., Sp. *agüero*, Pg. *agouro*, Pr. *auguri augur agur*, *aür*,
O. Fr. *eür heür*, Fr. *heur*, Wall. *aveure*, omen, luck; It. *augurare*, Sp. Pr. *augurar agurar*, Fr. *augurer* to *augur*, Pr. *ahu-
rar*, O. Fr. *heürer* to bless, Wal. *urà* to wish luck; from *augurium augurare*, the derivation of *heur* &c. from *hora* being suf-
ficiently disproved both by the gender and by the forms in
Pr., O. Fr., and Wallon, though the *h* may have been prefixed from a false notion of the etymology, cf. *heureux*, O. Fr.
eüreux = Pr. *aürós*, It. *auguroso*, L. L. *auguriosus; horosus* is
nowhere found. Hence we have Pr. *bonaür*, Fr. *bonheur, ma-
laür, malheur;* It. *sciagurato, sciaurato*, O. Sp. *xaurado*, Sp.
xauro wretched from *exauguratus*, It. *sciagura, sciaura* mis-
fortune; E. *enure;* It. *uria* is a plur. form from *augurium.*

Aujourd'hui — *oggi.*

Aullar Sp. (*alular* Berceo) to howl; from *ejulare* as *ayuno* from
jejunium.

Aumaille Fr. horned cattle (f., and generally in plur.); from *animalia* (cf. *merveille* from *mirabilia*, and v. *ora*). Rh. *armal*, Wall.
amà a bullock, Piedm. Parm. *animal* = a pig, Rom. *animela*
a sow, cow, mare, bitch &c.: v. Pott, Höfer's Zeitschr. 3, 161.

Aumône — *limosina.*

Aumusse — *almussa.*

Aun — *anche.*

Aune — *alna.*

Aunée — *enola.*

Auques — *algo.*

Aura ora It., Sp. Pg. Pr. Rh. *aura*, O. Fr. *ore* a breeze from
aura; hence the Pr. *aurat*, O. Fr. *ore';* Pr. *auratge*, O. Fr. *orage*
a breeze (*lo dous auratge, lo fer auratge*), Fr. *orage* a storm,
Sp. *orage;* Sp. *orear*, Cat. *oretjar* to refresh, *oreo oretj*, It.
oreggio, Pr. *aurei* a gentle gale. From *oreggio* is to be distinguished It. *orezzo rezzo* a cool, shady place, from a form *au-
ritium. Arezzo* is also found, *a* = *au* as in *ascoltare.*

Aurone Fr. the plant southernwood; from *abrotonum*, It. *abro-
tano.*

Aus N. Pr. (m.) al. *aou*, Champ. *ause* the fleece of a sheep; from
the Lat. *hapsus* (Celsus) on which the grammarian Caper
(Putsch p. 2249) remarks: *hapsum vellera lanæ non hapsus*, cf.
hapsum vellus lanæ Gloss. Isid. The *p* is lost as in *neipsum*,
Pr. *neus, malaptus malaut.*

Aussi Fr., O. Fr. *alsi ausine*, Florent. *alsi;* from *aliud sic.*

Autant Fr., O. Sp. *autan;* from *aliud tantum.*

Autel Fr.; from *alius talis.*

Autillo Sp. a screech-owl; from *otus* (ὠτός) a horned-owl, for *a-otilla.*

Auto Sp. a decree, edict; from *actum,* It. *atto.* Hence *auto de fe,* Pg. *auto da fé* a religious decree.

Autour — *astore.*

Autruche — *struzzo.*

Auvent Fr. a shed, awning; apparently the same as the Pr. *anvan amban* a projection or balcony to defend the entrance to a town; *an = au* as in *erraument = errannment. Anvan* may be from *an = ante* (cf. *angarda*) and *vannus* or *vertus.*

Avacciare It. to hasten, *avaccio (accio)* haste; a participial verb like *cacciare; abigere abactus abactiare;* hence O. Cat. adv. *yvaç,* v. Chron. d'Esclot.

Avachir Fr. to relax, give in, languish, to become weak, flaccid; from O. H. G. *weichjan* to *weaken,* the *a* prefixed as in *avilir, attendrir* &c. (Rom. Gr. 1, 296). Wall. *s'avachi* = to sink.

Avalange avalanche (cf. O. Fr. *fresenge = fresenche*), whence It. *valanga* an *avalanche;* from *avaler* to descend (O. Fr. *aval = down, amont = up,* whence *montare, monter, mount, amount*), which has also given *avalaison* a torrent. Another form is *lavange lavanche,* Pr. *lavanca* partly from *avalange,* partly from L. L. *labina* (Isidorus, who derives it from *labi*), Rh. *lavina,* G. *lawine.* Others derive these from G. *lauen* to thaw. *l'alance* is the same word.

Avancer avant avantage — *anzi.*

Avanid It. Pg., Fr. *avanie* oppression, exaction, prop. = a poll-tax extorted from the Christians by their Turkish rulers. Probably a Turkish word, M. Gk. ἀβανία.

Avannotto It. a fish of not more than a year old; from *ab anno* (Ménage).

Avanti avansare — *anzi.*

Avaria It. Pg., Fr. *avarie,* E. *average* prop. = damage at sea; from the G. *haferei;* Du. *haverij* = sea-damage, *haf* = sea (Scandin.).

Aveo Fr. prep. = It. Sp. *con,* O. Fr. *avoc avuec avec;* from O. Fr. *ab = apud* and *oc = hoc;* cf. O. Fr. *por-uec* "by means of this" Rom. Gr. 2, 405. Another form is *avecques.* Cf. *appo* and *o.*

Aveindre Fr. to take out, take forth, Occ. *avédre,* Champ. *avainder* (1st conj.); from *abemere* to take away (Festus: *abemito significat demito auferto*).

Avel O. Fr. Champ. (plur. *aviaux*) = anything precious; not from *velle* but from *lapillus,* It. *lapillo* (= bijou). The first syllable was mistaken for the article and thus the word became *avel*, cf. It. *arello* from *labellum*.

Avello It. a stone coffin, Mod. *larello*, Mil. *navell* a vessel of marble &c.; from *labellum* a vessel, L. L. (9ᵗʰ century), *lavellum* == a coffin, v. Muratori and Rom. Gr. 1, 240. *l'as* also in L. L. == a coffin.

Avenant Fr., Pr. *avinen* (hence It. *avvenante avvenente*) becoming, next; from *adveniens*, cf. *conveniens*, becoming, G. *bequem* from *biqueman* to come.

Averiguar — *santiguar*.

Avés abés O. Sp. adv. == *vix*; from *ad vix* like *assaz* from *ad satis*, Rh. *vess*. Hence *malavez*.

Avestrus — *struzzo*.

Aveu — *voeu*.

Aveugle — *avocolo*.

Avieso Sp., Pg. *avesso* perverse; from *averso*, O. Sp. *enresar* == *enversar*, cf. *rivescio*.

Aviron Fr. an oar, L. L. *abiro*. Perhaps from *ad gyrum* as moving circularly. This derivation is supported by the Lothr. *aiviron* an instrument which in working describes a circle.

Avis aviser — *viso*.

Avocolo vocolo It., Fr. *aveugle* blind, It. *avocolare*, Fr. *aveugler*, Pr. *avogolar* to blind. From *aboculus*, on the analogy of *abnormis amens* &c., cf. the L. Gr. ἀπ' ὀμμάτων or ἀπόμματος ἐξόμματος.

Avoi O. Fr. interjection expressing ill-humoured astonishment. Various derivations have been given: (1) *ah voie* == It. *eh via*, (2) Lat. *evoé*, (3) an ecclesiastical refrain *evovæ*, the vowels of *"seculorum amen!"* The true etymology is *ah voi* ah! see! == Span. *afé* (Cid 1325), where *v* == *f* (cf. *he*) == *ah ve*. Cf. O. Fr. *voici* and *veci*.

Avol Pr. bad, wretched, sbst. *avoleza*. The word occurs also, but very rarely, in O. Sp., O. Cat., and O. Pg. *Avolome* (Berceo) == *ladron* (Sanchez). In Pr. the word is commonly used as the opposite to *pros*, Fr. *preux*, and is written *aul*, cf. *freul* from *frevol*. It comes from a L. L. *adrolus* (== *advena*) mentioned by Ducange. *Adrolatus* would make *advolus arol*, just as *cordatus* gives Sp. *cuerdo*, *clinatus* Pr. *clin* &c. The first meaning would be stranger, homeless; cf. G. *elend* == (1) *peregrinus*, (2) *miser*.

Avoltore avoltojo It., Pr. *voltor*, Fr. *vautour*, E. *vulture*; from *volturius*, Sp. *biutre*, Pg. *abutre*, from *vultur*. Hence Sp. *buitron* a partridge-net, a fish-net; cf. Fr. *epervier* == sparrow-hawk and fish-net. Littré (hist. de la langue franç.), instead of *vulturius*, gives *vulturem* (for *vultürem*) as the original of the Fr. *vautour* &c.

Avorio It., Pr. *avori evori*, Fr. *ivoire* (m.) ivory; from *eboreus*.

Avouer Fr., Pr. *avoar*, E. *avow* to confess, own, acknowledge. not from *advotare* but from *adrocare*, as *avoué* = *advocatus*. Pr. Pg. *avocar* meant to call to one, own, acknowledge, L. L. *advocare ut filium suum*. Hence *areu*.

Avoutre O. Fr. Pr. a bastard, Bret. *avoultr;* from *adulter*, It. *avoltero* an adulterer, Wal.*votru* a pandar. Hence Eng.*avoutry*. For the *v* v. Rom. Gr. 1, 164. The Wall. *avotron arutron* has also the sense of a shoot, sapling.

Avutarda — *ottarda*.

Avvegnaché It. = Lat. *etsi;* from *avvenire* = prop. it might happen that.

Avvenente — *avenant.*

Avventare It. to throw. The Pr. *ventar*, O. Fr. *venter* = to throw to the wind, whence the It. word. *Aventare* to thrive is from *avvenire*, Sie. *abbentare* to find rest, *abento* rest = *adventus* (se. Christi).

Avventura It., Sp. Pg. Pr. *aventura*, Fr. *aventure*, E. *adventure*, G. *abenteuer*, accident, luck, peril (*aventure de mort* = death-aventure), particularly of knightly combat; from *advenire* to happen (cf. *arriver*).

Axedrez Sp., Pg. *xadrez enxadrez* the game of chess; from Ar. *ash-she'trang* chess-board, this from the Persian, which has taken the word from the Sanskrit *chatur-anga*, lit. "having four members", viz. the four sets of men with which the game was originally played in the East, or the four different arms of which each set was composed.

Axedrea — *satureja.*

Axenjo Sp., O. Sp. *enxenso* wormwood; from *absinthium*.

Axuar axovar Sp. bride's trousseau; from Ar. *ash-shuwar*.

Aye Fr. (also *aie*) interjection; from the old imperative *aie* "help"!

Ayer — *ieri.*

Ayo Sp. governor, tutor, *aya* nurse, It. *ajo aja*. The O. H. G. has *hagan haggjan* to nurse, hence *hagjo* and *heio* a warden; but the Sp. is more probably derived from the Basque *ayoa* "one who guards and attends", whence *zayu* a guardian, *seinzayu* a nurse. Is the It. word from the Sp.? Others derive *aya* from *avia*, *ayo* from a corresponding *avius*.

Ayunar — *giunare.*

Ayunque — *incude.*

Aza — *haza.*

Aza Pg. (1) a handle, ear of a pitcher &c. = Sp. *asa*, Cat. *ansa*, *nansa*, Lat. *ansa*, (2) a bird's wing = Sp. *ala* not used in Pg., perhaps also from *ansa*, the wing being regarded as a handle.

The Gloss. Isid. has: *acia ala*, but whence is this? Graevius mentions in connection with it *axilla*, whence *ala*.

Azada — *accia*.

Azafate Sp. Pg. a low basket, tray: from Ar. *al-safa't as-safa't*.

Azafran — *zafferano*.

Azagaya — *zagaia*.

Azaut adaut Pr. agreeable, *azautar* to cheer, enliven: from *adaptus, adaptare* (cf. *malaut* from *malaptus*), thus = It. *adatto* adopted, fitting, agreeable.

Azcona Sp., corrupted *fascona*, Pr. *ascona*, O. Cat. *escona* a dart: prob. from O. H. G. *asc*, G. *esche* an ash (*eschiner schaft* Nibel. 537). Pg. *ascona* = comet (Lat. *hasta*).

Azemar — *esmar*.

Azesmar — *esmar*.

Azevinho — *acebo*.

Azienda — *faccenda*.

Azinho — *elce*.

Azofar Sp. brass, latton: from Ar. *al-çofr aç-çofr*.

Azogue Sp., Pg. *azougue* quicksilver: from Ar. *al-zuway az-zuway* or *alzibaq azzibaq*, which comes from the Persian. Freyt. 2, 219.

Azor — *astore*.

Azote Sp., Pg. *açoute* a whip, *azotar, açoutar*, It. *ciottare* to flog: from Ar. *al-sau't as-sau't*.

Azucar — *zucchero*.

Azucena Sp. a white lily; from Ar. *al-susan assusan*, Heb. *shushan*, Gr. σοῦσον, Freyt. 2, 375, whence the name Susanna.

Azufaifa azufeifa Sp. Pg. jujube-tree, fruit of jujube-tree: from Ar. *al-zofaizef az-zofaizef*.

Azufre — *solfo*.

Azza — *accia*.

Azzardo It., Fr. *hasard* (*h* asp.), Pr. *azar*, Cat. *atsar hazard* chance, Sp. Pg. *azar* an unlucky throw, unforeseen accident, ill-luck; *jeu de hasard* = game of chance; It. *azzardare*, Fr. *hasarder*, to hazard, stake, wager, L. L. *ludere ad azarum*. O. Fr. *hazart* = a dice-player, *hazarder* to be fond of dice or hazard-playing. The Fr. *d* is epenthetical, and the It. is derived from the Fr. The original form is evidently the O. It. *zaro*, It. *zara* = a throw of 3 aces. Perhaps from the Ar. *zahr*, a die (root *zahara* to glisten, bo white Freyt. 2, 261). The Ar. article prefixed, *al-zahr az-zahr*, gives the commoner Rom. form, v. Mahn (Etym. Untersuch.).

Azzimare — *esmar*.

Azzuro assuolo It., Sp. Pg. *azal*, Pr. Fr. *azur*, dark blue *azure*: from Pers. *ldzuward*, whence *lapis lazuli* the sapphire.

B.

Baba bableca babosa — *bava.*

Babasorro Sp. a coarse, ill-bred fellow: prop = a sack of beans, a nickname of the Alabenses; from the Basque *baba* bean and *zorro* sack.

Babbacolo babbuasso — *babbeo.*

Babbeo, babbacolo, babbano, babbuasso It. a blockhead: Pr. *babau,* Pic. *baba* a fop, dotard; It. *babbole,* Fr. *babioles, baubles;* the root is seen in the Lat. *babulus* (Apuleius), *baburrus stultus* Gloss. Isid.; *baburra stultitia* Gloss. Placid.; cf. Irish, W. *baban* a child, Eng. *babe, babby.*

Babbo It. father, Dante Inf. 32 *nè da lingua che chiami mamma o babbo,* only used by children, but in Sard. *babu* is the proper word for father; so Rh. *bab,* Wal. fem. *babe* a midwife, Hung. *baba,* M. H. G. *babe.* The word belongs to many languages.

Babbuino It., Sp. *babuino,* Fr. *babouin,* Eng. *baboon;* probably akin to the Fr. *babine* an ape's or cow's lip, and to the G. provincial *bäppe* a mouth, v. *beffa.*

Babeurre Fr. buttermilk = *bat-beurre: battre le beurre* = to make butter.

Babil Fr. *babiller,* Eng. *babble,* G. *babbeln;* an onomatop.

Babine — *babbuino.*

Babioles — *babbeo.*

Bâbord Fr. larboard, left side of a ship; from Du. *bak-boord,* A. S. *bæcbord* back-board, because in steering the helmsman turns his back to that side.

Babouches Fr. (f. pl.) whence Sp. *babuches* Turkish slippers; from Ar. *bâbûg, bâbûsh,* this from Pers. *pâpûsh* foot-covering.

Bac Fr. a flat-boat, ferry-boat, Rouchi = a trough; cf. Du. *bak* a tray, trough, Bret. *bag bak,* v. *bacino.* Hence dim. *baquet* (E. *bucket*), and *baille (bac-ula),* whence Du. *balie,* Swed. *balja,* G. *balge.*

Bacalao — *cabeliau.*

Baccalare It., Pr. *bacalar,* Fr. *bachelier,* in later It. *baccelliere,* Sp. *bachiller,* Pg. *bacharel.* Diez is unable to fix the etymology: he mentions some attempts that have been made, e. g. Fr. *bas-cavalier,* Lat. *baculus,* or Gael. *bachall (= baculus).* Littré gives *vassal* as the etymon. Better from the celtic, W. *bach* little, *bachgen* a boy, *bachgenes, baches* (dim.) a little darling, *bachigyn* a very little thing. Hence Fr. *bacelle, bacelote, bachele, bachelette* a young girl or servant, *baceller* to make love, serve apprenticeship, commence a study; *bacellerie* youth; *bachelage* art and study of chivalry. Hence *bacheler, bachelard, bachelier* a young man, aspirant to knighthood,

apprentice in arms or sciences, v. Wedgwood. The L. L.
was *baccalarius*, which, in the sense of an academician not
yet admitted to his degree, was corrupted into *baccalaureus:
do baccharo e do sempre verde louro*, Lusiad 3, 97.

Baccello It. hull, pod, husk, also blockhead; from L. *bacca*.
The Sp. *baya* (from *bacca*) also means husk or pod.

Bacchetta It., Sp. *baqueta*, Fr. *baguette* a switch; from *baculus*
with a change of suffix, cf. Rom. Gr. II, 224.

Bachele — *bagascia*.

Bacheller — *bacca*.

Bachiller — *baccalare*.

Bacia Sp. Pg. a basin: L. L. *baccea*, v. *bacino*.

Bacino It., O. Sp. Pr. *bacin*, Fr. *bassin*, Eng. *basin:* first found
in Gregory of Tours: *pateris ligneis quas vulgo buchinon (buchi-
nos) vocant*, v. Ducange. The Isid. Glossary has *bacca vas
aquarium*. It cannot be from the G. *becken*, which would have
given *baquin* in French, v. s. *franco*. The Du. *bak* bowl,
trough, must be referred to the same root, which is, probably,
the Celtic *bac* a cavity, cf. *bacia*.

Bacio It. (a better but scarcer form is *bagio*), Sp. *beso*, Pg. *beijo*,
Pr. *bais*, E. *buss* a kiss; vb. *baciare* &c.; from *basium basiare*
(mostly poetical).

Bacio It. a site exposed to the North, adv. *a bacio* towards the
North. It is formed on the analogy of *solatio* a place exposed
to the sun (from *solata* sunshine with the suffix *ivus*), and
meant properly a shady place, *obacio* for *opac-io*; the Cat. has
obaga, N. Pr. *ubac*, Dauph. *lubac (= l'ubac)*, Com. *ovich* and
vagh, Romagn. *bègh*, Gen. *luvegu*.

Bacioceo a blockhead, = *baccello* with a change of suffix; cf.
Augustus using *baceolus = stultus* Suet. Aug. c. 27.

Bacler Fr. to bar, bolt; from *baculus*.

Baco It. a silk-worm, worm generally; from *bombyx* (βόμβυξ),
L. L. *bombax*, whence *bombáco baco*, Parm. *beg bega*. The
Wal. has *bambác* from *bombyx*. The form *big-atto big-attolo*
is best referred to *bombyx*, and so shortened from *bombigatto*.

Bacococo — *albercocco*.

Bacon O. Fr. Pr. E., from the O. H. G. *bacho*, Du. *bak*, E. *back*
a chine, but Wedg. from O. Du. *backe*, Du. *bigge* a pig.

Bacoro Pg. a one-year-old pig; perhaps from Arab. *bekr* the
first born, a young beast, Freyt. 1, 145ᵃ. Nothing to do with
the preceding word.

Badalucco It. a skirmishing (velitatio), a trifling or toying, Pr.
badaluc baluc, Ven. *badaloco*, Com. *barloch baloch*, It. *balocco*
a gaper (also = badalucco), It. *badaluccare baluccare baloc-
care*, Piedm. *badolè*. Ménage gives *badare* whence could come
only *baduccare*. Diez suggests Pr. *badalhar* to gape, *badaluc*

= *badalhuc.* A writer in the Journal of Classical and sacred Philology (June 1855) says that *badalucco,* if not from the Ostrogoths, is prob. of Etruscan origin. He compares is with the Rhæto-Rom. *badaish* fight, quarrel, which seems connected with the Goth. *baidjan* vexare, Sansk. *bâdh* or *vâdh* vexare.

Badana Sp. Pg. dressed sheep's leather; from Ar. *bi-'tânah.* Hence Fr. *basane,* adj. *basané* of the colour of tanned sheep's skin, tawny.

Badare It., Pr. Cat. *badar,* O. Fr. *baer béer,* Fr. *bayer* (in Berry *bader*), E. *bay.* The word meant (1) *to gape,* Pr. Cat. Fr. O. It, in Pr. also = to scoff, in Occit. *badado* = scoffing, (2) *to tarry,* loiter (stop with open mouth), It. Pr. O. Fr., (3) *to long after* a thing (to gape after), It., O. Fr.; Sbst. Pr. *bada* a sentinel, adv. *de bada, a bada,* O. Fr. *en bades* to no purpose, It. *stare a bada* to stay with open mouth, wait. It is probably an onomatop. from *ba* expressing the opening of the mouth, whence *ba-itare* or *ba-are, badare.* Hence It. *badigliare, sbadigliare, sbavigliare,* Pr. *badalhar,* O. Fr. *baailler,* Fr. *bâiller* to gape; Fr. *badaud,* Pr. *badau* gaper, fool, dotard; Pr. *badoc, baduel, badiu;* Fr. *badin* jester, *badiner;* It. *baderla* a simple, foolish woman, Com. *baderlà* to waste time, Rh. *baderlar* to prate, chatter.

Badaud, badiu — *badare.*

Baderla — *badare.*

Badigliare — *badare.*

Badile It., Sp. *badil, badila* a fire-shovel; from *batillum.*

Bafo O. Sp. Pg., Sp. *baho,* Cat. *raf* breath, steam; Sp. *avahar,* Pg. *bafar* to warm with the breath; an onomatop., cf. Mil. *banfà* to snort, Ar. *bakhara* to emit vapour.

Bafouer — *beffa.*

Bâfre Fr. a rich feast, *bâfrer,* N. Pr. *braffá,* Pied. *bafré* (and *balafré*) to gourmandize, Rouchi *bafreux,* Piedm. *bafron* a glutton. Perhaps of the same root as *bave* slaver, cf. Pic. *bafe* a gourmand, *baflier* a sloverer &c.; *r* is found in It. *bâvaro,* whence Ven. *bavarolo* a bib; v. *safre.*

Baga Sp. packthread, Pr. *bagua;* O. Fr. *bague* a bundle, cf. Lomb. *baga* a wine-bag; hence It. *bagaglia,* Pr. Fr. *bayage,* baggage. The word is Celtic, Gael. *bag,* W. *baich,* Bret. *beac'h* a bundle, bag, Gael. *bac* to hinder, Norse *bagu.*

Bagage — *buga.*

Bagarre Fr. a tumult, contention; from O. H. G. *bâga* strife (?).

Bagascia It., Sp. *bagasa* (by metath. *gavasa*), Pg. *bagaxa,* Pr. *baguassa,* O. Fr. *bagasse bajasse* &c., a prostitute, E. *baggage.* The term. *assa* = Lat. *acea,* in It. *ascia.* This would make it from *baga* a pack (for the connexion v. s. *basto*). Other derivations are (1) the Celtic *bach* (v. *baccalare*), *baisele*, *bachele*, a maid-servant, (2) the Arab. *bagl* a strumpet.

Bagatella It. a conjuror's trick, a trifle; Sp. *bagatela*, Fr. *bagatelle* a trifle. Muratori derives it from the Modenese *bagattare* to bungle, huddle, and both words, as well as *bagattino* a small coin, presuppose a sbst. *bagatta* or *baghetta* which may come from *baga* (supra), and so = a "small property" which meaning belongs to the Parm. *bagata*.

Bagliore It. a sudden and blinding splendour, a dazzling, *abbagliare* to dazzle, *abbaglio abbagliore* illusion, error, also *sbaglio sbagliare*, *barbaglio abbarbagliare*, where the *bar* is the same as that in *barlume* (q. v.). Menage derives it from *balluca* gold-sand, so of anything glimmering and dazzling, but this word was scarcely known in It. (v. *baluz*); perhaps it is of the same origin as the Fr. *berlue* (v. *bellugue*), so for *bargliare* = *bar-lucolare* (cf. *diluculum, anteluculus*); in *barbagliare* there is a *reduplication*. The Gen. *abbarlugá* has the same meaning, and comes nearer the original form.

Bagno It., Sp. *baño*, Pr. *banh*, Fr. *bain* a bath; *bagnare* &c., Fr. *baigner;* from *balneum* with elision of the *l*, *balgno* being impossible (Basque *mainhua*). The Wal. *bae* (fem. pl.) answers to the Lat. *baiæ*.

Bagordo bigordo It., O. Sp. *bohordo bofordo*, O. P. *hofordo bofardo*, L. L. *bufurdium*, Pr. *beort biort bort*, O. Fr. *bohort bouhourt behort* a sort of knightly exercise, a joust, also a lance or other weapon used therein; *bagordare* &c. to joust, break lances. In France the knights rode at the 'quintain' with the lance (v. Ducange s. *quintana*), in Spain the *bafordo* was used for throwing at the *tablado*, in Germany the *bühurt* was a sort of combat between two bodies of troops. The G. origin of *bohorder* (whence Fr. *bohort*) is almost demonstrated by the Sp. *f* (cf. *faraute* from *héraut*), and the It. *g* (cf. *gufo* for *huette*)=the aspirate. The latter part of the word is prob. not from *hurten* to thrust, for this gives in Fr. *hurter*, but from G. *hürde*, O. H. G. *hurt*, O. Fr. *horde*, vb. *horder*, the form *hordeïs* a fence, *hurdle* corresponding to *bohordeïs* = *bagordo*. *Hourdum* in L. L. = Sp. *tablado* = a scaffolding, *hoarding* = Rouchi *hourd*. Perhaps the first part of the word contains the root *botar (butt v. s. botta);* hence *bot-hort bohort* (*t* being dropped before the aspirate) = something to strike the stage or scaffolding.

Bague Fr. a ring set with precious stones, also = the ring of a circus; from *bacca* a pearl, link of a chain. Also from *baca bacca* is the Fr. *baie* a berry, Pr. *baga baca*, Sp. *baca*, Pg. *baga*, It. *bacca*.

Baguette — *bacchetta.*

Bahari Sp., Pg. *bafari* a kind of sparrow-hawk; = prop. *marine*, from the Ar. *ba'hr* sea (*ba'hri* marinus, Freytag 1, 88).

Bahut — *baule.*

Baie — *baja.*

Bagner — *bagno.*

Bailler — *bailo.*

Bâiller — *badare.*

Baillet — *bajo.*

Baillif — *bailo.*

Bailo bailo It., Sp. *bayle baile*, Pg. *bailio*, Pr. *baile*, O. Fr. *bail* (whence E. *bail*) a guardian, tutor, manager, *bailiff*, Fem. It. *baila balia*, Pr. Rh. *baila* a nurse; It. *balia*, Sp. Pr. *bailia*, O. Fr. *baillie* a bailiff's office or jurisdiction, bailiwick; It. *balivo*, Pr. *bailieu*, Fr. *bailli* a bailiff, or land-steward; It. *balire*, Pr. *bailir*, O. Fr. *baillir* to manage, take care of, so also the Pr. *bailar*, O. Fr. *bailler* to reach forth, present, Wal. *bëia* to foster, educate, *bëiat* a boy. From the Lat. *bajulus* (Dante *bajulo*) in L. L. = a tutor &c., prop. one who carries children, *baila* = a nurse. Hence = a warden, bailiff &c.

Baille — *bac.*

Bain — *bagno.*

Baïonnette Fr. a *bayonet;* so called from *Bayonne* where they were first made or used.

Baire It. to be astonished or amazed; O. Fr. adj. *baif*, Rouchi *bahi* astonish; hence It. *sbaire*, Pr. *esbahir*, Fr. *ébahir* to be astorended, Sp. *embair* to deceive, delude, prop. to amaze. From the sound *bah* (which is used in N. Pr. as an exclamation of astonishment). Thus it would be connected in origin with *badare*.

Baisele — *bagascia.*

Baja It., Sp. Pr. Sard. *bahia*, Fr. *baie*, E. *bay;* Isidorus quotes it as a Latin word: *hunc portum mercatores a bajulandis mercibus vocabant baias.* Frisch derives it from the Fr. *bayer* to open the mouth, so that *baie* = prop. an opening, and this seems to be confirmed by the Cat. form *badia* from *badar*, the *d* of which had disappeared from the Sp. before Isidore's time. Others make *bahia* a Basque word whence *Bayonne* (*baia* harbour and *ona* good); others refer it to the Gael. *bàdh* or *bàgh* with which the Rom. forms agree well enough.

Baja It., Sp. Pg. *vaya*, Fr. *baie* jest, jeer; whence It. *bajuca* a jest, a trifle. The Gk. βαιός and the Fr. *baie* a berry, have been proposed, but it is better to refer the word to the Pr. *bada*, O. Fr. *baie*, adv. *en bada* in vain, in jest, Fr. *donner la baie* = Sp. *dar vaya* to make light of one, v. *badare.*

Bajare abbajare It. to bark; from the O. Fr. *abayer*, which from *baubari*, or formed from the sound liko *baubari*. Tho Sard. is *baulai (baubulari)* and *beliai abeliai.*

Bajo It., Sp. *bayo*, Pr. *bai*, Fr. *bai*, Eng. *bay* (of colour); from the Lat. *badius* used by Varro of the colour of a horse. The Sp. has also *bazo* = brown *(pan bazo = pain bis)*. Hence Fr. *baillet* light‑red, chesnut, L. L. *badiolettus;* It. *bajocco* a copper‑coin, so called from its colour, like the Fr. *blanc*, G. *weisspfennig*. Tho Sp. *albazano*, Pg. *alvaçáo* chesnut = *albbazano?*

Bajocco — *bajo.*

Bajuca — *baia.*

Baladí Sp. mean, worthless. According to the Sp. etymologists, from Ar. *balad* a city, *baladi* civic; *baladi* would then be a word used by the country‑people who had been cheated in the towns.

Baladrar Sp. to bleat; prob. a corruption of O.Sp.*balitar* formed on the model of *ladrar* to bark.

Balafre Fr. a gash or scar in the face, Rouchi *berlafe*, Mil. *barleffi*, It. *sberleffe* (= grimace), vb. Fr. *balafrer*. Prob. a compound from the part. *bis* = bad, and the O. H. G. *leffur* = lip, so = bad lip, then of a gaping wound, like χεῖλος. In Champ. *berlafre* = a sore lip.

Balai Fr. a besom, *balayer* to sweep. The Pr. *balai* = a stalk, rod, switch, so too the O. Fr. *balais* (balai?), O. Eng. *baleis*, Pr. *balaiar* to whip. Prob. of Celtic origin: tho W. *bala* = a shoot plur. *balaon* = buds, *balant* a twig, Bret. *balaen* a besom, O. Fr. *balain* a whip, Bret. *balan*. But the Rom. has no substantival suffix *ai* so that the entire form must have been adopted, but W. *balai* means the tongue of a buckle.

Balais — *balascio.*

Balance — *bilancia.*

Balandre — *palandra.*

Balansa — *bilancia.*

Balascio It., Sp. *balax balaxe*, Pg. *balais balache*, Pr. *balais balach*, Fr. *balais* a precious stone, a sort of ruby, so called from *Badakschan (Balaschan, Balaxiam)* where it is found. Cf. Ducange s. *balascus.*

Balaustro It., Sp. *balaústre*, Fr. *balustre*, E. *baluster* (corrupted *banister* and *ballaster*), hence *balustrata* &c.; from L. L. *balaustium (βαλαύστιον)* the flower of the wild pomegranate, Sp. It. *balaústra.*

Balco palco It. a scaffold, stage, whence Sp. Pg. *palco;* hence It. *balcone*, Sp. *bolcon*, Pg. *balcão*, Fr. *balcon*, E. *balcony;* from the O. H. G. *balcho palcho*, G. balken, E. *baulk* a beam, Du. *balke* a loft, cf. O. N. *bálkr* an enclosure. In Picardy *bauque* retains the German signification. Others derive *balcone* from the Pers. *bálkána* a grated window or more probably from *bálá-khána*, "an upper chamber". See *barbacane*.

Baldacchino It., Sp. *baldaquino*, Fr. *baldaquin* a canopy; from It. *Baldacco*, Bagdad, whence was brought the peculiar stiff (woven of gold-thread and silk) of which they were made. Another form in O. Fr. is *boudequin*, E. *bawdekin* a rich embroidered cloth used for copes, palls &c., also the portable canopy borne over shrines in processions.

Baldo It., Pr. *baut*, O. Fr. O. Cat. *baud*, bold, wanton &c., Pr. *baudos;* It. abst. *baldore*, Pr. O. Fr. *baudor* wantonness, merriment, It. *baldória* a bonfire, feu de joie; O. It. *sbaldire*, Pr. O. Fr. *esbaudir* to be bold or wanton; from the Goth. *balths*, O. H. G. *bald* bold, frank, Goth. *balthjan* to be bold, to venture. The languages of the S. W. of Europe have a similar form *baldo* empty, bare, *de balde*, *em balde* in vain, to no purpose, *baldio* useless, refuse, uncultivated, *balda* a useless thing, a trifle, *baldar* to maim, *baldon baldão* = affront, insult (prop. = worthlessness, cf. O. Sp. *en baldon* = *en balde*), *baldonar baldoar* to insult. If from the Germ. the idea of wantonness must have passed into that of idleness and worthlessness, cf. the O. H. G. *gemeit* = insolent and idle. But this is improb. for the notion of boldness is nowhere met in the Sp., and the Sp. words stand quite apart from the rest. Prob. from the Arab. *ba'tala* to be useless, whence *balla balda*, just as *spatula* becomes *espalda*, *rotulus rolde*.

Baldonar — *baldo.*

Baldoria — *baldo.*

Baleno It. lightning, *balenare* to lighten; from βέλεμνον a dart (βελεμνίτης = a thunderbolt). The proper form would have been *belenno.* Hence It. *arcobaleno* rainbow, also called *arco celeste*, *arco piovoso*, Sic. *arcu de donno deu*, Ven. *arco de verzene*, Sic. *arcu de Nuè.*

Balèvre Fr. the lower lip; for *basse-lèvre.*

Balicare It. (Lomb. *balicà*), O. Fr. *baloier* to move to and fro, to flutter, Cat. *balejar*, Sp. Pg. *abalear* to winnow; perhaps from *ballare* to dance. The Pr. *balaiar* to flutter, to lash, is different in form.

Balija — *valigia.*

Balla It., Sp. Pr. *bala*, Fr. *balle* a ball; It. *ballone*, Sp. *balon*, Fr. *ballon*, a foot-ball (E. *balloon*). The It. has also *palla pallone* which leaves no doubt of the derivation from the O. H. G. *balla palla*, M. H. G. *bal*, O. N. *böllr* (which Benecke derives from the G.), E. *ball.* The G. is nearer than the Gk. βάλλειν πάλλειν, abst. πάλλα.

Ballare It., Sp. Pg. *bailar*, Pr. *balar*, O. Fr. *baler* to dance; It.

ballo, Sp. Pg. *baile*, Pr. Fr. *bal* a dance, E. *ball*. From *balla* a ball; the Sp. *bailar* is for an orig. *balear* (cf. *guerrear*, *manear*), whence *baelar bailar*, in O. Sp. also *ballar*, Pg. *balhar*. Ball-play in the Middle-Ages, as in ancient Greece, was often associated with singing and dancing. Hence Rom. *ballare* got to mean to dance; so in O. Sp. *ballar* meant to sing, whence It. *ballata*, Fr. *ballade* a ballad.

Balme O. Fr., Pr. Cat. *balma* (in the modern dialects *baumo*) a cave or grotto in a rock, Swiss *balm*. Some consider the word to be Celtic (Schmeller s. v. *balfen*), but in the above sense it does not occur in this family of languages. The G. has *barm* a bosom (for the change of *r* into *l*, cf. Pr. *Alvernhe albre*), which is found even in Rom. (v. Schott deutsche spr. in Piemont p. 242), but the sense of cavity, *sinus terræ*, seems foreign to the G. word. Steub (Rhæt. Ethnol.) considers the Rhæt. *palva* to be the original form (found in many names of places), hence Bav. Tyrol. *balfen*, Rom. *balma*, Rh. *bova*.

Balocco — *badalucco*.

Baloier — *balicare*.

Balordo — *lordo*.

Balourd — *lordo*.

Balsa Sp. Pg., Cat. *bassa* a pool, also a raft, Pg. also = strawmat, from the Basque *balsa* a collection or heap. Humboldt refers the name of the town *Balsa* in Bætica (Pliny) to this word.

Baluardo — *boulevard*.

Baluo — *badalucco*.

Balustre — *balaustro*.

Balus O. Sp. a small nugget of gold; Lat. *balux ballux* goldsand (Pliny), *balluca* (in later authors), prob. an old Sp. word, v. Pott, Etym. Forsch. 2, 419, 510. *Baluz* (also *baluce*) is formed by Rom. writers from *balux*.

Balsa It. the hem or border of a garment; from *balteus*, Wal. *baltz* a snare. Hence *balzano*, Pr. *bausan*, O. Fr. *bauçant*, white (prop. striped), generally used of animals, espec. as the name of the boar in fables, Fr. *balzan* a dark horse with white feet, E. *bawson* a name of the badger from the white streaks on its face.

Balsan — *balza*.

Balsare It. to jump, spring, bound upwards, Pr. *balsar*, It. *balzo*, Cat. *bals*, O. Fr. *baus*, a bound or leap, in It. also = a cliff (for which a fem. *balza* is also used); It. *sbalzare* to swing, vibrate, sbst. *sbalzo*. The word is prob. Italian, being chiefly used in that language (cf. *balzellare*, *balzelloni*): so, perhaps, from the Gk. βαλλίζειν to hop or bound.

Bambagio bambagia It. cotton, Milan. *bombás*, E. *bombast* prop.

= cotton-wadding; from *bombyx* (βόμβυξ) silk, cotton, M.Gr. βαμβάκιον, L. L. *bambacium.* Hence It. *bambagino,* Sp. *bombasi,* Fr. *bombasin basin,* E. *bombasin,* L. adj. *bombycinus.*

Bambin bamboche — *bambo.*

Bambo It. childish, silly, Sp. *bamba* a simpleton (Covarruvias); hence It. *bambino, bambolo, bambola, bamboccio* (Fr. *bamboche*), Sp. *bambárria* (m.) a child, baby, childish man &c., Austrian *bams* a child. The root is the same as that of *bambalio* (Cicero) and of βαμβαλός, βαμβαλίζειν, βαμβαίνειν to lisp &c. The Sp. *bamba* == a swing, *bambolear* to swing, Norm. *bamboler,* Wall. *bambi* to waver, Burg. *vambe* the swing of a bell; the It. *bamboleggiare* (*bambolo* a child) corresponds exactly with *bambolear:* cf. the cognate *babbeo.* It. *bimbo* is a weakened form of *bambo.*

Ban — *bando.*

Ban bana Pr., Cat. *banya* a horn, a stag's horn; prob. from the W. *bán,* cf. also O. H. G. *bain,* Bavar. *hirschbain* a stag's horn. Hence Occit. *banarut* horned, *banar(d)* a horned beetle.

Banasta — *benna.*

Banco It. Sp. Pg., Pr. Fr. *banc,* It. Sp. Pg. Pr. *banca,* Fr. *banque,* a bench; from O. H. G. *banc.* There is also a W. *banc* (Gael. *binnse*), but the It. form *panca* vindicates the G. derivation. Hence It. *banchetto,* Fr. E. *banquet,* Sp. *banquete,* prop. == a light ornamental dessert, from vb. *banchettare* to give a banquet, prop. to arrange tables and benches; *banchiere* &c., *banker.*

Banda It. Sp. Pr., Fr. *bande* a band, string, also a *band* == a troop; from the Goth. *bandi* (f.), O.H.G. *band* (n.). Hence It. *bandiera,* Sp. *bandera,* Pr. *bandiera baneira,* Fr. *bannière* (G. *panier,* E. *banner*), a standard, cf. Goth. *bandva* an ensign, and Paul. Diac. 1, 20: *vexillum quod bandum appellant;* the simple *bannum* is found only in O. Fr. *ban,* Pr. *auri-ban* (cf. *auriflamma*); hence, too, Sp. *bandear,* Pr. *bandeiar baneiar* float (as a banner), intrans. to pass to and fro, to pass across, O. Fr. *banoier, esbanoier,* M. H. G. *baneken,* whence orig. Rom. form *banicare,* still seen in Com. *bangà* to waver.

Bande bander — *benda.*

Bandibula Sp. the jaw; from *mandibula.*

Bando It. Sp. Pg., Pr. *ban,* Fr. *ban* a public proclamation, *bann;* It. *bandire,* Sp. Pr. *bandir,* Pg. *bandir banir,* Fr. *bannir* to proclaim, denounce, banish, whence It. *bandito* a *bandit* an outlaw. L. L. *bannum* == *interdictum, bannire* == *edicere, relegare.* The root is German, but G. *bannan* would have given *bannare banner;* so that it is better to derive *bandire* &c. from the Goth. *bandvjan, bannir* from another form *banvjan;* some G. dialects omit the *v.* The O. Fr. *arban* service == G.

hariban, *heerban*, whence by a corruption Fr. *arrière-ban*.
From *bando* comes the O. Fr. Pr. *bandon* generally with *à*
= (1) *ban: vendre gage à bandon*, (2) will, discretion (price):
prenez tot a vostre bandon. From this adv. *à bandon* is formed
a sbst. *abandon*, It. *abbandono* abandonment, *abbandonare* &c.
to *abandon*. Trench gets the sense of *abandon* differently,
viz. from that of denouncing: "what you denounce you
detach yourself from, you *abandon*". Another derivative is
O. Fr. *forbanir* to outlaw *(for = foras)*, It. *forbannuto* an outlaw, O. Fr. *forban* banishment, also = an outlaw, a pirate
(Fr. *forban*), L. L. *forbannitus*, *ferbannitus*. It. *contrabbando*,
Fr. *contrebande* = non-observance of an edict, smuggling.
Hence E. *contraband*.

Banlieue Fr. prop. = a league's jurisdiction, so a district under
such jurisdiction, suburbs, environs. So too O. Fr. *ban-molin*
mill-territory, v. Duc. s. *bannum leucæ*.

Banne — *benna*.

Bannir — *bando*.

Banque — *banco*.

Banse — *benna*.

Baquet — *bac*.

Bara It., Fr. *bar* usu. *bière*, Pr. *bera* a *bier*, Rh. *bara* a corpse;
from O. H. G. *bâra*, A. S. *bœr bère*, E. *bier*, Du. *berrie*.

Baracane It., Sp. *barragan*, Pg. *barregana*, Pr. Fr. *barracan* a
stuff made of goat's hair, *barracan*; from Ar. *barrakân* a dark
dress, Freyt. 1, 113, which according to Sousa comes from
the Persian *barak* a stuff made of camel's hair.

Baracca It., Sp. *barraca*, Fr. *baraque* a hut, tent, *barrack*; from
barra a bar, like It. *trabacca* from *trabs*.

Baragouin gibberish; from the two Breton words *bara* bread and
gwin wine coined by the French who heard these words often
uttered by the Bretons whom they regarded as barbarous, cf.
bretonner to talk unintelligibly. Wedgwood refers it along
with *barbarous*, *bargain*, *barter* &c. to the root *bar* signifying
confused noise, squabble, tumult.

Baraja — *baro*.

Baratto It., O. Sp. *barato*, Pr. *barat*, Fr. *barat*, O. Sp. Pr. *barata*,
O. Fr. *barate* a fraudulent bargain; It. *barattare*, Sp. Pr. *baratar*, O. Fr. *bareter* to cheat, truck, exchange *barter*, Sp.
baratear to cheapen, O. Pg. *baratar* to destroy; It. *sbarattare*,
Sp. Pr. *desbaratar*, O. Fr. *desbareter* to distroy, disorder; Fr.
baratter to churn (to mix up and stir confusedly); Sp. *bara-
teria* fraud, espec. by master of a ship, E. *barratry*. *Barratry*
acc. to Blackstone is the offence of stirring up quarrels.
Several derivations are given: (1) that from It. *barare* to cheat
(baro) would not be regular in form; (2) the Pers. *barâtel*

bribery could only have been introduced during the Crusades,
whereas the Rom. word occurs as early as the first half of
the 12th cent.; (3) the O. N. *bardtta* battle corresponds to
Dante's use of *baratta*, but this rather means the entanglement, and bustle, and tumult of a fight, O. Fr. *barate*, O. Sp.
barata; besides the meanings of 'combat' and 'fraud' (entanglement) could hardly be of common stock. It is best perhaps, to derive it from πράττειν (cf. *bolte* from πύξις), a word
which may have been introduced by the Gk. merchants.
Wedgwood gets it from the root *bar*, v. *barugouin* s. fin. The
Sp. *barato* = cheap, abst. cheapness, vb. *baratar* to buy
cheap.

Barba It. (m.) uncle, father's brother, Dante Par. 19, 37, Rh.
barba, L. L. *barbas*, It. *barbano*, L. L. *barbanus;* from *barba*
a beard. In Com. it is used generally as a title of honour, so
Neap. *zi* = It. *zio.*

Barbacane It. (m.), Sp. Pr. *barbacana*, Pg. *barbacão*, Fr. *barbacane* a barbican; from the Pers. *bálá-khána* upper chamber,
a word which also gives *balcony*, prob. brought from the East
by the Crusaders, Wedg.; but v. *balco.*

Barbasco Sp. a plant; from *verbascum*, like O.Sp. *bardasca* from
verdasca (viridis) a rod.

Barbassero — *vassallo.*

Barbecho Sp., Pg. *barbeito* a fallow; from L. *vervactum.* In the
North West the *v* (as in other instances v. Rom. Gr. I, 187)
has become *g;* thus Pr. *garag*, Fr. *guéret*, Valen. *guaret*, Cat.
guret.

Barbotar barbulhar — *borbogliare.*

Barca It. Sp. Pg. Pr., Wal. *barcé*, Fr. *barque* a small trading
vessel, a bark, barge, L. L. *barca.* The Pr. *barja*, O. Fr.
barge, Fr. *berge*, E. *barge*, requires an orig. *barica* (cf. *carrica*
charge, serica serge), which may be from βάρις (baris Proper-
tius) like *auca avica* from *avis.* Many marine terms are borrowed from the Gk. cf. *poggia, sesto, golfo, artimone.* Others
derive it from O. N. *barkr*, E. *bark*, prop. = a vessel made
of *bark.*

Barcar Sp. Pg. found in *abarcar* to embrace, *sobarcar* to carry
under the arm. Not from *brachiare* which would give *brazar*,
but from *brachicare*, like *caballicare.* Sp. *sobaco* = armpit is
the L. L. *subbrachium.*

Barda It. Sp., O. Fr. *barde* horse-armour of iron-plate, Pg.
barda, Fr. *barde* a saddle, also a slice of bacon so called from
its being placed round fowls before roasting: hence Fr. *bardeau* a shingle, It. *bardella*, Fr. *bardelle*, Pr. *bardel* a pad,
pillion, It. *bardotto*, Fr. *bardot* a saddle-mule (one which the

driver rides). Perhaps from the N. *bardi* a shield; though the Pg. *barda* a hedge. Sp. *barda* the fencing on a wall belongs to the Basque *abarra* "it is grafted" (Larramendi). Or all the above words may with the Sp. *abbarda* a saddle and a slice of bacon be referred to the Ar. *al-barda'ah* a pad or cloth put under the saddle to prevent its hurting the back. Freyt. 1, 106. The O. Fr. Champ. *barde* a carpenter's axe, Wal.*bardé*, Dauph. *partoua* bill is prob. from a different root, O. H. G. *barta*, Du. *barde* a pick-axe.

Bardascia It., Sp. *bardaxa*, Fr. *bardache* = pathicus; from the Ar. *bardag* a slave? Lomb. and Piedm. *bardassa* = merely "boy", the Sard. *bardascia* has both meanings. On the O. Fr. *bardache* a stake, v. Grandgagnage v. *bardahe*.

Bardeau — *barda*.

Bardosso — *bisdosso*.

Barga Sp. O. Pg., Fr. *berge* a steep slope; prob. from the Celtic, cf. W. *bargodi* to hang over, *bargod* the eaves of a house.

Bargagno It., Pr. *barganh*, Pg. Pr. *barganha*, E. *bargain*, O. Fr. *bargaine* (= ceremonie Roquefort); It. *bargagnare*, Pg. Pr. *barganhar* to bargain, Fr. *barguigner* (for *bargaigner*, cf. *grignon*) to hoggle, loiter. The L. L. *barcaniare* shows that the *g* is for *c*, so that the word prob. comes from *barca*, which, according to Isidore, was used for traffic, so that *bargagno* would be properly = trafficking. Wedgwood derives it from the root *bar* (in *barbarous* &c.) from the notion of squabbling and haggling. Genin derives it from Rom. particle *bar* = *bis*, *ber* and *gagner*, but the L. L. *barcaniare*, and the constant form *bar* and *gagn* for *guadagn*, are against him.

Bargello It., Sp. Pg. *barrachel*, O. Fr. *barigel* a police-officer, a bumbailiff; from L. L. *barigildus*, certainly a G. word, but of unknown derivation, cf. Grimm, Rechtsalt. p. 314.

Barigel — *bargello*.

Baril barile — *barra*.

Barioler Fr. to speckle, make a medley of; if from *variare*, *rariolare* the *b* must be due to the particle *bar* (= bis), for L. *v* does not become *b* in Fr. *(brebis* is from L. *berbex)*, or it may be from *bar* and *riolé* striped.

Baritono It. Sp., Pg. *bariton*, Fr. *baryton* (obsol.), E. *barytone*; from βαρύτονος.

Barlong Fr., O. Fr. *berlong* (a garment) of unequal length; for *beslong* = It. *bislungo*, *bis* = anything uneven &c., q. v.

Barnatge — *barone*.

Baro barro It. a rogue; whence *barone*, *barare barrare* to cheat. From the same root prob. come: Pr. *baran* fraud, It. *barocco* usury, O. Sp. *baruca* craft, It. *barullo* a fruiterer (cf. *treccare* to cheat, *trecca* a huckster); Sp. *baraja*, Pg. Pr. *baralha*,

O. Fr. *berele* a tumult, brawl, *barajar, baralhar* to throw into confusion. Perhaps from the root *bar*, v. s. *baratto*.

Barocco — *baro.*

Barone It., Sp. *varon*, Pg. *varão*, Pr. *bar* (acc. *baró*), O. Fr. *ber* (acc. *baron*), Fr. E. *baron* orig. = vir or maritus, next as adj. = manly, whence Pr. *barnatge*, O. Fr. *baronie barnie* prowess, *embarnir* to be courageous, next in L. L. = lord, *"gravis et authenticus vir"*, *barones* = nobles or vassals of the crown. L. *baro* = a fool, simpleton, in Scholiast on Persius is explained to be *"servus militum"* and is said to be of Gallic origin. We find a Gael. *bar* = champion, but words formed like *bar baron* are either from the L., as *drac dragon, laire lairon*, or from the G., as *fel fellon, Uc ugon;* so it is better to refer it to the O. H. G. *bero* (acc. *berun beron*) porter, from vb. *beran*, Goth. *bairan (bear);* others make it radically the same word as the L. *vir*, Goth. *vair*, A. S. *wer*, Gael. *fear* a man, v. Bopp. Gloss. s. *vira*. Com. Bergam. *bar*, Piedm. *berro*, Romag. *berr* = ram, Lorr. *bèrra (berard)*, cf. s. *marrone.*

Baroque — *barrucco.*

Barque — *barca.*

Barra It. Sp. Pr., Fr. *barre*, E. *bar;* hence Sp. *barrio*, Pr. Cat. *barri* a wall, a suburb, L. L. *barrium;* Fr. *barreau*, It. *barriera*, Sp. *barrera*, Fr. *barrière*, E. *barrier* &c.; Sp. *barrar barrear*, Fr. *barrer* &c. From the Celtic: W. *bar* = a bough; M. H. G. *bar barre* is used in Rom. sense. Hence Sp. *barras* a bar, Sp. *embarazo*, Fr. *embarras*, Sp. *embarazar*, Fr. *embarasser, débarrasser*, E. *embarrass* &c.; Sp. *barrica*, Fr. *barrique* a barrel, whence *barricata* a *barricade* (of casks &c.); It. *barile*, Sp. Pg. *barril*, Fr. *baril*, W. *baril*, Gael. *baraill*, E. *barrel*, Sp. *barral*. We find the same word in the Fr. names of places, e. g. *Bar-sur-Aube, Bar-le-duc.*

Barrachel — *bargello.*

Barragan Sp., Pg. *barragão* a companion, a bachelor. As it is used for a man of prowess (*buen barragan* Poem d. Cid), it may be identical with *barragan* (= *baracane* q. v.) which meant a strong durable stuff.

Barrette — *berretta.*

Barrica barril — *barra.*

Barriga Sp. Pg. the abdomen. Not from *barra* since the Sp. has no suffix *iga*. As *poitrine* prop. = breast-girdle, so *barriga* may = girth, from the O. H. G. *baldrich, baldriga barriga* (cf. Rodrich Rodrigo); *baldriga* appears in Parm. *bodriga* = belly (*o* = *al*). In Berry *baudru* = *ventru*, cf. *baudré.*

Barro Sp. Pg. mud, clay; from Ar. *barj* earth, potter's clay.

Barroch — *biroccio.*

Barrucco berrucco Sp., Pg. *barroco* a pearl of uneven shape

not round, in Pg. also = an uneven rock, Fr. *barroque* oval.
Three derivations are given, (1) *verruca* which Pliny uses to
express the unevenness of a precious stone; the Lat. *uca*,
however, is not exchangeable with Rom. *oc*, (2) *brochus* a
prominent tooth, (3) *bis-roca* an uneven rock (v. *bis*). *Brochus*
has the advantage in gender, *bis roca* in sense and sound.
Hence, perhaps, too the Pg. *barroca* an uneven stony district,
which some connect with the Ar. *borqah* Freyt. 1, 111.

Barruntar Sp. Pg. to foresee, guess, O. Sp. *barrunta* foresight,
barrunte a spy, a scout. Prob. = *barutar* with *n* inserted, cf.
garganta for *gargata*, *encentar* for *encetar*, *cimenterio* for *cimeterio*, *hedant* for *edat; barutar* = to sift, cf. *cernere*, χρίνειν,
v. *blutar*. The N. Pr. has the same word *barountá* to shake
which, doubtless, comes from the notion of sifting, cf. Sp.
mecer = to mix, to shake.

Baruffa — *ruffa*.

Barullo — *baro*.

Bas — *basso*.

Basane — *badana*.

Basca Sp., Pg. *vasca* disgust, nausea, O. Sp. *bascar* to feel disgust. Prob. from the Basque, v. Larramendi. The Rh.
baschizzi has the same meaning.

Bascule Fr. counterpoise belonging to a swipe or a weigh-
bridge, see-saw &c.; from *bas* and *cul* according to Frisch
and Scheler. The N. Pr. *leva-coua* (= *cauda)* is more clear.

Basin — *bambagio*.

Basire It. to die, N. Pr. Dauph. *basir;* from Gael. *bás* death,
basaich to die, N. *basa* to kill. The Com. has *sbasi* to die and
to grow pale, Piedm. *sbasi* in latter sense.

Basquiner O. Fr., Wal. *bosconi* to bewitch; from βασχαίνειν.

Bassin — *bacino*.

Basso It., Sp. *baxo*, Pg. *baixo*, Pr. Fr. *bas* low; It. *bassare* &c.
The Isid. Gloss. has *bassus crassus pinguis*, Papias *bassus curtus humilis;* the former is the earlier meaning; in fact, the It.
has *bassotto* thick = O.Fr. *bas* broad. The word is a genuine
Latin one, *Bassus* having been used very early as a family-
name, which, like many others, had reference to personal peculiarity. Perhaps, the orig. meaning of *bassus* was that which
extends in breadth not in height, whence the senses of "thick"
and "short". From the adj. comes It. sbst. *basso* the under-
part, Fr. *bas* stocking (prop. bas-de-chausse, cf. haut-de-
chausses), Sp. *baxos*, Pg. *baixos* (pl.) under garments, also
shoes, nothing to do with L. *baxea*, which would have given
baisse in Fr.

Basta It. Sp. Pg. Cat. a basted seam, O. Fr. *baste*, Occ. *basto* (a
coat-lap?); Fr. *bâtir*, Sp. *bastear*, It. *imbastare*, Sp. Cat. *em-*

bastar to *baste*; from O. H. G. *bestan* to repair, M. H. G. *besten*, which from sbst. *bast*.

Bastar — *basto*.
Bastare bastione — *basto*.
Bastilla — *basta*.
Bastille bât — *basto*.
Basto It. Sp., Pr. *bast*, Fr. *bât* (E. *bat*-horse) a pack-saddle; Pr. *bastar*, Fr. *bâter* to saddle. It is generally referred to the G. *bast* of which the materials for the fastenings might be made. Wedgwood refers it to *basta* (sup.) the pad being orig. a quilted (stitched) cushion. Diez is led from a comparison with *bastone* to attribute to *basto* the notion of "prop" "trestle" on which the burden rests, so that it would be akin to βασταζειν. *Basterna* a litter may be referred to the same root (but v. Grimm, Geschichte d. deut. spr. p. 461). But Gk. βάσταξ (βαστάζω) a porter is found in Pr. *bastais*, Cat. *bastax*, Sp. *bastage*, It. *bastagio*. Of the same origin are It. *bastone* (Fr. *bâton*, Wal. *běston* &c.), It. *bastire*, O. Sp. Pr. *bastir*, Fr. *bâtir* to build (prob. to prop?), whence O. Sp. Pr. *bastida*, It. *bastia*, *bastione*, Fr. *bastille* &c.; Sp. Pg. *basto* close, compact, Sp. also = thick, coarse (espec. in moral sense); It. *bastare*, Sp. Pg. Pr. *bastar* to be sufficient (prop. to fill out, cf. Sp. *harto* filled out, sufficient), Ven. *bastare* to hinder (stop up), O. Sp. *bastir* to furnish, provide for. Hence, too, probably comes It. Sp. Pp. *bastardo*, Pr. *bastart*, Fr. *bâtard*, O. Fr. E. *bastard*, also called in O. Fr. *fils de bast* and by corruption *fils de bas*, son of a pack-saddle. The termin. *ard* is common in a bad sense (cf. Kom. Gr. 2, 310, such E. words as drunkard, niggard &c.). The word prob. had its origin in Provence and Spain, where the licentious muleteers were accustomed to use the *pack-saddles* and furniture of their mules for bedding, cf. Don Quixote, p. 1, cap. 16, where the muleteer's bed is spoken of as being "fabricado de las enjalmas" "y de todo el adorno de los dos mejores mulos que traia". The rest of his story affords further illustration, cf G. *bankert*, *bankart* a bastard, from *bank*. Wedgwood derives *bastard* from the Celtic *baos* (Gael.) lust.

Batafalua, batafaluga Sp. (obsolete), with *m* for *b*, *matalahua*, -*huya*, -*huva*, Cat. Sard. *matafaluga* anise; from Ar. 'habbat-al-'halwah.

Bataille — *battere*.
Bâtard — *bastardo*.
Batassare It. to shake; prob. from the Gk. κατάσσειν to strike, to rattle, not from *battare*, for the It. has no suffix *ass*.

Bateau — *batto*.
Bâtir bâton — *basto*.

Battere It., Sp. *batir*, Pg. *bater*, Pr. *batre*, Fr. *battre*, Wal. *bâte*, Serv. *bátati*, E. *beat;* from *batuere*, shortened to *batere* (Rom. Gr. 1, 162). This, though rare in classical, occurs often in L. L. where, however, it takes a different flexion : pf. *battidi* (like *prendidi*, *ostendidi*), partic. *battutus*. Among the derivatives are It. *battaglia*, Sp. *batalla*, Fr. *bataille*, Wal. *bĕtĭe*, E. *battle;* It. *battaglio* and *batacchio*, Sp. *badajo* for *batajo* clapper of a bell; It. *battigia* epilepsy; Sp. *batan* a fulling-mill; Pr. *bataria* fray, *battery*, Fr. *batterie* mounted ordnance, a *battery*.

Battessone It. a coin bearing the image of John the Baptist, from *battezzare;* hence G. *batzen*, It. *bezzo*.

Battifredo It., Fr. *beffroi*, O. Fr. *berfroi beffroit* a tower, *belfry;* from M. H. G. *bercvrit bervrit* a tower for shelter or assault, L. L. *berfredus belfredus*. The It. word has a reference to *battere*. For similar secondary etymologies cf. *palafreno*, *baccalaureus*, *lanthorne* &c.

Batto It. a rowing-boat; hence *battello*, Sp. *batel*, Pr. *batelh*, Fr. *bateau* a boat; from A. S. *bât*, O. N. *bátr*, W. *bâd*, E. *boat*.

Bauçant — *balza*.

Bauche O. Fr. plaster-work on a wall, or a workshop; hence *ébaucher* to work in the rough, *embaucher* to engage a workman, *débaucher* to lead astray, to decoy a workman, E. *debauch*. Cf. Gael. *bale*, O. N. *bálkr* partition-wall, *baulk* between furrows.

Baud Fr. a stag-hound, also called *chien muet;* from Gael. *baoth* deaf, dumb, Goth. *bauth* κωφός, cf. Norm. *baude* numb.

Baudet Fr. an ass, fem. *baude*, in fables *Boudouin;* from *baud* frolicsome (v. *baldo*).

Baudré O. Fr., Pr. *baudrat*, Fr. *baudrier*, Pg. *boldrié*, It. *budriere*. From the O. H. G. *balderich*, O. E. *baldrick baudrik*. Hence O. Fr. *esbaudre* the waist, cf. *cinge* (cingulum). V. s. *barriga*.

Baule It., Sp. *bahul baul*, Pg. *bahul bahu*, Pr. *bauc*, Fr. *bahut*, *bahu*, a trunk, valise. From M. H. G. *behut* (used by Luther = magazine, repository) which is from *behüten* to cover, keep. The O. Fr. *bahud*, L. L. *behudum* is the orig. form: v. Mahn, Etym. Untersuch. p. 89. Diez wrongly refers it to *bajulus*.

Bausan — *bugia*.

Bausia — *bugia*.

Bava It., Sp. Pg. *baba*, Fr. *bave* spittle, slaver; Pg. Pr. *bavar*, Fr. *baver*, Sp. *bavear* to drivel. An onomatop., expressing prop. the drivelling of an infant (cf. βαβάζειν to stammer), hence E. *babe*, *baby*, Fr. *bave* = also childish talk, *baveux bavard* a gossip; Sic. *vava* = slaver and child. Hence Sp. *babieca* foolish (prop. = drivelling, foaming, whence its use as the name of the Cid's horse); Sp. *babosa* = a slug, &c., Cat. *emba-biecar*, Pg. *embabacar*, Sp. *embaucar* to cheat, impose upon.

Baxo, — *basso.*

Baya Sp. a berry; from *bacca baca*, Pg. *baga.*

Bayer — *badare.*

Bazo Sp. Pg. spleen, cf. N. Pr. *bescle*, O. Fr. *bascle.*

Bazo — *bajo.*

Bazza It., Sp. *baza*, Cat. *basa* good luck, trump in cards; from M.H.G. *bazze* gain *(baz=besser).* It was prob. introduced by the G. mercenaries. Hence It. *bazzica* a game at cards, *bazzicare* to have intercourse with, frequent.

Beau Fr. in *beau-père, beau-fils, beau-frère, belle-mère, belle-fille, belle-sœur*, N. Pr. *beou-pero, bela-mera*, father-in-law or step-father &c. Formerly there were words for each: *sogre, sogredame, gendre, bru* or *nore, serorge* (m. f.) to express relationship in law; for step-relationship *parastre, marastre, filiastre* (m.f.), *frerastre, sorastre.* When *marastre* got to mean a bad step-mother, *belle-mère* came into use ὑποκοριστικῶς, and then *beau-père* &c. The words were afterwards used for relations in-law. The Du. has *schoon* (fair), the Bret. *kaer* to express step-relationship. The Mil. *messee*, Ven. *missier* = father-in-law, *madonna* = mother-in-law.

Beaucoup Fr., whence It. *belcolpo* = multum; from *beau* fine, great (cf. *beau mangeur* = grand m.), and *coup* a stroke or throw, a heap, cf. Sp. *golpe* = a multitude. In O. Fr. we find *grandcoup*, Pr. *mancolp.*

Bécasse bêche — *beoco.*

Beccabungia It., Sp. Pg. Fr. *becabunga*, Russ. *ibunka*, a plant, brook-lime; from Du. *becke-bunge* (brook-clod), G. *bachbunge* one of the very few names of plants which the G. has given to the Rom. languages. The usual Fr. is *berle de rivière.*

Becco It., Pr. Fr. *bec*, Pg. *bico* beak, bill; Sp. *bicos* (pl.) small gold tags. A Celtic word: *cui Tolosæ nato cognomen in pueritiá Becco fuerat, id valet gallinacei rostrum* Suet. Vitell. c. 18; Gael. *beic*, Bret. *bek*, Du. *bek*, W. *pig.* Hence Pr. *beca*, Fr. *bêche* for *beche* a spade, though O. Fr. has *besche;* It. *beccare*, Pr. *bechar*, Fr. *becquer* to hack, *bécher* dig, G. *bicken picken*, E. *pick;* It. *beccaccia*, Fr. *bécasse*, Cat. *becada* a snipe; Fr. *béquille* a crutch, Fr. *abéquer* to feed young birds; Pg. *debicar* to eat daintily. It. *bezzicare* to pick with the beak may include the two, *becco* and *pizza* (q. v.).

Becco It. goat. This word is found in very old inscriptions. It cannot be of the same origin as the Pr. *boc*, Fr. *bouc*, but is connected with Fr. *bique* = *chèvre*, in the Jura *bequi* = chevreau, = Camp. *bequat*, Rouchi *béquériau* = lamb, Norm.

becard = a wether. The Serv. has *bèkawitza* sheep from *bè-knuti* to bleat, Serv. *bik* = an ox.

Becerro Sp. Pg. a calf, Pg. fem. *becerra;* from Basque *beicecorra*, from *beia* a cow (W. *biw*) and *cecorra* a calf. Hence Sp. *bicerra* a wild-goat, *bizerra* a roe.

Bedaine — *bedon.*

Bedeau — *bidello.*

Bedel — *bidello.*

Bedello — *betulla.*

Bedon Fr. a tambour, small drum, also = a big belly (= *bedaine*), Com. *bidon* fat and lazy, Rouchi *bidon* a fat lazy man, Fr. *bidon* a big-bellied pitcher. *Bed* = *bid* in *bidel* (p. v.). Rouchi *bèdene* = *bedaine* and *bidel.*

Béer — *badare.*

Befana It. a large doll with which children are frightened on the Epiphany (*befania*), whence the name. So in Germany an image of Bertha was used on the same day for the same purpose.

Beffa It., Sp. *befa*, O. Fr. *beffe*, O. Sp. Pg. *bafa* a scoffing, derision; It. *beffare*, Sp. *befar*, O. Sp. *bafar* to scoff, Fr. *bafouer* to treat shamefully; Sp. *befo* the underlip of a horse, also = thick-lipped (written also *belfo*), Cat. *bifi*, Occ. *befe*; Pic. *bafe* a glutton. Prob. from the G., cf. Bav. *beffen* to bark, to scold. Frisch refers to the Thuring. *bäppe* mouth, Mil. *babbi*, Com. *bebb*, Occit. *bèbo* a lip; the Gen. *fä beffe* = pout the lips at. From *beffa* comes the Fr. *beffler*, E. *baffle* (formerly = mock; put to scorn, espec. a recreant knight).

Beffler — *beffa.*

Beffroi — *battifredo.*

Befo — *beffa.*

Bègue Fr., Pic. *beique bique* a stammerer; hence O. Sp. *vegue*, Pic. Norm. Burg. *béguer*, Fr. *bégayer* to stammer, Fr. *begai* stammering. Perhaps contracted from the Pr. *barec* a silly babbler, Sp. *babieca* a booby, O. Fr. *begaud*, Norm. *begas.* For the contraction cf. Pr. *sageta*, O. Fr. *sette.*

Bégueule Fr. a booby, prop. a gaper: from *béer* and *gueule.*

Behetria Sp. Pg. a free town; from Basque *beret-iria* a town for itself, i. e. independent; according to others from *benefactoria* (A. D. 1020), *benfetria* (A. D. 1129).

Beignet — *bugna.*

Beira — *riviera.*

Belare It., Fr. *bêler* to bleat; from *belare* used by Varro for *balare.* Hence Romagn. *be* = bleating, Cat. *be* a sheep, Norm. *bai* a wether, cf. *bidet.*

Beldroega — *portulaca.*

Bele O. Fr. a weasel, Fr. (dim.) *belette*, Sp. *beleta*, Mil. *bellora*,

5*

Com. *bérola*, Parm. *benla*, Gen. *béllua*, Sic. *baddottula* (for *ballottula bellottula*). In form *bele* corresponds to the W. *bele* a pole-cat, O. H. G. *bille*, but it is more probably the same as the Lat. *bella* beautiful, so *bellora* = *bellula*, cf. the Bavar. *schönthierlein, schöndiglein*, Dan. *den kjönne* (pulchra), a propitiatory epithet for an animal which was thought to possess mysterious power, O. F. *fairy*. The Norm. word is *roselet* (red), Lorr. *moteile* (mustela), Norm. *bacoulette*.

Beleño Sp. henbane; from *venenum*, It. *veleno?* More probably connected with the A. S. *belene belone belune*, Russ. *belená*, Pol. *bielun*, Bohem. *bljn*, Hung. *belénd-fu*, O. H. G. *bilisa*.

Beller Fr. a ram, in fables *Belin*, whence Norm. *blin;* from Du. *bel*, E. *bell*, cf. Du. *bel-hamel*, E. *bell-wether*, in Fr. also *clocheman* and *mouton à la sonnette*, L. L. *aries squillatus*. The Fr. *belière* the ring on which a bell-clapper hangs, is of the same origin.

Belitre Fr. a beggar, a scoundrel, whence Sp. *belitre*, Pg. *biltre;* It. *belitrone*. Prob. from the G. *bettler*, the O. Fr. *belistre* having an *s* inserted before the *t*.

Bellaco — *vigliacco*.

Belleguin Sp., Pg. *beleguim* a bailiff; according to Sousa from Ar. *baleguin*, according to Larramendi from Basque *bella*=Sp. *vela*, watch.

Belletta It. sediment, mud. The Mil. has *litta*. It can hardly come from πηλός as Blanc suggests.

Belletto It. paint; from *bello*, cf. *fattibello* = *belletto*.

Bellesour O. Fr., Pr. *bellazor* a comparative from *bel*, Pr. nomin. *bellaire;* from the L. *bellatior*, from *bellatus* (Plaut. *bellatulus*): cf. *ebriolatus, pullatus, bifidatus. Bellatus* is found in O. Fr. *bele.* The O. Sp. had a peculiar form *belido (bellitus).* Connected with this is, prob., the Neap. *belledissemo*.

Bellico — *ombelico*.

Bellicone — *wilecome*.

Belliscar — *pellizcar*.

Bellota Sp., Pg. *belota bolola boleta* acorn; = Ar. *ballü't* Freyt. 1, 153, which answers to the Lat. *balanus*. Hence, too, It. *ballotta*.

Bellugue O. Fr., Pr. *beluga*, whence Norm. *heluette*, Fr. *bluelle*, Pr. *belugeiar (belugueiar?)*, Fr. *bluetter* to emit sparks. From the part. *bis* and *lux*, so = properly "feeble light" = It. *barlume*, Sp. *vis-lumbre*, Norm. *berluette. Beluga* = *bes-luga* as O. Fr. *beloi* = *bes-loi*. The Fr. *berlue* a dazzling is only another form of the same word, Berrichon *éberluette*, Pr. *abellucar*, Piedm. *sbaluché*, Ber. *éberluter*, Champ. *aberluder* to dazzle. In the Mil. *barluss* (= *berlue) lux* is preserved not altered to *luca*.

Benda It. Pr., Lomb. *binda*, Sp. *venda*, Fr. *bande* vitta, tænia, fascia, It. *bendare* &c.; from O. H. G. *binda*, O. H. G. Goth. *bindan* to *bind*. G. *bündel*, E. *bundle* = O. Fr. *boundle*.

Benna It. a basket-cart, Com. a cart, or basket for a cart, Rh. a carriage, Fr. *banne* a large covering for the protection of goods &c., a tarpaulin, Com. *beñola*, Rh. *banaigl*, Fr. *banneau benneau*, *banneton*. Festus says: *benna lingua Gallica genus vehiculi appellatur*, so in L.L.= vehiculum and also a kind of vessel. The Sp. Cat. N. Pr. *banasta* is connected, but it must be through the O. Fr. *banastre* as no ending *asta* is found. The Goth. *banst* is found in the prov. Fr. *banse* (f.) a large basket, L. L. *bansta*.

Beodo O. Sp.=drunken, from *bibitus*, cf. *comido* = one who has eaten, R. Gr. 3, 241. *Beo* = *bib*.

Béquille — *becca*.

Berbice It., Wal. *berbeace*, Pr. *berbitz*, Fr. *brebis*, Pic. *berbis* a sheep; from *berbex* a form used by Petronius for *vervex*, L. L. *berbix*. Hence Pr. *bergier*, Fr. *berger* a shepherd, L. L. *berbicarius*; O. Fr. *bercil* a sheep-cote = vervecile; Fr. *bercail* = *vervecale*.

Berbiqui — *vilebrequin*.

Bercail — *berbice*.

Berceau — *bercer* (2).

Bercer (generally *berser*) O. Fr. to shoot, also to hunt; O. Fr. *bersail*, It. *bersaglio*, *berzaglio* a butt, *bersailler bersciller* to hit. In an old It. chronicle we find: *trabs ferrata quem bercellum appellabant* i. e. a battering-ram, evidently from *berbex vervex*; from *berbex* would be formed It. *berciare (imberciare* is found), Fr. *bercer* = to pierce, cf. Wal. *berbecà inberbecà* to hit.

Bercer Fr., Pr. *bressâr*, O.Sp. *brizar* to rock; O.Fr. *bers* (whence Pic. *ber*), Pr. *bers bres*, O. Pg. *breço*, Pg. *berço*, O. Sp. *brizo*, whence Fr. *berceau* a cradle, L. L. *berciolum*. Prob. from *berbex* (v. preced.), the notion being got from the swing of the battering-ram, cf. L. L. *agitarium* in same sense. Fr. *berceau* = also an arch of vines &c., from the resemblance to the covering of a cradle. Besides *brizo* the Sp. has *brezo* and *blezo* = a wicker-work bed, *combleza* = concubine.

Bergante — *briga*.

Berge — *barca*.

Berla Mil. a waggon-basket; from O. H. G. *biral* cophinus.

Berlanga — *brelan*.

Berle Fr. a water-parsnip; Marc. Empiricus has: *herbam quam Latini berulam, Græce cardaminen vocant*. This may be the orig. of *berle* for though the plants are distinct, yet both are found growing in brooks, and both were used for salad.

Berlina It. Rh. a whipping-post. Muratori gets it from Fr. *pilori* as if for *pilorina;* but no It. dialect has the tenuis. Perhaps, from Bavar. *breche* pillory, whence *breche-lin berchlin berlina?* or from M. H. G. *britelin* a small bridle.

Berline Fr. a *berlin* (carriage); from *Berlin*.

Berlingare It. to feast, regale oneself, *berlingozzo* a tart, *berlingoccio* = Jeudi gras. From O. H. G. *prezilinc* a cake.

Berlue — *belluca*.

Berlusco It. squinting, Com. *balosc blusc;* for *bilusco* (v. *bis*) = Rouchi *berlou berlouque; warlouque* seems a different compound connected with Piedm. *galucé* to squint.

Berme Fr., whence Sp. *berma*, narrow path at the foot of a rampart; from Du. *breme*, A. S. *brymme*, E. *brim*.

Bermejo — *vermiglio*.

Berner Fr. to toss a ball, toss in a blanket, scoff. The Romans, says *Cujacius*, used the *sagum* for this purpose: *sagum* = O. Fr. *berne* (v. *bernia*), whence *berner*. The Neap. *bernare* to amuse oneself is from the French.

Bernia sbernia It., Sp. *bernia*, Fr. *bernie berne* a coarse stuff for cloaks &c., also a cloak made of it, a rug; from *Hibernia* where it was manufactured. Cf. Sp. *holanda*, holland, *cambric* &c.

Berretta It., Sp. *birreta*, Pr. *berreta barreta*, Fr. *barrette*, O. Sp. (m.) *barrete*, Fr. *birret* a cap; from the late L. *birrus (byrrhus)* a coarse cloth, v. *bujo*.

Berro Sp. water-cress; the same as the W. *berwr*, Bret. *béler*, whence L. *berula* used by Marcellus Empiricus: *herbam quam Latine berulam, Græce cardaminen vocant.*

Berroviere — *berruier*.

Berruier O. Fr., Pr. *berrovier* champion. Murat. (Ant. Ital. 2, 530) makes the *berruiers* = les hommes perdus du seigneur, little different from the ribaldi. Properly = a man of Berry. As in the case of *chaorcia* we have no means of determining how it came to be used as an appellative. Hence the It. *berroviere* a highwayman, a birro, police-officer, O. Gen. *berruel*.

Bersaglio — *bercer*.

Berser — *bercer*.

Berta It. bantering, railing, Lomb. Piedm. a magpie, chatterbox; It. *berteggiare* to jeer; Pr. *bertaut* a sorry wight? Rouchi *bertaud* an eunuch, *bertauder*, Fr. *bretauder* to castrate, Com. *bertoldà* to crop the ears or hair; It. *bertone* a crop-eared horse; *bertuccio* an ape. Is this root *bret* or *bert* (mutilating, deriding) from the O. N. *britian* to cut in pieces, or from *bretôn* in the lay of Hildebrand translated by Lachmann to mutilate? The It. *berta* has, however, another meaning, viz:

that of a rammer or beetle for driving posts into the ground,
Fr. *demoiselle*. The origin of this is clear enough when we
consider that the hideous and cruel *Bertha* of the German
tales also bore the name of *Stempfe*, from her *stamping* on
those obnoxious to her (e. g. refractory children who used to
be threatened with her vengeance). Whether the other Rom.
words are connected with this or not, is not clear.

Bertouser — *bis*.

Bertovello It. a weel, bownet. The L. L. *vertebolum* (L. Sal.),
a dim. of *vertebra*, but, in meaning, directly from *vertere*,
the neck of the weel being *turned* inwards, cf. It. *ritroso*
(= *retrorsus*) mouth or neck of a weel. Hence Ven. *bertevelo*,
Pied. Crem. Mil. *bertavel*, Com. *bertavelle bertarel*; It. *bertovello*, as *martello* from *martulus*, Fr. *verveux* (more correctly
verveu) is for *vertveu* = *vertovello*.

Berza — *verza*.

Bes N. Pr. Cat. a birch-tree; from the Celtic: Corn. *bes bezo*,
Bret. *bezô*, W. *bedw* = Lat. *betula*.

Besace — *bisaccia*.

Besaigre Fr. sourish; from part. *bis* and *acer*.

Besaiguē — *bicciacuto*.

Besant — *bisante*.

Bescio besso It. blockhead; from *bestia*, like Pr. *pec* from *pecus*,
cf. Com. *bescia* a sheep, Rh. *beschlar* to bleat.

Besi Fr. (in the W.) a wild pear; cf. Du. *bes besie* a berry.

Besicle Fr. (f. usu. plur.) spectacles. Not from *bis-cyclus*, but
= *bericle* (O. Fr. Pr.) = *beryllus* (used in L. L. = spectacles),
Occ. *mericle*, Gen. *bericle*, Wall. *berik*. The form *besicle* may
have originated in Paris, where *frèse* = *frère*, *misesese* = *mise-
rere*, cf. *chaise* and *poussière*.

Beso — *bacio*.

Besoin — *sogna*.

Bestemmia — *biasimo*.

Bestordre bestors — *tordre*.

Beta — *veta*.

Betarda — *ottarda*.

Beter O. Fr. to muzzle = A. S. *bœtan*, Du. *beeten*, M. H. G.
beizen to make bite (the curb), also to *bait*, M. H. G. *erbeizen*.
Hence L. L. *abettum*, O. Fr. Pr. *abet* deceit, trick, Pr. O. Sp.
abeiar, O. Fr. *abeter* to cheat, Norm. *abet* a bait, *abeter* to
bait, E. *abet*. The O. Fr. *betè*, Pr. *betat* often used with *mor*
= coagulatum; cf. M. H. G. *lebermer* from *liberen* to curdle,
E. *beestings* = colostrum. This, too, is prob. from G. *beizen*
to bite, be tart or sour.

Betula betulla It. Pg., It. *bedello* (Crem. *béddol*), Cat. *bedoly*,
Sp. *abedul*, Pic. Champ. *boule* (for *beoule*?), whence Fr. *bouleau*

a birch-tree; from *betula betulla*, which is of Celtic origin,
v. *bes*.

Beugler Fr. to bellow like an ox; from *buculus*, whence *beugle*
an ox.

Bévero It., Sp. *bibaro*, O. Sp. *befre*, Fr. *bièvre*, Wal. *breb*, N. Pr.
vibre a beaver, O. Norse *bifr*, A. S. *befor beofer*, O. H. G. *bibar*,
G. *biber*, Lith. *bebru*, Russ. *bober*, Gael. *beabhar*, Corn. *befer*
= L. *fiber*, the asp. of which, according to rule, becomes a
medial in German, Lithuanian, Sclavonic and Celtic, cf. Zeuss
1, 44. *Bebrinus* is found in scholia in Juv. 12, 34.

Bévue Fr. a false view, an error; from *bis* (q. v.) and *vue*.

Bezzicare — *becco*.

Biacca It. pale-white; from G. *bleich*.

Biadetto — *biavo*.

Biado O. It., Pr. Cat. *blat*, O. Fr. *bled bleif*, Fr. *bled blé*, It. *biada*,
Mil. Ven. Piedm. *biara* (cf. *Rovigo* = *Rhodigium*), O. Fr. *blée*,
L. L. *bladum blatum* corn. Hence Pr. *bladaria*, Fr. *blairie* rent
of pasture; It. *imbiadare*, Fr. *emblaver* (cf. *gravir, parvis, pouvoir*) to sow with corn. The usual derivation is from the A. S.
blæd (f.) fruit, but Romance terms of husbandry are not likely
to have come from so remote a source; rather is *blæd* from
the Rom. as G. *fruht* from Lat. *fructus*. Diez derives it from
the neut. plur. *ablata*, with the Rom. article *l' ablata l' abiada
la biada*, m. *biado* (ablatum); for the meaning cf. G. *getreide*
(produce) and G. *herbst*, Gr. καρπός = that which is gathered.
In L. L. *ablatum abladus abladium* occur = messis. The Crem.
biada = Fr. *oublie (oblata)*. Mahn makes the Pr. *blat* the original form and asserts its identity with the G. *blatt* a leaf, in
Bret. and W. *blot, bleud, bled, blawd* meal, all which belong
to the Sansk. root *phull, phal*, E. *blow*, whence also *folium*
and φύλλον.

Biais Fr. Pr. Val. O. Cat., N. Cat. *biax*, Sard. *biasciu* (m.), E.
bias, Pg. *viez* obliquity, It. *s-bescio* awry (cf. Piedm. *sbias*,
N. Pr. *es-biai*), Fr. *biaiser*, Pr. *biaisar*, Sard. *sbiasciai*. In the
Isidor. Gloss. we find *bifax duos habeas oblutus* double-sighted,
squinting, like the Sp. *bisojo*, cf. Buvar. *zweidugeln* to squint.
From *bifax (bis-fax* for *bis-oculus)* would come *bifais biais*
(cf. *refusar reusar profundus preon)* first used as an adj. (*via
biayssa* Choix 5, 64) afterwards as a substantive. L. L. *bifa-
cies bifaciare* = *biais biaiser*.

Bianco It., Sp. *blanco*, Pg. *branco*, Pr. Fr. *blanc* white; from
O. H. G. *blanch*, M. H. G. &c. *blanc* a shining white. Connected with *blinken* to glitter, E. *blink*. It was the common
word to represent the Lat. *albus* which became extinct in the
North-West, in the South-West (Sp. *albo*, Pg. *alvo*) = snow.-

white, in Italian dull-white, turbid, dull. *Albus* is retained in Rh. and Wal., where *blank* is not fonnd.

Biante It. a vagabond: for *riante* from *riare* to wander (Menage) or, perhaps = the Pr. *viandan (via andare)* wanderer. The l'arm. is *bigant*.

Biasciare biascioare It. to munch, mumble; perhaps from *blæsus* whence *blasare* (Com. *blassà*).

Biasimo It., O. Sp. *blasmo*, Pr. *blasme*, Fr. *blâme*, E. *blame*; It. *biasimare* &c.; from βλάσφημον (adj.), βλασφημεῖν. From βλασφημία, with a change of the *f* into *t*, comes It. *biastemma bestemmia*, Rh. *blastemma*, Pr. *blastenh*, O. Fr. *blastenge*, Wal. *blēstēm* blasphemy; It. *biastemmare* &c.; with loss of the *f* (as in *lacio* for *flacio*) Sp. Pg. *lastima* abuse, grief, lamentation, *lastimar* to abuse, move to pity.

Biastemma — *biasimo*.

Biavo Ven. It. (Boiardo 2, 37), O. Sp. *blavo*, Pr. *blau* (f. *blava*), Fr. *bleu* (like *peu* from *pau*), whence It. *biù*, E. *blue*; It. dim. *biadetto*; It. *sbiavato sbiadato*; from O. H. G. *bldo blaw*. The Rom. *blave* also = green, *blavoyer* = *verdoyer*. Hence Wedgwood derives *biada* (q. v.) first used for the *brilliant* green of young corn, then for *corn* itself. *Biavo* also = pale straw-colour. The word is widest spread in Pr.: *blavenc*, *blaveza*, *blaveiar*, *blavairú*, *emblauzir*.

Biassa — *bis-accia*.

Bica It. a circle of sheaves, a stook; *abbicare* to set up sheaves, to heap together (Dante Inf. 9, of frogs *crouching*); from O. H. G. *biga* a heap.

Bicchiere It., Rh. *bichér* a drinking vessel, E. *beaker*, also It. *pecchero* a goblet, Wal. *péhar*, Pr. O. Fr. *pichier pechier*, Sp. Pg. *pichel*, Basque *pitcherra* a tankard, *pitcher*; L. L. *bicarium picarium*; O. N. *bikar*, O. H. G. *pehhar*, G. *becher*. The radical *i* will not allow it to come from L. *bacar* (Festus). It may be from *becco* a beak = mouth of pitcher (cf. E. *beaker*), or from Gk. βίχος an earthen vessel, the *p* for *b* coming through the O. German.

Biciacuto It. two-edged; corrupted from *bisacuto*, O. Fr. *besaigu*.

Bicha bicho — *biscia*.

Biche Fr. a hind, O. Fr. E. *bisse*, Wall. *bih*, N. Pr. *bicho*, Piedm. *becia*. The form *bisse* will not suit the der. from *bique* a goat, N. Pr. *bico*, so it is better to refer it to L. *ibex*, O. Fr. *ibiche*.

Biche O. Fr. a bitch; from A. S. *bicce*, E. *bitch*, N. *bikkia*, cf. G. *betze*; but Frisch makes it for *babiche* = *barbiche (barbe)* a shaggy dog, whence It. *barbone*, Gen. *barbin*. From *biche* comes *bichon* a small long-haired dog.

Bicocca, biociocca, bicicocca It. a watch-tower, Ven. *bicoca* a ruinous house, Sard. *bicocca* a hut, stairs with two landings, terrace, Lomb. a reel, Sp. *bicoca* a sentry-box, a narrow chamber, small town, Fr. *bicoque, bicoq.* Cf. also Sp. *bicoquete* a bonnet, *bicoquin* cap with two lappets, Piedm. *bicochin* a priest's cap. The first syllable is, perhaps, *bis* (cf. *bicocca, bicoquin*), but the sense of *cocca* here is doubtful.

Bidello It., Sp. Pr. *bedel*, Fr. *bedeau*, E. *bedell;* corresponds exactly with the O. H. G. *petil* emissarius, less exactly with the A. S. *bydel* = O. H. G. *butil*, G. *büttel*, E. *beadle.*

Bidet Fr. E. a little horse, a nag, It. *bidetto.* From a Celtic root, Gael. *bideach* little, *bidein* a little creature, cf. W. *bidan* a weakling.

Bidon - - *bedon.*

Bieco abieco oblique, awry, squinting; from *obliquus* which should have given *obbico bico*, but the *e* is inserted as in *piego* = *plico.* Dante's plurals *bieci* Par. 5, 65, *biece* Inf. 25, 31, come immediately from *obliqui obliquæ.*

Bied O. Fr. the bed of a river, whence Norm. *bedière* (cf. *lit litière*); from A. S. *bed*, O. N. *bedr* = O. H. G. *betti*, whence Fr. *biez* mill-pool, L. L. *bieziam bietium.* From *bed* come Burg. *bief*, Norm. *bieu*, Piedm. *bial*, Gen. *beo*, L. L. *bedum.*

Bière — *bara.*

Bière — *birra.*

Biffera It. a woman who has two husbands; from *bivira*, cf. *fiasco.*

Bifolco It. one who tills with oxen; from *bubulcus* (*f* = *b*, cf. *tafano*).

Biga Piedm. a sow; Du. *big bigge* (f.), E. *pig.*

Bigarrer Fr. to variegate, Cat. *bigarrar*, Sp. *abigarrar* (from the Fr.). Menage derives it from *bis-variare*, but, perhaps, better from *bi-carrer* (carré square) properly = to make square, cf. G. *scheckig*, E. *checkered. Bis* here denotes irregularity (v. *bis*).

Bigatto — *baco.*

Bigio It., Pr. Fr. *bis* dark-grey, dark-coloured. Hence Piedm. Pr. *bisa*, Fr. *bise* the North-wind, Bret. *biz* North-East-wind (cf. *aquilo* from *aquilus*). The Pg. *buzio* and Sp. *bazo* dark *(pan bazo* = pain bis) are probably connected (but v. *bajo*), all coming from *bombycius bambucinus* or *bombacius.* Silk and woollen stuffs were dyed scarlet or purple before being imported to Europe, hence L. L. *bombicina* = scarlet, It. *bambagello* purple pigment, O. H. G. *sidin* = *coccineus.* The first syllable was dropped, probably, from its likeness to *bombus* (cf. L. L. *bacius*, It. *baco*, Fr. *basin*). Diez formerly derived the word from *bysseus:* Mahn refers it to the Basque *baza beza* = *baltza beltza* dark, but the radical *t* is an objection.

Bigle Fr. squinting, *bigler* to squint. Probably = Sp. *bis-ojo* from *bis-oculus*, when it would stand for *bisigle*, contr. *bisgle*, cf. *icle* in *bornicle bournicler* (Jura).

Biglia It., Sp. *billa*, Fr. *bille* a ball; probably from the M. H. G. *bickel* a knuckle-bone, Du. *bikkel* a bone with which children play. Hence Fr. *billard* (E. *billiard*) and *billot* a lay of wood.

Bigne — *bugna*.

Bigorne Fr. an anvil with projections like horns (incus cornuta); from *bicornis*, It. *bicornia*, Sp. *bigornia*.

Bigoncia It. a tub, a liquid measure; from *bis congius*.

Bigot Fr. E. *bigot*. In O. Fr. it was used as a nickname of the Norman, its modern sense being unknown before the 16ᵗʰ century. An old anecdote gives the following account of its origin. Duke Rollo when called upon to kiss king Charles' foot made answer: *ne se bi god* whence the Normans were termed *bigots*, cf. *sandio*. But we should in this case have expected *bigot* rather than *bigot* (cf. *bruth brui* v. *bru*). Others derive it from *Visi-gothus* like *cagot* from *canis gothus*. This is too artificial. Trench and others derive the modern sense of the word from the Pr. Sp. *bigote* a moustache, *hombre de bigote* a firm resolute (and so *bigoted*) man. It. *sbigottire* = frighten, disconcert, put out of countenance. We find also O. Fr. *bigole*, *bigotelle*, *bigoterre* a purse hanging at the girdle, *bigoter* to provoke. Wedgwood's etymology (from *bigio* grey) is untenable.

Bijou Fr. a jewel; from a compound *bisjocare*, *bijouer*, so = something doubly sparkling. Then, why not *bijeu*? no verb *bijouer* is found. Perhaps it is from the Celtic (O. Corn.) *bisou* "annulus", Bret. *bizou* = W. *byson* (from *bys* a finger?).

Bilancia It., Mil. Ven. Sp. *balanza*, Pr. *balans balansa*, Fr. *balance*, E. *balance*; from *bilanx bilancis*.

Bilenco It. crooked, askew; from G. *link?*

Billard bille — *biglia*.

Billet — *bolla*.

Biltre — *belitre*.

Bimbo — *bambo*.

Bindolo — *ghindare*.

Binoccolo It., Fr. *binocle* an opera-glass; from *bini oculi*.

Biocoolo It. flock; from *floccus*, cf. *bonte* (dialect.) for *fonte*.

Biondo It., Pr. *blon* (f. *blonda*), Fr. *blond*, whence, probably, the Sp. *blondo*, G. *blond*, E. *blond*. The A. S. has *blonden-feax* = of *blended-hair* grey-haired, but the transition from *grey* to *blond* is difficult. Perhaps it is from the O. N. *blaud*, Dan. *blöd* soft, weak (in colour or quality). The It. *biondella* (the plant centaur) is so called from its blond tresses.

Biotto It. wretched, Lomb. *biott blot*, Rh. *blutt* naked, Ven. *bioto*

simple, Pr. O. Fr. *blos* destitute, N. Pr. *blous* pure (of water
&c.), Mod. *bioss* naked, Basque *buluza*. Of German origin:
Bavar. *blutt*, Sw. *blutt* and *blutz*, vb. *blutten*, L. L. *blutare* to
empty, M. H. G. *blôz* (whence Pr. *blos*), G. *bloss*.

Bique — *becco*.

Birar — *virare*.

Birba birbone — *bribe*.

Bircio It. weak-eyed, *sbirciare* to blink, *bercilocchio* a squinter.
Perhaps connected with O. H. G. *brehan*, Bav. *birg-aug*.
Aust. *bir-augig* all of which express a defect in the sight.

Biroccio baroccio It. a two wheeled vehicle, Sp. *barrocho*, a
barouche; from *birotus* with the ending formed on the model
of *carroccio*. The Fr. is *brouette* for *bi-rouette*, Wall. *berwette*.

Birra It., Fr. *bière*, Wal. *bearè* beer. Another expression for the
O. Rom. word, It. *cervigia*, Sp. *cerveza*, O. Fr. *cervoise*, L. *cere-
visia*. The It. *birra* is from the G. *bier*, the Fr. *bière* from the
M. H. G. *bier* (as one syllable), a German-Celtic word; O. H.
G. A. S. *beor*, E. *beer*, O. N. *bior*, Gael. *beôir*, Bret. *biorch*.
The G. *bier* is, according to some, only the L. inf. *bibere*,
sbst. *biber*, It. *bévere*, *béere*, *bere*, Sard. *biere*, cf. Wal. *beu-
ture*, prop. = drink, F. *bever* = lunch; according to others
the H. G. *bier* is to be referred to Goth. *bius* and this to the
Sansk. *piv*, *pib* from *pâ* to drink.

Birracchio — *birro*.

Birreta — *berreta*.

Birro sbirro a serjeant, police-officer, whence Sp. *esbirro;* prob.
from *birrus* (v. *berretta*), the dark cloth with which he was
clothed. So Menage, who also derives *birracchio* a steer one
year old from *birrus* in its sense of *rufus*.

Bis (sometimes in the forms *ber bre bar*) a Romance particle used
in composition to denote that which is wrong, false, counterfeit &c.; It. *biscantare* to sing irregularly, trill, hum a tune,
Pr. *beslei* bad faith, It. *barlume* weak light (twilight), Fr. *ber-
louser berlauder* to shear unevenly, Piedm. *bertiché* to taste a
little, *berlaita* whey (poor milk = petit lait), cf. R. Gr. 2, 357.
Various derivations are given. The form is against the G.
mis, both sense and form against the Bret. *besk*. The Lat.
rice (= something *not-real, fictitious*) would suit the It. and
Sp. where *v* may become *b*, but not the Fr. Perhaps it is the
adv. *bis*, which from the sense of *double* passed into that of
oblique, awry (as in Sp. *bisojo* squinting, Fr. *biais*), and then
= wrong, counterfeit, bad, e. g. *besivre* badly drunk, *bes-
order* to pollute, *besancà* hip-shot, *bévue* (Fr.) an error. Of
the same origin is the Sp. *bisel*, Occ. *bizel*, Fr. *biseau* sloping
edge, oblique surface, E. *basil bezel*. When a joiner's tool is

ground away to an angle it is called a *basil* edge (Fr. *taillé en biseau*).

Bis — *bigio*.

Bisaccia It., Sp. *bisaza*, Fr. *besace* a wallet; from *bisaccium*, pl. *bisaccia* (Petronius). So Pr. Fr. *bissac*, Piedm. *bersac*, from *bis-saccus*. For *bisaza* is found also *biaza*, perhaps on the analogy of. *via viage*.

Bisante It., Sp. Pg. *besante*, Pr. *bezan*, Fr. O. E. *besant* a Byzantine coin, from L. L. *byzantius*, Gr. βυζάντιος.

Bisarma — *guisarme*.

Bisbiglio It. whispering, noise of talkers, *bishigliare*, G. *pispeln*, Pic. *bisbille;* formed from the sound.

Biscanto — *canto*.

Biscia It. a serpent, Lomb. *bissa*, N. Pr. *bessa*, O. Fr. *bisse*, Piedm. *biesso*, Lomb. *biss*, It. *biscio* a flesh-worm. Usually derived from *bestia*, but this would give *bescia*. Better, perhaps, from the O. H. G. *bizo* a biting creature = A. S. *bita*. The Lomb. has *bisià besià* to prick, *bisient* biting, *bistell* a bee's sting, *bisioce* an insect with sting. The Sp. *bicho bicha* a grub may also come from *bizo biza*.

Biscotto It., Sp. *bizcocho*, Pr. *biscueit*, Fr. *biscuit*, E. *biscuit;* from *bis-coctus*. So It. *guascotto* from *quasi-coctus*.

Bisdosso bardosso without saddle; *andare a bisdosso* to ride on the bare back, *bis* expressing the discomfort (v. *bis*).

Bise — *bigio*.

Bisel biseau — *bis*.

Biset — *bigio*.

Bislessare — *lessare*.

Bislungo — *barlong*.

Bismalva — *malvavischio*.

Bisogno — *sogna*.

Bisojo Sp. squint-eyed, prop. double-eyed from *bis-oculus*, cf. *biais*, Sard. *bisogu*, however, = one-eyed (Fr. *louche*, *luscus*).

Bisse — *biscia*.

Bissêtre bissestre O. Fr., Norm. *bisientre*, Piedm. *bisest* disaster; prop. = intercalary day, from *bissextus*, which was even with the Romans considered *unlucky*, v. Ducange.

Bistensar — *stentare*.

Bistondo — *tondo*.

Bitta It., Sp. Cat. *bita*, Fr. *bitte* a piece of wood, stake (*bitas* Sp., Fr. *bittes* = *bits* to belay the cable), from the O. N. *biti* a beam, E. *bit*, Sw. *bissen;* L. L. *bitus* = lignum quo vincti flagellantur.

Bivac bivouac Fr., E. *bivouac*, vb. *bivouaquer;* from G. *biwacht*, *beiwacht* an extraordinary watch, Sp. *virac vivaque*.

Bizco Sp., Pg. *vesgo* squint-eyed. The contraction from *bisoculus* (whence Sp. *bisojo*) would be harsh. Larramendi derives it from the Basque.

Bizerra — *becerro*.

Bizma Sp. (f.) a plaster, *epitima* (f.) a poultice; from *epithema*, It. *epittima*, *pittima*, Fr. *épithème*, E. *epithem*.

Bizoooo (Menage) It., *bizzoccone* a blockhead. From *bliteus* (Plautus) (cf. Papias. *blitea stultitia*) came *bizzo*, with suffix *bizzocco*.

Bizzarro It. irascible, capricious, sprightly, Sp. Pg. *bizarro* gallant, high-spirited, Fr. *bizarre* whimsical, extravagant. For the It. word a primitive *bizza* wrath is given which, if not of G. origin (cf. O. H. G. *bizôn* to gnash) must be from *bizzarro*, there being no suffix *arr*. The Sp. is found also in the Basque, where another word *bizarra* = beard (= *bizarra* "he is manly"), whence the wider sense in Sp.

Blafard Fr. pale; from the O. H. G. *bleih-faro* (G. *bleifarb*) pale-coloured, *d* epenthetic as in *homard*.

Blaireau Fr. a badger, also written *blereau*, *blereau*; from *bladarellus* (It. *biadarello*) dimin. of L. L. *bladarius*, It. *biadajuolo* (cf. O. Fr. *blairie* = Pr. *bladaria*) = corndealer. The E. *badger* is from the same word *bladarius (bladiar, bladger badger)* and in O. E. meant also *corndealer*. The badger is an "animal omnivorum" and lays up store for the winter. This store was popularly, but wrongly, supposed to be corn, hence his name "little corndealer". Diefenbach derives it from the W. *blawr* iron-grey (cf. E. *gray* = badger, Fr. *grisard*), but *aw* would not become *ai* in Fr. The It. *grajo* is not from E. *gray* but, probably, = *agrarius*. Another Rom. word for badger is *tasso* (It.), Fr. *taisson* &c. (q. v.). In O. Fr. it was called *bedoneau bedouan*, Norm. *bedou* = big-bellied.

Blâme — *biasimo*.

Blanc — *bianco*.

Blandir — *brando*.

Blasone It. blazonry, heraldry, Sp. *blason*, Pg. *brasào* also = fame, renown, Fr. *blason* coat of arms, escutcheon; It. *blasonare*, Fr. *blasonner* to paint arms, Sp. *blasonar* to blazon, extol. First found in Fr. where it meant a shield or scutcheon, Pr. *blezó blizó*. It is, doubtless, derived from the A. S. *blæse*, E. *blaze*, whence the sense of *"lustre"* would do both for the *device on an escutcheon* and for *fame, renown*; cf. O. H. G. *bldsa* a trumpet, Du. *blazen* to boast. The Pr. *blezon* takes its *e* from the A. S.

Blé — *biado*.

Blêche Fr. weak, weakly, Norm. *bleque* mouldering, decaying; from Gr. βλάξ βλαχός mollis (L. L. *blax* = *stultus*), cf. *moustache* from μύσταξ. Grandgagnage (v. *bléque*) derives it from G. *bleich* pale.

Bledo Sp., Pg. *bredo*, Cat. *bred* the wild amaranth, or a kind of watercress; for *blitum* (βλίτον).

Blême Fr. pale, *blêmer* to grow pale. The O. Fr. has *blesne* and *blesme*, the *s*, therefore, is inserted; from O. N. *blámi* blue colour (*blá* blue), cf. O. Fr. *blemir* to beat (prop. make blue), E. *blemish* (prop. of dark colour of lifeless flesh).

Blesser Fr. to wound, O. Fr. also to injure: *quant li quatre angles sont bleciet* Liv. de Job 503. The O. Fr. *c* often = G. *z*, so, perhaps, from M. H. G. *bletzen* to patch, *bletz* (O. H. G. *pletz*) cut leather, whence *blesser* to slash, M. H. G. *ze-bletzen* to hew.

Blet Fr. rotten, now only in the phrase *poire blette*, Pied. *biet*, Rouchi *blétir* to rot; cf. O. H. G. *bleizza* a livid spot from a bruise.

Bleu — *biavo*.

Bleso — *bercer*.

Bliaut, blisaut, blial, bliau (robe, habit, justaucorps), *blezo bleso* (tunique), O. Fr. *bliaut bleaut bliaus bliaux* (justaucorps, manteau), Sp. Pg. *brial* a rich petticoat, L. L. *bliaudus blial-dus*, *bliaus*. The M. H. G. *bliait bliât* denotes the stuff merely, so also in O. Fr. Diez suggests that the root *bli* or *blid* is oriental, and Mahn refers to the Pers. *baljad* a plain garment, from Ar. root *bald* to wear a garment. The Fr. *blouse*, Pic. *bleude*, Norm. *plaude* (cf. the forms *blizaut*, *bliaus* &c.) is the same word. Ducange derives *bliaud* &c. from the W. *bliand* a fine linen-stuff, O. E. *bleaunt*, *blehand*.

Blinder Fr. to cover, blind; from Goth. *blindjan*, O. H. G. *blen-dan*, G. *blenden*, E. *blind*. Hence subst. *blindes*, It. *blinde*.

Bloc Fr. a *block*, *bloquer* (It. *bloccare*), Sp. *bloquear* to *blockade*; from O. H. G. *bloc bloch*, G. E. *block*, which Grimm derives from *bi-loh* a bolt (Goth. *lukan* to shut). The Fr. *blocus* is the G. *blochus blockhaus*.

Bloi O. Fr. Pr. light-coloured, yellow, espec. of flowers and of hair, L. L. *bloius blodius*. Thus we find: *l'seut la blonda* and *Ysseultz ab lo pel bloy*. From A. S. *bleó bliü* colour, so light-colour as opp. dark, or better to consider *bloi* another form of *bleu*, both coming from the O. H. G. *blao* = flavus and cœru-leus, cf. *pol* and *peu* from *pau (paucus)*.

Blois O. Fr., Pr. *bles* = *blœsus*.

Blond — *biondo*.

Bloquer — *bloc*.

Blos — *biotto*.

Blostre O. Fr. a little hillock or mound; from Du. *bluyster*, E. *blister*.

Blouse — *bliaut.*

Blù — *biavo.*

Bluette — *bellugue.*

Bluter Fr. to *bolt* meal, separate it from the brau, *bluteau bluloir* a bolting-sieve. *Bluter* is for *bruter* (an O.Sp. *brutar* is found). *Bluter* is the L. L. *buletare*, Rouchi *bulter*, *bluteau* the L. L. *buletellum*. The O. Fr. *buretel* is nearer the original, and = It. *burattello* from *buratto* a sieve, prop. = a thin stuff, v. *bure*, and cf. *étamine*. From *buretel* came *buletel bulutel bluteau*. For *buratel* the Pr. has *barutel*, Dauph. *barìtel*, Bret. *burutel*, Occ. *harutá, baruteló*. Others derive the word from the G. *beuteln*, M. H. G. *biuteln.*

Bobine Fr. a spool, *bobbin*, Piedm. *bobina*. From *bombus* because of the *humming* noise it makes (accord. to Nonius).

Bobò Com., Gen. *bubù* drink (a word used by children). Varro has *bua* in the same sense, which onomatop. seems to have been reduplicated in the Rom. The words involve the same root as *bi-bo*. The It. *bombo bombare bombettare* is rather from Gk. βομβεῖν, *bombola* a flask from βόμβυλος.

Bobo Sp. Pg., Sard. *bovu* blockhead, simpleton; from *balbus*, It. *balbo*, Pr. *balb* &c., cf. Sp. *farfulla* a stammerer, Basq. *farfuilla* a blockhead, and for the form, cf. *popar* from *palpare*.

Boca It., Sp. Pg. *boga*, Pr. *buga*, Fr. *bogue* the sea-bream; from L. *box bocis* (m.) (Pliny), Gk. βόαξ βῶξ.

Bocage bois — *bosco.*

Bocca It., Sp. Pg. Pr. *boca*, Fr. *bouche* a mouth, from *bucca*. Hence Pr. *bucello* (L. *buccella* Martial), *bossi*, O. Fr. *boussin* a morsel; Sp. *bozal* a muzzle = a L. *bucceale*, from *buccea*.

Boccale It., Sp. Fr. Wal. *bocal* a mug, pitcher; from L. L. *baucalis*, which from Gr. βαυκάλιον a vessel, v. Journ. d. Sav. 1833, p. 478.

Boccia — *bozza.*

Boccar Sp. to move the lips, O. Sp. Pg. *bocejar* to gape, Sp. *bocezar* and *bostezar* (for suffix cf. *tropezar*); probably from Sp. *buz* a lip (q. v.).

Bocel — *buz.*

Bocha — *bozza.*

Bochorno Sp. Pg. a sultry East-wind; from *vulturnus.*

Bociare It. to cry, publish; from *vox*, It. *boce.*

Boda Sp. Pg. Cat. a wedding, nuptials. From *vota* pl. of *votum*, cf. Cod. Justin. *ad tertia vota migrare*. An O. Sp. word for vow is *vota*, It. *boto.*

Bode Sp. Pg. a he-goat; cf. Com. *bida* a goat.

Bofe Sp. Pg. lung; from *bufar* to blow, Pg. also *bofar* cf. πνεύμων from πνειν, It. *mantaco* wind - bag, lung; hence Sp. *bo-fena bohena* a pudding made of pig's lung.

Bofé O. Pg. adv. = L. *certo;* for *á boa fé.*

Bofeton — *buf.*

Boffice — *buf.*

Boga — *boca.*

Bogar — *vogare.*

Bohena — *bofe.*

Boisie boisdie — *bugia.*

Boisseau boiter — *boite.*

Boisson Fr. drink; from *boire (bibere); boisson = beison (bibitio).*

Boîte Fr., Pr. *bostia boissa,* also *brostia brustia* a *box.* From *pyxis* was formed L. L. *buxis,* whence the Pr. *boissa;* in the 10th cent. *buxidu* from acc. *pyxida (πυξίδα)* was corrupted into *buxdia bustia,* whence Pr. *bostia,* O. Fr. *boiste,* Bret. *boëst.* In a 9th cent. Glossary we find: *pyxides vulgo poxides.* From *boîte* come *déboîter* to wrench, sprain, *boîter* to limp, Rouch. *boîer.* Hence, too, Fr. *boisseau* (E. *bushel*) a dialectical form of which is *boisteau* L.L. *bustellus.* This is to be distinguished from the O. Fr. *boucel bouchiau,* Pr. *bossel* a liquid measure = It. *botticello* from *botte* (q. v.).

Boja O. It., Pr. *boia,* O. Fr. *buie* a chain, fetter; from *boja* (Plautus &c.); M. H. G. *boije.* The Sp. *boya,* Pg. *boie,* O. Fr. *boye,* Fr. *bouée,* G. *boje,* E. *buoy* is the same word, prop. = a floating piece of wood fastened by a rope or chain *(boja).*

Boja It. an executioner, O. Sp. *boya,* N. Pr. *boiou,* Wall. *boie,* Rh. *bojer.* The It. forms no masculine in *a* (though it uses some masculines as f., e. g. *il camerata, lo spia*), so the word must have existed before in a different sense. It is the O. It. *boja* a fetter, halter, cf. Papias: *boja tormenta damnatorum.* In Sp. the same word is used for *"rod"* and *"executioner",* v. *verdugo.*

Bojar Sp. to sail round an island or a promontory; from Du. *bogen,* G. *biegen beugen* to bend, cf. L. *flectere promontorium.*

Boldrone — *paltro.*

Bolegar — *bouger.*

Boleta — *bolla.*

Bolgia It., O. Fr. *boge* a sack, Fr. *bouge* a little room; hence Sp. *burjaca* a knapsack; Fr. *bougette* a travelling bag, O. E. *bogett bougett,* E. *budget,* which last has travelled back to France in its new sense. It is the Lat. *bulga* (Lucil.) which Festus mentions as a Gallic word; the O. Irish is *bolc,* Gael. *builg,* W. *bwlch* hole &c., O.H.G. *bulga* (*belgen* to swell). The Rom. forms come through a L. adj. *bulgea.*

Bolla bulla It., Sp. Pr. *bola bula,* Pg. *bolha bulla,* Fr. *boule bulle,* a bubble, bladder, ball, and, from the form, a seal affixed to

records (for which the form with *u* is generally used, E. *bull*);
from L. *bulla*. The Sp. *bola*, O. Fr. Pic. *boule* = brag, deceit
arose out of the meaning *"bubble"*, hence *bouler* (of pigeons)
to swell the crop. From *bolla* &c. come It. *bolletta bulletta*,
Fr. *billet* note (= *sealed* paper), It. *bulletino*, Fr. E. *bulletin*;
Sp. *bollon*, Fr. *boulon* a thick-headed nail, O. Fr. = bolt, cf.
L. *bulla* = head of a nail. From the same root, through L.
bullire, come It. *bollire*, Sp. Pr. *bullir*, Pg. *bulir bolir*, Fr.
bouillir to *boil*; hence It. *bollone*, Fr. *bouillon* broth (E. *bullion*),
cf. Sp. *caldo*, Pic. *caudiau*, O. Fr. *caudel*, E. *cauale*; Sp. *bulla*,
Pg. *bulha* noise, whence Cat. *esbulyar* to disturb, and, perhaps, Pg. *esbulhar* to search thoroughly, bereave, which is
gen. derived from *spoliare*.

Bolsa — *borsa*.

Bolso It. asthmatic, (of a horse) broken-winded, Mil. *sbolzà* to
cough; from *pulsus*, whence also Fr. *pousse, poussif*, Limous.
poussà to breathe with difficulty, Sw. *bülsi* have a dry cough.
Cf. Pr. *buls* "equus nimis pulsans".

Bolsone It., O. Sp. O. Fr. *bozon*, Pr. *bossó* an arrow with blunt
point, also a battering-ram; from *bulla* the head of a nail
with the suffix *cion* (cf. *boulon* Fr. a bolt, arrow), cf. *hameçon*
from *hamus*. There is no necessity to derive it from the G.
bolz bolzen.

Bomba Pr. O. Valen. brag, pomp, show; It. *bombanza* rejoicing,
O. Fr. *bombance* sumptuous cheer &c., *bobance*, Pr. *bobansa*
= *bomba*; Pr. *bobans* for *boban*, O. Fr. *bobant*. From *bombus*
buzzing, bustle, *bombicus* noisy, boastful (Venant. Fort.),
whence also *bomba bombarda* a noisy missile, a *bomb*, *bombar-
dare* to *bombard* &c.; It. *rimbombare* to re-echo.

Bomba Sp. Pg. Cat., Fr. *pompe*, E. *pump*. So called, according
to Adelung, from the noise which it makes, but, perhaps,
better from the Rom. *bombare* to drink, suck, which, however, is itself an onomatop., cf. *bobo*. In Italian it is called
tromba, which represented the L. *tuba*, and = a water-pipe.

Bombasin — *bambagio*.

Bombero It. a ploughshare, Ven. *gamiero*; for *vomero*, L. *vomer*.

Bomerie Norm. bottomry; from Du. *bodemerij*, G. *bodmerei*, E.
bottomry, these from *boden, bottom* (of a ship) = a ship.

Bonaccia It., Pr. *bonassa*, Fr. *bonace*, Sp. *bonanza* a calm; from
bonus, cf. Sp. *bonazo* peaceful, good-natured, Wal. *rěsbunĕ* it
clears up. *Malina* in O. Sp. = bad weather, a storm, from
malus.

Bonde Fr. a sluice, tap, *bondon* a bung (Pr.); from the Sw. *punt*,
Swab. *bunte*, O. H. G. *spunt*.

Bondir Fr. to *bound*, leap, *bond* a bound. The O. Fr. Pr. meant
to hum, sound, doubtless from *bombitare* to hum, *bondar*. As

is often the case in intransitives, *bondir* took the form of the 3rd conj., cf. *tentir* from *tinnitare*.

Bonete Sp. Pg., Pr. *boneta*, Fr. F. *bonnet*. It was orig. the name of a stuff, but whence derived is uncertain (Bonnet in Ireland?). J. Grimm connects with this *obbonis* (*obpinis abonnis* a sort of net or coif), Merkel, L. Sal. p. 54.

Bonheur — *augurio*.

Bonina Sp. Pg. ox-eyed camomile; prob. a corruption of Ar. *bábúnag* = Pers. *bábúnah*, Freyt. 1, 78.

Bor — *ora*.

Borbogliare It., Pic. *borbouiler* to mutter, Sp. *borbollar*, Pg. *borbolhar borbulhar* to bubble out, Cat. *borbollar* to cheat, confuse; Sp. *burbuja*, Pg. *borbulha* a bubble, a knob. The Sp. is prob. from a reduplicated form of L. *bullare*, the rest are more doubtful though the meanings "murmur" and "sputter" may easily be connected. Besides *borbogliare* there is another form *borbottare*, O. Fr. *borbeter*, Pic. *borboter*, and another word for the Sp. *borbollar* is *borbotar*, prob. formed from the sound like βορβνρίζειν, Gael. *borban* a muttering, It. *burbero* morose. Another form (influenced by *barba*) is Sp. *burbotar*, Mil. *barbottà*, Pic. *barboter*, Cat. *barbotejar*, hence It. *barbugliare*, Sp. *barbullar* to talk confusedly.

Borboleta Pg. a butterfly; from *borbolhar* to rumble, bound, cf. Rh. *bulla* = *borboleta*, *bugliar* = *borbolhar*, cf. also Loth. *bouble*, Du. *bobbeln* to rove, v. *mariposa*.

Borbottare borbotar — *borbogliare*.

Borchia It. a buckle on horse-trappings, a large head of a nail, a golden heart or similar ornament worn by women. Prob. from *bulla* though it is difficult to get *bul-cula* from *bullacula*. Cf. the O. H. G. *bolca* = Lat. *bulla*.

Borda Pr. Cat., O. Fr. *borde* a hut; from Goth. *baurd*, O. N. *bord*, O. H. G. *bort*, E. *board*, cf. Ir. Gael. *bòrd*, W. *burdh*. Hence It. *bordello*, Pr. Fr. *bordel*, Sp. *burdel*, O. Fr. *bordela* (fem.), E. *brothel*.

Borde Sp., Pr. *bort*, O. Fr. *borde* a bastard. Prob. the original of the late Lat. *burdo* a mule (*burdonem producit equus conjunctus asellæ*, Duc.), which some derive from the G. *beran* to draw.

Bordel bordello — *borda*.

Bordo It. Sp. (also *borde*) Pg., Fr. *bord*, O. Sp. Pg. *borda* hem, border, side (e. g. of a ship); from O. H. G. *bort*, O. S. *bort* rim, &c. Hence Sp. *bordar*, Fr. *border*, E. *border*. The Sp. verb also means to embroider, for which the others have a distinct form; Cat. *brodar*, Fr. *broder*, E. *broider*, W. *brodio*, cf. Gael. *brod*, O. E. *brode* a prick, a *prod*, embroidering and pricking (Fr. *brocher*) being cognate. Another form is the

6*

Wall. *brosder,* O. Sp. O. Pg. *brosdar* for brosdar (L. L. *brostus, brustus*), evidently from the O. H. G. *ga-prortôn* (from a Goth. *bruzdôn,* cf. A. S. *brord,* O. N. *broddr* a point).

Bordone It., Sp. Pr. *bordon,* Fr. *bordão,* Fr. *bourdon* a pilgrim's staff, which he might regard as his mule *(burdo)* from its supporting him. Cf. Sp. *muleta* = both *"mule"* and *"crutch".*

Bordone It., Sp. *bordon,* I'g. *bordão,* Fr. *bourdon,* E. *burden* (of a song), Fr. also = bumble-bee; Fr. *bourdonner* to hum. If it be true that this word meant orig. a long trumpet or organ-pipe, it may be the same as the preceding *bordone* from the resemblance to a staff. In this case the Gacl. *bùrdan* a humming, O. E. *bourdon* are of foreign origin.

Borgne — *bornio.*

Borgo It., Sp. I'g. *burgo,* Pr. *borc,* Fr. *bourg* a small town, a borough. The word is of G. origin, Goth. *baurgs,* O. H. G. *burg* (from *bairgan bergan* to shelter), E. *burgh borough. Burgus* was also a late L. word, cf. Veget. de re milit. 4, 10: *castellum parvum quem burgum vocant;* if this be from the G., it seems to owe at least its masc. form to the Gk. πύργος. It is from this L. word that the Rom. forms come, for the G. *burg* could not have given the soft *g* in It. *borgese,* Sp. *burges,* I'g. *burgel,* Fr. *bourgeois,* though its influence was sufficient to create other forms, It. *borghese,* I'g. *burguez,* Pr. *borgues,* O. Fr. *borgois.* The Sp. town *Burgos* is a relic of the same word, L. *Burgi-orum.*

Boria It. pride, arrogance, *boriare boriarsi* to be arrogant; perhaps from the O. H. G. *biurjan* to uplift, G. *em-pören* to rebel. According to others, from *Boreas* or from *vaporeus* (v. *brina*).

Borino It., Fr. *burin,* Sp. Pg. *buril,* O. Sp. *boril,* E. *burine* a graving-tool; perhaps from O. H. G. *bora* terebra, *borôn* terebrare, E. *bore.*

Borla — *burla.*

Borne Fr. (f.) a boundary-stone, L. L. *bonna,* O. Fr. *bonne boune bousne,* N. Pr. *bouino,* and L. L. *bodina bodena,* O. Fr. *bodne.* The oldest form is *bodina,* which would give both *bonne (bodna)* and *borne.* The root *bod* is found also in I'r. *boz-ola* (= *borne*) contr. *bola,* L. L. *bodida,* v. *bouder.*

Borni Sp. I'g. a kind of falcon; from Ar. *burni,* plur. *bardni,* said to come from the province of *Bornou* in Africa.

Bornio It., Cat. *borni,* Fr. *borgne* one-eyed; O. Fr. *borgnoier* to be one-eyed. Orig. = squinting, cf. *borniele* (E. *barnacles*) squint-eyed, Jura *bournicler* to squint; Sp. *bornear* to bend, twist, evade, is of the same origin; cf. *tuerto* = twisted, squinting, and one-eyed. The derivation is uncertain, the Bret. *born* seeming to come from the French. The Limous. has *borli.* Hence It. *borniola* a false sentence.

Borra It. Sp. Pr., Fr. *bourre* short wool, goat's hair, flock &c. It is the sing. of Ausonius' *burræ* = quisquiliæ, ineptiæ, in which sense It. *borre*, and Sp. *borras* (pl.) are also used (cf. *fiocco* in both senses). From this *burra* comes the L. L. *reburrus* rugged, rough. Hence come Sp. *borra borro* a lamb (with short wool) also *borrego;* It. *borraccia*, Sp. *borracha* a wineskin (of goat's skin?); Pr. *borrás*, Fr. *bourras* a coarse cloth; Fr. *bourrer*, It. *abborrare* to stop with wool, Sp. Pg. *borrar* to blot; Sp. *borron*, Pg. *borrão* a blot, cf. *burro*.

Borraccia borracha — *borra.*

Borrace It., Sp.*borrax*, Fr.E.*borax;* from Ar.*bûraq*, Pers.*bûrah*. It comes from China and Japan.

Borraggine It. (contr. *borrana*), Sp. *borraja*, Pg. *borragem*, Pr. *borrage*, Fr. *bourrache*, Wal. *borantzè*, E. *borage*, L. Lat. *borrago;* prob. formed from *borra* (q. v.), with the suffix *aggine* = L. *ago* (cf. *capr-*, *fus-*, *lent-*, *uliv-aggine*), because of the its rough hairy leaves, unless, indeed, the word be of Oriental origin. It is found in the Levant countries, espec. in the neighbourhood of Aleppo.

Borrasca — *burrasca.*

Borrego borro — *borra.*

Borrero — *bourreau.*

Borrico — *burro.*

Borro It. the bed of a mountain-stream, dell, clift, Moden. *budrione;* from βόθρυς βόθρον. Hence *burratto*(Dante) a broken precipice, *burrato* an abyss. Cf. Wal. *bûturè* a cave, Sp. town *Val-de-buron*, N. Pr. *bauri* a precipice.

Borrofler — *bouder.*

Borsa It. Pr., Sp. Pg. *bolsa*, Fr. *bourse*, E. *purse*, from L. L. *byrsa* (βύρσα) = leather. Hence, too, Wal. *boase*, Basque *molsa.*

Borzacchino It., Sp. *borcegui*, Fr. *brodequin*, E. *buskin;* from Du. *broseken*, *brosekin*, a dimin. of *broos* (f.), probably a corruption of *byrsa* leather, cf. *leerse* = boot from *leer* leather.

Bosco It., Sp. Pg. *bosque*, Pr. *bosc*, Fr. *bois*, L. L. *boscus buscus* a wood. J. Grimm refers this word to the G. *bauen* to build, whence *buwisc buisc* building-material, wood (cf. Fr. *bois*). The G. *û* has been shortened in the Rom. *bosco* for *busco*, cf. *busca*. The Fr. *bosquet* and *bocage* for the obs. *boschet boschage* are formed after It. *boschetto*, Sp. *boscage;* Fr. *bouquet* is for *bousquet* (for the meaning cf. L. *silva*). Hence It. *imboscare*, Sp. Pr. *emboscar*, Fr. *embusquer* (O. Fr. *embuscher* and *embuissier*) to lie in ambush, *embuche*, E. *ambush.*

Bosquet — *bosco.*

Bosse — *bozza.*

Bosseman Fr. from the Du. *bootsman, boosmann* a boatman.

Bosso It., Sp. *box*, Pg. *buxo*, Pr. *bois*, Fr. *buis*, E. *box* (tree);

from *buxus*. Hence It. *buscione*, Fr. *buisson*, Pr. *boisson* a *bush* (not from *bois* *bosc* which would have given in Pr. *boscun*); It. *bossolo* box-tree and a box, Sp. *bruxula* a compass (for the inserted *e*, cf. Pr. *brostia* with *boite*), Fr. *boussole*, also Sp. *buxeta*, Pr. *bosseta*, Fr. *bossette*.

Bossolo — *bosso*.

Bostar Sp., Pg. *bostal* an oxstall. The Gloss. Isid. has: *bostar locus ubi stant boves:* some compare the Gk. βουστάσιον, from which, however, the Rom. word could hardly come.

Bostezar — *bocear*.

Bot — *botta*.

Botequin Sp. a small boat; from Du. *bootje* (orig. ph. *bōtkin*), Ronchi *botequin bodequin*.

Botta It., O. Fr. *botte* (and *boz*) a toad, Champ. Dauph. *bote*; from a G. root which appears in *bōzen* to thrust, drive, so = that which is banished, driven out. Hence Sp. *boto* dull, Fr. *bot* (*pied bot* clump-footed) *botte* a lump, Rh. *bott* a hill, Wal. *butaciu* dull; the G. *butz butzen*, L. G. E. *butt* are connected.

Bottare It. (in *dibottare* to strike, agitate), *buttare* to bud (of trees), Sp. Pg. Pr. *botar*, Fr. *bouter*, E. *butt*; from M. H. G. *bōzen* to strike. Hence Mil. *butt* a bud, It. *botto*, *botta*, Sp. *bote*, Fr. *botte* a push &c., *bout* end, whence *debout*, *aboutir*, E. *abut*, *buttress*. Hence It. *bottone*, Sp. Pr. *boton*, Fr. *bouton*, E. *button*, ph. = O. G. *bōzo* a lump. The W. *bot bōth* a round substance is sometimes compared, but the It. forms with the double *t* and double *z* (v. *bozza*) seem to come from a G. source.

Botte It., Sp. Pr. *bota*, Fr. *botte boute*, Wal. *botē bute* tub, skin, *boot* &c. The word is common to many languages, cf. Gr. βοῦτις βύτις a flask, A. S. *butte*, G. *bütte* a butt (vessel), Gael. *bōt* a boot. Hence It. *bottiglia*, Sp. *botilla botiga*, Fr. *bouteille*, L. L. *buticula*, E. *bottle pottle* (cf. L. L. from *puticla*); It. *bottino* a cistern, O. H. G. *butin*, A. S. *byden* &c.

Bottega It., Sp. *botica*, Pr. *botiga*, Fr. *boutique*, E. *booth;* from *apotheca*, Neap. *potiga*, Sic. *putiga*.

Bottino It., Sp. *botin*, both, probably, from the Fr. *butin* booty; from N. *byti*, M. H. G. *biten*.

Bou O. Fr. a bracelet; from O. H. G. *boug* (from *biugan*), O. N. *baugr* a ring. The Pr. was *bauc*.

Bouc Fr., Pr. *boc* a he-goat, Rh. *buck* (E. *buck*), Com. *boech*, Cat. *boc*, Arag. *boque*, O. Sp. *buco*. A word common to the Celtic and German languages, but, according to Grimm, introduced into the G. from the Rom. The It. has instead *becco*, the Sp. *bode*. Hence Fr. *boucher* (= It. *beccaro*), Pr. *bochier*, E. *butcher*, pr. = one who kills goats (cf. It. *beccaro*), Fr.

boucherie, Pr. *bocaria*. Cf. *brecaria* a place for slaughtering sheep, *cabreria* for goats &c. The O. Fr. for *boucher* was *maiselier = macellarius*.

Bouche — *bocca*.

Boucher — *bouc*.

Boucher Fr. to stop up, *bouchon* a stopper, = Pr. *bocó*, It. *boccone* meaning prop. *mouthfull*, so = that which fills the mouth of bessels &c.

Boucle Fr. (f.) a metal ring, a lock of hair (Sp. *bucle*); O. Fr. *bocle blouque*, Pr. *boca bloca*, O. Sp. *bloca* = clasp of a shield, L. L. *bucula scuti*, M. H. G. *buckel*, E. *buckle*; hence Fr. *bouclier*, Pr. *bloquier*, It. *brocchiere*, O. H. G. *buckeler*, E. *buckler* a shield with a buckle; from *buccula* dim. of *bucca* a cheek.

Bouder Fr. to pout, *boudin* (com. *bodin*) a black-pudding (= E. *pudding*, W. *poten*), *boudine* a knot, O. Fr. the navel, N. Pr. *boudóti boudougno* a buckle, a tumour, Piedm. *bodero* thick-set; hence N. Pr. *boud-enflá boud-ouflá boud-iflá* to blow; Fr. *bour-souffler (= boud-souffler)*, *borrofler* (but cf. Wal. *bos-unflá* from *borsa* a tumour, and *inflare*). The root is *bod* which denotes something *projecting* (e. g. in *bouder* the underlip), and which also gives rise to *bódina* a boundary (v. *borne*), cf. G. *schwelle* a threshold from *schwellen*. The root *bot* is found in L. *bot-ulus*, v. *bottare*, *botte*.

Boudin boudine — *bouder*.

Boue Fr. mud, O. Fr. *boe*; prob. the W. *baw* (m.).

Bouée — *boja*.

Bouffler bouffon — *buf*.

Bouge — *bolgia*.

Bouger Fr., Pr. *bojar* to move, cf. Wall. *bogé* to retreat. From O. H. G. *biugan*, G. *biegen* (to give in, yield), or, perhaps, better from O. H. G. *bogén*, Du. *bogen*, Sw. *bojen*, O. N. *buga*, G. *beugen* to bend; the former would require a radical *u (buger)*. The proper Pr. word is *bolegar =* It. *bulicare*, from *bulir bolir* to boil, cf. Sp. *bullir* to move about, bustle, Pg. *bulir* to move a thing from its place (cf. *bouger*).

Bougie — *bugia*.

Bougran — *bucherame*.

Bougre Fr. = *Bulgarus*, and meant orig. a *heretic*, *Bulgaria* being the chief seat of the Manichæan heresy, *bougerie =* heresy. *Bougre = pædico*, the punishment of this and of the heretic being the same, Menage. V. Ducange, s. *Bulgarus*.

Bouhourt — *bagordo*.

Bouillir bouillon boule — *bolla*.

Boulanger Fr. a baker. Cf. Sp. *bollo* a roll, Com. *bulet* a sort of bread. The word is prob. from *boule*, whence would come a form *boulange* = bread in a round form. *Bulengarius* is found in the 12ᵗʰ century.

Bouleau — *betula.*

Boulevard boulevart Fr. (*boulever* Nicot) a fortification, hence It. *baluardo*, Sp. *baluarte;* from G. *bollwerk* a *bulwork*, cf. *Estrabort* from *Strazburc*. Roquefort has *bollewerque.*

Bouleverser Fr. prop. = to turn over like a ball *(boule)*. The Lim. has corrupted it into *polo-versá* (*polo* clunis).

Boulimie — *bulimo.*

Bouline Fr. (naut.) bow-line, O. Fr. *boline, boëline;* Du. *boelijne*, E. *bowline*, G. *bolcine.*

Boulon — *bolla.*

Boundle — *benda.*

Bouquer Fr. to yield, to truckle; from N. *bucka*, to stoop, G. *bücken.*

Bouquet — *bosco.*

Bouquin Fr. a bad book; from Du. *boeckin* (G. *buch-chen*). Cf. *mannequin, brodequin, hellequin,* Rouchi *pénequin* = bad bread, *verquin* a small glass.

Bourbe Fr. (f.) mud, Wall. *borbou;* cf. Gr. βόρβορος.

Bourde Fr., Pr. *borda* a lie, vb. *bourder.* The old sense of the word (jest, pastime) points to the Pr. *bort* for *biort* (v. *bagordo*); the O. Fr. *behorder* had the meaning "to sport, jest". From *behord* jest came the E. *boord*, Gael. *bùrd.*

Bourdon — *bordone.*

Bourg — *borgo.*

Bourgeon Fr., E. *burgeon.* Perhaps from the O. H. G. *burjan* to lift, so = something protruding, breaking out. In Langued. *boure* = the eye of a shoot.

Bournous — *albornoz.*

Bourrache — *borraggine.*

Bourras — *borra.*

Bourrasque — *burrasca.*

Bourre — *borra.*

Bourreau Fr., Pr. *borel* an executioner. The contraction from *bouchereau (boucher)* would be too violent. *Borel* might come from *boja* (q. v.) with the double suffix *er-el*, cf. Fr. *màtereau* from *màt*, thus = an hypothetical *boi-er-ello*, cf. Rh. *bojer*, O. Sp. *borrero.* From *bourreau* comes *bourreler* to torture. Or it is the same as the O. Fr. *borel, burel*, O. E. *borel* a clownish, common fellow, prop. = clad in *borel* or the undyed wool of brown sheep, v. *buio.*

Bourreler — *bourreau.*

Bourrer — *borra.*

Bourrique — *burro.*

Bourse — *borsa.*

Boursoufler — *bouder.*

Bouse Fr., Pr. *boza buza* cowdung. The Rh. has *bovatscha*, Com. *boascia*, Parm. *boazza*, so we might have a Fr. *bouasse;* but it is doubtful whether this could give *bousse bouse*, such a transposition of the accent from the suffix to the root being unknown in French. Better from M. H. G. *butze* clod, cf. *étron* s. *stronzare.*

Boussole — *bosso.*

Bout — *bottare.*

Boute bouteille — *botte.*

Boutique — *bottega.*

Bova It. (only in pl.), Lomb. *boga* fetters for the feet; from O. H. G. *bouga* an armlet, L. L. *bauca armilla* Papias: cf. *bou.*

Boveda — *volta.*

Box — *bosso.*

Boya — *boja* (2).

Boyau — *budello.*

Bozal — *bocca.*

Bozar — *versare.*

Bozza It., Pr. *bossa*, Fr. *bosse*, Pic. *boche* a lump, a boil, Eng. *boss*, Fr. *bossu* humpbacked, It. *boccia* a bud, ball, Sp. *bocha* ball, bowl, Pg. *bochecha* the cheek puffed out; the same word as, the H. G. *butze butzen* any blunt point or lump, cf. Du. *butse* a boil, from M. H. G. *bôzen* to thrust (protrude), v. *bottare.* The It. *bozzo* and *bozza* mean a rough unformed block of stone, whence *abbozzare* to work in the rough, to sketch, E. *boast*, Pg. *esboçar*, Sp. *bosquejar*, O. Sp. *esbozo* = *abbozzo*, Fr. *bossage* any stone indeed for sculpture. Other forms have a radical *u* instead of the *o:* thus It. *buzzo* a belly, a pincushion, Sp. *buche* crop, bosom, pad; Sp. *buchete* = *bochecha*; Fr. *but* a raised knob, a butt, whence *scopo*, design (cf. Gr. σκοπός, G. *zweck*), whence *début;* Fr. *butte* (f.) a raised mound. From *buzzo* in the Mil. *buzzecca*, Piedm. *buseca*, It. *busecchio* the bowels, cf. O. H. G. *gebuzze* exta. From Sp. *buche* seems to come *bucha* a bread-chest, money-box, *buchar* to hide. From *boccia* a bud prob. come *bozzacchio* and *bozzacchione* (Dante Parad.) a withered plum.

Braca It., Sp. Pg. *braga*, Pr. *braya*, O. Fr. *braie* breeches (usu. in pl.), Sp. *braga*, Fr. *braie* a child's napkin; from Lat. *braca* of Gallic origin, Bret. *brages.*

Bracco It., Sp. *braco brac*, Fr. *braque* a hunting dog, pointer; It. *braccare* to track; from O. H. G. *braccho*, G. *bracke*. The Sp. adj. *braco* = flat-nosed. From O. Fr. *bracon* came *braconnier* a poacher, *braconner* to poach.

Braconnier — *bracco.*

Bragia brascia bracia It., Sp. Pr. *brasa*, Pg. *braza*, Fr. *braise* glowing coal, Fl. *brase;* It. *abbragiare,* Sp. *abrazar,* Fr. *embraser,* O. Fr. *esbraser* to set on fire. From the O. N. *brasa* solder, whence A. S. *brǎsian* to *braze,* whence It. *bragiare; bracia* is like *cacio* from *caseus.* Mil. *brascà* == *embrasser.* Hence E. vb. *brase,* sbst. *braser* a pan of hot coals. E. *brass* is from the same.

Brago It., Pr. *brac* mud, mire, O. Fr. *brai* mire, whence *le pays de Bray,* Pr. == matter, Cat. *brac* ulcer, pitch, Fr. *brai* pitch whence Sp. *brea,* Pg. *breo breu,* vb. *brayer, brear,* cf. Wall. *briac* mire. From Gk. βραγός == ἕλος (Menage)?

Brague O. Fr. diversion, Fr. *braguer* to be merry, N. Pr. *bragà* to E. *brag,* O. Fr. *bragard,* E. *braggart,* Du. *braggaerd.* It is not found in O. Pr., hence prob. from the N. *brak* noise, *braka* to brag. Dief. Goth. Wörterb. 1. 268, derives it from the Celtic, W. *brag* == malt, *bragiaw* to swell, brew.

Brai — *brago.*

Braidif — *braire.*

Braie — *braca.*

Brailler — *braire.*

Braiman Pr. a freebooter; prop. == a man of Brabant, O. Sp. *breimante,* v. Duc. (s. *Brabanciones*).

Braion — *brandone.*

Braire Fr. E. *bray,* O. Fr. Pic. Norm. Pr. *braire* generally to cry, also to trill (of birds): *(lo rossinhols brai),* particip. *brait,* whence *brait* a cry. As O. Fr. *muire* from *mugire, bruire* from L. L. *brugire,* so *braire* from L. L. *bragire.* Prob. the same as *raire* (q. v.), cf. *bruire* from *rugire.* From *brait* comes Pr. *braidar,* Pg. *bradar,* whence Pr. *braidiu,* O. Fr. *braidif* impetuous, stormy; prob. also Pr. O. Fr. *braidir,* O. It. *bradire.* The Fr. *brailler,* Pr. *braillar* to blare (for *braailler?*), Piedm. *brajè* may come from *braire* as *criailler* from *crier, piailler* from a form *pier,* It. *piare.*

Braise — *bragia.*

Bramare It., Rh. *brammar* to long for, Sp. Pr. *bramar,* Fr. *bramer* to scream, N. Pr. *bramá* in both senses, cf. O. Cat. *glatir* to bark, N. Cat. to desire, and Festus has: *latrare Ennius pro poscere posuit.* It is the O. H. G. *breman,* Du. *bremmen* to roar, Gr. βρέμειν, L. *fremere,* Sansk. *bhram.*

Bramangiere It. a first course; from Fr. *blanc-manger* a blancmange, dish made with milk, M. H. G. *blâmenschier.*

Bran — *brenno.*

Branca It. O. Sp. O. Pg. Pr., Fr. *branche,* Pr. also m. *branc,* E. *branch,* Wal. *brěncě* a forefoot, L. L. *branca leonis* a plant. The L. *brachium* could only have give *brancia.* *Branca* was probably an old Rom. word, perhaps even used in the spoken Latin. The O. Gael. *brac,* Corn. *brech,* W. *breich* arm, are connected, the Bret. *branc* preserving the purer form. From *branca* comes It. *brancolare* to grope.

Branche — *branca*.

Brande Fr., N. Pr. *brando* brushwood, Berr. *brande* broom.

Brandir brandon branler — *brando*.

Brandistocco It. a javelin; from *brandire* to brandish and *stocco* a stick.

Brando It., Pr. *bran*, O. Val. *brant*, O. Fr. *brant branc bran* a sword-blade *(branc de l'espée)*; from O. H. G. *brant* a brand, O. N. *brandr* a sword, cf. Sp. *Tizon Tizona (tizio)* the sword of the Cid. This from G. *brennen* to burn. Hence come It. *brandire*, Pr. Fr. *brandir*, Sp. *blandir*, E. *brandish*; dimin. Fr. *brandiller*, cont. *branler*, *ébranler*, for *brandoler*, E. *brandle*, orig. used of waving a *brand* or sword. Hence too Pr. *brandó*, Fr. *brandon*, Sp. *blandon* a stake, a torch; O. Fr. *brander* to *brand*, N. Pr. *brandá*, Piedm. *brandé* to boil, O. Pr. *abrandar* to ignite. Thus Diez, but Wedgwood connects *brand* with the following word (*fire-brand* = prop. a splinter or faggot). *Brandish* &c. he gets from the Manx *brans* to dash. This is prob. related to the Sansk. *bhranç* cadere, in Caus. dejicere.

Brandone It., cont. *brano* a piece or collop of flesh, shred of cloth &c., O. Sp. *brahon* (for *bradon*) a patch of cloth, Pr. *bradon brazon braon*, O.Fr. *braion*, Lorr. *bravon*, Wall. *breyon*, E. *brawn* a lump or roll of flesh, the buttocks; It. *sbranare*, O. Fr. *esbraoner* to tear piece-meal, from the O. H. G. *brâto*, acc. *brâton* a lump of flesh, the calf of the leg.

Brano — *brandone*.

Braña — *brenno*.

Braque — *bracco*.

Braquer Fr. to bend, manage; from O. N. *bráka* to subdue (E. *break*).

Bras O. Fr. malt, L. L. *bracium*, Fr. *brasser* to brew, O. Sp. *brasar*, L. L. *braxare*; from Gallic *brace* (Pliny), Gael. *braich bracha*, W. *brag*. The Wallon form is *brá* or *brau*, Wal. *brahé* malt. From the L.L. comes the G. *brauen* (J. Grimm); whence E. *brew*.

Brasa — *bragia*.

Brasile It., Sp. Pg. *brasil*, Fr. *brésil* a wood furnishing a red dye; found in *Brazil* to which it has given its name. Some connect it with *brasa* glowing coal, because of its bright red colour, but Diez prefers to make the vb. *brésiller* to dye with Brazil-wood, the same word as *brésiller* (Pr. *brezilhar*) to break in small pieces, splinter *(briza)*, the wood being usually brought to Europe in splinters.

Brasse — *braza*.

Bratta Gen. dirt, whence It. *imbrattare* to soil (*Imbratta* a nickname in Bocc. Dec. 6, 10), *sbrattare* to purify. Diez gives no derivation. Perhaps it is shortened from *baratta* which = entanglement, trouble, v. s. *baratto*.

Bravo It. Sp. Pg., Pr. *brau* (f. *brava*), Fr. *brave* (G. *brav*, E. *brave*); Sp. Pg. *bravío*. Diez traces the meanings thus: *bravo* meant (1) unruly, stormy; O. It. *unde brave*; it was then used specially of wild animals or plants: L. L. *bravus bos*, It. *bue brado* (a young *untamed* ox), Sp. *ganso bravo* a wild goose, Pg. *uva brava* wild grape; thence it came to mean impetuous, valiant, fine. The Fr. preserves the orig. sense only in *ébrouer* and *rabrouer*. Diez prefers the derivation from O. H. G. *raw*, E. *raw* (cf. *bruire*, *brusco*, *braire*), and compares the senses of *crudus*. Wedgwood, however, refers it to the same root as *brag* (v. *braguer*), viz.: the N. *brak braka* crash, noise (cf. use of *crack* in O. Eng. = boast, brag). *Brag* = Gael. *breagh* fine, Sc. *braw*, Bret. *brao brav*, whence the Rom. words.

Brasa Sp. Pg., Pr. *brassa*, Fr. *brasse* a fathom; from *brachia* the (outstretched) arms, cf. O. Fr. *brace levée* with open arms.ı

Brea — *brago*.

Brebis — *berbice*.

Breccia — *brèche*.

Brecha — *brèche*.

Brèche Fr., E. *breach*, Pr. *berca* a notch, and from *brèche* It. *breccia*, Sp. *brecha*, Pr. *bercar enbercar*, Pic. *eberquer*, Fr. *ébrécher*; from O. H. G. *brecha* a breaking, cf. W. *brég* a breach. The It. *briccola*, Sp. *brigola*, Fr. *bricole* a battering-ram, belong to the M. H. G. *bréchel* a breaker.

Bredouiller Fr. to stutter; prob. from O. Fr. *bredir*, Pr. *braidir* to sing, warble (v. *braire*).

Bréhaigne Fr. barren (of animals), O. Fr. *baraigne*, Wall. *brouhagne*, Pic. *breine*, Burg. *braime*, Bret. *brechan*, O. E. *barrayne*, E. *barren*. Diez makes *baraigne* the orig., and derives from *baro* a man, cf. Sp. *machorra* from *macho*, Pr. *tauriga* from *taur*. Wedg. from the Du. *braeck* sterilis.

Brelan Fr. a game at cards, *brelander* to play at such game, *brelandier* a gamester. The O. Fr. form was *brelenc berlenc* = a dice-board; from the G. *bretlin* or *bretling* a little board. Hence Sp. *berlanga* a game of chance.

Breloque — *loque*.

Brème Fr. (E. *bream*) for *bresme*, from G. *brachsme*, *brassen*, N. Pr. *bramo*.

Breña Sp., Pg. *brenha* ground covered with brambles, L. L. *brenna* (Ducange). Perhaps from G. *brahne* a bush or hedge. Diez. May it not be connected with *bren* refuse (v. s. *brenno*)?

Brenna It. a jade, a sorry nag; cf. Serv. *barna* a nag, *brnja* a horse with a blaze or white mark.

Brenno Gen., Com. Piedm. Pr. O. Fr. O. Sp. *bren*, Piedm. also *bran* bran, Fr. *bran* refuse, Sp. *braña* dung, withered leaves; Fr. *bren* ordure, *berneux* snotty; a Celtic word, W. *brân*, Gael. *bran*, Bret. *brenn*, E. *bran*.

Brenta It., Piedm. *brinda*, Ronchi *brande* a wine-vessel, G. *brente*, *brânte* a wooden vessel.

Bresca Mant. Sard. Sp. Cat. Pr., Sic. *vrisca*, O. Fr. *bresche*, L. L. *brisca* a honey-comb. Prob. Celtic: Ir. *briosg*, W. *bresg*, Bret. *bresk*; Diez after Villemarqué. But the Ir. *briosg* = brittle, and no W. *bresg* exists. Mahn connects it with the Prov. *brusc*, L. L. *ruscus*, Fr. *ruche* a bee-hive, which is from the Celtic: W. *rhisg*, Bret. *rusk*, Gael. *rûsg* bark. Pott connects *bresca* &c. with βλίττειν, βλῖσαι, Brisæus (Kuhn's Zeitsch. Vol. 6, p. 328).

Bressin Fr. (naut), E. *brace*, Du. Sw. *bras*, G. *brasse*; all from Fr. *bras*, the rope having the appearance of an arm, *e* for *a* to distinguish it from *brassin* brewing.

Bretauder — *berta*.

Bret Pr. "homo linguæ impeditæ", Fr. *parler bret* or *bretonner* to stammer; prop. to speak *Breton*, cf. Sp. *rascuence*, *algarabia*.

Brete Sp. fetters, Pg. a snare for birds = Pr. *bret*, O. Fr. *bret*; hence O. Fr. *broion* a noose, Fr. *bretelle* a strap, brace, Com. *bretela bartela* a crupper, Sp. *bretador* a bird-call, Sp. *bretel* brace, N. Pr. *bretella*, *bratella*. From the O. G. *brettan* stringere, *gabrettan* contexere; A. S. *bredan breydan* to weave, braid; E. to *braid* and *braid* in O. E. = to deceive (Chaucer: *brede*). Wedg. connects *braid* with *bray* to make a noise (to rush, to bend, to twist).

Brette Fr. (f.) a backsword, vb. *bretailler*; cf. N. *bredda* a short sabre.

Brettine — *brida*.

Bretto O. It. unfruitful, poor. Cf. *bretauder*, s. *berta*.

Brettonica It., Sp. Pg. *bretonica*; from *betonica*. Fr. *bétoine*, E. *betony*, cf. s. *brida*.

Breuil — *broglio*.

Breuvage Fr. beverage; for *beurage*, Pr. *beuratge*, It. *beveraggio*, from *boire*, L. *bibere*; *abbreuver* for *abbewer*, Pr. *abeurar*, Fr. *embreuver* to moisten, soak, *embruer* = E. *imbrue*. *

Brezo — *bercer* (2).

Brezza It., Fr. *brise*, E. *breeze*, Sp. *briza brisa* a North-East-wind. Hence It. *ri-brezzo* a shudder. Perh. from It. *rezzo*. Wedgwood says that the origin is in the imitation of a rustling noise. He makes the Fr. *bise* the same word as *brise*, but v. *bigio*.

Brial — *bliaut.*

Bribe Fr. O. E. a lump of bread, Wall. *brib* alms, E. *bribe;*
Wall. *briber,* Pic. *brimber* to beg. For *bribe* the Pic. has *brife,*
whence O. Fr. *brifer* to be greedy, *brifaud* glutton, Bret. *brifa*
brifoad, It. *briffalda* a vagrant woman. Hence Sp. *bribar* to
be a vagrant, *briba,* It. *birba* a vagrant life; Sp. *bribon,* It.
birbone, birbante, O. Fr. *briban,* O. E. *bribour* a vagrant, a
rogue, a robber (v. Marsh, Lectures on the English language).
Diez suggests the derivation from O. G. *bilibi* bread, A. S.
bilifen; others derive it better from W. *briwo* to break, *briw*
a fragment, *bara briw* a lump of bread.

Bricoo It., Fr. *brique* a brick; from A. S. *brice* a bit or fragment,
E. *brick* (from *break*); *brique de pain* = A. S. *hlâfes brice* a bit
of bread. It. *briccolino briciolo* a crumb. Connected with these
are It. *bricca* a rough country, Piedm. *brich,* Com. *sbrich* a
precipice.

Bricoo It., in *sbricco,* whence *briccone,* Pr. *bric bricon* a rogue,
knave. Prob. from O. H. G. *brecho* a violator, *breaker,* A. S.
brica.

Bricoo — *burro.*

Bricoola — *brèche.*

Bricia briciolo — *briser.*

Brico Sp. a sandbank; from N. *breki* a sunken rock.

Brida Sp. Pg. Pr., Fr. *bride,* O. Fr. A. S. *bridel,* E. *bridle,* It.
predello; from the O. H. G. *brittil, pritil* (M. H. G. *briten*) to
weave. Another form is *briglia* (from *britl*) Wal. *breglê;* also
It. *brettine* (for *brettile?*). Wedgwood gets it from Icel. *bitill*
a bridle from *bit* (that which the horse bites) by insertion of
r, cf. *brettonica betonica, brulicame bulicame,* Du. *broosekens,*
E. *buskins* &c.

Brifer — *bribe.*

Briffalda — *bribe.*

Briga It. O. Pg., O. Fr. *brigue,* Sp. Pg. Pr. Cat. *brega* strife,
quarrel (It. also trouble, business, Cat. also tumult, Fr.
convassing); It. *brigare,* Fr. *briguer* to strive, Sp. *bregar,* Pg.
brigar to quarrel, Pr. Cat. *bregar* to rub; It. *brigante* a busy-
body, intriguer, pirate, Pg. *brigão* a quarreller, Sp. *bergante,*
Pg. *bargante* a rogue, Fr. *brigand* a skirmisher, a light-armed
trooper, a *brigand* (cf. *latro* and It. *malandrino*). The under-
lying notion of *briga* is *exertion,* trouble, from root *brak*
(brachium, break), whence : : business, so *brigata* = a company (engaged in same business), Fr. E. *brigade.* From *bri-*
gante a pirate come *brigantare* to rob, *brigantino* a pirate-ship,
a small two-masted vessel, E. *brigantine, brig,* Fr. E. *brigan-*
dine a sort of scale armour, so called because worn by the
Brigands.

Brigand — *briga.*

Brigantino — *briga.*

Briglia — *brida.*

Brignole — *brugna.*

Brigola — *brèche.*

Brillare It., Sp. Pr. *brillar*, Fr. *briller* to shine, hence *brilliant.* Diez refers it to O. Fr. *bericle* from *beryllus*, but Wedgwood, with more probability, to makes it the same word as *griller* to crack, crackle; *gresiller griller* corresponding to *breziller briller.* Words denoting light are commonly derived from those expressing sound, e. g. G. *hell* clear, from *hall* a sound, *étincelle* from *tinkle*, so *bright* in O. E. was used of sound.

Brimborion Fr. a trifle, bawble; ph. from *brimber* (v. *bribe*) to beg, with a Lat. ending *(brimborium)*.

Brin Arag. Pr., Pg. *brin*, Fr. *brin* a fibre, blade of grap &c. v. *brenno*, with which it is prob. connected.

Brin O. Fr. noise. Ph. from O. N. *brim* surf, roar of the sea, or connected with O. Fr. *bramer* to cry with desire, *bram* a cry, It. *bramare* (βρέμειν).

Brin d'estoc Fr. a leaping-pole; from G. *springstock.*

Brina It., Langued. *brino breino*, Mil. *prinna* rime, hoar-frost. From *pruina* the *b* for *p* being unusual but not unexampled; or, better, from *vapor*, through the Ven. *borina* (cf. *boricco, bricco*); cf. Ven. *borana burana* a cloud, Wal. *boré* steam, rime (Wal. *abor* = *vapor*). Sard. *borea*, Cat. *boira* a cloud come from *raporea* better than from *boreas.*

Brincar Sp. Pg. to leap, skip, dance, play, *brinco* a leap &. *brincos, jewels* (play things). Prob. from G. *blinken* to glitter, cf. *micare, coruscare* &c.

Brindar — *brindisi.*

Brinde — *brindisi.*

Brindisi It., Sp. *brindis* a health (propinatio); from G. *bring dir's.* Hence Fr. *brinde*, Lorr. *bringuei* to drink a health, Sp. *brindar.* The O. Sp. *caráuz* in the same sense Covarruvias derives from G. *gar-aus*, but more prob. it comes from Du. *kroesen krosen (kruyse* a cup, *cruse)* to tipple, whence *carouse.*

Brio It. Sp. Pg., Pr. *briu*, O. Fr. *bri*, vivacity, courage, spirit; hence Pr. *brivar abrirar* to press, partic. *abrivatz*, O. Fr. *abrivé* hasty, ph. also It. *abbrivo* way (of a ship), *abbrivare* to get underway, and not from *ab-ripare.* *Brio* is probably connected with the O. Ir. *brig*, Gael. *brigh* strength (βριᾷν to be strong), cf. Pr. *crau* from *crag.*

Brique — *bricco.*

Brisa Sp. (common in Aragon and Catalonia) skins of grapes; from L. *brisa* (Columella).

Brisa — *brezza.*

Briscar Sp. Cat. to embroider with gold twist (O. Fr. *broissier*).

Brise — *brezza*.

Briser Fr., Pr. *brisar brizar* to break, Fr. *bris* rubbish, Pr. *briza* a crumb, E. *breeze* dust &c., *briss brist* rubbish, It. *bricia* a crumb (cf. A. S. *brice* = a bit, E. *brick*), *briciola briciolo* (v. *bricco*), *sbriciolare* to crumble; hence Pr. *desbrizar, abrizar, desabrizar* to shatter, Fr. *débris* rubbish; Fr. *bresiller*, Pr. *brezilhar* to break up, Fr. *bresilles bretilles* little bits of wood. From a G. root *brist* found in O. H. G. *brëstan* (pres. *bristu*) O. N. *bresta* to break, G. *bersten* to burst, O. N. *brestr*, M. H. G. *brëste* a breach, O. E. *brise* to crush. The Fr. *bruiser* (q. v.), E. *bruise*, A. S. *brysan* are connected. There is also a Gael. *bris* to break. It. *bricia, briciola, briciolo* may be a form of Lomb. *brisa* (cf. *cucire* from *cusire*), Pr. *briga*, Lomb. *brica* &c., vb. Pr. *esbrigà* = *brizar* may belong to G. *brechen*, E. *break*.

Britar O. Pg. to break = A. S. *brittian* to break, whence *brit brittle*, connected with the former word.

Brive Fr. fragments a Celtic word found in *Samarobriva* (intersected by the Somme). Humboldt makes it the same as the Celtic *briga* (q. v.). Dauph. *briva brio* = road, cf. *route*, O. Fr. *bris* = fragment and road.

Brisar briso — *bercer* (2).

Brocard, broche, brocher — *brocco*.

Brocca It., Pr. Fr. a jug, Sw. *broke brôg* tub. Ferrari derives it from πρόχους, but more prob. connected with *brocco* (q. v.), so = a vessel with a projecting nose, a beaker. Dim. Prov. *broisson (broccio)* neck of a vessel, Pie. *brochon* also = vizor of a helmet, prop. something projecting. Hence Fr. E. *embrocation*.

Brocchiere — *bouclier*.

Brocco It. *(sbrocco sprocco)* a sharp stump, or spur of a tree, a snag, bud, peg, short, Parm. *broch* a bough, O. Fr. Pic. *broc* a point, spike, also Pied. *brocio* == It. *brocco*, Lomb. *broc* = *broch*, It. f. *brocca* a split stick, Sic. *brocca* also a shoot, sucker, Pied. Parm. Ven. *broca* a small nail, Lomb. a bough, Sp. *broca* a reel, drill, Pr. *broca*, Fr. *broche* a spit, skewer (v. Duc. *brocca*) &c., Sp. *brocha* a button, *broche* clasp, = E. *brooch;* dim. It. *broccolo*, Sp. *broculi*, E. *broccoli* (cf. It. *sverza* a cabbage sprout and splinter); It. *broccare*, Pr. *brocar*, Fr. *brocher* to prick, embroider (E. *broach abroach*), *broccato brocard brocade*, Sp. *brocado*, *brocadel*. *Brocard* Fr. == taunt may be the same word, though usu. derived from *Burchard* Bishop of Worms, author of treatise called *"Brocardica"*. The Lat. has *brocchus broccus* (Plaut. Varro) == a protruding tooth (whence the name *Brocchus*): from this we easily get the senses of the Romance words. Wedgwood traces all to the root *brak*, E. *break*. From *broche* comes Fr. *brocart*, E. *brocket* a hart 2 years old, because of the single snag on his antler. The fallow-deer was called a *pricket*.

Brochet Fr. a pike (fish); from *broche (brocco)*, because of its sharp head, cf. E. *pike* (in two senses), Fr. *bequet* a beak, bill, and also a *pike*, Fr. *lanceron* a young pike, from *lance*. The It. *brocchetto* (= *brochet*) means a small bough.

Broder — *bordo*.

Brodo, broda It., Sp. Pg. *brodio bodrio*, Pr. *bro*, whence Fr. *brouet* broth; from O. H. G. *brod*, A. S. *brodh*, G. *brühe*, E. *broth*, Ir. *broth*, Gael. *brot*, from G. *brühen* to pour boiling water, W. *brwd* hot.

Broglio bruolo It. (Dante *brolo* a crown), Pr. *bruelh*, Fr. *breuil*, fem. Pg. *brulha*, Pr. *bruelha*, O. Fr. *bruelle*, G. *brühl* a bushy place; It. *brogliare*, O. Sp. *brollar*, Pg. Pr. *brolhar*, Fr. *brouiller* (Pg. also *abrolhar*, sbst. *abrolho*, Sp. *abrojo*) to sprout, break out, rebel, raise a disturbance, It. *broglio*, E. *broil*. Prob. from the Celtic: W. *brog* a swelling, whence *brog-il* in O. G. From *brouiller* comes *brouillon* a disturber, a makebate, also = a sketch, rough copy.

Broigne brunie O. Fr., Pr. *bronha*, L. L. *brugna* (A. D. 813) a coat-of-mail; from Goth. *brunjô*, O. H. G. *brunjâ*, which from *brinnan brennen* to burn, glitter.

Broion — *brete*.

Broissier — *briscar*.

Broisson — *brocca*.

Broncher — *bronco*.

Broncio It. morose, angry look, *imbronciare* = *pigliar broncio* to wear such a look, L. L. *broccus* obstinatus, O. Fr. *embrons soucieux*, E. in a *brown* study (v. Wedgw.); perhaps connected with Sw. *brütsch* morose, vb. *brütschen*, G. *protzen*.

Bronco It. a stock, trunk, Sard. *bruncu* a shoot, Fr. f. *bronche* a bush, O. Sp. *broncha* a bough; It. *broncone* a broken bough, Fr. *broncher* to stumble (cf. It. *cespo* a bush, *cespicare* to totter), Pr. *abroncar* to knock at. Perhaps from Pr. *bruc* a stump, trunk, *burcar (brucar?)* to stumble, with inserted *n* (cf. Parm. *brocon* = *broncone*, Mil. *brocca* = *bronche*), so that *bronc* may be referred to the same origin as *brocco*, viz. Lat. *broccus broncus*. It may, however, be from O. H. G. *bruch*, Du. *brok* anything *broken*, a stump, v. *brocco* ad fin. The Sp. Pg. *bronco* = rude, coarse, morose, cf. L. *truncus*, G. *klotz*.

Bronde O. Fr., Piedm. *bronda*, Langued. *broundo* a twig, whence Pr. dim. *brondel brondill*.

Brontolare It. to murmur: βροντή?

Bronzo It., Sp. *bronce*, Fr. E. *bronze*, It. *abbronzare*, O. Sp.

bronzar, Fr. *bronzer* to scorch, *bronze*, Ven. *bronza*, It. pl. *bronze* glowing coals. The metal is so called from being used in soldering, an operation performed over hot coals, cf. *brass* from *brasa* embers. *Bronza* coals is prob. of same origin as G. *brunst* heat, *brennen* to burn. Connected with *bruno, brown.*

Brosse — *broza.*

Brote brota Sp., Pr. *brot*, Fr. *brout* a bud, sprout, Sp. Pr. *broton;* Sp. Pr. *brotar* to sprout; from O. H. G. *broz* a sprout, *brozzěn* to sprout.

Brouailles Fr., O. Fr. *breuilles* the entrails of birds or fishes, L. L. *burbalia* intestina (Gloss. Isid.). V. Dief. Celt. 1, 200.

Brouée Fr. mist; a participial form like *guilée, gelée*, Sp. *nevada.* Pic. *brouache* = fine rain, Berrichon *brouasser* to drizzle, *berrouée* = *brouée.* Ph. from A. S. *brodh*, G. *brodem*, Sc. *broth* = steam (from heated bodies): *brouillard* fog, from a form *brodel brudel* rising damp. v. *brodo.*

Brouet — *brodo.*

Brouette — *biroccio.*

Brouillard — *brouée.*

Brouiller brouillon — *broglio.*

Brouir Fr. to burn; from M. H. G. *brüejen*, Du. *broeijen*, G. *brühen.* Piedm. *broé brové*, Ven. *broare*, Mil. *sbroja.* Langued. *braouzi* = *brauzir* which is related to *brouir*, as *auzir* to *ouir*, *jauzir* to *jouir*, *blauzir* to *blouir.*

Brouques Pic. breeches; from Du. *broek* = O. H. G. *bruoch*, v. *braca.*

Broussaille — *broza.*

Brout — *brote.*

Brouter — *broza.*

Broyer — *briga.*

Broza Sp. fallen leaves, chips, rubbish, also a brush *(bruza)*, Pr. *brus* (but v. *bru*), Fr. *brosse* small bushes, heath, *brosse* also = a brush; hence Fr. *broussailles* brush-wood, It. *bruzzaglia* rabble. The O. Fr. *broce*, Pic. *brouche* shows that *ss* = *st*, so the Pr. *brostar*, Fr. *brouter (broüter)* to browse (O. Fr. *broust* fallen leaves &c., pasturage) belong here; the It. *brustia* = Sp. *bruza* points to the same fact. The origin is to be sought in the O. H. G. *burst brusta* a bristle, comb (something bristly), plainly seen in Fr. *rebours*, against the grain, *rebourser rebrousser* to stroke against the grain (stringere), L. L. *rebursus* bristly. The forms with *st* favour the derivation from the A. S. *brustian (burst)* to sprout, Bret. *broust* a bramble bush, *brousta* to browse.

Bru Pr. heath (only found in the nom. *brus*), Langued. Mil. *brug*, Gen. *brügo;* from the W. *bruy* bush, Bret. *brüg*, Sw.

brúch heath (but v. *broza*). Hence Fr. *bruyère*, Cat. *bruguera*, O. Fr. *bruerui*.

Bru Fr., O. Fr. *bruy* = belle-fille, a daughter-in-law. From Goth. *bruths*, O. H. G. M. H. G. *brùt*, G. *braut*, O. S. *brùd*, Du. *bruid*, A. S. *brýd*, E. *bride*, O. N. *brúdhr*, Swed. *brud*. Norm. Champ. *bruman* = *brùdhgumi* = bridegroom, Swed. *brud-man* a bridesman.

Bruces — *buz*.

Bruciare brusciare (in *abbrusciare*) It., Pr. *bruzar bruizar*, Rh. *brischar*; hence It. *brustolare, ab-brustiare*, Pr. *bruslar*, Fr. *brûler*, E. *broil*. Diez derives from Lat. *perustus* whence *perustare prustare brustare brusciare bruciare* (cf. *cacio* for *cascio*), Pr. *bruzar* = *brussar*; also from *perustulare brustolare* &c., which represent the O. Rom. *ustolare (ustulare)* found in O. Sp. *uslar*, Pr. *usclar (ustlar)*, Wal. *usturà*. Wedgw. makes all these words onomatopœia, and compares Sc. *birsle brissle* to broil, G. *prusseln*, E. *brustle* to crackle, also Fr. *griser, gresiller griller, grill*, It. *grullo* = *brullo* parched.

Brucio — *bruco*.

Bruco It. a caterpillar, Sp. *brugo* a worm, from *bruchus* (Prudentius), βροῦχος; hence *brucare* to strip off leaves. The form *brucio* points to an adj. *brucheus*. Cf. Wal. *brug* a cockchafer.

Brugna It., Pg. *brunho abrunho*, Sp. *bruno*, Fr. *brugnon*, Mil. *brugnocu*, Fr. *brignole* a plum, plum-tree. *Brugna* = *prugna*, *brugnocu* = *pruynudo* and *prugna* = *prunea*, cf. *ciriegia* = *cerasea*. The Sp. *bruno*, however, seems to connect itself with the adj. *bruno*. *Brignole* in Provence *(Broniolacum)* was noted for its plums.

Brugnon — *brugna*.

Bruine Fr., Pr. *bruina* cold fine rain. Not from *pruina*, but analogous to the Pr. forms *calina, plovina* &c. The root is perhaps found in *brugir bruir bruire*, which last in Champ. = to make a noise and to be foggy. Is it the same as the *bru* in *bruma* (not *brevima*).

Bruire It. Fr., Pr. *brugir bruzir*, Com. *brùgi*, O. Cat. *brogir* to rumble, make a noise; It. *bruito*, Fr. *bruit*, Pr. *brúit brúida;* from *rugire*, or ph. connected with Sansk. *brù* to speak, W. *brud* a chronicle, Sc. *bruidhean* to talk, E. to *bruit*.

Bruiser bruser O. Fr. to bruise, whence *combruisser, debruisier*, O. Sp. *abrusar*. From A. S. *brysan*, E. *bruise;* connected with *briser*.

Bruit — *bruire*.

Brûler — *bruciare*.

Bruma Sp. Pg. Pr., Fr. *brume*, Cat. *broma* vapour, mist, Wal. *brumè* hoarfrost; from *bruma* which in L. L. = hoar-frost.

Bruno It. Sp. Pg., Pr. Fr. *brun*, brown; from O. H. G. *brùn*,

G. *braun*, E. *brown*. Hence *brunire*, Sp. *bruñir broñir*, Pg.
bornir, Pr. Fr. *brunir*, E. *burnish*, cf. M. H. G. *briunen*.

Bruno — *brugna*.

Brusca — *busca*.

Brusco It. Sp., Fr. *brusc* (whence G. *brüsch*), Pg. fem. *brusca*
holly; from *ruscum*, cf. Pr. *brusc* bark, bee-hive from *rusca*,
It. *bruscare* to strip bark from Com. *ruscà*. Hence Pr. *brusca*
a rod (cf. Fr. *houssine* from *houx*).

Brusco It. sour (e. g. of wine), rude, abrupt, Sp. Pg. *brusco*
morose, gloomy, Fr. *brusque* passionate &c.; Fr. *brusquer* to
treat rudely. Prob. from O. H. G. *bruttise brutt'se* gloomy.
But Ferrari derives it from the Lat. *labruscus*, the It. dropping
the first syllable.

Brustolare — *bruciare*.

Brutto It. ugly, rude, misformed; from *brutus* senseless, shapeless.

Bruxa Sp., Pg. Cat. *bruxa* a screech-owl, a witch, cf. *striga* (It.
strega), *bruxo* a wizard, sorcerer. Perhaps another form of
bruza bristle, the *owl* being so calledfrom its shaggy head. A
rough-haired man is called in Sw. *huwel*=*owl*. Witches were
thought to take the form of owls (*convertidas en gallos*, "*lechu-
zas*", *o cuervos* Cervant. Nov. 6), v. Ducange, s. *bruxa*.

Bruxula — *bosso*.

Bruyère — *bru* (1).

Brusa — *broza*.

Bruzzaglia — *broza*.

Bubbola — *upupa*.

Bubbone It., Sp. *bubon*, Pg. *bubão*, Fr. *bubon*, Wal. *buboin* s
bubo, a tumour; from βουβών, L. *hubo*. Hence Sp. *buba bua*,
Pg. *bouba bubo*, Fr. *bube*, Wal. *bubě*, unless these are to be
referred to a lost Lat. primitive, cf. s. *manto*, *mazza*, *mozzo*,
fraya, *sap*.

Buo — *buco*.

Bucato It., Sp. Pr. *bugada*, Fr. *bucé buck*-linen, *bucking*, Burg.
buie, It. *bucata buck*-ashes; *bucatare*, Rh. *buadar*, Bret. *buga*,
Fr. *buguer buquer buer* to *buck*, G. *beuchen*, *buchen* &c. Diez
derives *bucato* from *buca* a hole, because the ashes were
strained through a pierced dish, cf. Sp. *colada* lye from *colare*
to strain. But *bucare* does not mean to strain, so Wedg.
would refer the word to the Celtic *bog* = moist, Sclav. *mok*
(whence L. *macero* to soak). In L. *imbuere* the guttural is lost
as in Fr. *buer*.

Buccio buccia bark, peel, skin. Perhaps from *lobuccio*, from
λοβός or λοπός peel. Cf. *loppa* and Rom. Gr. 1, 240, 253. The
lo was perhaps mistaken for the article, cf. *lierre*.

Bucha buchar buche — *bozza*.

Bûche — *busca*.

Bucherame It., Cat. *bocaram*, Pr. *bocaran boqueran*, Fr. *bougran*, E. *buckram* coarse stiffened stuff with open interstices; from It. *bucherare* to perforate. Others derive it from *boc* a goat (boc-ar-an) so = stuff made of goat's hair.

Buco buca It., Sp. *buco buque*, Cat. *buc* a hole, Pr. O. Fr. *buc*, Com. *bugh* a trunk, Pr. *buc* (which, however, Mahn makes = *brusc*) a bee-hive; It. *bucare* to perforate; from O. H. G. *bûh*, M. H. G. *büch*, O. N. *bûkr*, Du. *bûk buik* = belly, trunk. Hence Sp. Pr. *trabucar*, Fr. *trébucher* to fling to the ground, to stumble, prop. to overthrow in wrestling, cf. *tram-bustare* from *busto.* Hence Sp. *trabuco*, Pr. *trabuc*, *trabuquel*, Fr. *trébuchet* a catapult. The It. *traboccare trabocco trabocchetto* have reference to *bocca* (mouth); the Ven. *trabucare*, O. It. *trabucco*, Com. *trabuc*, Ver. *strabuco* preserve the original form.

Buda burda It. = Gk. τύφη, L. *tomentum.* Servius has: *ulvam dicunt rem, quam vulgus budam vocat.*

Budello It., O. Sp. *budel*, Pr. Fr. *boyau* (O. Fr. *boel*), E. *bowel*; from *botellus* (Martial) a sausage; L. L. *botelli* = bowels. Gellius 17, 7 gives *botulus* as a word used by the vulgar. Wedgwood says the word is probably derived from the rumbling of the bowels, but it would, perhaps, be better to connect it with It. *botte*, Sp. *bota* &c., A. S. *butte* = a hollow receptacle, v. s. *botte.*

Budget — *bolgia.*

Budriere — *baudré.*

Buega Sp. a boundary-stone; cf. G. *buk* a boundary, *buik*, Frisch 1, 151; cf. also E. *balk*, q. v. s. *balco.*

Buer — *bucato.*

Buf Pr. Fr. an interjection; It. *buffo*, Mil. *boff* a puff of wind; It. *buffa*, Sp. *bufa* a scoff (whence *buffone* &c.), O. Fr. *buffe* a *buff*, blow, *buffet* a box on the ear, a *buffet*, Wall. *bofet* a pin-cushion, Sp. *bofeton* = O. Fr. *bofet*, N. Pr. *buffo* the buttock; It. *buffare*, Parm. *boffar*, Sp. Pg. Pr. *bufar*, Fr. *bouffer bouffir buffer*, N. Pr. *buffà bouffà* to puff, blow, O. Fr. *buffier* a buffet; for the connexion in meaning cf. *blow* in its two senses, and Fr. *souffler soufflet.* From *buf* an imitation of the sound of a blow. The G. has *buf puf, puff, puffen, puffer*, Fr. *pouf, pouffer.* The It. *boffice* soft, yielding, is formed on the analogy of *soffice.* The Fr. *buffeter* meant to "mar wine by often tasting it" (Cotgrave) properly to let in air by taking out the vent-peg, then, generally, to tap, *vin de buffet* wine on tap, *buffetier* L. L. *bufetarius* (E. corr. *beef-eater*) a tapster. Hence *buffet* would = the *tap* of a tavern, next in E. any *sideboard*, in Sp. a *writing-desk*, in Fr. an office for business.

Bufera It. a hurricane; from the root *buf* v. supr.

Bugia It., Lomb. *busia* a lie, Pr. *bauzia* and *bauza*, O. Fr. *boisie*

deceit; *bugiare* to lie, *bauzar boiser* to deceive; Pr. *baussan*
(f. -*ana*) a deceiver; Sp. *bausan* an effigy. Prob. from the
O. H. G. *bôsi*, G. *bôse* wicked, *bôsa* = tricks (= Pr. *bauza*),
bôsôn to slander (cf. *nugari* = to lie). The It. *bugiare busare*
also = to perforate, *bugio* O. Sp. *buso* = a hole, It. *bugio*
buso = perforated, empty. These are referable to the same
word *bôsi* = vain, idle, empty. The Fr. *boisdie* (adj. *boisdif*)
is formed on the analogy of *roisdie* (v. *vezzo*).

Bugia It. Sp. Pg., Pr. *bogia*, Fr. *bougie* a wax-taper; from *Bugie*
in North Africa, whence the wax was imported (Menage).

Bugna Mil. Ven., Romagn. *bogna*, N. Pr. *bougno*, O. Fr. *bugne*,
Fr. *bigne* (Menage *beugne*) a bump (from a blow), boil &c.,
also in masc. Mil. *bugn*, Sard. *bugnu*, Romagn. *bogn;* Veron.
bugnon a blow, E.*bunion* a lump on the foot, *bunny* a swelling;
Crem. *bugnocca* a boil; E. *bun*, N. Pr. *bougneto*, Fr. *beignet*
bignet, Sp.*buñuelo*, Limous.*bouni* a small round cake, properly
a lump, cf. Gael. *bonnach* = *bannock*. The origin is in the
idea of striking, Bret. *bunta*, E. to *bunt*, Du. *bunsen* to strike.
The Manx *bun* = butt-end, Gael. *bun*, Ir. *bôn* = a root or
stump, Prov. E. *bun* = the tail of a rabbit, hence *bunny* =
rabbit.

Bugno It. a bee-hive, *bugna bugnola* a basket of straw-work,
O. Fr. *bugnon* = *bugno*, N. Pr. *bugno* = stump of a tree, v.
bugna (Celtic *bun*).

Buho Sp., Pg. *bufo*, Wal. *buhě* an owl; from *bubo* influenced,
however, by the O. H. G. *bûf hûf*.

Buie — *boja* (1).

Buis buisson — *bosso*.

Buitre — *avoltore*.

Bujo It. dark, Lomb.*buro (bur)*. From *bureus burius* for *burrius*
from *burrus* which Festus says = *rufus* (cf. *fujo* from *furvius*
for *furvus*). O. Fr. *bure buire*, Pg. Pr. *burel*, Sp. *buriel* dark-
brown, specially of sheep, then = a coarse woollen cloth
made of the fleeces of such sheep. This being worn by the
lower orders gave rise to the O. E. *borel* a layman, a boor,
cf. *griselle*. *Bureau* was properly a desk covered with such
cloth. The It. *buratto* a coarse cloth, *buratello* &c., *burella*,
bujose dungeons are from *bujo buro*. For the same L. word
in another form (*birrus* = a coarse mantle Vopiscus and Papias) v. *berretta*.

Bula — *bolla*.

Bulicare — *bouger*.

Bulimo sbulimo It. intense hunger; from βούλιμος, Fr.*boulimie*.

Bulla — *bolla*.

Bulletin — *bolla*.

Bullir — *bollire*.

Bulo Ven. Piedm. Lomb. a fop, beau, a fighter, bully; from G. *buhle* a lover.

Bulto vulto Sp., Pg. *vulto* a lump, bulk, pillow-case, also = form, figure. In the latter sense evidently from *vultus*, in the former from the Du. *bult*, E. *bulch bulk* a lump, cf. Wedgw. s. *bulge, bolster*, and v. *bolgia*. Diez refers it to *volutus*, so = volumen, cf. *volta*.

Buñuelo — *bugna*. ·

Buquer Fr. to knock; from the Du. *beuken*. Hence prob. *bouc*, E. *buck*, W. *bwch* from its *butting*. *Butt* and *buck* are connected, cf. *rebuter* with *rebuke*.

Bur Norm. a dwelling, O. Fr. *buron* a hut; from O. H. G. *bûr* a house, G. *bauer*.

Burat bureau — *bujo*.

Burbero — *borbogliare*.

Burbuja — *borbottare*.

Burella — *bujo*.

Burga Sp. a hot-spring; from Basque *bero-ur-ga* warm-water-spot, v. Larramendi.

Burgo — *borgo*.

Buriel — *bujo*.

Buril — *borino*.

Burin — *borino*.

Burjaca — *bolgia*.

Burla It. Sp. Pg., N. Pr. *bourlo* scoff, jest; It. *burlare*, Sp. Pg. *burlar* to scoff; Pr. *burlaire*, O. Fr. *bourleur*; It. *burlesco* &c. Ausonius has *burra* a jest, prop. = shaggy hair, cf. It. *fiocco* = *flock* of wool and *trick*; hence *burrula burla*, Sp. *borla* = a tassel. Wedgw., however, traces the word to the Celtic *burd burl* mockery, whence O. E. *bourd* a jest.

Burrasca It. (adj. *borrascoso*), Sp. Pg. Cat. *borrasca*, Fr. *bourasque* a storm, tempest. As Sp. *nieve* gave *nevasca*, so It. *borca*, Mil. Ven. Romagn. *bora* (= L. *boreas*) *borrasca burrasca*. Perhaps the double *r* shows a reference to *burrus* dark-red (of a tempestuous sky), v. *bujo*.

Burro Sp. Pg. an ass. Hence Pg. *burrico*, Sp. Neap. *borrico*, Fr. *bourrique*, Lomb. *borich*, It. *bricco* an ass. *Buricus* a nag is found as early as the 5th century. Isidorus has: *equus brevior quem vulgo buricum vocant*. So called either from its shaggy hair (v. *borra*), or from its dark colour (*burīcus* from *burrus*, v. *bujo*).

Burrone — *borro*.

Busare — *bugia*.

Busart — *buse*.

Busca Lomb. Piedm. Pr., Sic. *vusca*, O. Fr. *busche* a splinter, Cat. *brusca busca* a rod, Fr. *bûche* a log, Fr. *bucher* to hew

wood. Prob. connected with *bois bosc* (*v. bosco*), cf. O. F
embuscher with It. *imboscare*.

Buscare It. to catch, Sp. Pg. *buscar*, O. Sp. *boscar* to search,
track, Fr. *busquer* to seek after, It. Sp. Pg. *busca* search. From
the Sp., where *buscar* = It. *cercare*, Fr. *chercher*. The original
meaning was "to go through the bush" *(bosco)* (cf. *montar* to
go up a hill), hence to hunt, track; Sp. *busca* = a hunting
dog, O. Sp. *busco* = a track.

Buschetta — *busca*.

Buscione — *bosso*.

Buse Fr. a sort of falcon, also *busart*, Pr. *buzac*, It. *bozzago
abuzzago* = L. *buteo*, G. *buse*, *bufshart*.

Buseocchio — *bozza*.

Busquer — *buscare*.

Bussare It. to knock; from G. *buchsen* (E. *box*), cf. *bossen* to
knock, beat, Du. *buysschen*. Hence, too, the O. Fr. *buissier*,
which Roquefort refers to *busquer*.

Busse buse buoe O. Fr., L. L. *bucia buza*, Pr. (m.) *bus*, O. Sp.
buzo; from A. S. *butse* (*butse-carlas* = shipmen), E. *buss*, Du.
buyse, O. N. *bússa* a fishing-boat. A particular application,
says Wedgw., of the many-formed word meaning bulk,
trunk &c., v. *boss, box, butch, bust*. V. seq. and *bulto*.

Busto It. Sp. Pg., Pr. *bust*, Fr. *buste*, E. *bust*. L. L. *busta* =
arbor ramis truncata. Ph. connected with *busca* (*bùche* = a
log), E. *busk*, Sp. *bucha* = a chest, *buche* = breast, L. L.
busta = arca (from *buxida, pyxida, v.boîte*), cf. *arca*, It.*casso*,
E. *chest*, G. *rumpf*. Hence It. *imbusto* bodice, busk, Sp. *embuste* gewgaw, artful story &c., *embustero* an importer, It.
trambustare to fling, overthrow.

But buto — *bozza*.

Butin — *bottino*.

Buttare — *bottare*.

Bus Sp. Pg. a reverential kiss, Pr. *bus* lip, E. *buss*. From the
Celtic *bus* a mouth or lip. Sp. *buces* or *bruces* = upper lips,
bocel edge of a vessel, *bocera* crumbs sticking to the lips,
though the two last may be from *bocca*. The L. *basium* and
Pers. *bôs* are perhaps connected.

Busso — *bozza*.

C.

Ca O. It. O. Sp. O. Pg. = L. *nam;* from *quâ re* (Pr. Fr. *car*),
or from *quia*. O. It. *ca* after comparatives = *quam*.

Ça — *qua*.

Caable chaable O. Fr. a machine for throwing stones, from *cadable* L. L. *chadabula*. The Pr. is *calabre* (*l* for *d*). O. Fr. *caables* also = fallen branches of trees, Fr. *chablis*. Hence Fr. *accabler* to crush. The der. from χαταβολή would suit both form and meaning of *caable*. Wedgw. makes *calabre* the original form, and connects *cable*, cable, but v.*cappio, calibro.*

Cabal Sp. Pg. Pr. exact, perfect; from *cabo (caput).*

Cabala It. Sp. Pg., Fr. *cabale*, E. *cabal*; from the Hebr. *kabalah* a secret traditional interpretation of scripture. Hence the secondary meaning of a conclave of secret plotters.

Cabane cabinet — *capanna.*

Cabaña — *capanna.*

Cabas — *cava.*

Cabdal — *caudal.*

Cabe Sp., O. Sp. *cabo*, O. Pg. *cabe cabo* = juxta; prop. = *à cabo*, O. Fr. *à chief* at the end or side, sbst. *cabe* a shake. O. Sp. *cabear* = to adapt.

Cabellau Fr. a cod-fish; from Du. *kabeljaauw*, whence, too, perhaps with a reference to *baculus*, the Sp. *bacalao*, Basque *bacaīlàba*, Ven. Piedm. *bacalà.*

Cabestan Fr. (m.), E. *capstan*; from Sp. *cabrestante* = standing-goat *(cabra)*, cf. G. *bock*, E. *ram (aries).*

Cabeza — *cavezza.*

Cable cabo — *cappio.*

Caboral — *caporale.*

Cabos — *chabol.*

Cabrer Fr., N. Pr. *cabrá* (reflex.) to rear; from *caper.*

Cabus Fr. in *chou-cabus* a cabbage with a head; = It. *capuccio (caput)*, G. *kappes*, E. *cabbage.*

Cacáo cacoáo It., Sp. Pg. Fr. E.*cacao* fruit of a South American tree, Sp. Pg. *cacao-tree*; from the Mexican *kakahuatl*. The tree is also called in Sp. *cacaynal*, Pg. *cacaoeiro*, Fr.*cacaoyer, cacaotier.*

Caçapo — *gazapo.*

Cacolare It., Sp. Pg. *cazar*, Pr. *cassar*, O. Fr.*chacier*, Pic. *cacher* (whence E. *catch*), Fr. *chasser* (whence *chase*); sbst. *caccia, caza, cassa, chace chasse* &c. This word is the representative of the L. *venari*, and comes from *captus*, whence *captiare cacciare*, cf. *succiare (suctiare)* from *suctus*, *conciare (comtiare)* from *comtus*, *pertugiare (pertusiare)* from *pertusus.*

Cache cacher cachot — *quatto.*

Cacho — *quatto.*

Cacho Sp. a slice, a piece, *cachar* to break in pieces; from L. L. *capulare cap'lare* to cut off? Cf. *cacha* handle of a knife, from *capulus*, and cf. *ancho* = *amplus.*

Cachorro Sp. a whelp, cub. Prob. from *catulus cat'lus*, as *cachonda* from *catuliens*. The suffix is, however, of Basque form, and the word may be of Basque origin, B. *chakhuira* = dog.

Caco Pg. a potsherd; from *cacabus* (χάχχαβος), cf. *Jago* from *Jacobus*.

Cadahalso — *catafalco*.

Cadalecho — *cataletto*.

Cadastre — *catastro*.

Cadauno It. *caduno*, Sp. *cada uno*, Pg. *cada hum*, Pr. *cada un (cadun)*, O. Fr. *cadhun*, *cheun* = L. *quisque*. From *usque ad unum* (cf. Rh. *s-cadin* = s-cadun), or from *quisque ad unum* (cf. O. Sp. *quiscadauno*, O. Pg. *quiscadaun*). *Cada* was afterwards used as an independent pronoun; cf. N. Gr. χαθένας = *quisque*, from χαθ' ἕνα, χάθε like *cada* being used as an adj. χάθε δένδρον = Sp. *cada arbol*.

Cadeau Fr. a flourish of caligraphy, an ornament (hence = present), vb. *cadeler* (obs.); from *catellus* a dim. of *catena*, cf. It. *catenella* a chain-like ornament in needle-work.

Cadenas — *candado*.

Cadera Sp. Cat., Pg. *cadeira* hip, hip-joint; from *cathedra*. Hence Sp. *caderillas* (pl.) ladies' hoops.

Cadet Fr. E. the younger son of a family; from *capitettum* (caput), a little chief.

Cadimo Pg. crafty; from Arab. *kadem (kadim)* Freyt. 3, 409, which, however, has only the meaning of *valiant*. Pr. *caim* is the same word.

Cadran Fr., Pr. *quadran* a sun-dial; from *quadrans*, It. Sp. *quadrante*, a *quadrant*.

Cadre — *quadro*.

Caes — *cayo*.

Cafard — *cafre*.

Caffe It., Sp. Fr. *café*, *coffee*; from Ar. *qahwah* a sort of wine, a drink prepared from berries, the form following the Turkish pronunciation *kahve*.

Caffo It. an uneven number: *giuocare pari o caffo* = *ludere par impar*. From *capo* that exceeds measure (περισσός): *essere il caffo* = περισσός, sans pareil, unique; or from the L. *caput* in the formula *caput aut navem*.

Cafila a caravan; from Ar. *qâfilah*, a *coffle* of slaves.

Cafre Sp. Pg. rude, barbarous; from Ar. *kâfir* unbelieving, profligate. Hence Fr. *cafard* a hypocrite.

Cage — *gabbia*.

Cagione It. occasion, pretext (Pr. *ocaison*, O. Fr. *ochoison*); from *occasio*, cf. Wald. *cayson*, O. Pg. *cajão*.

Cagnard — *casnard*.

Cagot Fr. a hypocrite. The Goths and Arabs fled from Spain to Aquitaine, where they were protected by Charles Martel and his successors; by the French they were regarded as Arian heretics, and called *canes Gothi, cagots* (Pr. *cd* a dog and *Got* = Goth). From unbeliever the word came to mean hypocrite, cf. *cafard.* Frisch derives it from *cap-gott* = Caput Dei, an expression used in oaths.

Cahier Fr. pamphlet, copy-book, quire. Pic. has *coyer, quoyer*, E. *quire;* from *codicarium*, not from *quaternio* (Dante *gnaderno*), which gives *carrignon, quaregnon.*

Cahute Fr. a hut, O. Fr. *chahute* and *cahuette.* Perhaps a compound of *ca-hutte*, dimin. *cahuette* for *cahutette.* Or *cahuette* is the original form and *cahute* a contraction. Cf. Norm. *cavé* a ship (Due. s. *cayum*). *Cajute* is from the Du. *kajutt.*

Caille — *quaglia.*

Cailler — *quagliare.*

Caillou Fr., Pic. *calian*, O. Fr. *caillo chaillo*, Pr. *calhau*, Pg. *calhao* flint. Prob. from *cailler* to coagulate, so = a fixed mass of silex, cf. G. *kiesel* = any fused mass, stone or hail, *kes* = glacier-ice, both from *kisan* to coagulate. Littré makes *caillou* from *calculavus (calculus) caillo caillou*, cf. *Andigavus, Pictavus,* which give *Anjou, Poitou, clavus clou clo, travum trou tro, paparer papou.* The Berrichon *caille* preserves the simple form, cf. also W. *cellt.*

Cais — *casso.*

Caisse — *cassa.*

Cajoler — *gabbia.*

Calabasa Sp., Pg. *cabaça*, Cat. *carabassa*, Sic. *caravazza* a pumpkin, a *calabash*, Fr. *calebasse;* ph. from Ar. *qerbah (qerbat)*, Pl. *qerabat* a water-skin, with Rom. suffix.

Calabre — *caable.*

Calabrone scalabrone a hornet; from *crabro*, L. L. *scabro*, Papias: *carabrio genus animalis muscae similis.* The Occit. has *chabrian.*

Calafatare It., Sp. *calafatear*, Pr. *calafatar*, Fr. *calafater calfeutrer*, M. G. χαλαφατειν to caulk a ship; from the L. *calefectare.*

Calamandrea It., Sp. *camedrio*, Fr. *germandrée* a plant, *germander:* from *chamaedrys* (χαμαιδρυς).

Calambre Sp., Pg. *cambra* cramp; M. H. G. *klamphern* to suffer cramp, cf. O. H. G. *chlampheren.*

Calaminaria sc. *pietra* It., Sp. Pg. *calamina*, Fr. E. *calamine;* from *cadmia* (χαδμεία χαδμία) with adjectival suffix, G. *galmei.*

Calamita It. Sp. Pg., Pr. Cat. *caramida*, Fr. *calamite* a magnet.

From *calamus*, the needle being inserted in a stalk or piece of cork, so as to float on water.

Calan — *chaland*.

Calaña Sp. sample, quality; from *qualis*.

Calandra It. Pr., Sp. Cat. *calandria*, Pg. *calhandra*, N. Pr. *caliandro cariandro*, Fr. *calendre*, M. H. G. *galander* a tufted lack. From *galerita* with perhaps a reference to *caliendrum* (tuft). The Sp. *caladre* suits the Gk. χαραδριός, L. L. *caradrius* translated in the Glossaries by the O. H. G. *lerihha* (G. *lerche* lark).

Calandre Fr. a cylinder, E. *calander*, from *cylindrus*, prop. *celendre*; *calandre* is a corruption of *colendre*, cf. *coing* from κυδώνιον.

Calappio — *chiappare*.

Calare It., Sp. Pg. Pr. *calar*, Fr. *caler* to let down; from χαλᾷν to loose, let go, L. *chalare* (Vitruvius), Rh. *calar* to desist, Pic. *caler* to give way, withdraw, drop; Pg. Pr. *calar* also = to be silent, Sp. *callar*. N. Pr. *calá* unites both senses to drop and to be silent. Hence It. Sp. Pg. Pr. *cala*, Fr. *cale*, It. N. Pr. *calanca* a bay (*calare* = to drop anchor), Gael. *cala* a bay, *cal* to drop anchor. Hence, too, Sp. *cala* a peg, Sp. Pg. a notch, *calar* to penetrate, pierce, Fr. *cale* = a flat piece of wood, a trestle, unless these are from L. *cala* a piece of fire-wood (κᾶλον) in Lucilius.

Calavera Sp., Pg. *caveira* a skull; from *calvaria*.

Caldaja It., Sp. *caldera*, Pr. *caudiera*, Fr. *chaudière* a pot, L. L. *caldaria*; from *caldarius*; hence It. *calderone*, Sp. *calderon*, Fr. *chaudron*, *cauldron*.

Calèche — *calesse*.

Caleçon — *calzo*.

Caleffare It. to mock, jeer; from G. *klaffen* to yelp, bark.

Calentar Sp. to heat, from *calens*, *caleo*; hence Sp. *escalentar*, Pg. *esquentar*, *acaentar aquentar* (O. Sp. *calecer*, *escalecer*, Pg. *aquecer* from *calescere*). Hence Sp. *calentura* a fever, E. *calenture*.

Calere It., O. Sp. Pr. *caler*, O. Fr. *chaloir* verb impers. with dat. of the person, to be of importance, to concern; from L. *calere*, *non mi cale* = *non mihi calet*, cf. ἐμὲ οὐδὲν θάλπει κέρδος. Hence Fr. *nonchalant*, *nonchalance*.

Calesse calesso It., Sp. *calesa*, Fr. *calèche*, E. *calash caloch* an open carriage; from Bohem. *kolesa* wheel-work (Russ. *koleso* wheel).

Calha quelha Pg. a canal, from *canalicula*, cf. *funcho* from *fœniculum*.

Calhao — *caillou*.

Calibro It., Sp. Pg. Fr. E. *calibre*, E. *caliver calliper* (-compasses), the bore of a cannon. Diez derives it from the Arab. *qdlib* a model, pattern (O. Sp. has also *calibo*); Mahn from *qud librd*; Wedgwood makes *caliver* = an arquebuss or small cannon the original sense, and this from *calabre* (v. *caable*) an engine for casting stones, = *carabe* for *cabre* from *cabra* a goat, *calabre* orig. = a battering, ram, G. *bock*.

Calina Sp. dense vapour; ph. originally = steam, from *caleo*, cf. *bruine*. Diez suggests *caligo*.

Calma It. Sp. Pg., Fr. *calme* (m.) absence of wind, *calm*, Du. *kulm kulmte*; *calmare* &c. to *calm*, Fr. *chommer* for *chaumer* to make holiday. Sp. *calma* = heat of the day Gk. καῦμα, L. L. *cauma*. *Al* = *au* (v. *yota*), though, perhaps, in *calma* there was a reference to *calor*. The *noon-heat* was the time of *rest*. N. Pr. *chaume* = time when the flocks sought the shade, Rh. *cauma* a shady place for cattle.

Calpestare It. to tread under foot, sb. *calpestio*; from *calce pistare*, Pr. *calpisar*, v. *pestare*.

Calterire — *scalterire*.

Caluco It. poor, needy; from *caducus*.

Calzada Sp. Pg., Pr. *caussada*, Fr. *chaussée*, E. *causeway*. From *calceata* (*calx* chalk), prop. a pavement strengthened with mortar. Wedgwood from *calceata* because *shod* or protected with stone, Sp. *calzar*, Fr. *chausser* to shoe.

Calzo calza It., Sp. *calza*, Pr. *caussa*, Fr. *chausse*, whence *calzone* &c., Fr. *caleçon*; from *calceus*. Hence It. *discalzo scalzo*, Sp. *descalzo*, Pr. *descaus*, Fr. *déchaus*, Pic. *décaus*, Lor. *deichaux*, L. L. *discalcius* for *discalceatus*.

Cama Sp. Pg. a bed, a lair. Isidorus has: *in camis* i. e. in *stratis*. Ph. from χαμαί (cf. *acamar* to stretch on the ground) so = χαμευνή.

Cama Sp. (only in plur.) bridle-bits; from *camus*, χημός a halter, O. H. G. *chamo*.

Camaglio It., Pr. *capmalh*, O. Fr. *camail* the collar of a coat-of-mail, serving also to cover an head, Fr. *camail* a mantle; from *cap* and *malha* mail. Hence Sp. *camal* a halter, *gramalla* a coat-of-mail.

Camaieu, camée — *cameo*.

Camangiare It. pulse, vegetables; for *capo-mangiare* Menage.

Camarlingo It., Sp. *camarlengo*, Pr. *camarlenc*, Fr. *chambrelain*, *chamberlain*; from O. H. G. *chamarlinc*, G. *kämmerling*.

Camba — *gamba*.

Cambellotto ciambellotto It., Sp. *camelote chamelote*, Fr. *camelot*, E. *camlet chamlet* a stuff of *camel's* hair. It had a wavy or watered surface, hence Fr. *se cameloter* to grow wrinkled. Ph. from χαμηλώτη camel's skin.

Cambiare cangiare It., Sp. Pg. *cambiar*, Pr. *cambiar camjar*, Fr.

changer, E. *change;* L. L. *cambiare* from *cambire* in Apuleius
(χάμπτειν χάμβειν). Wedgwood, with less probability,
considers it to bo the nasalised form of E. *chap chop* (G. *kaufen*), cf. Chaucer's *champmen* for *chapmen.*

Cambrer Fr., N. Pr. *cambrá* to bend, curve: from *camerare* to
arch.

Cambron Sp., Pg. *cambrão* (only in pl.) buck-thorn; from
camurus?

Camedrio — *calamandrea.*

Camerata It. (m.), Sp. *camarada* (m., Pg. m. f.), Fr. *camerade*
(m. f.), E. *comrade;* formerly = a company occupying the
same chamber *(camera)*, thence = one of such company, a
tent-fellow. Cf. Piedm. *mascrada* (1) a company of maskers,
(2) one of them.

Camicia camiscia It., Sp. Pg. Pr. *camisa*, Fr. E. *chemise*, Wal.
cëmase, Alban. *cëmişe*, whence It. *camiciola*, Sp. *camisola*, Fr.
E. *camisole;* It. *incamiciata*, Sp. *encamisada*, Fr. E. *camisade*
a night-attack, the shirt being worn over the armour.
Hieronymus has: *solent militantes habere lineas quas camisias
vocant.* Various derivations are given: (1) O. H. G. *hamidi
hemidi* indusium, (2) *cama* a bed, Isidor: *camisias quod in his
dormimus in camis*, but neither of these account for the termination *isia*. That *is* is part of the root we see from It. *ca-
mice*, O. Fr. *chainse.* So it will be better to refer the word
either to the Gael. *caimis* a shirt, W. *camse*, or to the Ar.
qamiç an under-garment, which, however, is not found in
other Sem. dialects, and is prob. from the Rom.

Caminata camminata It. a room (prop. with a fire-place in it),
Fr. *cheminée*, E. *chimney.* L. L. *caminata* = a room with a
caminus. The E. *chimney* now = the gorge or vent of a furnace,
once = the fire itself, cf. Sir John Cheke, Matt. 13, 50: the
chimney of fire.

Camméo It. (Cellini in 16th cent.), Fr. *camée* (m.) and *camaïeu*,
Sp. *camafeo*, Pg. *camafeo, camafeu, camafeio*, E. *cameo*, G.
gamaheu, L. L. *camaheu, camahelus, camahutus.* Mahn's der.
is the most probable: from *gemma, gama, cama, cammaeus*
and from *cammaeus altus, camahutus.* But the hardening of the
g is without analogy. V. seq.

Cammino It., Sp. *camino*, Pg. *caminho*, Pr. *camin*, Fr. *chemin*,
L. L. *caminus* a way; from the Celtic, W. *cam* a step, *caman*
a way. Others derive this and the previous word from the
Slavonic *kamen* a stone, though neither are likely to have
come from such a source.

Camoscio — *camuso.*

Camozza It., Sp. *camuza gamuza*, Pg. *camuça camurça*, It. *ca-
muscio*, Fr. E. *chamois*, M. H. G. *yam-z*, G. *gemse.* Perhaps

the original word is seen in the Sp. Pg. *gamo gama* a deer (E. *gamut?*). This may be from L. *dama*, cf. *golfin* = *dulfin delfin*, *gragea* = *dragea*, *gazapo* = *dasapo (?)*. But a *g* is not thus hardered in Rom. It may be connected with Celtic *cam* crooked (-horned).

Campagna It., Sp. *campaña*, Fr. *campagne* (O. Fr. *Champagne*), E. *champain;* from *Campania*, first used as an appellative by Gregory of Tours. E. *campaign* = time an army serves in open field.

Campana It. Sp. Cat. Pr., Pg. *campainha* a bell; the Fr. has *cloche*, but the Limous. has *campano*, Berr. *campaine* a bell. From *Campania* where bells were first used in churches, v. Ducange. Isid. has: *campana (statera unius lancis) e regione Italiæ nomen accepit*, thus also = a *steel-yard* (Wal. *cumpěně*), which meaning, however, it soon lost.

Campeggio It., Sp. *campeche*, Fr. *campêche* log-wood; from *Campeche* in South America.

Campione It., Sp. *campeon*, Pr. *campion*, Fr. E. *champion;* from L. L. *campio*, which is from *campus* as *tabellio* from *tabella*. From *campus* also come It. *campeggiare*, Sp. *campear (campeador)*, O. Fr. *champeler* to be in the field, to encamp. The A.S. has *camp* a fight, Du. *kamp*, Du. *kempen* to fight &c. These may be from the L., though the Scand. *kapp* would seem an older form than *camp*. Ic. *kapp* = fight. So in vulgar E. to *cap* = to excel. W. *camp* = a feat, game, *campio* to strive, Sp. *campar* to excel.

Camuffare — *muffare*.

Camuso camosoio It.; Fr. *camus*, O. E. *camous* flat-nosed, Pr. *gamus camus* awkward, *camusat* = *camus*. The root is W. *cam* (cf. *cam-ard* = *camus*), and the 2nd part is prob. *muso* snout. Others derive it from *camurus* nothwithstanding the difference of accent. With It. *camoscio* cf. Fr. adj. *camoissié* bruised, black and blue, cf. Rou. *camoussé* pock-marked.

Canaglia It., Sp. *canalla*, Fr. *canaille*, O. Fr. *chienaille* rabble; from *canis*, cf. Sp. *perreria*.

Canapo It., Wal. *cěnepě*, Sp. *cañamo*, Pr. *canebe cambre*, Fr. *chanrre* hamp; from *cannabis cannabus*. Hence It. *canavaccio*, Sp. *cañamazo*, Pr. *canabas*, Fr. *canevas*, E. *canvas*.

Canapé — *canope*.

Canapsa Fr. a knapsack; from G. *knappsack* (*knappen* to eat, munch).

Canard — *cane*.

Canasto canasta Sp. N. Pr. a *canister;* from *canistrum*, It. *canestro*.

Canavaccio — *canape*.

Cancellare — *chance*.

Candado Sp. (vulg. *calnado*), O.Sp. *cañado*, *cadenado* a padlock; from *catenatum*; O. Sp. *candar* to lock. Cf. It. *catenaccio*, Fr. *cadenas*.

Cane O. Fr. a ship, Fr. *canot* a small boat (the E. *canoe* is from Sp. *canoa* an Indian word); Fr. *cane* a duck, *canard* a drake. Not from *canna* but from Du. *kaan*, G. *kahn* a boat.

Candire It., Fr. *se candir*, to candy, become candied, cf. It. *zucchero candito*, Sp. *azucar cande*, Fr. *sucre candi*, E. *sugarcandy*. The Ar. is *qand* or *qandah* and is from the Sk. *khanda* a piece, a piece of cristallized sugar (*khand* to break), v. Mahn, p. 47.

Canevas — *canapé*.

Canezou Fr. a light muslin jacket, worn by women. Orig. = hot weather, a corruption of *quinze août*, v. V. Hugo, Les Misérables 1, p. 356.

Canfora It. Sp., Fr. *camphre*, E. *camphor*; from Ar. *al-kâfûr* with inserted nasal, Sp. *alcanfor*; without the nasal It. *cafura*, M. H. G. *gaffer*. The word is of Indian origin, Sansk. *karpûra*.

Cangiare — *cambiare*.

Cangilon Sp., Pg. *cangirão* a liquid measure, a jar; from *congius*.

Cangrena It. Sp., Fr. *cangrène*, Sp. *gangrena*, Fr. *gangrène*, E. *gangrene*; from *ganyræna* (γάγγραινα), spelt with a *c* from a false reference to *cancer*.

Canho Pg. left, *canhoto* left-handed, sbst. a crooked piece of wood; from *cam* crooked (v. *gamba*).

Canif Fr. a penknife; from O. N. *knifr*, A. S. *cnif*, E. *knife*, G. *kneif*. Dim. *ganivet*, O. Fr. *cnivet*, Pr. *canivet*, whence O. Sp. *cañivete*, Pg. *canivete*.

Canivete — *canif*.

Cannamele It., Sp. *cañamiel*, L. L. *canamella* sugar-cane, prop. = honey-cane.

Cannella It., Sp. Pg. Pr. *canela*, Fr. *cannelle*, whence Du. *kaneel* cinnamon; from *canna*.

Cannibale It., Sp. *canibal*, Fr. *cannibale*, E. *cannibal*; prop. an inhabitant of the Antilles, a *Carib* or *Canibal*; the Sp. *caribe* is used in the same sense.

Cannone It., Sp. *cañon*, Fr. *canon*, a large pipe (*canna*), also = cannon.

Canopè It., Wal. *canapeu*, Sp. Fr. *canapé* (O. Pg. *ganapé*) a couch; E. *canopy*; from *conopeum* (κωνωπεῖον) a mosquitonet, then = a bed or couch protected by such a net, cf. *bureau* = (1) coarse cloth, (2) a desk covered with it.

Canova It. a store room, cellar; Isid. Gloss. *canava camera post cœnaculum*.

Cansare scansare It. to turn aside. From O. Lat. *campsare*

(Ennius); cf. *campsare Leucaten* with *cansar la morte* &c. Priscian derives it from χάμπτειν.

Cansar canso — *cass.*

Cantiere It., Pg. *canteiro*, Fr. *chantier* a stand, trestle, E. *gauntree.* Sp. *cantel* a rope for binding casks; from *canterius* a yokebeam, Bavar. *gander.*

Cantimplora — *chantepleure.*

Canto It. Sp. Pg., O. Fr. *cant* a corner, angle, Sp. Pg. also = stone, It. = side, region (Fr. *champ*, orig. *chant*). The word . is widely spread. Gr. κανθός = corner of the eye, or rim of a wheel (L. *canthus*). The W. *cant* = circumference rim, border. O. Fris. *kaed*, N. *kantr*, Dan. *kant*, G. *kante* = corner, rim; E. *cant canted* in carpentry used to express the cutting off the angle of a square. Hence It. *cantone*, Sp. Pg. Fr. E. *canton*, Wald. *canton* a partition; Sp. *cantillo* a small stone, Pr. *cantel*, Fr. *chanteau*, E. *cantle* a corner-piece, a piece (of bread &c.); It. Sp. *cantina*, Fr. *cantine*, E. *canteen* a winecellar (prop. = a corner). It. *biscanto* = a dark hole, Piedm. *bescant* = oblique, awry. Vid. Dief. Orig. Europ. p. 278.

Cañaherla Sp. a plant, fennel; from *canna* and *ferula*, Cat. *canyafera.* The Sp. *cañaheja* is from *cannafericula.*

Cañamo — *canape.*

Capanna It., Sp. *cabaña*, Pg. Pr. Piedm. &c. *cabaña*, Fr. *cabane*, E. cabin. Not from *capere* nor from *cappa* a mantle, since *anna* is not a R. term., but from W. *caban* (dim. of cab); hence E. *cabin*, Fr. *cabinet*, It. *gabinetto*, Sp. *gabinete.*

Capazo — *cappa.*

Capdel — *capitello.*

Capére It., Sp. Pg. Pr. *caber* to contain and (intrans.) to have room, cf. *verbum meum non capit in vobis* S. Joan. (χωρεῖ); sub. *locum.*

Capessale — *cavezza.*

Capitano It., O. It. *catanno*, Sp. *capitan*, E. *captain* from *capitanus* (caput); L. L. *capitaneus* gives Pr. *capitani*, Fr. *capitaine*, O. Fr. *chevetaine chataine*, E. *chieftain.*

Capitare It. to end (intrans.); from *caput*, v. *chef.* Scapitare, Pr. *descaptar* to lose in traffic, summam imminuere.

Capitello It. dim. of *capo*, Sp. *caudillo*, O. Sp. *capdiello*, Pr. *capdel* the captain of a troop; from *capitellum* dim. of *capitulum.* Sp. *acaudillar*, Pr. *capdelar* to head a troop, O. Fr. *cadeler. caieler.*

Capitolo It., Sp. *capitulo cabildo*, Pg. *cabido*, Pr. *capitol*, Fr. *chapitre*, E. *chapter* in the sense of an ecclesiastical (or secular) assembly; from *capitulum* a heading, chapter (principal section of a book): either because the *chapters* of statutes were read in the assembly, or because they were a *governing* body, cf. *capitol* in S. France = a town-council, *capitoul* an individual member of such a council.

Capocchia It. the knob of a stick, *capocchio* dull, stupid; from *capitulum* corrupted into *caputulum*.

Caporale It., Sp. Fr. *caporal*, Rouchi *coporal corporal*, E. *corporal*; from *capo*, *caporalis*, prob. formed on the analogy of *corporalis*, with which it was afterwards confounded.

Capot — *cappa*.

Cappa It., Sp. Pg. Pr. *capa*, Fr. *chape*, E. *cape*. A very old word, prob. used in the spoken Latin. Isidore has: *capa, quia quasi totum capiat hominem.* From *capere* as O. H. G. *gifang* a garment, from *fahan* G. *fangen* to hold. For the double *p*, cf. *cappone* from *capo.* Hence It. *cappello*, Fr. *chapeau* a hat, O. Fr. *chapel*, *chapelet*, E. *chaplet* a garland. Boccaccio has: *capello ghirlanda secondo il volgar francese;* It. *cappella*, E. *chapel* &c., are so called from the covering or canopy over the altar, the name being extended to the recess in which the altar was placed. Ducange derives the name from the chapel where St. Martin's cloak was kept. Hence *cappotto, cappuccio, capperone* &c., Fr. *chaperon;* Sp. *capazo*, Sp. Pg. *capacho* a fruit or basket.

Cappero It., Fr. *câpre*, E. *caper;* from *capparis*, Ar. *alcabar* whence Sp. Pg. *alcaparra*, Arag. *caparra*.

Cappio It. loop, knot, Sp. Pg. *cable*, Fr. *câble* (O. Fr. *chable cheable*), E. *cable*. From L. L. *capulum* (*funis a capiendo* Isid.), M. Gr. καπλίον, Du. *kabel*. The Sp. *cabo* is a contraction. For another der. v. s. *caable*.

Câpre — *cappero*.

Capre Fr. a pirate, pirate-ship. From Du. *kaper* which is from *kapen* to rob (Lat. *capere?*).

Capriccio It., whence Sp. *capricho*, Fr. E. *caprice;* from *capra*, cf. *ticchio*, *rerve*, and Com. *nucia* = kid, *nuce* = caprice. Thus Diez. Wedgw., however, makes *capriccio* = *arriccia-capo* = a shivering fit, a fantastical humour (making the hair to stand on end). It. *riccio* = a hedgehog, L. *ericius*, connected with *bricciare, gricciare,* Fr. *hérisser,* Gr. φρίσσειν.

Captener — *mantenere*.

Car *(quar)* Pr. Fr. O. Sp. O. Pg. particle = *nam;* from *quare*, Boeth.: *morz a me quar no vés* Death, *why comest thou not to me?* Dante's *quare* (Inf. 27, 72) is a Latinism, v. *ca.*

Cara Sp. Pg. Pr., O. Fr. *chiere*, Fr. *chère*, whence It. Rh. *cera*, O. Eng. *chear cheer. Faire bonne chère* = to make good cheer to. The word meant (1) *countenance* (cf. this word) (2) favour (3) favourable entertainment (4) banquet. Corippus (6th century) has: *postquam venere verendum Cæsaris ante caram* (face). Perhaps from the Gk. κάρα, κάρη. Hence Sp. *carcar acarar,*

O. Fr. *acarier* to confront; Fr. *acariâtre* stubborn, whimsical. Wal. *o-carê* affront from *a-carare?* Fr. *contrecarrer* to thwart is from *carrer* = *quadrare* to arrange, cf. *contrecarre* = *antisophisma*.

Caraba Sp. a vessel; from *carabus*, "parva scapha", χάραβος, Celtic *carbh* = plank, ship, *carbad* a chariot, whence *carpentum*, *carpenter*. Hence Sp. *carabela*, It. *caravella*, Fr. *caravelle*, E.*caravel*. The Ar.*qârib*, Anglo-Indian *grab* is perhaps, the same word.

Carabina It. Sp. Pg., Fr. *carabine*, E. *carbine*, Fr. *carabin* a carabineer, O. Fr. *calabrin*, It. *calabrino;* from Pr. *calabre* (v. *caable*), cf. E. *caliver*, a machine for casting stones. Cf. *musquet*, It. *moschetta* originally = a missile discharged from a machine, cf.*catapulta* used to translate *gun*, Sp.Pg.*espingarda* = the ancient *springald*.

Caracca It., Sp. Pg. *carraca*, Fr. *caraque*, E. *carack* a large ship, galleon, Du. *kraecke*. Not from Ar. *'harraqah* fire ship, the *'h* not = *c*, so *cable (cappio)* not from *'habl*.

Caracca — *carraca.*

Caraffa It., Sp. *garrafa*, Fr. *caraffe*, Sic. *carrabba* a pitcher; from Ar. *qirâf* a measure, *qarafa* to draw water.

Caragollo It., Sp. Pg. Fr. *caracol* a snail, winding-staircase, turn of a horse (E. *caracol*, It. *caracollo*). From Gael. *car* a twist, *carach* winding, A. S. *cerran* to turn.

Caramillo — *chalumeau.*

Caraque — *carraca.*

Caratello It. a small barrel; for *carratello* from *carrata* a car-load.

Carato It., Sp. Pg. *quilate*, O. Pg. *quirate*, Fr. E. *carat;* from Ar. *qirâ't* a carob-bean, from Gk. κεράτιον, Ven. *carato*. The bean was used for a weight. Isid. *cerates oboli pars media, siliquam habens unam et semis.*

Caraus — *trincare.*

Caravella, caravelle — *caraba.*

Carcame — *carcasso.*

Carcan Fr. Pr. a collar, pillory. From O. H. G. *querca*, O. N. *qverk* the throat. O.Fr. has *charchant cherchant*, Du.*karkant*.

Carcasso It., Sp. *carcax*, Pg. *carcas*, Fr. *carquois*, N. Gr. χάρχασι a quiver; It. Pg. *carcassa*, Sp. *carcasa*, Fr. *carcasse*, E. *carcass* a skeleton. Wedg. derives from W. *carch* restraint (whence *carcer*), so = a box or chest, v. *carcara*. But *-asso* is not a Rom. suffix, so Diez refers it to *caro* and *capsus* (v. *casso*), It. *carcame* being formed on the analogy of *arcame* from *arca*.

Carcava Sp. Pg. an enclosure, pit, ditch, vb. *carcavar*. Diez gets it from *concava* (1) *corcava* (v. *corcovar*) (2) *carcava*. But may it not be connected with *carcasso*, the latter part being *cavus*, and the former the *car* or *carc* of *carcer?*

Carciofo — *articiocco.*

Caroomer Sp. to gnaw, *carcoma* a wood-louse; according to Covarruvias, from *caro* and *comedere!*

Cardo It. Sp. Pg. a thistle, teasel for dressing cloth; from *carduus*; hence Sp. Pr. *cardon*, Fr. *chardon*, It. *cardare*, Fr. *carder* &c.; It. *scardo* a card, Fr. *écharde* a splinter, Sp. *escardar* to weed out thistles, Norm. *écharder* to scale. Rouchi *écard*, Wall. *hârd* a notch, vb. *écarder*, *harder* are from O. H. G. *scarti*, O. N. *skard*, O. H. G. *skertan*, O. N. *skarda* to notch.

Carême — *quaresma.*

Carestia It. Sp. Pg. Pr., L. L. *caristia* dearness, scarcity; from *carus*. Cf. Basque *garestia* = *carus*. The termination is not easily accounted for. Fin. *karista*, which Wedg. connects with *carus* and E. *care*, means to moan, to grumble (for want).

Caricare carcare It., Sp. Pr. *cargar*, Pg. *carregar*, Fr. *charger*, E. *charge*; It. *carico*, Sp. *cargo*, Pr. *carc*, It. *carica*, Sp. Pr. *carga*, Fr. *charge*, E. *cargo* (from the Sp.) *charge*. St. Jerome has *carricare* from *carrus*. It. *caricare* also = to overload, whence *caricatura*, *caricature* an overcharged representation.

Carmesino cremisi cremisino It., Sp. *carmesi*, Pg. *carmesim*, Fr. *cramoisi*, E. *crimson;* from Ar. *qermez* (= Sansk. *krimis*, L. *vermis*, W. *pryv*, Goth. *raurms*, E. *worm*), the cochineal insect, adj. *qermazi*. Pott refers the word to the Sansk. *krimi-ja* worm-born. Hence too It. *carminio*, Sp. Fr. *carmin*, E. *carmine.*

Carmin carminio — *carmesino.*

Carnasciale — *carnevale.*

Carnaval — *carnevale.*

Carne Fr. corner. Diez derives this from *cardo cardinis* a hinge (cf. Fr. *charnière* a joint), but it is better to connect the word with *cran*, E. *cranny*, *corner.*

Carnel carneler — *cran.*

Carnero Sp., Pg. *carneiro* a sheep, wether; from L. *crena* so = the notched or castrated animal (cf. Fr. *crenel* = *carnel*), cf. *montone*, *moltone*, *mouton (mutton)* from L. *mutilus*, and G. *hammel* = mutilated.

Carnevale carnovale It., whence Sp. Fr. E. *carnaval* (E. also *carnival*) the festive period before the Lenten fast; not from *carne vale* fare well flesh! but from *carnelevale* a corrupt form of the L. L. *carnelevamen* solace of the flesh. Other forms are L. L. *carnelevarium*, Sic. *carnilivari*, Pied. *car-lavé*. It. *carnasciale* is from *carne-lusciare*. Other expressions for the same thing are: *carnicapium, carniprivium,* Sp. *carnestolendas,* N. Pr. *carmentran* = *carême entrant.*

Carnicol — *carnero.*

Carogna It., Fr. *charogne,* Rouchi *carone,* E. *carrion;* from *caro, carnis,* by dissimilation for *carnogna.*

Carole querole O. Fr., whence It. *carola,* E. *carol* a circular dance, vb. *caroler* &c. Then = song (cf. *balade* from *balare,* and Gr. μολπή). The Bret. has *korolla* to dance, W. *coroli,* Gael. *coirioll,* Prov. *corola, corolar.* Diez derives it from *chorulus (a* for *o* as in *calandre, canapé),* and objects to *corolla* which does not suit the sense and would have given in Fr. *caroule.* Wackernagel gives a verb *coraulare* (from *choraula),* whence sbst. *coraula, carole.*

Carosello — *carriera.*

Caroube carouge — *carrobo.*

Carozza — *carriera.*

Carpa Sp., Fr. *carpe,* Wal. *crap,* Pr. *escarpa,* It. *carpione,* E. *carp,* G. *karpfen;* from L. L. *carpa* (Cassiodorus).

Carpentiere It. a cart-wright, *carpenter* (Sp. *carpintero),* Pr. *carpentier,* Fr. *charpentier;* from *carpentarius* in L. a cart-wright *(carpentum),* in L. L. = a worker in wood. Fr. *charpente* = carpenter's work. The word is of Celtic origin, Gael., *carbh* a plank, *carbad* a chariot.

Carpone adv. "on all fours". Properly = "on the hands", from *carpo* (L. *carpus)* the wrist, whence *carpiccio* a blow, N. Pr. *carpà* to strike.

Carrasca Sp. Cat., Sp. Pg. *carrasco* an evergreen oak; from L. *cerrus,* cf. *lagarto* for *lazarto, regalar* for *rejalar.*

Carré, carreau, carrer, carrière — *quadro.*

Carrefour Fr., Pr. *carrefore* a place where four roads meet; from *quadrifurcum.*

Carriera It., Fr. *carrière,* Sp. *carrera,* Pg. *carriera* a highway, street, *career.* From *carrus.* The O. Fr. *charrière* is better than *carrière,* which also means a stone pit *(quadro).* From *carrus* also come It. *carrozza,* Sp. *carroza,* Fr. *carrosse (carriage);* Fr. *carrousel* a tilt-yard, It. *carosello.*

Carrignon — *cahier.*

Carrillon Fr. a chime; properly of four bells, from a form *quadrilio.*

Carrizo Sp., Pg. *carriço* sedge; from *carex,* It. *carice.*

Carrobio It. = L. *quadrivium,* cf. *gabbia* from *cavea.*

Carrosse — *carriera.*

Carrouse — *trincare.*

Carruba It., Sp. *garroba garrofa algarroba,* Pg. *alfarroba,* Fr. *caroube carouge,* E. *carob;* It. *carrobo carrubbio,* Sp. *garrobo algarrobo,* Pg. *alfarrobeira* carob-tree; from Ar. *kharrúb.*

Carvi It. Sp. Fr., N. Pr. *charui*, E. *caraway;* from *careum* (χάρον) whence also Ar. *al-karriyâ*, which is nearer in form to the Rom. words, expec. to the Sp. *alcaravea*.

Casa It. Sp. Pg. Pr., Wal. *casě*, L- L. *casa* for the L. *domus*, Sard. *domu*. Hence Rh. *casar* to dwell, It. *casare*, Sp. Pg. Pr. *casar* to marry, prop. = to house.

Casacca It., Sp. Pg. *casaca*, Fr. *casaque*, E. *cassock;* from *casa* a hut (cf. *casipola*, and G. E. *hose*). For the suffix cf. It. *guarnacca*.

Casamatta It., Sp. Pg. *casamata*, Fr. E. *casemate*, L. L. *casamatta*. According to Mahn, from *casa - matta* a weak, poor hut hastily constructed, cf. *carro matto*, *penne matte* pen-feathers, *peli matti* down. According to Diez, from χάσμα, χάσματα. Wedgwood derives it from *casa-mata* (Sp. *mata* slaughter) so = slaughter-house, G. *mordkeller*, the *casemate* being properly a loop-holed gallery in a bastion, whence the garrison could annoy an enemy in possession of the ditch. May it not be connected with *mattone* a brick (q. v.)?

Casare, casar — *casa*.

Cascajo cascara casco — *cascar*.

Cascar Sp. to break, Pg. to bruise, Sard. *cascai* to maltreat = *quassicare* from *quassare*. Hence *casco* = potsherd, skull (cf. *testa*), cask, *casca*, *cascara* husk, peel, shell, *cascajo* broken potsherds, gravel. *Casco* Sp., Fr. *casque* a head-piece; but v. Wedgwood, s. *case*.

Cascare cascata — *casco*.

Cascio cacio It., Sp. *queso*, Pg. *queixo* cheese; from *caseus*, cf. Sp. *quepo* from *capio*.

Casco It. old, decaying; from *cascus* old (Ennius, and Ausonius). Hence, perhaps, It. *cascare* to fall, unless this be from *casare* (Plautus), *casicare*, or connected with *cascar* (q. v.) so = to fall with a crash. From *cascare* comes It. *cascata*, Fr. E. *cascade*.

Casoo — *cascar*.

Caserma It., W. *cěsarmě*, O. G. *casarm*, Sp. Pg. *caserna*, Fr. *caserne* a barrack; from *casa d'arme* (Mahn) or from *casa* like *caverna* from *cava* (Diez). Perhaps it will be best to take the former derivation, allowing that the form of the word was modified by its resemblance to *caverna*.

Casimiro Sp., Pg. *casimira*, Fr. *casimir*, E. *kerseymere;* from *Cashmire*.

Casipola casupola It. a little hut, hence Fr. E. *chasuble*, Sp. *casulla*, L. L. *casula; casipola* is prob. formed on the analogy of *manipulus*. For the connection of meanings, cf. *casacca*, and *cappa capanna*.

Casnard O. Fr. a flatterer, fawner. Quintilian has: *casnar* *assectator e Gallia ductum est. Casnard* is prob. for *canard* or *cagnard* (N. Pr. = loiterer), Pic. *cagne acagnardi* lazy. Berr. *cagnaud* = *casnard.* The origin is prob. the root *cagn* L. *canis.*

Casque — *cascar.*

Cass Pr. O. Fr. broken, Pr. *casser,* Fr. *casser* to break; from *quassus quassare.* It. *accasciare* to fail in strength, is from a form *quassiare.* With an inserted *n* we have Sp. *canso* weary, *cansar* to weary.

Cassa It., Sp. *caxa,* Pg. *caixa,* Pr. *caissa,* Fr. *caisse,* E. *case,* a chest, Fr. *châsse* a setting; from *capsa* (Diez), or from the sound of a blow *quash! cass!* whence *cassus* hollow, and *caisse, cask, casco* &c., in the sense of a hollow receptacle (Wedgwood). Hence It. *cassetta, cassettone, castone,* vb. Pg. *encaixar,* Fr. *enchâsser,* It. *incassare,* to enchase, chase; also Cat. *encastar,* Sp. *engastar,* It. *incastrare,* Pr. *encastrar,* and Pr. *encastonar,* Pg. *encastôar,* Sp. *engastonar,* cf. L. L. *incastratura.*

Cassero — *alcazar.*

Casserola casserole — *cazza.*

Casso It. Sp. Pg., Pr. *cass,* O. Fr. *quas* empty, void; from *cassus.* Hence *cassare, casser,* L. *cassare* for *cassum reddere* in Sidonius and Cassiodorus.

Casso It. the breast, chest, L. L. *cassum cassus;* from *capsus* a receptacle, cf. L. L. *arca.* Hence, also, Pr. *cais* the jaw, as *eis* from *ipse.* Wedgwood gives a different account (v. *cassa*). Related to *cais* are Pg. *queixo,* Cat. *quex,* where Pg. *queixada,* Sp. *quixada,* and perhaps Sp. *quixera.*

Casta Sp. Pg., E. *caste;* from *castus* pure?

Castaldo castaldione, Ven. *gastaldo* a steward, cf. Fr. *Gastaud* as a proper name; from L. L. *gastaldius gastaldio* which is from Goth. *ga-staldan* to acquire, possess.

Casulla -- *casipola.*

Catacomba It., Sp. Pr. *catacumba,* Fr. *catacombe,* E. *catacomb,* a subterranean burial-place. According to Diez, from Sp. *catar* to view and *comba* for *tomba* a tomb (cf. Mil. *catatomba,* O. Sp. *catatumba*). The Roman *catacombs* contained the remains of the martyrs, and were visited for purposes of devotion. In support of this der. cf. *catafalco, cataletto.* Others propose κατατύμβιον, or κατά and κύμβος a cavity, or the Sabine *cumba,* cf. Festus: *cumbam Sabini vocant eam quam militares lecticam.*

Catafalco It., Sp. *cadafalso cadahalso cadalso,* Pr. *cadafalc,* O. Cat. *cadafal,* Val. *carafal,* O. Fr. *escadafaut,* Fr. *échafaut,* M. Du. *scafaut,* G. *schaffot,* E. *scaffold.* The orig. form is *cata-falco,* Sp. *cadafalso* is from Pr. nom. *cadafalcs,* the *c* becomes *t* in Fr. as in *Estrabort* for *Estrabore (Strasbourg).*

Catafalco is from Sp. *catar* to view and *falco* = It. *palco* or *balco* (q. v.), cf. *catacomba*, *cataletto*. Fr. *catafalque* and Sp. *cadafalco* are from the Italian.

Cataletto It. a bed of state, prop. = show-bed, from *catar* and *letto*, v. *catacomba* and *catafalco*. The same word is found in Sp. *cadalecho* a rush-bed, N. Pr. *cadaliech*, Fr. *châlit* a tenter-bed, O. Fr. *calit*.

Catar O. Sp. to see, view, Sp. Pg. to search, examine, taste, *cata* inquiry (also = mine, cf. *μέταλλον*), *recatar* to taste again, to keep carefully, to hide, *recato* prudence, *acatar* to inspect, respect, &c. Menage gives a Fr. dim. *catiller* to spy out. Rh. Parm. Ven. *catar*, Lomb. *catà* = to find, seize. Its sense of to "view" is found in It. *cata-comba*, *cata-falco*, *cata-letto*, Sp. *cata-lecho*, *cataribera*, *cata-viento*. Wal. *cĕută* = to view, seek, keep. Isidorus has: *cattus* (a cat) *quod cattat i. e. videt.* It is from the L. *captare* (sc. *oculis*) to lie in watch.

Cataraña Sp. a sheldrake. Prop. a diver, from *catarractes?*

Catasta It. a wooden-pile; from L. *catasta* a scaffold.

Catastro It. Sp., Fr. *cadastre* a register of taxes, a tax; from *capitastrum* a poll-tax, cf. Sp. *cabezon* from *cabeza.*

Catir — *quatto.*

Catrame It., Pg. *alcatrão*, Sp. *alquitran*, Fr. *guitran goudron*, L. L. *catarannus* tar. From Ar. *al-qatrân.*

Cattivo It., Sp. *cativo*, Pr. *caitiu*, Fr. *chétif* a wretch, E. *caitiff*; from *captivus*, which is also found in its proper sense, It. *cattivo*, Sp. *cautivo*, Fr. *captif*, E. *captive.*

Cau caucala — *choe.*

Cauchemar Fr. a ghost, night-mare; from vb. *caucher* (obs.), Pic. *cauquer*, Burg. *côquai* = It. *calcare*, E. *cauk*, and G. *mar* in *nachtmar*, E. *nightmare*. Occ. has *chaouche-vielio* pressing-old woman, witch, also cf. *pesant peant peen*, *greou*, *ploumb* all = something weighty, an incubus, Sp. *pesadilla*, O. Sp. *mampesada*. Rouchi has *coquenoir*, Wall. *marke*, v. Grand-gagnage.

Caudal Sp. Pg., Pr. *cabdal*, O. Fr. *chaudel* superior, rich, sbst. power, wealth, capital, abundance; from *capitalis*. Sp. *caudaloso* = very rich.

Caudillo — *capitello.*

Causer — *cosa.*

Cautivo — *cattivo.*

Cava It. Sp. Pg. Pr., Fr. *cave* a cellar, E. *cave*; from *cava*. Hence Pg. *cabaz*, Fr. *cabas* a large basket, whence, ph. Sp. *capazo*, but v. *cappa*.

Cavallo It., Sp. *caballo*, Pr. *caval*, Fr. *cheval* (Fr. *chevale* a mare, *chevallerie*, *chivalry* &c.), Wal. *cal*, Alb. *calĕ callĕ* a horse;

from *caballus* (χαβάλλης). Hence *cavalcare*, Sp. *cabalgar*, Fr.
chevaucher (Fr. E. *cavalcade*) to ride (cf. *ἱππεύειν* from *ἵππος*),
L. L. *caballicare cavallum* = It. *cavalcare un cavallo*. *Equus*
remains only in Sp. f. *yegua*, Pg. *egoa*, Pr. *egua*, O. Fr. *aigue*,
Wal. *eapé*, Sard. *ebba*. From *caballus* we have also L. L. *ca-
ballarius*, It. *cavalliere* &c., and *cavalleria*, *cavallerie*, *cavalry*;
It. *cavalletta*, Sp. *caballeta* a field-cricket (cf. G. *heupferd* =
grass-hopper), Sp. *caballete* == a wooden horse, easel &c.

Cavare It. to take out; prop. to dig out, L. *cavare*.

Cavelle covelle It. (Boccaccio) = qualche cosa; perhaps fr. *quod
vellet*, so = *qualsi voglia?*

Cavesson — *cavezza*.

Cavezza It. a halter, O. Fr. *chevece* a collar, Sp. Pg. *cabeza* head,
Pr. *cabeissa*; also Sp. Pg. *cabezo*, Pr. *cabes* the top of a thing;
hence It. *cavezzone*, Fr. *cavesson caveçon*, E. *caveson* a nose-
halter, whence G. *kapp-zaum* spelt as if from *kappen* to cap
and *zaum* a bridle, Sp. *cabezon* = shirt-collar. From L. L.
capitium, so = (1) head (2) hood (3) collar. It. *scavezzare* to
sever = *scapezzare*, Sp. *descabezar*, prop. = to behead.

Caviale It., Sp. *cabial*, Pg. Fr. *caviar*, M. G. *χαβιάρι*, *caviare*
the salted roe of the sturgeon.

Cavicchia caviglia, cavicchio caviglio It., Pg. Pr. *cavilha*, Fr.
cheville a peg. From *clavicula claviela* for euphony *cavicla*.
The Sp. has *clavija*.

Cavolo It., Sp. *col*, Pg. *couve*, Pr. *caul*, Fr. *chou* cabbage; from
caulis whence also Bret. *kaol*, W. *cawl*, G. *kohl*, E. *cole*.

Caxa — *cassa*.

Cayado Sp., Pg. *cajado*, Cat. *gayato* shepherd's crook; from
χαῖος?

Cayo Sp. (usu. plur.), O. Fr. *caye* a sandbank, shoal, Pg. *caes*,
Fr. *quai*, Du. *kaai*, *kaje*, E. *quay*. Isidor. has: *kaij cancelli*.
It is the W. *cae* hedge, enclosure, Bret. *kaé* also == a dam,
ph. also the origin of the O. H. G. *cahot* munimentum.

Cayo Sp. a daw; cf. O. H. G. *kaha* a craw, Du. *kauie*; so called
from the noise it makes, cf. E. *caw*.

Cazar — *cacciare*.

Cazza It., Cat. *cassa*, O. Fr. Pic. *casse*, Rh. *cas*, Sp. *cazo* a
saucepan, a ladle; from O. H. G. *chezi (kezi)*, O. N. *kati*,
whence G. *kessel*, E. *kettle*. Hence It. *cazzuola*, Sp. *cazuela*,
Fr. *casserole* (cf. *mouch-er-olle*, *mus-er-olle* &c.) a frying-pan,
whence It. *casserola*, Pic. Champ. *castrole*, G. *castrol*.

Ce — *ciò*.

Céans — *ens*.

Cebada Sp., Pg. *cevada* barley, Cat. Pr. *civada* oats; from *cibare*,
Sp. *cebar* to feed; fatten. Sp. *cibera* corn is from *cibaria* (pl.).

Cebellino — *zibellino*.

Cece It., Sp. *chicharo*, Pr. *cezer*, Fr. *chiche* (usu. pl.) = L. *cicer*; It. *cicerchia* &c. from *cicercula*.

Cecero It., O. It. *cecino*, L. L. *cecinus*, *cico*; from L. *cicer*; which (in It. *cece*) = the knob or tubercle on the swan's bill, cf. *Cicero*. From *cecinus* rather than from *cygnus*, comes Sp. Pg. O. Fr. *cisne*, O. Pg. *cirne*.

Cedazo — *staccio.*

Cederno — *cedro.*

Cedilla oédille — *zediglia.*

Cedola It., Sp. Pg. Pr. *cédula*, Fr. *cédule* schedule; from L. *schedula*, as *cisma* from *schisma*. From another pronunciation arose the Sp. *esquela.*

Cedro It., Sp. Pg. *cidra*, Pg. also *cidrão*, Fr. E. *citron* (fruit); It. *cedro*, Sp. *cidro*, Fr. *citronnier* (tree); from *citrus*, *citreum*. It. has *cederno* on analogy of *quernus*. The usu. word is the foreign *limone*, q. v. The variable quantity of the L. accounts for the double form in *e* and *i*; hence It. *cedronella*, Sp. *cidronela*, Fr. *citronelle* balm, L. *citrago*; also It. *citriuolo*, Fr. *citrouille* pumpkin.

Ceffo It. a snout, muzzle, *ceffare*, Parm. *cifar* to snap, seize; Com. *zaf* = *ceffo*, *zafà*, Sic. *acciaffari* = *ceffare*, Piedm. *ciaflù* = *ceffuto*, Sic. *ciaffa* = claw, It. *zaffo* = bailiff. Prob. from a G. pronunciation of the root *tap* (v. *tape*), whence also It. *ciampa* = Sic. *ciaffa.*

Ceindre Fr. to gird; from *cingere*, as *peindre* from *pingere.*

Cejar Sp. (prop. *cexar* as in O. Sp.) to recede; from *cessare* which in It. = to escape.

Céladon Fr. sea-green (also lover, gallant); from the name of a shepherd (clad in green) in D'Urfé's Astræa (1610).

Celata It., Sp. *celada*, Fr. *salade* a helmet, O. Eng. *salet*, W. *saled*, from *cœlata* (*cassis cœlata* Cicero).

Celda Sp., O. Sp. *cella* cell; from L. *cella*, whence also Sp. *cilla* a granary; *cillero*, Pg. *cilleiro* from *cellarius.*

Céléri — *sedano.*

Celui — *quello.*

Cembel — *zimbello.*

Cencerro Sp. a bell; Basque *cincerria cinzarria*, a name derived from the sound.

Cenefa sanefa Sp., Pg. *sanefa* a frame, fringe, border; from Ar. *çanefah* the hem of a garment.

Cónelle Fr. the holly-berry; from *coccinella* (*coccina* for *coccum*) scarlet berry.

Cenno It., Rh. *cia* a nod, Sp. *ceño* a frown; It. *accennare*, O. Sp. *aceñar*, O. Fr. *acener* to nod, make signs. In the old Glossaries we find *cinnus tortio oris* and *cynnavit innuit*. It is prob. shortened from *cicinnus* (κίκιννος), so that *cinnare cennare*

would denote prop. some peculiarity in the "chovelure", cf.
Fr. *harlocher* to agitate, from *haarlocke*, v. *locher*.

Cenogil Sp. a garter; from It. *giavecchiello* prop. = kneeband.

Cenoura — *zanahoria*.

Centeno Sp., Pg. *centeio senteio* rye; from *centenus* as it was suppose to produce a hundredfold.

Centinare It., Fr. *cintrer* to vault or arch; abst. *centina*, Fr.
cintre, E. *centre centering* the wooden frame for building an
arch; from *cincturare (cinctura)*; It. *u* for *r* as in *cecino* from
cicer. The Cat. is *cindria*, the Sp. *cimbria cimbra*, *mb* from
cimborio a dome.

Centinela — *sentinella*.

Cenzaya Sp. a nurse; from Basque *seinzaya*, from *seña* a child
and *zaya* watch.

Cepillo Sp., Pg. *cepilho* a plane (tool), brush; from Sp. *cepo* a
block, L. *cippus*.

Ceramella cennamella a shawm; a corruption of Fr. *chalemel?*
v. *chalumeau*.

Cercare It., Wal. *cercà*, Pr. *cercar sercar*, Fr. *chercher* (by assimilation for *cercher*, O. Fr. *cerchier*, Pie. *cerquier*, cf. *Ciciglia*
for *Siciglia*), E. *search*. The orig. meaning is to "*search
through*", Dante, Inf. 1, 84: *che m' han fatto cercar il tuo
volume*, O. Fr. *cerchier les moutagnes* &c. Sp. Pg. *cercar* = to
enclose, but O. Pg. also to search through. *Cercare* is the
Propertian *circare: fontis egens erro circoque sonantia lymphis*
(4, 9, 35): Isid. *circat circumrenit*, L. L. *circator* a watchman,
cf. Alb. *khëreoig* to seek, from κιρχοῦν; W. *kyrchu*, Bret.
kerchat from the same root as *cercare*. Hence Pr. *ensercar* to
distinguish, Pg. *enxergar*; L. L. *cercitare*, Wal. *cercetà*.

Cerceau Fr. a ring, circle, O. Fr. *recercelé* encircled; from *cir-
culus circellus*.

Cerceta sarceta Sp. Pg., Pr. *serceta*, Fr. *cercelle sarcelle* a widgeon,
teal; from *querquedula*, It. also *cercedula*, *eercevolo*. The It.
gargauello (E. *gargane*) is a corruption.

Cercine It. a ring, Fr. *cerne* (= *cerc'ne*) a circle, Sp. *cercen*
(adv. = thoroughly), Pg. *cerce*; Fr. *cerner* to encircle, Sp.
cercenar to pare round; from *circinus* a circle, *circinare* to
circle.

Cercueil Fr. a coffin. *Sarcophagulus* would have given *sarfail*;
it is, therefore, better to derive from the O. H. G. *sark* (G.
sarg) a coffin, with suffix *el* = O. Fr. *sarqu-el sarqu-eu
carc-u*.

Cerda — *cerdo*.

Cerdo Sp. Pg. a hog; according to Larramendi, from the Basque
cherria a hog, but it may be derived from *sordidus* (*suerdo*

serdo v. *frente*). Sp. *cerda* (f.) = a hog's bristle, or horse's hair, ph. from *cerdo* so = (1) the hog's hide (2) the bristles.

Ceresa — *ciriegia.*

Cerfoglio It., Sp. *cerafolio*, Fr. *cerfeuil* a plant, *chervil;* from *caerefolium* (χαιρέφυλλον).

Cerise — *ciriegia.*

Cernada Sp. lie; = *cinerata*, Cat. *cendrada*, from *cinis.*

Cerne cerner — *cercine.*

Cernecchio It., Sp. *cerneja*, Pg. *cernelha* a fetlock. From *discerniculum* (*acus quæ capillos disseparat* Nonius), so = prop. parted hair.

Cerquinho Pg. in *carvalho cerquinho* a holm-oak; a corruption of *quercinho* = It. *quercino.*

Cerrar — *serrare.*

Cerre — *cerro.*

Cerretano — *ciarlare.*

Cerrion Sp. an icicle; from L. *stiria, st* = *c* (cf. *mozo* from *mustum*).

Cerro It. (1) a Turkey-oak, from *cerrus*, Fr. *cerre;* (2) a bob, toupet, from *cirrus.*

Cerro Sp. Pg., Pr. *ser* a hill, a backbone; from Basque *cerra* (which, however, may be from the Spanish word), or from L. *cirrus* = a top-knot, so = top.

Cers Pr. Cat., Sp. *cierzo* a north-east-wind; from L. *cercius circius* a word used in Gallia Narbonensis, v. Pott. Etym. Forschung. 2, 499. Hence, perhaps Sp. *cecina* dried beef, *cecial* dried fish (for *cercina cecial*).

Cervello It., Pr. *cervel*, Fr. *cerveau* brain, Pr. Rh. *cervella* (fem. = It. pl. *cervella*), Fr. *cervelle;* from *cerebellum*, L. L. *cerbellus.* From *cerebrum* come Sp. Pg. *celebro cerebro*, Wal. *crieri* (pl.), from *crecbrum.*

Cesoje It. (pl.) scissors; from *caesus* as *rasojo* from *rasus.*

Cespo It. a bush, shrub; from *cespes* turf, brush-wood; hence *cespuglio; cesto* is from *cespitem.* In Placidus we find *caespites frutices.* Hence It. *cespicare*, Wal. *ceaspetà.*

Cespuglio — *cespo.*

Cesso It. retreat, privy; from *secessus.*

Cesto — *cespo.*

Cet — *questo.*

Cetrero Sp. a falconer, = *accipitrarius*, cf. *accertello.*

Cetto It.. O. Sp. O. Pg. *cedo (encedo)* adv. from *cito.*

Cha — *tè.*

Chabasca Sp. a twig, rod; from *clava* a graft, whence also Sp. *chaborra* a young maiden.

Chablis — *caable.*

Chabot Fr. a fish, the miller's thumb, Pg. *caboz;* from *caput* because of its thick head, cf. L. *capito*, Gk. *κέφαλος*.

Chabraque Fr. a horse-cloth, housing; the G. is *schabracke;* both words come from the Persian *tschâbrâk*.

Chachara Sp. chatter; an onomatopœion, Sic. *ciacciara*, It. *chiácchiera*.

Chacona Sp. the name of a Spanish dance; from Basque *chocuna* neat, pretty.

Chacun — *ciascuno.*

Chagrin Fr. grief, *chagrin*. From the Fr. *chagrin*, *shagreen* the shark-skin, which, being used as a rasp, came to typify the gnawing of grief, cf. It. *lima*. Shagreen in It. was *zigrino*, Ven. Romagn. *sagrin*, Du. *segrein*, M. H. G. *zager*. Gen. *sagrinà* = to gnaw, *sagrindse* to fret, consume with anger.

Chainse — *camicia.*

Chaire Fr. a pulpit, Pr. *cadeira*, O. Fr. *chayere chair* seat; from *cathedra*, whence O. Sp. Cat. Basque *cadira*, Piedm. Com. *cadréga* seat.

Chaise Fr. a chair, seat. This is not found in the oldest dictionaries, so prob. a Parisian mispronunciation, cf. *bésicle*. Palsgrave's French Grammar (1530) mentions *chèze* as a faulty Parisian pronunciation of *chaère*.

Chaland Fr. a flat-bottomed boat, a transport, O. Fr. *chalandre*, O. Cat. *xelandrin*, L. L. *chelandium chelinda zalandria*, M. Gr. *χελάνδιον*. These boats were chiefly used by the Byzantines, and prob. derived their name from *χέλυδρος* a turtle. Fr. *chaland*, Sp. *calan* a trafficker are from *chaland* a boat, cf. *barguigner* from *barca*. Others derive *chaland* from *calo* (Papias: *calones negotiatores*) and make the sense of boat a secondary one. But the form will hardly suit this etymology.

Châlit — *cataletto.*

Chalonge chalenge O. Fr., *calonja* Pr. a disowning, disputing a claim, *chalongier*, *calonjar*, E. *challenge*, to call in question, claim; to *challenge* one to fight is to call on one to decide a disputed matter by combat; from *calumnia* a false charge, chicane.

Chaloupe Fr., hence Sp. *chalupa*, It. *scialuppa*, E. *shallop;* corrupted from the Du. *sloep* (from *sloepen* to glide, slope, as Du. *schuit* from *schieten* to shoot), E. *sloop*.

Chalumeau Fr. for *chalemeau*, O. Fr. *chalemel*, Pr. *caramel*, Sp. *caramillo* flute, E. *shaum;* from *calamus*, L. L. *calamel*.

Chamade Fr. E. a trumpet-signal calling to a parley; from Pg. *chamada* a shout *(chamar* = L. L. *clamare)*.

Chamar — *chiamare.*

Chamarasca Sp. a bundle of twigs, for fire-word; from Basque *chamar-asca* "very small", Larramendi.

Chamarra chamarrer — *zamarro.*

Chamborga Sp. a long, wide coat; so called from Marshal Schomberg (v. Seckendorf).

Chamois — *camozza.*

Chamorro Sp. Pg. shorn, *chamorra* a shorn or bald head; from *clavus* (for *calvus*) and Sp. *morra* crown of the head.

Champ — *canto.*

Champignon Fr. a mushroom; from *campus, agaricus campestris* (Linnæus), It. *campignuolo.*

Champion — *campione.*

Champis O. Fr. still used in Berry and South-East of France for a bastard, enfant trouvé (dans les champs); from L. L. *campilis* (O. Fr. also *champil*). Wall. *champi* = mener paître, comes from a form *campicare*, which would be in Fr. *champier.*

Chamuscar Sp. Pg. to singe, O. Sp. *xamuscar;* from *flamma,* Pg. *chama.*

Chanca chanclo chanco — *zanca.*

Chanco Fr., O. Fr. *cheance* (E. *chance*) from *cheoir* L. *cadere.* M. H. G. *schanze,* It. *cadenza* &c. Hence *chanceler* to totter, Pr. *chancelar,* whence It. *cancellare.*

Chancolor — *chance.*

Chancir Fr. to get mouldy; from *canescere,* Sp. *canecer.* Norm. *chanir* from *canere.*

Chancre — *granchio.*

Chancla chincla Sp. an overshoe, slipper = It. *pianella* from *planus.*

Change changer — *cambiare.*

Chanteau — *canto.*

Chanteplouro Fr. a watering-pot; from Fr. *chanter* and *pleurer;* hence It. Sp. *cantimplora.*

Chantier — *cantiere.*

Chanvre — *canape.*

Chanza — *ciancia.*

Chaorcin Pr. a usurer, L. L. *caorsinus caturcinus cauarsinus,* G. *kawartsch gawertsch kauwerz.* From *Cadurcinus,* Pr. *caorcin chaorcin* a native of Cahors, which Dante makes the abode of usury: *e però lo minor giron suggella del segno suo e Sodoma e Caorsa* Inf. 11, 49.

Chapa Sp. a plate of metal or leather, E. *chape* a plate of metal at the point of a scabbard, the white tip of a fox's tail. Hence *chapar* to plate, Pg. *chapear; chapeleta* de una bomba Sp. = Fr. *clapet,* the *clapper* or sucker of a ship's pump. From root *klap clap* the representation of the sound made by two flat surfaces striking together. Hence Sp. *chapin* a shoe with cork sole, E. *chopine* a clog, this last, perhaps, connected with Du. *kloppen* to knock, from the clumping sound of clogs.

Chaparra chaparro Sp. a kind of oak; from Basque *achaparra* a claw, its branches resembling claws.

Chape chapeau chapelle chaperon — *cappa.*

Chapitre — *capitolo.*

Chapler chapeler chaploier O. Fr., Pr. *chaplar* to cut down, sbst. Pr. *chaple*, whence O. Fr. *chapleis*, Pr. *chapladis*; from *capulus* a sword, sword-hilt, L. L. *capulare* to cut off. Or is it connected with *chapuiser?*

Chapuiser O. Fr., Pr. *capusar* to cut off, cut in pieces; *chapuis* = a carpenter. L.L. *capus capo* = a castrated cock, whence Sp. *capar* to geld. *Chapuiser* is formed on the analogy of its synonyme *menuiser;* cf. O. Fr. *chantuser* from *chanter.*

Chapuzar zapuzar zampuzar Sp. to dive, duck, cf. Cat. *cabussar*, Pr. *cacabustar;* perhaps from *capo cabo*, so = to plunge in over head, cf. *chapuiser;* zampuzar prob. took its form from *zampar* (v. *tupe*), the Pg. *chafundar* from *fundus.*

Chaque Fr., Pr. *cac* each. Rather from *chac-un (quisque unus)* than immediately from quisque, cf. *ciascuno* and *cadauno.* Pr. *quecs* is for *queses (quisque)*, Com. *ciusche*. There is no need to have recourse to the Ir. *cách*, Gael. *ceach*, where the *c* = *p*, cf. O. W. *poup*, Corn. *peb*, Bret. *pep.*

Charade Fr. E.; perhaps from Neap. *charada (-o)* = It. *ciarlata* chatter, whence "play on words".

Charco Sp. Pg. a standing-pool, puddle, slough; from Basque *charcoa* bad, disgusting.

Chardon — *cardo.*

Charge — *caricare.*

Charivari Fr. cat's music, clatter, L. L. *charivarium*, *chalvaricum*, O. Fr. *caribari*, *chalivali*, Pic. *queri-boiry*, Dauph. *chanarari*, N. Pr. *taribari.* Orig. used of the discordant music used on the occasion of a man's second marriage, Sp. *cencerrada* from *cencerro* a bell, Cat. *esquellotada.* The termination is common, e. g. *ourrari*, *hourvari* hunting cries, Pic. Norm. Champ. Gen. *boulevari*, Pied. *zanzivari*, Norm. *varivara*, Rh. *ririvari* (G. *wirrwarr* clatter). The former part of the word is made to rhyme with the latter (cf. *hurly-burly*), and may be the L. *calix* (cf. *chalivali* and Wall. *paillege* from *paill* = Fr. *poele*). Dante's *caribo* Purg. 31, 132 is, probably, from *charirarium.*

Charlatan — *ciarlare.*

Charme O. Fr. an incantation, Fr. a *charm*, It. *carme carmo*, Fr. *charmer* to charm, O. Fr. *charmeresse* = enchantress; from *carmen*, L. L. *carminare* to enchant. From *carmen* also comes O. E. *charm* a hum, murmuring noise of birds &c. A *charm*

of goldfinches = a flock. In O. Fr. *charraie charroie* =
witchcraft, *charroieresse* a witch, vb. *encharrauder*, Norm.
enquérauder for *charmeraie* &c.

Charme Fr. the horn-beam, Berr. *charne*, Rouchi *carne*; from
carpĭnus (carpĭnus), L. L. *carpenus*, It. *carpino*, Wal. *carpin*,
Sp. *carpe*.

Charnière — *cran*.

Charogne — *carogna*.

Charpa — *sciarpa*.

Charpente — *carpentiere*.

Charpie Fr. lint, It. *carpia*; participle of the O. Fr. verb *charpir*
(carpere) found in *escharpir descharpir*. This latter = O. F.
verb to *stickle*, to separate combatants (with *sticks*).

Charraie charroie — *charme* (1).

Charro Sp. Pg. a churl; from the Basque *charro* = bad (?).

Charrua — *aratro*.

Chartre charte Fr. a deed, record, E. *chart*; from *charta*.

Chartre O. Fr. (f.) prison; from *carcer* (m.), Sp. *carcel* (f.), It.
carcere (m. f.).

Chasco Sp. the lash of a whip; probably from the sound, G.
klatschen to clash, lash, cf. E. *lash*.

Châsse — *cassa*.

Chasser — *cacciare*.

Chasuble — *casipola*.

Chat — *gatto*.

Chat-huant chauans — *choe*.

Châtier Fr., F. *chastise*; from *castigare*, It. *gastigare*.

Chato — *piatto*.

Chatouiller Fr. to tickle; from *catullire* (neut.), whence *catulliare*
(act.) cf. *cambire, cambiare*.

Chaudière chaudron — *caldaja*.

Chauffer Fr., Pr. *calfar* to heat, whence *échauffer, escalfar*; from
calefacere.

Chaume Fr. (m.) stubble, whence *chaumière* a straw-hut; from
calamus, whence also L. L. *calma: vineas deplantassent aut
calmas rupissent*, G. halm, E. haulm.

Chaumière — *chaume*.

Chaupir caupir Pr. to take or seize a thing; from Goth. *kaupōn*,
O. H. G. *chaufan*, G. *kaufen* to buy, orig. to take in exchange,
exchange. For the connection between *taking* and *buying* cf.
L. *emere*, Fr. *acheter*.

Chausse — *calza*.

Chaussée — *calzada*.

Chauve-souris Fr. a bat, prop. = *bald* mouse, from the wings
being destitute of feathers. Grandgagnage suggests that it is
a corruption of *choue-souris* = *souris-hibou* mouse owl, the Wall.

being *chawesori, chausori, chehausori;* so the Pic. *casseuris* and *cateseuris* may be = *cave-seuris,* cavette-*seuris,* v. *choe.* Lorr. is *bo-volant* = flying-toad, Pr. *soritz-pennada* = G. *fledermaus.*

Chavirer Fr. to capsize; from *caput rirare;* It. *capo-volgere, capo-voltare.*

Chasa Sp. chace in ball-playing, point where the ball stops; *chazar* to stop the ball; from Fr. *chasse, chasser.*

Che It., Sp. Pg. Pr. Fr. *que* pronoun and conjunction; from *quid,* whence also Wal. *ce, cê, ca.* Fr. *quoi* from *que,* as *moi mei* from *mê.* It. *chi,* Fr. *qui* from *quis;* Sard. *chini,* Sp. *quien,* Pg. *quem,* from *quem,* v. *quien.*

Chef Fr. head, Sp. *xefe,* E. *chief;* from *caput.* Hence *chevir* = O. Fr. *venir a chief; chief* Pr. *cap,* It. *capo* = "beginning" and also "end", *de chief en chief; rechief, rechap* = recommencement. From *chevir* comes *chevance* profit, and It. *civire* to provide, *civanza* profit. *Chevet* (Fr.)=a pillow (for the *head*).

Chegar — *llegar.*

Cheirar — *flairar.*

Chelme (schelme) O. Fr. a disturber, makebate; from G. *schelm* rogue, knave.

Chêmer — *scemo.*

Cheminée — *caminata.*

Chemise — *camicia.*

Chenapan Fr. highwayman, G. *schnapphahn.*

Chêne Fr. (f.), O. Fr. *chesne,* Prov. Fr. *quesne,* Pr. *casser* (m.) for *casne* as *Roser* for *Rosne* from *Rhodanus,* Gasc. *casso* (m.), Born. *cassoura,* L. L. *casnus.* Prob. from *quercus, quercinus quercnus quecnus quesnus,* O. Fr. *quesne chesne;* for *qu* = *ch* cf. *chascun* from *quisque.*

Chéneau Fr. a gutter; from *canalis.*

Chenet Fr. an andiron, fire-dog; from *canis,* being usually made with feet like dog's paws. Langued. *cha-fuec.*

Chenille Fr. a caterpillar, Pr. *canilha.* From *canicula* a little dog, from a supposed likeness in the head or eyes; cf. Mil. *can cagnon* a silk-worm; in Lomb. it is called *gatta gattola* (cat), in Sp. *felpilla* (if not, as is more prob., from *felpa*) = *felis pilosa* hairy cat = Norm. *chatte pelouse,* whence E. (corrupted) *caterpillar.* The Pg. is *lagarta* (prop. lizard).

Chente It. pronoun, from *che ente (ens entis)* "what a thing" formed on the analogy of *niente.*

Chercher — *cercare.*

Chère — *cara.*

Chervis — *chirivia.*

Chétif — *cattivo.*

Cheto It., Sp. Pg. *quedo*, O. Fr. *coit coi recoi*, E. *coy;* from *quietus;* hence vb. It. *chetare*, Sp. Pg. *quedar* (also intrans.), Fr. *coiser* (whence E. *cosy* = *coisé*), like *hausser* from *altus*. Hence also Fr. *quitte*, O. Fr. *cuite*, Pr. *quiti*, Sp. *quito*, F. *quit*, G. *quitt* = *absolutus* (L. L. *quietus);* Sp. Pg. *quitar* to absolve make void, take away, Fr. *quitter* to release, let go, E. *quit*, It. *quittare chitare* to cede one's rights; sbst. *quitanza*, *quittance* &c. For *cheto* It. has *chiotto* prob. from Fr. *coit*, Neap. *cuoto*.

Cheval chevaucher — *cavallo*.

Chovet — *chef*.

Chevêtre Fr. a halter; from *capistrum*, It. *capestro*.

Cheville — *cavicchia*.

Chevir — *chef*.

Chevrette — *crevette*.

Chevron Fr., Pr. *cabrion cabiron* a beam, Sp. *cabrio* a rafter, *cabria* axle-tree, *cabrial* beam; from *capreolus (caper)*, cf. Wal. *cafer* = a rafter, G. *bock* = a block or piece of wood on which anything rests. A *chevron* in heraldry is the representation of two rafters.

Chez Fr. = L. *apud* for *en chez* = O. Sp. *en cas* = *in casâ*. Cf. O. N. prep. *hiâ* from *hi*, Dan. *hos* from *hus*.

Chi — *che*.

Chiamare It., Wal. *chiëmâ*, Sp. *llamar*, Pg. *chamar*, to call, Pr. *clamar*, O. Fr. *claimer* to call out, E. *claim;* from *clamare* L. L. *(si quis alterum vulpem clamaverit)* = nominare.

Chiappare It. to catch; from O. H. G. *klappen* to clap, clap to, *klappe* a trap; Com. *ciapà (cia* = *cla*, *ciamà* = *clamare)*. Hence, too, It. *calappio galappio* a trap. *Clap klappen* is, of course, an onomatopœion.

Chiarina, clarinetto, clarone It., Sp. *clarin, clarinete*, Fr. *clarinette clairon*, O. Fr. Pr. E. *clarion*, E. *clarionet;* from *clarus*.

Chiasso It. from the Pr. *clas* a crying, bawling, O. Fr. *glas (chlaz)* the sound of bells, Fr. *glas* a knell for the dead, Ir. *glas* wailing, Wal. *glas* sound, E. *clash*. These may be referred to the Sansk. *hlas* sonare (cf. *hlâd* and *glad*), and are, doubtless, derived from the sound. Diez, however, makes *chiasso* &c. = Lat. *classicum* a trumpet-signal, L. L. a sound of bells, cf. *conclassare conclamare* Isid. Gloss.

Chiavica It. sewer, conduit; corrupted from *cloaca*, L. L. *claraca*. *cloaca*.

Chiazza It. scab, *chiazzare;* from G. *kletz* dirty, *bekletzen* to soil.

Chibo — *ziba*.

Chicane chiche chicot — *cica*.

Chicchera — *xicara*.

Chiche — *cece*.

Chicharo — *cece.*

Chicharro — *cigala.*

Chico — *cica.*

Chiedere It. to demand, = poet. *cherere* from *quærere*, Sp. *querer* &c., *r* = *d* as in *fiedere* from *ferire* &c. *Conquidere* from *conquirere.*

Chien Fr. dog. *Canis* would give *chain*, as *panis pain.* The *i* must be euphonic *(chiain, chien)* as in *lieu* for *leu* &c., or must be from the fem. *chicnne* from *cania* (cf. It. *cagna*) as *Guienne* from *Aquitania.*

Chieppa cheppia It. a fish; from *clupea* v. Menage.

Chiffe Fr. poor stuff, *chiffon* rag, Pic. *chifer*, Fr. *chiffonner*, Champ. *chifouiller* to tear, rumple, Piedm. *cifogné.* Grand-gagnage makes *chiffonner* = Wall. *cafougni*, *chiffon* = Wal. *cafu*, Champ. *cafut* rubbish, from Du. *kaf* chaff. But cf. E. *chife* a fragment, *chibble* (to break in pieces) shiver, Du. *scheve*, E. *shives.*

Chiflo — *cinfolo.*

Chifre — *cifra.*

Chiglia It. *(chiela)*, Sp. *quilla*, Fr. *quille*, E. keel; from O. H. G. *kiol*, O. N. *kiölr.* Fr. *quille* also = G. *kegel*, O. H. G. *kegil.*

Chignon Fr. the nape of the neck, O. Fr. *chaaignon chaignon* for *chaignon* = ring or link of a chain and nape; from *chaîne* (O. Fr.), L. *catena.* Nicot has: *chainon du col* vertebra of the neck, Langued. *cadena daou col.*

Chillar Sp. to scream, cry &c.; from *sifflare* like *sollar* from *sufflare.* Cf. *cigolare.*

Chimera It., Sp. *quimera*, Fr. *chimère*, *chimera* whim; from *chimaera.*

Chimica chimie — *alchimia.*

Chinche Sp. Pg. a bug; from *cimex*, It. *cimice.*

Chinea — *haca.*

Chinquer — *escanciar.*

Chioccare It. to beat; O. H. G. *klochòn*, whence also *cloche*, clock, G. *glocke.*

Chiocciare crocciare It., Sp. *cloquear*, N. Pr. *clouchd*, Fr. *glousser*, Wal. *clocëi* to cluck, G. *glucksen*; an onomatop. as also L. *glocire*, cf. A. S. *cloccan*, E. cluck. It. *chioccia*, Sp. *clucea*, Pg. *choka*, Wal. *clocë*, G. *glucke* a brooding hen; hence It. *chioccio*, Sp. *clueco llueco* hoarse.

Chiocciola It. a snail; for *cloce-iola*, dim. of a form *cloccia* from *coclea.*

Chiodo chiovo It. a nail = *chiavo* from *clavus*, Sp. *clavo*, Fr. *clou* &c. From *chiavo* came first *chio-o* = Pr. *clau*, O. Fr. *clo*, the hiatus being filled up with *d* or *v*, cf. *padiglione* from *pa'iglione papiglione*, *Rovigo* from *Ro'igo Rhodigium.* The E.

9*

form is *clore* so called from its resemblance to a nail, It. *chiodo di girofano*, Fr. *clou de girofle*, Sp. *clavo di especias*.

Chioma It. the hair of the head, from *coma*, *i* = *l* inserted, v. Rom. Gr. 1, 269; cf. *fiavo* = *favo* &c.

Chiotto — *cheto*.

Chiourme — *ciurma*.

Chiovo — *chiodo*.

Chiquet — *cica*.

Chirivia Sp., Pg. *cherivia*, Fr. *chervis chiroui* (m.), E. *skirret*, a parsnep, L. *siser*.

Chirlar — *zirlare*.

Chisme Sp., Cat. *xisme* slander, malicious tale; a corruption of *schisma* (though *sch* does not regularly = Sp. *ch*), or from the Gk. σισμός a hissing?

Chitarra It., Sp. Pg. Pr. *guitarra*, Fr. *guitare*, E. *guitar*; from Gk. κιθάρα. From L. *cithara* come It. *cetera cetra*, Pr. *cidra citola*, O. Fr. *citole* &c.

Chito — *zitto*.

Chiudere It., Sp. *cluir* (in compos.), Pr. *claure*, Fr. *clore* to *close*; from *cludere* and *claudere*. Hence Pr. *esclaure*, Fr. *éclore* (*ex* and *claudo*); Pr. *esclure*, Fr. *exclure* (*excludere*).

Chiurlare — *urlare*.

Choc — *ciocco*.

Chocho Sp. Pg. of weak intellect, doting; prob. from *suctus* for *exsuctus*, cf. *sciocco*.

Chocolat — *cioccolata*.

Choe O. Fr., Pic. *cave*, Pr. *cau chau* = L. *bubo*. Hence Fr. *chouette*, Pic. *cavette* a screech-owl, whence It. *ciorella civetta*, Ven. *zovetta*, Wal. *cioricë*; Pic. also *caran*, Anj. *chouan*, Berr. *charant*, Pr. *chauana*, Bret. *kaouan*, L. L. *cavanus*, *cauanna*. The Fr. *chat-huant* (hooting-cat) is prob. a corruption of *chouan*. From the same root comes Pr. *caucala*, Fr. *choucas* a grey crow, also Sp. *chova* (= Fr. *choe*) a jay, Sp. *choya* a jackdaw. The root is found in the M. H. G. *chouh* an owl, cf. E. *chough*, Du. *kauw* a crow, cf. E. *caw*.

Choisir Fr., Pr. *causir chausir*, whence It. *ciausire*, O. Sp. *cosido* (adj.), O. Pg. *cousimento* = Pr. *causimen*, Pr. *escausir*, O. Cat. *scosir* to choose, Fr. *choix*, Pr. *causit*, E. *choice*; from Goth. *kiusan*, O. G. *kiosan kiesen*, A. S. *ceosan*, E. *choose*, or from Goth. *kausjan* to prove, try, which suits the form *causir* better?

Chommer — *calma*.

Chopine Fr. a liquid measure, Rouchi *chope*; from G. *schoppen*.

Chopper — *zoppo*.

Choque choquer — *ciocco*.

Chorlo Sp. iron-stone; from G. *schörl*.

Chorro Sp., Pg. *chorro* and *jorro* a gush of water; from *susurrus?*

Chose — *cosa.*

Chotar choto — *ciocciare.*

Chou — *cavolo.*

Chouan choucas chouette — *choe.*

Choupo — *pioppo.*

Chouvir — *chindere.*

Chova choya — *choc.*

Choza Sp. Pg. a hut. Perhaps, from *plutea* for *pluteum* L. L. a shelter; it is not the same word as Sp. *llosa*, Pg. *chousa* an enclosed place, L. *clausa.*

Chubarba — *jusbarba.*

Chubasco — *pioggia.*

Chucho Sp. a long-eared owl, so called from its cry, or from its being supposed to *suck* the blood of children, Pg. *chuchar* to suck, Piedm. *ciucé.*

Chuchoter chut — *zitto.*

Chufa — *ciufolo.*

Chulo Sp. Pg. a jester; cf. It. *zurlare* to jest.

Chumazo Pg. a pillow; from *pluma*, It. *piumaccio* and *pimaccio.*

Chupar — *sopa.*

Chus O. Sp. adv. of comparison, from *plus*, O. Pg. *chus, chos.*

Chusma — *ciurma.*

Chuva — *pioggia.*

Chuzo Sp. Pg. head of a spear, spear. Perhaps from *pilum piluzo pluzo chuzo.*

Ci — *qui.*

Cià — *tè.*

Ciabatta It., Sp. *zapata*, Fr. *savate* an old shoe, Sp. Pg. *zapato* a shoe. From Arab. *thabbât*, and perhaps the same word as Fr. *sabot* a wooden shoe. It. *ciabattajo ciabattiere*, Sp. *zapatero*, Fr. *savetier* a cobbler. But, according to Mahn, from the Basque *zapata* a shoe, *zapatu* to tread, root *zap*, G. *sappen* to tread heavily.

Ciacco It. a pig. Perhaps from Gk. σύβαξ σύβαχος whence *siacco ciacco*, cf. *camicia* for *camisia.*

Ciampa — *tape* (2).

Ciancia It. raillery, jest, trifle, *ciancare* to jest, mock, Rh. *ciuncia* tattling, Sp. Pg. *chanza* joke, facetiousness; formed from the sound, cf. Sp. *cháchara*, E. *chatter*, N. Gr. τζάτζαλα, E. *chaff.*

Ciarlare It., Sp. Pg. *charlar*, Val. *charrar*, Norm. *charer* to chatter, prattle, It. *ciarlatano*, Fr. E. *charlatan* a tattler, mountebank. Like *ciancia*, a word derived from the sound of chattering or chirping. Cf. Sp. *chirlar* to chirp, prattle, It. *zirlare*, Basque *chirchila* = *charlatan*. From Norm. *charer* is prob. formed *charade*. The It. *cerretano* = *ciarlatano* is said to be derived from the name of a town *Cerreto*.

Ciarpa — *sciarpa*.

Ciascuno It., Pr. O. Sp. *cascun*, Fr. *chacun*, from *quisque unus*, cf. *chaque*; It. *ciascheduno* from *quisque et unus*, or *quisque ad unum*, like O. Sp. *quiscadauno*, v. *cadauno*.

Ciausire — *choisir*.

Cibera — *ribada*.

Ciborio It. Pg., Fr. *ciboire*, the vessel for containing the consecrated elements, Pr. *cibori*, O. Fr. *ciboire*, Sp. Pg. *cimborio* the cupola or dome over the altar, L. L. *ciborium*, M. Gr. *κιβώριον*; from *κιβώριον* a seed-vessel of a plant, a "vessel".

Cica It. a trifle, adj. *cigolo* single, Sp. *chico*, Cat. *xic*, *chic* small, Fr. *chiche* parsimonious (cf. Gr. *σμικρίνης* parsimony). Fr. *chiquet* a morsel, *chicot* a sprig, stump, Sp. *chicote* end of a rope, *chichota* (Sp.) a trifle, Fr. *chichoter* to wrangle about trifles, Sp. *cicatear* to be parsimonious. From L. *ciccum (ciccum non interduim = non darei cica)*, *c* = *ch* as in Sp. *chicharo*, Fr. *chiche* from *cicer*. Hence also Fr. *chicane* (1) a crumb (2) hair-splitting, wrangling, E. *chicane*.

Cicigna It. blind-worm; for *ciciglia* from *caecilia*, with change of suffix to distinguish it from *Ciciglia* = *Sicilia*.

Cicisbeo It., from Fr. *chiche* (little) and *beau*.

Ciclaton Sp., Pr. *sisclaton*, O. Fr. *siglaton*, Sp. also *ciclada*, a woman's dress; from *cyclas cycladis*.

Cidra cidro cidronela — *cedro*.

Cidre — *sidro*.

Ciera — *cara*.

Cierge Fr., Pr. *ciri* wax-taper; from *cereus*.

Cierna Sp. the flower or best of anything, Pg. *cerne* the heart of wood, cf. It. *cerna* choice, and refuse; from *cernere* to sift, Sp. *cerner* to sift, to blossom.

Cierzo — *cers*.

Cifra cifera It. cipher (secret writing), Sp. Pg. *cifra* a numeral figure, Fr. *chiffre*, E. *cipher* in both senses. Orig. a figure denoting a blank or nought, *cifra figura nihili*, Wal. *cifré*, From Ar. *cifr* empty, nought, *cafira* vacuum esse. According to Mahn, it is the same word as Sp. Pg. It. E. *zero*, Fr. *zero*.

Cigala It. Pr. Cat., Fr. *cigale*, Sp. *cigarra* a grass-hopper; from *cicada*. The Sp. *chicharra* imitates the chirping noise it makes.

Cigarra — *cigala*.

Cigolare It., *scivolare* to creak; from *sibilare* (Ferrari). Cf. Ven.

cigare to creak, It. *cingottare* to chirp. These may be all onomatopœia.

Cigolo — *cica.*

Cigüeña Sp., Pg. *cegonha* a crane for pumping water &c.; from *ciconia.*

Cilla — *celda.*

Cima It. Sp. Pg. Pr., Fr. *cime* top. From *cŷma* a tender sprout, Wal. *chimë*, O. Sp. *cima* a twig, orig. = the top of a plant, cf. It. *vetta.* Hence It. *cimiero*, Sp. *cimera*, Fr. *cimier* a crest, Wal. *tzimiriu* a token, coat-of-arms, M. H. G. *zimier zimierde.*

Cimbel — *zimbello.*

Cimbra — *centinare.*

Cimbrar Sp. to brandish a rod (prop. to bend), *cimbreño* pliant; according to Larramendi, from Basque *cimela* pliant; but cf. *cimbra.*

Cimento It. proof, experiment, risk, *cimentare* to put to the proof &c., *cimentoso* hazardous, *cimento* also = cement, Sp. *cimiento* = foundation, *cimiento real* cement, prop. a composition of vinegar, salt, and brick-dust used in the refining of gold, *cimento* cement, *cimentar* to found, refine gold, Fr. *ciment*, *cimenter*, E. cement, L. L. *cimentum* fundamentum; *caementare* ædificare, *caementarius* qui muros struit. The Sp. and Fr. words are easily traced to the L. *caementum.* The It. *cimento* = proof, presents more difficulty. Diez follows Ferrari in deriving it from *specimen specimentum* (cf. *cantamen cantamentum* &c., for the rejection of the first syllable, *baco* for *bombaco*, *ciulla* for *fanciulla* &c.). The meaning, however, of "experiment" may without much difficulty be deduced from that of "a composition for refining gold", v. Mahn.

Cimeterio It., Sp. *cimenterio*, Fr. *cimetière*, O. E. *centric*, E. *cemetery*; from *caemeterium* (κοιμητήριον). For cemetery we have It. *carnajo*, Sp. *carnero*, Pr. *carnier*, Fr. *charnier*, E. *charnel*-house, O. H. G. *charnare*; from *carnarium.*

Cimeterre cimitarra — *scimitarra.*

Cinabro It., Sp. Pg. *cinabrio*, Fr. *cinabre*, Pr. *cynobre*, E. *cinnabar*; from L. *cinnabaris*; Wal. *chinovar* from χιvvαβάρις.

Cincel Sp., Pg. *sizel*, Fr. *ciseau*, chisel, Fr. *ciseaux* scissors; *ciseler* &c. to chisel. From *secellus* dim. of *secula* a sickle, or from *sicilicula (sicilis)* in Plautus, whence *sicilicellus*, *scilcellus.* This latter is supported by the wavering between *c* and *s*, and also by the Sp. *n* for *l*, cf. *zonzo* from *insulsus.*

Cincillo — *cencio.*

Cinghia It., Wal. *chingë*, Pg. *cilha*, Pr. *singla*, Fr. *sangle* a belt, *chingiare* &c. to gird; from *cingula*; It. *cinto cinta*, Sp. *cinto ciuta cincha*, Pr. *cinta* from *cinctus* (sbst.). From *cingere* It. *cigna*, Pr. *cenha*, O. Fr. *segue.*

Cinghiale It., Pr. *senglar*, Fr. *sanglier* a wild boar, L. L. *singularis epur.* So called from its solitary habits, cf. Gk. μόνιος, Sard. *sulone*, and cf. Gk. οἰωνός (bird of prey) from οἶος. *Cinghiale* for *singhiale* as *concistorio* for *consistorio*, *camicia* for *camisia.*

Cingler Fr. to whip, from *cingulum.* Berr. *sillon* = whipcord.

Cingler — *singlar.*

Cingottare — *cigolare.*

Cintre — *centinare.*

Ciò It., Pr. *aisso so*, O. Fr. *iço ço (ceo)*, Fr. *ce* from *ecce hoc*; Pr. *aquo aco* from *eccu' hoc.*

Cio — *zelo.*

Ciocciare It. to suck, G. *zutschen;* It. *ciotola* a drinking-cup, Sw. *zotteli*, G. *zaute;* Sp. *chotar* to suck, *choto* a sucking-kid, Com. *ciot* a child, *ciotin* a lamb, Rh. *tschutt;* Champ. *tuter* to suck the fingers. All onomatopœia.

Ciocco It. a block, O. Fr. *choque chouquet* a root, Fr. *choc*, Sp. *choque* a thrust, shock, *chocar choquer* to thrust, G. *schock schocken*, E. *shock;* cf. also It. *ciocca* a tuft with G. *schock* a heap. Cf. *toppo.*

Cioccolata It., Sp. *chocolate*, Fr. *chocolat*, E. *chocolate.* From Mexican *chocollatl.*

Ciofo It. wretch, base, mean fellow; from G. *schuft.*

Cioncare It. to break, mutilate, Rh. *ciuncar*, Wal. *ciung* mutilated, Hung. *tsonka;* from *truncare*, or from It. *ciocco?*

Cioppa — *giubba.*

Ciotola — *ciocciare.*

Ciottare — *azote.*

Ciriegia cillegia It., Sp. *cereza*, Pg. *cereja*, Pr. *scrisia*, Fr. *cerise*, Wal. *cerâse*, E. *cherry;* from adj. *ceraseus*, like many others names of trees *(faggio, prugna, quercia)*, It. *ciriegia* as *primiero* from *primarius.*

Ciro It. a pig; from χοῖρος?

Ciruela Sp. a plum; from *cereola*, cf. *prunum cereum* (Virgil).

Cirsir — *zurcir.*

Cisale — *cisoje.*

Ciseau ciseler — *ciucel.*

Cisemus O. Fr. corrupted from the O. H. G. *zisi-mûs*, A. S. *sise-mûs*, L. L. *cisimus*, G. *zieselmaus* a shrew-mouse.

Cisma It. Sp., Pr. *scisma*, O. Fr. *cisme*, schism; from *schisma.*

Cisne — *cecero.*

Citano — *zutano.*

Citriuolo It. a cucumber, Fr. *citrouille* a gourd; from *citreum*, v. *cidro.*

Citron citronnelle citrouille — *cedro.*

Città It., Wal. *cetate*, Sp. *ciudad*, Pr. *ciutat*, Fr. *cité*, Pr. nom. *ciu*, O. Fr. *cit*, E. *city*; from *civitas*.

Ciudad — *città*.

Ciuffo It. a top, top-knot; from G. *schopf*, or from *zopf*, Lomb. *zuff*, v. *zuffa*.

Ciufolo zufolo It., Sp. *chufa*, Pr. *chufla*; O. Fr. *chufle*, Sp. Pr. *chifla* whistle, taunt, jest; vb. *zufolare* &c. A word formed from the sound, influenced by the L. *sibilare* and *sufflare* v. *siffler*. Some make *zufolo* the same as the Etrurian *subulo* a flute-player.

Ciurma It., Sp. Pg. *chusma*, Pg. also *churma chulma*, Fr. *chiourme* the crew of rowers in a galley. From κέλευσμα the signal for the rowers, whence it came to designate the rowers themselves, cf. G. *commando*. From κέλευσμα came *cleusma chusma*, as from *clamare chamar*, Sic. *chiurma* for *clurma cluma*, It. *ciurma* for *chiurma* as *morcia* from *morchia*. Of the same origin is It. *ciurmare* to charm with mystical words and signs.

Civada — *erbada*.

Civaja It. vegetables; from *cibaria*.

Civanza — *chef*.

Cive Fr., *civette*, E. *chive*; from *cæpa* an onion.

Civeo — *civière*.

Civetta — *choe*.

Civire — *chef*.

Cizza — *tetta*.

Clabaud — *glapir*.

Claie Fr., O. Fr. *cloie*, Pr. *cleda* hurdle-work, basket-work, L. L. *clida*, *clia*, dim. *cletella*. It is a Celtic word, Fr. *cliath*, W. *clwyd*. L. L. *cretella* = *clitella* a pack-saddle (prop. of basket-work).

Clairon clarinette — *chiarina*.

Clamp Fr. Wall. a clamp, Norm. *acclamper* to clamp; from O. N. *klampi*, M. H. G. *klampfe*, G. *klammer*, E. *clamp*.

Clap Pr. a heap, mass, *clapiera*, O. Fr. *clapier*, *aclapar* to heap up; == W. *clap clamp* a heap, lump.

Clapier — *clapir*.

Clapir Fr. *(se clapir)* to run to burrow (of rabbits); *clapier* a burrow, prop. a heap of stones, E. *clapper*, from *clap* in Lang. == a stone, == W. *clap*, *clamp* a lump. Diez refers *clapir* to L. *clepere* to steal.

Claque Fr. a crack, sound of a blow &c., *claquer* to clack, clap, clatter; an onomatop., Du. *klack*, vb. *klakken*.

Clarinetto — *chiarina*.

Clatir — *ghiattire*.

Clavicembalo gravicembalo It., Sp. *clavecimbano*, Fr. *clavecin* a harpsichord; from *clavis* a key, stop (Fr. *clavier* a row of keys), and *cymbalum*.

Cleda — *claie*.

Cligner Fr. to wink, Pic. O. Fr. *cliner* *clinner*, sbst. *clin*, Fr. *clin d'œil*; from *clinare* to nod. For *cligner* for *cliner* cf. O. Fr. *crigne* for *crine*, Fr. *harpigner* from *harpin*. O. Fr. *clingier* is from a form *clinicare*.

Clinche Fr., Norm. *clanche*, Champ. Wall. *cliche*, O. Fr. *clenque*, Pic. *cliquet* a latch; from G. *klinke*, Du. *klink*, a word derived from the sound ("unlifted was the *clinking* latch"), or = a fastener, and connected with *cling*, *clench*, *clinch*, Du. *klinken* to fasten.

Clinquant Fr. tinsel, *clincaille* pots and pans, corrupted *quincaille* frippery, vb. *se requinquer* to bedizen oneself; from Du. *klinken*, G. *klingen*, E. *clink*, Fr. *quincailler* = a tinman.

Clique Pic. a slap, vb. *cliquer*, Fr. *cliquet* *cliquette*, E. *clicket* a clapper &c., vb. *cliqueter*. An onomatop. G. *klick*, E. *click*. The Fr. E. *clique* perhaps = a noisy conclave.

Clisse éclisse Fr., O. Fr. *clice* *esclice* a splint; from O. H. G. *kliozan* to split (*i* from *io* as in *quille* from *kiol*).

Cloche Fr. = *campana* in the south, a bell, Pr. *cloca* *clocha*, Piedm. Com. *cioca*, O. Fr. vb. *clocher*, Pr. *clocar*; from L. L. *clocca* *cloca* = A. S. *clucge*, N. *klucke*, O. H. G. *clocca*, *glocca*, G. *glocke*, E. *clock*, Ir. *clog*, W. *cloch*. *Clock* is a variation of *clack* and is imitative of the sound made by a blow.

Clocher — *clop*.

Clop O. Fr. Pr. lame, halting (W. *kloff*), sbst. O. Fr. *clopin*, *clopinet*, E. *cloping*, vb. *cloper*, *clopiner*, Fr. *éclopé*. L. L. *cloppus* = χωλός. More likely from the G. *klopfen* *kloppen* to knock (cf. *club-footed*), than, as Diez, from χολόιπους. Another word for *cloper* is *clocher*, Pic. *cloquer*, Pr. *clopchar*, from L. L. *cloppicare*, cf. It. *zoppicare*.

Clore — *chiudere*.

Clou — *chiodo*.

Coalla — *quaglia*.

Cobalto It., Sp. Pg. E. *cobalt*, Fr. *cobolt*; from G. *kobalt* (from Boh. *kow* metal, or = *kobold* mountain-goblin).

Cobarde — *codardo*.

Cobe — *cupido*.

Cobrar Sp. Pg. Pr. O. Fr. *combrer* to recover, O. H. G. *koborôn*; from *recuperare*, the simple form, preserved, like so many lost Latin words, in the Rom. *cuperare*, would be from *capere*, formed perhaps, on the analogy of *superare*, to which it is akin in meaning. The Lat. verb *recuperare* is preserved in the Rom. but with a different meaning: It. *ricovrare* to escape, Sp. *recobrarse*, Pr. *recobrar*, O. Fr. *recouvrer* to recover (from sickness); cf. L. L. *rex ægrotavit quo recuperante filius ægrotare caepit.* Cf. *ressortir* (v. *sortir*) and Gk. ἀναχομίζεσθαι.

Cocagne — *cuccagna.*

Coçar Pg. to scratch, tickle; perhaps from *coquere* to burn, *coctus, coctiare.* Hence, too, Sp. *coscar, cosquillas?*

Cocarde — *coq.*

Cocca It., Pr. *coca* (in *encocar*), Fr. *coche,* E. *cock* the notch of a cross-bow; It. *coccare* to *cock,* to lay the bowstring in the notch, *scoccare* to discharge an arrow, Fr. *encocher* &c. Of uncertain derivation. Wedg. derives the verb *cock, coccare* from the sound of a quick sudden motion imitated by the syllable *cock,* which word is also used to express sharp projections (*cog* of a wheel) or indentations (notch).

Cocca It., Sp. *coca,* O. Fr. *coque,* Fr. *coche,* E. *cock* = *cock-boat,* cf. *coxswain.* From *concha* as *cocchiglia* from *conchylium.* We have also O. H. G. *koccho,* Dan. *kog,* W. *cwch,* Bret. *koked.* From *concha* also come O. Sp. *coca,* Sard. *conca* head (cf. *testa,* Gk. κόγχη), Sp. *cogote,* Pr. *cogot* the occiput, also Fr. *coque* egg-shell, *cocon cocoon;* from *concheus* come It. *coccio* potsherd, *coccia* head, Sp. *cuezo cueza* basket.

Cocchio It., Sp. Fr. *coche* (m.), E. *coach.* According to some, from Hung. *kotczy* (Wal. *cocie,* Alb. *cotzi*); others make it etymologically the same word as *couch,* from Du. *koetse* = couch or coach (litter), which from *koetsen* = *coucher* to lie. Diez, however, makes *cocchio* a masc. dim. of *cocca* a boat, and from *cocchio* Fr. *coche,* Sp. *coche,* G. *kutsche,* cf. from It. *nicchia,* Fr. *niche,* Sp. *nicho.*

Coccia coccio — *cocca.*

Cocciniglia It., Sp. *cochinilla,* Fr. *cochenille,* E. *cochineal;* from Sp. *cochinilla* a wood-louse (dim. of *cochina* a sow); the Spaniards gave this name to the Mexican insect, which resembles a wood-louse. The It. spells the word as if from *coccinus.*

Cocear — *coz.*

Cochar — *coitar.*

Coche Fr. a sow, whence *cochon* and Sp. *cochino, cochastro, cochambre.* Perhaps the same word as *coche* a nick or notch (*cocca*), cf. Sp. *carnero* from *crena,* Piedm. *crina* sow, from *crena.*

Coche — *cocca.*

Coche — *cocchio.*

Cochenille cochinilla — *cocciniglia.*

Cochevis Fr. a tufted lark = Pg. *cotovia,* Sp. *totovia;* from the Bret. *kodioch,* v. Mahn Unters. p. 26.

Cochiglia It., Fr. *coquille* a mussel; from *conchylium,* as Sp. *coquina* from *concha.*

Cochino — *corhe.*

Cocon — *cocca* (2).

Cocu — *cucco.*

Coda It., Pr. *coa*, Fr. *queue*, Sp. Pg. *cola* (cf. *csquela* for *esqueda* = *scheda* &c., O. Sp. *coa*) a tail; from *cauda*. Hence It. *codione codrione* a bird's tail, O. Sp. *codilla* the rump, *codasta* the stern of a ship; vb. It. *scodare*, Fr. *écouer* to dock the tail.

Codardo It., Pr. *coart*, O. Fr. *coart coard couard* (whence E. *coward*), Sp. Pg. *cobarde*, O. Sp. *cobardo* (from *coardo* as *juricio* from *juicio*), Fr. *couard*. From *cauda* a tail, so = one who holds back, cf. O. Fr. *couarder* to retire. Or there is a reference to a terrified animal with his tail between his legs. In heraldry a lion so depicted is called a *lion couart*. Mahn, Unters. p. 76, says that *couart* was a name used by the old fabulists for a hare, *cod-ard-o* = badly-tailed, short-tailed, v. Rom. Gr. 2, 311.

Codaste — *coda.*

Codea, codena — *cotenna.*

Codeso Sp. from *cytisus*, corrupted *cutcsus.*

Codicia — *cupido.*

Codillo codo — *cubito.*

Codol Pr. Cat., Parm. Crem. *codol*, N. Pr. *códou* a sort of stone; from *cos cotis.*

Codrione — *coda.*

Coello — *coniglio.*

Cofano cofaro It., Sp. Pr. *cofre*, Fr. *coffre*, E. *coffer*, also Sp. *cuebano* a large basket, Sp. Pr. *cofin*, Fr. *coffin* a small basket, E. *coffin*; from *cophinus*. Bret. *kof* = the belly, A. S. *cof* a cave. Sp. *cofa*, *cofe*, It. *coffa* == the scuttle of a mast. The same root appears in *cavus.*

Cofe coffre — *cofano.*

Cofia — *cuffia.*

Coger — *cogliere.*

Cogliere It., Sp. *coger*, Pg. *colher*, Pr. Fr. *cueillir* (E. *coil*), Wal. *culeage* to collect; from *colligere*. Hence Sp. *escoger* to select; O. Pg. sbst. *escol* the best of anything, Pr. *escolh* species.

Coglione It. dial. *cojon*, Sp. *cojon*, Pr. Fr. *coillon* testiculus; from *coleus*, Pr. O. Fr. *coil*, Wal. *coiu*. *Coglione* also = coward, wretch, Sp. *collon*, Fr. *coyon.*

Cognato It., Sp. *cuñado*, Pr. *cunhat*, Wal. *cumnat* (fem. *cognata* &c.) brother-in-law; from *cognatus*. The Fr. has *beau-frère.*

Cogno It. a wine-measure; from *congius.*

Cogollo Sp. the heart of a cabbage &c.; perhaps a corruption of *cologlo* from *cauliculus.*

Cogoma It. a pot; from *cucuma*, whence also Fr. *coquemar.*

Cogoto — *cocca.*

Cogotz cogul — *cucco.*

Cogujada Sp., Cat. *cogullada* a crested lark, It. *cappelluta;* from *cogulla* a hood, L. *cucullus.* Hence also *cogujon* the corner of a pillow or bolster.

Cohue Fr. noise, bustle; perhaps from *cou* and *huer* to cry? The Berrichon has *cahuer* from *huer.*

Col — *cheto.*

Coiffe — *cuffia.*

Coillon — *coglione.*

Coin Fr. corner, wedge; from *cuneus,* It. *conio* &c. Hence *coguée* an axe; *quignon* for *cuignon* a lunch, whence Sp. *quiñon,* Pg. *quinhão* a share.

Coing — *cotogna.*

Cointe — *conto.*

Coitar cochar O. Sp. Pg. Pr., O. Fr. *coiter* to push, throng, press, hasten; sbst. O. Sp. Pr. *coita;* adj. *coitoso* hasty. From a freq. form *coctare (coquere).* Cf. O. Sp. *cochado = cocido,* O. Pg. *coito = coctus.*

Coitare O. It., Sp. Pg. Pr. *cuidar,* O. Fr. *cuidier,* Fr. *cuider* to care; from *cogitare.* O. It. *coto,* O. Sp. *cuida,* Sp. Pg. *cuidado* care. Hence It. *tracotanza,* Fr. *outrecuidance* presumption, = *ultracogitantia.*

Coite — *coltrice.*

Cojon — *coglione.*

Col — *cavolo.*

Colà It., Sp. *acullá,* Pg. *acolá,* Wal. *colea* adverb of place; from *eccu' illac.*

Cola — *coda.*

Colcare corcare coricare It., Wal. *culcà,* Pr. *colgar,* Fr. *coucher* to couch, Sp. Pg. *colgar* to suspend, Cat. to cover with earth, lay a shoot (It. *coricare*); from *collocare,* L. L. *culcare.*

Colcha — *coltrice.*

Colchete — *croc.*

Colgar — *colcare.*

Colla It., Sp. *cola,* Fr. *colle* glue; from χόλλα.

Collare It. to torture, *colla* a rope for torturing; prob. from M. H. G. *quellen, kollen* to fetter, punish (G. *quälen*); from the punishment of mast-heading, *collare* came to mean "to hoist sails".

Collazo Sp. a foster-brother; from *collacteus* for *collactaneus.*

Collon — *coglione.*

Collottola It. the nape; from *collum.*

Colmena Sp., Pg. *colmea* a bee-hive. Not, as Diez gives, following the Spanish etymologers, from the Arab. *kuwàra mia nahl* a hive of bees, but, probably, from the Basque *kólóenwenan* a bee-hive (*kólóen* a straw-fabric and *gwenan* bees), spelt *colmena* as if = *colmena* a well-stocked place *(colmar)*, v. Mahn, Unters. p. 54.

Colmillo Sp., Pg. *colmilho* a tusk, fang; from *columella*, so = *dens columellaris;* Sp. *columelares* = incisors. Isid. has: *dentes caninos vulgus colomellos vocant.*

Colmo It. Sp., Fr. *comble* heap, summit, vb. *colmare* &c., to heap up. From *cumulus* and *culmen*, the latter being found also in Sp. *cumbre*, Pg. *cume* summit, the former in Pg. *comoro combro*, L. L. *combrus* a mound, Pr. *comol* = It. *colmo* full; from *cumulus* also come Pr. Fr. *encombre*, It. *ingombro* an incumbrance, *encombrar*, *encombrer combrer*, *ingombrare*, E. *cumber incumber;* Fr. *décombres* rubbish. It. *sgombrare* to remove. G. *kummer*, E. *comber* grief, trouble are from the Rom.

Colodra Sp. milkpail, wine-vessel. Of uncertain origin. Probably, a compound with *uter*, Diez. Perhaps the *col-* is the same as in *colostrum*. From *colodra* comes Sp. *colodrillo* the occiput, cf. *testa.*

Colpo It., O. Sp. *colpe*, Sp. Pg. *golpe*, Pr. *colp*, Fr. *coup* a blow; It. *colpire* to strike, O. Sp. *colpar*, Fr. *couper* to knock off, cut off. From *colaphus*, which in L. L. appears as *colapus colopus.*

Coltrice It. (for *colcitre*), O. Sp. *colcedra*, Pr. *cousser cosser* a mattress; from *culcitra;* It. *coltra coltre* (f.), O. Fr. *cotre*, Fr. *coultre* from *culcitra;* Sp. Pg. *colcha* from *culcia* for *culcita*, whence also Fr. *coulte* (E. *quilt*), *coite couette*, O. Fr. *coute keute quieute* (for *colte* &c.), Pr. *cota* (for *colta* as *mot* for *molt*). From *culcita puncta* came Fr. *coulte-pointe*, *courte-pointe*, by corruption, *contre-pointe*, whence E. *counterpane*. *Culcita* is from the Celtic, W. *cylch* a circle, *cylched* bed-clothes. From *culcita* would be formed a dim. *culcitinum culçtinum*, whence It. *cuscino*, Sp. *coxin*, Fr. *coussin*, E. *cushion*, G. *küssen.*

Colul — *quello.*

Comadreja Sp. a weasel, properly = a little godmother, cf. *bele* and Grimm's Reinhart, p. 224.

Combagio It. a joining, *combagiare* to join = *combaciare (bacio)* to kiss, to join, perhaps with some reference to L. *compages.*

Comble — *colmo.*

Comblesa — *bercer.*

Combo Sp., Pr. *comb* bent, crooked; Sp. *comba* a bending, Pr. *comba*, O. Fr. *combe* a deep valley (cf. *Alta-comba*, *Combalonga*, *Como*), Piedm. *comba*, Com. *gomba;* Sp. *combar* to bend, Gen. *ingumbàse.* From W. *cwm*, E. *combe* a valley. There is no necessity to have recourse, with Diez, to the L. *concavus.*

Combrer — *colmo.*

Combro — *colmo.*

Come It., Sp. Pg. O. It. *como*, Sic. *comu*, O. Sp. O. Pg. Pr. O. Fr. *com cum*, Wal. *cum*, Fr. *comme*, Pr. *coma*; from L. *quomodo*. Hence Pr. *coment*, Fr. *comment*, Sard. *comenti*; also Pr. *cossi*, *coussi* from *quomodo sic*. The Pr. has also *co* for *cum* as L. *quo* for *quomodo*.

Comer Sp. Pg. to eat; from *comedere*.

Cominciare It., Sp. Pr. *comenzar*, Pg. *começar*, Fr. *commencer*, E. *commence*; from *cum* and *initiare* (Mil. *inzà*); O. Sp. *compenzar compezar*. Sard. *incumbenzai* from *in-cum-initiare*; Sp. *empezar* from *in-initiare*. Wal. has *incepe* from *incipere*, Rh. *antscheiver*.

Comment — *come*.

Comoro — *colmo*.

Compagno It., Sp. *compaño*, Pr. O. Fr. *compaing*, G. *companion*; *compagnia* &c. *company*; *compagnare accompagnare* &c. From the L. L. *companium*, from *cum* and *panis* on the analogy of the O. H. G. *gimazo*, *gileip* from *gi* = *cum* and *mazo* meat, *leip* bread. Thus Diez, who rejects the derivation from *com-paganus (pagus)*, there being, he alleges, no instance of a similar change of accent in derivatives from words in -*anus*. But the change of accent may have arisen from the growing usage of *pagano* in another sense, the commoner word naturally taking the shorter form. The *g* is found in the oldest L. L. *ubi habuisti mansionem huic nocte compagn*, cf. O. Fr. *compaing*. Moreover, the meaning of *compagnia* = confederation, points rather to *pagus* than to *panis*. The derivation from *pagus* would be further supported by the word *semipaganus* in Persius, if, as has been suggested, the meaning be not "half a clown", but "a poor half-brother of the guild" (Prof. Conington).

Compasso It. Pg., Sp. Fr. Pr. *compas*, E. *compass*; *compassare* &c. to *compass*. From *cum* and *passus* a step, Pr. O. Fr. *compas* = equal step, *compasser* to keep equal step, so in Sp. *compas* = time in music. Others der. from the W. *cwmp* circle, *cwmpas* compass.

Complot Fr. a plot, *comploter* to plot. From *complicitum complic'tum* = *complicatio*. *Complot* for *comploit*, as *frotter* for *froiter*.

Compote Fr. preserved fruit; for *compôte*, It. *composta* = *composita*.

Comprare — *parare*.

Compter — *contare*.

Comte — *conte*.

Concerto It., Sp. *concierto*, Fr. E. *concert* agreement; vb. *concertare* to agree. From L. *concertare*, or, better, from *consertare*; It. *conserto* = agreement, *consertare* to concert, agree.

Conserto afterwards borrowed the *c* of *concento,* with which it was confounded from the similarity both in sense and sound.

Conciare It. *acconciare* (Sp. *aconchar*) to attire, trim, adj. and subst. *concio acconcio,* Wal. *conciu.* A participial-verb from *comtus comtiare,* cf. *cacciare (captus), succiare (suctus).*

Concierge Fr., Pic. *conchierge* a jailor.

Condore It., Sp. Fr. E. *condor;* a South American word.

Confortare It., Sp. *conhortar,* Pr. *conortar* (cf. *preon* from *profundus*), Fr. *conforter,* E. *comfort* to strengthen; "an angel from Heaven *comforting* him (ἐνισχύων)"; from L. L. *confortare.*

Congé Fr., Pr. *comjat* leave; from *commeatus;* Fr. *congédier* from It. *congedo,* which from the O. Fr. *conget.*

Congédier, congedo — *congé.*

Congegnare It. to join; from *concinnare,* influenced by It. *genio,* Pr. *genh* art.

Congoxa — *angoscia.*

Conhecer Sp. = L. *cognoscere.*

Conhortar — *confortare.*

Coniglio It., Sp. *conejo,* Pg. *coelho,* Pr. O. Fr. *conil,* E. *coney;* from *cuniculus;* Fr. (with change of suffix) *connin, connine;* Fr. vb. *conniller* to have recourse to subterfuges.

Connétable — *contestabile.*

Conoochia It., Fr. *quenouille* a distaff; L. L. *conucula* for *colucula* from *colus,* O. H. G. *kuncla,* G. *kunkel.*

Conquidere — *chiedere.*

Consoude Fr., Sp. *consuelda* a plant; from *consolida.*

Contadino contado — *conte.*

Contare It., Sp. *contar,* Pr. *comtar* to count, Fr. *compter,* also to tell, narrate, Fr. *conter;* from *computare,* cf. the two senses of O. H. G. *zeljan* and E. *tell.* It. *computo, conto* &c. = L. *computus* (Firm. Maternus).

Conto It., Sp. Pg. *conde,* Pr. *coms,* O. Fr. *quens,* Pr. and O. Fr. *accus. comte,* Fr. *comte,* E. *count;* from *comes* = a companion of the prince; hence *contado* &c., *county, contadino* a countryman.

Contestabile connestabile It., Sp. *condestable,* Fr. *connétable,* E. *constable;* orig. = Master of the Horse, from *comes stabuli,* then = commander of the army or of a fortress (constable of the Tower &c.), then restricted to mean a petty officer of the peace.

Contigia — *conto.*

Contir O. Sp. to happen, *cuntir acuntir, contescer,* Sp. Pg. *acontecer;* from *contingere.*

Conto It., O. Fr. *cointe* acquainted, O. Fr. Pr. *cointe coinde* neat, pretty, E. *quaint;* from *cognitus* known, intimate, *agreeable,*

cf. M. H. G. *maere* known and agreeable. Hence Pr. *coindar
acoindar*, Fr. *accointer*, E. *acquaint* = L. *adcognitare*, Pr. *acoin-
dansa*, O. Fr. *accointance*, E. *acquaintance*. In L. L. we find
cogniter cognite benigne humane. From *comtus* comes It. *contigia* ornament, v. *conciare.*

Contrada It. Pr., Fr. *contrée*, E. *country;* properly = that which
lies over against one, from *contra* with suffix *-ata*, cf. G.
gegend from *gegen*. Pr. has also *encontrada* from *encontrar*.

Contreindre — *étreindre*.

Contrebande — *bando*.

Contrecarrer — *cara*.

Contrôle — *rotulo*.

Convier — *conritare*.

Convine Fr. behaviour, It. *convegno*, Sp. *convenio convention*, E.
corin a deceitful agreement; from *convenire;* for the loss of
the *n* in E. cf. *covenant*, O. E. *covent* (for convent).

Convitare It., Sp. Pg. Pr. *conridar*, Fr. *convier* to invite; *convito*,
Sp. *convite*, Pr. *convit*, O. Fr. *convi* invitation, feast. From
invitare, the *con* being taken from *convivium*.

Convoiter — *cupido*.

Convojare — *voyer*.

Convoyer — *voyer*.

Copeau Fr. a chip or splint; from *coupe* a slice *(couper);* or is
copeau the same word as O. Fr. *cospel coispel (cuspis?)* a thorn?

Copete copo — *coppa*.

Coppa It., Sp. Pg. Pr. *copa*, Fr. *coupe*, Wal. *cofé*, E. *cup;* from
cuppa a form of *cupa*, L. L. *cuppa* = cup. Hence also Sp. Pg.
Pr. *cubu*, Fr. *cuve*, O. H. G. *kupa*, E. *coop*. Hence Pr. *cubel*
a tub; Sp. *cubilete*, Pr. Fr. *gobelet*, L. L. *gubellus* a cup; also
It. E. *cupola*, Fr. *coupole, coupe*. The same root is found in
O. Fr. *cope*, Pic. *coupet couplet* a hill, W. *cop copa*, E. *cop*, Du.
kop, G. *kopf* and *kuppe* head, top; Fr. *coupeau*top, Sp. Pg.
copa copo bunch, *copete* top, tuft, v. *toppo*.

Copparosa It., Sp. Pg. *caparrosa*, Fr. *couperose*, E. *copperas;*
from *cupri rosa* = χάλκανθον.

Coppia It., Fr. E. *couple;* from *copula;* hence also O. It. *cobbola*,
Pr. *cobla*, Fr. E. *couplet*. The It. *scoppiare* to uncouple is to
be distinguished from *scoppiare* from *schioppo* (q. v.).

Coq Fr. = A. S. *cocc*, E. *cock*, Wal. *cocóš*, Rh. *cot;* so called
from its cry, cf. vb. *coqueriquer, coqueliner*, Du. *kokelen*. From
coq come *coquet*, E. *cocket* swaggering (from the strutting
pride of a cock); *cocarde*, E. *cockade*, Wall. *cockad* prop. =
the comb of a cock; O. Fr. *cocart coquart* vain. For *coq* the
Pr. and O. Fr. have the Rom. *gal, jal*, Norm. Berr. *jau, jollet*
Lor. *jau jallé*, Champ. *gau*.

Coque — *cocca*.

Coquelicot Fr., E. *cockle* wild poppy. From *coccum* χόχχος the kermes-insect, coque de kermes. By a false association *coquelicot* has taken the same form as the word for the cry of a cock = *coquelicot, coquericot*, the red comb of the fowl being the point of connexion. Cf. Occ. *cararaca* = crow of a cock and poppy, Pic. *corriacot* = cock and poppy.

Coquemar — *cogoma*.

Coquet — *coq*.

Coquille — *cochiglia*.

Coquin Fr. a beggar, rogue; according to some, a dim. of *coquus*, prop. = kitchen-boy, scullion. Others make it from O. N. *kok* throat, *koka* to swallow. The best way is make it a dim. of O. Fr. *cocs, queux* a cook, for L. *coquinus* would give *cuisin*.

Coquina — *cochiglia*.

Cor — *ora* (2).

Coraggio It., Sp. *corage*, Fr. E. *courage*; from *cor* the heart, *coraticum*, cf. *omaggio* &c. from *hominaticum (homo)*.

Corassa It., Sp. *coraza*, Pr. *coirassa*, Fr. *cuirasse*, E. *cuirass*; from *coriacea (corium)*, cf. L. *lorica* from *lorum*.

Corbacho Sp., Fr. *cravache* a scourge, prop. the Nubian lash of rhinoceros hide, G. *karbatsche*; borrowed from the Turk. *kyrbách*, Russ. *korbatsch*.

Corbata — *cravata*.

Corbeille Fr. a basket; from *corbicula* (Palladius).

Corbeta Sp., Pg. *corveta*, Fr. E. *corvette*; from *corbita* a merchant-vessel, with a Romanised ending.

Corcare — *colcare*.

Corchete — *croc*.

Corcho Sp. cork-tree, *corcha* a cork-receptacle; *corche* sandal; from *cortex*, as *pancho* from *pantex*.

Corcovar Sp. Pg. to bend, *corcova* a hump; from *con-curvare*, cf. Sp. *corcusir* for *concusir*. Pg. *corcos* = *corcovado* hump-backed.

Cordero Sp., Pg. *cordeiro* lamb; from *agnus chordus* (Varro and Pliny).

Cordoglio It., Sp. *cordojo*, Pr. *cordolh*, Rh. *cordoli* grief; from *cordolium* (Plautus and Apuleius). *Dolium* = Fr. *deuil*, It. *doglia*.

Cordonnier — *cordovano*.

Cordovano It., Sp. *cordoban*, Pr. *cordoan*, Fr. *cordonan*, E. *cordovan, cordwain* = Cordovan leather, Ar. *kortobani*. An older form was *cordovesus, cordebisus*, from L. *cordubensis*, Sp. *cordobes*. Hence *cordovaniere*, O. Fr. *cordoannier*, Fr. *cordonnier* a shoemaker, E. *cordwainer*.

Coreggia It., Sp. Pg. *correa*, Pr. *correja*, Fr. *courroie*, Wal. *curcá* a strap; from *corrigia*. Hence It. *scoreggia*, E. *scourge*.

Corgere It. in *accorgersi* (Rh. *ancorscher*) to *perceive*, and *scorgere* (1) to perceive (2) to escort. *Accorgere* = *ad-corrigere* expressed orig. the correction of an error. *Scorgere* = *excorrigere* got its sense of escorting, leading from that of ruling and guiding. From it is derived *scortare*, *scorta*, Fr. *escorter* *escorte*, E. *escort*, Sp. *escoltar escolta*.

Corine — *corruccio*.

Coriscar Pg. to lighten, *corisco* lightning, Sic. *surruscu*, from *coruscare*.

Corlieu O. Fr. Pr. runner; from *corre* to run, *lieu* light. Hence Fr. *courlieu*, *courlis*, E. *curlew*.

Corma Sp. fetter; from χορμός a block?

Cormano — *hermano*.

Corme Fr. Pg. a fruit, O. E. *corme*; from *cornum?*

Cormoran Fr., E. *cormorant*; from *corb* = *corvus* a crow, and Bret. *môr-vran* (*mor* sea, *bran* crow), thus a pleonasm like *loupgarou*. The Pr. is *corp-mari*.

Cornamusa It. Sp. Pg. Pr., Fr. *cornemuse* a bag-pipe; from *cornu Musæ*. Pr. *corna*, O. Fr. *corne* = a horn (musical instrument), Pr. *musa*, O. Fr. *muse* = pipe.

Cornard Fr. cuckold, = It. *becco cornuto* or *becco*, Sp. *cabron*. A derisive expression, a *cornut* or *bestia cornuda* (Pr.) being taken as synonymous with a fool. Cf. Pr. *soffren*, It. *bozzo* (prop. = a rough stone), Fr. *sot* all used in the same sense as *cornard*.

Cornia corniolo It., Sp. *cornizola*, Pg. *cornisolo*, Fr. *cornouille*, Wal. *coarne*, *cornel* plum; It. *cornio corniolo*, Sp. *cornejo cornizo*, Pg. *corniso*, Fr. *cornouiller*, *cornel*-tree; from *cornum*, *cornus*, or from *corneus corneolus* (cf. s. *ciriegio*), *corniculum (cornejo) cornuculum (cornouille)*.

Cornice It., Sp. *cornisa*, Fr. *corniche*, Wall. *coroniss*, G. *carnies*, E. *cornice*; from *coronis* (χορωνίς) a cornice, in Rom. confounded with *cornix*, cf. χορώνη = curve, crown, and crow.

Corniola It., Sp. *cornerina*, Pg. Pr. *cornelina*, Fr. *cornaline*, E. *cornelian*; from *cornu*, because in colour it resembles the *horny* nail of the finger, whence also its Gk. name ὄνυξ, v. *nacchera*.

Corral — *corro*.

Corredo — *redo*.

Corro Sp. a ring; from *currere*; *correr toros* to exhibit a bullfight; hence Sp. *corral* a court, yard &c.

Corroyer — *redo*.

Corruccio It., Pr. *corrotz*, Fr. *courroux* anger; for *colleruccio* &c.,

10*

from *cholera* gall. Hence It. *corucciare crucciare*, Pr. *corrossar*, Fr. *courroucer*. O. Fr. *corine* as if *cholerina*.

Corsare corsale It., Sp. *corsario cosario*, Pr. *corsari*, Fr. *corsaire*, E. *corsair;* from *cursus*, whence Sp. *corsa corso* a course or cruise at sea.

Corset Fr. E. bodice; from Fr. *cors* = *corpus*, cf. *cors-age*. The It. has *corpetto*, and also, from the Fr., *corsetto*.

Corte It. Sp. Pg., Pr. *cort*, Fr. *cour*, Wal. *curte*, E. *court;* from L. *chors chortis* a cattle-yard. From *corte* &c. in the sense of a prince's court, come It. *cortese*, Sp. *cortes*, Fr. *courtois*, E. *courteous (= cortensis);* Sp. *cortesano*, Fr. *courtisan*, It. *cortigiano*, L. L. *cortisanus;* It. *corteggiare*, Sp. *cortejar*, Pr. *cortejar cortezar*, Fr *courtiser* to court; It. *corteggio*, Fr. *cortége*.

Cortecoia It., Sp. *corteza*, Pg. *cortiça* rind, bark, from *corticea (cortex);* It. *scorticare*, Pr. *escorgar*, N. Pr. *escourtegá*, Fr. *écorcher*, Sp. Pg. *escorchar* to peel, flay, L. L. *escorticare*.

Cortége — *corte*.

Cortesa — *corteccia*.

Cortina It. Sp. Pr., Fr. *courtine*, Wal. *cortiné*, E. *curtain*, from *chors* as *aulæum* from *aula*. L. L. *cortina* = a little court, a hanging, a covering (L. *cortina*).

Cortir — *curtir*.

Corvée Fr. soccage, L.L. *corvada*. From *corrogata* like *enterver* from *interrogare*, Rouchi *courowée*, Lang. *courroe*. The orig. meaning was "summons", cf. O. Fr. *rover (= rogare)* to command.

Corveta — *corbeta*.

Corvetta It., Sp. *corveta*, Fr. *courbette*, E. *curvet;* from *curvus*.

Corvette — *corbeta*.

Corso corsa Sp. Pg. a roe; from ζόρξ ζορχός a form of δόρξ δορχός, or from *caprea caurea corea corja* (cf. *granea granja*) *corza*, cf. *arcilla*.

Cosa It. Sp. Pg. Pr., Fr. *chose;* from *causa*, in L. L. = a thing; the orig. L. form is preserved in the orig. sense, It. Sp. *causa*, Pg. *cousa*, Fr. *cause*, Wal. *causě*, the Pr. *causa* having both meanings. The same connexion of meanings is found in the G. *sache*, and the N. Gk. πρᾶγμα. From *causari* come It. *cusare* to assert, Pr. *chausar*, O. Fr. *choser* to dispute, Fr. *causer* to talk is from O. H. G. *chôsòn*, G. *kosen*.

Coscar — *coçar*.

Coscia It., Pg. *coxa*, Pr. *cueissa*, Fr. *cuisse*, Wal. *coapsě* the thigh; from *coxa* the hip. Sp. *caro* lame, Isid. *claudus coxus*. Hence Sp. *quixote*, Val. *cuixot* armour for the thigh, Fr. *cuissot*.

Coscojo Sp., Cat. *coscoly* the berry of the scarlet-oak, L. *cuscu-*

lium (Pliny). The tree is called *coscoja*, Cat. *coscolya*, Basq. *coscolla cusculla*. An old Spanish word.

Cosecha Sp. harvest; from *consecare consectus*. O. Sp. *cogecha* = Pg. *colheita*, L. *collecta*.

Cosensa — *cuire*.

Coser — *cucire*.

Cosi It. = O. Sp. *ansi*, O. Fr. *ainsinc* (Burg. *ansin*, Pic. *ensin*), Fr. *ainsi*, Sp. *asi*, Pg. *assim*, Pr. *aissi*, Wal. *asà*. From *æque sic*, *qu* = *cu*, whence *cusì cosi*, Sic. *accussi*. As the Sp. *aun* from *adhuc*, *nin* from *nec*, *sin* from *sic*, so *an* for *ac* or *ec*, whence *ansi*, *asi*. The Pr. has *acsi* for *aissi*, Romagn. *acsé*, Brescian *icsi*, Lomb. *insci* for *cosi*.

Coso Sp. a corso, place for a bull-fight; for *corso* from *cursus*, It. *corso*. Hence Sp. *coser* war-horse = It. *corsiere*, E. *courser*, Sp. *acosar* to pursue.

Cospel — *copeau*.

Cosse écosse Fr. (f.) a pod, husk or shell, *écosser* to shell &c. From G. *schote* pod (Du. *schosse*) = W. *côd cwd* a bag, Bret. *kôd*, E. *cod*. *Cosse* would be from *écosse*.

Cosser — *cozzare*.

Cossi — *come*.

Cosson Fr. a weevil; from *cossus*, Bret. *kos*.

Costa It. Pg. Pr., Sp. *cuesta*, Fr. *côte* (E. *coast*), rib, side, coast; from *costa* a rib; hence It. *costato*, Sp. *costado*, Fr. *côté* side; It. *costerella* a little hill, Fr. *coteau* for *côteau* a declivity, side of a hill; It. *accostare*, Sp. *acostar*, Fr. *accoster* to approach (cf. *costa* = *juxta*), Sp. *acostar* to incline, lay down, E. *accost*.

Costà, costi, costinci adverbs; from *eccu' istac*, *eccu' istic*, *eccu' istinc-ce*.

Costra Sp. crust; from *crusta*.

Costui — *questo*.

Costuma It. Pr., Sp. *costume*, Fr. *coutume* (all fem.), It. Pg. *costume*, Sp. *costumbre*, Pr. Cat. *costum*, Fr. *costume* (all masc., Cat. also fem.), E. *custom* (and in der. sense *costume*); from *consuetudin costudn*, through the medium of a form *consuetumen*, *ume* being a Rom. termination for expressing qualities, cf. It. *asprume*, Pg. *ciume*, Pr. *frescum*, and cf. from *mansuetudin* Sp. *mansedumbre*, Pg. *mansedume*, also Pg. *mansidão*, Pr. *mansueza*. The masc. *costume* is the earlier form, the fem. being formed from a neut. plur. *costumina*, O. Pr. *cosdumna*.

Cota cotar cotejar — *quota*.

Cota — *coltrice*.

Cotale It., Wal. *cutare* a pronoun, from *æque-talis?* Hence also Sp. *atal* = Pr. *aital*, O. Fr. *aintel itel*, Norm. *entel*, O. It. *aitale*, v. s. *cosi*.

Cotanto It. from *æque tantus?* O. Sp. *atanto*, Pr. *aitant*, O. Fr. *itant*, v. *cotale*.

Cotar — *cotc.*

Cote Pg. in *a cote de cote* adv. = daily; from *quotidie*, whence also *cotio* every-day, common, Sp. dia de *cutio* a work-day.

Cote coter coterie — *quota.*

Côte côté coteau — *costa.*

Cotenna codenna It., Pr. *codena*, Fr. *couenne* skin, Sp. *codena* thick cloth. *Couenne* is prob. for *couaine*, O. Fr. *codaine* (whence *codena*), from *cutaueus*. Pg. *codea* rind may be from *cutica*, whence It. *cotica* (Parm. *codga*, Ven. *coega*, Gen. *quiga*), and *cuticagna.*

Cotesto cotestui It. from *eccoti esto*, L. *eccu' tibi iste.*

Cotillon — *cotta.*

Coto Sp. an enclosure, boundary, Pg. *couto* asylum, sanctuary. From L. *cautum* an order, mandate (so in O. Sp.), whence = limit &c., L. L. *infra cautos, infra cautum, lapis cauti.*

Cotogna It., Pr. *codoing*, Fr. *coing*, E. *quince*, Wal. *gutuie;* from *cydonia*, κυδώνιον, L. L. *cotonium cottanum*, so called from *Cydon* in Crete.

Cotone It., Fr. *coton*, Sp. *algodon*, E. *cotton;* from Ar. *qo'ton, al-qo'ton.* Sp. *algodon* and *alcoton* also = wadding, whence Pr. *alcotò*, O. Fr. *auqueton*, Fr. *hoqueton.*

Cotovello — *cubito.*

Cotovia Pg. lark, whence Sp. *totovia* tufted lark, It. *tottovilla*, Fr. *cochevis;* from Bret. *kodioch.* V. Mahn, Unters. p. 25.

Cotta It., Sp. Pg. Pr. *cota*, O. Fr. *cote*, Fr. *cotte*, E. *coat*, *cotte de maille* a coat of mail, Pr. *cot* (m.); L. L. *cotta cottus;* hence Fr. *cotillon cotteron* &c. *Cottus cotta* = a coarse woollen mat, a monk's tunic, from G. *kotze* a shaggy covering, overcoat, E. *cot* = a matted lock, a fleece of wool. Others derive *cotta* &c. from E. *cote, cot* a hut, a covering.

Couard — *codardo.*

Couchant — *ponente.*

Coucher — *colcare.*

Coucou — *cueco.*

Coude — *cubito.*

Coudel — *capitello.*

Coudre — *cucire.*

Coudre Fr. hazel; from *corylus, cotrus, coldrus*, Com. *coler*, It. *corilo.*

Couenne — *cotenna.*

Couette — *coltrice.*

Couivre O. Fr. *cuevre cuivre*, E. *quiver;* from O. H. G. *kohhar*, A. S. *cocer*, G. *köcher.*

Couler Fr. to trickle, flow; from *colare.* Hence adj. *coulis*, Pr.

coladis, as if *colaticius*, sbst. *coulisse* a sliding-door, E. *cullis* a groove or channel, O. Fr. *coleïce* = E. *portcullis*.

Coulis coulisse — *couler*.

Coup — *colpo*.

Coupe coupeau — *coppa*.

Couper — *colpo*.

Couple — *coppia*.

Cour — *corte*.

Courage — *coraggio*.

Courbette — *corvetta*.

Courge — *cucuzza*.

Courroie — *coreggia*.

Courroux — *corruccio*.

Courtier — *cura*.

Courtine — *cortina*.

Courtisan courtois — *corte*.

Cous — *cucco*.

Cousin — *cugino*.

Cousin Fr. a gnat; dim. of *culex*, as if *culicinus*.

Coussin — *coltrice*.

Coûter Fr. E. *cost*, sbst. *coût cost*; from *constare*, to stand one in, It. *costare* &c. Hence O. Fr. *coste* a drug, M. H. G. *koste* victuals, cf. G. *speise* prop. = expense; O. Fr. Wall. *costenge* = expense.

Coutre Fr. a plough-share; from *culter*, It. *coltro*; Com. *coltra contra* a plough.

Coutume — *costuma*.

Couve — *cavolo*.

Couver — *covare*.

Covare It., Pr. *coar*, Fr. *couver* to brood; from *cubare* (= *incubare*). It. *covo cova* a den, lair, Sp. *cueva* a cave, from *cubare* in its proper sense.

Covone It. a sheaf, Lomb. *cov*, Piedm. *cheuv*, as much as can be held in the hollow of the hand, from *cavus*, cf. *chiovo* from *clavus*.

Coxa — *coscia*.

Coxin — *coltrice*.

Coyon — *coglione*.

Cozzare It., Fr. *cosser* to butt; sbst. *cozzo*. A participial verb, from *coctus* = *coictus* (*co-icere*), cf. *dirizzare*, *cacciare* &c., Rom. Gr. 2, 323. It. *cozzare con uno* = *co-icere cum aliquo*.

Cozzone It., Pr. O. Cat. *cussò*, O. Fr. *cosson*, Wal. *goson* a factor, dealer, espec. in horses, a groom. From *cocio* (Plautus and Gellius), *coctio* (Festus). Hence It. *scozzone*.

Crac Fr., vb. *craquer*; an onomatop., cf. O. H. G. *krac*, G. *krach*, E. *crack*, Gael. *crac*. Fr. *craquelin*, Du. *krakeling*, E. *crackling*.

Cracher — *racher.*
Craie Fr. chalk; from *creta*, Sp. *greda* &c.
Craindre Fr. to fear, O. Fr. *crembre*, *cremir*, *cremmoir*, pret.
creins cremi cremu, part. *craint crcmi crcmu*. Prob. from *tre-*
mere (cr = tr), cf. *empreindre* from *imprimere*, *geindre* from
gemcre, *raembre* (cf. *crcmbre*) from *redimere.*
Cramoisi — *carmesino.*
Crampe crampon — *grampa.*
Cran Fr. a slit, a notch, Rouchi *créner* to notch; hence Fr. *cre-*
neau, O. Fr. Pr.*carnel* an embrasure of a battlement, a *crenelle*
(whence *crenellated*), Fr. *carneler* to notch, sbst. *charnière* a
joint. From L. *crcna* (Pliny), Rh. *crenna*, Lomb. *crena*, Pied.
cran, cf. *carnero.* Cf. also Du. *karn*, vb. *karnen*, Bavar. sbst.
krinnen, v. Fr. *carne* a corner.
Crane — *granchio.*
Cranequin — *crone.*
Crapaud Fr., Pr. *crapaul grapaul*, Cat. *gripau*, Lim. *gropal* (for
grapal) a toad. From E. *creep grope*, A. S. *creopan*, Du. *kru-*
pen, O.H.G.*krifôn.* Or from *crape*=scales on the skin, so=
the blotched animal, cf. Pr. *graissant* from *graissa* = Fr.
graisse, *crasse.*
Craquer — *crac.*
Crau Pr. the name of a stony district near Arles, whence adj.
crauc stony, Norm. *crau* a peculiar sort of stone. The word
is Celtic: W.*craig*, Bret. *crag*, Gael.*creag crag*, E.*crag.* *Crau*
= *crag*, as *fau* = *fag*, *esclau* = *sclag.* ¦
Cravache — *corbacho.*
Cravanter — *crebantar.*
Cravatta It., Sp. *corbata*, Fr. *cravate*, E. *cravat;* introduced into
France in the first half of the 17th century. It was so called
from being worn by the Cravats (Fr. *Cravates*), or *Croatian*
soldiers. The It. is *croatta*, Rouchi *croate croyatte.*
Creanter O. Fr. to assure, *creant* bail; from *credentare* a form
from *credens;* other forms are *craanter cranter*, *graanter gran-*
ter, whence E. *grant.*
Crebantar Pr., O. Fr. *cravanter*, Sp. Pg. *quebrantar* to break;
from *crcpare* (*crepans*).
Crèche — *greppia.*
Crema It. Sp. Pr., Fr. *crème*, E. cream, L. L. *crema* n. (Venant.
Fort.); from L. *cremor.* Wedg. mentions the cognate words
kraumr kraum in Icelandic (= It. *cremore*, *crema*), A.S.*ream*,
E. *rime*, *grime*, G. *rahm.* The accent in Fr. prop. belongs to
cresme, *chrism*, χρίσμα, It. *cresima.*
Crémaillon crémaillère Fr., whence Sp.*gramallera* a pot-hanger,
Burg. *cramail*, Wall. *cramâ*, Champ. *cramille*, L. L. *crama-*
culus, *cramacula.* From G. *kram* an iron hook, v. *grampa.*

Crembre, cremir — *craindre.*

Cremisi — *carmesino.*

Crena quorens Pg. a keel; from *carina*, It. Sp. *carena*, Fr. *carène;* hence *carenare, carener*, E. *careen.*

Crencha crenohe Sp., Pg. *crencha*, Cat. *clenxa* a parting in the hair; from *criniculus*, or, better, from *crenicula (crena* a slit).

Créneau — *cran.*

Crepare It., Pr. *crebar*, Fr. *crever*, Sp. Pg. *quebrar* to break; from *crepare.*

Crêpe Fr., E. *crape* (O. Fr. *crespe* culled, frizzled); from *crispus.*

Crepore It. animosity, rancour; prop. of anger suppressed and eager to break out *(crepare).*

Crescione It., Fr. *cresson*, Cat. *crexen;* formed as if from *cresciare (a celeritate crescendi)*, but really derived from another source, A. S. *caerse*, Du. *kersse*, Sw. *crasse*, E. *cars, cress*, G. *kresse.*

Cresson — *crescione.*

Creuset creusequin — *crisuelo.*

Creux Fr. hollow, abst. *creux*, Pr. *cros* a hole, vb. *creuser*, Com. *croeuss.* From *corrosus.*

Crever — *crepare.*

Crevette Fr. a small crab; from *carabus*, or G. *krabbe*, E. *crab*, whence also Rouchi *crape. Chevrette* a shrimp is from *chèvre*, cf. G. *böckle.*

Criado Sp. Pg. a servant (It. *creato);* from *criar* to breed, bring up, from *creare*, so = prop. one brought up in the house (verna).

Crier — *gridare.*

Criquet Fr., N. Pr. *cricot*, E. *cricket*, Pic. *crequeillon; krekkel* a cricket, W. *cricell.* An onomatop., cf. Fr. *criquer*, Du. *krieken*, E. *creak*, Gk. κρίκειν, κρίζειν.

Criquet Fr. a small horse; from G. *kracke;* E. *cricket* prop. = a trestle, then = a wicket.

Cris Pg. an eclipse; from *eclipsis.*

Crisuelo Sp. a lamp, *crisuela* a lamp-pan; from Basque *criselua cruselua.* Hence also *crisol* a crucible. Diez. But the Basque is more probably from the Sp., which is the same as the Fr. *creuseul, croisel* a lamp, connected with G. *krus*, E. *cruse*, Fr. *cruche* (q. v.), Du. *kruyse*, whence also Fr. *creuset croiset* a crucible or *cruet*, Fr. *creusequin*, E. *cruskin*, Ir. *criusgin;* L. L. *crucibolum* = Fr. *creusseul, croissol.* V. Wedgwood, s. *crock.*

Croc Fr. Pr. Rh. a hook, whence *crochet crochu accrocher;* O. N. *krokr*, Dan. *krog*, E. *crook*, Du. *krooke*, W. *crôg;* hence L. L. *incrocare*, Fr. *encrouer*, E. *encroach.* From *crochet* comes Sp. *corchete*, Pg. *colchete.*

Crocchiare It. to clatter, from *crotalum* (κροτάλον), *cchi* = *tl* as in *vecchio.* Sp. *crotorar* to cry like a crane is the same word.

Croccia gruccia It., E. *crutch*, It. *cruccia* a spade, O. Sp. *croza*, Pr. *crossa*, Fr. *crosse*, E. *cross*, *crozier*. From *crux*, like *pancia pansa panse* from *pantex*, or perhaps better from adj. *crucea*, whence also O. H. G. *krukja*.

Crochet — *croc.*

Crogiare It. to roast. Connected with O. H. G. *chroste*, *roast*, cf. *agio asio.*

Croi — *crojo.*

Croissir croistre — *cruxir.*

Crojo O. It. stiff, rude, coarse, Pr. *croi*. From *crud-i-us* a by-form of *crudus*, as *bajo* from *badius*. For other instances of similarly lengthened adjectives, cf. s. *fujo*. The long vowel is shortened by its position *crudjus*, and passes into *o*.

Crollare It., Pr. *crollar crollar* to shake, Fr. *crouler* to fall to ruin, O. Fr. *croler crodler crosler*. The orig. form is *crollar* which is from *co-rotulare*, as *rollar* from *rotulare*. So Fr. *crouler* agrees with *rouler*, and we see the original sense in the phrase *crouler un bâtiment.*

Crone Fr. (m.) a crane (instrument); from Du. *krân*, E. *crane* = G. *kranich* a crane (bird), cf. Fr. *grue*, Gk. γέρανος. Hence O. Fr. *cranequin* (for crossbows), Wall. *crenekin* a crossbow.

Crosciare It., Sp. *cruxir*, Pr. O. Fr. *croissir*, Wal. *crohi* to gnash. The Goth. has *kriustan* to gnash, e. g. Mark 9, 18: *kriustith tunthuns* == Sp. *cruxe los dientes*, Pr. *cruis las dens* = τρίζει τοὺς ὀδόντας. The Rom. forms would not come directly from this, but from a form *kraustjan* (cf. *kiusan kausjan* Fr. *choisir*), *stj* = It. *sci* as in *angustia* = *angoscia*. We find also in the 2nd conj. Cat. *croxer*, Rh. *scruscer* (O. Fr. *croistre*).

Crotorar — *crocchiare.*

Crotte Fr., Pr. *crota* mud, dung of sheep, goats &c. Prob. from the L. G. Swed. *klöt*, G. *kloss*, E. *clod*, *clot.*

Crouler — *crollare.*

Croupe croupir — *groppo.*

Cruccia — *croccia.*

Crucciare — *corruccio.*

Cruche Fr., O. Fr. *cruye*, Gasc. *cruga*, Pr. *crugô*, Fr. *cruchon*, E. *cruse* (v. s. *crisuelo*); from W. *crwc* a pail, cf. O. H. G. *cruoc crôg*, O. Fris. *krôcha*, A. S. *crocca*, E. *crock* (whence *crockery*), G. *krug*, Rh. *cruog hruog.*

Cruna It. eye of a needle. From *corona*, as *crucciare* from *corrucciare;* for *u* from *o*, cf. *giuso*, *tutto.*

Crusca It. bran. O. H. G. *crusc* = *furfur*, Sw. *krüsch*, Swab. *grüsche*, Fr. *gruis*, Piedm. *grus*. N. Pr. vb. *cruscà* = to crush.

Cruxir — *crosciare.*

Cuajar — *quagliare.*

Cubebe It., Sp. Pg. Pr. *cubeba*, Fr. *cubèbe*, E. *cubeb* the name of an Indian plant which yields a sort of pepper; Ar. *kabâbat*.

Cubito It., Sp. *codo*, O. Sp. *cobdo*, Pg. *covado coto*, Fr. *coide code*, Fr. *coude*, Wal. *cot* elbow; from *cubitus*. It. has also *gomito gombito*, Rh. *cumbet*. Hence Pg. *cotorello* = *coto* by corruption from *covetello?* Sp. *codillo* knee of a horse &c., Sp. *recodo* an angle, cf. ἀγκών.

Cucar — *cucco.*

Cuccagna It., Sp. *cucaña*, Fr. *cocagne*, O. E. *cokaygne*, E. *cockney (cokenay coknay)*, Utopia or land of plenty, thence applied in E. to one brought up in such a land, pampered. The orig. meaning was Land of Cakes, from Cat. *coca*, Rh. *cocca*, Langued. *coco*, Pic. *couque* a cake, from *coquere* as *torca* from *torquere*. Wall. *cocogne* = Easter eggs. For a full discussion of the word, v. Notes and Queries, Vol. 4. Wedg. makes the orig. sense of *cockney* = rocked, dandled, cf. *coqneliner*, E. *cockle cocker.*

Cucchiajo It., O. Pg. *colhar*, Pr. *culhier*, It. fem. *cucchiaja*, Sp. *cucchara*, Pg. *colher*, Fr. *cuiller cuillère* a spoon; from *cochlearium cochlearia*. The Wal. is *lingurĕ* = L. *lingula.*

Cuccio It., Sic. *guzzu* (also *guzza cuccia*), Cat. Pr. *gos*, Fem. *gossa*, Sp. *gozque* a cur, Wall. *go* a dog. Cf. Sic. *guzzu*, It. *cucciolo* small, Sp. *cuco*, perhaps from It. *cucco* nestling, fondling. But the word is found in Illyr. *kutze*, Hung. *kuszi* a little dog.

Cucco It., Ven. *cuco*, Romag. *cocch* &c., Pg. *cuco* a cuckoo; from the Old Latin *cucus* (Plautus); It. *cuculo*, Pr. *coqul*, Fr. *cocu coucou*, E. *cuckoo*, from *cuculus*, Sp. *cuquillo*, *cuclillo*. In the derived sense of the Fr. *cocu* we have Pr. *cogotz* (cf. Cat. *cucut*) *coutz*, O. Fr. *cous*, E. *cuckold*. Sp. *cucar* to scoff is from the form *cucus.*

Cuchara — *cucchiajo.*

Cucina It., Sp. *cocina*, Fr. *cuisine*, Wal. *cocnĕ*, also O. H. G. *kuchina*, A. S. *cycene*, E. *kitchen*, O. Fr. *cugann*, W. *cegin*; from L. *coquina* for *culina*. Vb. *cucinare* &c., from *coquinare* (Plautus).

Cucire It. (prop. *cuscire*, *sc* = *s*), Sp. *coser cusir*, Pg. *coser*, Pr. *coser cusir*, Fr. *coudre*, Wal. *coasĕ* to sew; from *consuere*, L.L. *cusire*. Hence It. *costura* (for *consutura*), Fr. *couture*, whence *accoutrer*, E. *accoutre*. It. *sdrucire sdruscire* to unsew, is from *resuere* with privative *s* and euphonic *d*, *sdrecire*, then, on analogy of *cuscire*, *sdruscire.*

Cucuzza It. (1) a gourd (2) a head; corrupted from *cucurbita*. It. *zucca*, whence Pr. O. Fr. *suc*, Pr. *zuquet* head, is prob. corrupted from *cuzza* for *cucuzza*. The N. Pr. is *tuca*. From

cucurbita comos also Fr. *gourde, gougourde*, N. Pr. *cougourdo,*
E. *gourd,* Fr. *courge,* in the Jura *coudre.*

Cudir Sp. Pg. in *acudir* to help, *recudir* to return, assist. From
recutere to strike back, in reflexive sense, to sprink back,
comes *recudir* (cf. *sacudir* from *succutere, precudir* from *percutere*); *acudir* was formed on the analogy of *recudir.*

Cuebano — *cofano.*

Cueillir — *cogliere.*

Cuento — *contare.*

Cuerdo Sp., Pg. *cordo* prudent; for *cordado* from *cordatus* (Ennius, Plautus &c.); cf. *pago* from *pagado, manso = mansuetus.*

Cuesco Sp., Pg. *cosco* kernel, *coscorron coscorrão* a bruise, a blow
on the head, a crust (cf. Fr. *grignon* from *granum*). Basq.
coskha = butting (of a ram).

Cueva — *covare.*

Cueza — *cocca* (2).

Cuffia souffia It., Sp. *cofia escofia,* Pg. *coifa,* O. Pg. *escoifa,* Fr.
coiffe (cueffe), Wal. E. *coif,* Du. *coifie.* From O. H. G. *kuppa
kuppha kuphja =* mitra, F. *cap* (cf. *krippa kripja*) came L. L.
cofea cuphia. Kuppha = L. *cuppa* a cup (v. s. *coppa* &c.) cf.
L. *galeola* in both senses).

Cugino It., Pr. *cosin,* Fr. E. *cousin,* fem. *cugina* &c.; from *consobrinus,* Rh. *cusrin cusdrin.* The Sp. is *sobrino.*

Cuidado cuidar — *coitare.*

Cuider — *coitare.*

Cuiller — *cucchiajo.*

Cuirasse — *corazza.*

Cuire Fr. to cook, Pr. *cozer,* from *coquere; cuisson* pain from
coctio; cuistre a pedant, from *coquaster,* cf. Pr. *coguastró,* L. L.
cocistro; Pr. *cosenza* pain, from *coquentia,* Fr. *cusençon;* It.
cociore, Sp. *escozor* sharp pain.

Cuisine — *cucina.*

Cuisse — *coscia.*

Cuistre — *cuire.*

Cuivre Fr. copper, brass; from *cuprum,* adj. *cuprcum.*

Culantro Sp., from *coriandrum.*

Culbute Fr. a summersault, vb. *culbuter;* from *cul* rump, and
bute a projection.

Culla It. cradle; from *cunula,* as *lulla* from *lunula;* Neap. *connola,* Romagn. *conla.*

Culvert culvert O. Fr., Pr. *culvert* roguish, impious, infidel.
From *collibertus* a term which denoted one whose condition
was little above that of a slave inasmuch as he could be sold
and bought. Matt. Paris has: *sub nomine culvertatis et perpetuæ servitutis.* The association of ideas is obvious, cf. *knave,
villain* &c.

Cumbre cume — *colmo.*

Cundir Sp. Cat. to increase, spread (neut.). From Goth. *kuni* = γένος, O. N. *kynd*, A. S. *gecynd*, E. *kind.*

Cupido It., Pr. *cobe*; whence It. *cupidigia cupidezza*, Sp. *codicia*, O. Sp. *cobdicia*, Pr. *cobiticia cobezeza*, Fr. *convoitise* (for *covoitise*), (E. *covetousness*) from a Lat. *cupiditia (cupidus)*; It. *cubitare*, Pr. *cobeitar*, Fr. *convoiter*, E. *covet*. Pr. *cohir* = fall to one's share, e. g. *jois m'es cobitz;* from *cupere alicui* to wish one well, Rh. *cuvir;* Pr. *encobir*, O. Fr. *encovir* to covet.

Cupo It. hollow; from *cupa* a cask, v. Rom. Gr. 2, 232. Sard. has *cupudu* = *cupo.*

Cura Sp. Pg. (m.) a clergyman, prop. one who takes charge, in which sense *cura* was used even in Lat., and in L.L. as masc. From *cura* come It. *curato*, Fr. *curé*, E. *curate;* also It. *curattiere*, Pic. *couratier*, Fr. *courtier* a factor, one who has charge of business.

Curtir Sp., Pg. *cortir* to tan leather. From *conterere*, *coterere* with *r* transposed *corter cortir*, cf. *derretir.*

Cusare — *cosa.*

Cuso Pr. pure, clean, adv. *cuschement;* from O. H. G. *kûsc*, G. *keusch* pure, chaste.

Cuscino — *coltrice.*

Cusir — *cucire.*

Cuspir cospir Pg. to spit; from *conspuere.*

Cussó — *cozzone.*

Cuticagna — *cotenna.*

Cutio — *cote.*

Cutir Sp. to strike against, strike, defend. Perhaps from *competere cumplir cuplir cutir*, as from *conterere cuterir cutrir.*

Cutretta cutrettola It. a wagtail. From *coda retta (recta)*, so for *cudretta*, = Fr. *hochequeue;* It. *coditremola* = Fr. *branlequeue*, G. *wedelsterz*, E. *wagtail*, W. *tinsigl*, Gr. σεισοπυγίς, Lat. *motacilla* &c.

Cuve — *coppa.*

D.

Da — *a.*

Da Fr. in *oui-da*, *nenni-da.* The oldest form is *divá*, shortened *deá* (one syllable) used to express an urgent summons: *diva, ne me celer! diva tu m'as honi!* v. Rom. Gr. 2, 413. The orig. meaning was "say on!" from imperat. of *dire*, and *va* imp. of *aller.*

Dace — *dazio.*

Dadiva Sp. Pg. a present; = *dativa* L. L. for *donativa.*

Dado It. Sp. Pg., Pr. *dat*, Fr. *dé*, E. *die;* from *dare* = to throw *(dare ad terram).* The Fr. *dé* = *dez* thimble is from *digitus (?).*

Daga It. Sp. Pg. (also Pg. *adaga*), Fr. *dague*, E. *dag dagger,* Du. *dagge*, G. *degen*, also in the Celt., Gael. *daga* pistol, Bret. *dag dager* a dagger (cf. s. *pistola*). Fr. *daguet* = a spade. The root is *dag* to thrust = *dig*, O. E. *dag* to pierce.

Dagorne Fr. a one-horned cow; from *dague* and *corne*, cf. *bigorne* for *bicorne.*

Daguet — *guatare.*

Daim Fr. a deer, fem. *dainé*, O. Fr. *dain* (m.), whence It. *daino*, Pied. *dan*, O. Sp. *dayne*, Du. *deyn;* from *dama* (It. *damma*).

Daino — *daim.*

Daintié O. Fr. (m.), also *daintier, daintée*, E. *dainty* (sbst. and adj.). This is from the Celtic, W. *daintaith (daint = dens).* O. E. *deintee* value *(dainty* worthy) is the O. Fr. *deinetet deintet (= dignitas)*, which some indentify with the foregoing words.

Dais Fr. a canopy, E. *dais*, O. Fr. *dois*, Pr. *deis* a table, from *discus*, It. *desco* (E. *desk*), G. *tisch. Dais* was a corruption of *dois*, cf. *épais* and *espois.* The name was then transferred to the raised step (E. *dais*) on which the high table was placed, or the canopy over it. Wedgw. Others derive from *dorsum dossium*, which, however, could not give the form *deis;* the Sp. *dosel*, It. *dossiere* may be from the old form *dois*, or from *dorsale dorsarium*, E. *dorsal, doser, dosel* = hangings round the walls of a hall or church (at the *back* of the priests), v. Parker, Glossary of Architecture.

Dala Sp. Pg., Fr. *dalle*, a pump-*deal* (naut.). The Sp. *adala* points to the Ar. *dalla* ducere, *dalalah* ductus. Cf. It. *doccio* from *ducere.*

Dalle Sp., Pr. *dalh*, O. Fr. *dail*, Dauph. *dailli* a sickle; vb. Pr. *dalhar*, O. Fr. *dailler* to slash, fight, *s'entredalier.* Perhaps a dimin. from *daga.*

Damasco It. Sp., Fr. *damas*, E. *damask;* from *Damascus* where it was made; the It. has also *damasto. Damascus* was also noted for its sword-blades, whence It. *damaschino* &c., and also for its plums, whence Sp. *damascena* &c., E. *damascene, damson.*

Dame — *donno.*

Dame Fr. interjection; from *domine*, cf. *dame-dieu* = domine deus.

Damigello — *donno.*

Dandin Fr. a simpleton, *dandiner* to rock, dandle; cf. G. *tand, tändeln*, E. *dade, dandle, dandy*, It. *dondolare.* Wal. *tendalé* = It. *dondolo* a toy; v. Wedg. s. *dade.*

Danger Fr., E. *danger*. *Dangerium* or *domigerium* (*domager* or *damager*, from *damnum*, to fine or seize for trespass) was orig. a feudal word, and meant the right of inflicting fines for breach of territorial rights, *fief de danger* a fief held under strict and severe conditions, *sergent dangereux* the officer who looked after the *dangeria*. Wedgwood. *Se mettre en danger de quelqu'un* to be in the *danger* of one came to mean to be in his power, liable to a penalty, hence the present meaning. *Danger* also = difficulty, refusal: *faire danger de dire* to refuse, Lim. *dondzié* refusal. But Littré remarks that the O. Fr. *dangier* = authority, and thus corresponds better to a Lat. *dominiarium*, cf. *dominicellus*, *damoisel*, *dansel*.

Dans — *ens*.

Dansare It. (for *dansare*, as *anzare* for *ansare*), Sp. Pg. Pr. *dansar*, Fr. *danser*, Wal. *dëntzui*, E. *dance*, G. *tanzen*. It. *danza* &c.; from O. H. G. *dausón* to draw, extend; from *dinsan*, Goth. *thinsan*.

Dañar Sp., Pg. *danar* to hurt; from *damnare* to hurt, cf. L. L. *condemnare*, L. Sal.: *si quis terram alienam condemnaverit*, O. Fr. *condemner*.

Dardo It. Sp., Pr. *dart*, Fr. *dard*, Wal. *dardé*, Hung. *darda*; from A. S. *daradh darodh*, E. *dart*, O. N. *darradhr*, O. H. G. *tart*. Others from δόρυ δόρατος.

Darga — *targa*.

Darne Fr., N. Pr. *darno* a slice; from Bret. W. *darn* a fragment, Sansk. *darona* (*dṛi* to tear). Hence E. *darn* prop. = to patch.

Darse, darsena — *orsenale*.

Dartre Fr., Provincial Fr. *dertre* = A. S. *teter*, E. *tetter*, G. *zitter*. Pictet derives the word through the Celtic (W. *tarweden*) from the Sansk. *dardru* a tetter.

Datil datte — *dattero*.

Dattero It., Sp. Fr. *datil*, Fr. *datte*, E. *date* (fruit); from *dactylus*.

Daus — *a*.

Davanti — *anzi*.

Dazio It., Sp. *dacio*, Fr. *dace* (f.) impost, tax; from *datio*.

Dé — *dado*.

Débaucher — *bauche*.

Debloar — *becco*.

Débit Fr. sale, *débiter* to sell, prop. to enter as *debitum* (*debt*) in an account book, to *debit*.

Debonnaire — *aria*.

Debout — *bottare*.

Débris — *briser*.

Début — *bozza*.

Dec dech Pr. (1) command (2) government, province (3) tribute (4) fine, fault, deficiency, Fem. *deca decha* = (4); N. Pr. *decá*

to break off, O. Pr. *dechar* to deceive. From *edictum*. From
indictum come Pr. *endec* injury, defect, *endechat* defective, Sp.
endecha a dirge for the dead; O. Fr. *enditier*, to *indite* = *in-dictare.*

Decentar — *encentar.*

Dechado Sp. a sample; from *dictatum*, Pr. *dechat*, O. Fr. *ditié*,
E. *ditty*; Pr. *dechar* = *dictare.*

Dechat — *dechado.*

Déchirer — *eschirer.*

Déchouer — *échouer.*

Déciller desailler Fr. to open the eyes; from *cilium*, It. *disci-gliare.*

Décombres — *colmo.*

Défalquer — *falcare.*

Défaut — *falta.*

Défi défier — *disfidare.*

Défiler — *fila.*

Défrayer — *frais.*

Degré Fr., *degrat (degra)* Pr., Pg. *degrao;* for *gré* = *gradus*, the
preposition from *degradare* being added to distinguish it from
gré = *gratum.*

Déguerpir — *guerpir.*

Degun Pr. = nullus, O. Sp. *degun;* from the O. H. G. *dik-ein*,
cf. *maint.*

Deh It. interjection, Fr. *dey;* probably shortened from *deo* as *i'*
from *io.*

Dehesa Sp., O. Sp. *defesa*, Cat. *devesa* pasturage; L. L. *defensa
defensum*, O. Fr. *defois.*

Deitar — *gettare.*

Déjà — *già.*

Déjeûner — *giunare.*

Délabrer — *lambeau.*

Délai Fr., E. *delay;* from *dilatum*, It. fem. *dilata.* Hence vb.
dilayer, O. Fr. *delayer*, It. *dilajare* to *delay.*

Delante — *anzi.*

Délayer — *dileguare.*

Deleznar — *liscio.*

Délié Fr., O. Fr. also *deugié* delicate; from *delicatus*, as *plié* from
plicatus, Pr. *delguat*, Sp. *delgado* slender.

Demain — *mane.*

Demanois O. Fr., Pr. *demanes*, = statim. From *de manu* with
suffix *ipsum* = "off hand", Gk. ἐκ χειρός, M. H. G. *zehant.*
For *demanois; demanes* we also find *manois manes.*

Démarrer — *amarrar.*

Demas — *mai.*

Demoiselle — *donno.*

Demonio It. Pg., Sp. *demonio dimoño*, Pr. *demoni* a demon; from *dæmonion* (Tertullian).

Denaro danaro It., Sp. *dinero*, Pr. Fr. *denier* from *denarius*. Hence It. *derrata*, Sp. *dinerada* prop. = a sum of money or its worth, Fr. *denrée* commodity, food, cf. Bav. *pfennwerth*.

Dende — *indi*.

Dengue Sp. Pg. Cat., Sard. *denghi* prudery, affectation; from *denegare*, It. *diniego*.

Denier denrée — *denaro*.

Dentello It., Pr. *dentelh*, Sp. *dentellon* moulding of a cornice &c., It. *dentelli* (pl.), Fr. *dentelle* point-lace; from *dens* a tooth.

Denuedo Sp., Pg. *denodo* boldness, *denodarse* to be bold; from *nodus* knot, restriction.

Denuesto Sp., Pg. *doesto* insult, Sp. *denostar*, Pg. *doestar*, *deostar*; from *dehonestum*, *dehonestare*. Pr. *desnot* = *denost?*

Dépêcher — *pacciare*.

Dépens dépense Fr., from *dispendere dispensus*.

Dépêtrer — *pastoja*.

Dépit Fr., Pr. *despieg* displeasure; from *despectus* disdain, It. *dispetto*, Sp. *despecho*, E. *despite*. Adj. *despit*. Vb. *despire*, E. *despise* from *despicere*. Cf. *répit*.

Dépouille — *spoglio*.

Depuis — *poi*.

Dératé — *rate*.

Dernier — *retro*.

Dérober — *roba*.

Déroute — *rotta*.

Derramar Sp. Pg. to pour out, spread; for *des-ramar* to sever branches, divide, It. *disramare*, Pr. *desramar derramar*, Wal. *derëmà* to prune, Fr. *deramer desrasmer* to tear. Opposed to it is the Com. *ramà* to collect.

Derrata — *denaro*.

Derrear — *derrengar*.

Derrengar Sp., Pg. *derrear* (for *derrenar*), Pr. *desrenar, deregnar*, O. Fr. *éreiner*, Fr. *éreinter* to sprain the hip; from *ren renes*, the Sp. through *disren-icare*. It. has only sbst. *direnato*, but the Piedm. *derné* = Pr. *desrenar*.

Derretir Sp., Pg. *derreter* to melt. From *deterere* or *disterere.* Sbst. *derretimiento* = *detrimentum*. V. *curtir*.

Derribar Sp. Pg. to demolish, ruin; from *ripa* a bank, It. a precipice, Sp. *ribazo*; cf. *derrocar*.

Derrière — *retro*.

Derrocar — *rocca*.

Des O. Sp., O. Pg., Sp. Pg. *des-de*, Pr. *des deis*, Fr. *dès* = Lat. *ex* or *usque a*, It. *da*. From *de ex*, *dès lors* = *de ex illâ horâ*, *désormais* = *de ex horâ magis*; cf. O. Fr. *desanz* = *de exante*.

O. Sp. *desent* = *de exinde*, *desi* = *de ex ibi*, Sp. *despues* (v. *poi*) = *de ex post*; *exante* and *exinde* are found in Latin.

Descaptar — *capitare*.

Descer Pg. to descend, O. Sp. *decir*. From *desidere*.

Desde — *des*.

Deseo — *disio*.

Desguinzar — *esquinzar*.

Desi — *qui*.

Designare — *disegnare*.

Desinare disinare It., Pr. *disnar*, *dirnar*, *dinar*, O. Fr. *disgner*, *disner*, *digner*, L. L. *disnare*, E. *dine*. Among the etymons given are δειπνεῖν, *dignare* (the beginning of a grace), *decima* (hora). Diez derives it from *decoenare* (cf. *devorare depascere*), whence Fr. *deciner*, *desner*, *diner*, as from *decima*, *desme*, *dime*, from *buccina*, *busna*, cf. O. Fr. *reciner* a lunch, from *recoenare*, cf. also It. *pusigno* = *postcoenium*. But Mahn wishes to prove that it is merely another and earlier form of *sdigiunare*, *déjeûner* = *disjejunare*, so that *disinare* would be the orig. form. The *s* is radical as shown by the Pr. *diruar*. For the double form of the same word, cf. *sevrer* and *séparer*, *chose* and *cause*, *hôtel* and *hôpital* &c. But though "breaking the fast" would be a proper designation for the first meal in the day, it would not apply equally well to a later meal, nor would the same word be used for two distinct meals.

Desleir — *dileguare*.

Deslizar — *liscio*.

Desman — *ademan*.

Desmayar — *smagare*.

Desollar Sp., O. Sp. *desfollar*, Pg. *esfolar* to flay; from *follis*.

Désormais — *des*.

Despachar — *pacciare*.

Desparpajar — *parpaglione*.

Despedir Sp. Pg. to discharge, dismiss, *despedirse* to go away; from *de-expedire*. Hence also Pg. *despir* to strip.

Despejar — *specchio*.

Despertar — *espertar*.

Despir — *despedir*.

Despojo — *spoglio*.

Despues — *poi*.

Desrener O. Fr., O. E. *darraign*, *darreine*, *darreine the battle* Chauc. = fight it out, let the battle decide, *darreine by battle* = settle, but *darraign your battle* (Shaksp. H. VI) = array. It is from *derationare*, *rationes* = accounts, whence *aresner arraigner arraign* to call to account, *darraign* &c. to clear the account, settle the controversy.

Dessein, dessin, dessiner — *disegnare*.

Dessert — *serviette.*

Desso It., Wal. *dënsu* pronoun. According to Pott from *idem ipsus*, but the loss of the *m* is against all analogy. It is from the L. L. *id ipse, ille est id ipse, illa videtur id ipsa = desso, dessa* only used in the nom. case.

Dessous — *sotto.*

Dessus — *suso.*

Destare It. to awake; from *de-excitare*, Mil. *dessedà*. Cf. *dorare* from *deaurare.*

Destriero It., Pr. O.Fr. O.E. *destrier* a war-horse, L. L. *dextra-rius*, so called because led by the esquire on the *right* of his own horse, v. Ducange.

Destrozar — *torso.*

Deaver derver O. Fr. to be out of one's senses, rave; O. Fr. adj. *desvé dervé* frantic, sbst. *desverie derverie* madness. Fr. *endéver* to rage, rant, *faire endéver* to vex; prob. from *desipere*, with change of conjugation.

Dételer — *teler.*

Détraquer — *trac.*

Détresse Fr., Pr. *detreissa*, E. *distress*. Not from *destrictus*, Pr. *destreit*, whence It. *distrettezza* is regularly formed, but from a verb *destreissar* to *distress* L. L. *destrictiare*. The L. L. *distringere* (Fr. *distraindre*, E. *distrain*) was used for constraining a person to do something by exaction of a pledge &c. Hence *distrain for rent*. The pledge was termed *districtio distress*. The right of exercising such authority, and the territory over which it was exercised, were called *districtus*, It. *distretto*, O. Fr. *destroict*, E. *district.*

Détrier — *trigar.*

Détroit — *étroit.*

Dette Fr., E. *debt*: from pl. *debita*, Sp. *deuda.*

Deuil — *cordoglio.*

Devant — *anzi.*

Dovanar — *dipanare.*

Dévider — *vide.*

Devis — *diviso.*

Dévouer — *voeu.*

Dexar Sp., Pg. *deixar* to leave, from a form *desitare des'tare (desinere desitus)*. Cf. *quexar.*

Diamante It. Sp., Pr. *diaman*, Fr. *diamant*, E. *diamond*; from *adamas adamantis*, prob. influenced by *diafano* transparent. Another form is the Pr. *adiman, aziman, aiman*, O.Fr. *aimant*, Fr. *aimant*, Sp. Pg. *iman* a magnet, in which sense L. L. *adamas* was used.

Diana It. the morning-star, prop. *stella diana*, from an old adj.

11*

diuno (dies), whence the expression *battere la diana,* Fr. *battre la diane* to beat the reveille (milit.).

Diane — *diana.*

Diante — *anzi.*

Diantre Fr. interj., corrupted from *diable,* Rh. *dianser.*

Diansi — *anzi.*

Diapré — *diaspro.*

Diaspro It., Sp. *diaspero* a jasper; from *jaspis,* cf. It. (prov.) *diacere* from *jacere.* O. Fr. *diaspré diaspé* flowered stuff, Fr. *diapré* variegated, diapered, whence E. *diaper.*

Dicha Sp., Pg. *dita* luck; from *dictum,* pl. *dicta,* cf. *fatum* from *fari.* So also It. *detta.*

Die O. Fr., Pr. *dia* = henchman, feudal dependant? Prob. from the O. H. G. *deo* (for *theo, thio* = Goth. *thius,* A. S. *theov*) with a term. in *a* (like *bada, crida, uca, sira*) to distinguish it from derivatives of *Deus.*

Dieta It. Sp., Fr. *diéte,* E. *diet;* from *diaeta* (δίαιτα).

Dieta It. Sp., Fr. *diéte,* E. *diet* = day of assembly, then the assembly itself; from *dies,* cf. *dietim* L. L. for *quotidie.*

Dietro — *retro.*

Diga It., Fr. *digue,* Sp. *dique* a dam for stopping water; from Du. *dyk,* A. S. *dic,* E. *dike* (= ditch), v. Wedg. *dike.*

Dilayer — *delai.*

Dileggiare It. to deride = Pr. *desleyar* to decry, subst. *deslei* = *dis-lex.*

Dileguare It., Pr. *deslegar,* Fr. *délayer,* O. E. *delay,* to dilute; from *dis-liquare.* The Sp. *desleir* is prob. a corruption of the Pr. *deslegar.* The O. E. *delay* often = allay, cf. Surrey: the watery showers *delay* the raging wind; Holland speaks of the *delaying* of wines.

Dimanche — *domenica.*

Dinde Fr. a turkey-hen, *dindon* a turkey-cock; from *coq d'Inde* the Indian (American) bird, Cat. *gall diudi, indiot.*

Diner - *desinare.*

Dinero — *denaro.*

Dintel — *linde.*

Dio It., Sp. *dios,* O. Pg. Sard. *déus,* Pg. *déos (deós),* Pr. *diéu,* Fr. *dieu* (O. Fr. *deo*). In the South West *deus* was treated as a proper name, cf. Carlos, Marcos, Reynaldos &c. The anomalous pl. *dioses* is also found. Such anomalies are usual in sacred names, cf. It. *gli dei* and v. Grimm 1, 1071, Dief. 2, 416. The Wal. for God is *dumne-zeu* = It. *domeneddio,* Pr. *dame-dieu,* O. Fr. *dame-dieu, dombre-dieu.* From *domeneddio* comes the It. *iddio* for *eddio,* cf. *iguale* for *equale.* It. *addio* = Sp. *á dios,* Fr. *adieu,* Pr. *a dieu siatz,* O. Fr. *a dieu soyez,*

O. Cat. *a deu siau.* It. *madio,* Sp. *madios,* Fr. *maidieu* = *m'aide dieu,* O. Fr. *si m'ait dieus* = ita deus me adjuvet.

Dipanare It., Pr. *debanar,* Sp. *devanar* to wind off; from *panus* a bunch of wool for spinning.

Dirupare It., Pg. *derrubar,* Sp. *derrumbar* to precipitate from a rock *(rupes);* hence *dirupo* a precipice, O. Fr. *desrube, desruble,* also *desrubant* defile, Pr. *deruben;* O. Fr. *desrubison;* Sp. *derrubio* a fall of earth on the banks of a river, also = an overflow of water.

Discolo It. Sp. Pg. unruly, froward; from δύσχολος.

Disognare designare It. (1) to point out, mark out, (2) to draw, Sp. *designar,* O. Sp. *deschar,* Pr. *desegnar designar,* Fr. *designer,* E. *design* = (1), Sp. *diseñar,* Fr. *dessiner,* E. *design* = (2); abst. It. *disegno,* Sp. *diseño designio,* Fr. *dessein* = E. *design* (in both senses). From L. *designare.*

Disette Fr. want; from *desecta.*

Disfidare sfidare It., Pr. *desfizar,* Fr. *défier,* Sp. Pg. *desafiar,* O. Pg. *desfiar,* E. *defy* = to retract one's confidence *(fides)* in a person, to renounce, disclaim, cf. Henry IV, 1, 3. "All studies here I solemnly *defy.*"

Disfrasar — *farsa.*

Disio It., Sp. *deseo,* Pg. *desejo,* Pr. *desig* a longing; vb. *desiare* &c. Not from *desiderium,* but from *dissidium* (cf. Cat. *desilj*), so, like Pg. *saudade,* prop. = separation, then = the consequent longing.

Ditello It. the armpit = *ditale* a thimble, Rom. *didel,* O. Fr. *deel,* Fr. *deau* (prov.) *dé.* For *ditello* Neap. has *tetelleca,* from *tellecare* to tickle.

Diva — *da.*

Diviso It., Pr. Fr. *devis,* E. *device* plan, contrivance, It. *divisa,* Sp. *divisa devisa,* Fr. *devise,* E. *device* a distinction, distinguishing mark, cognisance; It. *divisare,* Sp. *divisar* to divide, arrange, dispose (O. Fr. *deviser*), E. *devise.* From *dividere,* Pr. *devire,* whence freq. *divisar.* Wedgw. makes 2 words (1) = a badge &c. from *dividere* (2) = a plan &c. from *viso (visum)* view, opinion. The expression *à point devise,* E. *point device,* = in a condition of ideal excellence, such as one can *devise* or imagine.

Docciare It. to *douse,* pour water on, abst. *doccia,* Fr. *douche,* Sp. *ducha* a spout &c., from *ductiare (ductus)* as *succiare* from *suctus.* Cf. *ductus* = O. Fr. *duit (conduit),* Norm. *doui,* from *ductio,* Pr. *dotz,* O. Fr. *dois,* whence *dusil,* E. *dosil* a spigot. But Wedgw. derives *doccia* &c. from (I. *docke,* E. *dock* a bunch, tap, whence the sense of spout, conduit &c. From Gael. *dos* a tuft, E. *doss* a hassock, *dossel* a plug; E. *dosil* a tent for a wound prob. from Fr. *dusil.*

Dodu — *dondon.*

Doga It. Pr. Cat., Wal. *doagē*, Alb. *dogē*, Fr. *douve*, Mil. *dore* the stave of a cask, Du. *duyghe*, *duig*, Sw. *dauge*, G. *daube* staff; hence Sp. *dovela ducla*, Pg. *aduela*, Norm. *douvelle douelle*, Lor. *doule.* The Pr. *doga*, Norm. *douve* also = a dam, a bank: L. L. *douvam sive aggerem* (Carpentier). It. *doga* = also a stripe, It. *dogare* to gird (Dante), Sp. *dogal* a halter, from the notion of hemming in, confining, like the staves of a barrel. Gregory of Tours has *doga* in the sense of conduit: *ne forte dogis oecultis lymphæ deducerentur.* From *doga* in Lat. = a vessel (Vopiscus) = Gk. δοχή a receptacle. From this it would come to mean a dam for holding in water, the staving of a cask, a stave. Wedgw. derives it from a different source, viz. the G. *docke*, E. *dock* a bunch, a plug, a stopple, a tap, whence *dock* an inclosed basin which keeps out the water by great *flood-gates.* From the sense of plug comes (1) that of dam (*doga*, *douve* &c.), (2) that of conduit (*doga*, *doccia*, *douche* &c.).

Dogana It., Pr. *doana*, Fr. *douane*, Sp. Pg. *aduana*, customhouse, excise, toll. From the Arab. *divân ad-divân* a statecouncil (for excise), whence *diuana doana duana* with inserted *g* in It., ph. with a reference to *doga* a cask-stave. The Sp. *duan* = *divân.* Or it may be from *divan* in the sense of an account-book, Freyt. 2, 74, cf. Boccaccio Dec. 8, 10: *i doganieri poi serivono in sul libro della dogana* &c.

Doge — *duca.*

Dolequin O. Fr. a short dagger; from M. Du. *dolekin*, dim. of *dolk*, G. *dolch.*

Domani — *mani.*

Dôme — *duomo.*

Domenica It., Sp. Pg. *domingo*, Pr. *dimenge dimergue*, Fr. *dimanche* sunday; It. from *dominica*, Sp. from *dominicus*, Pr. Fr. from *dies dominica*, whence O. Fr. *diemenche* = Gk. κυριακή.

Dominio It. Sp. Pg. lordship, possession, Fr. *domaine* (m.), E. domain, Pr. *domaine domeni*, O.Fr. also *demaine demenie*, E. demain demesne, O. It. *diminio*; from *dominium*, *ai* from *i* as in *daigner* from *dignari.* O.Fr.adj. *demaine*=own, L. L. *demainius.*

Dommage Fr., O. Fr. Wal. E. *damage*, Pr. *dampnatge*; from *damnum.*

Donaire Sp. Pg. grace, elegance, prop. = natural gift, from *donarium.* Adj. *donoso* graceful, from *don* = *donum.*

Donc — *dunque.*

Donde — *onde.*

Dondolare It. to rock, E. *dandle.* From the same root as the Fr.*dodiner dodeliner*, from *dodo* a word used in rocking children to sleep. *Dodo* is a child's word formed by reduplication from *dormir.* Wedgw. connects these words with E. *dade* = to teach a child to walk, *dading* strings = It. *dande*, Fr. *dada* = a child's hobby-horse; hence *daddle doddle diddle toddle*, with nasal *dande*, *dondle*, *dondeliner dodeliner* to rock, *dandiner* It. *dondolare* dandle, idle, *dandolo* a ninny, *dandolo dandola* a toy, doll, E. *dandy*, Sc. *dandilly.*

Dondon Fr. f. a plump woman; from E. *dump* in *dump-ling*, *dump-ty (donde)*. *Dondon* is connected with *bedon* (q. v.) *dondaine* = *bedondaine.* Perhaps *dodu* may be also referred hither, though the loss of the nasal is unusual.

Dongeon donjon Fr., Pr. *donjo*, E. *donjon*, *dungeon*, a strong lofty building in a fort, so called from its commanding the rest, *dominio domnio dongeo* (as *songer* from *somniare*) *donjon.* But Diez rejects this derivation, and refers the word to the Irish *dun* a fortified place (v. *duna*) whence *dunion*, O. Fr. *dognon donjon.* Zeuss 1, 30 gives as the orig. form *dangio* Fr. *daingean.* V. Murat. 2, 500.

Donno donna It., Sp. *don doña dueña*, Pg. *dom dona*, Pr. *don* (fem. *dons*), *dombre* (in *dombre-dieus*) *domna*, O. Fr. masc. *dame* (in *dame-dieu*) *dan dant*, O. E. *dan*, O. Fr. Fr. fem. *dame* (whence Pr. Fr. Sp. *dama*), Wal. *domn doamnĕ;* from *dominus domina* in inscriptions *domnus domna*, L. L. *donnus donna.* Hence Sp. *doncel doncella*, Pr. *donsel donsella*, O. Fr. *donciaus* (nom.) *dancel danzel* (oblique cases), *damoisiel, damoiseau, damoisele*, Fr. *demoiselle*, hence It. *damigello damigella*, Sp. Pr. *damisela*, as if from a L. *dominicillus*, Wal. *domnisor.* Vb. Pr. *domneiar*, O. Fr. *donoier* to court women, whence It. *donneare*, sbst. *domnei donnoi.* For the Fr. *a* = *o*, cf. *damesche* from *domesticus*, *danter (daunt)* from *domitare.* From *domen* for *domin* comes the Prov. and Cat. abbreviation *en*, used before proper names, e.g. *En Barral* (O. It. *Imberal*), from *domna Na* as *Na Maria* &c. For the degradation in meaning of *damoiseau* and *donzelle* in O. Fr. cf. *valet* (Berr. *valet* = a help), *vassal, varlet. Mesquin*, on the contrary, orig. = poor wretch, came to be used of *young* persons even of highest rank, the idea of youth being got from that of weakness, wretchedness.

Donnola It. a weasel; prop. = little woman, from *donna*, cf. Sp. *comadreja*, G. *jüngferchen*, M. Gr. νυμφύτα, Basq. *andereigerra* from *andrea* a woman. Cf. *bele.* The name was derived from the character usu. assigned to the weasel in the fables.

Dont — *onde.*

Dopo — *poi.*

Doppiere It. a taper; from *duplus*, the which being formed of double thread, cf. G. *zwirn* from *zwir.*

Dorca doro Pr. a jug; from *orca*, v. R. Gr. 1, 264.

Dorelot O. Fr. a darling, Fr. *doreloter dorloter* to fondle; from
A.S. *deórling*, E. *darling*, or from W. *dorlawd*, *dawr* dear and
llawd a boy.

Dorénavant Fr. = *dehine*; from *de hora in ab ante*.

Dorna Pr. a pot, N. Pr. *dourno*; from *urna*, cf. *dorca* from *orca*.
Hence Sp. *dornajo dornilla* a trough.

Dosel — *dais*.

Dossiere — *dais*.

Dotta — *otta*.

Douaire — *douer*.

Douane — *dogana*.

Douche — *docciare*.

Doudo Pg. a ninny; from the Eng. *doll*, *dold*, A. S. *dol*, connected with G. *tölpel*.

Douer Fr. to *endow*; from *dotare*; *douaire* (m.) Pr. *doari*, E.
dower dowry; *douairière* a widow who has a jointure, E.
dowager.

Douille doille O. Fr. weak; from *ductilis*, Pr. *ductil* &c.; Fr.
dim. *douillet* (not from *dulcis*).

Douille Fr. a tap, L. L. *ductile* a channel; cf. Com. *indoja* a
husk, from *inductile*, v. *andouille*. From *ducere* also comes
Fr. *dusil* a spigot, E. *dosel*, but v. *doga*, *docciare* for another
derivation.

Dour O. Fr., Pr. *dorn* of a hand's breadth, It. *dorone*; from the
Celtic, Gael. *dórn*, W. *dwrn*, Bret. *dorn* a hand. Pliny Nat.
Hist. 35, 14: *tegulæ apud Gallos didoron dictæ a longitudine
duorum palmorum*, *di* = Gael. *da* or *de*, W. *dau dwi*, Bret.
daou div two.

Douve — *doga*.

Dove — *ove*.

Dovela — *doga*.

Doyen dean; from *decanus*.

Dragée — *treggea*.

Drageon Fr. a shoot, sprig; from Goth. *draibjan* to push, O. H.
G. *treihjan* (Fr. *ge* = *bj*, cf. Rom. Gr. 1, 166), cf. *bouton* from
bouter, *pousse* from *pousser*.

Dragomanno It., Sp. *dragoman*, Fr. *drogman*, M. H. G. *trage-
munt*, E. *dragoman* an interpreter, also It. *turcimanno*, Sp.
trujaman, Fr. *trucheman truchement*, O. E. *truchman*; from Ar.
targomán, *torgómán* an interpreter, from *targama* to explain,
Chald. *targum* a translation.

Drague Fr. brewer's grains; from N. *dragg*, E. *dreg dregs*, which
Wedgw. connects with E. *draff*, G. *träber* brewer's grains, Pr.
draco dregs of the vintage, *drasche drêche* draff, husks (this
last, however, Diez derives from O.H.G. *drescan*, G. *dreschen*

to *thrash*), O. E. *drast drest*, G. *trestern*, A. S. *dresten* fæces, also A. S. *dros* fæx, whence E. *dross*.

Drague Fr., E. *drag* (for water).

Drappo It., Pr. Cat. Fr. *drap* cloth, whence *drappello*, *drapeau* a rag, a banner, L. L. *drappus*, Fr. *draper*, *drapier*, E. *drape*, *draper*. In Sp. and Pg. it has the tenuis: *trapo*, *trupaijo*, *trapero*, *traperia*, but also *drapero*, and *gualdrape* = *trappings* of a horse, *gualdrapazo* flap of the sail against the mast, *gualdrapear* to flap. Frisch derives from *trappen* to tread, so of closely-trodden or woven stuff (Sp. *trapa* = stamping), but ph. better from *trap* the sound of a *flapping* piece of cloth.

Drasche — *drague*.

Dredré — *trillare*.

Dresser — *rizzare*.

Dridviller — *trillare*.

Drille Fr. (m.) comrade; from O. H. G. *drigil* lad, servant, fellow, O. N. *thræll*, E. *thrall*, v. Grimm 3, 321.

Drille Fr. (f.)

Drizzare — *rizzare*.

Droga It. Sp. Pg. Pr., Fr. *drogue*, E. *drug* spices, aromatics &c., so called from their hot, dry nature, Du. *droog* dry, dried goods.

Drogman — *dragomanno*.

Droit — *ritto*.

Drôle Fr. facetious, droll; not found in the Fr. dictionaries of the 16th century. It is the same word as the E. *droll*, G. *drollig*, cf. Du. *drol*, O. N. *drioli*, Gael. *droll* a blunt, awkward man.

Dromon O. Fr. a large ship of war, O. N. *drômundr*, M. H. G. *tragmunt dragmunt* (but v. *dragomanno*); from *dromo* δρόμων "*genus navigii velocissimi*" Fulgent. Plancus. Pr. *dromô* = a platform. Wal. *drom* a street, course, from δρόμος.

Drudo druda It. O. Pg., Pr. O. Fr. *drut druda drue* a friend, a lover; hence O. Fr. *drugim druiun* intimate. The word is found both in the Celtic and the Teutonic: Gael. *druth* a harlot, O. H. G. *drùt trùt*, *drùd* (in comp. *Drudbald*, *Wieldrud*) friend, lover, fem. *triutin* (all related to *triuwi*, G. *treu*, *true*). In Rom. it is often found in connection with *ami* "mes amis et mes *drus*" &c. There is also an adj. It. *drudo* beloved, pretty, also = gallant, Fr. *dru* sprightly, wanton, luxuriant, vb. *endruir* to make thick, dense, Gen. *druo* thick, fat, *drueza* abundance, Piedm. N. Pr. *dru* luxuriant, fruitful. The adj. is best referred to the Gael. *drùth* wanton, W. *drud* vigorous.

Duca It., Wal. *ducë*, Sp. Pg. *duque*, Pr. Fr. *duc*, E. *duke*; It. *ducato*, Sp. Pg. *ducado*, Pr. *ducat*, Fr. *duché* (in O. Fr. fem. whence It. *ducea*) E. *duchy*, L. L. *ducatus* for *ductus*. *Duca* is not immediately from *dux*, which would have *doce* (Ven. *doge*), but from the Byzantine δούξ, δούχα, v. Ducange. From *duca* come It. *ducato ducatone*, Sp. *ducado ducaton*, Fr. G. *ducat*, first used c. 1140 by Roger II. of Sicily who held the duchy of Apuglia *(ducato d'Apuglia)*.

Ducha — *docciare*.

Duela — *doga*.

Duello It., Sp. *duelo*, Fr. E. *duel*; from *duellum*. The word introduced into the Rom. at a late period, and was adopted from a mistaken notion of the etymology of the L. word. *Battaglia* was used previously.

Duendo Sp., Pg. *dondo*, Pr. *domde* domestic, tame, vb. Pr. *domtar dondar*, O. Fr. *donter*, Fr. *dompter* (E. *daunt*); from *domitus domitare*. Hence, too, Sp. Pg. *duende* a fairy, ghost, prop. house-ghost (Sp. *duende de casa*). The words are not derived from *domus*.

Duiro O. Fr. Pr. to lead, instruct, pf. *duist*, part. *dozen*, O. Fr. Pr. adj. *duit* clever, sbst. *duison* neatness; from *ducere (duist = duril)*, cf. Sp. *ducir = duire, ducho = duit* and cf. G. *ziehen*, L. *educare*.

Duna It. Sp., from Fr. *dune* a sand-hill; from Dn. *duin* = A. S. *dùn* (f.), E. *down, don* in names of places, which from the Celtic, Fr. *dùn*, W. *din* a hill, a strong place *(dinas* a city), whence *dunum* in *Augustodunum, Lugdunum* = Ravenhill &c. The root of the Celtic words is in the Ir. *dunaim*, Gael. *duin* to shut in, surround, thus showing a community of origin with the G. *zaun*, O. H. G. *zim*, O. S. *tùn tyne* enclosure, O. N. *tùn* (E. *town*, O. E. *tune*) from G. source, A. S. *tynan* to enclose. V. Mahn, Diefenbach.

Dunque adunque It., O. It. *donqua adonqua, dunche adunche*, O. Sp. *doncas*, Fr. *donc* particle for L. *ergo*. O. Fr. *dunc, donques adunc*, Pr. *donc adonc* = L. *tum*; whence sense of "ergo", cf. *igitur* = inde and postea, Festus, E. *then*, Sp. *pues, luego. Adunc* is the orig. from for *a* or *ad* and *tunc. A tunc* and *ad tunc* are found in old documents.

Duomo It. a cathedral, = the house *(domus)* "par excellence", Fr. *dôme*, E. *dome* = cupola, most of the churches in Italy being built with cupolas.

Dupe Fr. (f.), E. *dupe*, vb. *duper, dupe*. Frisch connects it with the Swab. *düppel* a blockhead; Wedgw. makes it from *dupe duppe* a hoopoe (so called from the tuft on its head), cf. It. *bubbola* a hoopoe, *bubbolare* to cheat (E. *bubble?*).

Durare It., Sp. *durar*, Fr. *durer*, E. *dure*, G. *dauern* to hold out; from *durare* to harden, for which *indurare* was used.

Durazno Sp. a peach; from *persica duracina*, cf. It. *duracine* firm (of fruit).

Dureta Sp. a bathing-chair. Suet. August. 82; *insidens ligneo* *solto, quod ipse hispanico verbo duretam vocabat.* Larramendi refers it to the Basq. *ura* water.

Durfeü O. Fr. wretched, pitiable; from *dure fatatus* (cf. *malfeü* = Pr. *malfadat*, Sp. *malfadado*) with a substitution of the suffix *utus* for *atus*.

Dusil — *douille.*

Dusque — *jusque.*

Duvet Fr. *down* of feathers, O. Fr. *dum*, Provin. E. *dum*, Norm. *dumet*, L. L. *duma*, from O. N. *dún*. *Duvet* is a corruption of *dumet.*

E.

Ea Sp., Pg. *eia*, Sic. *eja jeja* interj., Lat. *eja*, O.Fr.*aye*, Basq. *ea.*

Eau Fr. (f.) water; from *aqua*, O. Fr. *aigue*, *eve* (cf. *yve* from *equa*), whence *évier* a vase, O. Fr. *aiguiére*, E. *ewer (aquarium)*, from *eve, iere iave eawe eau* (so *bel biel bial beau*). Gris. *awa.*

Ébahir — *bahir.*

Ébaubi Fr. astounded; from an old vb. *ébaubir abaubir*; from *balbus*, O. Fr. *baube*, prop. to make to stammer.

Ébaucher — *bauche.*

Ebbio It., Sp. *yedgo yezgo*, Pg. *engo*, Pr. *evol*, Fr. *hièble* (*h* asp.), Berr. *géble*, Ven. *gévalo* dwarf-elder; from *ebulus*. Sp. *d* for *t* as in *sendos* from *singulos.*

Ebbriaco imbriaco ubbriaco briaco It., O. Sp. *embriáco*, Pr. *ebriac*, Fr. (Berr.) *ebriat imbriat*; from L. *ebriacus* (Plautus) formed like *meracus* from *merus*. Hence Pr. *abriga*, Fr. *ivraie* darnel.

Èbe Fr. (f.) ebb; from Du. *ebbe*, E. *ebb.*

Éblouir Fr. to dazzle, Pr. *esbalauzir* for *esblauzir* to stun, *emblauzir* to dazzle. From O. H. G. *blôdi* weak, dull (Sc. *blait*, E. *blunt*), *blôdi* bluntness, whence G. *blöde, blödsichtig* weak-sighted. The O.H.G. verb was *blôdan*, Pr. *blauzir* = a Goth. *blauthjan.*

Ébranler — *brando.*

Ébrouer — *braro.*

Écaille écale — *scaglia.*

Écarlate — *scarletto.*

Écarter — *scartare.*

Ecco It., Wal. *eacě*, Pr. *ec*, O.Fr. *eke* an adv. from *eccum*, often with pronouns; It. *eccomi, eccoti, eccolo, eccola, eccoci* &c., Wal. *eacěmě*, Pr.*ecvos*, O. Fr. *ekevos*; Sp. *ele, elo, ela* (for *ec-le* &c.). Pr. *vec* = *ve* (imper. of *vezer*, L. *vide*) and *ec*, whence *vecvos, veus*; so, too, It. *vecco reccolo*. From *ecce* is Pg. *eis*,

O. Fr. *eis es ez* whence a verbal plur. *estes-vos*, cf. *eglino*. For other combinations cf. *qua, quello, questo, qui.*

Échafaut — *catafalco.*

Échalas Fr. a wine-prop, O. Fr. *escaras*, Pic. *écarats*, Borr. *charisson*, Piedm. *scaras.* From L. L. *curratium* (with prefix *es*), which from Gk. χάραξ (Wal. *hërác*).

Échalier Fr. a hedge, paling. From *scala*, from its resembling a series of ladders.

Échandole Fr. shingle; from *scandula*, Lorr. *chondre*, Wal. *scéndure*.

Échanson — *escanciar.*

Échantillon Fr. a sample, Rouch. *écautillou* a rule, ruler (Sp. *escantillon descautillon*), E. *scantling* = the dimensions of a piece of timber in breadth and thickness. From O. Fr. *cant chant* corner, piece &c. (v. *canto*), O. Fr. *eschantelet* = *chant.*

Échapper — *scappare.*

Échar — *gettare.*

Écharde — *cardo.*

Écharpe — *sciarpa.*

Échars — *scarso.*

Échasse Fr. stilts, O. Fr. *eschace*, Rouch. *écache*; from Du. *schaats*, E. *skate.*

Échaugette Fr. a watch-tower, O. Fr. *eschargaite eschirgaite* a spy, *eschargaitier* to watch; from G. *schaar-wacht* a night-patrol, also a watchman. The Fr. *échaugette* is a corruption of *escharguete eschalguete.*

Écheo — *scacco.*

Échemer — *sciame.*

Écheveau Fr. strong thread or yarn. Ph. from *scapus* = a twist or roll of paper, so = a skein or hank of thread (O. Fr. *eschevete*).

Échevin — *scabino.*

Échine — *schiena.*

Échiqueté échiquier — *scacco.*

Échome — *scalmo.*

Échoppe Fr.; from O. H. G. *schupfa*, G. *schuppen*, E. *shop*, Wal. *şopru.*

Échouer Fr. to strand, *déchouer* to set a float. From *caules?*

Éclair Fr. lightning; from *éclairer*, L. *exclarare*, like *fulmen* and *fulgur* from *fulgere*, Champ. *lumer* to lighten from *lumen.*

Éclater — *schiantare.*

Éclisse — *clisse.*

Éclore — *chiuderc.*

Écluse — *esclusa.*

Écope Fr. a water-can, from Sw. *skopa.*

Écorce écorcer — *scorza.*

Écorcher — *corteccia*.

Écore Fr. a steep part of the shore; from O. H. G. *scorro* a rock, A. S. *score*, E. *shore*, Du. *schorre schore*, cf. Gael. *sgòr*.

Écornifler Fr. to spunge (as a parasite), Norm. to pilfer; = *écorner (cornu)* to break off the horns or ends, to pinch off.

Écosse — *cosse*.

Écot — *scotto*.

Écoufle Fr. a kite (bird), Norm. a flying-dragon; O. Fr. *escofre escoufre* from G. *schupfer* (from *schupfen*) a missile. So, conversely, projectiles had their names from birds of prey (v. *terzuolo*).

Écourgée — *scuriada*.

Écouter — *ascoltare*.

Écouvillon Fr. a duster or small broom, Sp. *escovillon*; from *scopa*.

Écran Fr. a screen; from O. H. G. *scrauna*, E. *screen*.

Écraser to crush; a Norman word, from O. N. *krassa*, Sw. *krasa* bruise, E. *crash*. An onomatopœion.

Écrevisse Fr. a crab, O. Fr. *escrevisse* also armour, O. E. *creveys*, *crerish*, corrupted *craw-fish*; from O. H. G. *krebiz*, Du. *krevisse*, *krevitse*, G. *krebs*, Rouch. *grariche*, Wall. *grevess*, with *s* prefixed (perhaps from *scarabæus*). So called from the grabbing action of the animal, Sp. *escarbar* to scrabble, *escarabajo* beetle *(scarabæus)*, *escarabisse* a crayfish.

Écrou Fr. (m.) screw; from G. *schraube*, E. screw.

Écrouelles Fr. (f. pl.) scrofula; from *scrofella (scrofula)* a swelling in the throat.

Écu Fr. shield; from *scutum*, It. *scudo* &c., whence *écuyer*, Pr. *escudier*, It. *scudiere*, E. *esquire*, Fr. *écusson*, E. *escutcheon* (from a form *scutio* as from *arcus arcio arçon*).

Écueil — *scoglio*.

Écuelle Fr., Pr. *escudela*, E. *scull (scullion, scullery)* dish; from *scutella*, It. *scodella* &c.

Écume — *schiuma*.

Écurer — *sgurare*.

Écureuil — *scojattolo*.

Écurie Fr., *escuria escura* Pr. a stable; from O. H. G. *scùra skiura*, L. L. *scuria*, G. *scheuer*, whence also Wal. *suré*, Hung. *tsür*. Hence E. *equerry*. W. connects these words wrongly with *écuyer* (v. *écu*).

Écusson écuyer — *écu*.

Edera ellera It., Sp. *hiedra*, Pg. *hera*, Pr. *edra*, Fr. *lierre* (O. Fr. Pic. *hierre yerre* with the article, cf. *lendemain* &c., Neap. *lellira*, Gen. *lellua*) ivy; from *hedera*.

Effacer — *faccia*.

Effarer Fr. to perplex, surprise; not from *efferare*, but from *ferus* = shy, timid, cf. *farouche* from *ferox*, Pr. *esferar* to scare.

Effondrer — *fondo*.

Effrayer effroi — *frayeur*.

Effronté — *affrontare*.

Égarer — *garer*.

Eglantier — *aiglent*.

Egli It., O. It. *ello el*, Sp. *el*, O. Sp. *elle elli*, Pg. *elle*, O. Pg. *el elli*, Pr. *el elh*, Fr. *il*, Wal. *el*. Partly from *ille*, partly from *illic* (= *ille* Terence). It. Pr. Fr. Wal. *lui*, from *illujus* or from *illuic*, v. Rom. Gr. 2, 66; fem. It. Pr. Wal. *lei*, O. Fr. *lei* and *lié*, from *illae* or *illaec* for *illi*; pl. It. *loro*, Pr. Wal. *lor*, Fr. *leur*, from *illorum* (Sard. *insoru* = *ipsorum*). In It. pl. *eglino*, *elleno*, *no* is a verbal suffix: *egli-no*, *canta-no*.

Égout Fr. sewer; from *égouter* to drip, cf. Pr. *goteira*, Fr. *goutière* = *égout*.

Égraffigner — *greffe*.

Égratigner — *grattare*.

Égruger — *gruger*.

Eis ele — *ecco*.

Eissurar — *sauro*.

Eissernir — *scernere*.

Élaguer Fr. to prune, or thin trees. From O. H. G. *lah* incisio arborum, or from Du. *laecken* to lessen, impair. With *lah* is connected G. *leck*, our *leak*.

Élan — *laucia*.

Élan Fr., E. *eland*, from G. *elen-thier*, from O. H. G. *elaho*, M. H. G. *elch*, E. *elk*.

Elce It., Pr. *euze*, Fr. *yeuse* holm-oak, from *ilex*; It. *leccio*, from *ilicius*, *leccelo* from *ilicelum*. Another form of *elce* is It. *elcina*, Sp. *encina*, Pg. *enzinha aziuho*, *azinheira*, Pr. *olzina*.

Elohe Sp. Pg. an apostate; from Ar. *elg* a proselyte.

Électuaire — *lattovaro*.

Élingue — *slinga*.

Elissire It., Sp. E. *elixir*, Fr. *élixir*; from Ar. *al* and *iksir* the philosopher's stone, elixir, essence; cf. Chauc. "*The Philosopher's stone, Elexir cleped*".

Ella — *enola*.

Elmo It. Pg. O. Sp., Sp. *yelmo*, Pr. *elm*, Fr. *heaume* (*h* asp.); from O. H. G. *helm*, O. N. *hialmr*, Goth. *hilms*, E. *helm*. In O. Pg. the word meant "a covering" generally. Sp. Pg. *almete* for *elmete* = O. Fr. *healmet*, E. *helmet*; hence Fr. *armet* head-piece.

Eloendro — *oleandro*.

Elsa elso It. hilt; from O. H. G. *helza* hilt. O. Fr. *helt* (*h* asp.), also *heux* (nom.), O. N. *hiolt*, A. S. E. *hilt* (n.), whence vb. *enheldir.*

Émail — *smalto.*

Embair — *baire.*

Embalde — *baldo.*

Embarazo — *barra.*

Embargar Sp. Pg. Cat. to arrest, lay an embargo on, sbst. *embargo, embarc* a seizure; from *barra* (q. v.) a bar, whence It. *imbarricare.*

Embarras — *barra.*

Embaucar — *bava.*

Embaucher — *bauche.*

Embaxada — *ambasciata.*

Embeleñar — *beleño.*

Emblaver — *biado.*

Embler O. Fr., Pr. *emblar* to steal; from *involare* = *volato rapere* (Petron. &c.), L. L. *imbulare,* It. *involare,* Flor. *imbolare,* Grix. *ingular angular.* Shortened from *involare* in Fr. *voler.*

Embora — *ora.*

Emborcar — *volcar.*

Embraser — *bragia.*

Embronc O. Fr. Pr. bent, bowed, pensive, sad, Val. *enbronch* crooked, Pic. *embron* awkward, vb. *embroncher,* Burg. *rembroncher,* O. Sp. *broncar* to bend. From *pronus? embronc* = *impronicatus?* But in O. Fr. Pr. the vb. is used of covering, esp. the face. Wedgw. derives the E. phrase "brown study" from Fr. *embron,* which he refers to *broncio* anger, grief (q. v.), *imbronciare* = *embroncher.*

Embudo — *imbuto.*

Embusquer — *bosco.*

Embuste — *busto.*

Embutir Sp. Pg. Cat. to inlay, impress; from the same G. root as *botar* (v. *battare*), cf. M. H. G. *buz* a blow.

Émeraude — *smeraldo.*

Éméri — *smeriglio.*

Émérillon — *smerlo.*

Émeute — *meute.*

Émoi — *smagare.*

Émousser — *mozzo.*

Empachar — *pacciare.*

Empan — *spanna.*

Emparar emparer — *parare.*

Empecer O. Sp. Pg. to injure, with dat. or acc.; for *empedecer* from *impedire,* or, better, for *emperdecer* (*perda*).

Empêcher — *pacciare.*

Empeguntar — *pegar.*

Empeine Sp. tetter; from *impetigo*, It. *empetiggine*, Wal. *pecin-yine*. For *empeine* == groin, cf. *pettine*.

Empeltar Pr. Cat. to graft, sbst. Cat. *empelt*, Pr. *enpeut*, O. Fr. *enpeau* a graft; from *pellis* (= bark), or, better, from dim. Pr. *peleta* (E. *pell*, Fr. *pelletier*), so *empeletar* == to insert in the bark, E. *pelzen*.

Empeser empois — *peyar*.

Empêtrer — *pastoja*.

Empezar — *cominciare*.

Empiffrer — *pipa*.

Emplasto — *piastra*.

Emplâtre — *piastra*.

Emplear — *piegare*.

Emplette Fr. a purchase; for O. Fr. *emploite*, Norm. *empleite*, from *implicitus implic'tus*, *implicare* in Rom. sense to *employ*. O. Fr. *emploiter*, Pr. *empleitar* == *implicitare*. Cf. *exploit*.

Employer — *piegare*.

Empreinte — *imprenta*.

Emprunter — *improntare*.

En — *indi*.

En sbst. — *donno*.

Encan — *incanto*.

Encauser — *inculciare*.

Enceinte — *incinta*.

Enceltar — *encentar*.

Encentar Sp., Pg. *enceitar encetar* to begin, to cut (at a meal). From *inceptare* to begin. Sp. has also *decentar*.

Encher — *henchir*.

Encia — *gengiva*.

Encima — *cima*.

Encina — *elce*.

Enclenque Sp. weak, feeble; from *clinicus* bedridden, with *en* as in *endeble* from debilis.

Enclume — *incude*.

Encombre — *colmo*.

Encono Sp., O. Sp. *enconia* malevolence; *enconar* to irritate, inflame, *enconarse* (of a wound) to fester. Ph. from Sp. *malenconia* ill-will *(melancholia)*, wrongly supposed to be compounded with *mal*.

Encore — *ora* (2).

Encre — *inchiostro*.

Endecha — *dec*.

Enderezar — *rizzare*.

Endêver — *desver*.

Endica It. the buying up of goods to sell again, also == a storehouse (Murat.); from ἐνϑήϰη.

Endilgar Sp. to load away, persuade; from *indelegare* to send to, direct to, lead.

Endillar — *relinchar*.

Endivia It. Sp. Pg. Pr., Fr. E. *endive;* from *intybus* or adj. *intybea*.

Endro — *eneldo*.

Endroit — *ritto*.

Enebro — *ginepro*.

Eneldo Sp., Pg. *endro* dill; a corruption of *anethum?*

Enfoncer — *fondo*.

Enfreindre — *fraindre*.

Enfrum enfrun O. Fr., Pr. *enfrun* greedy, *s'enfrunar* to be greedy, to gorge oneself; from *frumen* the throat, wind-pipe, with *en = in*.

Engaño — *inganno*.

Engar — *enger*.

Engarrafar — *graffio*.

Engastar — *cassa*.

Engeance — *enger*.

Enger Fr. to pester, fill, surfeit: *Nicot a engé la France de l'herbe nicotiane*. From *enecare* to plague, *en'care*, as *vindicare*, *vin'care*, *venger*. The Pg. has *engar* to throng, press on hostilely, not from G. *eng*. O. Fr. *enger* also == to increase, prevail (of diseases &c.), *la peste enge fort*, hence *engeance* a brood, not from *ingignere*. Lim. *s'endzá* to produce, Sard. *angiai* to hatch.

Engle — *inguine*.

Engloutir — *ghiotto*.

Engo — *eppio*.

Engodar — *goda*.

Engouer — *gave*.

Engrant engrande O. Fr. greedy, desirous. Prob. a corrupt form from G. E. *hunger*. Gachet makes it from an O. N. part. *angraidr* disturbed.

Engreir Sp. to make proud; from *ingredi* used trans; cf. Sp. *escurrir* trans.

Engrès O. Fr. *engrais engrois* (f. *engresse*), Pr. *engres* hot, passionate, sbst. *engresté*, vb. *s'engresser*. Perhaps from *agrestis* wild, as *engrot* from *ægrotus*. Villemarqué derives it from Bret. *enkrez inkrez* unrest, grief. So Diez. The verb *engresser* may, however, come from *increscere* in It. == to be irksome, and the rest be thence derived.

Engrimanço — *grimoire*.

Engrudo — *glu*.

Enherdir — *yerto*.

Enhiesto Sp. erect, vb. *enhestar, enfestar*. From *fastigium* (O. Pg. *festo*), so *enhiesto == in fastigio*.

Enho Pg. a one-year-old fawn; from *hinnuleus* for *enhlo?* or from *ennhus* in *bi-ennius*, cf. *cobrar*.

Enio Pr. unwilling; from *iniquus*.

Enjóler — *gabbia*.

Enlear Pg. to fetter, hindor, O. Fr. *enloier;* from the O. Fr. *enlaier* = *inligare*.

Enne O. Fr. a particle of interrogation and exclamation: from interrogative *et* and the negative particle, Lor. *enne*.

Ennodio O. Sp. a young hart; from *enodis* branchless, hornless.

Ennui — *noia*.

Enojo — *noia*.

Enquar Pr. to begin; from *inchoare*, one of the few L. words confined to the Pr.

Enqui — *qui*.

Enrouer Fr. to be hoarse; from *raucus*.

Ens O. Fr., Pr. *ins;* from *intus;* O. Fr. *dens*, Fr. *dans*, *dedans*, Pr. *dins*, *dedins*, from *de intus*, *de de intus;* O. Fr. *saiens laiens*, Pr. *sains*, *laïns* (compounded with the Rom. particles *sai* and *lai*), Fr. *céans*, *léans*. Another O. Fr. form for *dens* was *deinz*, whence *deinzein*, opp. *forein (foraneus)*, E. *denizen*.

Ensalmar Sp., Pg. *enxalmar* to enchant; from *psalmus*.

Ensalzar — *alzare*.

Ensanchar — *ancho*.

Ensayo — *saggio*.

Enseigne — *insegna*.

Enseigner — *insegnare*.

Ensemble — *insembre*.

Ensoment — *esso*.

Ensenada Sp., Pg. *enseada* bay, creek; from *sinus*, *insinuare*, Sp. *ensenar*.

Enseña — *insegnare*.

Entamer Fr., Pr. *entamenar*, Piedm. *antamnà* to cut, notch, wound. Not from ἐντέμνειν, but from L. *at-taminare* to injure, with a change of preposition (R. Gr. 2, 391), cf. *convitare* for *invitare*, *atturare* for *obturare* &c.

Ente Fr. a graft, Piedm. Parm. *enta*, Mod. *entin*, Fr. vb. *enter* to graft. From ἔμφυτον, ἐμφυτεύειν, whence also O. H. G. *impitòn*, M. H. G. *impfeten*, G. *impfen*, E. *imp.* L. L. *impotus* = ἔμφυτον, cf. *colapus = colaphus*. Others derive from *in* and Du. *poot* = foot. hence *impitus*, Bret. *em-bouden*, but this der. will not suit the Fr. form, and the Bret. may come through the O. Fr. *emboter*. Pott derives the word from *im-putare*.

Entoado — *alnado*.

Enteco Sp. infirm, sickly; from *hecticus*, O. Pg. *eteyo*, It. *etico*. For *c* = Sp. *n*, cf. *anche*.

Entejar Pg. to loath, *entejo* loathing; from *tædium*.

Entercier O. Fr. to recognise, acknowledge, *par l'ivre l'entercad = æstimavit eam temulentam* Liv. d. Rois p. 3; from *intertiare* to put in a third person's hands. This was a legal phrase, and used of a person who, detecting his lost property in the possession of another, placed it, as by law permitted, in the hands of a third, till the right owner-ship should be proved. V. Ducange.

Entero — *intero*.

Enterver — *rover*.

Entibo Sp. a prop, *entibar* to prop; from *stipes*, Basq. *estiba*.

Enticher Fr. to infect (with disease &c.); from the G. *anstecken*.

Entier — *intero*.

Enton O. Sp., Pg. *então* = L. *tum*, from *in tum*; Sp. *entonces*, O. Sp. *estonze*, O. Pg. *entonces*, from *in tuncce*, *ex tuncce*.

Entrailles Fr., Pr. *intralias*, E. *entrails*. L. *interaneum*, pl. *interanea*, whence It. *entragno*, Sp. *entrañas*, O. Fr. *entraigne*, L. L. *intrania*. The Fr. has taken the collective suffix *aille*, following the analogy of *tripaille (trippa)*.

Entraver entraves — *travar*.

Entrechat Fr. a caper; from It. *capriuola entrecciata*.

Entregar Sp. Pg. Cat. give up, deliver, *entrego* delivered up, *entrega entrego* delivery; from *integer* for *entrego*, O. Pg. *entregue* = *entero*, *enteiro* = *integer*; prop. to make reparation, restore.

Entremes Sp. interlude; from It. *inter-mezzo* = L. *inter-medium*.

Entresait O. Fr., Norm. *antresiais*, Pr. *atrasait atrasag* unconditionally, entirely. From prep. *en*, *a*, and *tresait trasait = transactus*. In O. It. *trasatto: ben è ragione che 'l nostro amore si parta in trasatto* = unconditionally. Cf. It. *trasattarsi* to appropriate, make oneself master of.

Entroido antruido O. Sp., N. Sp. *antruejo*, O. Pg. *entroydo*, Pg. *entrudo* ·the last three days of the carnival; from *introitus* (sc. of Lent).

Envahir Fr. to seize forcibly, Pr. *envazir*; from *invadere*.

Envelopper — *viluppo*.

Envie Fr. envy, desire; from *invidia*; adv. *à l'envi* in emulation, with the final vowel elided, cf. *chez* for *chese*, or for *ore*. *À l'envie* was used up to the 16th century.

Environ — *virar*.

Envis and *à envis* O. Fr. adv. against one's will, Wall. *eviss*, Burg. *anvi*; from *invitus invite*, v. Sp. *ambidos*.

Envoisier — *vezzo*.

Envoûter Fr. to curse, imprecate evil on (by means of waxen images); Ovid, *devovet absentes simulacraque cerea fingit Et miserum tenues in jecur urget acus*. From *devotare* (Apul.) for

12*·

devovere. In L.L. we find *invultare* from a mistaken reference to *vultus.*

Enxada — *accia.*

Enralma — *salma.*

Enxambre — *sciame.*

Enxarcia — *sarte.*

Enxeco O. Sp., O. Pg. *enxeco eyxeco* difficulty, harm, punishment; from Ar. *esh-shaqq* difficulty.

Enxergar — *cercare.*

Enxerir Sp., Pg. to graft; from *inserere,* as *enxertar* from *insertare.*

Enxuagar Sp. to rinse, clean; from *ex-aquare,* It. *sciacquare.*

Enxugar — *suco.*

Enxullo — *subbio.*

Enxundia Sp. fat; from *axungia* cart-grease, Fr. *axonge,* cf. *sugna.*

Enxuto — *suco.*

Envoyer — *voyer.*

Epa It. belly; from *hepar.*

Épais — *spesso.*

Épancher Fr. to pour out; from *expandicare (expandere,* It. *spandere),* cf. *pendere pendicare pencher.*

Épanouir Fr. to unfold; a form of the O. Fr. *espanir* for *espandir = espandre (expandere),* cf. *tolir = tolre;* v. *évanouir.*

Épargner — *sparagnare.*

Éparpiller — *parpaglione.*

Épaule — *spalla.*

Épave Fr. a runaway. From *expavidus.*

Épeautre — *spelta.*

Épeiche Fr. = pic, O. Fr. *espeche,* Pic. *épéque;* from O. H. G. *speh,* G. *specht* a woodpecker.

Épeler Fr. to spell, O. Fr. *espeler* to say, mean, Pr. *espelar* to explain; from Goth. *spillôn,* O. H. G. *spellôn,* E. *spell.*

Éperlan Fr. (Sp. *eperlano esperlan*) a smelt; from G. *spierling.*

Éperon — *sperone.*

Épervier — *sparaviere.*

Épice — *spezie.*

Épier — *spiare.*

Épieu Fr. a spit, O. Fr. *espieil,* from *spiculum,* as *essieu* from *axiculus.*

Épinard — *spinace.*

Épinceler épincer — *pizza.*

Épingle — *spillo.*

Éplucher — *piluccare.*

Épois — *spito.*

Épouiller — *pidocchio.*

Épouvanter — *spaventare.*

Époux — *sposo.*

Épreindre — *preindre.*

Équerre — *quadro.*

Equi — *qui.*

Équiper — *schifo.*

Era It. Sp. E., Fr. *ère;* from L. *æra (æs)* counters, items in an account; hence L. L. *æra æræ* (cf. R. Gr. 2, 21) a number forming the basis of a calculation, an epoch.

Era — *ora* (2).

Érable — *acero.*

Ercer — *erguir.*

Éreinter — *derrengar.*

Ergo O. Pg. except; from L. *ergo?* Diez also suggests *prœter-quod*, cf. *algo = aliquod.*

Ergot — *argot.*

Ergoter Fr. to dispute about trifles, to caid; from L. *ergo*, which was much used in disputations.

Erguir Sp., Pg. *erguer* to erect; from *erigere.* Another form in *ercer*, cf. s. *arcilla* for *c = g.*

Erial erio Sp. a uncultivated piece of ground, from *era*, L. *area.*

Erizo — *riccio.*

Ermo It., Sp. *yermo* desert, sbst. a desert; from ἔρημος, L. *erĕmus* (Prud. *erĕmus*), L. L. *ermus hermus*, Eng. *hermit* from ἐρημίτης. Hence N. Pr. *hermás* a heath.

Erranment — *erre.*

Erre O. Fr. (f.) a way, O. E. *eyre* (Justices in *Eyre*) journey, *errer* to travel, also to treat, behave (*mes-errer* to ill-treat), hence *chevalier errant*, knight-*errant, juif errant*, adv. *erran erranment.* The oldest form is *edrar*, from L. *iter iterare.* The Prov. *errar*, however, is the L. *errrae.*

Ers — *ervo.*

Erto It. steep, partic. of *ergere = erigere*, sbst. *erta* an acclivity, *all'erta*, on the *alert*, prop. = on an eminence, hence adj. Sp. *alerto*, Fr. *alerte*, E. *alert*, Rh. *erti.*

Ervo and *Iero (= l'ervo)* It., Sp. *yervo*, Pr. Fr. *ers* tares; from *ervum, ers* conforming to the G. *erbse*, O. H. G. *arwiz.* From the der. L. *ervilia* (vetch) come Sp. *arveja alverja*, Com. *erbeja*, It. *rubiglia (r* transposed, as in *rigoglio = orgoglio)*, Mil. *erbion* (for *erviglione*).

Ervodo — *albedro.*

Esbahir — *badare.*

Esbalausir — *éblouir.*

Esbanoier — *banda.*

Esbosar — *bozzo.*

Esbulhar — *bolla.*

Esca It. Pr., O. Fr. *eche*, Sp. *yesca*, Wal. *eascē* tinder; from L. *esca*. Isidorus has: *esca vulgo dicitur fungus, quod sit fomes ignis*. Pr. vb. *escar* to bait, Pg. *iscar* to bait a hook for fish, Sard. *escai*, It. *adescare*, Sp. *enescare*. Sp. *esquero* = a leathern bag for fire-materials &c.

Escada Pg. stairs; a corruption of *escala* from *scala*, v. Rom. Gr. 1, 241; or from *escalada*.

Escadre, escadron — *quadro*.

Escai O. Pr. left, = Gr. σκαιός.

Escalin — *scellino*.

Escallo Sp. a fallow-field; from *squalidus*.

Escalmo — *scalmo*.

Escalona — *scalogno*.

Escamel Sp. Pg. a sword-maker's bench, Pr. *escaimel*, O. Fr. *eschamel*; not from *scabellum* (It. *sgabello*, Fr. *escabeau*, Cat. *escambell*), but from a form *scamellum* (al. *scamillum*, *scamnellum*) Priscian (from Apuleius).

Escamondar Sp. to prune; from *escami-mondar* to scale, cleanse; cf. *mani-atar, perni-quebrar*.

Escamoter Fr. to remove clandestinely, to juggle, whence Sp. *escamotar*. Perhaps from *squama*, Sp. *escamar* to scale fish, to clean, remove, cf. G. *wegputzen*, and v. *forbire*; Sp. *escamato* = tutored by experience, cunning.

Escanciar Sp., Pg. *escançar*, O. Fr. *eschancer* to pour in wine &c. (Rh. *schanghiar* to present); Fr. *echanson*, Sp. *escanciano*, Pg. *escançāo* a cup-bearer; from O. H. G. *scencan*, abst. *scenco*, orig. *scancjan, scancjo*, L.L. *scancio scantio*. From G. *schenken* comes Fr. *chinquer* to drink, tipple, Prov. Fr. *chiquer*. The It. has *scancia scansia* a tray for glasses or books, = L. L. *scancia*, Bav. *schanz*, G. *schenke*.

Escandallo — *scandaglio*.

Escandia — *scandella*.

Escantir Pr. to extinguish; from *candere* to glow, so for *escandir, can* glowing = *candidus*. Or from a G. source: O. G. *kenten*, O. N. *kinda*, E. *kindle*, O. N. *kindir* fire.

Escapar — *scappare*.

Escara It., Sp. Pg. *escara*, Fr. *escarre* scurf; from L. *eschara* (ἐσχάρα).

Escarabajo — *scarafaggio*.

Escaramuza — *scaramuccia*.

Escarapelarse Sp. Pg. to wrangle; from It. *scarpellare* to scratch, from *scarpello* = L. *scalpellum*.

Escarbar Sp., Pg. *escarvar*, Cat. *esgarrapar* to scratch; from Du. *schrapen*, M. H. G. *schrapfen*.

Escarbot — *scarafaggio*.

Escarcela escaroelle — *sciarpa*.

Escarcha Sp. Pg. hoar-frost, *escarchar* to congeal, curl; from B. *ecachea* fine rain.

Escarda — *cardo*.

Escargot Fr. a snail; probably from the same as *caracol*, with a strengthening prefix.

Escarir — *schiera*.

Escarlate — *scarlatto*.

Escarmentar Sp. Pg. to correct severely, warn, sbst. *escarmiento* warning. Three derivations are given, (1) *ex-carminare*, which, however, should give *excarmenantar*, (2) It. *schermo* = from G. *schirmen* to defend, but this has given Sp. *esgrimir*, (3) It. *scarnamento* a tearing of the skin, chastisement.

Escarmouche — *scaramuccia*.

Escarnio escarnir — *scherno*.

Escarpa escarpe — *scarpa*.

Escarpolo — *escopro*.

Escarzar Sp. to castrate bee-hives; from *ex-castrare*, by transp. *excarstare*.

Escaso — *scarzo*.

Escatima Sp. Pg. a diminution, *escatimar* to curtail, hoggle. From Basque *escatima* a quarrel.

Eschevi escavi O.Fr., Pr. *escafit* slender, Cat. *escofida* = a bodice. From O. H. G. *scafjan* to arrange, make, partic. *gascafit* for *wola gascafit*, cf. Fr. *molé* for *bien molé*, *séant* for *bien séant*, Lat. *compositus* for *bene compositus*, E. *cheap* for *good cheap* &c.

Eschiele — *schiera*.

Eschiele — *squilla*.

Eschirer O. Fr., Wall. *hiré*, Pr. *esquirar* to scratch; from O. H. G. *skêrran* to scratch, whence also Fr. *déchirer*, Pic. *dekirer*.

Eschiter O. Fr. to soil; from O. H. G. *skizan*, A. S. *scitan*, whence Wall. *hiter*. The G. word must also have influenced the formation of the Fr. *chier* which, if immediately from the L., would have given *chayer* (cf. *pacare payer*).

Escire It., commonly *uscire*, Wal. *esi*, O. Sp. *exir*, Pr. O. Fr. *eissir issir ussir*, E. *issue*; from *exire*. Hence It. *riuscire*, Fr. *réussir* to succeed, O. Fr. *rissir* to go out again. The *u* in *uscire, ussir* is derived from It. *uscio (ostium)*, O. Fr. *us* a door, cf. B. *athea* = *uscio*, *atheratu* = *uscire*, *forasire*, θυράζε έρχεσθαι.

Esclandre Fr. bustle, alarm, *slander*; from *scandalum*, O. Fr. better *eschandre*, v. Rom. Gr. I. 269.

Esclate — *schiatta*.

Esclave — *schiavo*.

Esclavin — *scabino*.

Esclavo — *schiavo*.

Esclenque O. Fr. left hand, *esclenge*, Wall. *hleing;* from O. H. G. *slinc*, Du. *slink* = G. *link*.

Esclet — *schietto.*

Esclier O. Fr. to split, slice; from O. H. G. *sclizan*, G. *schleissen* to split, A. S. *slitan*, E. *slice*.

Esclistre O. Fr. lightning, *écliste*, Rouchi *éclitre;* from O. N. *glitra*, Eng. *glitter, glisten.*

Esclo O. Fr., Pr. *esclau* track; from O. G. *slag slac, sclag*, G. *schlag* (hufschlag = track) a blow; cf. *fau* from *fagus*, and Sp. *batuda* = blow and track.

Esclusa Sp., Fr. *écluse* a sluice, L. L. *exclusa sclusa;* from *excludere*, not from G. *sliozan schliessen*, E. *sluice*, which would have given Fr. *éclusse écluce*.

Escodar Sp. Pg. to hew stones, prop. = to remove angles, from *codo* an elbow, corner. Hence *escoda* stone-breaker's hammer.

Escolh — *cogliere.*

Escolimoso Sp. hard, obstinato; from *scolymus* (σϰόλνμος) a sort of thistle.

Escollo — *scoglio.*

Escolta — *corgere.*

Escondire O. Fr. Pr. to excuse; L. L. *ex-con-dicere*, like ἐϰλογεῖσϑαι.

Escopeta escopette — *schioppo.*

Escoplo Sp., Pg. *escopro, estoupro*, Val. *escapre*, O. Fr. *eschalpre* a chisel; from *scalprum*, Sp. *escarpelo*, It. *scarpello*, from *scalpellum*.

Escorcer escorzar — *scorciare.*

Escorre — *scuotere.*

Escorte — *corgere.*

Escorzon — *escuerzo.*

Escola Sp. Pg. a sheet (naut.); from Du. *schoot*, E. *sheet* (from *schiessen, shoot*).

Escota — *scotta.*

Escote Sp. a round piece cut out in shaping a garment, vb. *escotar*. From G. *schoofs*, Goth. *skaut-s* &c. a lap.

Escote — *scotto.*

Escouade — *quadro.*

Escousse — *scuotere.*

Escosar — *cuire.*

Escramo O. Sp. a javelin. We find it in L. Wisig. 9, 2, 1: *scutis, spatis, sramis, lanceis, sagittis*, and with *sahs* a knife in Gregory of Tours: *cum cultris validis quos vulgus scramasaxos vocant*. Cf. Dief. Goth. wb. 2, 257.

Escraper O. Fr. to scrape; from Du. *schrapen*, E. *scrape*. From same source comes O. Fr. *escrafe, escreffe* a fish-bone, M. H. G.

schrapfen to scratch, Fl. *schraeffen*, cf. Langued. *escrafú* to scratch out, blot out.

Escregne escriegne escrienne O. Fr. a little house, summer-house &c., connected with L. L. *screuna* (from L. *scrinium* (Grimm) a subterranean chamber.

Escrimer — *schermo.*

Escroc — *scrocco.*

Escuchar — *ascoltare.*

Escudriñar Sp., N. Pr. *escudrinhá* to search, scrutinise; for *escru-diñar,* It. *scrutinare* from *scrutinium.*

Escuerso escorzon Sp. a toad, It. *scorzone* a sort of venomous snake; prop. = bark, It. *scorzo,* from the rough, bark-like skin.

Escuma — *schiuma.*

Escupir Sp. Pg., Pr. O. Fr. *escopir escupir,* Wal. *scuipă* to spit. A corruption of *exspuere.*

Ese — *esso.*

Esfolar — *desollar.*

Esglay — *ghiado.*

Esgrima esgrimir — *schermo.*

Esgrumer O. Fr., Cat. *esgrumar,* O. Fr. *esgrunier esgruner,* Pr. Cat. *esgrunar* to crumb, crumble; from Du. *kruim,* G. *krume,* E. *crum.*

Esguazo — *quado.*

Esguince — *sguancio.*

Esito It. sale of goods; from *exitus.*

Eslider O. Fr., Norm. *clinder* to slide; from A. S. *sliddn,* E. *slide.* Norm. *lider* = A. S. *glidan,* E. *glide.*

Eslingua — *slinga.*

Esmaier esmair — *smagare.*

Esmalte — *smalto.*

Esmar Pr., O. Fr. *esmer,* O. Sp. O. Pg. *asmar,* Gallic. *osmar* to estimate; sbst. Pr. O. Fr. *esme,* Cat. *esma,* Lang. *ime,* Lorr. *aume;* from *æstimare.* Hence Pr. *azesmar* = *ad-æstimare,* to reckon, aim: *a son colp azesmat* aimed his blow well, also *azermar, sermar.* From *azesmar* is O. Fr. *acesmer* to set in order (battle &c.), O. Gen. *acesmar,* Dante's *accismare* to set to rights, dress (not from *cisma*), also *azzimare,* Sp. *azemar* to adorn. *Esmar,* Pic. *amer* also gives E. *aim,* M. H. G. *âmen, aemen.*

Esmeralda — *smeraldo.*

Esmerar esmerer — *smerare.*

Esmeril — *smeriglio.*

Esmeril esmerejon — *smerlo.*

Esneque esneche O. Fr. a sharp-prowed ship; from O. N. *sneckia,*

Dan. *snekke*, O. G. *snaga*, *snecke*, probably connected with
G. *schnekke* a snail.

Espaciar — *spazzare.*

Espada — *spada.*

Espalda — *spalla.*

Espalhar — *paglia.*

Espalier — *spalla.*

Espantar — *spaventare.*

Esparcir Sp. to scatter, Pg. *esparzir*, O. Sp. Pg. *espargir*, from
spargere, Pr. *esparser.* Cf. *arcilla.*

Esparvel — *sparaviere.*

Espasmo — *spasimo.*

Espautar Pr. to be in anguish, Wall. *espawter*, Pic. *épauter*, abst.
Pr. *espaul;* from *ex-pavitare.*

Especia — *spezie.*

Espejo — *specchio.*

Espelh esplègle — *specchio.*

Espelta — *spelta.*

Esperir O. Fr. Pr. to awaken, *s'esperir* to awake, Pr. *resperir;*
from *expergere*, *re-expergere*, with elision of the *d*, as though
from *experrigere*, cf. *lire* from *legere.*

Esperlan — *éperlan.*

Esportar O. Sp. Pg. Pr. to awaken; from *espergitus.* Hence Sp.
despierto, Pg. *desperto*, vb. *despertar*, Wall. *dispierté.*

Esposo — *spesso.*

Espeto — *spito.*

Espiar — *spiare.*

Espiche Sp. a sharp-pointed weapon, goad, Pg. *espicho*, vb.
Sp. Pg. *espichar* to prick; from *spiculum spiclum*, *spiculare*, *cl*
= *ch* cf. *hacha (facula)*, *cuckara (cochlearium).*

Esplègle Fr. a wag, O. Fr. *Ulespiègle;* from G. *Eulenspiegel*
(owl-glass) the title of a collection of droll stories, v. Max
Müller, Lectures.

Espiet esple O. Fr., *espieut espiaut* Pr. spear; from O. G. *spioz*
sproz.

Espinaca — *spinace.*

Espineta — *spinetta.*

Espingarda — *springare.*

Esplon — *spiare.*

Espita — *spitamo.*

Esplinque Sp. bird-trap; for *esprinque*, O. H. G. *springa*, E.
springe. Hence also Lang. *esperenc* and Com. *sparangou.*

Espojo — *spoglio.*

Espolin — *spola.*

Espolon espuela — *sperone.*

Esponton — *spuntone.*

Esposo — *sposo.*

Espreitar — *exploit.*

Esprelle and *prêle* Fr. shave-grass (bot.), It. *asperella;* from *asper.*

Esprequer Fr. to prick; from Du. *prikken*, E. *prick.*

Espringuer — *springare.*

Esproher O. Fr. to besprinkle; from *spruejen*, M.H.G. *sprewen*, (†.*sprühen.* Sp.*espurriar* is, probably, a corruption of *espruyar.*

Esprohon O. Fr., Rouchi *éproon*, Wall. *sprew* a starling; from O.H.G. *spra*, G. *sprehe*, Du. *spreuwe*, O.F. *sparwe (sparrow).*

Espurriar — *esproher.*

Espurrir Sp. to stretch one's legs; from *exporrigere*, It. *sporgere.*

Esquadra — *quadro.*

Esquecer Pg. to cause to forget, *esquecerse* to forget; O. Pg. *escaecer* = *excadescere* used actively.

Esquela — *cedola.*

Esqueleto — *scheletro.*

Esquena — *schiena.*

Esquentar — *calentar.*

Esquero — *esca.*

Esquicio — *schizzo.*

Esquif esquife — *schifo.*

Esquila — *squilla.*

Esquille Fr. a bone-splint. Dim. from σχίδη or σχίδιον whence pl. *schidiæ* (Vitruv.). Cf. *scheggia.*

Esquilo — *scojattolo.*

Esquina Sp. Pg. corner, probably from *esquena* fish-spine, = sharp point, cf. It. *spigolo (spiculum)* = corner.

Esquinsar Sp., Pr. *esquinsar esquissar* to tear to pieces (rags &c.); from σχίζειν with *n* inserted? Sp. has also *desguinzar.*

Esquisse — *schizzo.*

Esquivar esquiver — *schivare.*

Essai — *saggio* (2).

Essaim — *sciame.*

Essart O. Fr., Pr. *eissart*, F. *assart* fresh land, *essarter*, *eissartar* to clear land; from *ex-saritum* hoed up, dug up, vb. *ex-saritare*, L. L. *exartum*, *exartare.*

Essere It., Pr. Rh. *ésser*, Fr. *être*, Sp. Pg. *ser* to be. The L. *esse* in L. L. took the regular inf. ending and became *essere* (impf. conj. *esseret*). From this was formed Fr. *estre être*, as from *tessere (texere) tistre titre.* The Sp. *ser*, however, orig. *seer* (in two syllables), is from *sedere* (1) to be situated: *Campo Nola sedet*, Dante: *siede la terra sulla marina* (2) remain (3) be. Cf. Goth. *visan* (G. *wesen*, E. *was*) to dwell (Sansk. *vas*), remain, be. The Sp. verb takes from *sedere* its imper. *sé* (or *sey*), gerund, partic. *sido* (or *seido*), infinitive, pres. conj. (*seu* or *seya*) impf. *sia* for *exa*.

Essieu Fr. axle; for *aissieu* from *axiculus*, like *épieu* from *spiculum*, It. *assiculo*.

Esso It., O. It. *isso*, Sp. *ese*, Pg. *esse*, Pr. *eis*, *eps*, Wal. *insu* from *ipse*, O. Sp. *essi* from *ips' hic*. Often in compounds, e. g. It. *lunghesso*, *sovresso*, Pr. *anceis*, *demanes*, cf. Lat. *nunc ipsum*, *isthuc ipsum* (Ter.), Sp. *ahora mismo;* Pg. *aqui eis* there, cf. G. *daselbst*. For L. *nunc* we have It. *adesso*, O. Sp. *adiesso*, Pr. O. Fr. *ades (ad ipsum);* O. It. *issa*, Rhæt. *ussa* from *ipsa* sc. *hora* = O. Sp. *esora*. Pr. *epsamen eissamen*, O. Fr. *esement*, *essement* = L. *pariter*, O. Fr. *ensement*, Pr. *ensament* (with inserted *n*). Cf. *des*.

Essoigne — *sogna*.

Essorer — *sauro*.

Essuyer — *suco*.

Est Fr., O. Fr. *hest*, whence Sp. *este*, O. Sp. *leste;* from A. S. E. *east*.

Estaca estache — *stacca*.

Estacha Sp. harpoon-rope; from B. *est-archa*.

Estacion — *stagione*.

Estafette estaflade — *staffa*.

Estala — *stallo*.

Estallar — *schiantare*.

Estameña — *stamigna*.

Estampar — *stampare*.

Estano — *stanco*.

Estancar — *stancare*.

Estancia — *stanza*.

Estandarte — *stendardo*.

Estaño — *stagno*.

Estarna — *starna*.

Estai — *étai*.

Esteil O. Fr. an arrow; from O. H. G. *stihhil*.

Estelo — *étai*.

Estera — *stoja*.

Estern Pr. track, *esternar* to follow; from A. S. *stearne*, E. *stern*.

Esters estiers O. Fr. Pr. without, except: e. g. *estiers mon grat* against my will. From *exterius*, by metathesis *extierus estiers*.

Estiar O. Sp. to remain still; from *æstivare*. Pg. *estiar* == to become clear, cease from raining.

Estivar — *stivare*.

Esto O. It., Sp. Pg. *este*, Pr. *est*, O. Fr. *ist*, Wal. *ist aist*, from *iste*. Hence *questo*, *cotesto* &c.

Estoc — *stocco*.

Estofa — *stoffa*.

Estopa — *stoppa*.

Estoque — *stocco*.

Estor — *stormo*.

Estorer Fr. to erect, build, furnish; from *instaurare; estorér, estorement*, L. L. *instaurum, staurum*, E. *store*, Gael. *stór*, W. *ystór*. The O. Fr. *estoire* (though in L. L. *instaurum*) belongs rather to *stuolo*.

Estout Pr. O. Fr. haughty, bold; from G. *stolz*, E. *stout*, It. *stolto*, from L. *stultus*. From *estout*, Pr. *estot* is the O. Fr. *estotoier* to maltreat.

Estovoir O. Fr. impersonal vb. to become, beseem, be necessary, pres. *m'estuet*, pf. *m'estut*. From *stare, ester* to stand near, become, which in pf. has *estut* = *stetit*, as *arestut* from *arester:* from pf. *estut* came pres. *estuet*, inf. *estovoir* like *muet, mut, movoir*. *Estovoir* was also used as a subst. = necessaries of life, E. *stover*, L. L. *estoverium* (cf. *manoir manerium*). But the Rhæt. has *stover stuver* = must, pf. *sturet*, conj. *stuvess*, and this could hardly come from *star* (pf. *stet*), nor is it likely to have been introduced from the Fr. It is better, therefore, to refer the verb to L. *studere, studuit* = O. Fr. Fr. *estut*, Rh. *stuvet, stuvess* = O. Fr. *esteust* = *studuisset*. What is desired or willed may be regarded as necessary, hence *studeo scire* = I must know, cf. Rom. Gr. 3, 204.

Estrac Fr. lean, meagre (of a horse); from G. *strack*, O. H. G. *strac* strictus = Fr. *étroit*, E. *strait*.

Estrada estrade — *strada*.

Estragão estragon — *targone*.

Estrago Sp. Pg. depravity, corruption, havoc, vb. *estragar*. From *strages*, cf. *gorga* from *gurges*.

Estraier — *strada*.

Estralar — *schiantare*.

Estrambote — *strambo*.

Estraño — *stranio*.

Estrapasar — *pazzo*.

Estraper O. Fr. to glean, cut down, hence Fr. *étrape* a sickle; from Sw. *strapen*, E. *strip*, Bav. *straffen* to cut. Cf. It. *strappare*. Or a form of *estreper* = *exstirpare?*

Estrayer O. Fr., Pr. *estraguar* to digress, E. *stray*; from *extravagare*, It. *stravagare*.

Estrazar — *stracciare*.

Estréer O. Fr. to give up, deliver; from Pr. *tradar* formed from *tra-dare, ex-tra-dare*.

Estregar — *fregare*.

Estreper — *estraper*.

Estriar — *strega*.

Estribo Sp. Pg., Cat. *estreb*, Pr. *estrenp estrieu estrep, estriub*,

O. Fr. *estrief*, E. stirrup: hence Sp. *estribera*, Pg. *estribeira*, Fr. *étrivière* and *étrier*. The It. uses *staffa* instead. From the M. H. G. *stege-reif*, L. G. *stircip* (E. *stirrup*), contr. *streep*. Hence Sp. *estribar*, O. Fr. *estriver* (*desestriver* = to throw from the stirrup). The O. Fr. *estriver*, E. *strive* is from G. *streben;* sbst. Pr. *estris*, O. Fr. *estrif*, E. *strife*. From *estribo* comes Sp. *costribo* support, vb. *costribar*. Sp. *estribo estribillo* = also burden of a song, refrain, properly a resting-place or stirrup. O. Sp. *estribote*, O. Fr. *estribot estrabot*, Pr. *estribot* a satire.

Estribot — *strambo*.

Estribord — *stribord*.

Estriga Pg. a portion of flax for spinning; from L. *striga* a streak, or swathe of mown corn.

Estrillar — *strecchia*.

Estringa — *stringa*.

Estrinque estrenque Sp., Pg. *estrinque estrinca* a rope, Pg. *estrincar* to twist; from G. *strick* a rope, with inserted *n;* E. *string* (v. *stringa*). Cf. Ven. *strica* a rope, Com. *striccà* to tie, and cf. *tricoter*.

Estriver — *estribo*.

Estro It. Sp. enthusiasm; from *œstrus* (οἶστρος).

Estrope — *stroppolo*.

Estropear estropier — *stroppiare*.

Estros Pr. O. Fr. with *ad, ad estros* unconditionally, immediately; from *extrorsum* (opp. *introrsum*) = outwardly, without reserve. *Par estros* was used, whence sbst. *la parestrusse* the extremity.

Estrovo — *stroppolo*.

Estrubar — *estribo*.

Estruendo Sp., Pg. *estrondo* noise, clamour; from *tonitrus* with *ex* and metathesis of the *r*, *extronitus*, cf. Fr. *estonner* from *extonare*. O. Sp. has *atruendo*.

Estrujar — *torchio*.

Estucho — *astuccio*.

Estufa — *stufa*.

Estuque — *stucco*.

Esturar — *torrar*.

Esturion — *storione*.

Esturleno Pr. a combatant; from O. H. G. *sturiline*, cf. *adelene* from *adaline* (E. *atheling*).

Esturman O. Fr. (also *estrumant*, *stieresman*); from Du. *stuurman*, A. S. *steorman*, E. *steersman*.

Établir Fr., E. *establish;* from L. *stabilire* (It.).

Étage — *staggio*.

Étai Fr., Sp. *estay* a stay (rope), Fr. *étaie* (Pg. *esteio*) prop, vb.

étayer; from Du. *staede staye* = A. S. *stede*, O. H. G. *stata*, M. H. G. *state*, vb. Du. *staeden*, E. *stead*, *stay.*

Étain — *stagno.*

Étal étalon — *stallo.*

Étamer — *stagno.*

Étamine — *stamigna.*

Étamper — *stampare.*

Étance — *stanza.*

Étancher étang — *staucare.*

Étangues — *stanga.*

Étape Fr., O. Fr. *estaple* a store-house, staple; from Du. *stapel*, E. *staple.*

Étau — *stallo.*

Éteindre Fr.; from *exstinguere*, It. *stinguere.*

Étendard — *stendardo.*

Éteule — *stoppia.*

Étincelle Fr. a spark (hence *'tinsel*); a corruption of *scintilla*, O. Fr. *escintele*, *stencele* (E. *stencil*).

Étiquette Fr. a stitched or pinned note or billet, Rouchi *estiquete* a pointed stick, Neap. *sticchetto.* From same root as It. *stecco* a thorn, prick, Rouchi *stique* a dagger, L. G. *stikke*, *stikken*, E. *stick*, cf. Champ. *stiquer* to put in, stick in, O. Fr. *estiquer* to beat with a *stick.*

Étoffe — *stoffa.*

Étonner Fr., O. Fr. *estoner*, E. *astony*, *astonish*; from *attonare*, *extonare.* O. Pr. has *estornar* for *estronar* (*tronar* = *tonner).*

Étouble — *stoppia.*

Étouffer — *tufo* (1).

Étoupe étoupin — *stoppa.*

Étourdir — *stordire.*

Étourgeon — *storione.*

Étrain Pic. sea-coast; from G. E. *strand.*

Étrange — *stranio.*

Étraper — *estraper.*

Être — *essere.*

Étrécir — *étroit.*

Étreindre Fr. from *stringere;* cf. *astreindre*, *restreindre* from *adstringere*, *restringere*, *contraindre* from *constringere.*

Étrier — *estribo.*

Étrille — *strecchia.*

Étriquet — *tricoter.*

Étrivière — *estribo.*

Étroit Fr., E. *strait;* from *strictus*, Pr. *estreit*, It. *stretto.* Hence *étrécir* to narrow, *rétrécir* to draw in, *retrench*, verbs of inchoative form and active sense, from a L. *strictescere*, Sp.

estrechecer. O. Fr. *estrecier* would = a L. *strictiare.* Hence *détroit* a narrow pass, from *destrictus,* cf. *détresse.*

Etron — *stronzare.*

Étrope — *stroppolo.*

Ette It. (m.) a trifle, Com. *eta,* Flor. *etti,* Rom. *etta ett,* Com. *m'importa on eta* = *m'importa un frullo;* from L. *hetta,* Festus: *res minimi pretii ... cum dicimus "non hettæ te facio".*

Étui — *astuccio.*

Étuve — *stufa.*

Évanouir Fr. (reflex.), Pr. *esvanuir* to vanish. It. corresponds to It. *svanire,* Rhæt. *svanir,* Pg. *esvair,* It. pres. *svanisco* = L. *evanesco. Ou* is inserted as in *épanouir,* O. Fr. *engenouir, amadouer, bafouer;* the *o* in Pr. *manoïr* = Goth. *v (manvjan).*

Évaser Fr. to enlarge an opening; from *vas,* or opp. *convasare* to pack together, *évaser un arbre* to give it room.

Eventail — *ventaglio.*

Évier — *eau.*

Exaucer — *alzare.*

Exploit Fr., Pr. *espleit esplecha* profit, vb. *exploiter espleitar* to perform, accomplish; from *explic'tum* drawn out, accomplished (E. *exploit*). Cf. *ploite* (O. Fr.) from *plicita,* as *plait* from *placitum.* Pg. *espleitar* to explore is also from *explicare,* but in a different sense, to unfold, find.

Esiandio It. = L. *etiam.* From *etiam deus;* cf. *avvegna dio che, macari dio che,* O. Ven. *quanvis-deo,* O. Gen. *quanvis-dè,* so *ezian dio che, ezian dio se, eziau dio.*

F.

Fabuco — *faggio.*

Faca — *haca.*

Faccenda It., Pg. Pr. *fazenda,* Sp. *hacienda,* O. Fr. *faciende* business; plur. *faciendum.* Sp. and Pg. = management of an estate, estate, whence It. *azienda.* So. Pr. *afar* (v. *affare*).

Facchino It., Sp. *faquin,* Fr. *faquin* a porter, also a knave. From Du. *vant-kin* a lad. Or, perhaps, from Ar. *faqir* poor. Sic. *facchinu* = *tavernaio.*

Faccia It., Wal. *fatzě,* Pr. *fassa,* Fr. *face,* Sp. *haz (facha* from the It.), Pg. *face face;* from *facies,* the first four forms from an old Rom. *facia,* Sp. *hacia* = L. *versus.* Hence It. *facciata,* Fr. *façade,* and Pr. *esfassar,* Fr. *effacer,* E. *efface.*

Facha — *faccia.*

Facha — *accia.*

Fâcher — *fastio.*

Facimola facimolo sorcery. According to Menage from *facere*

molam (Virg. *sparge molam et fragiles incende bitumine lauros*),
but we should expect *faci-mola* like *faci-mile*.

Façon Fr., Pr. *faissò*, E. *fashion*; from *factio* used passively, cf.
toison from *tonsio*.

Fade Fr. also *fat*, Pr. *fat* (f. *fada*) insipid, dull (E. *fade*); from
fatuus, cf. *vax* from *vacuus*. It. *fado*.

Faggio It., Sp. *haya*, Pg. Pr. *faya* a beech, O. Fr. *fage* a beech-
wood; from adj. *fageus fagea*. Fagus is found in Wal. *fag*,
Sic. *fagu fau*, Pr. Rh. Ronchi *fau*, O.Fr. *fo feu*, Lomb. Gen. *fò*.
Fr. *faine* beech-nut, O. Fr. Lorr. *faine*, from *faginus fagina*,
It. *faggiuolo*, Sp. *fabuco (= faguco)*, with the same suffix as
almendruco, Cat. *fatja (= fagea)*.

Fagotto fangotto It., Pr. Fr. *fagot*, Sp. *fogote*, E. *faggot*, W.
ffagod. From *fax* prop. = a bundle of split pine-wood (cf.
V. *jamque faces et saxa volant*), Gk. φάκελος (dimin.); *g* for *c*
as in It. *sorgo* from *soricem*, Sp. *perdigon* from *perdicem*, Pr.
lugor from *lucem*. Wal. *hac fagot* is from *fax* as *nuc* from *nux*.
The Sp. owes its form to a supposed connection with *fuego*.

Faide O. Fr. feud, hence *faidiu* hostile, Pr. *faidir* to persecute,
banish; from L. L. *faidu*, A. S. *fehdhe*, O. H. G. *gafêhida*,
G. *fehde*, E. *feud*.

Faille — *fiaccola*.

Faillir — *fallire*.

Faina It., Cat. *fagina*, N. Pr. *faguino fahino*, O. Fr. *fayne*, Fr.
fouine, hence Sp. *fuina*, Pg. *fuinha*, Ven. *fuina foina*, Lomb.
Piedm. *foin* a polecat, marten, O. E. *foin*. From *fouine*, *faine*
(v. *faggio*) beech-mast, cf. E. *beech-martin*. From sbst. comes
a vb. Genev. *fouiner*, Rouch. *founier*, Lomb. *fognà* to track,
cf. Fr. *fureter* to ferret out, from *furet*, It. *braccare* from
bracco. The E. *foumart = fouine* and *mart (= martin)*.

Faine — *faggio*.

Faint O. Fr., E. *faint*, partic. of *se feindre (de quelque chose)*,
Pr. *se fenher* to neglect; prop. to dissemble, from *fingere*,
O. Fr. *foindre = E. foin*. Hence *faignant* lazy (afterwards
written *fainéant [faire néant]*), cf. It. *infingardo* (1) dissembling,
(2) lazy, Murat.: qui aut nolunt aut cum pigritiâ faciunt, *simu-
lantes* sibi vires deesse.

Faire O. Fr., Pr. *far* to speak. Not from *fari* but from *facere*
(verba), cf. imperf. *fesoient* they spoke.

Faisca — *falavesca*.

Faisceau — *fascio*.

Faite Fr. (m.), O. Fr. *faiste, feste*; from *fastigium*, It. *fastigio*.
Fust in Devonshire = ridge of the roof.

Falaise Fr. a cliff, hence the name of a town in Normandy, O.
Fr. *falise*; from O. H. G. *felisa* (f.), G. *fels* (m.).

Falavesca It. embers, Pg. *faisca*, O. Sp. *fuisca* spark, vb. Pg.

faiscar. Another form is It. *farolesca* for *farillesca* from *fa-villa*, Veron. Parm. Crem. *faliva; fuisca* is for *foisca* for *forisca falvisca* (cf. *topo* from *talpa*). The O. H. G. *falawisca* is from the Rom. The same suffix is found in Fr. *flamm-èche* from *flamma*.

Falbalà It. Sp. Pg. Fr., Sp. also *farfalà*, Crem. Parm. *frambalà*, Piedm. *farabalà*, Rouchi *farbala*, F. *furbelow;* from G. *falbel* a plait, flounce, *falbeln* to plait? Or is this from the Rom.?

Falbo It., Pr. *falb*, Fr. *faure;* from O. H. G. *folo* (E. *fallow*), Gen. *falcwes*, G. *falb* yellow.

Falcare diffalcare It., Sp. Pg. *desfalcar*, Fr. *défalquer*, to defalcate, abstract. Usu. derived from *falx*, Sp. *falcar* to reap. But better from the O. H. G. *falgan* to rob, abstract. If the G. word came from the R., it would be *falchan falachan*.

Falco falcone It., Sp. *halcon*, Pr. *falcò*, Fr. *faucon*, O. H. G. *fulcho*, F. *falcon;* from *falco* (first used by Servius ad Æn. 10, 146), which is from *falx*, cf. *falcula* a claw. Festus says: *falcones quorum digiti pollices in pedibus retro sunt curvati.* Hence *falcone, falcon, fauçon* a gun, dim. *falconetto, falconcle, fauconneau* a *falconel*, cf. *moschetto, sagro, terzuolo.*

Falda It., Sp. *falda balda*, Pg. *fralda*, Pr. *fauda*, O. Fr. *faude*, the skirt or fold of a robe; from O. H. G. *falt*, A. S. *feald*, G. *falte*, E. *fold* (= Rh. *falda*). In It. Sp. Pg. it also = the brow, slope, or *skirt* of a hill.

Faldistorio It. Sp. Pg., Fr. *faldistoire* a fald-stool, Fr. *fauteuil*, O. Fr. *faudestueil* an arm-chair; from O. H. G. *faltstuol*, E. *faldstool* (= folding-stool). For *faldistorio* O. Sp. has *facistor facistol* = *falz-stuol*. Hence It. *palchistuolo* a penthouse (from *palco*).

Faldriquera faltriquera Sp. a pocket; from *falda*, whence *faldica*, then with inserted *r* as in *faltrero* a pickpocket, *faldriqu-era.*

Falla — *favola.*

Fallire It., O. Sp. O. Pg. *fallir falir* (Sp. *fallecer, falecer*), Pr. Fr. *faillir* to *fail;* from *fallere.* From *faillir* is derived the impers. pres. *faut*, pf. *fallut*, inf. *falloir*, O. Fr. *faldre faudre; il me faut* = me *fallit* it escapes me, I want it, I must have it. From *fallire* comes abst. It. *fallo falla*, O. Sp. *falla*, Pr. *falha*, O. Fr. *faille*, O. It. *faglia* fault; vb. It. *fallare* to fail, neglect, Sp. Rh. *fallar.*

Falò It. a bonfire, Fr. *falot* a lantern; from φανός a torch, or from φάρος a beacon, Piedm. *farò*, Ven. *fanò.* It. *falotico*, Fr. *falot* = odd, extravagant (prop. flaring?). From φανός also It. *fanale*, Sp. Fr. *fanal* a ship's lantern.

Falourde Fr. (f.) from *faix lourd.* It corresponds in form with the O. Fr. *falorde falourde* (f.) a merry tale, Sp. *falordia*,

Cat. *falornia*, vb. *falorder* to jest, *se falorder* to make oneself merry.

Faltare It., Sp. Pg. *fallar* to fail *(faller)*; hence It. Sp. Pg. *falta*, Fr. *faute*, E. *fault*, Sp. Pg. adj. *falto*, It. *diffalta*, Pr. *defauta*, O. Fr. *défaute*, *default*. *Faltare* is a freq. from *fallere (falli-tare)*.

Faluca — *feluca*.

Famiglio It., O.Sp. O.Pg. *famillo familio*, Rh. *famaigl* a servant; from *familia*, cf. Sp. *manceba* from *mancipium*.

Fanal fanale — *falò*.

Fanciullo — *fante*.

Fanello It. a linnet, Piedm. *fanin*, Mil. *fanett*; from the G. *hanf-il-ing (hemp-ling)?*

Faner Fr. to let dry, make into hay, *faner l'herbe*; O. Fr. *fener fanir* to wither, Pic. *fener*, L. L. *af-fenare*, Pr. *faner*, Rh. *fanar fenar*. From *faenum foenum*, cf. O.Fr. *fanoul* for *fenouil*, Lorr. *fouon* = Fr. *foin*, Lorr. *fouanná* = Fr. *faner*; Lim. sbst. *fe*, vb. *fená*.

Fanfa O. Sp. brag; It. *fanfano*, Sp. *fanfarron*, Fr. *fanfaron* a blusterer, *fanfare* blast of trumpet; Sp. *farfante*, Langued. *farfantaine* braggart; an onomatopœion.

Fanfaluca It. embers, trifles, Fr. *fanfreluche*, O. Fr. *fanfelue* trifles, gewgaws, Norm. *fanflue*. L. L. *famfaluca* a corruption of *pompholyx* (πομφόλυξ) (1) a bubble, (2) slag, scoria. Hence Mil. *fanfulla*, Com. *fanfola*, Sic. *fanfonj* (pl.) trifles; Fr. *freluquet* a fop, for *fanfreluquet*.

Fango It. Sp., Pr. O. Fr. *fanc*, fem. Lomb. *fanga*, Pr. *fanha*, Fr. *fange*, Norm. *fangue* mud. From Goth. *fani* (n.) gen. *fanjis* the *j* becoming *h (fanha)* or *g*, *c*, cf. from *renio* It. *vengo*, Pr. *venc*. Bret. *fank* from the O. Fr., which Pictet refers with the Ir. *fochall* to the Sansk. *panka*. *Fangoso*, *fangeux* might also come from *fumicosus* (Festus, according to O.Müller from *famex*, whence might come *fange [famicem]*).

Fanon O. Fr. a cloth, towel, Fr. *fanon fanion*; from O. H. G. *fano*, Goth. *fana* a piece of cloth, O. H. G. *hantfano* a towel.

Fante It. a boy, servant, foot-soldier, Sp. *infante* &c.; from *infans*. Hence *fanteria* infantry, *fantoccio* a doll, It. *fanciullo fanciulla* a child, Flor. Rh. *fancella*. For the loss of the 1st syllable, cf. *folto*, *scipido*, *stromento*, &c.

Fantôme Fr., E. *phantom*; from *phantasma*, It. *fantasima*, Pr. *fantauma* (from *fantalma*, cf. Cat. *fantarma*). O. Fr. vb. *enfantosmer*. Langued. *fantasti* a goblin, *phantasticus*.

Faon Fr., E. *fawn*, vb. *faoner*. O.Fr. *faon feon* = young espec. of lions, bears, dragons &c., *faoner feoner* to bring forth young. Connected with Pr. *feda* (q. v.), from *fetus*; *feon* from *fedon*, as *fea* from *feda*.

13*

Faquin — *facchino.*

Farandula Sp. Pg. Cat. profession of a comedian, also a wandering troop of comedians. Perhaps connected with the G. *fahrende* wandering people. *Farante* (Sp.) = a messenger, actor who speaks the prologue &c.; *farandula* from a form *farandu*, as *larandula* from *lavanda*, *girandula* from *giranda.*

Farapo — *arpa.*
Faraute — *araldo.*
Farce — *farsa.*

Fard Fr. paint, vb. *farder; fard* = *teinte*, L. *tincta*, which in O. H. G. would be *gi-farwit gi-farit* (from *farwjan* G. *färben* to colour).

Fardo Sp. Pg. a bale, pack, Sp. *fardillo*, Pg. Pr. E. *fardel*, Fr. *fardeau*; Sp. *farda alfarda* a notch, also a tax, Pg. *farda alfarda* a soldier's coat; Sp. *fardage*, Pg. *fardagem*, It. *fardaggio* luggage. Ar. *farda*, *al-fa'lda* pack tax, *fard* notch.

Farfalla It. a butterfly, a fickle man (Wal. *fĕrfalĕ*), Bas. *ulifarfalla* (*ulia* a gnat); Pg. *farfalhas* pl. cuttings of metal in coining, bragging, It. *sfarfallare* to cut through, become a butterfly, N. Pr. *esfarfalhà* to scatter (Fr. *éparpiller*). From *papilio* come It. *parpaglione*, then, perhaps through influence of the O. H. G. *fifaltra*, *farfaglione farfalla*. The Sw. has *farfall*. Com. *farfatola* a fickle person. Rh. *fafarinna* butterfly is = L. *fac farinam* "make meal", Sard. *fughe-farina*, because it is covered with a dust like that of meal.

Farfante farfarron — *fanfa.*

Farfogliare Neap., Lomb. *farfujà*, Sp. *farfullar*, Rouchi *farfouiller* to stammer; an onomatop. (= Fr. *farfouiller* to rummage) or = Ar. *farfara* to talk confusedly.

Farga — *forgia.*
Farinella — *fanella.*

Farnia fargna the broad-leaved oak, quercus robur; from *farnus* (Vitruv.) by some supposed to be contracted from *fraxinus*; the It. comes from the adj., Apicius has: *farnei fungi.*

Faro Pg. scent (of dogs), track, steam of meat &c.; from Ar. *fàrah*?

Farouche Fr., vb. *effaroucher*, from *ferox ferocis*, cf. *morduche* from *mordax*. Pr. Cat. *ferotge*. O. Fr. *harouche* = insolent.

Farpa farpão farpar — *arpa.*

Farsa It. Sp. Pg., from the Fr. *farce*, a farce, orig., as in French = a stuffing, thence a medley, farce, cf. *satira*: from *farsus* stuffed, whence also It. *farsetto* waistcoat, doublet; from *farsa* comes Pg. *disfarzar*, S. *disfrazar* to mask.

Fasolo It., Sp. *faxo*, *haz*, Pg. *feix*, Fr. *faix* bundle &c.; from *fascis*. Hence It. *fastello* for *fascettello*, Fr. *faisceau*. It. *fascina*, Sp. *faxina hacina* &c.; vb. Pr. *afaissar*, Fr. *affaisser*.

Fasquia Sp. Pg. a ledge; from Ar. *faschia* (Sousa), which is from vb. *fasacha* to separate.

Fastello — *fascio*.

Fastidio It., *fastio hastio* Sp., Pg. *hastio*, Cat. *fastig*, Pr. *fastig fastic*, O. Fr. *fasti*; from *fastidium*; vb. *fastidiare*. O. Sp. *hastiar*, Pr. *fastigar fasticar*, Fr. *fâcher*, E. *fash*; adj. It. *fastidioso*, Sp. *hastioso*, Cat. Pr. *fastigos*, Fr. *fâcheux*, L. *fastidiosus*. The guttural is due to a form *fast-icare*.

Fata — *té*.

Fata It., Sp. *fadu hada*, Pg. Pr. *fada*, Fr. *fée*, Dauph. *faye*, E. *fay*; vb. It. *fatare*, Sp. *hadar*, Pr. *fadar*, O. Fr. *féer*, *faer*, M. H. G. *feinen* to bewitch; from *fata* = Parca, on a coin of Diocletian, *fatis* = Dis manibus. *Fatus* is used by Petronius. Others derive it from *Fatua*.

Fatras Fr. booty; for *fartas*, from *fartus* (Menage).

Fattizio It. &c., artificial, *factitious*; from L. *facticius*; abst. Sp. *hechizo*, Pg. *feitico* enchantment (whence E. abst. *fetish*), like O. H. G. *zoubar* (G. *zauberei*) from *zouwau* to make; hence Sp. *hechicero*, Pg. *feiticeiro* a sorcerer, It. *fattucchiero*. *Factura* is used in the same sense, It. *fattura*, Pr. *faitura* (*feature*, cf. *feat* = *fait*, *fetish* = *faictis* well-made, neat), vb. It. *fatturare*, Pr. *faiturar*; abst. Pr. *fachurier*, Dauph. *faiturier*. Pr. *faitilha* enchantment is also from *facere*.

Fattuchiero — *fattizio*.

Faubourg Fr. suburb. For *faux-bourg* = *falsus burgus*, cf. *faux-frais*, *faux-bois*, *fausse-clef*. This der. is supported by the Wall. *fâ-bor*, Wall. *fâ* = Fr. *faux*. The O. Fr. form *forborg forsbourg* was spelt as though from *foris*.

Faucon — *falcone*.

Faude O. Fr. sheepfold; from A. S. *fald*, *falud*, E. *fold*, A. S. *faled*, cf. W. *ffald* dung.

Faute — *falta*.

Fauteuil — *faldistorio*.

Fautre fautrer — *feltro*.

Fauve — *falbo*.

Favola It., Sp. *fabla*, Fr. *fable*, Pr. *faula*, E. *fable*, Sp. *fabla habla*, Pg. *falla* speech, from *fabula*; It. *farella* language, from *fabella*, Sard. (m.) *fueddu* speech, word; dim. Fr. *fabliau*, O. Fr. Pr. *fabel* a short story; It. *farola farellare*, Sp. *hablar* (whence Fr. *hâbler*), Pg. *fallar*, Pr. *favelar faular*, O. Fr. *fabler* to narrate, speak, Wal. *hêblei* to make a noise; from *fabulari*. The It. *fola* = Pr. *faula*, *fiaba* = O. Fr. *flabe* with the trasposed.

Faxo — *fascio*.

Fazaleja — *fazzuolo.*

Fazzuolo fazzoletto It., O. Sp. *fazoleto* a pocket-handkerchief. The Sp. *fazaleja* is from *facies* (Sp. *faz*), L. L. *faciale.* Diez refers *fazzuolo* (by reason of its suffix) to another origin, G. *fetzen* a rag (cf. It. *pezzuola*). But the Sic. *fazzulettu* is from Sic. *facci (facies)*, and, doubtless, the It. is of kindred, perhaps dialectical, origin.

Fe (phe) O. Fr. = servus. It is tho O. N. *fœdd-r, fed,* brought up, cf. Sp. *criado.*

Feble — *fievole.*

Fechar Pg. to shut, hence *fecho* a bolt; prop. to close a letter &c. by dating it; from *factum* = date, Sp. *fechar* to date.

Feda Pr. Com., Piedm. *fea,* Dauph. *feia* a sheep; from *feta* = quæ peperit, spec. of sheep, cf. *cordero* and Virg.: *Non insueta graves tentabunt pabula fetus.* Bearn. *heda* = L. *feta* generally, Wal. *fēt* = child, *fatë* daughter, from *fetus,* vb. *fetà* = *fetare,* Sard. *fedu* = *fetus.*

Federa It. thick woven stuff, twill; from O. H. G. *fedara* feather, M. H. G. *federe* felt, L. L. *penna.*

Fée — *fata.*

Fégato It., Sp. *higado,* Pg. *figado,* Pr. *fetge,* Wall. *feûte,* Fr. *foie* (m.) liver; from L. L. *ficatum* (sc. jecur), prop. the fig-fattened goose's liver, *pinguibus ficis pastum jecur auseris albi* Hor. S. 2, 8, 88, cf. N. Gr. σιχότι from συκωτόν ήπαρ. The accent is thrown back, and we find also *figido* for *ficatum,* cf. *rogitus rogatus, dolitus dolatus, vocitus vocatus, provitus probatus* &c. Sard. is *figáu,* Ven. *figá,* Wal. *ficát.* For the importance of the goose, cf. its name It. *oca,* Fr. *oie (avica, avis) the bird.*

Feindre — *faint.*

Feira — *fera.*

Feloe It., Sp. *helecho,* Fr. *fougère* fern; (1) from *filix* (Lauguod. *frouze*), (2) from *filictum,* (3) from a form *filicaria.*

Fêler Fr. to split; for *fesler* from *fissiculare* (Apuleius).

Feligres Sp. parishioner; from *filius gregis.*

Fello It., Pr. O. Fr. *fel* impious, wicked; It. *fellone* wicked wretch, O. Sp. *felon fellou* = *fello,* Fr. *félon* perjured traitor, E. *felon;* It. O.Sp.*fellonia,* Pr.*felnia feunia* profligacy, wickedness, Fr. *félonie,* Sp. *felonia* treachery (espec. of a vassal), E. *felony.* From the A. S. E. *fell,* Du. *fel.* Pr. and O. Fr. nom. sing. *fel (fels)* acc. *felon,* whence the other forms, and fem. *felona.*

Felpa It. Sp. Pg. plush; from G. *felbel,* Swed. *fälp;* hence Fr. *feulpier.* The It. has also *pelpa,* Sic. *felba,* Sard. Cat. *pelfa.* O. Pg. *falifa* = a sheepskin.

Feltro It., Sp. *fieltro,* Pr. Fr. *feutre,* felt, L. L. *filtrum;* It. *feltrare,*

Sp. *filtrar*, Fr. *filtrer*, E. *filter*; from O. H. G. *filz*, A. S. E. *felt*, with *r* after *t*, R. Gr. 1, 323, hence O. Fr. *fautrer* to thrash, from *filzen* (to press), an *faultre* (= *feutre*) from filz.

Feluca It., Sp. *faluca*, Pg. *falua*, Fr. *félouque*, E. *felucca*; from Arab. *fulk* a ship.

Fenouil — *finocchio*.

Feo Sp. Pg. ugly; from *fa'dus*, O. Sp. *hedo*.

Ferlino It., O. Sp. *ferlin*, O. Fr. *ferling ferlin* a farthing; from A. S. *feordhling* (*farthing*).

Ferme Fr. (f.), E. *farm*, It. *ferma*, Sp. *firma* a signature, bond, confirmation, *fermare firmar* to sign &c. Fr. abst. *ferté* stronghold, for *fermeté fermté*, cf. *dortoir* for *dorm'toir*.

Fermillon fremillon O. Fr., Pr. *fremild*, perhaps = *haubert*; from *mailles de fer*, so = *fer-maillon*, cf. *grille* for *graille*, *provigner* for *provaigner*. Al. from *firmus*, *firmaculum*.

Ferrana It., Pg. *ferrãa*, Sp. *herren* (f.) a mixture of various chopped herbs for cattle, a mash; from *farrago*, Pg. also *farragem*.

Ferrant and *auferrant* O. Fr., Pr. *ferran alferan*, an adj. used to denote a light colour, e. g. of grey hair, of horses &c. From *ferro*, cf. It. *ferretto* = iron-grey, semicanus, also *ferrigno*, which answers to a Pr. *ferrene*, O. Fr. *ferrant* (cf. *flamene flamant*), whence Pr. *ferran*. *Al* is not the Arab. article, but for *alb-ferrant*, cf. *blanc-ferrant*, *chenu-ferrant*. Al. from the Ar. *al-fars*, Sp. *al-faraz* a Barbary horse.

Ferropea herropea arropea Sp., Pg. *ferropea* fetters, from *ferrum* and *pes*.

Ferté — *ferme*.

Forzare sforzare It. to scourge, abst. *ferza sferza*. Not from *ferire* (*feritiare*), since the 4th conj. does not form participial verbs. Perhaps from the O. H. G. *fillan*, whence an intensive *fillazan* = G. *filzen* to scold, hence *felzare ferzare* (cf. *scalmo scarmo*).

Fesse Fr. (f.) for Lat. *natis*; from *fissus fissa*, whence vb. *fesser*.

Fetta It. a bit, piece, shred, ribbon, O. Sp. *fita* ribbon; not from *vitta*, which gives It. *vetta*, but from O. H. G. *fiza* a ribbon, thread, perhaps connected with *fetzen* a shred (Rh. *fetza*):

Feu — *fuoco*.

Feudo — *fio*.

Feur — *foro*.

Feurre — *fodero*.

Feutre — *feltro*.

Fi O. Fr. Pr. sure, certain, adv. *fiement* confidently; from *fidus*, It. *fido*. O. Fr. adv. *de fi* = surely.

Fia fiata — *via*.

Fiaba — *farda*.

Fiacoo It., Sp. *fiaco*, Pg. *fraco*, Pr. O. Fr. *flac flaque* weak, languid, vb. *fiaccare* &c.; from *flaccus*. The Fr. *fiasque* must come from *flaccidus* = *flaxidus* == *flosquidus*, cf. *laxus lasque lâche*, Lorr. *fiâche*, Com. *fiasch*.

Fiaccola It., Sp. *hacho* (whence Rouchi *hache hace*), Pg. *facha*, Pr. *falha*, O. Fr. *faille* a taper; from *facula (fax)*. For the inserted *i* = *l* cf. R. Gr. 1, 269, and cf. *fiocina*, *rifiutare*.

Fiaore a late Fr. word, so called because the inventor's house in Paris bore the sign of *S. Fiacre*.

Fiadone It. honeycomb, Pr. *flauzon (flazon?)*, Sp. *flaon*, Fr. *flan* (for *flaon*), E. *flawn* a flat cake, a flat piece of metal for coining; L. L. *flado*, *flato* == O. H. G. *flado* f. *flada* (= laganum, placenta, libum, favus), Du. *vlade* (f.), connected with πλατύς, G. *platt*, E. *flat*.

Fiale — *fiavo*.

Fiama Pied., Sp. *fleme* (m.), Pr. *fleeme*, Fr. *flamme* (f.), E. *fleam*; from *phlebotomus*, whence also O. H. G. *fliedima*, M. H. G. contr. *fliede*, G. *fliete*.

Fiancer Fr. to *affiance*, Pr. *fiansar* to promise, It. *fidanzare*; from *fides*, *fidanza*.

Fianco It., Pr. Fr. *flanc*, Sp. *flanco* (milit. from the Fr.) flank. Diez derives it from *flaccus* inserting *n* as in It. *fangotto*, Fr. *ancôlie* &c., cf. G. for flank *weiche*, M. H. G. *krenke* both = weak. But it is more probably from the O. H. G. *lancha hlanca* (through the E. *flank*) to which D. objects that the G. *h* would not become *f* but *g*, v. *gufo* (but cf. It. *Fiovo* from *Chlodoveus*), and that *hlanca* is fem.; we find however It. *solcio* from *sulza*, Fr. *tin* from *tinna*.

Fiappo It. (prov.), Mil. Piedm. Ven. *fiap*, Crem. *fiapp* flabby; from G. *flap*, *flep*, *flabbe*, E. *flap*, *flabby*.

Fiasco It., Sp. *flasco frasco*, Pg. *frasco*, fem. It. *fiasca*, O. Fr. *flasche*, Fr. *flacon* for *flascon* (E. *flagon*), also found in the Germ. and Celtic tongues, E. *flask*, cf. Wal. *ploscĕ*, Hung. *palatzk*, Lith. *pleczca*. On the analogy of *fiaba (flaba)* from *fabula*, *pioppe* from *populus*, Sp. *bloca* from *buccula*, *blago* from *baculus* we may get *fiasco* from *vasculum* (cf. *f* for *v* in *parafredus*, *biffera*).

Fioccare It., O. Sp. Pg. Pr. *ficar*, Fr. *ficher*, O. Sp. O. Pg. *fincar* Sp. *hincar* to thrust or drive in (Pic. *hinquer*), It. *ficcarsi*, Sp. *fincarse* to insist on; It. *afficcare*, Pr. *aficar*, Fr. *afficher* to attach. Verbs in *ic* on the analogy of *fodicare*, *vellicare* are common in Rom. cf. *gemicare*, *vulvicare*, *pendicare*, *sorbicare*. So, perhaps, *figicare* from *figere* (dim. or frequent.).

Ficello Fr. f. packthread; from *filum* as if *filicellum*; for the change of gender, cf. *cervelle* from *cerebellum*, and for the lost *l*, cf. *pucelle* for *pulcelle*.

Fiche — *fitlo.*

Ficher — *ficcare.*

Fie fiée — *via* (1).

Fiedere It. to wound, from *ferire*, Sp. *herir* &c., *r* being changed to *d*.

Fief — *fio.*

Fiente Fr., Pr. *fenta* dung. From a form *fimitus* (cf. O. Fr. *friente* = *fremitus*) a corruption of *fimetum*. Cat. is *fempta*, N. Pr. *femto fiendo*, O. Sp. *hienda*.

Fiera It., Sp. *feria*, Pg. Pr. *feira*, Fr. *foire*, E. *fair*; from *feria* (*feriæ*), fairs being held on saint's days, cf. G. *messe*.

Fierce fierche fiergo O. Fr., Pr. *fersa*, O. E. *fers*, L. L. *fercia* queen at chess; from Pers. *ferz* a general. *Fierge* transformed into *vierge* gave rise to *dame reine*, Sp. *reyna*.

Fievole It., Sp. Pr. *feble*, Pg. *febre*, Fr. *foible*, O. Fr. *floible floibe*, E. *feeble*; from *flebilis*, the first *l* being dropped. Cf. G. *swach* (1) flebilis (2) debilis, and *wenig* (1) flebilis (2) parvus, paucus.

Fifre — *pipa.*

Figer Fr. to curdle, congeal; from *figere*. A late word, but found in Stephanus (1539) and Nicot.

Fignolo It. a pimple; from G. *finne.*

Fila It. Sp. Pg. Pr., Fr. E. *file* a row, prop. a thread, from *filum*. Vb. Fr. *filer*, *défiler*, E. *file*, *defile*, O. Fr. *pourfiler*, E. *purfile* to embroider(Chaucer), hence also sbst. *défilé*, E. *defile*. Hence It. Sp. *filo*, Fr. *fil* edge of a weapon (pr. thread); vb. *affilare* (1) to sharpen, (2) incite, Sp. *afilar* = (1), Pg. = (2); Pg. *enfiar* to thread, pierce, frighten.

Filhar O. Pg. to take; prop. to take into one's family, from *filius*.

Filipendula It. Sp. Pg., Fr. *filipendule* a plant, so called from the tubercles attached to its thread-like roots.

Filou Fr. a sharper, rogue, Piedm. Com. *filon*, Piedm. also *filuca*, • vb. Fr. *filouter*. The L. L. is *filo*; from O. H. G. *filön* to file, cf. *fourbe*, *fripon*, *polisson*, also slang Eng. *file* = rogue. The Fr. *filouter* may be from the part. *gi-filöt* = expolitus. The Du. has *fiell* good-for-nothing, sbst. *fielterye*. The Lorr. *affilou* = *filou* from a vb. *aiffilei* to deceive = Fr. *affiler* to polish. The difficulty lies not so much in the root as in the termination. May it be from E. *fellow?*

Filtrar filtrer — *feltro.*

Filza It. a row or string of things, vb. *infilzare*; from *filum*, through a form *filitium*.

Finanza It. a receipt, quittance, Pr. *finansa*, Fr. E. *finance*, plur.

It. *finanze,* Fr. E. *fmances;* from *finis.* Pr. *fin* = end, settlement, τέλος, specially of an adjustment of a legal quarrel, usu. by payment of money, L. L. *finis* = "finalis concordia, amicabilis compositio", *finem facere* componero de lite, E. *fine.* Hence vb. *finar finer finire* to pay a stipulated sum, which sum was prop. *la finance,* E. *finaunce* = *fine,* L. L. *financia* = generally "praestatio pecuniaria".

Fincar — *ficcare.*

Finoo Ven. a finch, Lat. fringilla; from O. H. G. *fincho,* G. *finke,* E. *finch.* Veneroni gives also a form *frinco.*

Findar Sp. to finish, conclude; from *finitus,* Pg. *findo.*

Fino It. Sp. Pg., It. also *fine,* Pr. Fr. *fin,* whence E. *fine,* G. *fein,* O. H. G. *finliho* (10th cent.). The fundamental meaning is: perfect, pure, sincere; Pr. *fin aur, fine* gold, *fin amor, fin vertalz,* O. Fr. *de fine ire* from pure anger. From *finitus* finished, perfect, cf. *clin* from *clinatus, cuerdo* from *cordatus, manso* from *mansuetus,* and for the sense cf. Sp. *acabado,* Lat. *perfectus,* Gk. τέλειος.

Fino infino It. particle = L. *tenus;* from *in finem, fine,* cf. Festus: *tenus significat finem.* In L. L. (A. D. 819) we find *de aliá parte fine flumen* &c. The Pr. has *fis,* N. Pr. Cat. *fins,* Bearn. *fens,* Sard. *finza, finzas.*

Finocchio It., Sp. *hinojo,* Pg. *funcho* (whence *Funchal*), Fr. *fenouil,* E. *fennel;* from *faeniculum,* L. L. *fenuclum.*

Fio It., Pr. O. Cat. *feu* (hence O. Pg. *fen*), Fr. E. *fief* from the O. Fr. *fien;* vb. Fr. *fieffer,* O. Fr. *fiever,* Pr. *affeuar* to *feoff.* It is the Lomb. *fiu* in *fader-fium* patrimony, O. H. G. *fihu fehu* (pecus), G. *vieh,* Goth. *faihu* possession, E. *fee* = O. Fries. *fia* in both senses. The *h* was lost (cf. R. Gr. 1, 312), the short *e* became *ie* as in Pr. *micu* from *meus,* and Pr. *u* = Fr. *f* cf. *juif* = Pr. *judeu,* Fr. *fieffer* for *fiever* as in *ensuifer* for *ensuiver.* Sic. *fegu* substitutes the regular *g* for *h,* R. Gr. 1, 311. From *fiu feu* came the L. L. *feudum feodum* (in the 9th cent.), the *d* being euphonic, as in *ladico* for *laico, chiodo* for *chio-o (clavus clauus).* The L. L. word spread into the Rom., It. Sp. *feudo* &c.

Fiocina It. a harpoon; from *fuscina* with *i* = *l* inserted, cf. *fiaccola,* and with *ci* for *sci,* cf. *cacio* for *cascio.* Sard. *fruscina,* Mil. *frosna* insert *r* = *l.*

Fioco It. hoarse, faint, weak. Diez derives it from *raucus (fraucus,* cf. *frombo, fruco, floco, fioco).* Mahn, however, maintains that the meaning of *weak (fioco lume* Dante &c.) ought to precede that of *hoarse,* and derives it from *flaccus* by means of a form *flaucus. Flaccus* is connected with βλάξ, E. *flag, flabby,* A. S. *wlaec* = E. *luke* (luke warm). The Pr. *frauc* makes the der. from *raucus* more plausible than that from *flaccus* which in Pr. is *flac.*

Fionda It., Pr. *fronda*, Fr. *fronde* a sling. From *funda* It. *fonda*, O. Fr. *fonde*, with inserted *i* = *l*, cf. *fiocina.*

Fioretto It., Sp. *florete*, Fr. *fleuret* a foil; so called from the button on the point, like the bud of a flower.

Florino It., Sp. Fr. E. *florin*, orig. a gold coin, stamped with the lily *(fiore)* of Florence, hence also in O. Pg. *frolença* for *florença.*

Flotta frotta It., Sp. *flota*, Pg. *frota*, O. Fr. *flote*, masc. It. *fiotto frotto* (cf. *fragello* from *flagellum*), Fr. *flot* a troop flood, tide; from *fluctus.* Vb. It. *fiottare* &c. to float, from *fluctuare.* From *frotta* comes *frottola* a vaudeville, Com. *frotola* jest.

Fischiare It. to whistle, from *fistula*, L. L. *fiscla.*

Fisga Sp. Pg. a harpoon, vb. *fisgar;* from Goth. *fiskòn* to fish, O. H. G. *fisker* a harpoon.

Fistella It. a basket, from *fiscella*, *fisc-ell-ella.*

Fita — *fetta.*

Fitta It. soil that gives way under the feet; from O. H. G. *fiuhti* moisture (G. *feucht* moist)? For *iu io* = passing into *i*, cf. R. Gr. 1, 287, and cf. Rhaet. *fiecht* from *feucht.*

Fitto It., Sp. *hito*, Pg. *fito* fixed; sbst. Sp. *hito*, Pg. *fito* a mark, target, landmark, *hita* a peg, nail, It. *fitto* rent (= *fixed* price). From the O. Lat. *fictus* (Lucret. Varro) = *fixus.* The Fr. *fiche* a peg may = Sp. *hita*, though *ficher* is better referred to *ficcare.*

Flucia fucia hucia O. Sp. confidence; from *fiducia.* Hence compounds such as: *afiuciar ahuciar, desfiuzar deshuciar, desahuciar.*

Flusso — *floscio.*

Fiutare — *flauto.*

Flaco — *fiacco.*

Flacon — *fiasco.*

Flageolet — *flauto.*

Flagorner Fr. to flatter meanly; from *flatter* and *corner* (aux oreilles) according to Le Duchat.

Flairar Pr. Cat., Fr. *flairer*, Pg. *cheirar* (*fl* = Pg. *ch*), = L. *fragrare*, changed to *flagare;* sbst. Cat. *flaira*, O. Fr. Pic. *flair*, Pg. *cheiro.* The It. and Sp. have only derivatives, such as *fragrante, fraganza fragancia.*

Flairer — *fragrare.*

Flambe Fr. the iris, flag, O. Fr. Pic. also = *flame;* from *flammula flamble flambe.* Hence *flamber, flambeau* &c.

Flamberge Fr. a sword, now only in the phrase: *mettre flamberge au vent* to draw swords; it is the G. *flamberg flamberge* from *flanc* flank and *bergen* to cover. Cf. *froberge* used as

the name of a sword, according to Grimm from *frô* (lord) and
bergen, or from the god *Fro* = N. *Freyr.*

Flan — *frignare.*

Flan — *fiadone.*

Flanc — *fianco.*

Flanella frenella It., Sp. *francla*, Fr. *flanelle*, E. *flannel.* The
primitive form is found in O. Fr. *flaine* a bed-covering (Roquefort), cf. W. *cüraing* (1) bed-covering, (2) flannel. *Flaine* may
be from *vclamen v'lamen*, as *flasca* from *vlasca.* The Pg. form
farinella is quite anomalous.

Flaon — *fiadone.*

Flaque Fr. a puddle, slough; from Du. *vlacke* a lagoon. Cf.
Ducange, *flaco flactra.*

Flasque — *fiacco.*

Flatir — *flatter.*

Flatter Fr., Pr. *flatar*, E. *flatter*; from A. S. O. N. E. *flat*, O. H.
G. *flaz.* Hence also O. Fr. *flat* a blow, *flatir* to strike to the
ground.

Flauto It., Wal. *flautĕ*, Sp. Pr. *flauta*, Fr. *flûte*, E. *flute*; vb. Pg.
frautar, Pr. *flautar*, Fr. *flûter* to *flute.* The old form was *flahute*
flaüte which form it still keeps in Pic., also with an *s* *flahuste*,
vb. *flahuter flaüter.* *Flaüter* is for *flatuer* (cf. *reude* for *ridue*,
Pr. *teune* for *tenue*), from *flatus*, the *u* being kept as in *flatu-*
eux. From *flauta* is Pr. dim. *flautol flaujol* (*flautiolus*), O. Fr.
flajol, Fr. E. *flageolet.* It. *fiutare* to smell is from an old form
flautare, cf. *rubare* from *rauben.*

Flavelle O. Fr. flattery; from *flabellum* a fan.

Fléau Fr. a scourge, O. Fr. *flael*, E. *flail*; from *flagellum.* With
r for *l* the It. has *fragello*, W. *ffrowyll*, O. Fr. *srogell.*

Flecha flèche — *freccia.*

Flèche de lard Fr. flitch, O. Fr. *flique flec*, Pr. *fleca.* From A. S.
flicce, E. *flick flitch*, G. *flick.*

Fléchir Fr. Pr. to bend. From *flectere*, *réfléchir* = *reflectere*,
though *ct* is not usu. changed to *ch* in Fr. (cf. *pacciare*), O. It.
fettere, It. *flettere* is a Latinism.

Fleco flueco Sp. fringe; from *floccus*, v. *frenc.*

Fleis — *fléchir.*

Flome — *fiama.*

Flete flette Fr. a ferry-boat, from Du. *vleet*, E. *fleet.*

Flote — *fret.*

Flétrir Fr. to wither, Berr. *flatrir*, O. *flaistrir.* From the O. Fr.
adj. *flaistre flestre* withered, which is a contraction from
flaccaster.

Flourer — *fragrare.*

Flibot Fr. from E. *fly-boat.* Hence Sp. *flibote filibote.*

Flin Fr. a thunderbolt, whetstone; from O. H. G. *flins*, A. S. E. *flint*.

Floc — *froc.*

Floresta — *foresta.*

Florin — *fiorino.*

Floscio It., Sp. *floxo*, Pg. *frouxo*, Pr. *fluis* lax, slothful, weak; from *fluxus*, whence It. *fiusso* transient.

Flot flota — *fiotta.*

Flotar — *frottare.*

Flotta It., Sp. *flota*, Pg. *frota*, Fr. *flotte*, E. *fleet*. The O. Rom. words for *classis* are It. *armata*, Sp. *armada*, Pr. *estol*, Fr. *estoire*. The O. Fr. *flote (fluctus* v. *fiotta)* had a wider sense, e. g. *flote de gens* as well as *flote de nefs*; the later word is prob. through the Du. *vloot* or the Sw. *flotta.*

Flou Fr. languid, feeble, O. Fr. (fem. *flaire*), O. Pic. *flau*, Rouchi *flau*. This latter is the orig. form, cf. O. Fr. *poi po pou* from *pau*. From *fluccus* corrupted into *flaucus*. (Cf. *suif* for *suev* from *sevum*). From *flou* comes the adj. *fluet* for *flouet*.

Floxo — *floscio.*

Fluet — *flou.*

Flûte — *flauto.*

Focaccia It., Sp. *hogaza*, Fr. *fouasse fouace* a cake, bun; from *focus*, Isidor: *cinere coctus et reversatus est focacius*. Cf. *focalia, fouaille, fuel.*

Focile — *fuoco.*

Fodero It., Sp. Pg. *forro*, Fr. *feurre* (E. *fur*), O. Fr. *fuerre foerre foarre* (the *Rue au Fouarre* = *Vico degli strami* of Dante Par. 10). The meanings are, in It. sheath, lining, fodder, in Sp. Pg. lining, sheathing, Pr. O. Fr. sheath, Fr. fodder; hence Fr. *fourreau;* Sp. *forrage*, Fr. *fourrage, fourrure fourier* &c., E. *forage;* vb. It. *foderare*, Sp. *forrar*, Pr. *folrar*, Fr. *fourrer*. From Goth. *fôdr* a sheath, O. H. G. *fustar* sheath, fodder, O. N. *fôdr* sheath, lining.

Fofo Sp. Pg. spongy, soft. The same root appears in Ven. *fofo* asthmatical, breathless, soft, weak, abst. *fafa*, Lomb. *fafa* fright (breathlessness), Com. *fofa* a spongy substance; it is the Du. *pof*, vb. *poffen*, G. *puffen*, E. *puff, f* for *p* by assimilation.

Foga It. violence, impetuousness, whence Fr. *fougue, fougueux;* vb. It. *fogare*. From *fuga*, Sp. *fuga* = liveliness, quickness; this is supported by the Romag. Crem. *fuga. Focus* would have given *fuoca.*

Foggia It. fashion, shape, manner, vb. *foggia;* from L. *forea* a hole (Pg. *fojo*, Sp. *hoyo hoya*). For the connexion of meanings, cf. It. *caro*, Gk. τύπος. The Ven. form is *foja*, so the word cannot come from Fr. *forge* = Piedm. *forgia* a *forge*; Sard. *forgiai* = Fr. *forger*.

Fogna It. conduit, *fognare* to draw off water; from *siphon* (Menage)?

Foible — *fievole*.

Foie — *fegato*.

Foin Fr. hay; from *foenum faenum*. The regular *fien* = It. *fieno* would have been confused with *fien* = *fimus*, and *ae* sometimes becomes *oi*, cf. *blois*. O. Fr. Pic. *fein* answers to a L. *fenum*.

Foire Fr., Rh. *fuira* diarrhœa; from *foria*.

Foire — *fiera*.

Fois — *vece*.

Foison Fr. E., Pr. *foisô*; from *fusio*, It. *fusione*.

Foja It. heat (sexual); from *furia*, Rh. *foia*.

Folc fouc O. Fr., Pr. *folc*, Com. *folco* a flock, troop, crowd; from O. H. G. A. S. *folc*, O. N. *fôlk* a crowd, E. *folk*; A. S. *floc*, E. *flock*, is O. Fr. *floc* (*flou*).

Folego — *holgar*.

Folla — *fullare*.

Follare It., Sp. *hollar*, Pr. *folar*, Fr. *fouler* to tread on, E. to *full*; It. *folla fola*, Sp. *folla*, Fr. *foule* (Pg. *fula*) a throng, cf. It. *calca*, also Sp. *huella* a footstep, *huello* a tread; hence It. *fullone*, Fr. *foulon* a *fuller*. The L. has not preserved the vb. *fullare*, but has the sbst. *fullo*. Hence It. *affollare*, O.Sp. *afollar*, Pr. *afolar*, Fr. *afoler*, to spoil.

Folle It., O. Sp. *fol*, Pr. *fol*, fem. *fola*, Fr. *fou folle*, sbst. and adj. droll, *fool* (Cat. *foll* = choleric); hence Fr. *affoler* to make a fool of (whence E. *foil*), Pr. *afolir* to be a fool. *Folle* is the L. *follis* used as an adj. (cf. R. Gr. 2, 232); it does not, however, denote the empty-headedness of the fool but his *instability*, Lat. *follere* (Jerome) meaning to move in and out, up and down, so a *restless* ghost, a hobgoblin, is termed It. *folletto*, Pr. Cat. Fr. *follet*, Bearn. *houlet*, cf. Fr. *fen follet* = ignis fatuus. In an O. Fr. psalter we find for *de mandatis tuis non erravi de les commandemenz ne foliai* from *folier* to err. Sp. *follon* = indolent, rogue, braggart (O. S.); Burg. *feulteu* = a beneficent spirit that guards cattle at night = a Fr. *folletot*.

Follon — *folle*.

Folto It. thronged; not from *folla*, but = *infultus*, Sic. 'nfultu.

Fona Pg. flake of fire. Goth. *fôn*, O. N. *funi* glowing coal, embers, whence G. *funke* spark.

Foncer — *fundo*.

Fonda Sp. a tavern, O. Sp. sling = Sp. *honda*; from *funda* a purse, L. L. place of rendezvous for market-people, cf. *bursa borsa* in both senses.

Fondaco It., Sp. *fundago*, O. Fr. *fondique* a warehouse; from Ar. *fondoq alfondoq* (whence Sp. *alhondiga*, Pg. *alfandega*) a tavern for merchants, also a store-house (from πανδοχεῖον πανδόχιον). The suffix *ic* in Rom. is so unusual as to forbid the der. from L. L. *funda*, v. *fonda*.

Fondefie O. Fr., = L. L. *fundibalum fundibulum*, Sp. *fundibulo*.

Fondo It. Cat., Sp. *hondo*, O. Sp. Pg. *fundo* deep. From *fundus* an old adj. found iu *profundus*, or from sbst. *fundus* Sp. *fondo*, Pg. *fundo* &c., sbst. being used as an adj. cf. R. Gr. 2, 232, and cf. *folle*. From *fundus* we have in Fr. (besides *fond*) *fonds*, Pr. *fons*, cf. *fils* from *filius*; hence Pr. *fonsar fondar*, Fr. *foncer*, *fonder* E. *found*, Pr. *afonsar* (cf. *preonsar* from *preon* = *profundus*), Fr. *enfoncer*, O. Fr. *afonder*. In the Pr. *esfondrar*, Fr. *effondrer* the *r* corresponds to the *l* of the It. *sfondolare*.

Fonil Sp., Pg. *funil*, Basq. *unila*; from *fundibulum* for *infundibulum*, Lim. *enfounil*. It is the same as the E. *funnel*, Bret. *founil*.

Fonsado O. Sp. O. Pg. *fosado*; from *fosar* to surround with a foss, thus prop. = a fortified camp.

Fontaine — *fontana*.

Fontana It. Sp. Pr., Fr. *fontaine*, Wal. *fēntēnē*, E. *fountain*; from *fons*, L. L. *fontana* (sc. *aqua*).

Forain — *fuora*.

Forban — *bando*.

Forbire It., Pr. *forbir*, Fr. *fourbir*, E. *furbish*; from O. H. G. *furban* to purify: *da lor costumi fa che tu ti forbi*, Dante. Hence It. *furbo*, Fr. *fourbe* rogue, cf. *fripon* from *friper*, Sp. *limpiar* (1) to clear (2) to clear out, rob, cf. also *escamoter*, *filou*.

Force O. Fr., Fr. *forces* (only plur.), Pr. *forsa* shears; from *forpex forpicis*.

Force — *forza*.

Forcels — *fuora*.

Forcené — *senno*.

Foresta It., Sp. Pg. Cat. *floresta*, Pr. *forest foresta*, Fr. *forêt* (f.), E. *forest*. The Sp. *floresta* has adopted itself to *flor*, and bears also the meaning of a flowery mead. We find in L. L. (f. whence Fr. *forêt*), *foreste* (n.), *forestus*, *forestum forastum*, *foresta forasta*, in the sense of unenclosed land, opp. *parcus* = enclosed land. The O. G. *varst*, G. *forst* is from the Rom. Some derive from the O. H. G. *foraha* a fir, *forehahi* a fir-wood. But, besides the loss of the *h* (usu. *g* in Rom., cf. *arguer* from *arahôn*), the termination *ast est* is very unusual, though found sometimes, cf. *brumasto brumesto*. From L. L.

forasticus = exterior (Placidus) came L. L. *forastis forestis*
(furas foris) = outlying land, open, unenclosed, cf. *forestiere*
= *exter extrarius*. *Forasticus* is also found in It. *forastico*,
Sic. *furestico*, Pr. *foresgue*, Cat. *ferresteg* wild, savage, Wald.
forest strange. Pic. *hors-ain* country people, prop. = those
outside the town. Zeuss derives *foresta* from W. *fforest*, which
is, however, from the E.

Forese — *fuori*.

Forfaro O. It., Pr. Fr. *forfaire*, la L. *foris facere* = *offendere*,
nocere prop. to err, do wrong, cf. *foris consiliare* to mislead.
In O. Fr. *se forfaire envers quelqu'un* = *se méfaire vers q.*;
with acc. = to lose, *forfeit* a thing, *forfaire son fief*, M. H. G.
verwürken, A. S. *forgyrecan*. Part. *forfatto forfait* = (1) an
evildoer, L. L. *forisfactus*, Goth. *fravaurhts* (2) an evil deed,
L. L. *forisfactum*, Goth. *fravaurhts (f.)*, E. *forfeit* = a thing
forfeited. The prefix is the same as the G. *ver*, E. *for* in *forget*,
forswear &c.

Forgia Piedm., Sp. Pg. *forja*, Fr. *forge*, E. *forge*, Pr. *farga*,
Sp. *fragua*; from *fabrica*, vb. *forgiare* &c., *fabricare*. O = au
from *ab*, Pr. *faur* = *faber*, O. Fr. *fevre*, Fr. *orfèvre* = *auri-
faber*.

Formaggio It., Pr. *formatge fromatge*, Fr. *fromage*, Pic. &c. *formage*, Sp. *formage* cheese. From Lat. *formaticus* from *forma*
a press: *liquor in fiscellas vel in formas transferendus* Columella.
Pr. *fourmo* = *forma*.

Fornire It., Sp. Pg. Pr. *fornir*, Fr. *fournir*, E. *furnish*. The Pr.
has also the form *formir furmir* to perfect, finish = It. *fornire*,
also *fromir* (It. *fronire*); it is from the O. H. G. *frumjan* to
further, perfect.

Foro It. Pg., Sp. *fuero* law, statute, jurisdiction, Pr. *for*, O. Fr.
fcur statute, tax; from *forum*. Hence Sp. Pg. Pr. *aforar*, O.
Fr. *afeurer* to tax, rate, guage. From *forensis* is Sp. *forense*
foreign, It. *forese* countryman, influenced by *foras*.

Porro — *fodero*.

Forza It., Sp. *fuerza*, Pr. *forsa*, Fr. E. *force*, vb. *forzare* &c.
L. L. *forcia* from a L. *fortia (fortis)*, prob. used in the spoken
L., if formed later we should have expected *fortia* as from
falsus falsia. Or *forcia* may be from the vb. *fortiare*, from
fortis as *graviare* from *gravis*, *leviare* from *levis*. Hence It.
sforzare, Sp. *esforzar*, Fr. *efforcer*, whence sbst. It. *sforzo*,
Sp. *esfuerzo*, Pr. *esfortz*, Fr. *effort* (E. *effort*) for *effors*, the *s*
being rejected as though it had been a mere case suffix.

Forziero It. a coffer, from φορτίον (Ferrari), or better = O. Fr.
forcier, L. L. *forsarius* (for *fortiarius*) strong-box = Fr. *coffre-
fort*, from *forza*, *force*.

Fouasse — *focaccia*.

Foudre Fr., Pr. *foldre folzer*, O. Fr. *esfoldre*, from *fulgur fol're foldre*, It. *folgore*, Wal. *fulger*.

Foudre Fr. a tun, from G. *fuder*, E. *fudder*.

Fouet (pron. *foit*) Fr., Mil. *foett*, Cat. *fuet* a whip, scourge, vb. *fouetter;* from *fou = fagus*, Rouchi *fouet = a* fagot, bundle of twigs, whence == rod, whip.

Fouger Fr.; from *fodicare*, Romag. *fudghè.* Hence *fouiller*, Pr. *fozilhar*, from a form *fodiculare*, whence Wall. *foyan* a mole. Hence also, by assimilation, *far-fouiller* to rummage. Lang. *fourfouliá* seems compounded with *furca*, cf. *frugar*.

Fougère — *felce.*

Fougue — *foga.*

Fouiller — *fouger.*

Fouine — *faina.*

Foule fouler — *follare.*

Fourbe fourbir — *forbire.*

Fourgon Fr. a wagon; prop. a wagon with a thill, from *furca*, It. *forcone*, Sp. *hurgon.*

Fourmiller Fr. to swarm; == *formiculare* from *formica*, O. Fr. *formier = formicare.* Sp. *gusanear*, from *gusano* a worm, has the same meaning, cf. also M. H. G. *wibelen* from *wibel (weevil).*

Fourrage fourreau fourrer — *fodero.*

Fouteau Fr. beech, Pic. *fo-iau;* from *fagus*, the *t* being a late insertion, cf. *sureau* dim. from O. Fr. *seu (salix).*

Foyer Fr., Pr. *foguier* hearth; from adj. *focarius*, Sp. *hogar.*

Foxa Sp. == anas torquata, coot; from φῶτξ (Covarruvias).

Fra — *tra.*

Fracassare It., Sp. *fracasar*, Fr. *fracasser* to smash, sbst. *fracasso, fracaso, fracas*, Rh. *farcas.* The Pr. *frascar* is from *fracsar* as *lasc* from *laxus.* From *fra-cassare* == Lat. *interrumpere.*

Fracido It., corr. *fradicio*, putrid; from *fracidus*, which occurs once in Cato de Re Rust., but which, corrupted and widely spread in It., must have been common in the spoken Latin.

Fraga Pg. rough stony ground, Sp. Pg. *fragura* roughness. From the root of L. *frag-osus*, cf. *bibbone.* Sp. *fraga* == bramble, blackberry (from *fragum* strawberry), cf. Pg. *fragoso* wild, uncultivated. Perhaps the Pg. word is the same as the Sp., taking a modified meaning through *fragosus.*

Fragata — *fregata.*

Fragua — *forgia.*

Frai — *fregare.*

Fraiditz fraidel fradel Pr., O. Fr. *fradons* wretch; from O. H. G. *freidi freidic* a deserter, apostate, M. H. G. *vreidec* faithless.

Fraile — *fraire.*

Fraindre O. Fr. to break, from *frangere*; Fr. *enfreindre* from *infringere*.

Fraire freire O. Sp., Pg. *freire*, Sp. *fraile freile* = Fr. *frère*, E. *friar*, contr. Sp. *fray* (It. *frà*), Pg. *frei*, fem. Sp. *fraila* &c. a nun; from *frater*, prob. through the Pr. (where *fraire* is regular), as the forms are not Spanish.

Frairin frarin O. Fr., Pr. *fraire* poor, miserable; from *frater* a monk (Gachet).

Frais Fr. (pl.) costs, expenses; from L. L. *fredum* (= *mulcta qua reus pacem exsequitur*, Duc.), O. H. G. *fridu*, G. *friede* peace, *friede-brief* a letter of acquittance, cf. *pagare = pacare*. Hence vb. *défrayer*, E. *defray*.

Frais — *fresco*.

Fraise Fr., Pr. *fraisa* strawberry, hence Sp. *fresa?* Prob. from *fragum*, whence Wall. *freo*, Parm. *fro*.

Fraise fraiser — *fregio*.

Fralda — *falda*.

Framboise Fr., whence N. Pr. *framboiso*, Sp. *frambuesa*, Com. *frambrosa*, Piedm. *flanboesa* raspberry. From Du. *braambezie*, O. H. G. *brâmberi* = E. *bramble-berry*. The *b* was changed to *f*, perhaps from *fraise*.

Frana It. fall of earth, vb. *franare*; from *fragmina*, *framna*, cf. *baleno* from βέλεμνον.

Franco It. Sp. Pg., Pr. Fr. *franc*, E. *frank*, N. Pr. *fran cuomo l'or* pure as gold. Usually derived from the name *Francus*, O. H. G. *Franco*, and this from the A. S. *franca* a dim. of *framea* a spear (Tacitus). J. Grimm, however, derives it from the Goth. *freis* = G. *frei*, E. *free*, whence the name of the people, who gave their name to the national weapon. There are two sets of forms, one with a soft *c*, the other with a *k* (*ch, qu*); It. *francese*, Sp. *frances*, Fr. *françois*, from the L. *Francia*; It. *franchezza*, Sp. *franqueza*, Fr. *franchise* (where the *ch* = It. *ch*, cf. *duchesse*, *sachet* &c.), from G. *Franco*, the G. guttural being invariably retained in derivatives, cf. *borgo*.

Frangia It., Sp. *franja*, Fr. *frange*, whence Du. *frangie*, G. *franse* fringe. From *framea* would be regularly formed *frange*, as from *vindemia vendange*, cf. *gherone*. But *framea* was an uncommon word, so it is better to refer it to *fimbria* whence *fringe* (E.), *frange*, cf. Wal. *fimbrie*, O. Pr. *fremna* = a form *frembia*. Rouchi *frinche* (*frimbia*), Sic. *frinza* from an O. Fr. *fringe*.

Fransir — *froncir*.

Frappa — *arpa*.

Frapper Fr., Pr. *frapar*. Like *friper* from the Norse, where *hrappa* means to scold, E. *frape*, adj. *hrappr* violent, E. *fraple* to make a noise (cf. *increpare*), whence *frape* a crowd, O. Fr.

frapin frapaille. Cf. also the E. *flap*, Du. *flappen*, Fr. (Rheims) *frapouille* = E. *flap* (subst.).

Frasca It. Rh. leafy branch, whence Sp. *frasca*, Rh. *sfrascar* to strip off boughs. Diez derives it from *virere, virasca vrasca frasca*, as *fuggiasco* from *fuggire*, cf. Sp. *verd-asca*. But it is better to connect it with Goth. *frasts* a child. *Frasche* = tricks, whence Fr. *faire des frasques.*

Frassugno — *fresange.*

Fratta It. a hedge; from φράττειν, N. Gr. φράκτη = φράγμα.

Fray freile — *fraire.*

Frayer — *fregare.*

Frayeur Fr., O. Fr. *froior*, Pr. *freior* fright; hence Fr. *effroi*, O. Fr. *esfroi*, Pr. *esfrei*, vb. Fr. *effrayer*, Pr. *esfreyar esfrei-dar.* From *frigidus, frigus*, shivering being the effect of fright as well as of cold, cf. φρίσσειν, *horrere, schaudern, farsi di gielo* &c. Others derive the word from E. *fray, fright*, but these are prob. from the Rom.

Frazada — *fregio.*

Freccia It., O. Sp. Pg. *frecha*, Sp. Pg. Pr. *flecha*, Fr. *flèche* (E. *Fletcher* = an arrow-maker), Piedm. Sard. *flecia*, also *frizza*, Wall. *fliche* an arrow; from Du. *flits* an arrow, M. H. G. *vliz, flitsch* a bow.

Fredon Fr. a shake in singing; vb. *fredonner*; from the root *frit* in *fritinnire* to chirp?

Fregare It., Sp. Pg. Pr. *fregar*, Fr. *frayer*, O. Fr. *froyer* (cf. *plicare ployer*), E. *fray* (*freak* = streak), rub; from *fricare.* Hence It. *frega* lust (E. *freak*), Fr. *frai* spawn, O. Fr. *fraye*, Rh. *frega*, It. *fregola.* Sp. *refregar, refriega*; It. *sfregare*, Pg. *esfregar*, Sp. *estregar.*

Fregata It., Sp. Pg. Cat. Neap. *fragata*, Fr. *frégate*, E. *frigate*, orig. = a small boat. From *fabricata*, cf. *bastimento bateau.*

Fregio It., Sp. *friso freso*, Fr. *frise fraise* fringe, E. *frieze* (= a horizontal broad band occupied with sculpture); vb. It. *fre-giare*, Fr. *friser fraiser* to curl, frizzle, Sp. *frisar* to raise the nap on cloth, *frisa* = E. *frieze* (stuff), It. *frisato*, Fr. *fraisette frizzet* ruffle, Sp. *frezada frazada* a blanket. Prob. from the German name *Frisa Fresa* = curly, whence Fries. *frisle*, E. *frizzle.* We find in L. L. *frisii panni, saga fresonica, vestimenta de Fresarum provincia.*

Fregola — *fregare.*

Frelater le vin Fr. to adulterate wine; from Du. *wyn verlaten* to pour out wine.

Frêle Fr., E. *frail*; from *fragilis*, It. *fraile.*

Frelon Fr. a hornet; from *frêle*, cf. Berr. *grelon* from *grêle* = *gracilis*, and Gr. σφήξ connected with σφίγγω, and = the slender (compressed) insect. O. Fr. *froilon* is from O. Fr.

form *fraile (oi = ai)*. The G. *horniss*, E. *hornet*, has reference to the humming *horn*-like sound of its flight.

Frelore O. Fr., and still in Fr. dialects, lost, forlorn, from the G. *verloren*. The form *forelores* = A. S. *forloren*, E. *forlorn*.

Freluquet — *farfaluca*.

Frêne Fr. (f.) an ash, O. Fr. *fresne fraisne*; from *fraxinus*, Pg. *freixo*.

Frente Sp. forehead; a euphonic contraction of *fruente (frons)*, cf. *fleco* from *fluero*, *estera* from *storea*.

Fresaie Fr. a screech-owl, Poit. *presaie*, Gasc. *bresague*, from *præsaga*, the bird being regarded as one of ill omen, also called *effraie*, *oiseau de la mort*, G. *todtenvogel*, *leichhuhn*.

Fresange fresanche fraissenque O. Fr. a young pig, N. Pr. *fraysse*; from O. H. G. *frisking*, G. *frischling* a shoot. The It. *frassugno* = *frisking friskung*, but derives it meaning from *sugna*, *frassugno (fraysse sugna)* = swine's fat. The Sic. *frisinga* is prob. from the Fr.

Fresco It. Sp. Pg., Pr. *fresc*, Fr. *frais*, f. *fraiche*, Wall. *friss*; from O. H. G. *frisc*, A. S. *fersc*, E. *fresh*, W. *fresg*, Bret. *fresk*.

Freso — *fregio*.

Freste O. Fr. (m.), Pr. *frest* a gable; from O. H. G. *first* top, gable.

Frestele O. Fr. flute, vb. *fresteler*, Pr. *frestelar*, from *fistella* for *fistula*.

Fret Fr., Pg. *frete*, Sp. *flete*; from O. H. G. *freht*, E. *freight*.

Fretes — *frette*.

Frétiller Fr., Pr. *frezilhar*. From a L. *fritillare (fritillus)* to shake, though this should have given *frediller*. *Frictillare* would suit the form better.

Fretin Fr. parings, refuse, fry; from *frictum*.

Frettare It., Pr. *fretar* to rub, It. *fretta*, N. Pr. *freto* haste; from *fricare frictum*. Fr. has *frotter* for *froiter*, Burg. *fretter*. From *frotter* comes the Sp. *frotar flotar*, and Fr. dim. *fröler (frotler)*, Norm. *freuler (= friculare)*.

Frette Fr. (E. *fret* in heraldry) iron hoop, pl. grating, hence Sp. *fretes*; for *ferrette*, from *ferrum*.

Freux Fr. rook; from O. H. G. *hruoch*, A. S. *hróc* (cf. *corus queux*), O. N. *hrókr*, Dan. *roge*, L. G. E. *rook*, H. G. *ruech*. For *f* = *h* cf. *frimas friper*.

Frezada — *fregio*.

Frezar — *frizzare*.

Friand fricandeau fricasser — *frique*.

Friche Fr. (f.) a fallow; from G. *frisch*, E. *fresh*, cf. *novale* from *novus* according to Ducange, but *frisch* gives *fraiche*, so it is better to derive *friche*, with Grimm, from *fractitium*, cf. Langued. *roumpudo*, Norm. *briser* to break up land.

Frionte O. Fr. : : L. *fremitus*, It. *fremito*. Le Duchat writes *frainte* and derives from *frangere*.

Frignaro Lomb. to whine, whimper, also to jeer, Com. *frigna* a whimpering woman, Crem. nice, captious. Prob. for *flignare* from G. *flennen* to make wry faces, Sw. *flina*, Dan. *fline*, E. *frine*, whence also Lomb. *frigna* = a ravine (prop. a grinning mouth), O. Fr. *flan* an embrasure (opening in the walls), G. *flans* a wry face. From *frignare* come It. *infriguo infrignato* wrinkled, morose, Dauph. *se deifrinà* to be morose, cf. Fr. *se refrogner se renfrogner*, E. *frown (refrogner* for *refroigner*, *oi* = *i*).

Friloux Fr. frosty; *frigidulosus*, from L. *frigidulus*.

Frimas Fr. rime, vb. Pic. *frimer*. From O. N. *hrim*, A. S. *hrim*, E. *rime*, Du. *rijm*, Bav. *reim pfreim*. Pic. *rimée* has lost the *h*.

Fringuollo — *fringuer*.

Fringuor Fr. to move quickly backwards and forwards, Bret. *fringa*, Langued. *fringò* to caress. From a root found in Lat. *fringutire* to trill, *fringilla* a finch, *frigutire*, *frigulare*, W. *ffreg* chatter. Bret. *fringol* a shake, trill, Fr. *fringoter*, It. *fringottare* to trill, are from *fringuer*, *frigoter* from *frigutire*. From *fringilla*, root *fring*, is It. *fringuello*, corrupted into *filunguello*, Crem. *frangol*, Piedm. *franguel frangoi*.

Friper Fr. to wear out, consume greedily, Berr. *friper* = to lick a plate, Anj. *fripe* = Gk. ὄψον; *fripper* to eat greedily, hence Fr. *fripon* a purloiner, rogue, *friperie*, E. *frippery* (prop. stolen property). Fr. *fr* = N. *hr* (cf. *frimas*), *friper* = N. *hripa* to do hastily.

Fripon — *friper*.

Friquo O. Fr., Pr. *fric*, N. Pr. *fricaud* brisk, lively, Dauph. *fricandela* a sprightly damsel. From Goth. *friks*, O. H. G. *frēh* eager, greedy, M. H. G. *vrēch*, A. S. *frec* bold, O. E. *frek* sprightly; for the connexion between boldness and sprightliness, cf. *gaillard*. Hence also N. Pr. *fricaud* dainty, costly, *fricot* a dainty dish, Fr. *fricandeau*, vb. *fricasser*, the notion of *daintiness* being derived from that of *greediness*. Mahn, however, derives *fricasser* from *frictus (frigere)*, whence *fricare* for *frictare*.

Frire Fr., E. *fry*; from *frigère*, It. *friggere*. Hence also *friand* dainty, nice, Norm. *frioler* to be eager, greedy, Rouchi *frider* to hiss, sputter (of meats on the fire), Fr. *affrioler* to entice, allure.

Frisato friso — *fregio*.

Frisol frisuolo frejol Sp. a kidney-bean; L. L. *fresa*, Gloss. Plac.: *defresum detritum, unde udhuc fresa faba, quæ obtrita*

frangitur, fubu fresa dicla quod eam frendant i. e. frangant.
Papias.

Frisone frosone frusone a sort of finch; from *frendere fresus.*

Frisson Fr. shivering, L. L. *frictio;* from a form *frigitio* contr.
frictio friçon, from *frigēre,* O. Fr. Pr. *frire.*

Frizzare It. to gnaw, smart, Sp. *frezar* to consume, rub, dig
up, N. Pr. *frizá* to grind, crash; sbst. Sp. *freza,* Pr. *fressa*
track.　Partly from *frictus frictiare,* partly from O. H. G.
frezzan, G. *fressen* to cat, consume.　Fr. *froisser* to crush,
O. Sp. *fresar* to murmur, may be referred to *frendere* gnash,
part. *fressus,* or from *frictus* (cf. Pic. *froicher*).

Froo Fr., E. *frock.* From L. *floccus,* Pr. *floc* with both L. and
Fr. meanings, L. L. *floccus froccus.* Perhaps also connected
with the O. H. G. *hroch,* G. *rock,* though, usually, only the
N. *hr* becomes *fr* in Fr. (cf. *frimas, friper freux*), and we find
no N. form *hroekr.*

Froisser — *frizzare.*

Fròler — *frettare.*

Frollo It. tender (of flesh-meat), weak.　L. *fluida caro* = It.
carne frolla: fluidulus, flollo, frollo, cf. *stridulus strillo.*

Fromage — *formaggio.*

Frombo — *rombo.*

Fronoher O. Fr. to snarl, snort; from *rhoncare* (Sidonius), v.
roncar.

Froncir O. Sp., Sp. *fruncir,* Cat. *frunsir,* Sard. *frunziri,* Pr.
froncir, Fr. *froncer* to gather into plaits, wrinkle, *frounce,*
Sp. *fruncir las cejas* to frown; O. Fr. sbst. *froncc,* E. *flounce,*
Sard. *frunza. Froncer* = *frontiar (frons)* prop. to contract
the brows.　Pg. *franzir* is a corruption.

Fronde — *fionda.*

Frotar — *frettare.*

Frotta frottola — *flotta.*

Frotter — *frettare.*

Frouxo — *floscio.*

Frugare It., Sp. *hurgar,* Pg. *forcar,* N. Pr. *furgá,* O. Fr. *furgier*
to stir with a stick, sound, probe, search, with inserted
vowel, Ven. *furegare,* Sard. *furogai.* Cf. It. *rinvergare* from
verga, Piedm. *fustignè* from *fustis,* L. *percontari,* which is,
perhaps, from *contus.*

Frullare It. to whistle, whizz, rustle: perhaps from *fluctuare*
dim. *fluctulare flullare frullare,* cf. *frollo,* but more prob. a
mere onomatop., *frullo* = the whirring noise made by par-
tridges when they rise.

Frusto It. = L. *frustum; frustare* to whip, scourge, prop. (as
Pr. *frustar*) to slash, cut in pieces, hence *frusta* a whip.

Fucar Sp. a rich man; from a German name *Fugger*, v. Schmeller 1, 516.

Fucia — *fiucia*.

Fucile — *fuoco*.

Fucina It. a forge, smithy. From *focus*, cf. *fucile*.

Fuero — *foro*.

Fuerza — *forza*.

Fulna — *faina*.

Fuisca — *falavesca*.

Fujo It. dark. From a Lat. form in -*ius*, *furrus furvius furvjus*, cf. Sp. *agrio*, *curvio*, *crasio*, *soberbio*, *novio*, and v. *crojo*, *mezzo*, *rozzo*, *vizzo*, *bujo*.

Fula — *follare*.

Fulano Sp., O. Sp. *fulan*, Pg. *fulano fuão* = L. *quidam*; from Arab. *fôlan*.

Fulo Pg. = L. *fulvus*; for the loss of the *v*, cf. *polilla*.

Fulvido It. shining; from *fulgidus*, with the *v* of *fulvus*.

Fumier Fr. dung, O. Fr. *femier*; from *fimus*, cf. O. Fr. Pic. Champ. *fumelle* for *femelle*, O. Fr. *frumer* for *fermer*.

Fummosterno It. a herb; corrupted from *fumus terræ*, Fr. *fumeterre*, E. *fumitory*.

Funcho — *finocchio*.

Fuoco It., Sp. *fuego*, Pg. *fogo*, Pr. *fuec*, Fr. *feu*, Wal. *foc*; from *focus* used for *ignis* in L. poets, and in L. L. *focum facere* = *facere ignem*. Hence It. *focile fucile*, Fr. *fusil* a steel, firelock, musket (*fusil*), cf. G. *flinte*.

Fuora fuori It., Sp. *fuera*, O. Sp. *fueras*, Pg. *fora*, Pr. *foras fors*, Fr. *hors* (*h* asp.), O. Fr. *fors*, Wal. *fërë*, = L. *extra*; from *foras foris*. Hence, too, Rh. *ora* or. Pr. *forceis* for *forseis* = *foras ipsum* (cf. *anceis*, *ainçois*); Fr. *hor-mis* = *foras missum*; Sp. *foraneo forano*, Fr. *forain*, O. Fr. *deforain*, E. *foreign*.

Furação — *uracano*.

Furbo — *forbire*.

Furo Sp. wild, shy, also *huraño*; like the It. *furo* from L. *fur*, cf. *hacer furo* to conceal a thing artfully.

Furolles Fr. (f. pl.) exhalations; for *furoles* from *feu*, formed like It. *focajuolo*, cf. *flammerole* ignis fatuus.

Furon O. Sp., Sp. *huron*, Pg. *furão*, O. Fr. *fuiron*; It. *furetto*, Fr. *furet*, Du. *furet foret fret*, *ferret*, Langued. *fure* a mouse; vb. Sp. *huronear*, Sard. *furittai*, Fr. *fureter* to *ferret*, search. Prob. an old L. word; Isidore has: *furo a furvo unde et fur*; *tenebrosos enim et occultos cuniculos effodet*. From *fur* a thief, It. *furone*, L. L. *furo*; cf. G. *maus* (*mouse*), Sansk. *mushika*, from *mausen*, Sansk. *mush* to steal.

Fusaggine It. the spindle-tree; from *fusus*.

Fuscello It. a fescue, straw; from *fustis*, for *fusticello*.

Fusil — *fusco*.

Fusta It. Sp. Pg., Fr. *fuste* a kind of galley, a *foist;* from *fustis*, Sp. *fuste*, Pr. *fust*, L. L. *fustis* wood, cf. It. *legno* a ship, from *lignum*. Hence Fr. *fût* = stock, cask &c., *futaie* a forest, *affût* gun-carriage (*être à l'affût* to be on the watch), *affûter* to mount, set, It. *affustare*.

Fustagno frustagno It., Sp. *fustan*, Pr. *fustani*, Fr. *futaine*, E. *fustian;* from *Fostât* in Egypt, where it was made.

Futaine — *fustagno*.

G.

Gabardina — *gabbano*.

Gabbano It., Sp. O. Fr. *gabau* a coarse cloak; prob. from the same root as *cabana*, *gabinetto (capanna);* hence also Sp. *gabardina*, *gavardina*, E. *gaberdine*.

Gabbia gaggia It., Sp. Pg. *gavia*, N. Pr. *gavi* (m.), Fr. E. *cage*, O. Fr. *caive*, Ven. Sard. *cabbia;* from *cavea*. Hence dim. It. *gabbiuola*, Sp. *gayola*, Pg. *gaiola*, O. Fr. *gaole jaiole* (Sp. *jaula*), E. *gaol jail*, Fr. *geôle*. Hence *cajoler*, E. *cajole*, Fr. *enjôler* to wheedle, coax, inveigle, Sp. *enjaular* to imprison. *Gabbione* gives Fr. E. *gabion*.

Gabbiano — *gavia*.

Gabbo It., Pr. O. Fr. *gab* gap banter, jest, vulg. E. *gab;* vb. *gabbare* &c.; from N. *gabb* jeering, vb. *gabba*.

Gabella It. Pg., Sp. Pr. *gabela* tax, excise, Fr. *gabelle* salt-tax, vb. *gabellare* &c. From the A. S. *gaful gafol*, E. *garel* (which is from *gifan*, Goth. *giban*, *give*), whence L. L. *gabhum gabulum*, *gabella* (prop. a plur. of *gabellum*).

Gabinetto gabinete — *capanna*.

Gable Fr. (f.) E. From L. *gabalus* a cross, Varro: *gabalum crucem dici veteres volunt*. The Norm. *gable* is m. O. H. G. *gabala*, G. *gabel* is, perhaps, nearer than the L. word. Cf. L. *furca* = gable.

Gaburo It., Crem. *gabeurr* a boor; from O. H. G. *gaburô*.

Gacha — *quatto*.

Gâcher Fr. to row, move, *gâche* an oar, from O. H. G. *waskau* to wash; hence *gâchis* puddle, O. Fr. *waschier* to soil.

Gado — *ganado*.

Gafa Sp. Pg., Fr. *gaffe*, E. *gaff* a hook, Sp. *gafo* cramped (of the nerves), leprous; vb. Sp. *gafar*, Fr. *gaffer* to hook; from Celt., Gael. *gaf*, H. G. *gaifung* an iron ring, *gaifen* to cut crookedly.

Gafar — *gabella*.

Gago — *gaggio.*

Gaggio It., Sp. Pg. Pr. Fr. *gage* pledge, wages *(gages)*, Pr. *gudi gazi* will, testament; vb. Pr. *gatjar*, O. Fr. *guger* to pledge, Fr. to wager; It. *engaggiare*, Pr. *engatjar*, Fr. *engager* to pawn (E. *engage*); Fr. *dégager*. L. L. has *vadium wadium* bail pledge, f. *radia*, vb. *wadiare*, *invadiare*, *disvadiare*, *cevadiare*. Hence N. Gr. βάδιον, Bax. *bahia*. Not from the L., for the *v* would remain soft, but from the Goth. *vadi* (partly from *ridan* to bind, partly from *vas vadis*), O. H. G. *wetti*, M. H. G. *wette*, O. Fris. *ved* pledge, G. *wette* wager, vb. Goth. *gavadjôn* to promise, M. H. G. *wetten*, G. *wetten* to bet.

Gagliardo — *gala.*

Gaglio — *quagliare.*

Gaglioffo It., Sp. *gallofo gallofero*, E. *loafer*, a beggar, rogue; Rouchi *galoufe* a glutton, Wall. *galofa gaioufe;* Sp. *gallofa* a bit of bread, Rh. *gagliaffa*, Lomb. *gajoffa*. From *Galli offu* alms given in the monasteries to the French pilgrims to S. Jago. Cat. *galyofol = Galli offula.*

Gagliuolo It. husk, pod, Com. *gajum* a nutshell. From L. L. *galgulus bacu* πυρήν Isid.? The Wall. has *gaille géie* a nut, v. Grandgagnage, who derives it from *callum.*

Gagner — *guadagnare.*

Gagnolare It.; from *gannire.*

Gago — *gaaguear.*

Gai — *gajo.*

Gaif Fr. = E. *waif*, vb. *guever;* L. L. *wayfium, res vaivæ, wayriare. Gaif* = E. *waif* orig. = *animal errans* or *vagans*, from E. *wave waive*, A. S. *vafian.*

Gaillard — *gala.*

Gaimenter waimenter O. Fr. (Chauc. *waymentynge*), Pr. *gaymentar*, Danph. *gucimentá* to lament, bewail. From the interj. *guai*, on the analogy of *lamenter*. In Fr. *guermenter* we see the Celtic root, Gael. *gairm*, W. *garmis*, Bret. *garmi* to cry, Du. *kermea*. Fr. *se gramenter*, however, points to G. *gram.*

Gaine — *guaina.*

Gaita Sp. Pg. Cat. flageolet, bag-pipe; from Pr. *gaita* a watcher, so = watcher's pipe. Or better from Arab. *gaïtah* flute.

Galvão galvota — *gavia.*

Gajo It., O. Sp. *gayo*, Pg. *gaio*, Pr. *gai jai*, Fr. *gai*, E. *gay* from O. H. G. *gâhi* rash, G. *jähe*. Hence Sp. *gayo gaya*, Pr. *gai jai*, O. Fr. Pic. *gai*, Fr. *geai*, E. *jay*, Sp. *gayar* to variegate.

Gal O. Fr. a stone; hence Fr. *galet* a pebble, *galette*, Pr. *galeta* a flat cake, It. *galetta*, Sp. *galleta* a biscuit; prob. an old Gallic word, connected with W. *calen* (f.) a whetstone.

Gala It. Sp. Pg., O. Fr. *gale* show, parade, munificence, charming address &c.; vb. O. Fr. *galer;* hence It. *gallone,* Sp. *galon,* Fr. *galon,* E. *galloon,* lace; Fr. *galant,* Sp. *galante galan galano* (elegantly-dressed), E. *gallant;* O. Fr. *galois gallois* &c. From O. H. G. *geil* proud, A. S. *gál* lively, O. H. G. *geili* pride. It. *gagliardo,* Sp. *gallardo,* Pr. *galhart,* Fr. *gaillard* = A. S. *gagol geagle* wanton, cf. also W. *gall* strength, O. Gael. *galach* strength, hardihood.

Galanga It. Sp. Pg., O. Sp. *garingal,* O. Fr. *galange, garingal,* E. *galingal,* G. *galgan galgant* a root imported from China and Java; from Ar. *khalangan* which is from the Persian.

Galant — *gala.*

Galapplo — *chiapparc.*

Galardon — *guiderdone.*

Galaubia It. costliness, expenditure; from Goth. *galaubs* costly.

Galbe Fr. (m.) the slope or arch of a roof; from M. H. G. *walbe* (m.) = G. *walm* slope, hence G. *gewölbe* arch, vault. The *al* (for *au*) of the Fr. shows the late origin of the word.

Galbero It., Mil. Com. *galbé* a gold-hammer (bird); = L. *galbula* (Mart. Plin.). From the later form *galgulus,* come Sp. *galgulo,* It. *ri-gogolo, rigoletto* = *aurigalgulus.* Parm. *galbeder,* Crem. *galpeder* = *galb-icterus.* In Sp. the bird is also called *oro-pendola,* in Fr. *loriot.*

Galdre Sp. a loose overcoat; introduced from *Guelder*-land.

Gale Fr. itch, *se galer* to itch. From the G. *galle,* E. *gall* to gall, It. *galla,* Sp. *agalla* a tumour, all, perhaps, from L. *galla* a gall-nut, It. *galla;* Pictet refers to Irish *galar galradh* a malady.

Galea It. O. Sp., Pg. *galé,* Pr. *galea gale galeya,* O. Fr. *galée, galie,* E. *galley;* It. *galeotta,* Sp. Pg. *galeota,* O. Fr. *galiot;* It. *galeazza,* Sp. Pg. *galeaza,* Fr. *galéasse,* E. *galleass;* It. *galeone,* Sp. *galeon,* Pg. *galeão,* Fr. *galion,* E. *galleon.* It. Sp. Pg. Pr. Lomb. *galera,* Fr. *galère* = *galea* and in Sp. Pg. a covered wagon. Probably from the Gk. (like so many other nautical words) where γάλη = ἐξίδρας εἶδος (Hesych.) a gallery, which may well have given its name to a large ship with covered rows of seats; this would account for the accent *(galéa).* From *galé* = γάλη, or from *galera* comes *galleria* &c., *gallery.*

Galora galère — *galea.*

Galerno Sp. Pg., Pr. *galerna,* Fr. *galerna* a North-West wind, cf. Bret. *gwalern gwalarn gwalorn.* From Celtic *gal,* E. *gale* with a Pr. termination, cf. *bolerna, buerna, suberna.*

Galgo Sp. Pg. a greyhound; from *canis Gallicus,* cf. Ov. Met. 1, 533. *Ut canis in vacuo leporem cum gallicus arvo vidit.*

Galgulo — *galbero.*

Galima Sp. pilfering, booty. From Ar. *ghanima.*

Galimatias Fr. nonsense, a confused heap of words. The etym. is unknown. Cf. E. *gallimaufrey*, Fr. *gallinafrée* a confused heap of things, a hodge‑podge, which Wedgw. makes an onomatop.

Gallare It. to swim, exult, *essere a galla* to float. Not from the floating of the *gall* nut, but, prob. from *gallus*, cf. Sp. *tener mucho gallo* to be very arrogant, It. *galloria* exultation.

Galleria It., Sp. *galeria*, Pg. *galaria*, Fr. *galérie*, E. *gallery*. In L. L. *galeria* = an ornamental building, hall, and a court-yard. V. s. *galea*.

Gallofo — *gaglioffo*.

Gallone — *gala*.

Galocha galoche — *galoscia*.

Galon — *gala*.

Galoppare It., Sp. Pg. *galopar*, Pr. *galaupar*, Fr. *galoper*, E. *galop*, abst. It. *galoppo* &c. It is the Goth. *hlaupan*, O. H. G. *gahlaufan*, A. S. *gehleápan* (E. *leap*), G. *laufen* to run, Pr. *au* = G. *an*, cf. *annir* = *haunjan*, *raubar* = *raubôn*, *raus* = *raus*. The Du. *walop* is from the Fr. *walop*, *waloper*, It. *gualoppare*, *w*=*g*, cf. *garçon warçon*, *gaignon waignon*, *gaquière waquière*. It. *galopo*, It. *galuppo*, Fr. *galopin* (in fables = the messenger hare) a foot-boy, varlet = O. H. G. *hloufo*.

Galoscia It., Sp. *galocha*, Fr. *galoche*, E. *galosh*; from L. *gallica* a slipper. The Sp. is *haloza*. Wedg. makes it a lengthened form of *clog*.

Galtera — *gola*.

Gamache — *gamba*.

Gamarra Sp. Pg. a martingale; also found in the Basque, whence like most words in *arra*, it is derived. But. cf. O. H. G. *gamarjan* to hinder *(mar)*, A. S. *gemearra* a hindering.

Gamba It. Sp. Cat., Pr. *gamba* in *gambaut*, Pg. *gambia*, Fr. *jambe* leg. We find forms with the tenuis, O. Sp. Pr. Sard. *camba*, Rh. *comba*, Alb. *khĕmbĕ*, and without the *b*, O. Sp. *cama*, O. Fr. *jame*. From the root *cam* or *camb* found in *cam-urus* *cam-erus* crooked, *can-era* an arch, *cam-erare* to arch, Celt. *cam* crooked, *camineg* a felloo, Pg. *camba*, which form prob. existed in L. = Gk. χαμπή, Celt. *cam* for *camb* (cf. *Cambodunum* &c.). Besides Pg. *camba* a felloe, we find *cambaio* crooked, O. Sp. *encamar* to bend, Burg. *camboisser*. Hence, also, Sp. *jamba* = E. *jamb*, It. *gambo* stalk, *gambone*, Fr. *jambon*, Sp. *jamon* a ham, *gammon*, O. Fr. *gamache* a leg-covering, E. *gamashes*. Hence, also, Fr. *gambiller* to leap, E. *gambol* = O. E. *gambaud*, Fr. *gambade*.

Gambais gambaison Pr., O. Fr. *wambais*, *gambeson*, O. Sp.

gambax, O. Pg. *canbas* a waistcoat, M. H. G. *wambeis*, G. *wams*, from O. H. G. *womba* belly.

Gambero It., Sp. *gambaro*, O. Fr. *jamble*, N. Pr. *jambre*, Dauph. *chambro* a crab; from *cammarus*.

Gambo — *gamba*.

Gamella Sp. Pg., Fr. *gamelle* a wooden trough = *camella* a drinking vessel.

Gamo gamusa — *camozza*.

Gana It. Sp. Pg. Cat. appetite. From O. H. G. *geinôn* = to gape, cf. *badare*, *hiare*, χαίνειν, and v. *guadagnare*.

Ganache — *ganascia*.

Ganado Sp., Pg. *gado* flock, herd; from *ganar*, so = the gained, acquired, cf. O. Fr. *proic* = herd, Pr. *aver*, N. Pr. *aver* (f.) = sheep. Basq. *atcienda* a head of cattle = Sp. *hacienda* possession.

Ganar gançar — *guadagnare*.

Ganascia It., Fr. *ganache* a jaw. Augmen. from *gena*.

Ganchir guenchir Pr. O. Fr., Rh. *guinchir* to give way; from O. H. G. *wankjan wenkjan*, G. *wanken*. From sbst. *wank* comes Com. *gnonch* a fault.

Gancio It., Sp. Pg. *gancho* a hook, Fr. *ganse* a loop for holding a button. Prob. from root *cam gam*, v. *gamba*.

Gandir O. Fr., Pr. *guandir* to give way, retire, O. Fr. also *gandiller*; from Goth. *vandjan*, O. H. G. *wantjan wentjan*, G. *wenden* to go, E. *wend*.

Gangamu Sic. a net; from γάγγαμον.

Ganghero It. a hinge, Sard. *cancaru*, Mil. *canchen*, Pr. *ganguil*, Hesych. κάγχαλος. Hence It. *sganghcrare* to unhinge, Pg. *escancarar* to open wide.

Gangrône — *cangrena*.

Gangucar Sp. to speak through the nose, adj. *gangoso*. An onomatop.

Ganivet — *canif*.

Ganse — *gancio*.

Ganso — *ganta*.

Gant — *guante*.

Ganta Pr. also *ganto*, a wild goose, O. Fr. *gante*, *gente*, Wal. *gênscê gênsac* (Pol. *geska*, Russ. *gusak* dim.). Pliny has *ganta*, and Venant. Fort. distinguishes *anser* and *ganta*. It is the L. G. *gante*, Du. *gent* (E. *gander*), M. H. G. *ganze*, O. H. G. *ganazzo*, whence Sp. *ganso*.

Ganzua Sp., Pg. *gazua* a picklock; from B. *gaco-itsva* a false key.

Gañon gañote Sp. windpipe; from *canna*.

Gara It. contest; from Fr. *gare* = ware! It. *garare* to vie = Fr. *garer* to beware.

Garabato Sp., Pg. *garavato* a pothook. From the Ar. *garb (girab)* the edge of a sword? Hence *garabo garabato*, cf. *horca horcate*; or from Ar. *kullâb* a pothook. Larram. derives it from a Basque word *gorobatu* to seize.

Garabia — *garbino*.

Garabito Sp. a stall or booth; from B. *garau* a chamber and *itoa* damp (Larramendi).

Garance Fr. (hence Sp. *granza*), Pic. *waranche*, L. L. *garantia*, *warentia* madder; the Greeks called 'red' ἀληθινόν, on the analogy of which may have been formed from *verus rerare*, *rerantia rarantia*.

Garañon — *guarugno*.

Garant garante — *guarento*.

Garba · *gerbe*.

Garbanzo Sp. chick-pea; according to Larram., from B. *garau* corn and *antzua* to dry.

Garbillo Sp. a sieve, *garbillar* to sift, E. *garble*. The Ar. has *girbâl*, vb. *garbala*, but the Rom. word is, perhaps, from the L. *cribellum*, cf. *carnero* for *crnero*, *bergante* for *brigante*. *Garbin* a hair-net = *cribrum?*

Garbin — *garbillo*.

Garbino It. Sp., N. Pr. *garbin* a south-west wind; from Ar. *garb* west, vb. *garaba* to set (of the sun), whence also Pg. *garabia* west. It. has also *agherbino*.

Garbo It. Sp. Pg. behaviour, elegance, E. *garb*: vb. It. *garbare* to please, Sp. *garbar* to show affectation; Pr. *garbier* a braggart; from O. H. G. *garawi garwi* ornament, G. *gerben*, Du. *guerwen* to deck, *b = w*, cf. *falbo = faluwer*.

Garbo Ven. Com. *garb gherb* (It. *garbetto* Veneroni) bitter; from O. H. G. *harw*, G. *herbe* sour.

Garbuglio It., Sp. *garbullo*, O. Fr. *garbouil grabouil* tumult, confusion. From *garrire* and *bullire*, cf. Sp. *bulla*, It. *buglione*, Cat. *bulyanga* a noise.

Garco garçon — *garzone*.

Garde garder — *guardare*.

Garenne Fr., also *varenne* for *warenne*, E. *warren*, L. L. *warenna*. Perhaps from O. Fr. *garer warer* to guard, be *ware*, *enne* for *ene = ine*, cf. *gastine*, *guerpine*, *haïne* from G. roots. Du. has *warande*.

Garer Fr., Pr. *garar* to take care, *beware*; from O. H. G. *warôn*. Hence Pr. *esgarar = garar*, but Fr. *égarer*, whence It. *sgarrare* to mislead.

Garño — *graffia*.

Garfo — *greffe*.

Gargamela — *gargatta*.

Garganta — *gargatta*.

Gargatta It., O. Fr. Pic. *gargate*, Rh. *gargata*, Genev. *garga-*

taine, Jura *garguelotte* &c., Bret. *gargaden*, O. E. *gargate*, Sp.
Pg. Cat. *gargauta* throat; from *gurges* with suffix *att*, and the
onomatop. *gargarizzare* to *gargle*, Sp. *gargara* a gargling noise
in the throat = Ar. vb. *gargara*, cf. It. *gorgogliare gorgozzo*,
gurgagliare gargozza &c. Hence also Sp. *gargola*, Fr. *gar-
gouille*, E. *gargoyle gurgoyle*, also Pr. *gargamela*, Fr. *garga-
melle* (Rabelais) throat, Pg. *gorgomilos* (pl.), Sp. *gorgomillera*.

Gargo It. cunning, malicious, Piedm. *gurgh* idle; from O. H. G.
karg crafty, cf. O. N. *hargr* obstinate, idle.

Gargote gargotte Fr. cook-shop. From Pic. *gargoter* to seethe,
an onomatop.

Garlar Sp. to chatter; from *garrulus*.

Garlopa — *varlope*.

Garnache garnir garnison — *guarnire*.

Garofano It., Sp. *girofle girofre*, Pr. Fr. *girofle* a clove, pink
(O. E. *gillofer*, *gelofer*, Shaks. *gilly-ror*, *gilly-flower*); from
caryophyllum with the Gk. accent, χαρυοφυλλον, but Wal.
carofil garofil, Ar. *garanful*.

Garone — *gherone*.

Garou — *loupgarou*.

Garra Sp. Pg. a claw, talon, Pr. *garra* hough? (cf. *squarar couper le jarret*), Lim. *jaro*, Genev. *jaire*. Hence It. *garretto*, O.
Fr. *garret*, Fr. *jarret*, Sp. Pg. *jarrete* hough, ham (whence
jarretière, *gartier*, E. *garter*), N. Pr. *garrou*, Sard. *yarroni*;
Fr. *garrot* joint, cudgel, Sp. *garrote*, whence Fr. *garrotte*, E.
garotte. From W. *gâr* shank, Bret. *gar* shin; cf. W. *cámes
gâr* hough. V. Dief. Celt. 1, 129.

Garrafa — *caraffa*.

Garrama Sp. Pg. tax, plunder; Ar. *gharâma*.

Garrio Pr., Cat. *garrig* the ilex. From *garra*? cf. *chaparra*.

Garrido Sp. Pg. neat, pretty; from Ar. *gari* with Rom. suffix
as in *florido*.

Garrobo — *carrobo*.

Garulla Sp. ripe grapes; from B. *garau-illa* dead grain Larr.

Garza — *garzone*.

Garzo (*yarz*) Lomb. heart of a cabbage (It. *garzuolo*), Mil. *gar-
zoeu* bud of vine, Ven. *garzólo* bunch of flax on the distaff,
Lomb. *garzon* milk thistle. From L. *carduus* through a form
cardeus cardeare, cf. *orzo* from *hordeum*; we have *cardare* and
garzar, *garzolo* and Parm. *carzoeul*, *garzon* and Sic. *cardedda*.
Fr. *carde* (*carder*, E. *card*) = It. *cardo* = L. *cardus* for *carduus*. V. *garzone*.

Garzo Sp. Pg. blue-eyed, a corruption of *zarco*, for *carzo*, cf.
gurasa for *bagasa*.

Garzo Sp. agaric; corrupted from *agaricus*.

Garzone It., Sp. *garzon*, Pg. *garção*, Fr. *garçon*, Pr. also *gartz*,

O. Fr. *gars* a lad, f. *garce* a prostitute. Orig. = a servant
boy, *garce* a servant maid, *garçon* also = a rascal, the first
meaning being simply boy *(puer)* and girl, cf. Jura *gars* son,
garse daughter. Prob. from the same root as *garzuolo, garzo,*
from *carduus,* in the sense of a bud, stalk &c., cf. It. *toso,*
Fr. *petit trognon,* G. *kleiner bützel,* Gr. χόρος, Gael. *gas,* cf.
Mil. *garzon* = *garzone* and *carduus.* For the medial cf. Lorr.
gade = *carde, gadā* = *carder.* Sp. *garza* a heron is prob. the
same word as *garce,* and alludes to the tuft hanging down the
heron's neck like a girl's hair, cf. *garceta* = a young heron
and a lock of hair.

Gas Fr. It. &c., E. *gas;* from Du. *geest,* G. *geist* spirit, E. *ghost.*

Gasa — *gaze.*

Gasalha gasalha Pr., O. Fr. *gazaille,* L. L. *gasalia* a company;
hence Pg. *agasalhar,* Sp. *agasajar gasajar* to treat in a friendly
way, divert, O. Pg. *agasalhar se com huma mulher* to marry.
From O. H. G. *gisello, gasaljo,* G. *gesell* companion. L. L.
gasalianes=Goth. pl. *gasaljans.* O. Pg. *gasilhado* = *gasailhado.*

Gaspiller Fr. to lavish, Pr. *guespillar,* Wall. *caspoui;* from A. S.
gespillan (E. *spill*), O. H. G. *gaspildan* to consume.

Gasto It. in Com. *gast* a lover; from G. *gast,* E. *guest.*

Gate Rouchi Wall., Lorr. *gaie,* Champ. *gaiette,* Jura *gaise;* from
Goth. *gaitei,* Du. *geit,* O. H. G. *geiz,* G. *geifs* drivel, slaver.

Gâteau Fr., O. Fr. *gastel* (Sic. *guasteddu*), Pr. *gastal* cake; from
M. H. G. O. E. *wastel* (Chaucer).

Gâter — *guastare.*

Gatto It., Sp. *gato,* Cat. *gat,* Pr. *cal,* Fr. *chat,* f. *gatta, gata,
cata, chatte,* N. Gr. γάτα a cat, not in Wall. which has *mëtzë,
pisicî* instead. From the Celtic and German; Ir. *cat,* W. *câth,*
A. S. E. *cat,* O. N. *köttr.* The Lat. *catus* is late, v. Freund.

Gauche Fr. left, O. E. *gauk,* E. *gawk gawky.* G = G. w, for
Rouchi *frère wauquier* stepbrother = Fr. *frère gaucher.* From
O. H. G. *welk,* E. *weak,* cf. It. *mano stanca* the tired, *manca*
the maimed, Sp. *zurda* the deaf, *redruña* the giving way,
N. Pr. *man seneco* the aged = the weak. Cf. M. H. G. *tenc*
left with Sw. *tckngy* weak. The Pr. E. *gaulic* requires a Fr.
gale. Sp. *gaucho* unlevel from *gauche?* Others, however,
derive *gauche* from *gawk* and this from *awk (awkward)* with
prefix *ge;* v. Garnett's Philol. Essays p. 66.

Gaucher — *gualcare.*

Gaufre Fr., Pic. *waufe,* O. Sp. *guafla,* L. L. *gafrum* a cake;
from G. *waffel* (E. *wafer*), connected with *wabe* honey-comb,
so prop. a honey-comb (in texture) cake, this from vb. *weben,*
E. *weave.*

Gauge O. Fr. in *nois gauge* walnut; from O. H. G. *walah wale*
foreign (G. *wälsch, welsh*) whence *gauge,* as from *del'catus*

deugé. A. S. was *veal-hnut*, O. N. *val-hnot*, G. *wallnuss*, E. *walnut.*

Gaule Fr., Rouchi *waude* a pole; from Goth. *valus* (= L. *rallus* whence the *au*), Friesl. *walu*, not from L. *vallus*, which would be against the rule.

Gaupe Fr., Burg. *gaupitre* a drab, dirty, ugly woman, perhaps from O. E. *wallop* a lump of fat.

Gausser Fr. *(se gausser de)* to be merry about anything; perhaps from Sp. *gozar*, which is also used reflexively.

Gaut gualt gal O. Fr., Pic. Norm. Rh. *gualt*, Pr. *gau gaut*; from G. *wald* wood. Hence O. Fr. *gaudine*, Pr. *gaudina* a thicket, Pg. *gudinha* an estate?

Gavasa — *bagascia.*

Gave Pic., Wall. *gaf*, Champ. *gueffe* a bird's crop, vb. Pic. *se gaver*, N. Pr. *se gavá*, Champ. *gueffer*, Fr. *s'engouer* to cram oneself, Pic. *engaver* to cram, Fr. *gavion* throat, Langued. *engavachá* to throttle, Mil. *gavasgia*, Com. *gavazza* a large mouth. Perhaps from *carus carea.* In the South of France *gava gave* = a mountain-stream, cf. *Gave de Pau, Gave de Couterets* &c., which, according to Mahn, is the O. Fr. *gave* = *eau, aqua*, Goth. *ahva.*

Gavela Pg., Sp. *garilla*, Pr. *guavella*, Fr. *javelle* sheaf, bundle, handful. From *capulus capellus capella*, N. Pr. masc. *gavel*, Pic. *gaviau*, cf. *martulus, scrophula*, which give *martellus scrophella (écrouelle).*

Gavotta It., Sp. *gabata*, Fr. *jatte* a wooden bowl; from *gabata* an eating-vessel, O. H. G. *gebita*, L. L. *capita*, cf. N. *jata* a manger. Fr. *jatte* from *gabata*, as *dette* from *debitum.* Pic. has *gate*, Norm. *gade jade*, O. Fr. *jadeau.* Sp. *gareta* a drawer is from the same.

Gavia Sp. a sea-mew, Pliny's *gavia.* Hence Sp. *gaviota*, Pg. *gaivota;* Sp. Pr. Neap. *gavina;* It. *gabbiano*, Pg. *gaivão* a sort of swallow.

Gavia — *gabbia.*

Gavilan Sp., Pg. *gavião* a sparrow-hawk, Mil. Com. *gavinel*, *ganivel*, Pr. *garanh.* From L. L. *capus (capere)*, cf. G. *habicht* from *haben.* Isid. *(capus) capys italicâ linguâ falco dicitur*, Serv. Æn. 1, 20, *falco qui Tuscâ linguâ capys dicitur.* Cap-el-an = *gav-il-an* from a dim. *capellus*, cf. *genellus gemelo gemeo;* cap = gav as in *gav-ela* from *cap-ulus.*

Gavina gaviota — *gavia.*

Gavion — *gave.*

Gayo — *gajo.*

Gayola — *gabbia.*

Gazápo Sp., Cat. *calxap*, Sard. *gacciapu*, Pg. *caçapu* a young rabbit. Perhaps from *dasypus* Pliny (δαούκους), *g* for *d*, cf. *camozza*, *apo* for *epo* being a commoner termination.

Gaze Fr., Sp. *gasa*, E. *gauze*; from *Gaza* in Palestine.

Gazmoño Sp. a hypocrite, a tartuffe; from B. *gazmuña* one who kisses (sc. images and relics of saints).

Gason Fr. turf, Arag. Crem. *gason*; from O. H. G. *waso*, G. *wasen*. A. S. *vase*, Du. *wase* = also mud, whence Fr. *vase* f., Pg. *vasa*, Norm. *gase*, *enguser* = *envaser*.

Gasouillor — *jaser*.

Gazuza Sp. great hunger; from B. *gose - utsa*.

Gazza It., Pr. *gacha*, *agassa*, Fr. *agace* a magpie; from O. H. G. *agalstra*, whence also It. *gazzera*.

Gazzella It., Sp. *gazela*, Fr. *gazelle algazelle*, E. *gazelle*; from Ar. *yazâl*.

Gazzetta It., Sp. *gazeta*, Fr. E. *gazette*: prop. the name of a Venetian coin (from *gaza*), so in Old English. Others derive *gazette* from *gazza* a magpie, which, it is alleged, was the emblem figured on the paper; but it does not appear on any of the oldest Venetian specimens preserved at Florence. The first newspapers appeared at Venice about the middle of the 16th century during the war with Soliman II, in the form of a written sheet, for the privilege of reading which a *gazzetta* (= a *crazia*) was paid. Hence the name was transferred to the news-sheet.

Geai — *gajo*.

Géant Fr. a giant, Pr. *jayan*; from *gigas gigantes*.

Gecchire It. in *aggecchirsi* to humble oneself, O. It. *gicchito*, *giachito*, Mil. *gecchiss* = *gecchirsi*, Pr. *gequir*, O. Sp. *jaquir* to let pass, O. Cat. *jaquir* to permit, O. Fr. *gehir* to grant, say, confess. From O. H. G. *jehan*, Goth. *aikan* to utter, to concede. *Aggecchirsi* = to give in to a person, *ch* = *h* as in *annichilare*.

Gehir — *gecchire*.

Geindre Fr. to groan, sigh; from *gemere*.

Geira Pg. as much land as could be ploughed in a day; for *jugeira*, L. *jugarius*.

Geitar — *yettare*.

Geito Pg. figure, shape, gait; from *jactus*.

Geldra It. rabble, Pr. *gelda*, O. Fr. *gelde* a troop espec. of footmen; from L. L. *gelda*, G. *gilde*, A. S. *gild*, E. *guild*. O. Fr. also *gueude: gueude marchande* = merchant's guild.

Gelso It. mulberry tree; for *moro gelso* = *morus celsa* as opp. the *morus humilis* the blackberry; Sic. *ceusu*, Gen. *sersa* = L. *celsus celsa*.

Gelsomino — *gesmino*.

Gencive — *gengiva*.

Gêne Fr. (f.), O. Fr. *gehene* torment, vb. *gêner;* from Heb. *gehenna.*

Genèvre — *ginepro.*

Gongibre — *zenzovero.*

Genglovo — *zenzovero.*

Gengiva It. Pg. Pr., Sp. *encia,* Fr. *gencive,* Wal. *gingie* gum; from *gingiva;* cf. Sard. *senzia,* Pr. *angiva,* Cat. *geniva,* Berr. *gendive.*

Genh, génie — *ingeyno.*

Genia It. offspring, Sic. *jinia;* from γενέα.

Génisse Fr., Pr. *juneya* a heifer; from *junix junicis;* cf. *genèrre* from *juniperus.* Jura *gegna = juneya;* Com. has *gioniscia,* Rh. *gianitscha.*

Genou — *ginocchio.*

Gens ges Pr., O. Fr. *gens giens,* N. Pr. *ges* or *gis,* Cat. *gents =* Fr. *point.* From *gentium,* as *pretz* from *pretium; non gens = non gentium = minime gentium;* or from *genus, non genus =* in no kind, not at all.

Gente O. It., O. Sp. *gento,* Pr. *gent,* f. *genta,* O. Cat. *gint ginta,* O. Fr. *gent gente* handsome, fine, genteel; vb. *agenzare agensar agencer* to please; probably from *genitus* a man of birth, *homme de naissance.*

Geôle — *gabbia.*

Gequir — *gecchire.*

Gerbe Fr. O. E., O. Fr. *garbe,* Pr. Cat. Arag. *garba* a cheaf, vb. *gerber,* Arag. *garbar;* it is the O. H. G. *garba,* G. *garbe,* Du. *garve,* E. *garb* (in heraldry).

Gercer Fr. *jarcer* to chap, crack, *gerce* a moth, a book-worm. From a form *carptiare (carptus), ge* for *ca,* cf. *carcola geôle.*

Gergo It., Sp. *xerga;* It. *gergone,* Fr. E. *jargon;* O. Sp. *girgonz,* Sp. *gerigonza,* Pr. *gergonz* unintelligible chatter. In O. Fr. we find for *jargonner gargoner* and in O. E. *gargoun.* Perhaps from the root *garg* (v. *gargatta*). Cf. also Sp. *guirigay.*

Gerigonza — *gergo.*

Gerla It., N. Pr. *gerlo,* O. Fr. *geurle jarle* a basket; from *gerulus* a porter.

Germandrée — *calamandrea.*

Germanía Sp. gibberish, language of the Gipsies, who called themselves *germani* brothers, also *hermania* from *hermano.*

Ges — *gens.*

Gèse O. Fr. a pike, from the O. Gallic *gæsum,* or O. Gael. *gais* (f.), L. L. *gesa,* B. *gesi.*

Gésier Fr., E. *gizzard* (O. Fr. also *jusier*); by dissimilation from *gigeria* bird's entrails (Lucil. Petron. Apic.). Pie. *giger, gigier.*

Gesmino It. (corrupt. *gelsomino,* Laug. *gensemil*), Sp. Fr. *jas-*

min, E. *jasmine jessamine;* from the Arab. *yàsamün* or *yàsamin* Freyt. 4, 514ᵇ.

Gesta It., O. Fr. *geste*, Pr. *gesta* lineage, stock. Lat. *gesta* used in the sing. = (1) exploits of a people (2) the chronicle of these exploits (3) lineage, stock.

Geto — *gettare.*

Gettare gittare It., Sp. *jitar*, Pr. *getar gitar*, Fr. *jeter*, Sp. *echar* to throw; from *jactare* (in comp. *jectare*), sbst. Fr. E. *jet*, Pr. *get*. It. *geto*, E. *jess.* Pg. *deitar* (O. Pg. *geitar*) = *déjeter*, *de- jecture.*

Gheda — *ghiera.*

Gheppio It. a kestrel; from γύψ *γυπός.*

Ghermire — *gremire.*

Gherone garone It., Sp. *giron*, Pg. *girão*, Fr. *giron*, a *gore* or gusset in a garment (in heraldry a triangle), a lap. From O. H. G. *gêro* acc. *gêrun*, M. H. G. *gêre*, O. Fries. *gare*, from *gêr* a spear, cf. L. L. *pilum vestimenti*, so called from the shape.

Ghezzo It. black or moorish; from *ægyptius*, cf. *gheppio*, *ghe = gy.*

Ghiado It. extreme cold, Pr. *glay* fright, Pr. Cat. *esglay*, O. Sp. *aylayo*; vb. It. *agghiadare* to benumb, O. Sp. *aglayarse* to be astonished, Pr. *esglayar.* Pr. *glay*, It. *ghiado* also = *gladius*, cf. *desglayar* to kill *desglaziar* = *degladiare;* O. Fr. *glaire* = shriek of death as well as sword (E. *glaive*). Cold and fright are so named from their *piercing* effects.

Ghiaja It. gravel; from *glarea*, O. Sp. *glera.*

Ghiattire schiattire It., Fr. *clatir*, O. Fr. *glatir*, Sp. Pg. *latir* to yelp, bark; sbst. Pr. *glat*, O. Fr. *glai (?)* cry, shriek; an onomatop. like G. *klatschen*, Du. *klateren*, E. *clatter*, Gr. κλά- ζειν, L. *lat-rare.*

Ghiazzerino It., Sp. *jacerina*, Pg. *jazerina*, Pr. *jazeran*, O. Fr. *jazerant jazerene*, whence Pg. *jazerão* a coat of mail; N. Pr. *jaziran*, Burg. *jazeran* a necklace. The word was orig. an adj., Sp. *cota jacerina*, Fr. *haubere jazerant.* Prob. from Sp. *jazarino* = Algerian, from Ar. *al-juzäir* (or *al-ǵazäir*) Algiers.

Ghiera It. an arrow, from O. H. G. *gêr* a missile. The Lomb. *gaida* a speer is the same word as the Piedm. Parm. *gajda*, Crem. Mil. *gheda*, Sard. *gaja* a gusset, cf. *gherone.*

Ghignare and *sghignare* It. to snigger, Sp. *guiñar*, Fr. *guiguer* to wink, leer, peep; from A. S. *ginian* to gape, O. H. G. *ginen*, or from O. H. G. *kinan* adridere, though G. *k* does not usu. = *g.*

Ghindare It. (for *guindare*), Sp. Pg. *guindar*, Fr. *guinder* to wind up; from O. H. G. *windan*, E. *wind.* Hence It. *guindolo (bin- dolo)*, Sp. *guindola*, Fr. *guindre;* Sp. Pg. *guindaste*, Fr. *guindas*

15*

and *vindas*, from the Du. *wind-as*, G. *wind-achse* (axle), whence Bret. *gwindask*, F. *windlass*.

Ghiotto It., Pr. O. Fr. *glot* a glutton; from *glitus*, *gluttus (gluttire)*. It. *ghiottone*, Sp. Pr. *gloton*, Fr. *glouton*, E. *glutton*, from *gluto* (Fest. s. v. *ingluvies*); vb. It. *inghiottire*, Pr. *englotir*, Fr. *englouter* from *gluttire*. From the same root are the Pr. *glot* a bit, morsel, and It. *ghiozzo*.

Ghiova It. for *ghieva*, L. *gleba*, cf. *piovano* for *pievano*.

Ghiozzo — *ghiotto*.

Ghirlanda It., Sp. Pg. *guirnalda*, O. Sp. *gnarlanda*, Pg. also *grinalda*, Pr. Cat. *garlanda*, E. *garland*, Fr. *guirlande*. Prob. from a form *wierelen* of the M. H. G. *wieren* to bind, O. H. G. *wiara* a wreath.

Ghiro It., Pr. *glire*, Fr. *loir* a dormouse; from *glis gliris*. Hence Fr. Sp. *liron*, Pg. *lirão*. The N. Pr. *greoule* is from *glirulus*.

Già It. Sp. O. Pg. *ya*, Pg. Pr. O. Fr. *ja*, from *jam*. Fr. *déjà* for *dejà* = It. *di già*.

Giaco It., Sp. *jaco*, Fr. *jaque* f., dim. *jaquette*, E. *jacket*, prop. a soldier's jacket, whence G. *jacke*. According to Ducange from *Jaque* the name of a Count of Beauvais c. 1358. But v. Wedgw., who says the *jack* was a homely substitute for a coat of mail, being the familiar name used so generally for mechanical contrivances, e. g. *boot-jack*, *roasting-jack* &c.

Gialda — *geldra*.

Giallo It., Sp. *jalde*, Pg. *jalde jalne*, Fr. *jaune* yellow. The Fr., orig. *jalne*, is from *galbinus* (Wal. *galbin*) and from *jalne*, *jalde*, Lomb. *giald*. The It. *giallo* suits the O. H. G. *gelo* (G. *gelb*), E. *yellow*, *a* for *e* as in *gialura* from *gelo*. Fr. *bejaune* gull, ninny == *becjaune*, properly of a young unfledged bird; so *gull* Sw. *gul* yellow.

Giannetta — *ginete*.

Giara It., Sp. Pg. Pr. *jarra*, Fr. *jarre*, E. *jar*; It. m. *giarro*, Sp. Pg. *jarro* &c.; from Ar. *jarrah* a water-vessel. In O. Pg. we find also *zarra*, *z* = Ar. *j*.

Giardino It., Sp. *jardin*, Pg. *jardim*, Pr. *jardin gardin jerzin*, Fr. *jardin*, *gardin*, f. Pr. *giardina*, E. *garden;* from O. H. G. *garto* (gen. dat. *gartin*), or, as the form *giardina* would seem to hint, a Rom. der. from O. H. G. *gart* (orig. *gard*), E. *yard*, Goth. *gards*, Gael. *gart*, W. *gardd*, E. *garth*. Wal. *gard* enclosure is the Goth. *gards*.

Giavelotto It. prob. from the Fr. *javelot*, O. Fr. *gavelot*, Bret. *garlod*, M. H. G. *gabilôt;* also It. *giavelina*, Sp. *jabalina*, Fr. *javeline*, E. *javelin*, Bret. *gavlin*. The root is found in the E. *gavellock*, A. S. *gaflac*, from the O. N. *gefja* a spear, N. *gaflok gafeloc gafeloc* (Grimm); or from Ir. *gabhla* a spear, W. *gafl*

(Pott, Diefenbach). The O. Fr. has an unintelligible form *gaverlot garlot.*

Gibet — *giubbetto.*

Gibier O. Fr. in *aller engibier* to hunt, Fr. *giboyer*, subst. *gibier*, O. Fr. *gibelet* (E.*giblet*), Fr. *gibecière*, E.*gipciere gipser* (Chauc.) a hunting-pouch, a purse. Perhaps connected with *gibet gibbet* (halter), whence *gibier* to catch birds in a noose?

Gier gieres giers a particle found the oldest Fr. monuments = L. *ergo;* from *erg ierg* whence *ger gier* as from *ego ieo jeo gie.*

Gieser — *gèsc.*

Giga It. O. Sp. Pr., O. Fr. *gigue* a string-instrument, Sp. *giga*, Fr. *gigue*, E. *jig.* From M. H. G. *gige*, vb. *gigen*, G. *geige* a violin, vb. *geigen.* Hence Fr. *gigot* a leg of mutton (from the shape), Sp. *gigote* minced meat.

Giglio It., Sp. Pg. *lirio*, Pr. *lili liri lis*, Fr. *lis*, Piedm. Mil. *liri*, Sard. *lillu*, O. Sp. *lilio*, Rh. f. *gilgia*, M. H. G. *gilge*, Sw. *jilge ilye* a lily. A notable instance of the principle of dissimilation, the *g* and the *r* being used to prevent the repetition of the *l.* The Fr. requires a form *lilius*, cf. O. H. G. *lilio*, M. H. G. *gilge* (m.). V. Pott, Forsch. 2, 99.

Giler Norm., N. Pr. *gilhá* to hasten away; from O. H. G. *gilan giljan* (Pr. *h = j*) for *gi-ilan* to hasten, G. *eilen.* The Com. is *zelà* cf. Com. *zerlo*, *zoja* = It. *gerlo*, *gioja.*

Gilet Fr. a waistcoat; from *Gille*, the name of the first maker (Menage).

Gina — *agina.*

Ginepro It., Sp. *enebro*, Pg. *zimbro (z* rare for *g)*, Fr. *genièvre;* from *juniperus.* The *e* for *u* is Fr. (cf. *génisse*), whence Du. *jenever*, Dan. *enebar.*

Gineta Sp. Pg., Fr. *genette*, E. *genet* a wild-cat, civet-cat (in the Levant). Of Eastern origin.

Ginete Sp. Pg. a light-armed trooper, *gineta*, It. *giannetta* a short spear carried by such, Sp.*gineta ginete*, It. *ginnetto giannetto*, Fr. *genet*, E. *jennet.* Probably from γυμνήτης.

Gingembre — *zenzovero.*

Ginocchio It., Wal. *genunche*, Sp. *hinojo*, O. Sp. *ginojo*, Pg. *giolho joelho*, Fr. *genou* (from *genoil*) knee; from *genuculum* for *geniculum.*

Giocolaro giullaro It. from *jocularius;* Sp. *joglar juglar*, Pr. *joglar* from *jocularis;* It. *giocolatore*, O. Fr. *jogleor*, O. E. *jogelour*, E. *juggler*, Fr. *jongleur*, from *joculator;* O. Fr.*jongler* from *joculari.*

Gioglio It., Sp. *joyo*, Pg. *joio*, Pr. *jueth* darnel, from *lolium*, cf. *giglio* from *lilium.* It. has also *lolio*, Arag. *luello* &c. Hence Pg. *jocira* a winnowing-sieve.

Gioja giojello — *godere.*

Giorno It., Pr. O. Cat. *jorn*, Fr. *jour;* from *diurnum*, L. L. *jornus; dies* is found in It. *di*, Sp. Pg. Pr. *dia*. Hence It. *soggiorno*, O. Sp. *sojorno*, Pr. *sojorn*, E. *sojourn*, Fr. *séjour* &c.

Giostrare — *giusta*.

• **Giovedi** It., Fr. *jeudi*, Pr. Cat. *dijous;* from *Jovis dies*, *dies Jovis;* Sp. *jueves*, Pr. *jous*, from *Jovis*, Wal. *joi*, Ven. Romag. *zobia*. Pg. *quinta feira* = $\pi \acute{\epsilon} \mu \pi \tau \eta$ in Mod. Gr., M. H. G. *pfinztac*, v. Schmeller 1, 321.

Giraffa It., Sp. *girafa*, Fr. *girafe*, E. *giraffe;* from Ar. *zarrâfah*.

Girandola girandula girandole — *giro*.

Gire It. to go, defective; from *de-ire(?)*, cf. L. L. *de-ambulare*.

Girfalco gerfalco It., Sp. *gerifalte* (from the Fr.), Pr. *girfalc*, Fr. *gerfaul*, E. *jerfalcon;* the *gir ger* is prob. the O. H. G. *gir*, (G. *geier* = Sansk. *grighra* a vulture, and this was afterwards connected with *gyrare* so that we have in L. L. *gyrofalco* (a gyrando Albert. Mag.). Cf. It. *ruola*, Ven. *ronda*, Gr. $\varkappa \acute{\iota} \varrho \varkappa o \varsigma$.

Giro It. Sp., Pr. *gir* a circle, round; from *gyrus*. O. Fr. *gires* pangs of labour, Berr. *girande gerente* a woman in labour, It. *girare*, O. Fr. *girer* from *gyrare;* It. *girandola*, Sp. *girandula*, Fr. *girandole* a fire-wheel, girandole, from a lost *giranda* = Fr. *girande;* Fr. *girouette* for *girotette* (cf. It. *girotta*) a weathercock.

Girofie — *garofano*.

Giron — *gherone*.

Gisarme — *guisarma*.

Giu — *giuso*.

Giubba giuppa It., Sp. *al-juba*, Pr. *jupa*, Fr. *jupe*, Com. Crem. *gibba*, Mil. Rh. *gippa*, M. H. G. *gippe joppe;* It. *giubbone*, Sp. *jubon*, Pg. *jubão gibão*, Cat. *gipó*, Pr. *jubon*, Fr. *jupon*, Wal. *jubeà*. From Ar. *al-jubbah* a woollen petticoat. Hence also Sp. *chupa*, It. *cioppa(?)*, G. *schaube*.

Giubbetto giubbetta It., Fr. *gibet*, whence E. *gibbet*. The It. is a dim. of *giubba*, a little jacket, a collar, a halter. For *i* from *u*, cf. *génisse*.

Giuggiola It., Sp. *jujuba*, Fr. E. *jujube;* from *zizyphum*. The usu. Sp. word is *azufaifa*.

Giulebbe It., Sp. *julepe*, Pr. Fr. E. *julep;* from Ar. *julab*, from Pers. *gul* rose, and *âb* water.

Giulivo It., Pr. O. Fr. *joli* for *jolif*, E. *jolly*, Fr. *joli* pretty; vb. O. Fr. *joliver jolier* to enjoy oneself. Not from *Jovialis*, but from O. N. *jol* a Christmas festivity (E. *yule*), Swed. Dan. *jul*, Goth. *jiuleis*.

Giullaro — *giocolaro*.

Giumella It. as much as can be held in the two hands placed together; from L. *gemella*. For the *u* from *e*, cf. Fr. *jumeau*.

Giunare It., Wal. *ajunà*, Sp. *ayunar*, Pg. *jejuar*, Pr. *jeonar*, Fr.

jeûner to fast; from *jejunare* (Tertull.); the *je* is lost in Fr. *jeûner*, Sp. *a-yunar* (cf. *ayer* from *heri*). For *giunare* we have It. *digiunare*, Pr. Cat. *dejunar*, adj. *digiuno dejun (jejunus)*. Fr. *déjeûner*, Sp. *desayunar*, Wal. *dejună* break-fast.

Giunchiglia It., Sp. *junquillo*, Fr. *jonquille*, E. *jonquil;* from *juncus*, its botanic name being *narcissus juncifolius.*

Giusarma — *guisarme.*

Giuso It., contr. *giu*, O. Sp. *yuso ayuso jus*, O. Pg. *juso*, Pr. *jos jotz jus*, O. Fr. *jus*, Wal. *din jos* for L. *infra*. From *deorsum* for *deorsum*, L. L. *josum jusum* as *jornus* from *diurnus*, O. Sp. also *diuso.*

Giusquiamo It., Sp. *josquiamo*, Fr. *jusquiame* (f.) henbane; from *hyosciamus* (ὑοσκύαμος), corrupted into *jusquiamus* by Palladius.

Giusta giusto (cf. *contra contro*), Pr. *josta*, O. Fr. *joste juste;* from *juxta* also = secundum in Rom., which meaning it had often in L. L., and occasionally also in L. Hence It. *giustare giostrare*, Sp. Pg. *justar*, Pr. *jostar justar*, Fr. *jouter*, O. Fr. *joster juster*, E. *joust* orig. = to bring together; sbst. *giostra*, Pr. *josta justa*, Fr. *joute*, E. *joust*, M.H.G. *tjost*, M. Du. *joeste;* Cf. Berr. *mon champ joute au sien* adjoins. Hence Pr. *ajostar*, Fr. *ajouter* to add, E. *adjust*. The E. *jostle* is a frequentative form.

Givre Fr. (f.) a snake in heraldry, O.Fr. *givre* snake; for *guivre* from *vipera*, O. H. G. *wipera*, whence also O. Fr. *wivre*, W. *gwiber*, Bret. *wiber*, E. *viper*. *Givre* also = a snake-like missile and an icicle, Burg. *gèvre*, Pr. *givre, gibre*, Cat. *gebre* hoar-frost, vb. Pr. *gibrar*, Cat. *gebrar.*

Glaba It. a layer, shoot; from *clava;* for the *b*, cf. the form *clabula.*

Glacier O. Fr. *(glaçoier)* to glide. From *glacies*, so to slip like ice, cf. *brillare*, to shine like beryl, *corbare* to cry like a raven, *formicare* to swarm like ants.

Glai — *ghiattire.*

Glaïeul — *glaive.*

Glaire (f.) Fr., Pr. *glara* humeur visqueuse, Sp. *clara (de huevo* = *glaire d'œuf)*, It. *chiara*, E. *glare, gleire, glere (gleyre* Chauc.). Not (as Grimm) from A. S. *glaere* amber, which = L. *glaesum*, O. N. *gler* glas, Dan. Sw. *glas*, E. *glass*, nor (as Mahn) from the Celtic: Bret. *glaour*, W. *glyfoer* drivel, slaver, connected with Br. *glao glav*, W. *gwlaw* rain (connected with L. *pluvia*), Br. *gleb*, W. *gwleb gwlyb* wet; but from *clarum ovi*, cf. Pr. *clara d'un hueu*, It. *chiara*, Sp. *clara*, M. H. G. *eierklâr*. It borrows the gender of *glarea* gravel (It. *chiara* also = sand-bank).

Glaise Fr., Pr. *gleza* clay; from L. L. *glis glitis* = *humus tenax*, adj. *gliteus = cretaceus. Glis* is, perhaps, connected with Gk. γλία glue, γλιοχρός.

Glaive Fr. (m.), Pr. *glavi* a sword, E. *glaive*, It. *glave* a sword-fish. From *gladius* came Pr. *glazi (z = d)*, *glai glavi*, cf. from *adulterium azulteri aülteri avulteri, vidua veuza veuva. Glaive = glavi* as *saive = savi*, O. Fr. *glai* (whence *glaïeul*) == Pr. *glai.*

Glaner Fr., Pic. Champ. *gléner*, N. Pr. *glenâ*, E. *glean*, Fr. *glane* a handfull of ears of corn &c.; L.L. *glenare*. From the Celtic, W. *glain glân = cleau*, vb. *glanhau* to clean up, to glean.

Glapir Fr. to yelp; Du. *klappen*, M. H. G. *klaffen*, O. H. G. *klaffôn*. Hence Fr. *clavaud*, cf. Du. *klabbaerd*, E. *clapper.*

Glas — *chiasso.*

Glasto — *guado.*

Glatir — *ghiattire.*

Glave — *glaive.*

Glay — *ghiado.*

Gleton O. Fr., also *gletteron*, Fr. *glouteron* a burdock; from the G. *klette*, O. H. G. *chletto*, acc. *chlettuu, chlettos.*

Glette Fr. litharge; from the G. (silber-) *glätte.*

Glisser Fr. to slip; from G. *glit-sen glitschen*, Du. *glitsen*. We find in It. *glisciare*, O. Fr. *glinser*, N. Pr. *liusâ*, Burg. *linzer.*

Gloriette Fr., Sp. *glorieta* a bower, prop. == a fine, handsome chamber *(gloria).*

Glousser — *chiocciare.*

Glouteron — *gleton.*

Glouton — *ghiotto.*

Glu Fr. (f.), Pr. *glut*, Pg. *grude* bird-lime, E. *glue*; from *glus glutis* (Ausonius). Hence Pic. *englui*, Pr. *englut*, Sp. *engrudo*, vb. *engludar engrudar.*

Glui Fr., Pr. *glueg* straw; from Flem. *geluye gluye*, or from W. *cluig.*

Gnaffè It. interj.; from *mia fè.*

Gobbe Fr., Norm. *gobet*, E. *gobbet*, Norm. *gobine* a meal, Fr. *gober* to gobble, E. *gob* a mouthful. Cf. Gael. *gob*, W. *gwb* a beak, v. Dief. Goth. Wb. 1, 169.

Gobbo It., Rh. *gob* a hump, Fr. *gobin*, from *gibba gibbus*, L. L. *gybbus* (χῦφος). Al. from W. *gob* a heap.

Gobelet — *coppa.*

Gobelin goblin Fr., E. *goblin hob-goblin*. From κόβαλος, whence also G. *kobold?* V. Grimm Myth. p. 420, Diefenb. Goth. Wb. 1, 150, who compares Bret. *gobilin* an ignis fatuus. But the Bret. *gobilin* is doubtless the W. *coblyn* (properly = one who knocks, from *cobio* to knock), v. Wedgwood.

Goccia It., Crem. (m.) *gozy gouzy* a drop. Not immediately from *gutta*, but prob. from vb. *gocciare*, for *gotteggiare* = Pr. *go-teiar*, Pg. *gotejar*.

Goda N. Pr. a dirty slut, O. Fr. *godon* a rake, Fr. *gouine* a whore, for *godine*, dim. Burg. *godineta*, Rouchi *godinete*, Burg. *gaudrille*, O. Fr. *gouérois* (cf. O. E. *guudery* sprightliness); *godemine* pleasure; vb. O. Fr. *goder*, Fr. *godailler*, Berr. *gou-ailler* to feast, revel; also Sp. (gipsy) *godo godeño*, *godizo* dainty, *goderia* a drinking-bout, Pied. *gaudineta*, Pg. *engodar* to allure, cf. Rouchi *godan* lure, bait. Basq. *godaria* = chocolate (enticing drink) from the Rom. From the L. *gaudere(?)* but the sbst. *goda*, adj. *godo*, can only be referred to the W. *god* wantonness. Hence, perhaps, also the Fr. *goinfre* a rake, the rare termination being found also in *goudiafre*. The verb *godailler* is referred by some to a sbst. *godale* = E. *good ale*.

Godailler godon goinfre — *goda*.

Godere gloire It., O. Pg. *gouvir*, Pr. *gauzir janzir*, Fr. *jouir*, Pic. *se gaudir*, from *gaudere*; sbst. Pg. *goivo*, Pr. *gaug joi*, Wald. *goy*, E. *joy*, also f. It. *gioja*, Sp. *joya*, Pg. Pr. *joia*, Fr. *joie*, Sp. Pg.=*jewel*, Fr.=*joy*, It. Pr.=*joy, jewel*, from *gaudium*, *gaudia*; hence It. *giojello*, Sp. *joyel*, Pr. *joiel*, O. Fr. *joel*, Fr. *joyau*, E. *jewel*, L. L. (wrongly) *jocale* for *gaudiale*. Pr. *jau-zion*, f. *jauzionda* from *gaudibundus* Apuleius and L. L.

Godet Fr. a pitcher, for *gotet* = *gottet* from *guttus*, It. *gotto*.

Godo — *goda*.

Goëland Fr. a gull; from the Celtic, Bret. *gwelan*, W. *gwylan* (E. *gull?*), Gael. *foilenn*, from vb. *gwela* Bret., *gwylaw* W., to cry.

Goffo It., Sp. *gofo*, Fr. *goffe*, E. *gof guff* (prov.) stupid, clownish. Perhaps the same word as L. L. *gufa (vestis = villata)* thick, coarse. Some derive it from the Gk. κωφός. It is connected with the Bav. *goff* a blockhead.

Gogna It. pillory, halter; shortened from *vergogna*, cf. Sp. *ver-güenza*, and *gogna* = dilemma.

Gogues Fr. (pl.) merriment, *goguettes* tricks, *se goguer*, *gogue-nard*, *gogaille*, Lang. *gougalios* = *goguettes*. Bret. has *gôgéa* to mock, W. *gogan* satire, or *gogues* may be from G. *gauch* cuckoo, cf. O. N. *gauka* to be merry = *goguer*. Fr. *gogue* also = plentiful supply of good things to eat, *être en gogo* to live in clover, *goguelu* one so living, insolent, from W. *gog* super-abundant.

Goi O. Fr. in *vertu-goi* = *vertu de dieu*, *mort-goi*, *sang-goi*, N. Pr. *tron de goi* = morbleu, from G. *god goi*. *Vertu-quieu* is for *vertu-dieu*. Similar corruptions are frequent in oaths.

Goitre Fr. (m.), O. Fr. Pr. *goitron*; from *guttur gutter*, whence *goetr goitre*. We find L. L. *gutturnia* for *gutturnea*, cf. *roburnea* from *robur*, whence L. L. *gutturnosus*, Pr. *gutrinos*.

Goiva — *gubia.*

Golafre — *goliarl.*

Goldre Sp., Pg. *coldre* a quiver; from *corýtus.*

Goliart O. Fr. Pr., O. Pg. *goliardo*, L. L. *goliardus*, O. F. *goli-ardeis* (Chauc.) a low jester, parasite, It. *goliare* to long for, from *gula*, whence also Fr. *gouliafre*, Sp. *golafre* greedy, for term. cf. *goinfre (goda).*

Gollizo Sp. gorge of mountains &c.; from *gula*, Sp. *gola.*

Golondrina — *rondine.*

Golpe It., O. Sp., Rh. *guolp, golp*, whence O. Sp. *gulpeja*, O. Fr. *goupille gourpille*, usu. m. *goupil gourpil*, also *wourpille werpille werpil* a fox; vb. O. Fr. *goupiller* to creep, slink away; Fr. *goupillon* a tail, brush (prop. of the fox), *goupille* the body of a nail as opp. the head. From *vulpes*, *v = gu* sometimes, cf. R. Gr. 1, 157. Other names of this animal, so well known in the fables of the middle ages, are *renard*, Pr. *guiner*, Cat. *gnineu*, Sp. *raposa, zorra*, O. Sp. *marota, gulhara*, Sard. *margiani*, Lang. *mandro.*

Gomia Sp. (f.) a prodigal, glutton; from *gumia (grunia?)* Lucil. and Apuleius.

Gomito — *cubito.*

Gómona gómena gúmina It., Sp. Pg. *gúmena*, Fr. *goumène* anchor-cable; from Ar. *al-gomal* or *gomol.*

Gond — *gonzo.*

Gonda góndola It., whence Sp. *góndola*, Fr. *gondole* a gondola. From *κόνδυ =* a drinking-vessel (Fr. *gondole*), or from an O. L. *gondus = scyphus patera* (Menage from an old Glossary).

Gonfalone It., O. Pg. *gonfalão*, Pr. O. Fr. *gonfanon*, Fr. *gonfalon* a banner; from O. H. G. *gundfano (gundja* battle and *fano* cloth). From the form *cundfano* come Pied. Sp. *confalon*, Pr. *confaño*, O. Fr. *confanon*, Sic. *canfaluni*, Ven. *confaloniero.*

Gonfiare It., Fr. *gonfler*, W. *gënfü* to swell; from *conflare* for *inflare* (N. Pr. *couflà*). It. *gonfio*, Genev. *gonfle =* Fr. *gonflé*, as *enfle = enflé*. N. Pr. *gofe* full, vb. *goufà*, Genev. *goffet* thick, come from the same, not from *goffo.*

Gonna It. a petticoat, O. Sp. Pr. *gona*, O. Fr. *gone* a coat, monk's habit, L. L. *gunna*, L. Gr. *γοῦνα*, Alb. *guné*. Varro mentions a L. *gaunacum* a shaggy covering, but the form does not suit the Rom. word. Prob. the L. and Rom. are both from the Celtic, W. *gún*, E. *gown*, though Diez says these may be from the Rom. (*gún* from *gone* as *fiel* from *fol*), v. Duc. s. *guna*, and Marsh, Origin and History of English, pp. 56, 512.

Gonzo engonzo Pg., Sp. *gonce gozne*, Fr. *gond*, Pr. *gofon* for *gonfon* a hinge. *Gonzo* from L. *contus*, *gofon* from *gomphus*, *gond* from *contus* and Lorr. *angon = ancon.*

Gonzo It. rude, sottish. From Sp. *ganso?* or from Ven. *gozzo* = It. *ghiozzo.*

Gora (*o aperto*) an aqueduct, mill-leat; from the Sw. *wuor*, Rh. *vuor* (so = *guora*), v. Frisch 2, 459°.

Gorbia — *gubia.*

Gordo Sp. Pg., Pr. *gort* fat, thick, Fr. *gourd* stiff, *engourdir* to benumb; from L. *gurdus* (Laberius in Gellius, and Quintilian) stupid, doltish; Quintilian says of *gurdus: ex Hispaniâ ducrisse originem audivi*, cf. O. Sp. = stupid. The It. *ingordo* greedy is rather from "*in gurgitem*", cf. O. Fr. adj. *enfrun* (It. *ingordarsi* = *se ingurgitare*).

Gore — *gorre.*

Gorge — *gorgo.*

Gorgia gorgogliare — *goryo.*

Gorgo It., Pr. O. Fr. *gore gort*, Fr. *gour* whirlpool; It. Sp. Pr. *gorga*, Fr. E. *gorge*, also It. *gorgia*; from *gurges*. Pr. *gorgolh* from *gurgulio*, vb. It. *gorgogliare* &c.

Gorgojo Sp. weevil; from *curculio.*

Gormar — *gourme.*

Goro — *huero.*

Gorra Sp. Pg. It. a cap, Sp. also *gorro.* From the Basque *gorria* red, a favorite colour for caps. Articles of clothing are often named from their colour, cf. *bujo.* It. *gorra* = also an osier, prop. the red osier. O. Fr. *gorres* = *rubans, livrées des nouveaux mariés* Roquefort, *gorrer gorrier gorrière* = *homme et femme magnifiquement parés.* O. Fr. *gorre* vérole, mal vénérien.

Gorupo — *groppo.*

Gos — *cuccio.*

Gosier — *gueux.*

Gota It., Pr. *gauta*, Fr. *joue* (whence E. *jaw?*) cheek, jaw; Cat. *galta*, Mod. *golta*, Rh. *gaulta*; Sp. has only *galtera* = cheek-piece of a helm. Pr. *au* gives *o al ou*; *gauta* is the L. *gabatu*, L.L. *gavata* (Bret. *gaved*) *gauta*, as *parabola paravola paraula.* *Gabata* = an eating-vessel (Langued. *gaouda*).

Goto Pg. throat; from *guttur.*

Gotta It., Sp. Pg. *gota*, Fr. *goutte*, E. *gout*; Wal. *gutê*, It. *gocciola* apoplexy; from *gutta*, G. *troph: tropfen apoplexia* in a Dict., date 1445. These diseases were supposed to be caused by drops of water from the brain, v. Ducange. Hence Fr. *esgout égout* a drain, *gouttière* a gutter.

Goudron — *catrame.*

Gouffre — *golfo.*

Gouge — *gubia.*

Gouge Fr. a wench, N. Pr. *gougeo* a maid; whence Fr. *goujat*; from Heb. *goy* people; the Jews called a Christian maid *goye.*

Gouine — *goda*.

Goujon Fr., E. *gudgeon*, from L. *gobio* (It. Sp.).

Goullafre — *goliart*.

Goupil goupillon — *golpe*.

Goupillor — *volpilh*.

Gour — *gorgo*.

Gourd — *gordo*.

Gourde — *cucuzza*.

Gourme Fr. glanders; Pg. *gosma* foul humours, *gosmar* Sp. *gormar* to vomit; Rouchi *gourmer* to sip, Fr. *gourmand* a glutton, Norm. *gourmacher* to be foul; Fr. *gourmer* to beat with the fists, to bit a horse, *gourmette* a bit, *gourmander* to maltreat, fall foul of. From N. *gormr* dirt *(gor)*, E. *gorm* to soil (cf. Berr. *eau gourmie* dirty water), W. *gorm* repletion, whence *gormes* a burden, *gormail* oppression. Others make a separate word *gourme* found in Bret. *gromm* and in *gourmette*, *gourmer*, *gourmender*, and coming from Celtic *crom (cromm)* bent, cf. E. *curb* from Fr. *courbe* = *curvus*.

Gourmette — *gourme* and *grumo*.

Gousso — *guscio*.

Goutto — *gotta*.

Gozne — *gonzo*.

Gozo Sp. Pg. pleasure, mirth, vb. *gozar*, O. Val. *gozar*, Cat. *gosar*, N. Pr. *gausá*. From *gaudium*, Cat. *gotj*, O. Val. *gotjar*, cf. *mitj* from *medius*, *ratj* from *radius*. From *jozo* is Sp. *regocijo*.

Gozque — *cuccio*.

Gozzo It. crop, craw, Lomb. *goss*. Shortened from *gorgozzo* from *gurges*; we have f. *gorgozza* and also *corgozzo*. For the loss of the 1st syllable, cf. *cenno*. *Sorgozzone sergozzone* = *sub guttur pugnus inflictus* Ferrari. *Trangugiare* = *trangorgiare*.

Graal greal grasal O. Fr., Pr. *grazal*, O. Cat. *gresal* a cup or bowl of wood, earth or metal. In South France *grazal grazau grial grau* are used for various kinds of vessels, Fr. *grassule* = a bowl. From *greal* comes O. Sp. *grial greal*, Pg. *gral* (a mortar), O. Ven. *graellino*. The *Saint graal* of the Romances was the dish which was used at the institution of the Holy Eucharist, M. H. G. *grâl*. The *d* of the L. L. *gradalis* answers to the *z* of the Pr., which, therefore, would appear to be the earliest form. Two of the various derivations given may be mentioned as probable: (1) *gratialis* from *gratia* in L. L. = the Holy Supper, which, however, does not suit the Fr. *graal*; (2) *crater*, L. L. *cratus* whence *cratalis*, *grazal*, *graal*.

Grabar — *graver*.

Grabuge Fr. a quarrel, brawl, Rouchi *grabuche*, O. Fr. *gra-*

béuge. Prob. a compound word, Pr. *grahusa,* vb. *grahusar,* O. Fr. *gréuse,* Jura *greuse.*

Gracco gracculo gracchia It., Sp. *grajo graja,* Pg. *gralho gralha,* Pr. *gralha,* O. Fr. *graille* a jay, jacdaw; from *graculus,* L. L. *gracula.*

Gracidare It. to croak (of frogs), Sp. Pg. *graznar* (of ravens).

Grada It. Sp., Pg. *grade* (f.), E. *grate,* Sp. Pg. also = *harrow,* from *crates;* It. *gradella.* From dim. *craticula* (L. L. *graticula*), come It. *graticola,* Fr. *grille, gril,* E. *grill,* Mil. *grella,* Fr. vb. *griller,* E. *grill,* for *graille graille (i* for *ai,* cf. *chignon grignon)* O. Fr. also *graïl,* vb. *graelier, grauillier,* Berr. *griller.*

Grado It. Sp. Pg., Pr. *grat,* Fr. *gré,* O. E. *gree* will, liking; from *gratum.* Hence It. *malgrado,* Pr. *malgrat,* Fr. *malgré,* E. *maugre* (sc. *a mal grado*), cf. L. *male gratus.* Vb. It. *gradire,* Pr. *gradir;* It. *aggradire aggradare,* Sp. *agradar agreiar,* Fr. *agréer* to please, approve, E. *agree;* It. *agraderole,* Sp. Pr. *agradable,* Fr. *agréable,* E. *agreeable.*

Graffio It., Sp. *garfio garfa,* Pr. *grafio* a hook, claw; vb. It. *graffiare,* Burg. *graffiner* (sbst. *graffin*): Fr. *agrafe* a brooch; It. *aggraffare,* Sp. *agarrafar engarrafar,* Wall. *agrafer* to grasp. From O. H. G. *krapfo krafo* a hook, E. *grab.*

Gragea — *treggea.*

Graille graja — *gracco.*

Grama Sp. Romag., It. *gràmola,* Pg. *gramadeira* a brake (for hemp), Sp. *gramilla;* vb. Pg. *gramar,* Romag. *gramé* to prepare hemp, Sp. *gramar* to knead dough, It. *gramolare* in both senses. Perhaps from *carminare.*

Gramalla — *camaylio.*

Gramallera — *crémaillon.*

Grammaire Fr., Pr. *gramaira gramáiria,* E. *grammar;* formed from the Pr. *gramádi* = *grammaticus,* whence *gramadaria gramáiria, d* being vocalized into *i.* O. Fr. masc. *gramaire* = *grammaticus (grammaticarius),* Basque *gramaticaria,* O. H. G. *gramatichare;* hence Fr. *grammairien.* Cf. L. L. *judicarius* from *jude.c.*

Grana It. Sp. Pr., Pg. *grãa,* O. Fr. *graine* (whence E. *grain*) a scarlet berry, *coccus ilicis,* scarlet cloth, in Sp. also = cochineal *(coccus cacti),* L. L. *grana,* M. H. G. *gran;* from *granum,* cf. κόκκος, v. onn. Marsh, Lectures on Eng. Lang. Hence It. *granata* = a *granate* or *garnet* stone, and = Sp. *granada* a *pome-granate.*

Granchio grancio It., Pr. Cat. *cranc,* W. *cranc,* Bret. *krank,* Wall. *cranche* a crab, Fr. *chancre* a cancer; a corruption of *cancer cancri.* Hence Pg. *granquejo garanquejo,* Sp. *cangrejo* from a dim. *cancriculus.* Hence, too, It. *grancire* to seize?

Granciporro It. cancer marinus; from *cancer* and *pagurus.*

Grancire — *granchio.*

Grange — *granja.*

Grangear — *granja.*

Granguejo — *granchio.*

Granito It., Sp. *granido*, Fr. *granit*, E. *granite;* from *granum* because of its *grained* appearance; *granito* prop. a participle of vb. *granire.*

Granja Sp. Pg. Pr., Fr. E. *grange;* from *granea* L. L., which has also a form *granica*, whence O. Fr. *granche*, Pr. *granga.* Sp. has the special sense of farm, whence *grangear* to till, gain.

Granter — *créanter.*

Grappa It., Sp. Pg. *grapa* hook, claw, Sp. *grapon;* Fr. *grappin* an anchor, Ven. *grapeia* bur; vb. It. *grappare aggrappare,* Norm.*grapper*, Pic.*agraper (agrape*, Wall.*agrap*=Fr.*agrafe).* From O. H. G. *krapfo*, G. *krappen*, W. *crap*, E. *grab.* Hence also It. *grappo grappolo*, Fr. *gruppe*, O. Fr. Pic. Champ. *crape* grape-stalk, grapo, Du. *grappe krappe*, E. *grape.*

Grascia It. provisions, *grascino* inspector of markets; from ἀγοϱασία. *Grascia* also = Fr. *graisse* fat.

Graspo — *raspare.*

Grasso It., Sp. *graso*, Pg.*graxo*, Pr. Rh. Wal. Fr. *gras* fat; from *crassus*, L.L. *grassus;* also It. Pg.*crasso*, Sp.*crassio crasio*, Fr. *crasse*, E. *crass* (usu. in metaph. sense).

Grasta It. a flower-pot; a Sicil. word, from γάστρα a big-bellied vessel.

Grattare It., Sp. Pr.*gratar*, Fr. *gratter* to scratch; from O.H.G. *chrazon*, Du. *kratsen* &c. Hence Fr. *gratin, égratigner;* It. *grattugio*, Dauph. *gratusi* a rasp, cf. It. *grattugiare*, Pr. *gratuzar*, O. Fr. *gratuser.*

Gratusi — *grattare.*

Gravelle gravier gravois — *grève.*

Graver Fr., E. *grave*, Sp. *grabar* (from the Fr.); from G. *graben* rather than from γϱάφειν, φ == *ff*, cf. γϱαφίον *greffe.*

Gravir Fr. to climb; from *gradus*, It. *gradire*, Fr. *gra-ir, gravir;* cf. *emblaver, parvis, pouvoir.*

Grasnar — *gracidare.*

Gré — *grado.*

Grodon — *gretto.*

Greffe Fr. (m.) an office, bureau, O. Fr. *grafe*, Pr. *grafi* = L. *graphium*, cf.*bureau* for a similar extension of meaning. Hence Pr. *grafinar* to scratch, N. Pr. *esgraffá*, O. Fr. *esgraffer* to scratch out, Fr. *égraffigner* to blot, soil.

Greffe Fr. (f.), *greffer* = E. *graff graft*, M. Du. *grafie, grafien.* Identical with the former word, f. from n. plur.; the shoot would be sharp and pointed like the stylus, cf. Sp. *mugron.*

Grègues Fr. breeches; from W. *guregys* girdle.

Grêle Fr., Pr. *graile* slim, thin, shrill; from *gracilis.* Hence O. Fr. sbst. *graisle grelle,* Pr. *graile* a wind-instrument, cf. *clairon* from *clair.*

Grêle grêler — *grès.*

Grelo - · *grillo.*

Grelot Fr. a bell; from *grelle* (v.*grêle*), or from *crotalum* a rattle, *grelotter* to chatter with the teeth.

Grembo lap; from *gremium, grembio* (whence *grembiata*), *grembo;* cf. *combiato* from *commeatus,* Mil. *scimbia* for *scimmia, rendembia* for *vendemmia.*

Gremire ghermire to claw; from O. H. G. *krimman.*

Grenon — *greña.*

Grenouille Fr., Pr. *granolha* a frog = It. *ranocchia* from a Lat. *ranucula,* O. Fr. *renouille, rane raine* in several dialects. For the *g* prefixed cf. *grenouillette* for *ranunculus,* It. *gracimolo* = *racimolo.*

Greña Sp. tangled hair, Pg. *grenha* hair of the head, Pr. *gren* (m.) beard; whence O. Sp. *greñon griñon,* Pr. O. Fr. *grignon grenon guernon* beard or mustachio. From L. L. *granus* (*videmus granos et cinnabar Gothorum* Isid.) = O. H. G. *grani* (pl. whence the Rom. forms with the weak *n*), M. H. G. *gran,* O. N. *grön* beard, G. *granne* bristle, also Gael. *granni* long hair, W. *grann* "cilium". The Rom. *i* is prob. due to *crinis.*

Greppia It. (*creppia*), Pr. *crepia crepeha,* O. Fr. *crebe, greche,* Fr. *crèche* a crib; from O. H. G. *krippa krippea,* O. G. *cribbia,* E. *crib.* From the kindred L. G. form *krubbe* come the Pr. *crupia,* Piedm. Ven. *grupia,* Gen. *groeppia,* Romagn. *gropia.* The B. has a similar form *khorbua.* The Sp. uses a L. word, *pesebre,* Lomb. *parseiv, presef.*

Greppo It., Rh. *grip,* Ven. *grebano,* Com. *grip crap* (= Rh. *crap carp* gravel) *cip* (from *clip*) cliff; from O. H. G. *klëp,* G. *klippe,* E. *cliff,* W. *clip.*

Grès Fr. (m.) sand-stone, N. Pr. *gres* coarse sand, whence Pr. *greza gressa (graissa),* Fr. *grêle* hail-stones, vb. *grêler;* dim. Fr. *grésil* fine hail, Pr. *grazil,* vb. *grésiller, grazilhar.* Cf. N. Pr. *grezo* grit = O. Pr. *greza* hail, G. *kieseln* to hail from *kies* gravel. *Grès* comes from O. H. G. *griez grioz,* G. *gries,* E. *grit,* cf. *grêle (gresle)* from M. H. G. *griezel* a grain, granule.

Grésil — *grès.*

Grésillon O. Fr. a cricket; from *gryllus,* for *grécillon,* cf. *oisillon* from *avis, pucelle* from *pulla.*

Greto It. sandy shore; from O. H. G. *grioz,* O. N. *griot,* E. grit.

Gretto It. greed, or adj. greedy; M. H. G. *grit,* adj. *gritec* greedy. With the L. G. *d* for *t* we find Fr. *gredin,* Pic. *guerdin,* Lorr. *gordin,* cf. Goth. *gredus,* O. N. *grád,* E. greed.

Greve It., Pr. *greu,* O. Fr. *grief* (Fr. sbst. E. *grief*), Wal. *greu:*

from *gravis*, whence It. *aggrevare*, O. Fr. *ayrever*, Pr. *agreujar* (as if *aggraviare aggreviare*), O.Fr. *agregier*, O.E. *agregge*, = *aggravate*, Fr. *rengréger* to make worse; *grevis* for *gravis*, being often paired with its opp. *levis*, cf. Pr. *ni greu ni leu*. O. Fr. *grieté* = *gravitas*.

Grève Fr. (f.) a flat sandy shore, Pr. Cat. *grava* gravel, Rh. *grava greva* sand-flat, Ven. *grara* bed of a mountain stream, Fr. *gravier*, *gravelle*, *gravois*, E. *gravel*. Bret. has *kraé grac*, *kròa gròa*. Perhaps from *crau*, W. *cray*.

Grioclare It. to scowl, to long for; Com. *syriza* to gnash; from same origin as Fr. *grincer* (q. v.), O. H. G. *grimizón* to gnash. It. *griccio gricciolo* = shivering fit.

Gridare It., Sp. Pg. *gritar*, Fr. *crier* (E. *cry*); sbst. It. *grido grida*, Sp. *grito*, Fr. *cri (cry)*: Parm. *cridar*, Ven. *criare*, Mil. *criâ*, O.Sp. *cridar gridar*, *crida grida grido*. The root is found in the Goth. *gretan*, E. *greet*, Du. *kryten*, also in the Celtic, but the immediate etymon is L. *quiritare* whence *kiritare critare gridare*, cf. Fr. *Cricq* from *Quiricus*, *triaca* from *theriaca*. It. *sgridare*, O. Fr. *escrier* have been influenced by the O. H. G. *scrian*.

Grief — *greve*.

Grietar Sp., Pg. *gretar* to split, burst, sbst. *grieta greta*, Lomb. *cretto*; from *crepitare*.

Griffo Fr. a claw, *griffer* to claw; from O. H. G. *grifan*, G. *greifen*, E. *grip*, sbst. *grif*, *grip*. Piedm. has *grif*, Com. *grif sgrif* a claw, Rh. *grifla*; It. *grifo* a snout. Connected with these is It. *griffo grifone*, Sp. *grifo*, Pr. *grifó*, Fr. *griffon*, E. *griffin* from L. *gryphus*, Fr. vb. *griffer*. It. *grifagno*, O. Fr. *grifaigne* expressed, in the latter language at least, not so much the rapacity of a bird of prey as a malignant threatening aspect: *Charlle à la barbe grifaigne*, cf. Dante: *Cesare armato con gli occhi grifagni* (falcon eyes).

Grifo — *griffe*.

Grignon Fr. crust of bread, Norm. *grigne*, Pic. *grignette*. N. Pr. *grignoun* = grape-stone &c. From *granum*, *grignon* for *greignon* or *graignon*, cf. *chignon* for *chaignon*, *barguigner* for *bargaigner*. From *grignon* comes Fr. *grignoter*.

Grigio — *griso*.

Gril grille — *grada*.

Grillo Sp., Pg. *grilho*, Pr. *grilhó*, Fr. *grillet* fetter, manacle; from the clanking sound like the note of the cricket *(gryllus)*, cf. O. Fr. *gresillon*, which has both senses.

Grillo It. Sp. caprice, whim; from the sudden leap of the cricket *(grillo)* cf. *capriccio*, and Rh. *grilla* in both senses. Vb. *grillare*.

Grillo Sp., Cat. *grily*, Pg. *grelo* shoot, sprout, vb. *grillar* &c. From *gracilis*, through the O. Fr. *grel*.

Grim Pr. afflicted, *grima* affliction, *grimar* to be afflicted; from O. H. G. *grim* furious, E. *grim*, cf. *gram* (*gramo*).

Grima Sp. fright (at seeing something dreadful), Pg. aversion. From A. S. *grima* ghost, from same root as the preceding word, v. *grimoire*.

Grimace — *grimoire*.

Grimo It. wrinkled; from O. H. G. *grim*, E. *grim*. Sbst. *grinza* a wrinkle, *grinzo* wrinkled, *aggrinzare* from O. H. G. *grim-mison*.

Grimoire Fr. a conjuring-book, unintelligible talk (E. *gramary*); from O. N. A. S. *grima* a ghost (whence Fr. E. *grimace*), *grimoire* like *exécutoire*, *monitoire* &c. There are others words from the Norse mythology, e. g. *cauchemar*, *loup-garou*, *truiller*. Génin finds a form *gramare* for *grimoire* and refers them to *grammaire* (i. e. Latin). Then, the form must have been adapted to *grima*. O. Fr. *ingremance*, Pg. *engrimanzo* gibberish are corruptions of *nigremance*, Pr. *nigromancia*, Wall. *egrimancien* from *nécromancien*. Littré (Hist. de la langue française) approves of Génin's derivation, which is, moreover, supported by the E. form *gramary*.

Grimper Fr. to climb; from O. H. G. *kliniban*, E. *climb*, G. *klimmen*, or from Du. *grijpen* (G. *greifen*) to seize, Norm. Wall. *griper* = *grimper*; Berr. *grimper* = to seize.

Grinar Pr. to grin; from O. H. G. *grinan*, G. *greinen*, E. *grin*; hence It. *di-grignare*, Com. *grignà*, Champ. Pic. *grigner les dents*, from an O. H. G. form *grinjan* = A. S. *grinian*. Sbst. Rh. *grigna* grimace.

Grincer Fr., Pic. *grincher* to gnash; from O. H. G. *gremizôn* = A. S. *grimetan*. Cf. It. *gricciare*.

Grinta Lomb. a grim sullen look, haughtiness; Ven. *grinta* rage, scorn; from O. H. G. *grimmida* grimness.

Grinza — *grimo*.

Gripo — *gripper*.

Gripper Fr. to seize; Goth. *greipan*, E. *grip*, O. N. *gripa*, Du. *grijpen*, = O. H. G. *grifan*, G. *greifen*. Lomb. *grippà* to rob, It. *grippo* a pirate-ship, Sp. *gripo* a trading vessel.

Grippo — *gripper*.

Griso grigio It., Sp. Pg. Fr. *gris*, grey, also sbst. Sp. Pg. O. Fr. *gris*, O. E. *grys* (Chauc. = grey fur). Hence It. *grisetto*, Sp. *griseta*, Fr. *grisette* a sort of grey stuff, Fr. also a person of the lower orders, cf. E. *borel* folk, from *buja*. From O. S. *gris* canus, M. H. G. *gris grise*, L. L. *griseus*, whence It. *grigio*, Rh. *grisch*, O. Sp. *grisco*.

Gritar — *gridare*.

Grive Fr., Cat. *griva* a thrush; an onomatop. (Menage).

Grogner groin gronder — *grugnire*.

Grole Fr. (f.) a rook. The form *acul* ought to give *acle* or *ail*, *graculus gracula graille* (v. *gracco*), but as *seule* from *seculum* so may have been formed *graule grole*, v. *meule*. It. *grola*, Du. *grol* from the Fr.

Gromma It. crust (of wine); cf. Sw. *grumlete* sediment, Swed. *grums grummel*.

Grommeler Fr., Wall. *grouml*; G. *grumeln grumen*, E. *grumble*, cf. W. sbst. *grwm*.

Gronda It., Rh. *gronda*, Fr. *séveronde*, E. *severans*, Rouchi *souvronte*, O. Fr. *souronde* eaves; from *subgrunda* (Varro). Hence *grondare* to drip, *grondaia* stillicidium.

Grongo gongro It.; from *congrus*, γόγγρος, Fr. *congre*, E. *conger* &c.

Groppo gruppo It., Sp. *grupo gorrupo*, Fr. *groupe*, E. *group*; It. *groppa*, Sp. *grupa*, Pg. *garupa*, Pr. *cropa*, Fr. *croupe*, E. *croup* (cf. Fr. *trousse* in both senses); vb. O. Fr. *croupir* to squat, Fr. to prop. The root is found both in the Germ. and the Celt. prop. = something compressed, O. H. G. *kropf*, Norse *kryppa* a heap, bunch, O. H. G. *krupel*, G. *kräppel*, E. *cripple*, vb. N. *kriupa*, L. G. *krupen* to cower, Gael. *crup* to contract, W. *cropa*, E. *crop*. Hence *groppone*, *croupion* rump, O. Fr. *crepon* (c from N. *krippa*); E. *crupper*.

Grosella Sp. Cat., Fr. *groseille*, Com. *crosela*, Pg. *groselheira*, Rouchi *grusiele*, Wall. *gruzale*; from *grossus* coarse, G. *krausbeere kräuselbeere*, Sw. *krusbar*, Du. *kruisbezie*, Eng. (corrupt) *gooseberry*, = It. *uva crespa*, G. *kraus* = rough.

Grosso It. Pg., Sp. *grueso*, Pr. Wall. Fr. *gros* thick, sbst. *gros* the name of a coin. L. L. *grossus*, G. *grôz* grandis, crassus, which latter, however, should have given Pr. *graut*, and is found in Berr. *grot grout*, E. *groat*. Hence E. *engross*, *grocer* = Fr. *marchand grossier* one who sells by the *gross*.

Grotesque — *grotta*.

Grotta It., Sp. Pg. *gruta*, Fr. *grotte*, Pr. O. Fr. *crota crote* a cavern, E. *grotto*, hence Burg. Genev. *encrotter* to bury; from *crypta* (κρύπτη), Wal. *cripte*; adj. It. *grottesco*, Fr. E. *grotesque* prop. like a grotto, fantastical in shape &c.

Grouiller Fr. to crawl, stir; from O. H. G. *grubilôn*, L. G. *grubeln* to grabble, G. *grübeln*, cf. O. N. *grufla*. Cf. also O. H. G. *crewelin*, Du. *krevelen*, E. *crawl*, Berr. *gravouiller*.

Gruau Fr. groats; for *grucau* = O. Fr. *gruel* which is for *grutel* from A. S. *grut*, O. H. G. *gruzi*, G. *grütze*, whence also E. *gruel*, W. *grual*. Champ. *gru* = bran.

Gruccia — *croccia*.

Grude — *glu*.

Grueso — *grosso*.

Grufolare It. to grunt, to turn up the soil as a pig; from *grifo* snout, and *grugnire* to grunt.

Gruger Fr. to chew a hard substance (O. F. *grudge*), *égruger* to pound small, hence E. *gurgeons*. Perhaps from M. H. G. *grôz*, O. E. *grut*, Pr. *gru*, E. *groats*, with suffix *icare* = Fr. *ger (viudicare venger)*. N. Pr. *gruci* = to make groats. Cf. *gruan*.

Grugnire It., Sp. *gruñir*, Pr. *gronhir gronir*, Wall. *grogni;* from *grunnire*. Also It. *gruguare*, Fr. *grogner*. Hence sbst. It. *grugno*, Pr. *gronh*, Fr. *groin*, O. Pg. *gruin* the snout. Cf. O. H. G. *grun*, *grunni*, E. *groan*, W. *gruen*. From *grundire* is Pr. *grondir*, O. Fr. *grondir grondre*, Fr. *gronder*. O. Fr. *groncer* = O. H. G. *grunzen*, E. *grunt*.

Grulla Sp. a crane; from *gruicula*.

Grumeler — *grumo*.

Grumo It. Sp. Pg. a lump, clot, O. Fr. *grume* divers sorts of corn, It. *grumolo* heart of cabbage, Sp. *grumete* a boy, ship's boy (cf. *garzone*), whence Fr. *gourmette;* Fr. *se grumeler* to clot together, curdle; from *grōmus grumulus* a heap.

Grupo — *groppo.*

Gruta — *grotta.*

Gruyer Fr. forester. As *verdier* from *viridis*, so *gruyer* from G. *grün*, E. *green*, M. H. G. *gruo* = pratum.

Gruzzo gruzzolo It. heap, mass of things, Wal. *gruetzi;* of G. origin, cf. Sw. *grütz*, M. H. G. *grüz*.

Guacharo — *guado.*

Guadagnare It., Rh. *gudoignar*, Pr. *gazanhar* for *gadanhar*, Fr. *gagner* for *gaagner*, E. *gain;* O. Sp. *guadañer* to mow; sbst. It. *guadagno*, Pr. *gazanh*, Fr. E. *gain;* Sp. *guadaña*, Pg. *guadanha* a scythe. The orig. meaning is prob. found in O. Fr. *gaaigner* to cultivate land (*gaagnage gaaignerie* profit of land), whence the sense of acquiring. From O. H. G. *weidanôn* or *weidanjan* (G. *weiden*) to hunt, pasture. From *guadagnare* we have Pg. *ganhar*, Cat. Val. *guanyar*. Sp. O. Pg. *ganar* (L. L. *ganare*) is too old to be a mere contraction, and is prob. connected with *gana* (q. v.). From *ganar*, Pg. *ganancia*, *gança*, vb. *gançar*, O. Pg. *guaançar* from *guadagnare*. Dante Inf. 24, 12 has *ringavagnare* from O. Fr. *regaagner.*

Guado It., Pr. *guó*, Fr. *gué* ford, from O. H. G. *wat*, O. N. *vad;* vb. It. *guadare*, Pr. *guazar (guasar)*, Fr. *guéer*, from *watan*, G. *waten*, E. *wade*. Sp. has *vado vadear* from the Latin; *esguazo esguazar* from the Pr., It. *guazzo guazzare. Guazzo* = a drinking-place, Sp. *guacharo* = dropsical, *guachapear* to paddle in the water.

Guado It., Fr. *guède* (f.), O. Fr. *gaide waide*, provinc. *vouede* woad; from O. H. G. *weit*, A. S. *wâd*, E. *woad*. From an O. Fr. *guesde* came L. L. *waisda*, *guasdium*, *guesdium*, Wall.

waiss royal-blue (for *waist* as *cress* for *crest*, L. *crista*, *aouss* for *aousí*, L. *augustus*). Sp. Pg. *glasto* = Gallic *glastum*.

Guai It. Sp. Pg., O. Fr. *wai*, Fr. *ouais*; sbst. It. *guajo*, Sp. Pg. *guaya*; from Goth. *vai*, O. H. G. *wê*, E. *woe*, W. *gwae*, L. *vae.*

Guaime It., O. Fr. *gaim*, Wall. *wayen*, Lorr. *reyen*, Fr. *re-gain* aftermath; from O. H. G. *weida* pasture, (G. *weide*, or from vb. *weidôn*, with Rom. suff. *ime guad-ime guaime*; cf. It. *guastime* from *guastare*. Rouchi has *waimiau*, Norm. *rouin* (for *gouin gain*), O. Fr. *vuin.*

Guaina It., Fr. *gaine*, O. Fr. *gaîne*, Rom. *waine*, W. *gwain* a sheath; from *ragina*. Mil. has *guadinna*, Ven. *guazina.*

Gualcare It., Rom. *gvalché*, O. Fr. *gaucher*, Dauph. *gouchier*, = O. E. *welk* to full; from O.H. G. *walchan*, G. *walken*, E. *walk*, (*walker* = a fuller). Hence *gualchiera*, O. Fr. *gouchoir.*

Gualcire It. to pull to pieces; from O. H. G. *walzjan* volvere, vellicare, G. *wälzen* to roll, to waltz.

Gualda Sp., Pg. *gualde*, Fr. *gaude*, It. *guadarella* a plant for dyeing yellow, *weld*, whence Sp. *gualdo*, Pg. *gualde*, O. Sp. *guado* yellow; from E. *weld*, G. *wau.*

Gualdana It. an incursion of soldiery, a troop of soldiers (Dante); from M. H. G. *woldan* a storming.

Gualiar gallar Pr. to deceive, *gualiart* scornful. From a G. source, Goth. *dvals* foolish, A. S. *dvala* error, *dvelian dveligan*, to err, Du. *dwalen*. For the loss of the *d* cf. *guercio*.

Guancia It. cheek; from O. H. G. *wanga wanka*, G. *wange*. Neap. *guoffola ruoffola* is from L. *offula* a bit of meat [cf. *bucca* (1) cheek (2) bit], or from O. H. G. *hiufila.*

Guanto It., Sp. Pg. *guanto*, Pr. *guan*, Fr. *gant*, dim. Sp. *guante-lete*, E. *gauntlet*. Beda has: *tegumenta manuum quæ Galli wantos vocant*. From a G. source: O. N. *vöttr* = *vantr*, Swed. Dan. *vante.*

Guañir Sp. to grunt; from A. S. *vânjan*, O. H. G. *weinôn*, E. *whine.*

Guappo Neap., Mil. *guapo* haughty, Com. *vap* vain (*v* for *gu*), Sp. Pg. *guapo* bold, elegant, Gasc. *gouapou*; sbst. Sp. *guapeza* ostentation; vb. Norm. *gouaper* to sport. From a G. root, found in A. S. *vapol* a bubble, vb. *vapolian*, Du. *wapperen.*

Guaragno It., Sp. *guarañon*, O. Sp. *guaran* (Val. *guará*), Pr. *guaragnon* a stallion; from L. L. *waranio*, which is from O. L. G. *wrênjo*, Du. *wrêne*, O. H. G. *reineo*, cf. E. *wren* = lascivus, the root being found in Sansk. *vâra* tail (*veredus?*).

Guardare It., Sp. Pg. Pr. *guardar*, Fr. *garder*, E. *guard*; from O. H. G. *warten* to take care, W. *gwara*, Sk. *vri* to protect; sbst. It. Sp. *guardia* (f.), Pr. *guarda* (f.), Fr. *garde* (f. m.), E. *guard*, from Goth. *vardja*, O. H. G. *warto* (m.), *warta* (f.). Hence also It. *guardiano*, Sp. Pr. E. *guardian*, Fr. *gardien*;

It. *guardingo*, Sp. *gardingo*; It. *squardare*, O. Sp. *esguardar*, O. Fr. *esgarder*.

Guardingo — *guardare*.

Guarento O. It., Sp. *garante*, Pr. *guaran guiren*, Fr. *garant a guarantee*, L.L. *warens*, E. *warrant*, O.Fries. *werand warand*; from O. H. G. *wёrёn* to give bail for, *warrant*. The Pr. *guiren* is the orig. form, vb. It. *guarentire* &c.

Guari It., Pr. Cat. *gaire*, Fr. *guère guères* == L. *multum*. Besides *gaire*, Pr. has *grauren gauren* (== *grandis res*), used with or without a negative. Both were used adjectively: *ganren vegadas*, *gaire companhós*, cf. It. *gnan tempo*. *Guari* is from O. H. G. *wäri* == L. *verus*, Pr. *guaire gaire*; for the sense cf. L. *probe*, *gawdri* == *probitas*. Fr. *naguère* == *il n'a guère*, *non ha guari* non est multum (temporis); Piedm. *pa-vaire* not much == Pr. *pas guaire*. O. Fr. *guersoi* great thirst == *guère soif*. Com. *gerr* is from O. It. *gueri*. Or from O. H. G. *weiger* (== O. Pr. form *gaigre*) "much" only found in *unweiger* == "not much".

Guarire guerire It., O. Sp. O. Pg. *guarir* (Sp. *guarecer*), Pr. O. Fr. *garir*, Fr. *guérir*; from Goth. *varjan*, O. H. G. *werjan*, G. *wehren* to defend. Hence Pg. *guarita*, Sp. *garita*, O. Fr. *garite*, Fr. *guérite* a safe place (E. *garret*, Chauc. *waricé*, *warish*), sentry-box &c.; formed from an It. participial form *guarita*, cf. *reussite* from *riuscita*. Piedm. *garita*, Ven. *gareta*, Crem. *garetta* are from the Fr.; the pure Sp. is *guarida* a lurking place. Cf. Dief. Wb. 1, 205.

Guarnaccia — *guarnire*.

Guarnire guernire It., O. Sp. *guarnir*, Sp. *guarnecer*, Pr. Fr. *garnir*, E. *garnish*; from O. H. G. *warnòn*, G. *warnen* (*warn*), or from A. S. *varnian* to take care of, O. Fries. *wernia* to protect, whence Rh. *varniar*, but Lomb. *guarnà* suits the O. H. G. word. O. Fr. *garnir* also == inform, admonish, as O. H. G. *warnòn*, A. S. *varnian*, E. *warn*. Hence It. *guarnaccia guarnacca*, Sp. *garnacha*, Pr. *gaunacha*, Fr. *gamache* a robe, cf. O. H. G. *warna*; It. *guarnello* an undergarment; It. *guarnimento*, Fr. *garnement*, E. *garment*, and It. *guarnigione*, Fr. *garnison*, E. *garrison*.

Guascotto — *biscotto*.

Guastare It., O.Sp. O.Pg. Pr. *guastar*, Sp. Pg. *gastar*, Fr. *gâter* to spoil, waste. From *vastare* or from O. H. G. *wastjan* (from sbst. *wastjo*, M. H. G. *wasten*, E. *waste*)? From the L., with the influence of the G. *w*; cf. adj. It. *guasto*, Pg. *gasto*, O. Fr. *guaste* == *vastus*; *diguastare*, *deguastar*, *degâter* == *devastaer*. O.Fr. *gastir* is from *wastjan*. O. Fr. *guastine* == waste, desert, adj. *gastin*.

Guatare guaitare It., Pr. *guaitar*, Fr. *guetter* to watch; sbst.

Crem. Pr. *guaita*, O. Fr. *guette*, Fr. (m.) *guet*; from O. H. G. *wahtèn*, sbst. *wahta*, G. *wacht*, Goth. *rahtvò*, E. *wateh*. Hence It. *agguatare*, Sp. Pr. *aguaitar*, O. Fr. *aguetier* = *guatare*; It. *aguato*, Sp. *agait*, Fr. *aguet* (usu. in pl.), ambush, whence *daguet* = *d'aguet*.

Guattora — *guêtre*.

Guazzo — *guado*.

Gubia Sp., Pg. *guiva*, N. Pr. *gubio*, Fr. E. *gouge*. L. L. *gubia gubia* and *gulvia gulbia*. From the Basque *gubia* a hole, *gubioa* a throat. Larr. derives *gubia* from *gurbia*, cf. It. *gorbia sgorbia*, L. L. *gulbia*.

Gudazzo It., Crem. Com. *gudazz* a godfather, f. *gudazza*; from O. H. G. *gotti*, f. *gota*, G. *gothe*.

Gué — *guado*.

Guèdo — *guado*.

Guedeja — *redija*.

Guédor Fr. to satisfy (only in partic. *guédé*); from O. H. G. *weidon*, G. *weiden* to pasture, whence also Wall. *waidi*.

Guenillo Fr. rag, rugged coat; from Flem. *quene* woollen overcoat, or like *souquenille* from *gonna* q. v.

Guenipe Fr. a dissolute woman, slut, Dauph. *ganippa*; from Du. *knipje* trap, cf. *knip* brothel, G. *kneipe* ale-house.

Guenon Fr. female ape; from *quena* woman, E. *queau, queen*; or from O. H. G. *winja* amica. Cf. It. *monna* a female ape, from *madouna*.

Guêpe Fr. a wasp; from *respa*, the *gu* from the O. H. G. *wefsa*, G. *wespa*, E. *wasp*, cf. Lorr. *voisse* (*vo* = O.H.G. *w*), Champ. *goupe*, Berr. *gêpe*.

Guer guerle — *guercio*.

Guercho — *guercio*.

Guercio It., Com. *sguere*, Rh. *guersch (wiersch)*, O. Sp. *guercho*, Pr. *guer guerle*, Dauph. *guerlio* squinting. From O.H.G. *twer dwerch*, G. *quer* oblique, E. *queer*.

Guerdon — *guiderdone*.

Guèro — *guari*.

Guéret — *barbecho*.

Guérir guérite — *guarire*.

Guermontor — *gaimenter*.

Guerpir O. Fr., Pr. *guerpir gurpir* to give up, desert, resign, Fr. *déguerpir*; from Goth. *rairpan*, O. H. G. *werfan*, G. *werfen* to throw. From an old German custom of throwing a straw into another's lap on ceding any property to him. V. Ducange.

Guerra It. Sp. Pg. Pr., Fr. *guerre*, E. *war*; from O.H.G. *werra*, O. E. *werre*, vb. O. H. G. *werran* to bring into disorder, so *guerrier* in O. Fr. = enemy, make-bate.

Guet guetter — *guatare.*

Guêtre Fr. (f.), E. *gaiter*, Lang. *gueto*, Wall. *guett*, Champ. *guête*, Piedm. *gheta*, Rouchi *guetton*, Bret. *gweltrea.*

Guoude — *gheldra.*

Gueux Fr. (f. *gueuse*) beggar, vb. *queuser*, Sw. *gösen.* Perhaps connected with *gueuse* throat. Whether *gueuse* be from It. *gozzo*, or Fr. *gosier* from It. *gozzaju = gozzaria* is doubtful. Others make *guenx* the same word as *queux (coquus)*, cf. *coquin.*

Gufo It. an owl; from O. H. G. *hûf hûvo.*

Gui Fr. mistletoe. From Celtic *gwid*, *gue*, *guy*, L. *viscus* (It. *visco vischio*).

Guiar — *guidare.*

Guiche guige O. Fr. a ribbon thong (espec. of a shield), It. *guiggia.* From O. H. G. *windicas*, plur. of *windine (fasciola "viudinca"* Gl.). Hence also Provin. *s'aguincher* to deck oneself (with ribbons).

Guichet Fr., O. Fr. *wiket guischet*, Pr. *guisquet*, E. *wicket*, Du. *winket;* from O. N. *rik*, A. S. *vic.*

Guidare It., Sp. Pg. *guiar*, Pr. *guidar guizar guiar*, Fr. *guider*, E. *guide;* sbst. It. *guida*, Sp. *guia*, Pr. *guida gult*, O. Fr. *guis*, Fr. E. *guide.* Perhaps from O. H. G. *vitan* to watch, cf. It. *scorgere*, and for the medial O. Fr. *hadir haïr* from *hatan;* sbst. *guida =* Goth. A. S. *vita* counsellor. From *guidare* is Fr. *guidon.*

Guiderdone It., Pr. *guazardon* (for *guadardon*) guiardon *guierdon*, O. Fr. *guerredon guerdon*, E. *guerdon*, Sp. *galardon*, Pg. *galardão*, O. Cat. *guardó*, L. L. *widerdonum;* vb. *guiderdonare* &c. *Widerdonum* is a corruption (through *donum*) of the O. H. G. *widarlôn* recompensation, A.S. *widherlean*, G. *wider* back, *lôn = loan.* Sp. *galardon* is for *gadardon.* Pr. Synon. *guazardinc* is through Lomb. *thinx garathinx.*

Guidon — *guidare.*

Guiggia — *guiche.*

Guigne — *visciola.*

Guigner — *ghignare.*

Guijo Sp. *guija* gravel, *guijarro* pebble-stone. From Basque *eguiya* angle, *guijarro* from *eguijarria* angular stone, v. Larramendi.

Guile O. Fr. E., Pr. *guila*, m. *guil*, vb. O. Fr. *guiler*, Pr. *guilar*, E. *beguile.* From A. S. *vile*, E. *wile*, cf. W. *gwill*, Bret. *gwil* a thief.

Guilée Fr. a shower of rain, Wall. *walaie* for *waslaie;* from O. H. G. *wasal* rain; *guilée* like *ondée* &c.

Guilena Sp. a plant, columbine; from *aquilina.*

Guilha — *guiler.*

Guilledin Fr., from E. *gelding.*

Guimauve — *malvavischio.*

Guimple guimpe O. Fr. f., E. *wimple;* from O. H. G. *wimpal,* G. *wimpel* a pendant, streamer. Sp. *impla* a veil may come from *wimpal* as well as from *infula,* cf. *Andalucia* from *l'au-dalitia.*

Guindar guindor — *ghindare.*

Guingois Fr. unevenness; from O. N. *kingr kengr* a bend, for *quingois,* by assimilation. For suff. *ois* v. R. Gr. 2, 314.

Guiñar — *ghignare.*

Guiper O. Fr. to work with silk thread, whence Fr. *guipure* a sort of lace; from Goth. *reipan* to festoon, O. H. G. *wiffan* to weave, G. *weifen* to reel. Cf. *aggueffare.*

Guirlande guirnalda — *ghirlanda.*

Guisa It. Sp. Pg. Pr., Fr. E. *guise;* vb. Sp. *guisar;* Pr. *desguisar,* Fr. *déguiser,* E. *disguise;* from O. H. G. *wisa,* G. *weise.*

Guisarme O. Fr., Pr. *gasarma,* O. Fr. *gisarme jusarme,* Pr. *ju-sarma,* It. *giusarma,* O. E. *gisarm gysarn,* also Fr. *wisarme risarme,* whence O. Sp. *bisarma* a sort of light weapon, L. L. *gisarma,* often found with epith. *esmolue* sharpened, ground. It is often found in connection with *falx falcastrum,* which is translated by the O. H. G. *getisarn* (G. *jäteisen* a hoe). This may have become *getsarna gisarna,* and then, through *arma, guisarma.* The form with *w* follow the analogy of such words as *guivre givre wivre, gachière jachière waquière.* Dief. derives it from *gesara,* v. *gése;* others from *gæsum* and *arma,* which would be too artificial.

Guiscart guichard O. Fr., Pr. *guiscos* sharp, acute; from O. N. *risk-r.* Others make it = *wizard, wiz* and *hart, wise-heart.*

Guita Sp. Pg. packthread; from *vitta* through O. H. G. *wita.*

Guitarra guitarre — *chitarra.*

Guitran — *catrame.*

Guivre — *givre.*

Guizzare sguizzare, Ven. *sguinzare,* Mil. *sguinzà* to quiver as fish do; from G. *witsen witschen.*

Guizzo — *rizzo.*

Gume Pg. (m.) acuteness; from *acumen,* whence, perhaps, Sp. *gumia,* Pg. *gomia agomia* a poniard.

Gurrumina Sp. uxoriousness; from Basque *gur-mina* evil inclination.

Gusano Sp. Pg. a worm; from *cossus,* whence also Rh. *coss.*

Guscio It. shell of nuts, eggs &c., Fr. *gousse* (f.) husk, pod, Mil. *guss* (m.) *gussa* (f.), Romag. *goss gossa;* hence Fr. *gousset* fob, E. *gusset.* Placidus has: *galliciciola cortex nucis juglan-*

dis, perhaps for *galliciola* from *gallicia (nux gallica* a walnut), which might become It. *galcia galscia guscio,* Fr. *gausse gousse,* Com. *s-gausc* for *s-galsc.*

II.

Habla hablar habler — *favola.*

Haca Sp., O. Sp. Pg. *faca,* O. Fr. *hague (h* asp.) a nag; O. Fr. *haquet,* Sic. *acchettu* a nag, Pic. *haguette* a little mare; Fr. *haquet* a dray. From E. *hack; hackney* = Du. *hakke-nei* (E. *nag,* Du. *negg,* G. *nickel),* whence Fr. *haquenée,* O. Sp. Pg. *facanca,* Sp. *hacanca,* It. *acchinea, chinea.*

Hacha hache — *accia.*

Hacha — *faccola.*

Hacia — *faccia.*

Hacienda — *faccenda.*

Hacina — *fascio.*

Hacino Sp. stingy, niggardly; from Ar. *'hazīn.*

Hagard Fr. (*h* asp.) stubborn, espec. of falcons, E. *haggard,* G. *hagart;* from E. *hawk* with depreciative suffix *ard* (as in *busart* &c.). The E. adj. *haggard* is a different word (from G. *hager* lean).

Haie Fr. (asp.) hedge; from M. Du. *haeghe,* Du. *haag* (whence the *Hague*), O. H. G. *hag* a town (cf. *town* &c.). Vb. O. Fr. *hayer,* O. H. G. *hagun,* G. *hagen.*

Haillon Fr. (asp.) rag; from M. H. G. *hadel,* G. *hader.*

Hair Fr. (asp.), O. Fr. *hadir,* from Goth. *hatan,* or, better, from A. S. *hatian,* O. Fris. *hatia,* O. S. *hetian,* E. *hate.* O. Fr. *hé* from Goth. *hatis,* A. S. *heti hate;* hence *haior haïne,* Fr. *haine,* whence *haineux,* E. *heinous.* Pr. has a comp. *azirar airar (adirare),* sbst. *azir air.*

Haire O. Fr. (asp.) haircloth; from O. H. G. *hara,* O. N. *haera* hair-stuff. Norm. *hair* (m.), E. *hair* = O. N. O. H. G. *hār.*

Haise *(hese)* O. Fr. (asp.), L. L. *hesia,* Norm. *aiset,* Rouch. *asiau* a small door or grating, Norm. *haisier* a cart-rack, Basque *hesia* a hedge. From *hirpex* a barrow, Fr. *herse,* E. *hearse.*

Hait O. Fr. (asp.) pleasure, joy, *haitier* to animate, cheer, *dehait* dejection, low spirits, vb. *dehaitier,* Fr. *souhait* wish, *souhaiter.* From Goth. *ga-hait,* O. H. G. *ga-heiz,* O. N. *heit* promise, vow, cf. L. *votum* (1) vow (2) wish; *à hait* = according to one's wish, *souhait* = secret desire. Wedg. connects *hait* with E. *hey-day* (= G. *heyda*), to *hoit, hoity-toity.*

Halagar Sp., O. Sp. *falagar afalagar,* Val. *falagar,* Cat. *afalegar,* Pg. *afagar* to cajole, caress, sbst. *halago* &c. From a form *flaihan* of the Goth. *thlaihan* to caress (or O. H. G. *flëhòn* to fawn), whence *flag falg falag*.

Halar Sp., Fr. *haler* (h asp.), Pg. *alar*; from O. N. *hala*, O. H. G. *halôn*, E. *haul*.

Halbran Fr. (asp.), *albran* Sp. Fr. a young wild duck, *halbrené* broken-winged, vb. *halbrener* to shoot ducks. From G. *halb-ente* (half-duck) = anas querquedula, so called from its small size, for *halber ent* (M. H. G. *ant* masc.) cf. *halber ampfer*. Hence, perhaps, E. *auburn*. Wedg.

Halbrené — *halbran*.

Halcon — *falcone*.

Hâle Fr. (asp.) summer-heat, vb. *hâler* to burn up, dry. The circumflex is not for a lost *s* (cf. O. Fr. *haller*), the word being from Du. *hael* dry.

Haleine — *alenare*.

Haler — *halar*.

Haligote harligote O. Fr. (asp.) rag, vb. *haligoter harigoter*; from E. *harl* a filament, O. H. G. *harluf* licinum.

Hallar Sp., O. Sp. *fallar* (still used in the sense of finding a verdict = Fr. *trouver*) to find. The obs. form *falar* might be from Pg. *aflar* (O. Sp. *ajar* v. *achar*), cf. Sp. *sajar* and *jasar*, *garzo* and *zarco*, *facerir* and *zaferir*. From *aflar* is Sp. *ajar* = to maltreat, cf. *offendere* (1) meet with (2) hurt.

Halle Fr. (asp.), whence It. *alla*; from O. H. G. *halla*, A. S. *heal*, E. *hall*.

Hallebarde — *alabarda*.

Hallier Fr. (asp.), E. *hallier*, Pic. *hallo* a bush. L. L. *hasla in hasla i. e. in ramo.*

Halot Fr. (asp.) a rabbit's hole; from O. H. G. *hol*, A. S. *hal*, E. *hole*.

Halt O. Fr. (asp.) abiding-place, Fr. *halte*, E. *halt*, It. Sp. *alto*; from G. *halt*, E. *hold*, O. H. G. fem. *halta* halt.

Hamac hamaca — *amaca*.

Hambre Sp. hunger; from *fames* (G. *faminis*, cf. O. Sp. *fame*, Sard. *famini*, v. Rom. Gr. 1, 190. The Pg. has *fome*, Com. *fom*, Wal. *foame*.

Hameau Fr. (asp.) hamlet, O. Fr. Pic. *ham*; E. *ham*, Goth. *haims*, O. H. G. *heim*, E. *home*.

Hameçon — *anciuo*.

Hampa — *rampo*.

Hampe Fr. (asp.) handle of a weapon; from O. H. G. *hant haba*.

Hanafat O. Fr. a vessel for honey; Du. *honig-vat*, O. S. *hanig-fat*, E. *honey-vat*.

Hanap — *anappo*.

Hanche — *anca*.

Hanebane henebane Fr. (asp.), from E. *heubane* = Fr. *mort aux poules.*

Hangar — *angar.*

Hanneton Fr. (asp.) a cockchafer; prob. a dim. of the G. *hahn* in *weiden-hahn* (meadow-hen) a name of the insect in provincial G., cf. E. *cock-. chafer. Eton* is a double dim. *et-on,* cf. *banneton, cancton, clocheton, feuilleton, brocheton, moineton, œilleton, sommeton.* From its buzzing-noise it is called in Lorr. *hurlat,* Pic. *hourlon, bruant,* Champ. *equergnot,* Wall. *biése-à-balouc.* Genin refers it to *ane* a duck, from a supposed likeness.

Hansacs O. Fr. a knife. From A. S. *hand-seax* a hand-knife. Hence Fr. *hansart* a garden knife.

Hanse Fr. (asp.) a trading-company; from O. H. G. *hansa* a band.

Hante hanste O. Fr. a spear-shaft; from *ames amites* (v. *andas*).

Hanter Fr. (asp.), *hantise* O. Fr. *hant,* E. *haunt,* G. *hantieren.* From the O. N. *heimta* to long after *(heim home),* Dan. *hente,* Cf. its intrans. use: *les seraines en la mer hantent* Brut. 1, p. 37.

Happe Fr. (asp.) a cramp-iron, *happer* to pack; from O. H. G. *happa* a sickle, G. *happen* to pack, Prov. E. *happ.*

Haquenée haquet — *haca.*

Haraldo — *araldo.*

Harangue — *aringo.*

Harapo — *arpa.*

Haras Fr. (asp.) a stud (of horses), L. L. *haracium.* From Arab. *faras* a horse (Sp. *alfaras*), the Arab. breed being famous, (farii equi Ducange). We should, however, have expected an O. Fr. *faras,* L. L. *faracium.*

Harasser Fr. (asp.) = E. *harass.*

Haroeler — *herse.*

Hard hart Fr. (f. asp.) string, *harde* rope, herd, pl. *hardes* articles of clothing &c.; cf. Sp. Pg. *fardas,* Fr. *fardeau,* O. Fr. *hardel.*

Hardi — *ardire.*

Hardier O. Fr. (asp.) to provoke; from same G. root as *hardi,* L. L. *anharden* to incite.

Hareng — *aringa.*

Harer harier O. Fr., hence O. E. *to hare* and *harie;* from *har haro* a cry for help *(halloo!),* cf. O. H. G. *hâren* to cry out. Connected is the O. Fr. *haraler* to plague, sbst. *harale* uproar. Some refer *harer harier* and *harasser* to an O. Fr. *har* withy, rod, scourge, but this is for *hard* or *hart,* and the dental could hardly be lost in derivatives.

Hargne O. Fr. peevishness, surliness, adj. *hergne,* Lorr. *harégne* quarrel, Fr. *hargneux (h* asp.) quarrelsome, Norm. *harigneux* stubborn, vb. O. Fr. *harguer* to quarrel, Pic. to scoff, *herguer* to complain. Some suit the O. H. G. *harmjan* (E. *harm*) "objurgare".

Haricot Fr. (*h* asp.) small bean; Pic. *haricotier* a retailer. Genin shows that the orig. meaning was anything minced small, e.g. "*haricot de mouton*". He refers it to *aliquod* (for haligote)!

Haridelle Fr. (asp.) a jade, Rouchi *hardele*, E. *harridan*, cf. Wall. *harott*, Norm. *harin*.

Harija Sp. mill-dust; from *farriculum?*

Harlot — *arlotto*.

Harnacher harnois — *arnese*.

Haro (asp.) a loud cry. From O. S. *herod* (O. H. G. *hera hara*) = L. *huc*, whence also vb. *haroder*, and the compounds *har-loup*, *harlevrier*, and vb. *harer harier*, O. H. G. *harēn* to cry out. The word was orig. used in such expressions as: *harou harou! à l'ors!*

Harouche — *farouche*.

Harpe harper harpon — *arpa*.

Harto Sp., O. Sp. Pg. *farto* satiated, adv. Sp. *harto*, O. Pg. *farte* enough, whence *hartar fartar*; from *farcire fartus.*

Hasard — *azzardo.*

Hascas fascas fasces O. Sp. adv. = L. *pæne*; from Sp. *hasta-casi.*

Haschière O. Fr. (asp.) (whence *haschie*, Pic. *haskie*) pain; from O. H. G. *harmscara* smart, L. L. *hascaria*, O. Cat. *aliscara.*

Hase Fr. (asp.) female hare; from O. H. G. *haso*. Norm. *heri* is from O. N. *hēri.*

Hasple — *aspo.*

Hasta Sp., O. Sp. O. Pg. *fasta* = L. *tenus;* from *haria* and *ata?* V. *té.* Or, from the Arab. '*hatta?* Hence vb. *hastar.*

Hastio — *fastio.*

Hâte Fr. (asp.) for *haste*, vb. *hâter*, adj. *hâtif*, Pr. *astiu*, O. It. adv. *astivamente;* from O. Fr. *haste*, N. *hastr*, E. *haste*, vb. N. *hasta*, M. H. G. *hasten*, E. *haste.*

Haterel O. Fr. (asp.) nape, *hasterel*, Pic. *hatéreau*, Wall. *hatrai.* From O. H. G. *halsadura*, M. H. G. *halsadar*, whence *halsterel halterel haterel hasterel;* cf. *contraindre*, It. *poltro* (for *polstro*) for the loss of *s* between a liquid and a *t.*

Hato Sp., Pg. *fato* clothes, effects, provisions, herd; from O. H. G. *fazza* or *faz* (n.) a bundle, O. N. *fat* = garment, pocket, cf. Swed. *fate-bur* store-house.

Haubans Fr. (asp.) shrouds, O. Fr. *hobenes;* from O. N. *höfud-bendur* (pl.); cf. M. Du. *hoband* for *hoofdband.* It would be more correct to write *hobans.* From Du. *raa-band* is Fr. *raban.*

Haubert — *usbergo.*

Hausser — *alzare.*

Haut Fr. (asp.), O. Fr. *halt hault;* from *altus*, the aspirate from N. *hā* or O. H. G. *hôch*, E. *high*.

Have Fr. thin and pale; from A. S. *hasva*, M. H. G. *heswe* torridus pallidus.

Haver O. Fr. (asp.) to draw to oneself; from O. H. G. *habên*, E. *have* = hold. From same root is O. Fr. *havet* a hook, from *haba* or *haft* with Fr. suff. *et*, cf. Wall. *haveter* from *haften*.

Haveron havron· averon Fr. wild oats; from O. H. G. *habaro*, or, since *h* is silent, for *aveneron (avena)*.

Havir Fr. (asp.) to singe; from O. H. G. *heiên* to burn.

Havre Fr. (m. asp.), O. Fr. *havene havle hable* harbour; from A. S. *häffen*, E. *haven*, O. N. *höfn*.

Havresac Fr. (asp.); from G. *habersack* provision-bag.

Haya — *faggia*.

Haz - *fascia*.

Haz Sp. Pg. (f.) array of soldiers &c.; from *acies*.

Haza aza Sp., O. Sp. *faza* a piece of garden or cultivated land; = Pr. *faissa (fascia)* a strip of land.

He Sp. in *he-me he-te he-lo* &c. = L. ecce; for *feme = veme = vide me*, so *helo* = It. *vello*. For *f* = *v*, cf. O. Sp. *femencia = vehementia*, Sp. *hisca = fisca* from *viscum*, *referentia* for *reverentia*, R. Gr. 2, 387.

Hé Fr. in *hélas* (*h* silent) = L. *ai* (*ai*); Pr. *ailas*, E. *alas*. *Las = lassus*.

Heaume — *elmo*.

Hebilla Sp. buckle, Galic. *febilla;* dim. of *fibula*, Pr. *fivela*.

Hebra Sp. thread, fibre; from L. It. *fibra*.

Hechicero hechizo — *fattizio*.

Hediondo Sp. fetid; = *fœtibundus*, Rom. Gr. 2, 310.

Hedrar Sp. to dig twice; from *iterare*.

Heingre O. Fr., Wall. *hink* slender, lank, Norm. *haingre* sickly; from *æger*, *n* inserted. Hence Fr. *mal-ingre* sickly, Picd. Mil. *malingher*, O. Fr. Norm. *miugrelin*, It. *miugherlino*. From *ægrotus* O. Fr. *engrol*, *engrote*.

Hélas — *lasso*.

Helecho — *felce*.

Hellequin O. Fr. (asp.) from G. *helle*, E. *hell* (with depreciative term. as in *bouquin, mannequin*), dim. Du. *helleken hellekin*, a ghost, in the form of a wild hunter, v. Carpentier. Hence Dante's *Alichino* (name of a devil), Inf. 21, 118.

Helt heux — *elsa*.

Henchir Sp., Pg. *encher*, O. Pg. *emprir* to fill, stuff, abst. O. Sp. *encha;* from *implere*, It. *empiere*. For the *h*, cf. R. Gr. 1, 264.

Hendrija — *rendija*.

Hendure O. Fr. (asp.) handle of a dagger, *hendé* provided with a handle; from O. N. *henda*, O. E. *hend* to seize.

Henir Sp. to knead dough; from *fingere*.

Héraut — *araldo*.

Herde O. Fr. (asp.), Pic. *herde*, O. Wall. *hierde* herd; from O. H. G. *herda*, Goth. *hairda*, E. *herd*. O. Fr. *herdier*, Champ. *hairdi*, Du. *herder*, M. H. G. *hertaere*.

Hère Fr. (asp.) *pauvre hère* = poor fellow. From G. *herr*.

Herigaut O. Fr. (asp.) an over-garment, also *hergaut*, L. L. *herigaldus*, cf. *harigola* (Ducange).

Hérisser hérisson — *riccio*.

Hermano Sp., Pg. *irmão*, Cat. *germà*, f. *hermana*, shortened Pg. *mano mana*; from *germanus* in oldest L. L. = *frater (fraite)*, which was used for a friar. Hence Sp. *cormano*, Pg. *coirmão* step-brother = *con-germanus*.

Hermine — *armellino*.

Hermoso Sp., Pg. O. Sp. *fermoso fremoso*, Wal. *frumos*; from *formosus (fuermoso fermoso)*.

Heron — *aghirone*.

Herpe Sp. Pg. Cat. a tetter, skin-eruption; from ἕρπης a sore.

Herpé Fr. (asp.); for *harpé* from *harpe*, Pr. *arpa* a claw. Cf. Norm. *herper* to seize.

Herren — *ferrana*.

Herrin Sp. rust; from *ferrugo ferruginis*. Sp. *herrumbre* for *ferrumen*.

Herse Fr. (f. asp.) harrow, O. Fr. *herce*, L. L. *hercia*; from *hirpex hirpicis*, It. *erpice*, N. Pr. *erpi*, Wal. *ipre ipe*; vb. Fr. *herser*, cf. E. *hearse*, A. S. *hersta*, O. H. G. *harsta* a gridiron. Hence *harceler*, O. Fr. *herceler* (asp.) to provoke, tease, cf. *harrow*.

Herupé hurcpé O. Fr. Norm. rough, shaggy. Perhaps from A. S. *hriopan* to pull, tear.

Hervero Sp. throat; from Basque *erbera*, v. Larramendi.

Hétaudeau hestaudeau O. Fr. (asp.) a young capon; a dim. from O. H. G. *hagastalt* caelebs, tiro, L. L. *haistaldus*.

Hêtre Fr. (m. asp.) beech; from Du. *heester heister* a bush, L. G. *hester* a young beech, G. *heister*.

Heur — *augurio*.

Heurt heurter — *urtare*.

Heux — *elsa*.

Hibou Fr. (asp.) an owl; an onomatop., cf. O. Fr. *houpi*, Sw. *hibuchen*.

Hidalgo Sp., O. Sp. Pg. *fidalgo* nobleman; also *hijodalgo* pl. *hijosdalgo* for *hijo de algo* (aliquod.)

Hide hisde O. Fr. (f. asp.) fright, horror, *hideur hisdeur, hideux* (Fr.) *hisdeux*, E. *hideous*. *Hispidosus* (Catull.) 'rugged' would hardly suit the O. Fr. *hide* which should be more primitive than *hisde*. Perhaps *hide* for *hede* is from O. H. G. *egidi* "horror".

Hie O. Fr. (asp.) power, stress; from Du. *hijgen* to strive, A. S. *hige (hyge)* zeal, vb. *higan*, E. *hie*. Fr. *hie* == a rammer, beetle.

Hiéble – *ebbio*.

Hienda – *fiente*.

Hier — *ieri*.

Higado — *fegato*.

Hijo Sp. son; from *filius*, Pg. Gal. *filho*, O. Sp. *fijo*.

Hillot Fr. a servant (Marot); for *fillot*, Bearn. *hils* == *fils*.

Hilvan Sp. basting; from *hilo vano* useless stitches.

Hincar — *ficcare*.

Hinchar Sp., Pg. *inchar* to inflate; from *inflare*, It. *enfiare* R. Gr. 1, 210. Hence sbst. *hincha incha* hatred.

Hiniesta Sp. Spanish broom; from *genista*, It. *ginestra*.

Hinojo — *finocchio*.

Hinojo — *ginocchio*.

Hipo Sp. hiccough, an onomatop.

Hisca Sp. birdlime; from *viscum*, pl. *visca*, Pg. It. *visco*, *v* being changed first to *f*, then to *h*, v. *he*.

Hisser — *issare*.

Hita hito — *fitto*.

Hiver – *inverno*.

Hober O. Fr. *(obier)* to stir, move away (neut.). Celt. *ob* departure?

Hobereau — *hobin*.

Hobin O. Fr. (asp.) a nag, whence It. *ubino*; from E. *hobby* (Dan. *hoppe* a mare), a small horse, also a small falcon. Hence O. E. *hobeler* one who rides a hobby, O. Fr. *hobereau* (asp.) a squire, also a small hawk, L. L. *hobellarius hoberarius*, cf. Sp. *tagarote* a small falcon, and a poor nobleman.

Hoc O. Fr. Pic., *hoquet* (h asp.), vb. *hoquer*, *ahoquer*; from A. S. *hoc*, E. *hook*, Du. *hoek*. Fr. f. *hoche* a notch, cf. *broc broche*, *croc croche*. Sp. *hueca* == *hoche*.

Hoche — *hoc*.

Hoche O. Fr. (asp.) a long garment; from M. Du. *hoicke*, Fries. *hokke* a mantle, W. *hug*.

Hocher Fr. to shake; Du. *hotsen hutsen*, Wall. *hossi*.

Hogaza — *focaccia*.

Hoge O. Fr. (asp.) a hill, Norm. *hogue*, L. L. *hoga*; from O. N. *haug-r*, O. H. G. *hôha hôhi*.

Holgar Sp., Pg. Cat. *folgar* to rest; from L. L. *follicare* to breathe like bellows *(follis)*, to respire, rest, sbst. Pg. *fôlego* respiration. Cf. It. *sciulare*.

Holgin — *jorgina*.

Hollar — *follare*.

Hollejo Sp. peel; from *folliculus*, It. *follicolo*.

Hollin Sp. soot; from *fuligo fuliginis*, It. *fuliggine*.

Homard Fr. (asp.) crab; from Swed. *hummer*.

Hombre homenage hommage — *uomo*.

Hondo — *fondo*.

Honnir honte — *onire*.

Hontem ontem Pg. adv. = L. *heri*. From *ante-diem*, Sp. *antedia* = pridie, L. L. *antedie*, v. Ducange.

Hopo — *houppe*.

Hoquet Fr. (asp.) hiccough; an onomatop.; cf. Wall. *hikètt*, Bret. *hak*, *hik*, E. *hic*-cough.

Hoqueton — *cotone*.

Horde O. Fr. a hoard, hoarding, vb. *horder* to protect, Fr. *hourder* to rough-cast; from O. H. G. *hurt*, G. *hürde*, E. *hoard hurdle*.

Horde — *orda*.

Hore, vieille hore Norm. = an old woman; from O. H. G. *hôra huora* meretrix, E. *whore*.

Horion Fr. (asp.) a hard blow (Norm. *horgne*), O. Fr. Norm. pest, contagion (Norm. *horique*), vb. Lorr. *hôrié* to cudgel.

Hormazo Sp. a dry wall; Pliny, H. N. 35, 14 *parietes quos appellant formaceos*.

Hormis hors — *fuora*.

Hornabeque Sp. hornwork; from the G. *hornwerk*.

Horro Sp., Pg. *forro* free, *alforria* freedom, from Ar. *'horr* free, sbst. *al-'horriyah*.

Hose — *uosa*.

Hostigar Sp. to molest, Pg. Pr. *fustigar*, from *fustis*.

Hôte — *oste*.

Hoto O. Sp., O. Pg. *foto* safety, Pg. *fonto afouto* sure, vb. *afoutar*, O. Sp. *ahotado*, *enhotado*; from *fotus* nourished, supported.

Hotte Fr.; from Sw. *hutte*, G. *hotze* a cradle.

Houblon Fr. (asp.). From O. Wall. *hubillon*, from Du. *hop*.

Houe hoyau Fr. (asp.) hoe, vb. *houer*, Rou. *hauwer*; from O. H. G. *houwa*, *houwan*, G. *hauen*, E. *hew*, *hoe*.

Houle O. Fr. (asp.) a pot; from L. *olla*, Sp. *olla*.

Houle O. Fr. brothel (*en taverne ou en houle* Fabl. 3, 283), *holier houlier* a brothel-frequenter or = Bret. *houlier* a pander. Hence O. E. *holard* a lewd fellow, O. Fr. *holerie*. From O. H. G. *hôli* fem., O. N. *hola*, E. *hole*, G. *höhle*.

Houle — *ola*.

Houpée Fr. (asp.) the rise of a wave; from A. S. *hoppan*, O. H. G. *hupfan*, E. *hop*.

Houppe Fr. (asp.) a tuft, Sp. *hopo* a tufted tail. From Du. *hoppe*.

Houret Fr. (asp.) a poor hunting-dog; cf. A. S. *horadr* thin.

Houseaux — *uosa.*

Houspiller Fr. (asp.) to touse; connected with A. S. *hosp* injury.

Housse Fr. (asp.) saddle-cloth, *housing;* from O. H. G. *hulst,* L. L. *hulcia, hulcitum.*

Houssine houssoir — *houx.*

Houx Fr. (asp.) holly; from O. H. G. *hulis* ruscum, L. G. *hulse,* Du. *hulst,* O. E. *holme, hulver* (Chauc. *hulfere*). Hence *houssoir* a besom, *housser* to brush, *houssine* a switch.

Hoy — *oggi.*

Hoya hoyo Sp., Pg. *fojo* hole; from *fovea,* cf. *foggia.*

Hoz Sp., Pg. *fouce* a sickle; from *falx,* Fr. *faux;* hence O. Sp. vb. *hozar* to cut off.

Hoz Sp., Pg. *foz* a narrow pass, mouth of a river; from *faux,* It. *foce.* Hence Sp. *hozar,* Pg. *foçar* to turn up the ground (of pigs), *hocico,* Pg. *focinho* snout.

Hu O. Fr. a cry, E. *hue* (in *hue* and cry), vb. *huer, huard, huette* (owl), Norm. *huant* (all asp.). An onomatop. Bret. *hù,* W. *hw,* cf. O. H. G. *hûwo* owl.

Huata — *ovata.*

Huche Fr. (asp.) chest, Sp. O. Pg. *hucha,* O. Fr. *huge,* L. L. *hutica* as *nuche* and *nage* = *natica.* From G. *hütte,* E. *hut?* From *huche* or *hutica* comes E. *hutch* (or from A. S. *hrŭcca*).

Hucher O. Fr. (asp.), Pr. *uchar* to cry loudly. *Hucher* = *hucar,* cf. Pr. *ucar,* Pic. *huquer,* Pied. *uché,* cf. L. L. *qui ad ipsos huccos cucurrerunt.* From L. *huc;* M. Du. *huuc,* W. *huchw,* Serv. *uka.* From *hucher* comes *huchet* a hunter's horn. Cf. Norm. *houder,* Rou. *hutier,* E. *hoot.*

Hucia — *fiucia.*

Huebos — *uopo.*

Huebra Sp. (a form of obra) a day's work; from *opera* often used by Columella (a Spaniard) in this sense.

Hueco Sp., Pg. *ouco* hollow, sbst. cavity, vb. *ahuecar* to excavate from *occare,* though *ouco* points to Goth. *halk-s* empty, v. R. Gr. 1, 327.

Huella — *follare.*

Huer — *hu.*

Huero Sp. empty, barren (of eggs), wind-egg; from οὔριος = οὔρινος whence *niro, uero, huero* also *güero* (cf. *huerto* and *güerto*), whence Pg. *goro,* cf. *enguerar* = *enhuerar.*

Huesped — *oste* (2).

Hueste — *oste* (1).

Huis huissier — *uscio.*

Huitre Fr. (asp.) oyster; from *ostrea,* Sp. *ostra,* It. *ostrica.*

Huivar — *urlare.*

Hulla — *houille.*

Hulotte de lapin Fr. (asp.) a rabbit's burrow; from O. H. G. *hulla*, G. *hülle*, cf. W. *hül* a covering.

Hulotte — *urlare*.

Humer Fr., Pic. *heumer* (asp.) to sup; an onomatop.

Humilde Sp. humble; from *humilis* R. Gr. 1, 266.

Huna — *hune*.

Hune Fr. (asp.) scuttle of a mast, whence Sp. *huna*; from O. N. *hün* (m.), M. Du. *hime*.

Huppe — *upupa*.

Hura — *hure*.

Huracan — *uracano*.

Huraco Sp. hole, *horacar (horadar)* to pierce; from *forare*.

Hurano — *furo*.

Hure Fr. (asp.) rough hair, wild boar's head, in O. Fr. = muzzle of the wolf, lion &c., whence O. Sp. *hura*, O. E. *hure*. Hence Fr. *ahurir* to perplex, Norm. *huré* rugged, Rou. *hurée* rough earth. Sw. *huvel* (O. H. G. *hiuwila*) = a long-eared owl. Perhaps *hure* is for *hule* = *huvel*, as O. Fr. *mure* from *mule* (*mula*), *navire* from *navile*.

Hurepé — *herupé*.

Hurgar — *frugare*.

Husmo — *orma*.

Huta — *hutte*.

Hutte Fr. (asp.), Sp. *huta*; from O. H. G. *hutta*, E. *hut*.

Huvot O. Fr. mitra; from O. H. G. *hūba*, O. N. *hūfa*.

I.

Ici — *qui*.

Iddio — *dio*.

Ieri It., Sp. *ayer*, Pr. *her*, Fr. *hier*, Wal. *eri*, from *heri*. Sp. *a* before *y* is enphonic, cf. *ayantar ayuso* for *yantar yuso*; Cat. *ahir*, Sic. *ajeri*.

If — *iva*.

Ijar Sp. (m.) flank, Pg. *ilhal* side, O. Fr. *iliers*; from L. *ile ilia*. Hence also Sp. *ijada*, Pg. *ilharga*.

Il lo la It., Sp. *el lo la*, O. Sp. *ello ella*, Pg. *oa*, O. Pg. *el lo la*, Pr. *lo la (il)*, Fr. *le la*, O. Fr. *li lo la*, Wal. *le (l) la (oa a)* article, from *ille illum*, R. Gr. 2, 14 &c. Sard. *su sa* from *ipse*.

Ilhal — *ijar*.

Iluco iloques O. Fr. adv. of place, from *illoc*, Pic. *ilo*; hence *icilec cilec*.

Iman — *diamante*.

Imbastare — *busto*.

Imbuto It., Sp. *embudo*, Cat. *embut* a funnel; from *butis* a vessel, cf. Fr. *entonnoir*, It. *imbottatojo* from *botta*.

Immantinente It., Pr. *mantenen*, Fr. *maintenant*, = L. illico, Fr. = nunc. From *in manum tenens*. Pr. also *de mantenen*, O. Fr. *de maintenant*, Wald. *atenent*.

Impacciare — *pacciare*.

Impeciare impegolare implocare impicciare — *pegar*.

Imprenta impronta It., Sp. Pr. *emprenta*, Fr. *empreinte*, E. *imprint*; vb. It. *imprentare*, *improntare*, Sp. *emprentar*, whence Du. *printen*, E. *print*. From the Fr. partic. *empreint*, rather than from a freq. form *imprimitare*, the verb not being found in Fr. and Pr. Such a corruption as *impronta* would more easily take place in a borrowed word.

Improntare It., Fr. *emprunter* to borrow, sbst. *emprunt*. The Wal. *inprumut*, vb. *imprumutà* point to the L. *promutuum*, *inpromutuum*, *in-promutuare (improntare)*.

Inaffiare — *achar*.

Incalciare incalzare It., O. Sp. *encalzar*, Pr. *encausar*, O. Fr. *enchaucer* to pursue; whence sbst. O. Sp. *encalzo*, O.Pg. *encalço*, Pr. *encaus*, O. Fr. *enchauce*; from *calx*.

Incanto It., O.Sp. *encante*, Pr. *enquaut encant*, Fr. *encan* auction, M. H. G. *gant*; from *in quantum*; vb. It. *incantare*, Pr. *enquantar*, Fr. *encanter*.

Incastrare — *cassa*.

Inchar — *hinchar*.

Inchiostro It., O. Mil. *incostro* ink; from *encaustum* (ἔγκαυστον) red ink, used by the Greek Emperors; the It. and the Pr. *encaut* keep the Latin, the Fr. *encre*, *enque*, Wall. *enche* the Gk. accent (ἔγκαυστον), Sic. *inga*, Du. *inkt*, E. *ink*. *Atramentum* is found in Pr. *airamen*, O. Fr. *errement*. *Tinta* is used in Sp. Pg. Cat. Sard., O. H. G. *tinctâ*, *dinctâ*, G. *tinte*. The Wal. has borrowed from the Slav. *cerneale* = *black*.

Inciampare — *tape* (2).

Incinta It., Pr. *encencha*, Fr. *enceinte* pregnant; from *incincta*, i. e. *sine cinctu*, *discincta*. Fr. sbst. *enceinte* is from *incinctus* in its classical sense.

Increscere rincrescere It. impers. vb. = L. tædet, Rh. *ancrescher*. From L. *increscere*, *incresce* = it grieves, prop. = is too much for me, M. H. G. *mich berilt*. We find the word in O. Fr. *mult li encroist* Brut. 2, 215, and in L. L. *ejus dissoluta conversatio omnibus increverat* Act. SS. Oct. 1, 468.

Incude incudine, ancude ancudine It., Sp. *yunque ayunque*, Pg. *incude*, Pr. *encluget*, Fr. *enclume* anvil; from *incus incudis*. Piedm. *ancuso*, Cat. *enclusa* from nom. *incus*.

Inda ainda Pg. adv. for L. adhuc, from *inde ad*, *abinde ad*.

Indaco It., O. Sp. *endico*, Fr. E. *indigo*, Pr. *indi endi*; from L.

indicum blue Indian pigment. Hence an O. Sp. adj. *yndio*, Pr. *indi*, O. Fr. *inde*.

Indarno It. == frustra; from the Slav. adv. *darmo darom* gratis, (Grimm 3, 107, cf. Wal. *in dare*, O. It. *a dono*. The Fr. also has: *en dar* or *en dort*, so that it is hardly necessary to have recourse to the Slav.

Indi It., O. It. *ende enne*, whence *en* and *ne*, O. Sp. O. Pg. *ende*, Pr. *en* and *ne*, O. Fr. *int*, *ent*, Fr. *en*, Wal. *inde*. Nearer the orig. than the Fr. *en* is Ronchi *end* in *endaler* == *en aller*. O. It. *ende* == It. *ne*, whence *nonde campo* == *non ne campo*, *nullande* == *nulla ne*, *peronde* == *però ne*. Sp. *dende* for *desde*, O. Sp. *dent*, O. Pg. *dende*, O. Fr. *den* from *de-inde*.

Infingardo — *faint*.

Infino — *fino*.

Infrigno — *frignare*.

Inganno It., Sp. *engaño*, Pg. *engano*, Pr. *engan* deceit; vb. *ingannare*, *engañar*, *enganar*, O. Fr. *enganer* to deceive, Wal. *ingĕnă* (from It.?) to mock. In L. L. we find *gannat χλευάζει*, sbst. *gannum* scoff, *gannatura*. Not from *ingenium* but prob. from O. H. G. *gamon*, A. S. *gamen* (E. *game*) *gamn*, cf. *danno* from *damnum*, Sp. *daño*, Pg. *dano*, Pr. *dan*. For the meaning cf. E. to make *game* of, It. *giuoco* game, trick, Com. *gioruch* deceit, Fr. *jouer quelqu'un* to deceive.

Ingegno It., O. Sp. *engeño*, Pr. *engeinh* grinh *engin*, Fr. *engin* genius and *engine*; from *ingenium*; O. Fr. *engignier* to outwit, Pr. *engenhar* to entrap, It. *ingegnarsi*, Fr. *s'ingénier* to strive, use one's wits; sbst. Pr. *enginhaire*, Fr. *ingénieur*, It. *ingegnere*, E. *engineer*, L. L. *ingeniosus*.

Ingombro — *colmo*.

Inguine It., Sp. *engle* (for *egne*), N. Pr. *lengue* (for *engue*), Fr. *aine* flank; from *inguen*. It. *anguinaglia* from *inguinalia*.

Innanzi — *anzi*.

Innaverare — *naverare*.

Innesto nesto It. a graft, *innestare nestare* to graft; from *insitus*, whence It. *insetare inestare* (for *ins'tare*).

Insegna It., O. Sp. *enseña*, Fr. *enseigne*, E. *ensign*; from L. *insignia* pl. of *insigne*. From *signum* Sp. *seña*.

Insegnare It., Sp. *enseñor*, Pg. *ensinar*, Fr. *enseigner* to teach. From *insignare (signum segno seña senh)*, cf. Wal. *insemnă* to inform, from *semn* == *signum*.

Insembre insembra It., O. Sp. *ensembra ensemble*, O. Pg. *ensembra*, Fr. *ensemble*, also It. *insieme*, Pr. *ensems*, O. Wald. *ensemp* == L. *una*; from *insimul*, *l* being rejected or changed to *r*; Wal. *aseamene* from *ad simul*. O. Fr. *semps* == *simul*. Cf. *sembrare*.

Insetare — *innesto*.

Insieme — *insembre.*

Insino — *sino.*

Inteiriçar — *intero.*

Intero It., Sp. *entero*, Pg. *inteiro*, Pr. *enteir*, Fr. *entier*, E. *entire;* from *integer integri*, Lomb. Wall. *intreg.* Hence Pr. O.Fr. adj. *enterin* perfect, vb. O. Fr. *enteriner* to approve. *Intero* also = straight, upright, whence vb. *intirizzare*, Pg. *inteiriçar* to benumb, adj. *inteiriço* perfect (prop. rigid). Cf. G. *steif*, E. *stiff* used both in physical and moral sense. With a change of prefix we have O. Pg. Sp. *aterir aterecer*, Sp. *ateritar.*

Intirizzare — *intero.*

Intrambo entrambi It., Sp. *entrambos*, Pr. *entrambs* both together, a compound with *inter* O. Rom. for L. *una*, v. R. Gr. 2, 405; 3, 374.

Intridore It., from *interere*, cf. *conquidere*, from *conquirere.*

Introoque — *mentre.*

Intuzzare rintuzzare It. (1) to blunt (2) to quench, check. Prob. a participial verb *tutiare*, from *tutus*, its latter meaning corresponding with that of *at-tutare.*

Inverno verno It., Sp. *invierno* (*ibierno* O. Sp.), Pr. *iveru*, Fr. *hiver*, Wal. *earnё;* from *hiberaus hibernum.*

Investire It., Sp. *embestir*, Fr. *investir*, to invest a place; from *investire* (cf. *forum iarestire* Maecen., *scrupeo investita saxo* Enn.).

Io It., Sp. *yo*, Pg. Wal. *eu*, Pr. Galic. *ieu eu*, O. Fr. *eo ieo jeo jo*, Fr. *je;* from *ego* by syncope *eo*, Fr. *i* added before short *e* as in *dieu* from *deus.*

Iqui — *qui.*

Irmão — *hermano.*

Isard Languеd., Cat. *isart* and *sicart* an *izard;* from Gr. ἴξαλος (Salmasius)?

Ischio eschio It. from *asculus.*

Isnel — *snello.*

Issa — *esso.*

Issare It., Sp. Pg. *izar*, Fr. *hisser* (asp.), from Swed. *hissa*, L. G. *hissen* (E. *hoist*).

Itant — *cotanto.*

Itel — *cotale.*

Iva Sp. Pg., Fr. *if* (m.) yew; from O. H. G. *iwa*, G. *eibe*, A. S. *iv*, E. *yew*, W. *yw*, Corn. *hivin.*

Ivi vi It., O. It. *i*, O. Sp. O. Pg. Pr. *hi y*, Fr. *y*, Sp. Pg. *ahi;* from *ibi.*

Ivoire — *avorio.*

Ivraie — *ebbriaco.*

Isaga Sp. a reedy place; from B. *izaga* (*iza* reed, *aga* fullness).

Izquierdo esquerro Sp., Pg.*esquerdo*, Cat.Pr.*esquer* (f. *esquerra*) left. From the B. *ezquerra ezquerdo*, Sp. *i* for *e* when next syllable has *ie*, cf. *cimiento, hiniestra, tiniebla, sintiese (sentir) mintiera (mentir).

Izza It. anger; from O. H. G. *hiza*, G. *hitze*. *Ad-izzare a-izzare*, Com. *ezzà*, O. Fr. *hesser* to incite (esp. dogs), G. *hetzen*, L. G. *hitsen*, as Ven. *uzzare*, Veron. *uzzà* from the prov. form *hutzen*.

J.

Jabali Sp., Pg. *javali* wild boar, Sp. *jabalina* wild sow. Ar. *khinzir gabali* = Sp. *puerco montes* mountain- or wild-boar.

Jabot Fr. crop of a bird, *jaboter* to murmur. Perhaps for *gibot* (cf. *jaloux* for *geloux*), from *gibba* a bump, cf. G. *kropf*, E. *crop* = orig. a swelling, or, according to others, connected with Fr. *japper* and E. *jabber*.

Jacerina — *ghiazzerino*.

Jaco — *giaco*.

Jadis Fr. from *jamdiu* as *tandis* from *tamdiu*, Pr. *tandius*.

Jaez Sp. Pg. harness; from Ar. *gahâz* implements.

Jaillir Fr. to shoot forth; for *jailler* from *jaculari*, cf. *bondir*.

Jalde jalne — *giallo*.

Jale Fr. a tub, measure; O. Fr. *jalon galon*, E. *gallon* (L. L. *galo, galetus*), Rou. *galot*. Beside *jale* O. Fr. has *jaille* (Duc. v. *galo*) = L. *galea*, dim. *galeola vas vinarium* Papias.

Jalon — *jauger*.

Jaloux — *zelo*.

Jamba jamon, jambe jambon — *gamba*.

Jangler O. Fr., Pr. *janglar* to insult, scoff, N. Pr. *janglà* to whine, O. Fr. *jangle*, Pr. *jangla* mockery; from L. G. Du. *jangelen janken* (E. *jangle*) to scold, whine, a *jangler*, Chauc. babbler.

Jante Fr. (f.) felloe of a wheel. Not from *canthus* (m.), but from L. L. *cames camitis* from root *cam* crooked, bent (v. *gamba*); as *jambe* from *camba*, so *jante* from *camitem*. Wall. *chame* = nom. *cames*.

Japper Fr., Pr. *japar* to yelp; an onomatop., cf. G. *jappen*.

Jaque — *giaco*.

Jardin — *giardino*.

Jargon — *gergo*.

Jarra jarre — *giara*.

Jarret jarreto — *garra*.

Jars Fr. gander. The orig. form is found in the Pic. *gars*, Bret. *garz*, Wall. *gedr*. Probably from the O. N. *gassi* = gander (which is connected with the G. *gans*, E. *gander*, L. *anser*, Gk. χήν, Sansk. *hansa*). Pictet, however, derives the Fr. from the Bret. *garz* which he gets from the Sansk. *varata* (protector of geese from *vri* to protect), cf. W. *gwart* (qui garde), vb. *gwara gwared* tegere *(vri)*.

Jaser Fr., O. Fr. *gaser*, Pr. *gasar* to chatter, Pic. *jaser*. From O. N. *gassi* a gander, or chatterer, cf. Bav. *gänseln* to babble. Hence, prob., *gazouiller*, O. Fr. *gaziller* to chirp, chatter.

Jasmin — *gesmino*.

Jasse — *se*.

Jatte — *gavetta*.

Jauger Fr., Wall. *gauger*, E. *gauge*, Fr. *jauge* a gauging-rod. From a Rom. *æqualificare egalger* (cf. O. Fr. *niger* from *uidificare*) *egauger gauger* (cf. s. *mine*). Ronchi *cauque gauque* point to a form *calc (calfc)*, cf. G. *eichen* = Du. *ikjen* from *æquare*. From *æqualis* also Fr. *jalon* a gauging-rod, pole.

Jaula — *gabbia*.

Jaune — *giallo*.

Javelina javelot — *giavelotto*.

Javelle — *gavela*.

Jausion jausir — *godere*.

Jaserant — *ghiazzerino*.

Je — *io*.

Jeudi — *giovedi*.

Jeûne — *giumare*.

Joglar — *giocolare*.

Joie — *godere*.

Joindre Fr., E. *join;* from *jungere*, It. *giugnere*.

Joli — *giulivo*.

Jongleur — *giocolaro*.

Jorgina jorguina Sp. witch; from B. *sorguña sorguína* which from L. *sors*, Sp. *suerte*, B. *zorteu*, and *guiña* making. Hence *enjorguinar* to cover with soot, as witches coming down chimneys, *jorguin* soot; *holgina holgin* from *jorgina*.

Joubarbe — *jusbarba*.

Joue — *gota*.

Jouer Fr. to play, from *jocari; jeu* from *jocus*.

Jouir — *godere*.

Jour — *giorno*.

Joute jouter — *giusta*.

Joya joyel joyau — *godere*.

Joyo — *gioglio*.

Jubon — *giubba*.

Juc Fr., Wall. *joc* a perch, vb. Fr. *jucher*, Pic. *juquer*, Wall. *joquer*, N. Pr. *s'ajoucá*, E. to *juke*, to roost, Berr. sbst. *gueuche*, vb. *gueucher*. The Norm. has *hucher*, which points to the Du. *hukken*, G. *hocken* to squat, cower.

Jueves — *giovedi*.

Juge Fr., Pr. Cat. *julge*, whence O. Sp. *juge*, B. *yuyea*. Not from *judex* which would give *jus*, but from *juger (judicare)*, prob. the only example, in the Rom., of a personal noun derived from a verb without suffix.

Juillet Fr. July. In O. Fr. this month was called *juinet* or little June, cf. A.S. *aerra lidha áftera lidha* (1ˢᵗ mild month, 2ⁿᵈ mild month) = June, July. From *juinet* came *Juillet* through L. *julius*. Sic. (prob. through Norm.) *giugne* June, *giugnetto* July. In Neap. the former is called *jon cerasiaro* (cherry June), the latter *julo messoro* (harvest July). In Sard. July is called *mesi de treulas* (threshing-month). Rh. *zareladur* (weed-month) = June, *fenadur* (hay-month) = July. In Prov. Cat. they are called *junh*, *juliol*, in B. *garilla*, *garagarilla* (barley-months).

Jujube — *giuggola*.

Julep julepe — *giulebbe*.

Jumart Fr.; prob. a corruption of *jumentum*, though the Langued. *gimère gimérou* points to *chimaera*.

Jumeau Fr. twin; from *gemellus*, Pr. *gemel*, cf. *fumier* from *fimus*. Hence E. *gimmal (= annulus gemellus)*.

Jupe — *giubba*.

Jusant Fr. ebb; from O. Fr. adv. *jus* down, formed on the analogy of *courant*.

Jusarme — *guisarme*.

Jusbarba Sp. butcher's broom, Fr. *joubarbe*, Pr. *barbajol* a leek; = L. *Jovis barba* (Pliny), It. *barba di Giove*. Sp. *chubarba* stone-crop is prob. the same word, cf. *chupe* = Fr. *jupe*.

Jusque Fr. from *de-usque*, O. Fr. *usque dusque*, Pr. *duesca*, *juscas*, O. Fr. also *jesque* from *juesque* (as *tresque* from *truesque*). Cf. *devers* = versus. Pr. *truesca*, O. Fr. *trosqu'a* = *intro usque ad*, Rh. *troqua autroqua*.

Jusquiame — *giuschiamo*.

Justar — *giustare*.

K.

Kermesse Fr. a fair; a corruption of the G. *kirch-messe (church-mess)* orig. = a church-ale, wake, festal gathering, cf. *fiera*.

L.

Là It., Sp. *allà*, O. Pg. *alà*, Pg. *là*, Pr. *la lai*, Fr. *là*; from *illac*.

Labarda — *alabarda*.

Labareda lavereda Pg. flame; from *labarum* a banner, cf. *oriflamme*.

Labaro It. Sp. Pg., Fr. *labarum*, L. *labarum* the banner of the Roman Empire from the time of Constantine. *Labarum* = prop. the voice or oracle (Bret. *lavar*, W. *llafar*, Ir. Gael. *labhrad*, Corn. *lavar*, whence Celtic name *Labarus* in Silius Ital.) &c. of God, alluding to the inscription on the standard of Constantine, *ἐν τούτῳ νίκα* V. Mahn, Etym. Unters. p. 65.

Labech — *libeccio.*

Labriego Sp., Pg. *labrego* a peasant; from *labor* = field-labour (Duc.).

Lacayo Sp. Pg., Fr. *laquais*, whence It. *lacchè*, E. *lackey* pedissequus. O. Pr. has *lecai* dainty, wanton (v. *leccare*), N. Pr. *laccai* a shoot (parasite) also = lackey, cf. Gk. ἄοζος, ἀοσσητήρ (Donaldson). O. Pg. *lecco* = Pr. *lec* (whence *lecai*) the same as *lacayo*. Wedgw. makes it the same word as the O. Fr. *naquet*, *naquais* (cf. *lirello*, *nirello* &c.) a ball-catcher at tennis.

Lacca It., Sp. Pr. *laca*, Fr. *laque*, E. *lake* (whence *laquer*, *lacquer*) an Indian resin; Pers. *lāk* (Sansk. *lāxā*, root *lākh* ornare).

Lacca It. a hole (Dante); from Gk. λάκκος.

Lacchetta — *racchetta.*

Laccia It., Sic. *alaccia*, N. Pr. Sp. *alacha* shad, Andal. *lacha*, G. *alse*; prob. corruptions of *halec*, according to Diefenbach = Celt. *alausa*. From *halec* we have It. *alice* (f.), Sic. *aleci* anchovy, Sp. *aléce* (m.) fish-ragout, Sp. *haleche* a sort of mackerel.

Laccio It., Sp. Pg. *lazo*, Pr. *latz*, Fr. *lacs*, Wal. *latzu*, E. *lace*; from *laqueus*; vb. It. *lacciare* *allacciare* &c., Fr. *lacer*, E. *lace*.

Lacerta It. *lucerta* *lucertola* (Sard. *caluscerta* *caluxertula*), Sp. Pg. *lagarto*, Fr. *lézard*, Burg. *lézarde* f., Rh. *lusciard*, E. *lizard*, Pg. *lagarta* caterpillar; from *lacerta*, with (in Sp. &c.) a change of ending to the suffix *ard* often found in names of animals. Hence It. *alligatore*, Sp. *alegador*, Fr. E. *alligator* (Sp. *el lagarto*), spelt as if from *adligare adligator*.

Lâche lâcher — *lasciare.*

Lacio Sp. faded, languid; from *flaccidus* (also written *lhacio* = *llacio* Berceo), cf. *llama* from *flamma*, *Lainez* from *Flainiz*.

Lacra Sp. scar, fault, vb. *lacrar* to hurt; from M. Du. *laecke*, O. E. *lake*, E. *lack*.

Lacs — *laccio.*

Ladino — *latino.*

Ladre — *lazaro.*

Ladrillo Sp., Pg. *ladrilho* brick; from *laterculus.*

Lagar Sp. Pg. wine-press; from *lacus.*

Lagarta — *lacerta.*

Lagnarsi It., O. Sp. *lañarse*, Pr. *se lauhar*, O. Fr. *laigner* to lament; sbst. It. *lagna*, Pr. *lanha*; from *laniare se* prœ dolore, cf. Pg. *carpirse (== carpere se)*, L. *plangere*, Gk. κόπτεσθαι.

Lagot Pr. flattery, Sp. *lagotear* to flatter; cf. Goth. *bi-laigón* to lick.

Lague O. Fr. law; from A. S. *lag*, E. *law*, hence *utlague ullage* outlaw, A. S. *út-lag*, E. *out-law*, cf. *ex-lex*.

Lai lais O. Fr., Pr. *lais* lay, E. *lay*, It. plur. *lai*. From O. N. *lag* law, melody (cf. νόμος), or from W. *llais* melody, Fr. Gael. *laoith* song.

Laiche — *lisca*.

Laido It. O. Sp. O. Pg., Pr. *lait*, Fr. *laid* ugly; from O. H. G. *leid* odious, O. N. *leidhr*, A. S. *láðh*. O. Fr. sbst. *lait*, Rh. *laid*, B. *laidoa*. Vb. It. *laidare*, O. Sp. *laizar*, O. Pg. *laidar*, Pr. *laizar*, O. Fr. *laider* to vex, injure; from *leidón*, *leidén*; also It. *laidire*, Pr. O. Fr. *laidir* from *leidjan*, A. S. *láðhjan*. O. Fr. *laidenge* (vb. *laidengier*), Pr. *ledena* for *laidenha* vexation, cf. O. H. G. *leidunga* accusation.

Laie Fr. O. Pg. *lada?* a way through a wood, vb. *layer un lois*; from O. N. *leid*, A. S. *lád*, M. Du. *leie*, L. L. *leda*. Hence S. Germain en laye.

Laisse leese Fr. = E. *leash*, It. *lascio*, E. *lasso*; from *laxus laxare*, cf. O. H. G. *láz* from *lázan*, G. *lassen*, cf. L. L. *laxamina habenæ*.

Laisser — *lasciare*.

Laiton — *ottone*.

Laivo Pg. spot, stain; from *labes*, whence an adj. *labeus?*

Lam Pr. lame, one-armed; O. H. G. *lam*, G. *lahm*, E. *lame*. Piedm. *lam* == slack.

Lama It. Sp. Pg., Dauph. *lanma* marsh, bog, mire; from L. *lana* Hor. Festus: *aquæ collectio quæ lamam dicunt*; found in Dante in the same sense.

Lama It. Pr., Fr. *lame* plate, blade, O. Sp. *laña* a slice, a band; from *lamina*. Hence O. Fr. *lame* grave-stone, and O. Fr. *lemele alemele* (from *l'alemelle* for *la lemele*), Fr. *alumelle*.

Lamaneur — *locman*.

Lambeau Fr. shred or tatter, Com. *lampel*, Sp. *lambel*, Berr. *lambriche* fringe, L. L. *lablellus*, O. Fr. *labeau*, E. *label*; Fr. vb. *délabrer* for *délabler*. The *m* is prob. inserted, so *délabrer* from *labrum (lèvre* cf. *cabrer*, *chèvre)*, *label* from *labellum*. The Com. form, however, approaches the G. *lappen* (shred), which is found also in Celtic, Gael. *leah*, W. *llabed* (E. *lappet*), Bret. *labasken*. Fr. *lambrequin* = Du. dim. *lamperkin* from *lamper lanifer* a veil, cf. *mannequin* = Du. *mannekin*.

Lambel — *lambeau*.

Lambicco limbicco It., Sp. *alambique*, Pg. *lombique*, Pr. *elambic*, Fr. *alambic*, E. *alembic*; from Ar. *al-anbiq*.

Lambre O. Fr. wainscot, from *lamina* a board, cf. *marbre* from *marmr*. Hence Fr. *lambris* (m.).

Lambrequin – *lambeau*.

Lambrija Sp., Pg. *lombriga* a worm; from *lumbricus*, It. *lombrico*, Sp. also *lombriz*.

Lambris — *lambre*.

Lambrusca It. Sp., Fr. *lambruche*, from *labrusca*.

Lamicare It. to drizzle; perhaps for *lambicare* to lick, cf. Sp. *lamer* from *lambere*. B. *lambroa* drizzling-rain.

Lampione lampone It. raspberry, Pied. *ampola*, Com. *ampòi*, Rh. *ompchia*; it is the Sw. *ombeer (hombeere himpel-beere)*.

Lampo It. Sp. Pg., Pr. *lamp lam*, N. Pr. *lau* blaze; from root *lamp* in *lamp-as*, cf. *capo* frow *cap-ut*. Hence Cat. *llampey*, Sp. Pg. *re-lamp-ago* flash.

Lampreda It., Sp. Pg. *lamprea*, Fr. *lamproie* (E. *lamprey*); usually derived from L. L. *lam-petra* (lick-stone), because this fish clings to stones with its mouth. The Bret., however, is *lamprez*, which Legonidec derives from *lampr* slippery, shining.

Lance — *lancia*.

Lancha — *lasca*.

Lancia It., Sp. *lanza*, E. *lance*, from L. *lancea*, according to Varro (Gellius) a Spanish, according to others, a Gallic or German word; vb. It. *lanciare* and E. *launch*, L. *lanceare* (Tertullian); hence It. *lancio*, Sp. *lance*, Pg. *lanço*, Pr. *lans* throw, cast; It. *slonciare*, Pr. *eslansar*, Fr. *élancer* to spring; Fr. sbst. *élan* for *élans*.

Landa It. Pr., Fr. *lande* plain, heath, O. Fr. *lande* saltus, B. *landa* field. Not from Goth. E. *land*, but from Bret. *lann* a thorny bush, pl. *lannou* a heath, cf. Fr. *brande* bush, pl. *brandes* heath. *Lann (land)* is pure Celtic, v. Zeuss 1, 168.

Landier Fr., O. Fr. *andier*, B. *landera*, E. *andiron*, Wall. *andi*, L. L. *andena*. Wedgw. makes *andiron* the same as Flem. *wendijser (wenden* to turn) prop. a rack for the spit; *verutentum, idem hoc andena* v. Ducange. *Landier* for *l'andier*, cf. *loriot*, *lendemain*, *lierre*.

Landit Fr. fair of St. Denis; for *l'endit* from *indictum*, the day being openly proclaimed, cf. *feriae indictivae*.

Landra slandra It., Dauph. *landra* prostitute; N. Pr. *landrin landraire* a loiterer; Com. *slandron* a vagabond, Ven. *slandrona* a prostitute; vb. Pr. *landrà* to walk the streets. Hence It. *malandrino*, Sp. N. Pr. *malandrin*, Rou. Lim. *mandrin* a pickpocket, vagabond, for *mal-landrino* &c., Com. f. *malandra* meretrix, Occ. *mandro* (f.) a fox, *mandrouno* a bawd, Sp. *molondro* a mean fellow; adj. Pr. *vilandrier* for *vil-landrier* a vagabond. From It. *slandra* is Wal. *ṣuleandré*. From O. H. G. *lantderi* (for L. *latro*) = a land-plague.

Lange Fr. m. a blanket, O. Fr. a woollen garment; from *laneus*.

Laniero It., Pr. Fr. *lanier*, E. *lanner*, a small falcon, a merlin; = *laniarius*, a *laniandis avibus*. Adj. *lanier* greedy.

Lanquan Pr. = Fr. *lorsque*, for *l'an quan*, an used as in *oyan*, *antan*.

Lanza — *lancia*.

Lanzichenecco It. (shortened *lanzo*), Sp. *lasquenete*, Fr. *lansquenet* a German foot soldier; from G. *landsknecht*; it also means a game at cards played by these soldiers, lansquenet.

Lanso — *lanzichenecco*.

Laña — *lama*.

Lapa Pg. an excavation; from Gk. λάπαθον a hole.

Lapa Sp. scum; from Gk. λάπη λάμπη. B. *lapa* leos.

Lapin Fr. a rabbit, dim. *lapereau*, cf. Du. *lampreel*. The *p* of *lepus* would require a *r* in Fr. (cf. *leveret*); *lapin* is prob. for *clapin*, from root *clap*, whence *se clapir* to hide (of rabbits), *clapière* a rabbit-burrow (q. v.), cf. *loir* for *gloir*.

Lapo Sp. blow with a flat instrument; from O. H. G. *lappa*, G. *lappen*, cf. G. E. *flap*. Hence also Com. *lapina* a box on the ear, Berr. *lapigne* a rag, *lápeau* a lazy fellow, Rh. *lapi* a simpleton = G. *lappa* slack. Sp. *solapar* to button one lappet over another, then to conceal.

Lappare It., Fr. *laper*, Pr. *lepar*, Cat. *llepar* = G. *lappen*, E. *lap*, O. N. *lepia*, W. *llepio*, Gk. λάπτειν &c.

Laquais — *lacayo*.

Lar Sp. Pg. Occ., Cat. *llar* hearth; the L. *Lar*, found also in It. *alare* andiron, Sp. *llares* pot-hangers.

Laranja — *arancio*.

Larcin Fr., E. *larceny*; from *latrocinium*, Pr. *laironici*, Sp. *ladronicio*, It. *ladroneccio*. From *latro* we have *ladrone*, *ladro*, *larron*.

Larigot Fr. a pipe or flute. The form *arigot* might come from the Gallic *arinca* (Pliny)=rye, cf. L. *avena*. *Arinca* becomes *riguet* in Dauph. Frisch derives *larigo* from *largo* (musical term).

Larmo Fr. from *lacrima*. In O. Fr. *lairme (lerme)* the *g* is vocalized into *i*.

Larris O. Fr. Pic. an untilled field, L. L. *larricium*, from Du. *laer laar* an open place in a wood, v. Dief. Goth. Wb. 2, 129.

Lasca It. a fish, barbel; from Gk. λευκίσκος.

Lasca Sp. a plate, thin flat stone, strip of leather; a corruption of *laxus laxa* (which is also found in Sp. *laxa* or *laja* = *lasca*). Pg. *lasca de presunto* = slice of ham. Sp. *laucha* = *laxa*.

Lasciare lassare It., O. Sp. *lexar leixar*, Pg. *leixar*, Pr. *laissar*, Fr. *laisser*, Wal. *lĕsà* (E. *lease* in *release*); from *laxare* (Sp.

luxar), influenced by the G. *lassen* = E. *let*, v. Max Müller (über deutsche Schattirung romanischer Worte). Hence Pr. *s'eslaissar*, O. Fr. *s'eslaisser* to rush in, sbst. *eslais* fall, rush, It. *slascio*; It. adj. *lasco*, Pr. *lasc lasch*, Fr. *lâche*, Rou. *lake* indolent, vb. Sp. *lascar*, O. Pg. *laixar*, Pr. *lascar laschar*, Fr. *lâcher*, O. Fr. *lasquer*, from *lascus* for *laxus*, cf. Gael. *leasy*, Ir. *leisy*, W. *llesg* = L. *laxus*, Gael. *asgall*, Corn. *ascle* = L. *axella*, Champ. *fisquer* for *fixer*, *lusque* for *luxe*.

Lascio — *laisse*.

Lasco — *lasciare*.

Lasso It. Pg., Sp. *laso*, Fr. *las*, It. *ahi lasso*, f. *ahi lassa*, Pr. *ai las*, O. Fr. *ha las* (E. *alas*), Fr. *bélas* (v. *hé*), from *lassus*; vb. It. *lassare* &c., from *lassare*. Hence also O. Fr. sbst. *laste*, *lasté*, O. Sp. *lasedad* weariness.

Lastar Sp. Pg. to pay for another, sbst. *lasto*. From O. H. G. *leistèn*, G. *leisten* to bail.

Laste — *lasso*.

Lastima — *biasimo*.

Lasto It., Fr. *laste lest* a ship's burden; from O. H. G. *hlast*, O. Fris. *hlest*, N. *lest*, G. *last*, A. S. *hläst* (E. *last* = boat-load). Fr. *balast*, Du. G. E. *ballast* is a compound of *last* and *bal*, Ir. *beal* sand *(garbheal* = gravel). W. *bal* in *balasarn* ballast, Bret. *bili* caillou rond, plat et poli que la mer pousse sur quelques rivages, L. *sa-bul-um (saburra* ballast), Sk. *bálukâ* sand, v. Bopp, Glossary. For Sp. *lastre*, Pg. *lastro*, which are confounded with this word, v. *astre*.

Lastra lastre — *astre*.

Latino It., Sp. *latin*, Pg. *latim* (1) Latin (2) knowledge (3) cunning: Sp. *saber mucho latino* to be cunning. Sp. Pg. adj. *ladino* cunning. What the Latin was to the learned, that their mother tongue was to laymen; hence *latino* was used for any dialect, even Arabic and the language of birds, cf. Dante: *gli augelli ciascuno in suo latino*, next it came to mean comprehensible, accessible, easy, convenient, Dante, Par. 3, 63: *si che m' è più ladino; ladino della mano* promptus, Rh. *ladin* swift. From *latin* is Pr. O. Fr. *latinier* linguist, interpreter, O. E. *latynere*, *latymer (Latimer)*.

Latir — *ghiattire*.

Laton — *ottone*.

Latta It., Sp. Pr. *lata*, Fr. *latte*; from O. H. G. *latta*, A. S. *lätta*, E. *lath*, W. *llàth* (f.). Wal. has m. *latz*.

Lattovaro lattuaro It., Sp. *electuario*, O. Sp. *lectuario*, Pr. *lactoari lectoari*, Fr. *électuaire*, O. Fr. *lectuaire*, E. *electuary*, O. E. *lectuary letuary*; from L. *electarium electuarium (elingo)*.

Laud — *liuto*.

Laudemio *lusinga*.

Launa Sp. a metal-plate &c.; not from *lamina* but from *laganum*, *g* changed to *u*, as in *sagma salma sauma (soma)*.

Lava It. E., Fr. *lave*; = Neap. *lava* a torrent, from *lavare*.

Lavagna It. slate, for *la-agua*, from G. *leie (ei* = R. *a)*, O. S. *leia*, Du. *lei*, W. *llech*, Gael. *leac*.

Lavanco Sp. Pg. wild duck; from *larare*, cf. E. *duck* (= diver).

Lavanda lavendola It., Sp. *lavandula*, Fr. *lavande*, E. *lavender*, G. *lavendel*; from its being used in washing (*lurare*, It. *laranda* = washing, whence Sp. *lavandera*, It. *lavandaia*, Fr. *lavandière* (E. *laundress*), *lavanderia* = E. *laundry*.

Lavange — *avalange*.

Laveggio It. a pan; = *lebetium* from *lebes*.

Lavello — *avello*.

Laya Sp. Pg. (1) two-pronged fork for digging (2) kind, nature, vb. *layar* to dig. From B. *laya* spade; the soil in Biscay being very hard requires a peculiar two-pronged instrument to work it. This is called *laya*, and the labour *layaria*. The word was so commonly used as to pass into proverbs: *son de una misma laya* = they are of the same sort; hence meaning (2).

Layette Fr. chest; from Du. *laeye*, G. *lade*.

Lazaro Sp. beggar, Mil. *lazzer* dirty, Pie. *lazaire* poor, Pr. O. Fr. *ladre*, *lazer* (also O. E.) a leper; hence O. Sp. *lacéria* poverty; It. *lazzeretto*, Sp. *lazareto*, E. *lozaretto*; It. *lazzerone*. From the *Lazarus* of St. Luke ch. 16. *Ladre* for *lazer*, as *madre* from *masar*, S. *Ludre* from S. *Lusor*.

Laso — *laccio*.

Lazzo It. sour; from *laciduus* for *acidulus*, cf. B. *latzá*, *laclui*.

Le — *il*.

Léans — *ens*.

Leardo — *liart*.

Lebeche — *libeccio*.

Lebrel — *levriere*.

Lebrillo Sp. an earthenware tub, pan; from *labrum*.

Leccare It., Pr. *liquar lichar lechar*, Fr. *lécher*, Rh. *lichiar*, Wal. *lichi* to lick; besides It. *leccatore*, O. Fr. *lecheor* a glutton, parasite (E. *lecher*), we find Pr. Lomb. Pied. *lec*, Sic. *liccu*, It. *leccone*; Pr. adj. *lecai licai* (sbst. *licai-aria*) and *licaitz* (sbst. *licaz-aria*). We have L. L. *lecator leno*, *lecacitas lenocinium*, cf. Pr. *lecaitz (lecax)*. From O. H. G. *lecchôn*, A. S. *liccôn leccôn*, A. S. *liccian*, E. *lick*: *lec leccone* = an O. H. G. sbst. *lecco*. Fr. *relécher* gives E. *relish*.

Leccio — *elce*.

Lèche — *lisca*.

Lécher — *leccare*.

Lechino Sp., Pg. *lichino* a tent of lint, lint; from *licinium* (from *licium*) Vegetius de arte vet.

Lechon Sp. a sucking-pick, from *leche* milk. Hence also *lechazo* a suckling (colt &c.).

Lechuzo — *lechon.*

Lega It. Pr., Pr. Sp. *legua*, Fr. *lieue*, Pg. *legoa*, L. L. *leuca, leuga, lega, leuca*, E. *league.* Gloss. Isid. *mensuras viarum nos milliaria dicimus, Galli leucas.* A word of Celtic origin, prop. == a stone (mile-stone, L. *lapis*), Ir. Gael. *leac*, W. *llech* a flat stone, slate. Gr. λᾶας, λεύς, L. *lap-id* may be connected, v. Pott, Forsch. 1, 218. O. Fr. *loie* == a league's distance.

Lega It., Sp. *ley*, Fr. *loi aloi* standard of metals; *alloy*; vb. It. *allegare*, Sp. *alear*, Fr. *aloyer*; from *lex, ad legem*, cf. Pr. *aleyalar* to justify.

Legamo Sp. slime, mud; from *uligo uliginis*, not from B. *legamia* == Fr. *levain*, E. *leaven.*

Lège léger — *lieve.*

Lège Fr. not laden (of a ship); from Du. *leeg* for G. *ledig* empty.

Leggiadro It. sprightly, pretty; for *leggiardo* from *levis*; so *bugiadro bugiardo, linguadro linguardo.*

Leggiero — *lieve.*

Leggio It. a reading-desk, L. L. *legivum*; from *legere*, cf. λογεῖον from λόγος.

Legs Fr. legacy; from *lego*, the *s* added to form a sbst. Cf. It. *lascio* from *lasciare*, O. Fr. *lais.*

Leixar — *lasciare.*

Lella — *enola.*

Lelo Sp. ignorant, stupid. From the B. *lelo, leloa* == insulsus. *Lelo* was the name of a Biscayan, notable as a cuckold and famous in the ballads of the country, one of which begins: *Lelo! il Lelo, Lelo! il Lelo, Leh a!* v. Mahn, Unters. p. 58.

Lembrar — *membrare.*

Leme Sp. Pg. tiller (naut.). Cf. Sp. Fr. *limon* shaft of a cart; from O. N. A. S. *lim*, E. *limb.* Wall. *limon* == Fr. *solive*, is prob. the L. *limen.*

Lendemain — *mane.*

Lendine It., Sp. *liendre*, Pg. *lendea*, Pr. *lende*, Fr. *lente* a nit; from *lens lendis (lendinis)*; Fr. *lente* from *lendine* (Wall. *lindiné*) as *page* from *pagina.* Cat. *llemena* is a corruption of *llenema* for *llendema*, *m* being from the acc. case.

Lendore Fr. (m. f.) an idle drowsy fellow, vb. Norm. *lendorer.* A purer form is the Bret. *landar* idle, vb. *landrea, landreant* a sluggard, whence O. Fr. *landreux*, Fr. *lendore*, which took its form from *il endort.* From Du. *lenteren* to loiter, sbst. *lenterer* == G. *schlendern, schlenderer.*

Lente — *lendine.*

Lenza It. a linen band, Sp. *lienzo* a handkerchief; from *lintea linteum*. Hence It. *lenzuolo*, Sp. *lenzuelo*, Pg. *lançol*, Pr. *lensol*, Fr. *linceul* a sheet &c., L. *linteolum*.

Lercio It. dirty, *gua-lercio gualerchio* (1) dirty (2) squinting; the latter sense points to the M. H. G. *lerz* left (*gua* = *guala*), but whence the sense of "dirty"?

Lerdo — *lordo*.

Léri Pr. gay, sprightly, N. Pr. *leri* (f. *leria*) pretty, wanton. From *hilarius (hilaris)*, which was used as a Christian name.

Lero — *ervo*.

Lès O. Fr., Pr. *latz* for L. *juxta*; from *latus*, It. *allato*; still found in names of places, e. g. *Passy-lès-Paris, Plessis-lès-Tours.*

Lésina It., Sp. *lesna*, better O. Sp. *alesna*, Pr. *alena*, Lim. *lerno*, Fr. *alène* an owl; from O. H. G. *alansa, alasna*, Sw. *alasme*. It. *lesina* (whence Fr. *lésine*) also = parsimony. "*Lésine*", says Ménage, "du livre Italien, intitulé Della famosissima Compagnia della Lesina; l'auteur feint que cette Compagnie fut ainsi appelée di certi Taccagnoni, i quali, per marcia, miseria, et avarizia, si mettevano a rattacconar le scarpette colla lesina, onde presono questo nome della *Lesina.*"

Lessare It. to boil; L. L. *lixare* to steep, *lix* lie. Hence *bislessare* to boil.

Lessive — *lisciva*.

Lesto It. Pg., Fr. *leste*, Sp. *listo* active, It. also clever; vb. It. *allestare*; from Goth. *listeigs*, O. H. G. *listic* clever, G. *listig* artful, suffix dropped as in It. *chiasso* from *classicum*, O. Fr. *ruste* from *rusticus*. Sbst. Rh. *list* (m.).

Lest — *lasto*.

Letame It. O. Sp. dung; from *letamen* (Pliny), L. L. *latare* to make fruitful (cf. Virg. quid *latas segetes*).

Lettiera It. bedstead, Sp. *litera*, Pr. *leitiera*, Fr. *litière*, E. *litter*; L. L. *lectaria*, from *lectus*.

Leu — *lere*.

Leude O. Fr., Pr. *leuda leida leddu lesda*, O. Sp. *lezda*, Arag. *leuda* a tax or toll on goods or on carriages; Lang. *ledo* = Fr. *hovage*. From *levitus* partic. of *levare* (as *cubitus* of *cubare*) in such phrases as *levare tributum* = *lever des impôts*. V. *lievito*.

Leudo — *lievito*.

Lour — *egli*.

Leurre —- *logoro*.

Levain Fr., Pr. *levam*, E. *leaven*; from *levare*, whence E. *lever* (= Fr. *levier*) *lery*, v. *lievito*.

Levantar Sp. to raise; a participial verb from *levare*.

Levante It. Sp. Pg., Fr. E. *levant; ore il sole si leva*, cf. Pg. *nascente*, Cat. *sol-ixent*, participles like *oriens, occidens*, cf. s. *ponente*.

Leve Pg., Pr. *leu*, Rh. *lev*, Pr. *levada* lights; from *levis*, cf. E. *lights*.

Levistico libistico It., Fr. *livèche* (*levesse* Menage), E. *lovage* a plant; from *ligusticum*, Veget. de re veter. *levisticum*.

Levriere It., Sp. *lebrel*, Fr. *lévrier* a greyhound; from *teporarius*.

Lexos Sp. *(lejos)* adv. for L. *longe*, also adj. *lexo*. From *laxus*.

Lézard — *lacerta*.

Lezia lezio It. affectation; from *delicia*, cf. *delicias facere*.

Lezzo It. stink, *lezzare* to stink; the form *olezzare* shows the der. from *olere; lezzo* is from the root *ol*, with term. as in *rezzo* for *orezzo* from *ora aura*.

Li It., Sp. *alli*, Pg. *alli* adv.; from *illic*.

Lia Sp. husk of grapes, Pg. *lia*, Pr. *lhia*, Fr. *lie* (E. pl. *lees*), Bret. *ly* (Ven. *lea* mud), Papias: *lia "amurca"*. *Lix licis* lye, would require a Sp. *liga* (cf. N. Pr. *ligo*, B. *liga*), though Fr. *lie* may = *licem*, as *ber-lue* from *lucem*. Dief. derives it from *levare* as G. *hefe* from *heben, bärme (barm)* from *beran*, cf. *levain*.

Liaison Fr., Pr. *liazò*, from *ligatio* (Scribonius Largus).

Liart O. Fr. (f. *liarde*), Pr. *liar lear* (hence It. *leardo*) of horses white, light-grey; from W. *llai* dark-grey, or from *lætus*, cf. It. *gajo*, Fr. *gai*, Gk. φαιδρός. Fr. *liard* a coin is the S. Fr. *li hardi*, Sp. *ardite*, q. v.

Libeccio It., Sp. *lebeche*, Pr. *labech (abech)*, O. Fr. *lebeche lebech* South-west wind; from λίψ λιβός, Alban. *livé*.

Libello It., Pg. Pr. *livel nivel*, Sp. *nivel*, Fr. *niveau*, Bret. *liré*, Wall. *livai*, E. *level;* vb. Sp. *nivelar*, Fr. *niveler* to level; from *libella*, R. Gr. 1, 241.

Liccia lizza It., Sp. *liza*, Pr. *lissa*, Fr. *lice*, E. *lists (lista?)*, a course, a place for combat &c.; from *licia* pl. of *licium* = girdle in the phrase: *per lancem et licium*. There may also be some reference to the M. H. G. *letze* a fence *(letzen* to keep off, *let)*.

Lice Fr., O. Fr. *leisse*, Pic. *liche*, Pr. *leissa* a hunting-bitch for breeding; from the name *Lycisca* or rather *Lycisce (multum latrante Lycisca* Virg.).

Licorno alicorno It., Pg. *alicornio*, Fr. *licorne* f.; a corruption of *unicornis*, Sp. *unicornio*, unicorn.

Licou Fr. a halter; from *lie-cou*.

Lie Fr. gay, in the phrase *faire chère lie;* from *lætus*, O. Fr. *lié* f. *liée* and *lie*, It. *lieto*.

Liége Fr. cork; from *léger* (Pr. *leuge*).

Liendre — *lendine*.

Lienzo — *lenza*.

Lierre — *edera*.

Lieue — *lega*.

Lieve It., Sp. Pg. *leve*, Pr. *leu* light, from *levis;* Fr. instead of *lief* has *lége* empty (of ships), cf. *neige* = Pr. *neu*. It. *leggiero*, Pr. *leugier*, Fr. *léger*, from a form *leviarius;* vb. Pr. *leujar* = L. L. *leviare* for *levare*, also *aleujar aleviar*, It. *alleggiare*, Sp. *alivier* (sbst. *alivio*), Fr. *alléger*, O. E. *allegge (= alleviate*, cf. *abridge = abbreviate*, *agredge aggravate*).

Liévito It., Romng. *leud*, Sp. *leudo (liebdo)*, Pg. *léredo* risen, fermented (of dough); vb. It. *levitare*, Sp. *leudar lleudar*, *aleudar alevadar*, Pg. *levedar* to ferment dough with leaven. From *levitus* a partic. for *levatus (levare)*, cf. *cubitus* from *cubare*, *domare domitus*, and unclass. *dolitus* for *dolatus* Varro, *vocitus* for *vocatus*, *provitus* for *probatus*, *rogitus* for *rogatus*, cf. also s. *segato*. So *levitare* is not a frequentative from *levare*. Another form is Pr. *levat*, Cat. *llevat*, Wal. *aluat* leaven; Neap. *levato*, Piedm. Mil. *levà* = It. *lievito*. Rh. *levont* from the pres. participle.

Lige Fr., Pr. *litge*, whence It. *ligio*, E. *liege*, L. L. *ligius*, sbst. O. Fr. *ligée*, *ligesse*. The fundamental meaning seems to be unlimited, perfect. The *homme lige* had to render *unrestricted* service to the *lige seigneur*, who, in return, was bound to afford *unconditional* protection. Hence *ligia potestas*, *ligia voluntas* unbounded. Three derivations are given: (1) from the Rom. *liga* bond, but we cannot have a non-Latin adj. formed with *-ius* or *-eus;* (2) O. N. *lidi* a companion, whence *lidi-us*, *lige*, but here the sense scarcely suits; (3) from G. *ledig* free: *ligius homo, quod Teutonice dicitur ledigman* Document of 13th century.

Ligio — *lige*.

Lilao It. Sp. E., Pg. *lilá*, Fr. *lilas;* from the Pers. *lilac*.

Limace limace limaçon — *lumaccia*.

Limande Fr. a plaice; from *lima* a file, by reason of its rough skin. It is called *lima* in It.

Limier Fr. a hunting-dog, E. *lime-hound*, O. Fr. *liemier loiemier loiemer*, Bret. *liamer;* from Fr. *lieu*, O. Fr. *loien*, L. *ligamen*, so prop. = a leash-hound.

Limon — *leme*.

Limone It., Sp. Pr. *limon*, Pg. *limão*, Fr. *limon*, E. *lemon*, also It. Sp. Pg. *lima*, It. *lomia*, Sic. *lumiuni;* from Pers. *limù* or *limùn* = tree and fruit, which is from Ind. *nimbàka*, Beng. *nimbu niba;* hence also Ar. *laimùn*.

Limosina It., O. Sp. Pr. *almosna*, Sp. *limosna*, Pg. *esmola (for elmosa)*, Fr. *aumône*, E. *alms;* from *eleemosyna;* hence Fr. *aumônerie*, E. *awmery*, almonry.

Linceuil — *lenza*.

Linde Sp. O. Pg. (m. f.), Pg. *linda* a boundary; from *limes limi-*
tis, Pr. *limit* &c.; vb. *lindar* from *limitare;* Pr. *lindar* lintel,
from *limitaris.* Hence also Sp. *lintel dintel,* E. *lintel.*

Lindo It. Sp. Pg., N. Pr. *linde* neat, fine, pretty, from *limpidus*
clear, whence in Piedm. == sincere. It. also *limpido,* Sp. *lim-*
pio, cf. *nitido* and *netto, torbido* and *torbo.*

Linea It. Sp. line, lineage, O. Val. *linia,* B. *leinua,* L. L. *linea*
sanguinis. Hence Fr. *lignée,* O. Pg. *linhada,* O. Fr. *lignage,*
E. *lineage,* Pr. *linh* (m.) from *lineus,* cf. Sp. *liño* row; O. Fr.
lin is L. *linum* thread.

Linge Fr. m., Pr. *linge,* B. *linca;* from *lineus,* as *lange* from
laneus.

Lingot Fr. (whence *ingot,* the *l* being taken for the article); from
lingua, cf. *lingula.* Or E. *ingot* may be the original word;
in-got (Chauc. == a mould), == G. *ein-guss* anything poured
into a mould (*giessen* to pour).

Linot linotte Fr., E. *linnet;* from *linum,* cf. G. *leinfinke flachs-*
finke (flax-finch).

Lippe Fr. underlip, O. Fr. *lepe,* Rou. *liper* to eat delicacies;
from L. G. *lippe,* A. S. *lippa,* E. *lip* (Gael. *lip liop* f.); Com.
leff lip, *liffia* mouth, from O. H. G. *lefs, leffur.*

Lira It. a coin; from *libra* (Fr. *livre*), cf. *bere* from *bibere.*

Lirio — *giglio.*

Liron — *ghiro.*

Lis — *giglio.*

Lisca It. stalk, festuca, Piedm. *lesca,* Mil. *lisca,* Fr. *laiche* (for
lèche) fish-bone; O. H. G. *lisca* fern, reed, Du. *lisch.* It. *lisca,*
Piedm. *lesca,* Cat. *llesca,* N. Pr. *lisco lesco,* Fr. *lèche* (not *laiche*)
a small piece of anything; vb. Cat. *llescar* to cut in pieces.
An old L. G. glossary has: *lesc scirpus, papirus.*

Liscio It., Sp. Pg. *liso,* Pr. *lis,* Fr. *lisse* smooth, with numerous
derivatives, v. It. *lisciare ligiare,* Sp. *alisar,* Fr. *lisser* to polish
(perhaps connected with *glisser* q. v.). The Gk. has λισσός
smooth, the O. H. G. *lisi,* G. *leise* soft. Hence Sp. *deslizar* to
slip, Cat. *lliscar.* From O. H. G. *leisanón* to follow a track,
is O. Sp. *deleznar* to glide, adj. *lizne* smooth, and perhaps
Rh. *laischnar.*

Lisciva It., Wal. *lésie,* Sp. *lexia,* Fr. *lessive,* Pr. *lissiu* (m.) lye,
W. *lisiu;* from *lixivia lixivium,* L. L. *leciva* (Vocab. S. Gall.).

Lisera lisière — *lista.*

Lisiar Sp. to lame, maim, Cat. *lesiar,* Pg. *lesar;* from *lædere*
læsus, O. Sp. *lision* == L. *læsio.*

Liso — *liscio.*

Lista It. Sp. Pr., Pg. *lista listra,* Fr. *liste* slip, stripe, border,
E. *list;* from O. H. G. *lista,* G. *leiste.* Hence Fr. *lisière* (whence
Sp. *lisera*) hem, for *listière.*

Listo — *lesto.*

Litera litiére — *lettiera.*

Liúto leúto liúdo It., Sp. *laúd*, Pg. *alaúde*, Pr. *laut*, *lahut*, O. Fr. *leut*, Fr. *luth*, Wal. *lântĕ alëutĕ*, N. Gr. λαοΰτο, G. *laute*, E. *lute*. From the Ar. *'ûd* with article *al-'ûd.* The Sp. *laud (a* for the Ar. *ain)* gave rise to the other Rom. forms.

Livêche — *levistico.*

Liverare livrare It., Pr. *liurar*, Fr. *livrer* to deliver, Sp. *librar*, Pg. *livrar = dar* or *entregar*, L. L. *liberare* (e. g. *dona*); also Fr. *livrée*, It. *livrea*, Sp. *librea*, E. *livery* (prop. something furnished or given, orig. something given as a livelihood), L. L. *liberata*, *liberatio;* hence Fr. *délivrer*, E. *deliver*, L. L. *deliberare;* from *liberare* to free, let go, give up, cf. Sp. *soltar.* The L. meaning is found in It. *liberare*, Sp. *librar*, Pr. *liurar*, Fr. *délivrer*, E. *deliver.*

Lisa — *liccia.*

Lisne — *liscio.*

Llamar — *chiamare.*

Llanten Sp. plantain; from *plantago*, It. *piantaggine*, E. *plantain.*

Llares — *lar.*

Llegar Sp., Pg. *chegar* (1) to bring near (2) intrans. to approach, hence Sic. *ghicari.* From *plicare*, cf. It. *piegare come il vento a noi gli piega* Dante Inf. 5, 79. The O. Sp. was *plegar*, and the meaning arose orig., perhaps, from the use of *applicare* (navem &c.).

Loba Sp. Pg. surplice; from Fr. *l'aube.*

Lobe O. Fr. scoff, vb. *lober;* from G. *lob* praise, vb. *loben*. cf. Pr. *gabar* to jeer, Pg. to praise.

Lobrego Sp. Pg. sad, gloomy; from *lugubris*, It. *lugùbre.*

Loo O. Fr., whence O. Fr. *loquet*, It. *lucchetto;* from A. S. *loc*, E. *lock*, O. H. G. *bi-loh (bloch)* bar, block, Goth. *ga-lukan* to shut.

Looco It. (Neap. Sicil. Crem. *loucch*) fool, Sp. adj. *loco*, Pg. *louco*, N. Pr. *locou* mad, foolish. Servius (ad Virg. Ec. 8, 55) mentions a L. *alucus* or *ulucus = ulula*, hence It. *alocco* (Com. Piedm. *oloch*) = owl and blockhead, as Parm. *ciò;* this was shortened into *locco* &c.

Loche Fr., Sp. *loja*, E. *loach.*

Locher Fr. to shake; *eslochier* to loosen (e. g. *les dents*), *s'eslochier* to rise up; Rom. *harlocher* to agitate. Perhaps from O. H. G. *loc*, O. N. *lockr*, *hârlockr (lock, hairlock)*, cf. *froncer* from *frons.*

Locman Fr. a pilot; from Du. *loods-man*, E. *loadsman*, O. E. *lodeman lodesman* (cf. *lodestar*). Hence, by corruption, Fr. *lamaneur*, formed after *gouverneur* helmsman.

Loco O. It. for L. *hic* (adv.), Sp. *luego*, Pg. *logo*, Pr. *luec luecx*, O. Fr. *lnes*, Wal. *de loc* = L. *statim*; from *locus loco*.

Lodier Fr. blauket; cf. O. H. G. *lodo* over-garment, O. N. *lód*, L. *lodix*. O. Fr. *lodier loudier* a sluggard, f. *lodiere*, N. *loddari* (M. Du. *lodder*, G. *lotter-bube*) are from the same root, cf. *poltro*.

Lodola — *allodola*.

Loendro — *oleandro*.

Lof Fr. wind-side of a ship; from E. *loof*, Du. *loef*. Hence vb. *louvoyer* to tack, G. *lavieren*, cf. *bordayer* = Sp. *bordear*, It. *bordeggiare* from *bord*.

Loge loger logis — *loggia*.

Loggia It., Pg. *loja*, Pr. *lotja*, Fr. *loge*, Sp. *lonja*, E. *lodge* &c.; from O. H. G. *lanbja*, L. L. *laubia*, G. *lanbe* bower, shed, whence also O. Fr. *loge* a tent, hut. *Laubja* from *laub* folium, as O. Fr. *foillie* from *fenille*. Nearer to the G. orig. is the Rh. *laupia*, Lomb. Pied. *lobia* a church-gallery. Hence Fr. *loger*, It. *alloggiare*, E. *lodge*; Fr. *logis* &c.

Logoro It. (for *logro?*), Pr. *loire* (whence Fr. *lorimier* a saddler, E. *lorimer*), O. Fr. *loitre*, Fr. *leurre* (m.), E. *lure*, prop. a bit of leather used by falconers to lure back hawks; from M. H. G. *luoder* (G. *leder*, leather) lure, It. *g* for *d* as in *ragunare* from *radunare*. Vb. Pr. *loirar*, Fr. *leurrer*, E. *lure*, *allure*; It. *logorare* to feast, revel = M. H. G. *luodern*.

Logro Sp. Pg. gain, usury, Pr. *logre*, Sp. Pr. *lograr* to gain, Sp. *logrear* to lend on interest, *logrero* usurer; from *lucrum lucrari*. Hence, with *malo*, Sp. *malogro*, Pg. *maliogro* failure, disappointment, vb. *malograr*, *mallograr*.

Loir — *ghiro*.

Loisir Fr., E. *leisnre*; from *licere*, cf. *plaisir* from *placere*.

Loja It. mud; perhaps from *allavies*, cf. *Bojano* from *Bovianum*. But the B. has *loya* in same senso.

Lolla — *loppa*.

Lombard Fr. a pawn-shop, a *lombard* (whence *lumber*), Du. *lombaerd*, O. Fr. adj. usurious, cf. Sicil. *lambardu* an innkeeper; from the *Lombards* (= Italians, cf. Dante Purg. 16, 125: *che me' si noma francescamente il semplice Lombardo* = Italiano), who were noted in France and other countries as merchants and usurers, cf. Lombard Street.

Lomia — *limone*.

Lomo Sp., Pr. *lom* loin, chine; from *lumbus*, It. *lombo*.

Lona Pr. a lake, marsh; from *lacnna la'nna*, N. *lón*.

Longa — *loggia*.

Longaniza Sp. a sort of long sausage; from L. *longáno* (Cælius Aurel. and Veget. de re vet.), gut, *longanum* Varro, *longabo* (Apicius) a sausage.

Longe Fr. loin, O. Fr. Wall. *logne*, É. *loin*, Sp. *lonja* a slice of ham; from an adj. *lumbea (lumbus)*.

Longe Fr. f. rope of a halter; = *alonge* a lengthening, *l'alonge* = *la longe*.

Lonja — *longe* (1).

Lontano It., Pr. *lonhdá*, Fr. *lointain;* from a L. *longitanus*, cf. forms with *t, longiter, longitudo, longitrorsus* (Festus, whence O. Müller conjectures an adj. *longiterus*).

Lontra It. Pg., Sp. *lutria nutria*, Pr. *loiria luiria luria*, Fr. *loutre* an *otter* (cf. *hierre, ingot, ottone* &c.); from *lutra* Gk. ἐνυδρίς (Sp. *nutria*).

Lonza It., Sp. Pg. *onza*, Fr. *once*, E. *ounce*. From λύγξ, o for *v* as in *borsa, tomba, torso* from βύρσος, τύμβος, θύρσος. From the L. *lynx* we have It. *lince*, Sp. *lince*, Fr. *lynx* (m.). Others from λεόντιος lion-like.

Lonza It. fleshy parts of an animal; from O. H. G. *luntussa* fat.

Lonzo It. slack; cf. M. H. G. *lunz* drowsiness, Bav. *lunzet* drowsy, M. Du. *lompsch* lazy, G. *luntsch*.

Loppa It., Lomb. *lop* (m.) husk, dim. *lolla* for *loppola;* from λοπός.

Loque Fr. shred, not directly from G. *locke* (v. *locher*) but from N. *lókr* a lock of hair or any appendage. Hence, perhaps, Fr. *breloque*, Rou. *berloque*, N. Pr. *barlocco* f., an appendage, charm, Rh. *bargliocca* a lock of hair, cf. Rou. *berloquer*, Rh. *balucar* to dangle, cf. also It. *badolucco*. Hence also Fr. *pendeloque*, Rou. *pendreloque* an earring, from *pendulus, r = l*.

Loquet — *loc.*

Lordo It. also *lurido* filthy; from *luridus, lurdus lordo*, R. Gr. 1, 113. Hence also Fr. *lourd*, Pr. *lot* for *lort* (E. *lout*), cf. *Bernal* for *Bernart*, Sp. Pg. *lerdo* for *luerdo* as *frente* for *fruente*, slow, dull, stupid (O. It. *lordo*). For the transition from "dirty" to "stupid", cf. Fr. *pourri* rotten, Wall. *pourri* sluggish, O. H. G. *fúl* putridus, Du. *ruil* = E. *foul*, G. *faul* lazy. The der. from *horridus* It. *ordo* with prefixed article, is unsupported by analogy v. *lazzo*. Hence Fr. *balourd* dolt, whence It. *bulordo*, Rh. *balurd*, Sp. *palurdo vilordo*, ba from *baer béer*, so *balourd* = gaping blockhead; cf. *badaud*.

Lorgner Fr., Norm. *loriner* to spy, view, *lorgnette* a spying-glass; from G. *lauern* to lurk, watch, Sw. *loren luren*.

Loriot Fr. a yellow-hammer, E. *oriole*, O. Fr. *oriouz*, Pic. *oriot*, Pr. *auriol*, Sp. *oriol*, from *aureolus*, with article *loriol*, corrupted O. Fr. *lorion*, Fr. *loriot*. Cf. *lendemain, landier, lierre* &c.

Loro Sp., Pg. *louro* tawny. Perhaps from *aureolus*, though there seems to be no instance of the article prefixed to an adj., cf. *lazzo, lrodo*.

Loro — *egli*.

Lors — *ora* (2).

Losa Piedm. Sp., Pg. *lousa*, Pr. *lausa*, O. Fr. *lauze*, B. *arlauza* (*arri stone*) a gravestone, flat stone, prop. an epitaph, from L. *laudes*, cf. Sp. *lauda* tombstone. For the form cf. *lusinga*.

Losenge — *lusinga*.

Lot — *lotto*.

Lotto It. lottery, Pg. *lote* m. kind, sort, number (*lot*), Fr. *lot* share (*lot*), Pg. *lotar* to fix the number, tax (*allot*), Fr. *lotir* to share; *loterie*, E. *lottery*, cf. Fr. E. *lot*, Sp. *lote*; from the G., Goth. *hlauts*, O. N. *hlutr*, O. H. G. *hlôz*, G. *loofs* κλῆρος κορς, O. H. G. *hluz* something gained by lot, O. N. *hlut* share.

Louange — *lusinga*.

Louer Fr. to praise; from *laudare*.

Louer Fr. to hire, from *locare*; *loyer* rent, pay, from *locarium*, Pr. *loquier*.

Loupe Fr. a round swelling, a wen, also a lens; from *lupa* a she-wolf, cf. Sp. *lupia lobanillo* a wen, Rh. *luppa*, G. *wolfsgeschwulst*. O. Fr. *lope* = grimace, prop. thick lip.

Loup-garou Fr. a man who could assume a wolf's form, a were-wolf, G. *währwolf* prop. = man-wolf, λυκάνθρωπος, Pg. *lobis-homem*, L. L. *gerulphus* (from A. S. *verewolf*). From *gerulphus* came O. Fr. *garou garou*, cf. *Raoul Raou* from *Radulphus*, in Marie de Fr. 1, 178, *garwall*. So *loup-garou* is a pleonasm, like the Bret. *bleiz-garð* (*bleiz* = *loup*), cf. *cormoran*, It. *Mongibello* (*gibello* from Ar. = It. *mon*). We have also O. Fr. *loup-beroux*, Pr. *leberoun leberou*, Berr. *marloup*, *louara*, *birette*, Norm. *lubin*, O. Fr. also *millegroux* and *leuwasté*; It. *lupo mannaro*. From *yarou* is Norm. *varouage* nightly flitting about. Pic. *garou* = sorcerer.

Loura Pg. a burrow; from *laurex* a young rabbit, whence also *lousa* (*s* from *c* in *lauricem*).

Lourd — *lordo*.

Loure O. Fr. bag-pipe, Fr. a dance; from O. N. *lûdr*, Dan. *luur* a shepherd's pipe.

Loutre — *lontra*.

Loyer — *louer*.

Losa Sp. an earthen vessel; from *luteus lutea*, whence also Rh. Com. *lozza*, Romag. *lozz* clay.

Lozano Sp., Pg. *louzão* luxuriant; from Goth. *laus*, O. H. G. *lôs* empty, light (G. *los*, E. *loose*), Pic. Wall. *loss* = jocular.

Lua Sp., Val. *luga*, Pg. *luva* a glove; from Goth. *lôfa* m., O. N. *lôfi* the flat hand, A. S. *glôfa* m., E. *glove*.

Lucarne Fr. a dormer-window; from *lucerna*, cf. Goth. *lucarn*, Ir. *luacharn*, W. *llygorn*.

Lucchetto — *loc*.

Lucerta — *lacerta*.

Luchera — *luquer.*

Lucherino It., Ven. *lugarin;* from L. *ligurinus.*

Luchina Mod. a false tale; from O. H. G. *lugina* a lie, G. *lüge.*

Lucillo Sp. tomb, sarcophagus, O. Fr. *luseau;* from *locellus* dim. of *loculus* = coffin in L. L.

Luego — *loco.*

Luette Fr. uvula; a dim. of L. *uva*, with article prefixed; It. *úgola* for *uvola*, Com. *uga* for *uva.* Lang. *nivouleto.*

Lueur Fr., Pr. *lugor*, O. It. *lucore;* from *lucere*, with the hard *c* of *lucanus, luculentus*, or the O. L. *lucus* = *lux;* from *lucere* we have Pr. *luzor*, It. *luciore* (as *cuciore* from *cuocere*). The same root in Pr. *lug-ana* light, *alucar*, O. Fr. *alucher* to light.

Lugánega Mil. Ven. a sort of sausage, Pied. *luganighin;* from L. *lucanica (Lucanian)*. B. *lukhainca.*

Luglio It. July; from *Julius*, altered in form so as to distinguish it better from *giugno* June, cf. Pied. *giugn, lügn*, and v. *Juillet.*

Lui It. a wren; perhaps so called from the cry.

Lui — *egli.*

Lulla It. stave at the bottom of a cask, in the shape of a half-moon; from *lunula.*

Lumaccia It., Sp. *limaza*, Pg. *lesma*, Fr. *limace, limaçou*, It. *lumaca*, Rh. *limuga*, Ven. *limega*, Cat. *llimac* a snail; from *limax.*

Lunedi It., Fr. *lundi*, Pr. *dilús*, Cat. *dilluns* Monday, *Lunæ dies;* Sp. *lunes*, Pr. *luns* (cf. *martes*), Wal. *lúni*, Ven. *luni*, Romag. *lon.* The Pg. has instead *segunda feira*, cf. N. Gr. δευτέρα.

Lunes — *lunedi.*

Lunette Fr. eye-glass; It. *lunetta* aperture in a vault for light, from *luna.*

Luquer Norm., *louqui* Wall., Fr. *reluquer* to ogle, leer; prob. from O. H. G. *luogén, luokën*, A. S. *lokian*, E. *look.* Do the It. *luchera* look, *lucherare* to look awry, belong here? The Lomb. *lughera* spark is from O. H. G. *loug* flame.

Luseau — *lucillo.*

Lusinga It., Sp. *lisonja*, Pr. *lauzenga lauzenja*, O. Fr. *losenge* flattery (O. Fr. Sp. E. *lozenge*, Sp. also *losange* orig. an heraldic term), B. *lausengua;* vb. *lusingare, lisonjar, lauzengar, losenger;* abst. *lusinghiere, lisongero (losengero), lauzengador lauzengier, losengeor.* Pr. *lauz-enga* from *lauzar* = *laudare* with same suffix as in O. Fr. *laid-enge, cost-enge*, Fr. *vid-ange.* The *s* of *losenge* is radical, cf. *los* (m.) praise, acc. *los*, from *laudes* (used as sing. = hymn), *aloser* to praise. The Sp. and It. are from the Fr. and Pr.; the It. has also Genev. *loso*, Ven. *lox* = *los.* The Fr. *louange, louanger, louangeur* are regularly formed from *laudare*, which in its peculiar Rom. sense = to consent, arbitrari, has given rise to *laudemium laudemia* (which Pott compares to *vindemia* and makes to mean the purchasing *laus* or permission from a feudal lord, cf. E. *allow, allowance*) from which juristic word come Pr. *laudeme lauzimi lauzisme*, It. Sp. *laudemio* dues paid to a feudal lord. O. Fr. *los* is found in the juristic formula *los et rentes* v. Ducange, *laudare*.

Luth — *liuto*.

Lutin Fr. a hobgoblin, vb. *lutiner*; O. Fr. *luiton*, Belg. *nuiton*, Wall. *nuton*. Grimm Myth. p. 475, derives it from *luctus*, so = a wailing ghost, which the *lutin* is not; Grandgagnage from Flem. *luttil*, E. *little*, as being dwarfish. Perhaps it is best to take *nuiton* as the orig. form, and derive it from *nuit*.

Lutrin Fr. a lectern, reading-desk, for *létrin, lectrinum*, from L. L. *lectrum "analogium, super quo legitur"* Gloss. Isid. Gen. has *letterin* for It. *leggio*; E. *lectern*.

M.

Ma — *mai*.

Maca — *amaca*.

Macabre, danse Macabre Fr. death's dance; from (1) S. *Macarius* (2) *chorea Macabœorum* (3) Ar. *maqábir* grave-yards? Cf. Lorr. *maicaibré* a grotto.

Macári magari magara It. interj. for L. *utinam*; from μαχάριος (N. Gr. μαχάρι), voc. μαχάριε. In O. It. it was used as a concessive particle, since; so Wal. *macár cé*, Serv. *makar*, Alb. *mácar*; perhaps also O. Sp. *maguar maguer maguera* = though, O. Pg. *maguer* (which are by some derived from Fr. *malgré maugré*).

Maccherone It., Ven. *macarone* (commonly used only in the plur.), *maccaroni*. Partly from *macco* or *maccare* (q. v.), partly from μαχαρία (Hesychius) βρῶμα ἐχ ζωμοῦ χαὶ ἀλφίτων, prop. = happiness, hence delicious food. The Gk. word was known to the It., cf. *macári*; to give *maccherone macco* would require an intermediate form *maccaria*, which is found in Neap., though in a different sense, v. *macco*.

Macchia It., Sp. Pg. *mancha* (for *macha*) stain &c., bushy ground *(La Mancha)*, Wall. *mégure* a woody hill, cf. G. *flecken*, E. *spot* (of land &c.); also It. *maglia*, Sp. Pg. Pr. *malla*, Fr. *maille*, E. *mail (coat-of-mail)*; from *macula*; also Pg. *mágoa* spot, vb. *magoar*. Hence Sp. *mancilla* spot, sore, *ill* for *ul*; Fr. *maillot* swadling clothes. From *macchiare*, Sp. *macar* or *manchar*, comes Fr. *marqueter* (formed after *marquer*) to stipple, put in the lights and shades of a picture, whence *marqueterie* chequered inlaid work.

Macco It. bruising (whence It. *ammaccare* to pound), a mash of bean food, Com. *mach* bruised barley, Sp. *maca* bruise on fruit, stain (perhaps an old Lat. word, whence *macula*), O. Fr. *maque* a hemp-bruiser, Rou. *maca* a large hammer, *maquet* a sort of bolt, Wall. *maclott* a club, E. *mace*; vb. It. *maccare maccare*, *am-maccare*, *s-maccare*, Rh. *smaccar*, Sp. Cat. *macar*, Pr. *macar machar*, O. Fr. *maquer* to bruise, press; sbst. Neap. *maccaria*, O.Fr. *macheure* butchery. The Bret. *macha* to press is from the same root. Some derive it from the Heb. *maccah* to slay, but the root is widely spread; cf. Gk. μάσσειν, L. *mac-ula*, *mac-ellum*. It. *macco macca* plenty, O. Fr. *maquet* a heap, Wall. *a make* in plenty, perhaps orig. = something pressed down, and heaped up.

Maccu Sard. simpleton; from *maccus* (Apuleius) the fool in the Atellanæ.

Machacar machucar machar — *macho*.

Mâcher — *masticare*.

Macho Sp. Pg. man, male. Not from *musculus* which gives in O.Sp. *masclo maslo muslo*, but, prob., the same word as *macho* a hammer (whence *machar machacar machucar* to hammer, pound, *machado* a hatchet, *machete* a chopping-knife), cf. It. *marcone* a husband. *Macho* from *marcus* (*marculus*) *malleus major* Isid. Gloss., O. It. *marco* (Lat. proper name *Marcus*).

Machurer — *maschera*.

Macigno — *mâcina*.

Mâcina mâcine mill-stone, *macinare*, Wal. *macinà* to grind; from *machina*, whence a form *machineus* gives It. *macigno* quarry-stone.

Macio Pg. malleable, pliant; Sousa derives it from Ar. *masih*, but why not from the same root as Sp. *macho?*

Maciulla It. a mace for bruising hemp, O. Fr. *maque* (v. *marco*) which = an It. *macca*, dim. *macchi-ciulla*, *maciulla*, cf. *fauti-cello fanciullo.*

Maçon Fr., Pr. *massô*, E. *mason*, Isid. *machio*, perhaps for *marcio* from *marcus* a hammer (v. *macho*), cf. *tabellio* from *tabella*. Sp. has an old verb *mazonar*. *Maçon* = *machio*, as *bracel-et* = *brachiale*. Or is the word from the root *mac*, v. *macco?*

Madera madoro Sp., Pg. *madeira* timber (hence *Madeira*); from *materia*.

Madexa — *matassa*.

Madia It. kneading-trough; from L. *magis magidis*, *magida*, Fr. (Jura) *maid*, Norm. *met*, Wall. *mai*, Pic. *maie*. Neap. *matra*, Mil. *marna*, N. Pr. *mastra* are from μάκτρα, vb. Wall. *mairi* to knead.

Madiò madios — *dio*.

Madraoo — *materasso*.

Madré Fr. spotted, sbst. Norm. *maire* spot (on the skin), O. Fr. *mazre madre* a spotted kind of wood, L. L. *scyphi maserini*,

O. Fr. adj. *mazelin*, *madelin maderin* a drinking-vessel; from O. H. G. *masar*, G. *maser* speck, speckled wood.

Madrigale It., Sp. Fr. E. *madrigal*, O. It. *mandriale*, Sp. *mandrial;* from *mandria*, L. *mandra* a flock, herd; so = a herdsman's song, a pastoral.

Madrugar Sp. Pg. to rise early, O. Sp. *madurgar* = a L. *maturicare*, from *maturus*.

Maestro mastro It., Sp. *maestro maestre*, O.Sp. *maese*, Pg. *mestre*, Fr. *maitre* (from the O. Fr. *maistre*), Wal. *mester*, E. *master;* from *magister*. Hence It. *maestrale*, Sp. *maestral*, Cat. *mestral*, Fr. *mistral* North-west wind, Pr. *maestre*, so called from its violence.

Magagna It., O. Fr. Wall. *méhaing* m., Crem. Mil. Pied. *mangagna* a defect, bodily failing, maim; vb. It. *magagnare*, Pr. *maganhar*, O. Fr. *méhaigner* to maim. L. L. has *mahamium mahamiare* (E. *maim?*). Perhaps from a Germ. *man-hamjan (man-maim)* formed like *man-slago* (manslayer). In Com. we find besides *magayn* also *màga* which would point to a root *mag (= mac v. macco?).* Muratori derives *magagno* from *manganum* a catapult.

Magazzino It., Sp. *magacen almagacen almacen*, Pg. *armazem*, Fr. *magasin*, E. *magazine;* from Ar. *makhan al-mazan* a shed.

Maggese It. fallow; from *maggio* May, in which month the fields were ploughed up, Mil. *maggenh*.

Maglone It., Pr. O. Sp. *mayson*, O. Pg. *meisom*, Fr. *maison* (whence Sp. *meson*); from *mansio (mansion)*. Hence It. *masnada*, Sp. *mesnada manuada*, Pr. *mainada*, O. Fr. *mesguée mesnie*, E. *meiny* (whence It. *menial*), household, retinue, body of armed men &c., from a form *mansionata* (It. *manata*, Sp. Pr. *manada* a handful, from *manus*); from *masnada (masnadino)* is It. *mastino*, Sp. Pr. *mastin*, Pg. *mastim*, Fr. *mâtin*, E. *mastiff* a house-dog, prop. = a member of the household (O. Fr. *mastin*). Further, from *manere* we have *manoir*, E. *manor*, Fr. *masure (mansura)*, mas *mès*, E. *manse (mansus)*, Fr. E. *messuage* (L. L. *man-suagium*).

Maglia — *macchia*.

Maglio It., Sp. Pg. *mallo*, Fr. *mail*, Wal. *maiu*, E. *mall;* from *malleus;* vb. It. *magliare*, Sp. *majar*, Pg. Pr. *malhar*, Fr. *mailler* to hammer; from *malleare (malleatus)*.

Magnano — *maña*.

Magoa — *macchia*.

Magone Mod. crop; = O. H. G. *mago*, G. *magen*, E. *maw*, Rh. *magun;* Ven. Pied. *magon*, Gen. *magun* = grudge, ill-will, cf. *stomachus*.

Magrana emigrania It., Sp. *migraña*, Fr. *migraine;* from ἡμιxρανία ache on one side of the head.

Maguer — *macari.*

Mai ma It., O. Sp. Pg. Pr. *mais*, Sp. Pg. Pr. *mas*, Fr. *mais;* from *magis*, It. *ma*, Sp. Pg. *mas*, Fr. *mais* used for L. *sed*, cf. Goth. *mais* for *magis* and *potius*, L. L. *sed magis = sed potius*. Hence Sp. *demas* cæterus, L. *de magis* in Festus (but = minus); adj. Sp. *demasiado* nimius.

Maidieu — *dio.*

Mail — *maglio.*

Maille — *macchia.*

Maille — *medaglia.*

Main Fr. in *main menue* poor folk; from *manus.*

Main adv. — *mane.*

Mainada — *magione.*

Mainbour mambourg O. Fr. guardian (Pr. *manbor*), vb. *mainbournir*, whence sbst. *mainbournie*. From O. H. G. *muntboro*, A. S. *munbbora*, Du. *momboor*, L. L. *mundiburdus* tutor, patronus; L. L. *mundiburdis mundiburdum*, O. H. G. *muntburti* = tutela; from *munt* hand and *beran (bear)*, cf. *main-tenir*. *Munt* is altered to Rom. *main* (cf. *manovaldo*), *burt* to *bournir*. For similar adaptations cf. *battifredo, guiderdone, candelabre, orange* &c.

Maint Fr., Pr. *maint mant* (N. Pr. *mant-un*), hence It. *manto* for L. *multus*. Three derivations are proposed: (1) W. *maint* multitude, cf. *troppo* from *truppus* (2) O. H. G. *managôti*, Du. *menigte* a multitude (3) O. H. G. adj. *manag*, G. *manch*, in which case we should have to suppose a neut. from *managaz managat*. Froissart has *ta-maint* (= Sp. *tamaño*), whence It. *tamanto.*

Maintenant — *immantinente.*

Maintenir — *mantenere.*

Maire Fr., E. *mayor;* for *major*, O. Fr. *moire*, G. *meier*, cf. *major domus.*

Mais — *mai.*

Maison — *magione.*

Maitre — *maestro.*

Maiz Sp., E. *maize;* an American (Haitian) word.

Majada Sp., Pg. *malhada* sheep-cote, inn; from *magalia (magaliata magliata)*. Cf. *naguela.*

Majar — *maglia.*

Majo It., Sp. *mayo*, Fr. *mai*, Pr. f. *maia* a sort of birch, May-tree, so called because it flourishes in May; also any green tree, or branch of a tree, such as on May-night it was the custom for lovers to plant before the doors of their mistresses. Rh. *maig* a bunch of flowers.

Majólica It. counterfeit porcelain; from the island *Majorca*, where it was made.

Majorana maggiorana It., Sp. *mayorana*, Pg. *maiorana mange-rona*, Fr. *marjolaine*, E. *marjoram*, G. *majoran*; corrupted from *amaracus*. Sp. *almoradux*, Cat. *moradux* are from Arab. *mardaqûsch* which is from the Persian *murda-gôsh*. *Majorana* may have been assimilated to *major*.

Mal — *ora* (1).

Mala Sp. Pg. Pr., Fr. *malle*, E. *maul* trunk; Gael. *mala*, O. H. G. *malaha* sack, Du. *maal maale*.

Malade — *malato*.

Malaise — *agio*.

Malandrin malandrino — *landra*.

Malart Fr. male of the duck, Pic. *maillard*, E. *mallard*; from *mâle (masculus)*.

Malato It. O. Sp., Fr. *malade*, Pr. *malapte malaut*, Cat. *malalt*; It. *malattia*, Fr. *maladie*, E. *malady*, Pr. *malaptia malautia ma-latia*, Cat. *malaltia*. The Pr. forms point to the der. from *male aptus*, cf. G. *unpässlich* from *passen* aptare, and E. *in-disposed*; Cat. *malalt*, as *galta* from *gauta*. The Fr. and It. (which, from aptus, should have been *malate*, *malatto*) may have taken their form from a part. *malatus* from *malum*, as *barbatus* from *barba*, or from *ammalato (ammalare)*.

Malaves — *avieso*.

Malgré — *grado*.

Malhour — *augurio*.

Malia It. sorcery, *maliardo* sorcery; from *malus* magical, Virg. Ec. 7, 28. *ne vati noceat mala lingua futuro*.

Malingre — *heingre*.

Mall-publio O. Fr. public justice; L. L. *mallum publicum*, Goth. *mathl*, O. H. G. *mahal* justice.

Malla — *macchia*.

Malle — *mala*.

Mallevare It. to bail, Sp. Pr. *manlevar*, O. Pg. *malevar* to bail, to borrow; from *manum levare* to lift the hand, promise so-lemnly, cf. *mallurium* for *manluvium*.

Mallo It. the green husk covering nuts &c.; = Fr. *malle (maul* chest) a repository?

Malogro — *ogro*.

Malotru — *astro*.

Malsin Sp., Pg. *malsim* tale-bearer, makebate, vb. *malsinar*. The verb might come from *male signare*; since, however, names of agents are rarely, if ever, derived from verbs with-out suffix, it may be better to derive the verb from the noun, and to make this a contraction of *mal-vecino* (bad neighbour), cf. It. O. Fr. *malvicino malvoisin*.

Malt Fr. m.; from E. *malt*, O. H. G. *malz*.

Malta It. mud; = L. *maltha* cement, Rh. *maulta molta*.

Maltôte Fr. f. extortion; from O. Fr. *toute tolte* (partic. of *tollir* from *tollere*) a levying of taxes, with *mal*, cf. It. *maltolto mala-tolta: guarda ben la mal tolta moneta* Inf. 19, 98; O. Pg. *malla-tosta maltosta* duty on wine. V. Duc. v. *tolta*.

Malvagio It., Pr. *malvais*, Fr. *mauvais;* It. *malvagità*, Pr. *mal-vastat malvestat*, O. Fr. *mauvestie*, O. Sp. *malvestad*. Goth. has a sbst. *balvavései* badness, adj. *balvavesi-s* bad = an O. H. G. *balvási*, hence *balvais*, altered to *malvais* so as to connect it with *mal;* for similar instances cf. *guiderdone*, *mainbour*, R. Gr. 2, 229 note. But is it unconnected with *malvar?*

Malvar O. Sp. to deprave, Sp. *malvado*, Pr. *malvat* wicked, *mal-vadesa* wickedness. From *mal-levar* (cf. *malograr* for *mal-lograr*), and so = prop. to bring up badly.

Malvavischio It., Sp. *malvavisco* (Fr. *maurisque*) marsh-mallow; from *malva ibiscum* (ἴβισκος); L. L. *bismalva* from *ibiscum malva*, Fr. It. *guimauve* for *vimauve*, *v* = *b*.

Malvis — *mauvis*.

Mamma It., Sp. *mama*, Fr. *maman*, Wal. *mamè* = E. *mamma*, Gen. &c. = nurse; from L. *mamma* (1) breast (so It. Sp. Pg.) (2) mother (Varro). *Maman* has an accusative form, which differs, however, from other forms such as *non nain*, *Evain* &c., probably in order to make it less unlike *papa*. Sp. *mamar* is to suck (L. L. *mammare*). The G. *memme* coward corresponds to Neap. *mammamia* (m.). V. H. Stephani lex. Graec. v. πάπ-πας.

Mammone It. prop. *gattomammone* a baboon; = Gk. μιμώ, M. Gr. N. Gr. μαϊμοῦ, Wal. *moimê meïmucê*, Alban. Turk. *maimûn*, Hung. *majom* ape.

Mamparar Sp. Pg. to shelter, defend; from *manu parare* to guard with the hand, v. *parare*.

Manada — *magione*.

Manaier O. Fr. to protect, save, sbst. *manaie*, Pr. *manaya*, from *manu adjutare*, hence also a form with *d*, *manaide*, *menaide:* cf. *mantenere*, *mallevare*, *mamparar*.

Manant Fr. a native, a peasant; partic. pres. from O. Fr. *manoir maindre* = *manere* L. L. to dwell; adj. O. Fr. *manant*, Pr. *manen* wealthy, *manantie* wealth; Gen. *manente* ploughman.

Mancebo Sp., Pr. O. Fr. *mancip massip* young man, f. *manceba mancipa;* from L. *mancipium*, L. L. *mancipius*.

Mancha manchilla — *macchia*.

Manche — *manico*.

Mancia It. drink-money, gratuity. From L. L. *manicia* pl. of *manicium (manica)* a sleeve, glove. Cf. *guanto*, *paraguanto*, Sp. *guantes*, Fr. *gants*, Pg. *luvas* = *mancia*. Cf. also Sp.

mangas perquisites, from *manga* a sleeve, costly sleeves having been used as presents. From *mancia manciata* handfull.

Mancip — *mancebo*.

Manco It. Sp. Pg., Pr. O. Fr. *manc* maimed defective; from *mancus*. Hence Fr. *manchot* = It. *manco d'una mano*, also Sp. *manca* the left hand, cf. *gauche;* vb. It. *mancare*, Sp. Pr. *mancar*, Fr. *manquer* to fail. It. *monco*, vb. *moncare* (cf. Rh. *muncar*=*mancar*) seems to borrow the *o* of the Lomb. *mock* blunt, broken off (O. H. G. *far-muckit* hebetudo, M. H. G. *mocke* mass, O. E. *mock* blunt), cf. It. *moncone* = Romag. *mucôn*.

Mandil Sp. Pg. apron, saddle-cloth; from *mantile*, Ar. *mandil* a towel.

Mandola mandore — *pandura*.

Mandorla It. *(mandola)*, Sp. *almendra*, Pg. *amendoa*, Pr. *amandola*, Fr. *amande*, E. *almond*, Du. *amandel*, G. *mandel;* corrupted from *amygdala* (ἀμυγδάλη), Wal. *migdalë* as well as *mandulë*. Contracted forms are Pr. *mella*, N. Pr. *amello* (Lang. *amentou*).

Mandragola It., Lat. *mandragoras;* by corruption, Fr. *main-de-gloire*, E. *mandrake*.

Mandria Sp. m. a coward; from B. *emandrea* a weak woman, cf. Pg. *mandrião* a woman's house-dress.

Mane It., O. Sp. *man* f., Pr. *man*, O. Fr. *main*, Wal. *mëne* morning; from *mane*, cf. Pr. *lo bè ma* = *bene mane*. Hence It. adv. *dimani domani*, Pr. *deman*, Fr. *demain*, Wal. *de mëne*, for which Sp. has *mañana*, Pg. *á manhãa*. Hence Fr. *lendemain*, Pr. *lendeman*, for *le en demain*, cf. O. Cat. *l-en-de-mig* meanwhile. From *matutinum* is It. *mattino*, Pr. *mati*, Fr. E. *matin*. For *domani* Sic. and other dialects have *crai* = *cras*.

Manége Fr. (m.); from It. *maneggio* which is from *maneggiare* to *manage*, v. R. Gr. 2, 327.

Manovir in *amanevir* O. Fr., Pr. *amanoïr amanarir amarvir, marvir*, to be ready, willing, hence O. Fr. partic. *manevis amaneris*, Pr. *amanoïtz amarvitz* ready, fervid, Lang. *amarbit* lively. From Goth. *maurjan* = *manoir (v = o)*. So Pr. adv. *marves* without hesitation, adj. *marvier* ready = Goth. adj. *manvus*.

Mángano It. a sling; hence *manganello* a cross-bow, Pr. *manganel*, O. Fr. *mangoneau* a sling for stones, Wal. *mënyëlëu* a mangle; from μάγγανον, O. H. G. *mango*, G. *mangel*, E. *mangle*. Hence also Sp. *manganilla* sleight of hand.

Manger — *mangiare*.

Mangiare It., O. Pg. Pr. *manjar*, Fr. *manger*, It. also *manucare manicare*, O. Fr. *manuer*, Wal. *mëncù mënêncà* to eat, Pr. O. Fr. *menjar menjiar*, Lim. *mindzá;* from *manducare* used in late Lat. = *edere: manducat et bibit* = ἐσθίει καὶ πίνει Vulg.

Matt. 11, 19; Pr. *manjuiar*, O. Fr. *manjuer* (pres. conjunct. *manjuce*) from *mandcuare*; Norm. *moujuer manjusser*. Fr. *démanger*, Pied. *smangè* to itch, cf. Sp. *comer (comedere)*.

Mangil manchil Pg. a butcher's cleaver; from Ar. *menjal* a sickle, which meaning is also given to the Pg. word by Constancio.

Mangla O. Sp., Pg. *mangra* mildew; from *melligera* honey-dew?

Mangual Sp., Pg. *mangoal* a flail, also a warlike instrument; from *mannalis*; for the inserted *g*, v. *menovare*.

Mánico It., Sp. Pg. *mango*, Pr. *margue*, Fr. *manche* (m.) handle. The suffix *ic* forms only feminines (v. *oca*), so it is best to make *manico* not directly from *manus*, but a variation of *manica* a sleeve (It. *manica* = also handle). In Lomb. Ven. *mánega*, Sp. Pg. *manga* troop, body of men, we have a meaning of the L. *manus*.

Manicordion — *monocordo*.

Manier — *menear*.

Maniero It., Sp. *manero*, Pr. *manier* handled, tame; from *manarius* for *manuarius*, cf. *maunaja*. Hence sbst. It. *maniera*, Sp. *manera*, Pg. Pr. *maneira*, Fr. *manière*, E. *manner*, prop. handling.

Maniganoe Fr. trick, knack; from *manica (manicare)*, jugglers making use of their *sleeves* in performing tricks. Cf. Papias: *maniculare dolum*.

Maniglia smaniglia It., Sp. *manilla* a bracelet, Fr. *manille*; from *monilia (monile)*, *a* for *o* coming O.H.G. *mánili* a moon-shaped ornament.

Manigoldo It. a hangman (Sp. *manigoldo*). The same word as the O. H. G. proper name *Manogald Managolt* (whence G. E. *mangold* a plant), which is probably, through the Rom., from *mano-wald* one who administers *(walten)* the halter *(menni* plur., Com. *men*, Gen. *menu)*: G. *mangold* is Com. *menegold*, Mil. *meregold*, Pied. *manigol* lettuce.

Maniqui — *mannequin*.

Manir Sp. to keep meat to make it tender; from *manere* used in trans. sense, to let remain.

Manlevar — *mallevare*.

Manna — *maña*.

Mannaja It. an executioner's axe, Lomb. *manara*, Rh. *manera*; from adj. *manuaria*, because two-handed.

Manne Fr. a basket, Pic. *mande*; from Du. *mand mande* (f.), A.S. *mond*, E. *maund*; so also *manne-quin* from Du. *mande-kin*.

Mannequin — *manne*.

Mannequin Fr., hence Sp. *maniqui* mannikin; from M.Du. *mannekin*, E. *mannikin*. Wall. *maniket* dwarf.

Mano — *hermano*.

Manoir — *mas.*

Manojo Sp., Pg. *manolho molho* a handfull; from *manupulus* for *manipulus*, It. *manipolo* &c.

Manópola It., Sp. Pg. *manopla* a gauntlet; from *manipulus (manupulus)*, cf. L. *manipula* a towel.

Manovaldo — *mondualdo.*

Manovra It., Sp. *maniobra*, Fr. *manoeuvre;* from *manus opera.*

Manser Sp. son of a prostitute; from the rabbinical *mamser* Buxtorf p. 1154.

Manso It. Sp. Pg. tame; shortened from *mansuetus* (v. *fino*). Hence Sp. *manso* an ox or sheep that guides the herd, It. *manzo* ox.

Mantaco mantice bellows, Papias: *follis vulgo mantacum fabri;* from *mantica* wallet. Cat. has *mancha* = Sp. *fuelle.*

Manteca Sp., Pg. *manteiga*, Cat. *mantega* butter; hence Neap. *manteca* butter from sheep's milk, Sicil. fat of cheese, It. pomade. From *mantica*, or, perhaps, a very old word, connected with the Sanskrit *manthaja* (root *math*, *manth* agitare) butter.

Mantenere It., Sp. Pr. *mantener*, Pg. *manter*, Fr. *maintenir*, S. *maintain;* from *manu tenere*, cf. G. *hand-haben;* cf. *mallevare* and L. *manstutor.* Cf. Pr. *cap-tener*, O. Sp. *cab-tener*, from *caput tenere;* Wall. *men-tni* from *manu-tueri.*

Manto It. Sp. Pg., It. also *ammanto* mantle, f. Sp. Pr. *manta*, Fr. *mante* a covering, contracted from *mantelum;* It. *mantello*, Fr. *manteau*, Sp. *mantilla*, E. *mantle* from *mantellum;* It. *mantile*, Sp. *mantel* from *mantile mantele.* Isid. has: *mantum Hispani vocant.*

Manto — *maint.*

Manzana Sp., O. Sp. *mazana*, Pg. *mazãa* apple; L. *malum Matianum* a peculiar kind of apple named after a person of the Matian gens. Cf. Col. 5, 10, 19; Suet. Dom. 21.

Maña Sp., Pg. *manha* readiness, handiness; from *machina mach'na* = craft. Hence also It. *magnano* (Cat. *manyá*, Fr. *magnan magnier*, Wall. *mignon*) a lock-smith, prop. artifex. It. *manna*, Sp. *maña* a bundle (It. *ammannare ammannire* to tie into bundles, to bring together, set in order) is the Gael. *mam* a handfull (pl. *maim*), Com. *man.*

Mañana — *mane.*

Maquereau Fr. for *moclereau* from *mocula*, prop. spotted fish, hence E. *mackerel*, Du. *makreel*, W. *macrell;* Champ. *maquet.*

Maquereau Fr. a pander; probably the same word as the preceding, cf. Donatus: *leno* (sc. in comœdiis) *pallio rarii coloris utitur.* It is, however, difficult to suppose that a word derived from the Roman stage would have been preserved only in the Fr.; so Diez derives it from Du. *maker*, from *maken* to negotiate, go between, O. H. G. *mahhari* from *mahhòn* machinari, *huor-mahhari* leno.

Maquila Sp., Pg. *maquia* miller's fee; from Ar. *mikyàl* a measure.

Mar Fr. adv. — *ora* (1).

Marais — *mare*.

Marangone It. a diver, Lomb. *maryon;* from *mergus maragone marangone*, cf. *fagotto fangotto*.

Marasca It. wild cherry, *amarasca*, from *amarus;* also *amarina*.

Maraud Fr. a beggar, scamp, *maraude* dissolute woman, *marauder* to plunder; hence *maraudeur* a marauder, plundering soldier, vb. *maroder*, abst. *marode* (through Sp. *merode marodear*). Several derivations have been given, (1) Ar. *marada* audax esse, (2) *male ruptus*, = Sp. *mal-roto*, Pg. *maroto*, vb. *malrotar marlotar*, (3) *maraudeur* from *morator* (Mahn), (4 and best) from *marrir* (q. v.) to stray, trouble, abst. *marauce, marison* grief, with the depreciative ending *aud* as in *badaud, clabaud (clabauder clabaudeur), nigaud, ribaud, richaud*.

Maravedi Sp. Pg., Pr. *marabotin* a Sp. coin; from Ar. *muràbîti* belonging to (coined by) the Almoravides *(al-muràbîtin)* an Arab. dynasty in Spain.

Maraviglia It., Sp. *maravilla*, Pg. *maravilha*, It. Pr. (better) *meraviglia*, Fr. *merveille*, E. *marvel;* from pl. *mirabilia*.

Marasso — *mare*.

Marc Fr. husks, grounds; Pic. *merc;* from *amercum (amurca)* found in Pliny and Columella, cf. *mina* from *hemiua*.

Marca It. Sp. Pg. Pr., Fr. *marque* marche (O. E. *march*), bound, limit, It. Sp. Pg. *marco*, Pr. Fr. *marc*, O. Fr. also *merc* mark, measure; vb. It. *marcare marchiare*, Sp. Pg. Pr. *marcar*, Fr. *marquer merker* to mark; abst. It. *marchese*, Sp. Pr. *marques*, Fr. *marquis*, E. *marquis*, L. L. *marchio*. From Goth. *marka* boundary (Sk. *màrga* a road, *màrg* quærere), O.H.G. *marcha*, A. S. *mearc*, E. O. N. *mark*, M. H. G. *marc*, vb. O. H. G. *markòn*, G. *merken*, E. *mark*.

Marcassita It., Sp. *marcasita marquesita*, Fr. *marcassite, marcasite* a sort of stone; from Ar. *marqashàtà* (Freytag).

Marchant — *marché*.

Marchar — *marcher*.

Marche — *marca*.

Marché Fr. market, from *mercatus; marchaud* (E. *merchant*) from O. Fr. *marcheant (marchedant)* = It. *mercatante*, partic. from *mercatare*, Pr. *mercadar*, L. L. *mercadantes;* also O. Fr. *marchant markant* = It. *mercante* from *mercari*.

Marcher Fr., abst. *marche*, hence It. *marciare*, Sp. *marchar*, E. *march*. From *marche* = bound (v. *marca*); *marcher* = O. Fr. *aller de marche en marche*. Cf. Sk. *udry* quærere, quæsitum ire.

Marchese — *marca*.

Marchito Sp. withered; prob. a dim. of a lost adj. *marcho* = It. *marcio*, Pr. *mar-cit*, *-ida*, from *marcidus*. Pg. is *murcho* q. v.

Marciare — *marcher*.

Marcotte — *margotta*.

Mardi — *martedi*.

Mare O. Fr. f. any collection of water, a pond, = Du. *maar*, E. *mere*. From *maar* come Du. *maerasch maersche*, L. G. *marsch*, A. S. *mersc*, E. *marsh*, whence O. Fr. *maresq*, Pr. *marex* (for *marsex*), O. Fr. *marescal, maresquel, marescage*, Fr. *marécage* &c.; Fr. *marais*, It. *marese*, E. *marish* may also come from *marasch*, or through *mare*; Fr. *marage*, It. *marazzo* are pure Rom. derivatives. V. Dief. Goth. Wb. 2, 44.

Marécage — *mare*.

Maréchal — *mariscalco*.

Maremma It. a maritime province, O. Fr. *maremme*; from *maritima*.

Marese — *mare*.

Marfil Sp. Fr., Pg. *marfim* ivory; from Ar. *nâb* tooth, *fil* elephant?

Margolato — *margotta*.

Margotta It., Champ. Rou. *margotte*, Fr. *marcotte* a shoot, layer; from *mergus*. Hence also It. *margolato*.

Margue — *manico*.

Marguillier Fr. churchwarden, O. Fr. *marreglier*; from *matricularius* one who keeps a list of the poor (*matricula*, whence Fr. *matricule, immatriculer*, E. *matriculate* to register, enrol).

Marionnette Fr. a puppet, dim. of *Marion* (dim. of *Marie*) = a little girl. Hence Fr. *marotte* (for *mariotte*).

Mariposa Sp. a butterfly, Pg. an ornament in the shape of a butterfly, Sp. also a rushlight. Prob. from the *flickering* motion, like the rise and fall of the sea *mar i posa* sea and calm (Mahn), which is almost too poetical, though *mar* is often used metaphorically in Spanish. The Sp. name is *borboleta* (q. v.).

Mariscalco maniscalco maliscalco It., Sp. Pg. *mariscal*, Pr. *manescalc*, Fr. *maréchal* a smith, farrier; from O. H. G. *marahscalc* (horse-attendant) a groom, G. *marschall*, E. *marshal*. Cf. *siniscalco*.

Marjolaine — *majorana*.

Marlotar — *maraud*.

Marmaglia — *merme*.

Marmelo Pg. a quince, whence *marmelada*, E. *marmalade*; from *melimelum*, Gk. μελίμηλον a sweet apple, apple grafted on a quince. The Sp. is *membrillo*.

Marmita It. Sp. Cat., Fr. *marmite* a pot, saucepan; hence It. *marmitone*, Sp. Fr. *marmiton* a scullion; *marmiteux* poor, hungry, wretched. Perhaps an onomatop. from boiling water, cf. *marmotter* to hum, sing. Some derive it from Ar. *marmi'd* a hole dug in the ground for cooking.

Marmotta marmotto It., Sp. Pg. *marmota*, Fr. *marmotte*, E. *marmot*. In Rh. it is *montanella* and *murmont*, O.H.G. *muremmnto murmenti*, Sw. *murmel*, which are from *mus montanus*, by gradual corruption, *marmotta*.

Marmotter Fr., Com. *marmota* to murmur, hum; an onomatop.

Marne Fr., O. Fr. *marle merle*, Pic. *marle*, E. *marl*, vb. *marner marler* to marl; from *marga*, according to Pliny a Gallic word: *quod genus terræ vocant margam (Galli et Britanni)*, whence *margula*; O. H. G. *mergil*, contr. *marle marne* as *posterle poterne*. The orig. form is found in It. Sp. *marga*, Bret. *marg* m., the derivative word only being found in the other Celtic tongues: W. *marl*, Ir. Gael. *merla*.

Maronier O. Fr. a seaman; from *marinier* as *chardonal* from *cardinal*, *vilonie* from *vilenie* &c., prob. through *maron*, a der. of *mare* as *pion* of *pes*, whence *maronnel* pirate.

Maroto — *maraud*.

Marotte — *marionnette*.

Marque marquis marques — *marca*.

Marra — *marron*.

Marraine Fr. godmother; Pr. *mairina*, It. Sp. *madrina*; Fr. is for *marrine*, being assimilated to *parrain*.

Marrano Sp. (It.) cursed; espec. of baptized but suspected Jews. From *marrar* to deviate, go wrong *(mar)*; *marrana* a sow, = accursed (sc. by Jews) animal? May it not be connected with the N. Test. *maranatha* (Chaldee *mdran athd* = our Lord is come), Sp. *maranata*?

Marrir Pr. O. Fr. to lose one's way, to err, hence *esmarrir*, It. *smarrire* to confuse, perplex, Rh. *smarir* to lose; from Goth. *marzjan*, O.H.G. *marran*, A. S. *meurrian (mar)* to scandalize, hinder; L. L. *legem, bannum, vel præceptum marrire* (L. *marra* a clod-breaker?). In 1st conj. Sp. *marrar* to go astray, partic. *marrido omarrido* cast-down, melancholy = Pr. *marrit*, Pied. *mari*, Pic. *amari*. From same root Sp. *maraña* maze, *marañar* to entangle.

Marritto — *ritto*.

Marrochino It., Sp. *marroqui*, Fr. *marroquin*, E. *morocco*, from *Marrocco*, *Morocco*.

Marron Sp. a ram, Cat. *marrá*, Lang. *marra mar-mouton*, B. *marroa*; vb. Pg. *marrar* to butt. According to Diez from *mas maris*, cf. Sard. *masca* ram. Of the same origin he says is *marra* a hammer (cf. *macho*). But *marra* = a pick-axe and = L. *marra*, cf. *marrir*. May not *marron* rather come from this? v. *macho*. *Morueco* ram may be for *marueco*, the o being to distinguish it from the name *Marruecos*, or it may be for *murueco* (in O. Sp. = battering-ram) from *murus*, cf. *marueca* a heap of loose stones.

Marrone It., Fr. *marron* a chestnut, Eustat. μάραον. Prob. an old Latin word the same as the L. name *Maro*.

Marsouin Fr. (in Belgium) a porpoise *(porkpisce = porcus piscis)*; quasi *maris sus*, O. H. G. *merisuin*, G. *meerschwein*, O. E. *meresuine*, Champ. *marsouin* = a dirty fellow.

Marteau — *martello*.

Martedi marti It., Fr. *mardi*, Pr. Cat. *dimars*; from *Martis dies*, *dies Martis*; Sp. *martes*, Pr. *mars* (from gen. *Martis*), Wal. *mártzi*, Ven. *marti*, Romag. *mert*. Pg. uses *terza feira*, N. Gr. τρίτη.

Martello It. Pg., Sp. *martillo*, Fr. *marteau* a hammer; from *martulus (marculus)*, *martellus* (in *Carolus Martellus*).

Martes — *martedi*.

Martin pescatore It. a sea-fish, Sp. *martin pescador*, and *paxaro de San Martin*, Sard. *puzone de Santu Martinu*, Fr. *martinet pêcheur* kingfisher, Sp. *martinete* a small white heron, Fr. *martinet* a kind of swallow (E. *martinet*), a *martin*, also a lamp with a handle like a martin's tail, It. *martinetto* a cross-bow windlass; all from the name *Martinus*, v. Grimm, Mythol. 1083, 1233.

Martora It., Sp. Pg. *marta*, Pr. *mart*, Fr. *marte martre*, E. *marten*; from L. *martes* (Martial), *martora martre* taking a G. form *(marder)*.

Marza It. a graft, scion; from *Martius*, the operation of grafting being chiefly performed in that month.

Marzapane It., Sp. *mazapan*, Pg. *mazapão*, Fr. *massepain*, E. *marchpane*, L. L. *marcipanis panis martius*, Neap. *marzapane*, Sic. *marzapanu* a little box (prob. from the shape). *Marchpane* = sweet-bread, macaroon. Some derive it from a man's name *Marci panis* (v. Mahn). The forms without *r* are prob. orig., the *r* being found first in the E. (Sydney 1554—1586, Shakspere &c.). Perhaps from *maza (panis)* Gr. μάζα (prop. what is kneaded, from μάσσειν) barley-bread. *Maza* according to Forcellini = farina hordeacea, vel panis lacte, sero, aut aqua subactus. Ducange: *maza ex farinâ oleo et aqua*. Or is it connected with Sp. *mazar* to churn, knead?

Mas Pr., O. Fr. *mas mes* house, farm, Cat. *mas*; from L. L. *mansus mansum*, from *manere*, whence Pr. *maner*, O. Fr. *manoir*, E. *manor*; Pr. *manen*, O. Fr. *manant* opulent, L. L. *manens colonus*. Hence also Sp. *masa*, Mil. *massa*, O. Fr. *mase* farm, L. L. *mansa massa*; It. *massaro massaio*, O. Fr. *mansiaire* housekeeper, with several more derivatives.

Mas — *mai*.

Masa — *mas.*

Mascar — *masticare.*

Mascarra — *maschera.*

Maschera It., Pied. *mascra*, Sp. Pg. *máscara*, Fr. *masque*, E. *mask* (1) a mask (persona) (2) a masked person. From the Arab. *maskharah* joer, laugh, laugher, object of laughter, buffoon, a man in masquerade, from the root *sakhira* irrisit (v. Mahn). From the same come Wal. *mĕscáré* blot, disgrace, Pg. *mascarra* dark spot, vb. Pg. *mascarrar*, Fr. *mascurer*, *machurer* to blacken. The L. L. *mascus masca*, Fr. *masque*, E. *mask* are shortened forms. Diez, however, considers them the orig. forms, and mentions 2 derivations (1) from *masticare*, Sp. *mascar* (Neap. Gen. *masca* a check), cf. L. *manducus*, (2) O. H. G. *masca* a net, G. *masche* (E. *mesh*), cf. Plin. 12, 14: *persona adjicitur capiti densusve reticulus.*

Masnada — *magione.*

Masque — *maschera.*

Massacrer Fr., O. Fr. *maschacler*, sbst. *massacre*, E. *massacre*, L. L. *massacrium mazacrium.* From G. *metzgern* to butcher, *metzger* a butcher (O. Fr. *massecrier*, cf. Piedm. *massuera* a maimer), this from *metzen* to hew, connected with *meizan* to cut, Goth. *meitan* = L. *metere.* Sk. *mă*, *măd.* L. L. *mazaccara* = *salsutiœ factœ de tritis carnibus intestinorum;* It. *mazzacara* = the entrails of poultry, *mazzachera* = an eel-spear. V. Mahn.

Massaro — *mas.*

Masse massue — *mazza.*

Massima It., Sp. *maxima*, Fr. *maxime*, E. *maxim* (prop. principle); from *maxima* sc. *sententia.*

Masso It. a huge stone; from *massa.*

Masticare It., Wal. *mestecà*, Sp. Pg. *masticar mastigar mascar*, Pr. *mastegar maschar*, Fr. *mâcher*, Rh. *mastiar*, B. *mascatu* to chew, *masticate;* from *masticare* (Apuleius &c. = μασταζειν). Neap. Gen. *masca* = check.

Mastin mastino — *magione.*

Masto mastro Pg., Pr. *mast*, Fr. *mât*, Sp. *mastil muste* mast; from O. H. G. E. *mast*, O. N. *mastr*, A. S. *măst.*

Mastranto mastranzo Sp. wild mint; a corruption of L. *mentastrum* (wild mint, from *menta*), It. *mentastro.*

Mastuerzo — *nasturzio.*

Mât — *masto.*

Mata Sp. (1) copse, thicket, (2) bush; Pg. *mata mato* = (1). Perhaps from Goth. *maitan* to hew, so orig. a cleared place in a forest. Ducange: *ipsum forest vel ipsam matam.* But *mata* also = lock of tangled hair; so from *matassa?*

Matar Sp. Pr. Pg. to kill; from *mactare*. Hence *rematar* to end, *remate* an end.

Matar — *matto*.

Matassa It., Sp. *madexa*, Pr. *madaisa*, O.Fr. *madaise* hank, lock of hair &c., Wal. *metase* silk; from *mataxa* raw-silk, also thread; from L. Gk. μάταξα μέταξα.

Matelas — *materasso*.

Matelot Fr. sailor; from *matta* a mat, *mattarius* one who sleeps on mats, *matelot* for *materot*, as *matelas* for *materas;* or from Du. *maat*, E. *mate*, but this is doubtful as the simple word is not found in Fr.

Materasso It., Fr. *materas matelas* (E. *mattrass*), Pr. *almatrac*, Sp. Pg. *almadraque*. From Ar. *al-ma'tra'h*. Hence Pg. *madraço* a sluggard? cf. *poltro*.

Matin — *mane*.

Mâtin — *magione*.

Matiz Sp. m. shading, shade (of colours), vb. *matizar* to shade; from *mata* a bush, cf. It. *macchia* (1) bush (2) shading.

Matois Fr. sly, cunning. Cf. *enfant de la mate*, the *mate* being a place in Paris, where thieves used to congregate.

Matraca Sp. Pg., hence It. *matracca* rattle; from Ar. *mi'traqah*, hammer, rattle.

Matras O. Fr., Pr. *matratz matrat* a missile weapon, O. Fr. *matrasser*, Pr. *matrasseiar* to crush; from Gallic L. *matara* (Cæsar), (*mataris* Livy), with suffix *as*, v. Zeuss 1, 97.

Mattino — *mane*.

Matto It., Sp. Pg. *mate*, Fr. *mat*, E. *mate*, Pr. O. Fr. also = sad, cast-down, G. *matt* languid; shortened from *scaccomatto*, Sp. *xaquimate*, Fr. *échec et mat*, E. *check-mate;* from the Pers. *shâh mât* "the king is dead". Cf. It. *mattare*, Pr. *matar*, Fr. *mater* to *mate*, to make feeble, humble, O. Fr. *amatir*.

Matto It. silly. From L. *mattus* or *matus* (Petron. *plane matus sum, vinum mihi in cerebrum abiit*) = Sansk. *matta* drunk, from *mad* lætari, inebriari, cf. Gk. ματᾶν μάταιος, E. mad &c.

Matto It. boy, *matta* girl, espec. in Northern Italy and Rhætia; from O. H. G. *magat*, M. H. G. *maget* f. (G. *magd*).

Mattone It., Fr. (prov.) *maton* brick, Cat. *mato* cream-cheese. From G. *matz matte* curds, cheese, Pic. *matte*, a brick being shaped like a cream-cheese, cf. O. Fr. *maton* (1) brick (2) cheese-cake.

Mauca Pr., Cat. *moca* belly; Sw. *mauck* a-fat person, Du. *moocke* belly.

Maufé O. Fr. a name of the devil; from *male factus*, It. *malfatto*, cf. Neap. *bruttofatto* (ugly) = demonio. Wal. *cowe* = caudatus.

Maussade — *sade*.

Mauvais — *malvagio.*

Mauvis Fr. (m. O. Fr. f.) a beccafico, turdus iliacus, E. *mavis.*
Sometimes derived from *malum vitis,* cf. Fr. *grive de vendange,*
G. *weingartsvogel, weindrossel.* It is of Celtic origin, like so
many other names of birds (v. *allodola*), Bret. *milfid milvid,
milc'houid;* Corn. *mel-huez* == lark (*mel huez* sweet breath).
From *mauvis* comes *mauviette* a lark, Rou. *mauviard* turdus
merula.

Mayota Sp. strawberry; prop. May-fruit from *majus;* cf. Mil.
magiostra, Lang. *majoufo.*

Mazette Fr. a poor mare, a jade; from G. *matz* awkward.

Masmorra Sp. Pg. a dungeon; from Ar. *ma'lmirah* a pit, cave.

Massa It., Sp. Pg. *maza,* Pr. *massa,* Fr. *masse,* E. *mace;* It.
mazzo, Sp. *mazo* a mallet, bundle; vb. It. *mazzare* (in *mazza-
sette* &c., Com. *mazà*), Rh. Sp. *mazar,* Pr. *massar* to cudgel,
knock down, It. *ammazzare;* O. Pg. *massuca massua,* Fr.
massue, Pic. *machuque* a club, N. Gr. ματζοῦχα, Wal. *meciucè.
Mazza* is from a L. *matea* (cf. *piazza* from *platea*), whence
mateola a mallet in Cato de Re Rust., It. *mazzuola,* Pr. *mas-
sola.* For similar lost L. primitives, cf. *bubone, claie.*

Mear Sp., Pg. *mijar,* from *meiere,* changed to 1ˢᵗ conjugation.

Mecer Sp. to stir, rock; from *miscere,* Pg. *mexer,* It. *mescere.*

Mecha mèche — *miccia.*

Méchant Fr., O. Fr. *mes-cheant,* partic. from *mes-cheoir (minus
cadere),* abst. O. Fr. *mescheance,* E. *mischance.* Cf. O.Sp. *mal-
caido* unfortunate.

Méchef — *menoscabo.*

Meda megano — *meta.*

Medaglia It., Sp. *metalla,* Fr. *médaille,* E. *medal;* augm. *meda-
glione* &c. L. L. *medalia* = half a denarius, the same word
as O. Pg. *mealha,* O. Sp. *meaja,* Pr. *mealha,* Fr. *maille.* Like
so many Rom. substantives, from an adj. in -*eus, metalleus
metallea,* Sp. *metalla* gold-leaf, cf. also Fr. *métail* for *métal,*
Pr. *metalh.*

Medes O. Pg. Galic., Pr. *medeis meteis medeps;* from *met-ipse
met-ipsum.* Hence a superlative form, Pr. *smetessme, medesme,*
O. Fr. *meïsme,* Fr. *même,* O.Sp. *meismo,* Sp. *mismo,* Pg. *mesmo,*
It. *medesimo,* Rh. *medem,* Wald. *meseyme,* from a Lat. *semet-
ipsimus* for *semetipsissimus,* v. R. Gr. 2, 421.

Media Sp., Pg. *meia* a stocking; prop. *media calza.*

Medrar Sp. Pg. to improve; for *meldrar* from *meliorare.*

Mege menge O. Sp., O. Pg. *mege,* Pr. *metge,* O. Fr. *mege* (Lim.
medze) a physician; from *medicus.* Hence O. Sp. *mengia* medicine.

Mégie Fr., *mégissier* (which supposes a form *mégis mégisse,* cf.
tapissier from *tapis, saucissier* from *saucisse*) leather-dressing,

leather-dresser. The Du. *meuk* softening would give Fr. *mé-guie*, cf. Pic. *méguichier* = Fr. *mégissier*.

Mego Sp., Pg. *meigo* soft, mild. From O. N. *makr* quiet, calm, E. *meek*, O. H. G. *gi-mah*, or, better, from *mitigatus*, cf. *santiguar* from *sanctificare*, and *cuerdo* from *cordatus*.

Mégue Fr. (f.) whey (Pic. *mègre*); from *maigre*, or from the Celtic, Gael. *meog*, W. *maidh*. L. L. has *mesga*, N. Pr. *mergue* whey, Wall. *mésgé* soft.

Méhaing — *magagua*.

Meiminho — *mimo*.

Mélange mêler — *mischiare*.

Melarancia — *arancio*.

Meliaca muliaca It. apricot; from *armeniaca*.

Mellizo Sp. twin; from a form *gemellicius (gemellus)*.

Melma It. mud; from O. H. G. *melm* dust, Goth. *malma*.

Melo It. apple-tree; from *malus*, the *e* being to distinguish it from *malum* (bad), cf. Gk. μῆλον.

Melsa — *melza*.

Membrare It., O. Sp. Pr. *membrar*, O. Fr. *membrer*, O. Sp. Pg. Pr. *nembrar*, Pg. *lembrar*, Lang. *lembrá* (E. *re- member*); from *memorare*, whence also adj. *membrado*, *membrat*, *membré* prudent, learned.

Même — *medes*.

Mena — *menare*.

Menace — *minaccia*.

Ménage Fr., vb. *ménager;* for *mesnage*, L. L. *mansionaticum*, v. *masnada*.

Menare It., O. Sp. Pr. Cat. *menar*, Fr. *mener* to lead, abst. It. Pr. *mena*. Diez derives it from a L. L. *minare* to drive with threats *(minari)* Apuleius: *asinos minantes baculis; agasones equos agentes i. e. minantes* Paulus ex Festo; cf. Wal. *menà* to drive, Papias: *minare = ducere de loco ad locum*, so *prominare* (Apuleius) = O. Fr. *se pourmener*, Fr. *se promener*, whence the Italianized *promenade* for O. Fr. *pourmenoir*. Others point to the O. Fr. *mainer* and derive from *manus*, cf. *menottes* handcuffs; hence Fr. *demener* to move about, conduct, E. *demean*, *demeanour*, cf. sq.

Menear Sp. Pg. to move from place to place, manage; from *manus* (for *manear*) It. *maneggiare*, Fr. *manier*, E. *manage*.

Menester menestral ménétrier — *mestiero*.

Menguar — *menovare*.

Ménil Fr. a farm-house; for *maisnil (mansionile)*.

Menino — *mina*.

Menno It. castratus; from *minimus?*

Menoscabo Sp. Pg., O. Pg. *mazcabo*, Pr. *mescap*, Fr. *méchef*,
E. *mischief;* from *cabo* end, *caput;* vb. *menoscabar, mescabar,*
O. Fr. *meschever (mescaver),* E. *mischieve.*

Menotte Fr. handcuff; from *main (manus),* cf. It. *manetta,* v. *menare.*

Menovare It., Sp. *menguar,* Pg. *mingoar,* Pr. *minuar,* Cat. *minvar,*
Fr. *di-minuer* to diminish; Sp. *mengua,* Pg. *mingoa* decay.
From *minuere* altered to the 1st conjug., L.L. *minuare.* In Sp.
menguar, ua becomes *gua* as if it had been a G. *wa,* cf. *mangual* from *manualis.*

Mensonge — *menzogna.*

Mentar Sp. Pg., O. Fr. *menter* to mention (orig. a abst.); It. *ammentare rammentare,* O. Pg. *amentar;* from *mens, ammentare*
being, probably, the oldest derivative. Pr. *mentaure amentaver,* O.Fr. *mentoivre mentevoir, amentoivre amentevoir, ramentevoir* (Molière), from *mente, ad mentem habere,* It. *avere a mente,* the orig. meaning "to think of" having passed into a
factitive one "to mention" cf. R. Gr. 3, 103. From *mentevoir*
comes, probably, the It. *mentovare.* Hence also It. *dementare,*
Sp. *dementar* to make mad, *demented,* O. Fr. *dementer* to rant,
dementare (Lactantius); It. *dimenticare* to forget.

Mente It. Sp. Pg. (O. Sp. *mientre*), Pr. *men,* Fr. *ment* adverbial
suffix added to the feminine adjective, v.It. Gr. 2, 382. From
the Lat. *mente,* cf. *bona, placida, devota, celeri mente,* hence
gradually assuming a wider meaning, *breve-mente, perfettamente, attra-mente,* cf. M. H. G. *ahte* (1) mind, intention
(2) kind, manner. In Sp. we find such expressions as *bella y
sutilmente,* in Pr. *sanctament e devota,* O. Cat. *fellonament et
desordenada.*

Mentira — *menzogna.*

Mentoivre — *mentar.*

Mentovare — *mentar.*

Mentre It. Pr. O. Fr., Sp. *mientras,* O. Sp. *mientre,* O. Pg. *mentres* = L. *dum,* interim or intra; O. It. *domentre,* Sp. *demientras,* Pr. *domentre dementre,* O. Fr. *dementre dementres, endementres,* O. Pg. *emmentres* &c. Muratori considers *domentre*
the orig. form and derives it from *dum interim,* the interchange
of *do* and *de* being also found in *domani domandare.* Others,
from the O. Ven. *domente,* Gen. *demente* take the derivation
dum mente. The O. Fr. *dementiers dementieres* seems to be from
dum interea, O. Fr. *entremente* from *interea mente,* but Piedm.
tramantre reproduces the *r.* Pott Forsch. 2, 100 makes *mentre*
from *in inter,* cf. Ven. *mintro (= infino).* O. It. *introeque* Inf.
20, 130 = *inter hoc* with euphonic suffix.

Menu menuet — *minuzzare.*

Menuiser — *minuzzare.*

Menzogna It., Pr. *mensonga mensonja*, Fr. *mensonge*. From *mentitio*, Pr. *mentizó*, formed on the analogy of the word which it replaced, *calogna calonja chalonge (calumnia)*. The Pr. *mensonega* is from *mentitionica*. The Sp. Pg. *mentira* is for *mentida* (Catal.), cf. *lampara* for *lampada*.

Mercé It., Sp. *merced*, Pg. Pr. *mercé*, Fr. *merci* = E. *mercy* and thanks. From *merces* = mercé in L. L. Hence Pr. *merceiar*, O. Fr. *mercier*, Fr. *remercier*.

Mercoledi mercordi It., Fr. *mercredi*, Pr. *dimercres*, Cat. *dimecres;* from *Mercurii dies*, *dies Mercurii;* Sp. *miercoles*, Pr. *mercres* like *martes (martedi)*, It. also *mércore*, Wal. *miércuri*. It. (prov.) *mez-edima* = *media hebdomas*, Rh. *mez-eamda*, cf. G. *mittwoch*. Pg. has *quarta feira* = N. Gr. τετράδη.

Mercorella marcorella a herb, mercury; from *mercurialis*, Sp. *mercurial* (Fr. *mercoret*).

Mercoredi — *mercoledi*.

Merino Sp., Pg. *meirinho* a circuit-judge, inspector of sheep-walks (hence adj. *merino* moving from pasture to pasture, whence the name of the *merino* sheep); from *majorinus*, v. Ducange.

Merir to pay, recompense; L. L. *suum servitium vult illi merere* Cap. Car. Calv., v. Ducange. In O. Fr. *diex le vos mire*, *mire* = *miere* (conjuctive, as *fiere* from *ferir*).

Merlan Fr. a whiting, O. Fr. *merlenc mellenc*, Rou. *merlen merlin*, Bret. *marlouan*, Du. *molenaar*.

Merlin Fr. = Du. *marlijn, meerling*, E. *marline*, vb. Du. *marlen*, E. *marl*.

Merlo merla It., whence Sp. *merlon*, Pg. *merlão*, Fr. E. *merlon;* vb. It. *merlare*, Pr. *merlar*. Bolza derives it from a L. *mærus* (for *murus*), whence *mærulus merlo*, but the open *e* does not represent the L. *oe*. Menage refers it to the L. *mina (minula mirula)*. The Sic. has *mergula* a merlon (from *merga* a fork), whence *merla* may be contracted, cf. G. *gabel* a fork = E. *gable*.

Merluzzo It., Pr. *merlus*, Sp. *merluza*, Fr. *merluche* (f.) a cod; from *maris lucius* a sea-pike, cf. Cat. *llus* = *merlus*.

Merme O. Fr. little; from *minimus*, like *arme* from *anima*. Hence Sp. *merma*, Pr. *mermaria* a lessening, Com. *marmaria*, It. *marmaglia* poor folk, Com. *marmel*, Crem. *marmelecn* little finger; vb. Sp. Pr. *mermar* to lessen, decrease.

Merode — *maraud*.

Merrain Fr., Pr. *mairam* staves; from *materiamen*, L. *materia*.

Merveille — *maraviglia*.

Mésange Fr. (f.) a titmouse. A G. word with a Rom. suffix as in *louange, laidenge* &c., and a corruption of the L. G. dim. *meeseke*, Pic. *maisaingue*.

Mesar Sp. to pull out the hair; from *metere messus*, cf. *barbam metere forcipe* (Juvenal).

Meschino It., Sp. *mezquino*, Pr. Fr. *mesquin*, O. Fr. also *meschin* poor, wretched. From Ar. *miskin*, which is from a vb. *sakana* Freyt. 2, 335. In Pr. O. Fr. also ═ feeble, *meschin* ═ boy, *meschine* girl, It. *meschina*, Wall. *meskéne*.

Mesel O. Fr. leprous, O. Sp. *mesyllo* leper; from *misellus*, in L. L. ═ a leper; hence also G. *miselsucht*.

Mesle O. Fr. medlar, *meslier* medlar-tree; from *mespilus*. Hence E. *medlar*, cf. s. *mischiare*.

Messa It., Sp. *misa*, Fr. *messe*, E. *mass*; from the words *missa est concio*, with which the congregation was dismissed.

Mest Pr. prep. for L. inter; from *mixtum*, cf. Dan. *i-blandt* from *blande* (blending), E. *a-mong*.

Mestiero mestiere It., Sp. O. Pg. *menester*, Pg. *mister*, Pr. *menestier mestier*, Fr. *métier* business, trade, craft (E. *mystery*, but v. Marsh, Lectures); from *ministerium*. Hence Sp. Pr. *menestral*, Pg. *menestrel*, O. Fr. *menestrel*, *menestrier ménétrier* artisan, workman, *minstrel*, L. L. *ministerialis* a house-servant (so in O. Fr.). As *mestiere* ═ *opus*, so It. *é* or *fa mestiere*, Sp. *es menester* ═ *opus est*.

Mestizo Sp., Pr. *mestis*, Fr. *métis* a mongrel; from *mixtieius*.

Meta It. a heap of dung, Lomb. *meda* a hay-cock &c., Sard. a heap, Sp. Pg. *meda* a stack of corn, O. Fr. *moie* a heap, E. *mow*; from L. *meta*. Hence Pg. *meddo* a heap, Pg. *medaño médano* a sand-hill (also *megano* cf. s. *camozza*); Sp. *al-mear* (for *al-medar*) a hay stack.

Metà — *mezzo*.

Métairie — *mezzo*.

Métal — *medaglia*.

Métayer — *mezzo*.

Métell Fr. meslin, mixed corn; ═ *mixturdum (mixtum)*.

Métier — *mestiero*.

Métis — *mestizo*.

Metralla — *mitraille*.

Mets Fr. (O. Fr. *mes*), E. *mess*; from *missura* that which is served up, It. *messo*; cf. *minestra*. *Mets* has taken the *t* of *mettere*.

Mettere It. &c. to put. From *mittere* to send, in later L. ═ ponere, cf. Seneca *manus ad arma mittere*, Lactantius *fundamenta mittere*. The L. sense is preserved in derivatives.

Meugler — *mugghiare*.

Meule Fr. (prov. *mule*) a heap of hay, corn, or dung, hence *mulon*, L. L. *mullo*, Rou. vb. *muler*. From *metula* dim. of *meta*, cf. O. Fr. *seule* from *saeculum*, *reule* rule from *regula*. Pic. *moie* ═ *meta*.

Meunier — *molino*.

Meurtre Fr., O. Fr. *meurdre mordre*, murder, vb. *meurtrir* to crush, O. Fr. *mordrir* to murder; from Goth. *maurthr*, G. *mord*, E. *murder*, vb. Goth. *maurthrjan*, O. H. G. *murdjan*. Com. *mórdar* = wicked, O. H. G. *murdreo* thief, *mord* crime, Rh. *morder* = G. *mörder* a murderer.

Meute O. Fr. = *motus*, rising, insurrection, Fr. G. *meute* = a pack of hounds. From *morere* (cf. *émeute* from *émouvoir*) through an old partic. *moritus*, cf. Sard. *movida* = It. *mossa*. From *meute* come *mutin* a *mutineer*, Sp. *motin mutiny*, Fr. *mutiner*, Sp. *amotinar*, It. *ammutinare* to cause to *mutiny*.

Mesclar — *mischiare*.

Mezzo It., Wal. *mez*, Sp. *medio*, Pg. *meio*, Pr. *mieg*, from *medius*; Fr. *parmi* = It. *per mezzo*, Pr. *enmiei*, O. Fr. *enmi* = It. *in mezzo*. Hence It. *mezzano*, Sp. *mediano*, Pr. *meian* (E. *mean*), Fr. *moyen* from *medianus*, whence also O. Fr. *menel*, Fr. *meneau*, O. E. *munial, moynal, moynel, monion, munion, mullion* prop. = qui est au milieu, the slender pier which forms the division between the lights of windows; It. *metà*, Sp. *mitad*, Pr. *meitad*, Fr. *moitié*, E. *moiety* from *medietas* (Cicero), hence Fr. *métayer*, N. Pr. *meytadier* a farmer who gives half the produce of his farm *(métairie)* to the owner, L. L. *medietarins*. The O. Fr. *mitan* a tenant-farmer, Fr. *mitaine*, E. *mitten* (half-glove) are rather from the G. *mitte* (O. H. G. *mittamo*). From It. *mezzana* come Fr. *misaine*, E. *mizen* (because amidship).

Mezzo It. (with close *e* and sharp *zz*) soft, decayed, withered; from *mitis* through a form *mitius mitjus*, v. *fujo*. Crem. *mizz*, Neap. Gen. *nizzo*, Mil. *nizz*.

Mica miga It. Pr., Fr. *mie* a particle used with negatives; from *mica* a crumb; whence also Wal. *ni-mic* = nihil, Fr. *miche* = a piece of bread.

Miccia It., Sp. Pg. Pr. *mecha*, Pr. also *mecu* (cf. *coca cocha*), Fr. *mèche* (E. *match*) a wick. From *myxa myxus*, Gk. μύξα a lampnozzle, also = a wick. The Fr. word was the original one (cf. *laxus lâche*), whence the other forms were derived.

Micio micia It., Sp. *micho mizo miza miz*, Wal. *metzu metze*, O. Fr. *mite* cat; an onomatop. like G. *mieze*. Hence Fr. *mitou matou* a male cat, Wal. *metoe;* Fr. *chatte-mite* a flatterer, cf. proverb: *si l'une est chate, l'autre est mite* to denote perfect similarity. It. has also *muci mucia muscia*.

Miche — *mica*.

Micmac Fr. trick, roguery; from G. *mischmasch*, E. *mishmash*.

Mielga Sp. a plant, lucern; from *medica*, cf. *julgar* from *judicare*.

Mien, tien, sien Fr. pronouns. From *mi, ti, si* with suffix *en* = L. *anus* as *ancien* from *anz*, cf. G. *meinig* from *mein*.

Miercoles — *mercoledi*.

Mies mies O. Fr., L. L. *mezium* = O.H.G. A.S. *medo*, E. *mead*, G. *meth*, Gr. μέθυ, Sk. *madhu* &c.

Miglio It., Fr. *mille* (m. from the It.), Sp. Pr. f. *milla* = O. H. G. *mila*, G. *meile*, E. *mile*; from *mulia* (passum), It. pl. *miglia*, whence the sing. *miglio*.

Mignard — *mignon*.

Mignatta — *miniare*.

Mignon Fr. neat, delicate, as sbst. darling, whence It. *mignone*, E. *minion*, hence Fr. *mignard*, *mignoter* &c. From O. H. G. *minni* or *minnia* (= *minja*) love, so from the Gael. *min*, v. *mina*.

Migraine migraña — *magrana*.

Milagro Sp., Pg. *milagre* a wonder; a corruption of *miraculum*.

Milano Sp., Pg. *milhano*, Fr. Pr. *milan* kite; from *miluanus*, a derivative from *miluus* (later *milvus*), B. *mirua*. Vb. Sp. *amilanar*, v. *astore*.

Milano and *vilano* Sp. thistle-down, from *villus*, cf. *mimbre*.

Milgrana mingrana O. Sp. pomegranate (thousand-grains).

Milieu Fr. from *medius locus*, cf. It. *miluogo*, Wal. *mijloc*.

Mille — *miglio*.

Milsoudor missoudor O. Fr., Pr. *milsoldor* = *caval misoldor* a valuable war horse; from *caballus mille solidorum*, cf. a poor horse = *bidet de quatre-vingt sous*. For a similar formation cf. O. Fr. *quartenor* = *quatuor annorum*.

Milza It., Sp. *melsa*, N. Pr. *melso*, Dauph. *milza*, Burg. *misse*; from O. H. G. *milzi* (n.), G. *milz*, E. *milt*, cf. Alb. *meltzi* liver, Mil. *nilza*, Rh. *snieulza*, N. Pr. *melco melfo*. Hence It. *smilzo* empty.

Mimar Sp. Pg. to coax, caress, *mimo* caress, adj. *mimoso*; perhaps from *minimus* little, darling, whence It. *mimma* a doll, Pg. *meiminho* little finger.

Mimbre Sp. also *vimbre* osier-twig; from *rimen*, cf. *milano*.

Mimma — *mimar*.

Mina It. Sp. Pg., Pr. *mina meina*, Fr. E. *mine*, Wall. *meinn*; vb. It. *minare*, Sp. Pg. Pr. *minar*, Fr. Wall. *miner*, E. *mine*. Hence O. Sp. *minera*, Pr. *meniera*, Fr. *minière* a mine, whence It. *minerale*, Sp. Pr. E. *mineral*, Fr. *minéral*. From L. *minare* Rom. *menare* to lead, conduct, prepare, L. L. *minare consilium* to prepare a plan, *minas parare* to lay an ambush. Hence *mina* a passage under the walls of a town, passage, *mine*, cf. *doccia* a canal from *ducere*. The *i* for *e* was perhaps to distinguish the meanings. Fr. *mine* = E. *mien*, G. *miene*, also comes from *menare* (Pr. *mena*), like *gestus* from *gerere*; Pr. *se menar* = to behave oneself. But v. s. *menare*.

Mina O. Lim., Gasc. *menina*, Pg. *minino menino*, f. *minima menina*, Sp. *menino menina* boy, girl, N. Pr. *menig* little, Berr. *menit* a child, Norm. *minet minette*; also Fr. *minon minette* a cat, Rou. *minette* a girl, Cat. *minyo* a little boy (cf., however, Fr. *mignon*). From Gael. *min* little.

Minaccia It., Sp. *a-menaza*, Pr. *menassa*, Fr. E. *menace;* from *minaciæ* for *minæ* (Plautus).

Mince Fr. small, fine (whence E. *mince*). From O. H. G. superlative *minnisto* = G. *mindeste*, *mince* for *minse*, as *rincer* for *rinser*.

Minchia It., L. *mentula;* hence *minchione* a dolt, as *pincone* from *pinco*, *coglione* from *coglia*.

Mine Fr., Pr. *mina* a measure; from *hemina*, whence Pr. *emina*, O. Fr. *emine*, Sp. *hemina*.

Minéral — *mina* (1).

Minestra It. soup, pottage, *minestrare* to prepare soup &c.; from *ministrare* to serve, so *minestra* == something served up. Cf. *mets*.

Minette minon — *mina* (2).

Mingherlino — *heingre*.

Miniare It. to paint with vermilion *(minium)* illuminate manuscripts &c., hence to paint in miniature, *miniate.* Hence It. *miniatura*, Fr. E. *miniature.* Menage also derives *mignatta* a leech, from *minium*.

Minugia minugio It. intestines; prop. = anything chopped small (Sp. *menudo);* from *minutia*, L. L. *minutia porcorum*.

Minuto minute — *minuzzare*.

Minuzzare It., Pr. *menuzar*, O. Fr. *menuiser* to make small, *minish;* from a form *minutiare*, from *minutus*, Fr. *menu*, Sp. *menudo*, Pg. *miudo* &c., whence It. Sp. *minuto*, Fr. E. *minute*, prop. *minuto primo* first division; *minuto secondo*, Fr. *seconde*, E. *second* = second division; *minuto terzo*, Fr. *tierce* (f.) the 60th part of a second. Hence Fr. *menuisier* a joiner, and (from Fr. *menu*) *menuet*, E. *minuet* a dance with short steps.

Mirabella It., Sp. *mirabel*, Fr. *mirabelle* a kind of plum; a corruption of *myrobalanum* μυροβάλανος the ben-nut; It. also *mirabolano*, Fr. *myrobalan*.

Mire O. Fr. Norm. a doctor, surgeon: *qui court après le mière, court après la bière* (Dumeril), vb. *mirer* to heal. Perhaps from *medicarius (medicus)*, which would not be so strange a word as *medic-ianus* (whence O. Fr. *medecien*, Fr. *médecin*), cf. *grammaire* from *grammatic-arius (grammaticus)*. Veneroni gives It. *medicaria* == *medecina*.

Miroir Fr., O. Fr. *mireor*, E. *mirror*, Pr. *mirador;* for *miratorium*, Sp. *mirador* a spectator, watch-tower, It. *miradore* a mirror. Another form is found in Pr. *miralh*, It. *miraglio*, Basq. *miraila* == L. *miraculum*.

Mis It., Fr. *mes mé*, Pr. *mes mens*, Sp. Pg. *menos* in comp. = L. *male* or, better, G. E. *mis*, from which, however, it is not derived, but, as shown by the Sp. Pg. from *minus;* e. g. *mis-*

pregiare, mens-, mes-*prezar*, mé*priser*, menos-*preciar*, E. mis-*prize*. The E. *mis* has, thus, a double origin.

Misa — *messa*.

Mischiare It., Sp. Pg. Pr. *mezclar mesclar*, O. Fr. *mesler medler*, E. *meddle*, Fr. *mêler* = L. L. *misculare*, sbst. It. *mischia* &c.; from *miscere*. Hence sbst. Fr. *mêlée*, E. *mellay* (Tennyson), cf. *volley* from *rolée*; Fr. *mélange* f. (O. Fr. m.), Pr. *mesclanha*, cf. *louange*, *laidange*.

Mismo — *medes*.

Mistral — *maestro*.

Mita Sp., Fr. *mite*; from O. H. G. *miza*, A. S. *mite*, E. *mite*.

Mitad — *mezzo*.

Mitaine — *mezzo*.

Mitraille Fr. (whence Sp. *metralla*), small pieces of metal, grape-shot; from O. Fr. *mite*, E. *mite* a small coin, so for *mitaille*.

Mo It., Neap. *mone*, Com. *ammò*, Sard. *moi immoi* (cf. *immo?*), Wal. *amù* : even now, from *modo*; Ven. *mojà* = *modo jam*.

Moccio It. from *mucceus* an adj. from *mucus* (μύξος); hence *mocceca* and *moccicone* a driveller, simpleton; from *mucus muccus* also *smoccare*, Fr. *moucher*, It. *moccolo* candle-end, prop. candle-snuff *(moccolaja)*. Sp. *moco* = mucus and snuff, Piedm. *moch*, N. Pr. *mouc mouquet* snuff.

Mochin mocho — *mozzo*.

Modano modine It., Sp. Pg. *molde*, Pr. *molle*, Fr. *moule*, mould pattern; from *modulus*, whence also It. *modello*, Fr. *modèle*.

Modèle — *modano*.

Moderno It. Sp., Fr. *moderne*, E. *modern*; from *modernus* (Priscian and Cassiodorus) from *modo*, on analogy of *hesternus*, *hodiernus*, *sempiternus*.

Modorra Sp. Pg. drowsiness, adj. *modorro* drowsy, vb. *modorrar* to make drowsy, sbst. *modorria* folly; from Basque *modorra* = stump of a tree; so O. Pg. *modorra* a heap.

Moelle Fr. marrow; for *mcolle*, Pr. *meula*, It. *midolla*, L. *medulla*. Cf. Pg. *joelho* for *jeolho*.

Mofa Sp. Pg. Cat., vb. *mofar* to mock; O. H. G. *mupfen* to wrinkle the nose, jeer = Du. *moppen*, E. *mop*.

Mofletes — *muffare*.

Mofo mofino — *muffo*.

Moggio It., Sp. *moyo*, Pr. *muei*, O. Fr. *moi* (= O. H. G. *mutti* Gloss. Cass.), Fr. *muid* a bushel; from *modius*.

Mogio — *murrio*.

Mogo O. Pg. a boundary-stone, Sp. *mogote* an insulated rock; from B. *muga* a boundary, or is this from Sp. *buega?* Larramendi derives *mogotes* tops of deer's horns, from B. *mocou* a point.

Moho mohino — *muffo*.

Moie — *metà.*

Moignon — *muñon.*

Moineau Fr. sparrow. Not from *moine* (in allusion to the στρουθίον μονάζον of Psalm 101), though we have It. *mouaco,* Sp. *fraile,* Fr. *nonnette,* G. *dompfaffe* used as names of birds. The Norm. is *moisson,* Wall. *mohon,* Cat. *moxú* from L. *musca (muscio),* cf. G. *grasmücke,* Rou. *mouchon,* N. Pr. *mousquet* a small bird, Norm. *moisserou* a finch; Pr. *moizeta,* Cat. *moxeta* a bird of prey. From *moison* came *moisonel moisnel* Fr. *moineau.*

Moire Fr. (f.), O. Fr. *mohère mouaire;* from E. *mohair,* v. Weigand 2, 184.

Mois — *moscio.*

Moisir Fr., Pr. to become mouldy; from *mucere* or *mucescere.*

Moison O. Fr. measure; from *mensio.*

Moisson Fr., Pr. *meissó;* from *messio.*

Moite Fr., O. Fr. *moiste,* E. *moist.* Not from *madidus,* but from *humectus,* cf. Pr. *mec* and Isid. Gloss.: *mactum est, humectum est,* or from *musteus* fresh, new, cf. *udus, ὑγρός,* molle, for the connexion between tender, soft and moist. V. also s. *moscio.*

Moitié — *mezzo.*

Moja It., Fr. *muire* brine, Sp. *murria* an ointment; from *muria.* Hence It. *sala-moja,* Sp. *sal-muera,* Pg. *sal-moura,* Fr. *saumure,* like ἀλμυρίς.

Mojar moje — *molla.*

Mojon Sp., O. Pg. *moiom,* Sard. *mullone* heap, landmark: from *mutilus?*

Molde — *modano.*

Molho — *manojo.*

Molino — *mulino.*

Molla It., Pg. *mola,* Sp. *muelle* (m.) spring, in plur. tongs, Sp. *molla* crumb, calf of the leg; hence It. *molletta,* Sp. *molleta* snuffers, *molledo,* Fr. *mollet* fleshy part of a limb, Sp. *molleja* sweet bread, It. *mollica* crumb &c.; from *mollis* soft, pliant. Also It. adj. *molle* moist, from *mollis* soft, vb. *mollare* to yield, *ammollare* to soak, Pg. Pr. *molhar,* Cat. *mulyar,* Fr. *mouiller,* Sp. *mojar* = *molliare* (cf. *leviare, graviare*); abst. Pg. *molho,* Sp. *moje* sauce. Hence also Sp. *mollera,* Pg. *molleira* crown of the head.

Mollet — *molla.*

Molo It., Sp. *muelle,* Fr. E. *mole* a dam; from *moles.* For Sp. *ll* = *l,* cf. R. Gr. 1, 241.

Molondro — *landra.*

Momer O. Fr. vb., abst. *momerie;* from G. *mummer mummerei,* E. *mummery mummer.* The word is derived from the name of a ghost *mumel,* v. Grimm's Mythol. p. 473.

Mon O. Fr. particle = quite, actually, surely: *c'est mon* it is quite so, Molière Malad. Imag.: *ça-mon ma foi.* From L. *munde,* like It. *pure:* the O. Fr. adj. was *monde* true, certain, masc. *mon mond.*

Monceau — *mucchio.*

Monco — *manco.*

Mondualdo manovaldo O. It. guardian, tutor; from L. L. *mundualdus* = O. H. G. *muntwalt* administrator, cf. G. *anwalt* proxy. *Manovaldo* for *monovaldo* takes its spelling from *mano,* cf. *mainbour.*

Monjole O. Fr. a hill; (1) from *mons Joris* (this should give *monjoi*); (2) *meum gaudium* the name of Charlemagne's sword (this should give *majoie*); (3) *mons gaudii* (in allusion to the hill on which St. Denis was martyred).

Monna It., Sp. Pg. *mona,* N. Pr. *monno,* Br. *mouna* she-ape, Fr. *monnine.* From *madonna* the meaning of which it also bears.

Monocordo It.; then, as if from *manus,* Sp. Pg. *manicordio,* Fr. *manicordion* a *manichord;* cf. μονόχορδον a one-stringed instrument.

Monseigneur monsieur — *signore.*

Montare — *avalange.*

Montero Sp., Pg. *monteiro* huntsman; from *mons.*

Montone It., Pic. *monton,* Ven. *moltone,* Pr. Cat. *moltó,* Pr. O. Sp. *moton,* Fr. *mouton* a wether, sheep (whence *mutton*), L. L. *multo, multones et verveces wideri* in a Glossary of the 8th century. The O. Fr. *molt* vervex, Gael. *mult,* W. *mollt,* Corn. *molz,* Bret. *maout* seems to have no root in the Celtic: so, perhaps, all may come from the L. *mutilus* (others connect the word with *multa* a fine), which der. is strengthened by the N. Pr. *mout,* Com. *mot,* Rh. *mutt* = *mutilus.* Cf. the G. *hammel,* and O. Fr. *castrois.*

Moquer O. Fr., Pr. *mochar,* E. *mock.* From Gk. μωχᾷν. Hence Sp. *mueca* a grimace.

Mora It. a stack of brushwood &c., Sp. *moron* a hill, Fr. *moraine* a heap of stones; cf. Bav. *mur* loose stones, and O. N. *mor,* whence G. *mürbe* brittle.

Morbleu Fr., O. Fr. *morbieu;* euphem. for *mort dieu.*

Morbido morvido It. soft, mellow, tender, effeminate, delicate. From *morbidus,* Sp. *morbido* having both the Lat. and the It. meanings.

Morbiglione morviglione It. measles; from *morbus.*

Morceau Fr., O. Fr. *morcel* (E. *morsel*), Fr. *amorce* bait, vb. *amorcer;* from *morsus,* It. *morsello, c* for *s* as in *percer, rincer, sauce* &c.

Morchia morcia It., Sp. *morga,* Cat. Mil. *morca* = L. *amurca.*

Morcon Sp. black-pudding; from B. *morcoa* bowel.

Mordache Fr. tongs; from *mordax mordacis;* Sp. *mordacilla.*

Morello It., O. Fr. *morel moreau,* Sp. Pg. *moreno* dark-brown; from *morus.* Hence It. Pr. *morella,* Fr. *morelle* night-shade, E. *morel* (cherries), v. *morille.*

Morfire It. to eat gluttonously, *morfia* mouth; from Du. *morfen,* M. H. G. *murpfen* to bite, eat. Hence It. sbst. *smorfia* = a wry face, if not from μορφή.

Morfondre Fr. to catch cold; from *morve fondre,* v. *mormo.*

Morga — *morchia.*

Morgueline — *coq.*

Morille Fr., Pic. *merouille meroule* an edible fungus, Du. *morilje,* E. *morel,* O. H. G. *morhila,* G. *morchel,* Swed. *murkla;* from its dark colour when cooked, v. *morello,* and cf. *merula* a blackbird, with the Pic. form.

Morione It., Sp. *morrion,* O. Sp. *murion,* Pg. *morriào,* O. Fr. *morion,* E. *morion.* Perhaps from Sp. *morra* crown of the head, cf. *moron, morro.*

Mormo Pg., Sp. *muermo,* Pr. *vorma,* Fr. *morve* (f.) (E. *mur*), Sic. *morvu* slime from the nose &c., Sp. Pg. also = glanders. From *morbus,* cf. It. *morviglione* measles, L. L. *morbilli.* Pr. *vorma* may be connected with Fr. *gourme.* From *mormo* comes O. E. *mormal* a gangrene (= morve mal).

Morne Fr., Pr. *morn* dejected, gloomy; from Goth. *maurnan,* O. H. G. *mornèn,* E. *mourn.* Pg. *morno* languid, feeble.

Moron Sp. a hill; from B. *murua* a heap, hill. Hence the city *Moron.*

Morondo Sp. bald; prop. = shaved like a moor. For the suffix *ondo* v. R. Gr. 2, 310.

Morro Sp. a round substance, small rounded rock or stone (Pg. *morro* a round hill), also protuberant lips (B. *muturra*); v. *moron.* Hence Pr. *mor morre,* O. Fr. *mourre* a snout.

Mortajo It., Sp. *mortero,* Pr. Fr. *mortier,* Wal. *mojériu,* E. *mortar;* from *mortarium.*

Mortella myrtle; from *myrtus,* whence also *mirtillo* myrtle-berry.

Mortier — *mortajo.*

Morue Fr. a cod-fish, *gadus morhua,* Prov. Fr. *molue.* From *moruda* as *barbue* from *barbuda barbuta.* Pr. *morut* (f. *moruda*), Sp. *morrudo* = thick-lipped. But, as this is scarcely a distinguishing characteristic of the cod, others connect it with Sp. *morros* = round lumps or collops of the salted fish.

Morueco — *marron.*

Morve morviglione — *mormo.*

Moschetto It., Sp. *mosquete,* Fr. *mousquet,* E. *musket,* O. Fr. *mouschete,* L. L. *muscheta;* orig. a sparrow-hawk, Pr. *mosquet mosqueta,* Fr. *émouchet,* It. *moscardo.* Cf. s. *terzuolo.* The *mosquet* was so called from its speckles *(mouches),* cf. Fr.

moucheter to speckle (Diez). But the A. S. is *mushafoc*, and the origin is more probably Du. *mossche mussche* a sparrow (E. tit-*mouse*).

Moscio It., Sp. *mustio*, Cat. *mox* faded, withered, gloomy, Pr. *mois* sullen, O. Fr. *mois*, Wall. *muss* dejected. From *mucidus (muçdius mustius)*? Cf. *muffo*. Perhaps from the same root come Cat. *mustig* lax, Lim. *mousti*, Rh. *moust*, Lomb. *moisc*, E. *moist* (but .v. *moite*), It. vb. *ammoscire*, Pr. *amosir*.

Moscione It., Ven. *musson*, Romag. *musslen*, Lim. *moustic* a gnat; not from *musca*, but from *mustum (musca cellaris* Linn.), cf. *moscione* also = a winebibber. Isidor has: *bibiones sunt qui in vino nascuntur quos vulgo mustiones a musto appellant.*

Mostacoio It., Sp. *mostacho*, Fr. E. *moustache;* from μύσταξ, Alban. *mustáke.*

Mostarda It. Pg. Pr., Fr. *moutarde*, E. *mustard*, Sp. *mostaza;* from *mustum*, It. *mosto*, *must* being originally used in preparing it.

Mostrenco mostrenca Sp. unowned goods, waifs and strays; from *mostrar*, as the owner, in order to claim them, must point them out.

Motin — *meute.*

Motta It. a sloping bank of earth, Sp. Pg. *mota*, Fr. *motte* clod, O. Fr. *mote*, O. Pg. *mota* raised earthwork for defence, E. *moat.* Of G. origin, Bav. *mott*, Sw. *mutte* a peat-stack, Du. *mot* turf, Fr. *mote* tan. Sp. *mota* knot, loose thread on cloth, from B. *motea* = Du. *moet*, *mot* spot = E. *mote;* Pg. *mouta* bush, cf. It. *macchia.* It. *mota* = *malta* q. v.

Motto It., Sp. Pg. *mote*, Pr. Fr. *mot;* from *mutire* (E. *mutter*), L. L. *muttum* (Cornutus ad Persium).

Mou Fr. lung (of animals); from *mollis*, opp. heart and liver, called in Norm. *le dur.* O. Fr. *mol* = *mollet* calf of the leg. .

Moucher Fr., L. L. *muccare* to wipe the nose; from *mucus muccus.* Hence *mouchoir* &c.

Moue Fr., E. *mow, mowe.* If from the E., it will, prob., be connected with *mouth, mund.* But D. derives the E. from the Fr. and refers it to the Du. *mouwe*, O. H. G. *mauwe* pulpa, then used of a protruding underlip, cf. *faire la moue* = *faire la lippe.*

Mouette Fr., Pic. *mauwe* a mew, sea-gull. Fr. G. *möwe mewe*, O. H. G. *meh*, A. S. *maev*, O. E. *mow*, E. *mew*. It. *mugnajo* is from the Sax. form *meum.*

Moufette — *muffo.*

Moufle moufler — *muffare.*

Mouiller — *molla.*

Moule Fr. muscle. Occ. *muscle*, Cat. *musclo*, O. H. G. *muscla;*

A. S. *muscel*, E. *muscle*. The form *moule* lies between *musculus* and *mutilus*. V. *nicchio*.

Moule — *modano*.

Moulin — *molino*.

Mousquet — *moschetto*.

Mousse Fr., Pr. *mossa*; from O. H. G. *mos*, G. *moos*, E. *moss* (It. Sp. *musco*, Wal. *muschiu* from *muscus*). Hence vb. *mousser*, *émousser*, sbst. *mousseron* (whence *mushroom*), so called because grown in moss.

Mousse — *mozzo*.

Mousse — *mozo*.

Mousseline — *mussolo*.

Mousser mousseron — *mousse*.

Moustache — *mostaccio*.

Moutarde — *mostarda*.

Moutier Fr. church, monastery, O. Fr. *moustier*; from *monasterium*. Lorr. *mote* = *église*.

Mouton — *montone*.

Moyen — *mezzo*.

Moyeu Fr., Pr. *muiol* nave of a wheel; from *modiolus*, cf. *mozzo*.

Moyeu Fr., Pr. *muiol mugol moiol*, Gasc. *mujou* yolk of an egg. From *medium ovi*, Fr. *moyeuf*? Or from *mytilus*, *mutulus* a muscle (*mutulus* cf. *scandula échandole*) which resembles the yolk of an egg in size and colour and is, like it, enclosed in a shell. From *mutulus* would come Pr. *muiol*, Fr. *moyeul*, cf. *crayon* for *creton*. The L. is *vitellus*, It. *tuorlo* (muscle), Sp. *yema* (bud), O. N. *eggia-blomi* (flower). E. *yolk*, *yelk*, G. *ei-gelb* are from the colour.

Moyo — *moggio*.

Mozo Sp. Pg. young (hence It. *mozzo*, Fr. *mousse*); from *mustus* young, fresh, sbst. *mozo* = *mustum*.

Mozzetta — *almussa*.

Mozzo It., Sp. *mocho*, Pr. *mos* (f. *mossa*), Fr. *mousse* maimed, lopped; from Du. *mots*, Sw. *mutz*, Du. vb. *motsen mutsen*, G. *mutzen*. From Fr. *mousse* comes It. *smussare*, *smusso*. Hence Sp. *mochin*. The root is the same as in *mut-ilus* if, indeed, the Sp. *mocho* be not immediately thence, as *cachorro* from *catulus*. Cf. B. *mutila* = a boy.

Mozzo It. nave of a wheel; from *modius* for *modiolus* L. L. *mozolus*. Cf. *moyeu*.

Mucchio It. a heap. Usually derived from *monticulus* (*monticellus* gives Fr. *monceau* a heap), cf. *cochiglia* from *conchylium*. But a L. L. *mutulus* is found and cf. Sp. *mojon*.

Muceta — *almussa*.

Muchacho Sp. a boy; for *mochacho* from *mocho* (*mozzo*).

Mucho Sp., Pg. *miuto*, Bearn. *much*, E. *much*; from *multus*, It. *molto*, cf. R. Gr. 1, 215. Shortened *muy*.

Muoi — *micio*.

Mueca — *moquer*.

Muella — *molla*.

Muelle — *molo*.

Muer Fr., E. *mew* to moult, O. Fr. to change, sbst. *mue*, E. *mew mue* moulting, also = cage, prison; from *mutare*, Pr. *mudar* &c. Fr. *remuer*, Pr. *remudar* from *re-mutare*.

Muffare It. in *camuffare* for *capo-muffare* to muffle the head; from G. E. *muff*, from *mou mouwe* ermine. Hence Fr. *moufle*, L. L. *muffula*, Du. *moffel* a muff, G. vb. *muffeln*, E. *muffle*; Pr. adj. *moflet*, Pic. *mouflu*, Wall. *mofnes* soft, elastic; Fr. *moufler* to puff out the cheeks, Sp. *mofletes* fat cheeks, Rouch. *moflu*.

Muffo It. musty, Com. Romagn. *moff* pale; sbst. It. *muffa*, Pg. *mofo*, Sp. *moho* mould, moss, Fr. *moufette* damp vapour, mephitis; from Du. *muf* musty, G. *muff* mould, vb. *muffen*. Hence also in moral sense Sp. *moho* laziness, *mohino*, Ven. *muffo* peevish, Pg. *mofino* niggardly, cf. G. *faul* = putridus, piger, in Sw. *malus*.

Mufle Fr. snout, muzzle. Cf. G. *muffel* dog with hanging lips, *muffeln* to pout, mumble (*muffle?*), Norm. *moufler* to pout. V. also *muffare*.

Mugavéro It., Sp. *almogarare*, Pg. *almogaure*, O. Cat. *almugaver*, O. Val. *almuguaber*, *almugavar* predatory soldier, partisan; from Ar. *al-mughâvir* a combatant. It. *mugavero* also = a weapon, cf. *partigiana*.

Mugghiare It., Fr. *mugler meugler* to low; L. L. *mugulare* from mugire.

Muggine It., Sp. *mujol mugil*, Pg. *mugem*, Fr. *muge* a mullet; from *mugil*. Fr. *mulet*, E. *mullet* from *mullus*.

Mughetto — *mugue*.

Mugnajo — *mouelle*.

Mugnajo — *molino*.

Mugre Sp. grime, dirt, grease; from *mucor?*

Mugron Sp. shoot of a vine; from *mucro* cf. *pua* = point and shoot. Cat. *mugró* = stalk.

Mugue N. Pr. hyacinth, Fr. *muguet* lily of the valley, It. *mughetto*, *mugherino* may-flower, O. Fr. *musguet*. From *muscus* musk, so = sweet-smelling. Hence also Fr. *muguette*, *noix muguette*, G. *muscat nuss*, E. *nutmeg*, v. Wedgwood.

Muid — *moggio*.

Muir — *mungere*.

Muito — *mucho*.

Mula It., Fr. *mule*, Sp. *mulilla* a slipper; from *mulleus?*

Muladar Sp., Sp. Pg. *muradal* a dust-heap; so called because rubbish was thrown just outside the walls *(muri)*.

Mulato Sp. Pg., Fr. *mulâtre*, E. *mulatto* orig. = a young *mule* (dim.). Engelmann derives it from the Ar. *muwallad* a half-breed.

Mulet — *muggine*.

Muleta Sp. Pg. a crutch, prop. a mule; v. *bordone*.

Mulilla — *mula*.

Mulino It., Sp. *molino*, Pg. *moinho*, Fr. *moulin* mill; from *molina* for *mola* Ammianus Marcell. Hence *mulinaro mugnajo*, Sp. *molinero*, Fr. *meunier;* It. *rimolinare*, Sp. *remolinar*, Pg. *remoinhar*, O. Fr. *remouliner* to whirl round, It. Sp. *remolino*, Pg. *redomoinho (retro)* whirlwind, Sp. *remolino*, O. Fr. *remoulin* a lock of hair in form of a star on a horse's forehead; It. *mulinello* whirlwind. From *re-molere*, *re-moudre* comes Fr. *remous* (m.) *remole* (f.) a whirlpool.

Mulot Fr. a large fieldmouse; from Du. *mul*, A. S. *myl* (= E. *mould*) dust. Cf. Du. *mol*, E. *mole*, perhaps shortened from G. *maulwurf (maul = mul)*, E. *mouldiwarp*. *Meal* is perhaps connected.

Mumiar Moden. = G. *mummeln*, E. *mumble*.

Mummia It., Sp. *momia*, Fr. *momie mumie* (E. *mummy*); from Pers. *mòm*, *mùm* wax, v. Pott in Lassen's Zeitschrift 4, 279. Sp. adj. *momio* lean. The Pers. and Ar. have also *mùmiyà* as the name of a mineral substance.

Muneca — *muñon*.

Mungere mugnere It., Sp. (Arag.) *muir*, Pg. *mungir*, N. Pr. *mouzer*, Wal. *mulge* to milk; from *mulgere*. The usual Sp. word is *ordeñar*, Fr. *traire*, but O. Fr. *mulger*, Pic. *moudre*. Other forms are Lomb. *molg*, Pied. *monse*, Sard. *mulliri*, Rh. *mulger*, Cat. *muñir*. From *mungere* comes It. adj. *munto smunto* emaciated, not from *emunctus*.

Muñir Sp. to summon; from *monere*, Pg. *monir*.

Muñon Sp., Cat. *munyo*, Sic. *mugnuni*, Fr. *moignon* muscle of the arm, brawn, stump of an arm &c.; vb. Com. *mugnà* to mutilate. From Bret. *moñ mouñ* maimed, B. *muñ* yolk of an egg (cf. *torulus*, It. *tuorlo*). Hence Sp. *muñeca* wrist, doll (also *muñeco*), Romag. *mugnac* block, stump.

Mur O. Sp. O. Pg. (m.), Rh. *mieur* (f.) mouse. From *mus muris*. Hence Pr. *murena* or *mureca* (better), N. Pr. *murga* formed like *oca* from *avis;* Pg. *murganho*, Sp. *musgaño* a shrew-mouse. Sp. *morcillo murecillo* muscle, is like *musculus* from *mus*, M. Gk. ποντικός (from μῦς ποντικός).

Mûr Fr., O. Fr. *meur maur* ripe; from *maturus*, Pr. *madur*. Hence E. *demure*, cf. Fr. = discreet *(de mure conduite)*.

Murcho Pg. weak. From *murcidus*.

Murciego O. Sp., Sp. *murciegalo*, Pg. *morcego* a bat; from *mus cæcus*, *mus cæculus*.

Murganho musgaño — *mur*.

Murria — *moja*.

Murrio Sp. melancholy, sbst. *murria;* from *morus* stupid. It. *mogio* may be from *murrio morjo mojo*, cf. *pejus peggyio* &c.

Musaico It., Sp. Pg. *mosaico*, Pr. *mozaic*, Fr. *mosaique* (E. *mosaic*); a corruption of *musivum* (μουσειον), Pr. also *musec*.

Musaraña Sp. Pg. Pr., Fr. *musaragne (museraigne* Rabelais), Rh. *misiroign*, Com. *mus-de-ragn* shrew-mouse; from *mus araneus*.

Musco amusco Sp. brown; *musk*-colour, from *muscus*.

Musco muschio It., Sp. *musco*, Pr. Fr. *musc*, L. L. *muscus*, E. *musk;* from Pers. *muschk*, Ar. *al-misk* whence the more usual Sp. *al-mizcle*, Pg. *almiscar*, Cat. *almesc*.

Museau musel — *muso*.

Muso It. O. Sp., Pr. *mus*, Fr. *museau*, Pr. *mursel* (E. *muzzle*, Gael. *muiseal*); vb. It. *musare*, O. Sp. Pr. *musar*, O. Fr. *muser*, E. *muse* to gape, Fr. *amuser*, E. *amuse* to make to muse, divert. *Muso* is from *morsus* (mouth for bite) as *giuso* from *deorsum deosum;* cf. Pr. from *mursel*. For the sense (to make a mouth, stand with open mouth) cf. G. *maulaffe* and s. *badare*.

Musser Fr. to hide, also *mucer* == Pic. *mucher*, whence Sic. *aumucciare;* Gris. *micciar*. From the M. G. *sich muzen*, G. *sich maussen* to hide like a mouse, L. *mus*, G. *maus*, which is from Sk. *mush* to steal.

Mussolo mussolino It., Sp. *muselina*, Fr. *mousseline*, E. *muslin;* from *Mausil* or *Mosul* a city in Mesopotamia where the fabric was first made.

Mustio — *moscio*.

Mutin — *meute*.

N.

Na — *donno*.

Nabisso — *abisso*.

Nabot Fr. a dwarf. Perhaps from O. N. *nabbi* (E. *knob*).

Nacar — *nacchera*.

Nacchera gnacchera It., Sp. *nacara*, Fr. *nacre*, O. Fr. *nacaire*, M. Sp. *nacar*, It. *naccaro* mother of pearl, pearl-oyster shell, It. O. Fr. also cymbal, castanet, Pr. *necari;* an oriental word, Kurd. *nakara* (Sk. *nakhara* a nail?). V. Pott, Höfer's Zeitschr. 2, 354.

Nacelle Fr. a little boat; from *navicella*.

Nache — *natica*.

Nacre — *nacchera.*

Nada Sp. Pg., Occ. *nado* = L. *nihil.* From res *nata*, O. Fr. *riens née*, cf. It. *nulla* for *nulla cosa*, once commonly used with *non* whence its negative force, cf. *rien* &c. Sp. *nadie*, O. Sp. *nadi* = *nemo*, to the plur. form (cf. O. Sp. *essi* for *esso* &c.) from *nado.* The Gasc. has *nat* fem. *nada.* Sp. Pg. *nonada* (f.) a trifle = *non-nihil.*

Nage Fr. in phrase *être en naye* to swent = *être en age*, *age* = un old form of *eau* q. v.

Nager Fr. to swim, O. Fr. also to sail; from *navicare.*

Naguela O. Sp. hut; from *magalia magaila maguela*, n for m, cf. *nappe.*

Naibo — *naipe.*

Naie O. Fr. = O. N. *nei*, G. *né*, E. *nay.*

Naïf Fr. natural, artless, ingenuous, *natif* native; from *nativus*, It. *nativo natio* natural. *Naïf* also = foolish, cf. silly, innocent, simple &c.

Naipe Sp. Pg. (m.), It. *naibo* a playing-card; from the initials of the inventor Nicolao Pepin, or, according to Mahn, from the Arabic *naib* a representative, the four suits (spade, coppe, donari, bastoni) being representatives of the four classes of warriors, priests, merchants and labourers?

Nalga — *natica.*

Nans (pl.) O. Fr. pledges, furniture, also *namps*, L. L. *namium*, hence *nantir* to give a pledge, *nantissement* security; from O. N. *nâm* seizure, M. H. G. *nâm* (G. *nehmen* to take) cf. Sp. Pg. *prenda* from *prendere.*

Nappe Fr. tablecloth (E. *napkin*, *napron* = *apron*), from *mappa* (cf. *naguela*). Only in the Fr.; Sp. has *manteles*, the It. *tovaglia*, but Piedm. *mapa*, Neap. *mappina* a towel.

Naranja — *arancio.*

Narguer Fr. to mock; = *naricare.* Sbst. L. L. *nario* subsannans, whence O. H. G. *narro*, G. *narr* a fop, Com. *nar*, cf. Basq. *narra* foppish. Ron. *naquer* to smell is for *narquer.* *Narquois* sneering is from *narquois* slang (prop. nasal, sneering talk) with same suffix as *pat-ois*, *clerqu-ois.*

Narquois — *narguer.*

Narria Sp. sledge; from B. *narra.*

Nasitort — *nasturzio.*

Naspo — *aspo.*

Nastro It. ribbon, Com. *nastola*, Wall. *ndle;* from O. H. G. *nestila*, G. *nestel* band.

Nasturzio It. &c., L. *nasturtium*, Ven. *nastruzzo*, Fr. *nasitort*, N. Pr. *nastocen*, Sp. *mastuerzo*, Pg. *mastruço*, Sic. *mastrozzu*, Sard. *martuzzu.* Piedm. *bistorce*, L. *nasturtium* = *nasitortium* *quasi a naso torquendo.* Cat. is *morritort (morro* = nose). It. also *crescione*, Sp. *berro.*

Nata Sp. Pg. Cat. cream. Plin. 28, 9. quod *supernatat*, butyrum est. It should have a *d*, but it might then have been confused with *nada* nought.

Natica It., Sp. *nalga*, Pr. *nagga*, O. Fr. *nache nage* buttock, L. L. *natica;* from *natis*, as *cutica* from *cutis, anca* from *avis* (v. *oca*).

Natte Fr. a mat, O. Fr. *nate;* from *matta* L. L. Hence also Du. *natte*, It. *matta.* Cf. *nappe.*

Nauclero — *nocchiero.*

Naut Pr. high, sbst. *nauteza;* from *in alto*, cf. Wal. *nalt* and *inalt*, and *ninferno.*

Nava Sp. Pg. a plain. A pure Basque word found in *Nararre.*

Navaja Sp., Pg. *navalha* razor; from *novacula.*

Naverare It. in *innaverare inarerare* to bore, wound, Pr. Cat. *nafrar*, Fr. *navrer* (espec. in metaph. to break the heart); sbst. Pr. *nafra*, Norm. *narre* a wound; from O. H. G. *nabagér*, G. *näber*, Du. *neviger neffiger*, N. *nafar* an auger.

Navot Fr. a turnip; from *napus*, It. *navone.*

Naviglio navillo navile It., Pr. *navili*, O. Fr. *navile (navilie)*, Fr. *navire* (cf. *concire* from *consilium, Basire* from *Basilius*), O. Fr. also *navirie* f. *Navile* from *navis*, as *civilis* from *civis.*

Navio Sp. Pg. a large ship; from *narigium*, Pr. *navigi navei. Navio* in the Gipsy language = body, cf. It. *cassero.*

Navire — *narilio.*

Ne Fr. from O. Fr. *non. Nenni* = O. Fr. *nen-il* = Pr. *non il* = *non illud*, v. *oui* and R. Gr. 2, 401.

Ne — *indi.*

Néanmoins néant - *niente.*

Nebli Sp., Pg. *nebri* a falcon, Ar. *nabli.* Perhaps from Ar. *nabl* arrow or *nabil* noble.

Nec — *nido.*

Nedoo — *netto.*

Neol — *niello.*

Néfle — *nespola.*

Nogaça — *añagaza.*

Negare Ven. (Mil. Gen. *negá*), Pr. *negar*, Fr. *noyer*, Rh. *nagar* to drown; from *necare* which in L. L. has the Rom. meaning. Cf. E. *starve* from *sterben.* It. has *annegare*, Sp. Pg. *anegar* from *enecare*, Wal. *innecà.* The Sansk. *naç (= neco)* has also the special sense of perishing by drowning.

Negromante nigromante It., Sp. Pg. *nigromante*, Wald. *nigromant*, Pr. *nigromanciá*, Fr. *necromancien*, E. *necromancer;* It. *negromancia*, Pr. *nigromansia*, O. Fr. *nigremance, ingremance*

&c.; from νεκρόμαντις, νεκρομαντεία. The form with *i* points to *niger*, cf. Sp. *magia nagra (= nigromancia)* black art.

Neguilla — *niello.*

Neige Fr. snow, from adj. *niveus nivea;* O.Fr. *neif,* Pr. *neu* from *nix nivis.*

Nels — *nessuno.*

Neleit neleg Pr. fault, mistake; from sbst. *neglectus.*

Nema Sp. a seal; from νῆμα thread, on which, when wrapped round the letter, the seal was placed.

Nomon Sp. hand of a sun-dial; from *gnomon.*

Nemps Pr. adv. from L. *nimis.*

Nenhum — *niuno.*

Nenhures Pg. adv. for L. *nusquam;* from *nec ubi* as *nenhum* from *nec unus.* Cf. *algures.*

Nenni — *ne.*

Neo It. mole; from *nævus.*

Nervio Sp., Cat. *nirvi,* Pr. *nerri* nerve, Sp. *nervioso,* Cat. *nirrios.* Pr. *nervios* nervous; from *nervium (νευρίον)* used by Varro and Petronius.

Nesga Sp. Pg. gore, gusset; from *nexus.*

Nespera — *nespola.*

Nespola It., Sp. Pg. *nespera,* Cat. *nespla,* Fr. *nèfle (f = p)* a medlar *(= meslar);* from *mespilum,* with the common change of *m* to *n,* cf. *nappe* &c. O.Sp. has *mespero,* B. *mizpira,* Wall. *mess.*

Nessuno It., O. It. *nissuno,* Pr. *neis-un,* O. Fr. *nes-un nis-un* = L. *nullus.* From Pr. *neis,* O. Fr. *neis nis,* from *ne ipsum,* and *un unus,* so = not even one.

Netto It., Sp. *neto,* Pg. *nedeo,* Pr. Fr. *net* clear pure; from *nitidus.*

Nials — *nido.*

Nibbio It. kite, Dauph. *nibla;* from *milvus milvius, m* passing into *n, v* into *b.*

Nicchio It. oyster; from *mytilus,* or *mitulus,* as *secchia* from *situla, vecchio* from *vetulus, n* for *m* as in *nespola* &c. In the fem. we have It. *nicchia,* Fr. E. *niche,* whence Sp. Pg. *nicho,* G. *nische.* Hence It. vb. *rannicchiare* to shrink in like a muscle, *se recoquiller* to crouch.

Nice Fr. fool; from *nescius,* Pr. *nesci,* Sp. *necio.* For E. *nice,* v. *nido.*

Niche — *nicchio.*

Niche — *nique.*

Nicher Fr. to nestle, O. Fr. *niger nigier;* from *nidificare, de (nidfcare nidcare)* = both *ch* and *g.* N. Pr. *nisa* from *nis = nidus.*

Nichetto niccolino It. a precious stone; from *onyx onychis,* Sp. *onique,* Cat. *oniquel.*

Nicho — *nicchio.*

Nido It. Sp., Fr. *nid,* Pr. *niu nieu,* Rh. *ignieu* nest, from *nidus;*

It. *nidio*, from *nidulus nid'lus;* Pg. *ninho*, Com. *nin* from dim. *nidimus.* Hence also It. *nidiace* nestling, dolt, Fr. *niais*, E. *nice* (or = Fr. *nice*), *nias*, = a L. *nidax*. The Pr. *niaic* is formed with the suffix *ac*, so too, probably, with suffix *eg*, the Sp. *niego* (for *nidego*), Pg. *ninhego*. From the Sp. comes Pr. *nec*, whence Fr. *nigaud*.

Nièce Fr., E. *niece*. L. *neptis*, to give it a more decided f. aspect, became *nepta* in Rom., Pr. *nepta*, Sp. *nieta*, Pg. Cat. *neta*. The Fr. took a form *neptia*, *nièce*, Pr. *netsa*, It. *nezza* (rare). From the m. *nepos* come f. *nepota*, Pr. Cat. *neboda*, Wal. *nepoate*.

Niego — *nido*.

Niello It., Sp. Pr. *niel*, O. Fr. *neel*, Fr. *nielle* (m.) dark inlaid work, enamel on gold or silver, L.L. *nigellum;* vb. It. *niellare*, Sp. Pr. *nielar*, O. Fr. *noeler*, E. *anneal*, L. L. *nigellare;* from L. dim. *nigellus*. Hence also It. *nigella*, Sp. *neguilla*, Fr. *nielle* (f.) smut, blight, in Fr. and Sp. also = fennel-flower.

Niente It., Pr. *neien nien*, Fr. *néant* = L. nihil; from *ens entis* with negative prefix *ne* or *nec*. Hence Fr. *néanmoins* = It. *niente dimeno*.

Niffa niffo niffolo It. (Flor.), Rh. *gniff* beak, Pr. *nefa;* from ? *A. S. E. Du. *neb*, L. G. *nibbe nif*, O. N. *nebbi nef*. Hence Lim. ? *niflà*, Pie. *nifler*, Fr. *renifler* to sniff, Rou. *niflete* snuffler, Lim. *niflo* nostril, Sw. *niffen* to turn up the nose, Bav. *niffeln*, Piedm. *nufiè* = G. *s-nüffeln*, E. *snuffle*.

Nigaud — *nido*.

Nimo It. (Prov.), Sard. *nemus* (cf. *cummegus* = con meco), Wal. *nime nimenea* nobody, from *nemo*.

Ninferno — *abrigo*.

Ninguem Pg. nobody; from *nec quem*.

Ninguno — *nimo*.

Ninho ninhego — *nido*.

Ninno ninna It., Sp. *niño niña* a child, infant. It. *ninna nanna* (also in Sp. and Pg.) = a lullaby, It. *ninnare* to rock to sleep with a lullaby, N. Pr. *ninà* to go to sleep. Lomb. *nana* = child and cradle (Fl. *andare a nanna* to go to bed), Sp. *hacer la nana* to sleep, Sp. *nana* also = nurse, mother; Cat. *nen nena* infant, Ven. *nena* nurse, Lim. *naina* cradle. Words of the nursery are very primitive, and with the series under review may be compared νύννιον = a lullaby (Hesychius). For forms like *ninna-nanna* cf. Lomb. *ginna-gianna* a child's game, *litta-latta* swing. Like χόρη and L. *pupilla* so Sp. *niña*, Cat. Pr. *nina* = the pupil of the eye; cf. Pg. *menina*, Ven. *putina*, Romag. *bamben*, Sic. *vavaredda* (from *vara* v. *bara*), Pie. *papare*, Pr. *anha* the pupil = prop. little lamb.

Nippe Fr. (only in plur.) ornaments, apparel, *nipper* to fit out; from Du. *nijpen*, E. *nippers*, *nip*.

Nique Fr. in *faire la nique* to nod at, laugh at, jeer; from G. *nicken* to nod. So also *faire une niche* to play a trick.

Nitrire It. to neigh; from *hinnitus (hinnitrus), anitrire* from *adhinnire.*

Niuno It., Sp. *ninguno*, Pg. *nenhum*, Pr. *negun nengun neun*, Wal. *nici un*, = *nec unus*, in Wal. *neque unus*. In O. It. *neuno*, O. Sp. *nenguno*, O. Pg. *neun*, Cat. *ningú*, Rh. *nayin*, Com. *negun nigun*. O. Fr. *nun*, Champ. *nune part* = *nulle part;* from *ne unus.*

Niveau nivel — *libello.*

Nocca It. knuckle; from M. H. G. *knoche*, G. *knochen.*

Nocchiere It., Sp. *nauclero*, O. Sp. *naochero nauchel*, Pr. *naucler nauchier*, Fr. *nocher* pilot, ferryman; from *nauclerus (ναύκληϱος)* used by Plautus.

Nocchio It. kernel, knot; from *nucleus*, Sp. *nucleo.*

Nocher — *nocchiere.*

Noël Fr. Christmas, from *natalis*, Pr. O. Sp. *nadal*, for *naël* as *poële* for *paële* R. Gr. 1, 164.

Noer — *notare.*

Noise Fr., Pr. *nausa*, Cat. *nosa* quarrel, bustle, *noise*. From *nausea* disgust, vexation, or, better, from *noxa.*

Noja It., Sp. *enojo enoyo*, Pg. *nojo*, Pr. *enuei enoi*, Fr. *ennui;* vb. It. *nojare* &c., E. *annoy*. From *in odio* in the phrase *est mihi in odio*, cf. It. *bajo*, Sp. *bayo*, Pr. *bai* from *badius*. The O. Ven. has: *plu te sont a inodio* = It. *più ti sono a noja*. Cf. It. *nabisso, ninferno, ingordo.*

Nolo naulo It. whence *nauleggio*, Fr. *nolis*, O. Sp. *nolit* freight; vb. *noleggiare*, Fr. *noliser;* from *naulum.*

Nomble Fr. (f.) haunch of venison; from *lumbulus*. V. Pott. Etym. Forsch. 2, 100.

Nombre Sp. name, O. Sp. *nomne;* from *nomen*, cf. *hombre.*

Nombril — *ombelico.*

Nonada — *nada.*

Nonnain — *nonno.*

Nonno It. grandfather, *nonna* grandmother, Pr. *nona*, Fr. *nonne nonnain* = E. *nun*, Lorr. *nonnon*, N. Pr. *nounnoun* uncle; from L. L. *nonnus nonna* (Hieronym.). Fr. *nonnain* is from an acc. *nonnam*, as *putain* from *putam*. Sp. *ñoño* = decrepit.

Norabuena — *ora* (1).

Nord Fr., whence It. Sp. *norte;* from A. S. *nordh*, E. *north.*

Norvis O. Fr. Norwegian, from the name of the people *Norvegr*, also = proud, insolent. From the Fr. Normans we have *réponse normande* = equivocal, ambiguous answer.

Nosche O. Fr. (also *nusche*), Pr. *noscla* buckle; from O. H. G. *nusca.*

Notare It., O. Fr. *noer*, Rh. *nudar*, Wal. *iu-notà* to swim; *o* for *a*, hence It. diphthong in pres. *nuoto*.

Nourrain Fr. brood, fry; from *nutrimen*, Pr. *noirim*, so for *nourrin*.

Novero It., vb. *annoverare*; from *numerus*, *numerare*.

Novio Sp., Pg. *noivo*, Cat. Pr. *novi* newly married man, f. *noria* *noira*; from *novus nova (nova nupta)*. Pr. sbst. *novias*, L. L. *nobia* is used only in pl. after the analogy of *nuptiæ*.

Noyau Fr. kernel; from *nucalis*, Pr. *nogalh*. Ducange derives it from *nodus nodellus*, cf. *boyau* from *budellus*, O. Fr. *nou*, *novel*, *noiel*, *noyal*, *noyau*, E. *newel*, *noel*, *nowel* the column round which the steps of a circular stair case wind, Fr. *noyau d'escalier*.

Noyer — *negare*.

Nualh Pr. worthless, only found in comp. *nualhor*, O. Fr. neut. *nualz* and *nuallos*, O. Fr. *nueillos*; from *nugalis* (Gellius) *nugalior*.

Nuance — *nuer*.

Nuca It. Sp. Pg. Pr., Fr. *nuque* nape of the neck. (*Cervix* is found in all the languages, but not in common use. Instead, various words have been introduced: It. *collottola*, *cottula*, Sp. *cogote*, *pescuezo*, *pestorejo*, *tozuelo*, Pr. *nozador*, Fr. *chignon*, O. Fr. *haterel*, Wall. *hanet*, Wal. *ceafę gut* &c.) Not, perhaps, from *nux nucis* though the Sicilians call it *nuci* (*noce*), *duca* from *dux* being peculiar. There seems to be a connexion between *neck*, *nuca* &c. and *nick*, *notch*, Du. *nocke*, cf. *cran*. *Nuca* may, however, be from *nux* and have taken its form to distinguish it from *noce*, for Du. *nocke* is rather = It. *nocca* knuckle, Lomb. *gnucca* nape (It. *denoccolare* to behead).

Nuer Fr. to shade; from *nue* = *nubes*. Hence *nuance*.

Nuitantre O. Fr. adv. = noctu, L. L. *noctanter* on the analogy of *cunctanter*. As *soventre* from *sequente*, so *nuitantre* from *noctante*, cf. *nuitamment* = *noctante mente*. It. has *nottare annottare*, Fr. *anuitier*.

Nuora It., Sp. *nuera*, Pg. Pr. *nora*, O. Fr. *nore*, Wal. *noré*. From *nurus* with fem. termination, L. L. *nora*.

Nuque -- *nuca*.

Nutria — *lontra*.

O.

O od It., Sp. *o ú*, Pg. *ou*, Pr. *o oz*, Fr. *ou*. Wal. *au*, from *aut*. Hence It. *orrero* = *aut rerum*.

O O. Fr. Pr. pronoun from L. *hoc*: in comp. O. Fr. *avoc* (cf. *avec*), *paroc*, *sinoc*.

Obbliare It., Pr. O. Sp. *oblidar*, Fr. *oublier*, Sp. Pg. *olvidar*; frequentative form from *oblivisci oblilus*. Sbst. It. *obblio*, Pr. *oblil*, Fr. *oubli*, Sp. *olvido*, fem. It. *obblia*, Pr. *oblida*. As the It. does not usu. syncopate a *l*, it probably got the word from the Fr. *Scordarsi* and *dimenticare* are more commonly used.

Obsequias Sp. Pr., Fr. *obsèques*, E. *obsequies*; from *obsequiæ* for *exsequiæ*, some reference being made to the *obsequium* of the attendant friends.

Obus Fr. (hence Sp. *obuz*); from G. *haubitze* (E. *howitzer*), in 15th cent. *haufnitz*, from Bohem. *haufnice* a sling.

Oca It. Sp. Pg., Fr. *oie*, with more primitive form Sp. Pr. Rh. *auca*, O. Fr. *oue*, Wall. *awe*, Berr. *oche* goose. From *avica* (*uvis*), cf. *natica*, L. L. *cutica*, *caudica*, It. *mollica*. In the Glossaries we find πτηνόν. As the most useful domestic bird was called the bird "par excellence", so oxen were designated by the term *aumaille = animalia*. For other transitions from the general to the specific, cf. *jument*, *monton*. Fr. dim. *oison*, cf. *clerçon* from *clerc*. In Limous. we find a masc. *aue*, Veron. *oco*, Crem. *ooch*; Lim. also *ooutzar* = a Fr. *oisard*.

Octroyer — *otriare*.

Oeillot Fr. a pink; from *oeil*.

Oes — *uopo*.

Ogan — *uguanno*.

Oggi It., Rh. *oz*, Sp. *hoy*, Pg. *hoje*, Pr. *huei*, O. Fr. *hui* adv. from *hodie*. Hence It. *oggimai omai* (= *oimai*, cf. *oi* in *ancoi*) not for *ormai*; Pr. *hueimais*; It. *oggidi*, Sp. *hoy dia*, Fr. *aujourd'hui*; O. It. *ancoi* v. s. *anche*.

Ogni It., O. It. *onni*, from *omnis*, O. Ven. *omia*. The *gn* originated either in *ogn-uno = omnis uuus*, or in *ogna = omnia*.

Ogre ogro — *orco*.

Oibò It., Com. *aibai* an interjection, perhaps the Gk. αἰβοῖ.

Oio — *oca*.

Oignon Fr., Pr. *uignon*, E. *onion*. From *unio* (Columella).

Oille — *olla*.

Oindre Fr. part. *oint*, whence E. *anoint*, *ointment*; from *ungere*. It. *untare*, sbst. *unto* from *unctus*.

Oiseau — *uccello*.

Oisif Fr. idle; from *otium*, with adjectival term. *-ivus* instead of *osus*.

Ola Sp. Cat., Fr. *houle* (*h* asp.) wave, surge; from the Celtic, W. *hoewal*, Bret. *houl*. O. Fr. vb. *holer* to surge, sway.

Oleandro It., Sp. *oleandro eloendro*, Pg. *eloendro loendro*, Fr. *oléandre*, E. *oleander*. In L. L. *lorandum* a corruption of *rhododendrum* through *laurus*, *l* being afterwards mistaken for the article and dropped.

Olifant O. Fr. (1) elephant (2) ivory (3) a wind-instrument, Pr.

olifan = (1), Du. *olifant*, Bret. *olifant*, Com. *oliphans*, W. *oliffant*. Corrupted from *elephas, -antis*, as also is It. *liofante*.

Olla Sp. an earthen pot, whence Fr. *oille;* from L. *olla*, Pr. *ola* &c., *olla podrida (pudrida* putrid, ripe, seasoned) = Fr. *pot pourri*.

Olore It., Sp. Pr. *olor*, O. Fr. *olour* odour; from L. *olor* (= *odor)* Varro and Apuleius.

Olvidar — *obbliare*.

Olzina — *elce*.

Omai — *oggi*.

Ombellco belllco bilico, Wal. *buric*, Sp. *ombligo*, Pg. *umbigo embigo*, Pr. *ombelic umbrilh*, Fr. *nombril* navel; from *umbilicus*. From *umbiliculus* come *umbrilh* and *nombril* (by dissimilation for *lombril* with article, cf. Cat. *llombriyol*). Cat. has a 2nd form *melic*. Navel = centre, so It. *bilico* = point of *equilibrium*, *bilicare* to balance.

Omelette Fr.; from *œufs mêlés*.

Ommaggio — *uomo*.

On — *uomo*.

One onques — *anche*.

Once — *lonza*.

Oncle Fr. Pr. whence E. *uncle* (Wal. *unchiu*, Alban. *unki*). From *a'unculus*, not from *unculus* (for *avunculus*), such aphaeresis not being permissible in Fr. *Avunculus* was early used for *patruus*, so G. *oheim*, A. S. *eme* = mother's brother.

Onde It., O. Sp. *ond*, Pg. *onde*, Pr. *ont on*, Wal. *unde;* from *unde*. Hence It. Sp. Pg. *donde*, Pr. *don*, Fr. *dont* = *de unde*.

Onire It., Pr. *aunir*, O. Fr. *honnir* (*h* asp.) to insult, shame; from Goth. *haunjan*, O. H. G. *hônjan*, G. *höhnen* to scoff. Sbst. It. *onta*, Pr. *anta* (for *aunta*), Fr. *honte*, O. Sp. *fonta;* from O. H. G. *hônida*, O. Sax. *hônda* shame, hence It. *ontare*, O. Sp. *afontar*, Pr. *antar*, O. Fr. *ahonter*, *hontoier*.

Onta — *onire*.

Ontano It. alder. Perhaps from the collective *alnetum*, Sp. *alnedo*, Fr. *aunaie*, through a form *alnetanus*, cf. *talpa topo*, Sp. *helecho* from collective *filictum*. Ven. is *onaro*, Mil. *olnizza*, *onise*.

Onza — *lonza*.

Oppio It. a sort of poplar; from *opulus* (Varro) for *populus?*

Oqueruela Sp. a tangled thread; from Basque *oquertzea* to twist.

Ora It. &c., L. *hora*. L. L. *bona hora, mala hora* = It. *in buon' ora, in mal' ora*, Sp. *en buena hora, en hora buena, norabuena* good luck, *noramala* ill luck, Pr. *en bon' hora*, O. Fr. *en bonc heure, bone heure;* so, at last, *bona* and *mala* alone, It. *mal* Inf. 9. 54, Purg. 4. 72, Par. 16. 140, Sp. *en buena*, Pr. *bona*, O. Fr. *bon bor mal mar*, O. Pg. *bora*, Pg. *embora* (the *r* from *hora). Hora* and *augurium* meet, e. g. *en bona ora (à la bonne heure)* = *en bon aür.*

Ora It., Sp. Pg. *hora*, O. Sp. *oras*, Pr. *ora oras or*, O. Fr. *ore ores or*, Fr. *or*, adv. from *hora.* The Pr. has the forms *ara aras ar, era eras er*, Rh. *er.* Among the compounds are: Sp. *ahora*, Pr. *aoras adoras*, O.Fr. *a ore*, It. *a ora* from *ad horam;* Fr. *alors*, It. *allora* from *ad illam horam;* Fr. *lors* from *illa hora;* O. Sp. Pg. *agora* from *hac hora;* It. *ancora*, O. Sp. *encara*, Pr. *encara enquera*, Fr. *encore*, from *hanc horam;* O. Fr. *unquore uncore*, from *unquam hora;* O. Sp. *esora*, from *ipsa hora;* Pr. *quora quor*, Rh. *cura cur*, from *quæ ora*, O. Fr. *cor.*

Ora oreggio oresso — *aura.*

Orafo It. goldsmith; from *aurifex.*

Orage ore orear oreo — *aura.*

Orange — *arancio.*

Orbacca It. laurel berry; for *lorbacca* from *lauri bacca*, R. Gr. 1, 240.

Orbo It., Pr. *orb dorp*, O. Cat. O. Fr. Wal. *orb* blind, a meaning which Isidorus considers to be the original one of the L. *orbus.* Cf. Apul. *en orba Fortuna.*

Orco It., Neap. *huorco*, O. Sp. *huergo uerco*, Sp. *ogro*, Fr. E. *ogre*, A. S. *orc;* from *Orcus.* Sp. *huerco* = mournful, and abst. = skeleton.

Orda It., Fr. E. *horde* (*h* asp.) a roaming body of Tatars; G. *horde*, Alban. *hardi*, Russ. *orda* &c.; an Asiatic word, *ordù* or *urdù.*

Ordalie (f.) Fr. ordeal; from L. L. *ordalium*, which from A. S. *orddl* (n.) = G. *urtheil* (*ur* out and *theil* part = a setting forth of parts). O. Fr. had *ordel* (m.).

Ordenar Sp., Pg. *ordenhar* to milk; another form of *ordenar* to put in order, so = prop. to bring a cow into good order or condition, cf. Lim. *odzustà* to milk = Fr. *ajuster.*

Ordo It., Pr. *ort*, O. Fr. Pic. *ord* ugly, dirty; Pr. *ordeiar*, O. Fr. *ordoier* to soil; It. Pr. *ordura*, Fr. E. *ordure.* From *horridus*, cf. Pr. *orre* (f. *orreza* i. e. *orreda*) = *ort*, vb. *orrezar* = *ordeiar.* But W. makes *ordo* = *lordo (luridus).*

Ordonner Fr. from *ordinare (donner* from *donner l'ordre);* O.Cat. *ordonar*, but O. Fr. *ordener*, N. Cat. Pr. Sp. Pg. *ordenar.* *Ordnance* = ordinance.

Orecchia orecchio It., Wal. *urcache ureche* (f.), Sp. *oreja*, Pg. Pr. *orelha*, Fr. *oreille* ear; from *auricula* oar-lap, ear.

Oreille — *orecchia.*

Orendroit O. Fr., Pr. *orendrei* temporal adv., from *or en droit.*

Orfèvre — *forgia.*

Orfraie Fr. (f.) osprey; from *ossifraga*, It. *ossifrago*, Sp. *osifrago*, Fr. *ossifrague*, E. *ossifrage*, *osprey* (with a reference to *prey*).

Orfroi Fr., better *orfrois*, O. Fr. *orfrais*, O. E. *orfrays*, Pr. *aur-fres*, O. Sp. *orofres* a stuff worked with gold, gold lace, dim. O. Fr. *orfrisiel*, vb. *orfroiseler*. The L. L. has *auriphrigium*, formed from *aurum* Fr. *or* and *fraise frise*, v. *fregio*.

Orge — *orzo*.

Orgoglio It., O. It. *argoglio*, also *rigoglio*, Sp. *orgullo*, O. Sp. *arguyo ergull*, Pr. *orgolh erguelh*, O. Cat. *argull*, N. Cat. *orgull*, Fr. *orgueil* pride; from O. H. G. *urguoli*, which from *urguol* insignis, cf. O. Sp. adj. *urgulloso*. The root is found in the Sk. *gur* tollere.

Orgueil — *orgoglio*.

Oricalco It., Sp. *auricalco*, Fr. *archal;* from *aurichalcum*, *ori-chalcum* Gr. ὀρείχαλκος.

Oriflamme Fr., O. Fr. also *oriflambe oriflant*, Pr. *auriflan*, E. *oriflame*, orig. the banner of St. Denis' monastery, a red flag on a gilded lance, then = the banner of an army. From *aurum* and *flamma* = a pendant, streamer (so called from its shape) cf. Veget. *flammula*.

Orilla — *orlo*.

Orin — *ruggine*.

Oripeau — *orpello*.

Oriuolo It., Mil. *reloeuri*, Sp. *relox*, Pg. *relogio*, Pr. *relotge* clock, watch; from *horologium*, Fr. *horloge* clock, *montre* watch (prop. indicator).

Orlo It., Sp. *orla orilla*, O. Fr. *orle* border, edge; a dim. from *vra*, which to distinguish it from *hora*, is in some languages treated as masc., Sard. *oru*, Lomb. *oeur*, Pr. *or*, O. Fr. *or ur*, Rh. *ur* (W. òr f.). Vb. It. *orlare*, Sp. *orlar*, Fr. *ourler* to hem, border, *ourlet* a hem. Another word for rim is Pr. *vora*, Cat. *bora*, Val. *vora*, O. Fr. *vore;* perhaps *la vora* = *la ora*, cf. Cat. *llavors* = Sp. *á la hora*, Fr. *lors*.

Orma It., Wal. *urmë* a track; vb. *ormare*, Wal. *urmă*. *Orma* = perhaps, the Sp. *husmo* scent, track, *husmar* to track, O. Fr. *osme osmer*, Lomb. Ven. *usma usmare;* from Gk. ὀσμή, ὀσμᾶσθαι. The change of *s* to *r* in It. is unusual, but not more so unusual than the aphæresis of *f*, which would be necessary in deriving it from *forma*, cf. s. *ciurma*.

Orme Fr. elm; from *ulmus*.

Orne O. Fr. adv. *a orne* "all together"; from *ad ordinem*.

Ornière Fr. rut, track; from O. Fr. Pic. *ordiere*, wh. from *orbitaria (orbita)*, Wall. *ourbire*.

Orondado Sp. undulatory (*orondo* pompous); from *undulatus ondorado?* Or from *ol-andado (ola* wave).

Orpello It., Sp. *oropel*, Pr. *aurpel*, Fr. *oripeau* gold-leaf, tinsel; from *aurum* and *pellis*, gold-skin.

Orpimento It., Sp. *oropimente*, Fr. *orpiment*, *orpin*, E. *orpiment;* from *auri pigmentum.*

Orteil — *artiglio.*

Oruga — *ruca.*

Orvalho Pg. dew; from *rorale roralia?* The Gallic and Astur. have *orbayo* cold drizzling rain.

Oscle O. Fr. Pr. a present (Burg. *ocle*, *octage*); L. L. *osculum "donatio propter nuptias, quam solet sponsus interveniente osculo dare sponsæ"* Ducange.

Oseille Fr. sorrel; from ὀξαλίς or ὀξάλιος sour.

Osier Fr. E., Berr. *oisis*, Bret. *aozil;* from Gk. οἶσος, which is connected with *ἰτέα*, *ἴτυς*, *vitex*, *with*, Sk. *viṭika*, from root *ve (rieu).*

Oso Sp. bear, for *orso* from *orsus*, R. Gr. 1, 249.

Ostaggio It., Sp. *hostaje*, Pr. *ostatge*, Fr. *ôtage*, E. *hostage;* L. L. *hostagium hostaticum*, It. *statico;* from *obsidaticum*, which is from the L. *obsidatus (obses).*

Oste It., Sp. *hueste*, Pg. *hoste*, Pr. O. Fr. *ost*, Wal. *oaste* an army, *host*, Pic. *ost* (pron. *o*) a flock. From *hostis* in L. L. = a host. The change of gender is remarkable; L. L. fem., It. masc. and fem., Sp. Pg. Wal. fem., O. Fr. fem. seldom masc. The fem. was perhaps used to distinguish it from the following word.

Oste It., Sp. *huesped*, Pr. *hoste*, Fr. *hôte* (E. *host*), Wal. *ospet* = host and guest; from *hospes*. Hence It. *ospitale, ospedale, spedale, spitale* (whence G. E. *spital*, Sp. Pr. E. *hospital*, Fr. *hôpital*, L. L. *hospitale;* It. contr. *ostale*, Sp. Pr. *hostal*, O. Fr. E. *hostel (hosteller = ostler)*, It. *ostello*, Fr. *hôtel*.

Ostico disagreeable or sour to the taste, sour, morose; from αὐστός (αὐστηρός).

Ostugo Sp. (1) track (2) corner, hiding-place. From B. *ostuguia* stolen (Larram.).

Ótage — *ostaggio.*

Oter Fr., Pr. *ostar* to take away, E. *oust*. Ducange derives it from *obstare*, *obstare viam* = *ôter le chemin*, the notion of *hindering* easily passing into that of *depriving*. Others from a L. *haustare* a frequent. of *haurire*, N. Pr. *austá*, cf. O. Fr. *doster*, Berr. *dôter*, Lim. *dousiá* from *dehaurire*. *Haustare*, however, is not found in L. L., and N. Pr. *austá* is usu. connected with *hausser*.

Otero Sp., *outeiro* Pg. hill; L. L. *oterum auterum*, from *altus*, = *altarium* raised altar, cf. It. adj. *altiero*.

Otorgar — *otriare.*

Otriare It., Sp. *otorgar*, Pg. *outorgar*, Pr. *autorgar*, *autreyar*, Fr. *octroyer* to allow, grant; from *auctoricare* (for *auctorare*) to authorise; the Fr. is thus nearer tho orig. than tho O. Fr.

otroier. Hence Sp. *ortogo* (contract), Pr. *autore autrei*, Fr. *octroi* (grant, toll).

Ottarda It., Sp. *avutarda*, Pg. *abetardu betarda*, Pr. *austarda*, Fr. *outarde*, Champ. *bistarde*, E. *bustard.* Not from *otis* (ὠτίς) with suffix *ard*, but from *avis tarda*, which Pliny (II. N. 10, 22) gives as the name of the bird in Spain. Sp. *avutarda* contains a repetition of *avis*, *u-tarda* for *o-tarda* and *ave*, as in *av-estruz.*

Ottone It., Sp. *laton alaton*, Cat. *llautó*, Fr. *laiton*, Norm. *latùn*, O. E. *latoun*, *latten.* From It. *latta* a plate of metal, cf. Sp. *plata plate*, silver. In Piedm. Mil. Com. Ven. *loton;* the *l* has been mistaken for the article and dropped in It. *ottone.* Some derive it from ἔλατρον (ἐλαύνω), cf. *lamina.*

Ou — *o.*

Où — *ove.*

Ouaiche Fr. (m.) course, track of a ship. Also *ouage* = Sp. *aguage* current = *aquagium.*

Ouaille Fr. sheep; from *ovicula*, Sp. *oveja*, Pr. *orelha oelha.* *Ovis* is found in the O. Fr. *oue* wether, Wal. *oae.* *Ouaille* is now used only in fig. sense, being superseded by *brebis*, It. *pecora.*

Ouais — *guai.*

Ouate — *ovata.*

Oublie Fr. a cake; from *oblate* (for *oublaie*), from its resemblance to the sacramental wafer.

Oublier — *obbliare.*

Ouche ousche O. Fr. terra arabilis; L. L. *olca*, prob. a primitive L. word: *campus tellure fecundus, tales enim incolæ olcas vocant* Greg. Tur.; cf. ὦλκα (acc.), ὦλαξ a furrow.

Ouest Fr. (O. Fr. *west*), whence Sp. *ovest;* from A. S. *vest*, E. *west.*

Oui Fr., Pr. *oc* affirmative particle. Pr. is from L. *hoc*, which, shortened into *o* becomes, with the addition of *illud*, the O. Fr. *oil*, whence Fr. *oui*, used by Molière and others as a dissyllable. With this use of *hoc* cf. L. *ita, sic* (from demonstr. roots), Gk. ταῦτα. In O. Fr. we also find *oie*, Wall. *awoi*. *Oil* corresponds to *nenil* v. *ne.*

Ouragan — *uracano.*

Ourler — *orlo.*

Outarde — *ottarda.*

Outil Fr., O. Fr. *ostil ustil*, Wall. *usteie* (= a Fr. *outille*). L'ustensile would have given *ousil.* Is it from *usatellum* a dim. of It. *usato*, cf. Com. *usadel*, Mil. *usadei* (kitchen utensils), O. Fr. *ustil* = Pic. *otieu (ieu* = *ell).* Rou. *otil* = knitted work = *opus textile?*

Outrecuidance — *coitare.*

Ouvrir Fr., Pr. *obrir, ubrir,* O. It. *oprire* to open. Whence the *o?* the It. has *aprire,* Sp. *abrir* from *aperire. Ovrir (= ourrir)* is prob. a shortened form of O. Fr. *a-ovrir, a-uvrir,* this for *adubrir,* which, with pref. *a* (as in *ablasmar afranher*), is from *de-operire* to uncover, open (Celsus), cf. N. Pr. *durbir,* Piedm. *durvi,* Wall. *drovi.* Mil. Com. *dervi,* Crem. *darver = de-aperire.*

Ovata It., Fr. *ouate* (Sp. *huata*) wadding, padding. From *ovum,* cf. *lombo lombata, giorno giornata,* -*ata* denoting extension. The E. *wad* is rather from *ouate* than the reverse, for the E. *d* would not become *t* in Fr. But Du. G. has *watte,* Swed. *vadd.*

Ove It., O. It. *o, u,* O. Sp. *o,* O. Pg. *ou,* Pr. *o,* Fr. *où* where; from *ubi.* Hence It. *dove,* Fr. *d'où.*

Ove Fr. from *ovum,* It. *uovolo,* Sp. *orillo.*

Ovvero — *o.*

Oxalá Sp., Pg. *oxalà* interj. = L. *utinam;* from Ar. *inschd alldh (in* if, *schd* wills, *alldh* God); *n* was lost, and *i* took the interjectional form *o.*

P.

Pabellon — *padiglione.*

Pabilo Sp., Pg. *pavio,* Sard. *pavilu,* Pr. *pabil,* Rh. *pavaigl,* W. *pabwyr* wick of a candle, snuff; from *pabulum,* cf. *esca* = tinder. Mil. *pabi* = L. *pabulum.*

Pacciare It. in *impacciare,* Sp. Pg. Pr. *empacher,* Fr. *empêcher* (E. *impeach*) to hinder; sbst. It. *impaccio,* Sp. Pg. *empacho,* Pr. *empach,* Rh. *ampaig;* It. *dispacciare spacciare,* Sp. Pg. *despachar,* Fr. *dépêcher* to release, despatch. *Impactare,* a freq. of *impingere,* would give Sp. Pr. *empachar,* and Fr. *empêcher* (cf. *fléchir* from *flectere, delécher* from *delectare);* It. *impacciare* would require *impactiare.* This deriv. is supported by the Pr. forms *empaitar empaig* (cf. *faita faig* from *facta factum*) and by the meaning "to ingraft" *(impingere).*

Pacco It., Fr. *paquet,* Sp. *paquete* a packet; from Du. *pak* or E. *pack* = Gael. *pac.* V. *baga.*

Pada Pg. a loaf; from *panada, padeiro* baker = Sp. *panadero.*

Padiglione It., Sard. *papaglioni,* Sp. *pabellon,* Pr. *pabalhô,* Fr. *parillon,* E. *pavilion,* W. *pabell,* O. Fr. *pupall;* from *papilio* = pavilion in L. L. The O. Fr. *paveillon* has the meaning "butterfly". For the It. form cf. R. Gr. 1, 164.

Padule It. marsh; a corruption of *paludem,* L. L. *padulis.* O. Sp. has *paul* (cf. Sard. *pauli), paular,* Pg. *paul.* Wal. *padure* forest = *padule.*

Paese It., Sp. Pg. *païs* (from the Fr.?), Pr. *paes*, Fr. *pays*, from a form *pagensis* (pagus); O. Sp. *pages*, Pr. *pages*, L. L. *pagensis* a farm. Hence It. *pacsano*, Sp. Pg. *paisano*, Fr. *paysan*, E. *peasant*.

Paffuto — *papa*.

Paflon — *plafond*.

Pagano It. Sp., Pg. *pagão*, Pr. *pagan payan*, Fr. *paien*, Wal. *pégén*, Bohem. *pohan*, E. *pagan;* from *paganus*, prop. = a countryman, rustic; the name was given in the time of Constantine to those of the old creed who, to avoid persecution, fled to the country, cf. G. *heide*, O. H. G. *heidan*, Goth. fem. *haithnô*, E. *heathen*, from Goth. *haithi*, E. *heath*.

Pagare It., Sp. Pg. *pagar*, Pr. *pagar payar*, Fr. *payer*, E. *pay*, abst. It. Sp. Pg. Pr. *paga*, Fr. *paie*, E. *pay;* from *pacare* to appease, settle, cf. a. *cheto*.

Paggio It., N. Pr. *pagi*, Fr. E. *page* (Sp. *page* from the Fr.); from *παιδίον*. Brought to Italy by the Byzantines, or Crusaders. L. L. is *pagius*.

Paglia It., Sp. *paja*, Pg. Pr. *palha*, Fr. *paille*, Wal. *paie* straw; from *palea*. Hence Pr. *paillola* bed; E. *pallet;* Fr. *paillasse;* *paillard* lewd; Pg. *espalhar* to strew, scatter.

Paillard paille — *paglia*.

Pairar Pg. to hold out, endure a storm, distress &c., to hesitate, be irresolute, temporise, naut. to tack, lie to (also Sp.). Not from *parar* to parry, though *a* may become *ai* in Pg., cf. *plaina, mainel, esfaimar*, but from Basque *pairatu* to bear, endure, hold out, whence the notion of temporizing &c. Com. *pairà*, Piedm. *pairé, apairé*, Gen. *apajá*, O. Ven. *apairar* to be at leisure (hold off from business). These It. words would rather support the der. from *parar*.

Paisseau Fr. vineprop; from *paxillus*.

Paja — *paglia*.

Palabra — *parola*.

Paladino Sp. public, open, plain, O. Sp. vb. *espaladinar*. O. It. *paladino* open, fair (Ciullo d'Alcamo); from *palam*, though the mode of formation is not clear. The *Paladins* of Charlemagne were those, whose names were public and famous, or = *Palatines (palatium)*.

Palafreno It., Sp. *palafren*, Pr. *palafrei*, Fr. *palefroi*, E. *palfrey;* from *para-veredus* side-horse, *παρά* and *veredus* (cf. *παράσειρος*), L. L. *parafredus*, whence also G. *pferd*, O. H. G. *pheril*, O. Sax. *pererd*. *Palafreno* got its spelling from *frenum*. Fr. has *palafrenier* groom.

Palais Fr. palate. Not directly from *palatum*, but from *palatium*, in which was involved the notion of an arched roof. It. has *il cielo della bocca*, Sp. *el cielo de la boca*, Du. *het gehemelte* *des monds*, E. *roof of the mouth*, Gk. οὐρανίσκος. Conversely, Ennius has *cæli palatum* = sky.

Palandra It., Sp. Pg. *balandra*, Fr. *balandre* a small ship for coasting, or for river or canal navigation; from L. G. *binnen-lander* (an *inland*-trading ship).

Palascio It. a kind of sabre, O. Fr. *palache;* = Russ. *paläsch*, Wal. *palos*, Hung. *palos*, cf. Bavar. *plotzen*.

Paloo — *balco.*

Palefroi — *palafreno.*

Paleron Fr. shoulder-bone; from *pala*, through an adj. *palarius*, so = a Pr. *palairò*. Sp. has *paleta* (also = *palette*).

Paleto Sp. a fallow-deer. From *pala*, Sp. *paleta*, from its flat *shovel*-like antlers, hence its name in G. *schaufel-hirsch*.

Pallo It. Sp., Pr. *pali*, O. Fr. *pali paile*, E. *pall;* from *pallium*, also = the woollen or silken stuff, from which palls were made; cf. *ciclaton*, O. H. G. has *phellol*, M. H. G. *pfellel pfel-ler (palliolum).*

Palla — *balla.*

Palletot Fr., O. Fr. *palletoc*, Sp. *paletoque*, Bret. *paltók*, Burg. *pal-toquai* a clown (Fr. *paltoquet*); from *palle-toque* (hooded-coat).

Palmiere It., Sp. *palmero*, O. Fr. *paumier*, E. *palmer; qni de Hierosolymis veniunt, palmam ferunt.* Ducange.

Paltone It. a beggar, vagrant, Pr. *paltom;* hence It. *paltoniere*, Pr. O. Fr. *pantonier*, whence M. H. G. *paltanaere*. For *pali-tone* from *palitari* (a frequentative of *palari*) used by Plaut. Bacch. 5, 2, 5, and, probably, in the vulgar speech. Cf. *ciar-lone* from *ciarlare*, *castrone* from *castrare* &c.

Paltoquet — *palletot.*

Palurdo — *lordo.*

Pámer — *spasimo.*

Pampre Fr., Pr. *pampol;* from *pampinus.*

Pan O. Fr. Pr. a piece of cloth (L. *pannus*, It. *panno*, Sp. *paño*), in O. Fr. also = something taken or seized, vb. *paner*, Pr. *panar*, Sp. *apañar* to take, seize, whence E. *pawn* and O. H. G. *phant*, O. Fris. *pant* a seizure (G. *pfand* a pledge, mort-gage), vb. *penta* G. *pfänden* to distrain, *pound*, M. Du. *pant* harm, loss. The Sp. verb, which also = to patch and to unwrap, clearly connects *pan* with *pannus paño*. Besides *paner* we find *panir paneïr, espanir espaneïr espanoir espenir espenoir* to pay penalty, *espanisseur* an officer of justice. *Pfand* &c., according to Pott, are from L. *panctum* for *pactum*. From *pan* we have E. *pane*, dim. *panel*, Fr. *panneau*, It. *pannello.*

Pana — *panne.*

Panache (m.) a tuft of feathers, a plume; from *penna*, Sp. *pe-nacho*, It. *pennacchio.*

Panca — *banco.*

Pancia It., Sp. *panza pancho*, Pr. *pansa*, Fr. *panse*, E. *paunch;* from *pantex pauticis*, Wal. *pëntece*. Hence It. *panciere*, Sp. *paucera*, O. Fr. *panchire*, G. *panzer*.

Pandura pandora It., O. Sp. *pandurria*, Fr. *paudore*, Sp. also *baudurria* (Pg. *bandurra*), *bandola*, It. *mandola*, Fr. *mandole mandore* a stringed instrument, *banjo;* from *pandura pandurium*, Gk. πανδοῦρα, L. also *pandorus*, *pandorium*, according to some = *Πανὸς δῶρον*.

Paniere It., O. Sp. *panero*, Pr. Fr. *panier*, E. *pannier;* from *panuarium* a bread-basket *(panis* whence also *paueterie*, E. *pantry* and *pantler).*

Panne Fr. whence Sp. *pana* velvet, O. Fr. *pene*, Pr. *penne pena*, O. Sp. *peña* fur; from *penna* a translation of the M. H. G. *federe* (feather) which was used for both *pluma* and *penua*.

Panneau — *pan.*

Pannocchia It., Sp. *panoja;* from *panucula* (Fest.) *panucla* (Non.) for *panicula* a tuft, panicle *(panus).*

Panse — *pancia.*

Panser — *peso.*

Pantalone It. a character on the Italian stage, Fr. *pantalon*, E. *pantaloon*, also = a garment worn by him; the name was brought from Venice, where *pantalone* (a common Christian name, L. Pantaleon, Gk. *Πανταλέων)* was used as a nickname.

Pantano It. Sp. Pg. marsh, swamp; L. L. *pantanum*. Perhaps from πάτος πάτημα with *n* inserted as in *pantofola*. The Lomb. has *palta* (Piedm. *pauta*), *paltan* = *pantano*, which may be a corruption of *polta* pap (from *puls*), for *poltiglia* = *palta* and *polta*, Rh. *paulan* = *pultan.*

Panteler — *pantois.*

Pantofola pantafola It., Wal. *pantoflë*, Sp. *pantuflo*, Fr. *pantoufle* (f.) a slipper. The first part is, perhaps, *patte* a foot, since forms are found without the *n*, Du. *pattufel*, Piedm. *patofle;* in the sense of a man of awkward, shuffling gait, Genev. *patoufle*, Roue. Norm. *patouf*, Fr. *pataud*. The Cat. has by a false deriv.*plantofa (planta)*. The termination is prob. the same as in Pr. *man-oufle* a glove from *manupula* (v. *manopola)*, as *fondëfle* from *fundibulum*, cf. Fr. *emmitoufler (amictus?)* to muffle.

Pantois Fr. breathless, sbst. Pr. *pantais*, Val. *pantaix*, Cat. *pantex* breathlessness, Pr. also = distress; vb. O. Fr. *panteiser*, Pr. *pantaisar*, *panteiar*, N. Pr. *pantaiyeu*, Val. *pantaixar*, Cat. *pantexar* to be breathless, distracted, Fr. *pantoiment* asthma, *panteler* to cough. From E. *pant*, which from W. *pautu* to press down, *paut* pressure (akin to Sk. root *pad panth* to go, tread), From the Pr. the O. It. has vb. *pantasare*, Ver. *pantesar*, Ven. *pautezare*, Crem. *panselaa* (for *pantaselaa)* = Fr. *panteler.*

Pantorrilla Sp., Pg. *panturrilha* calf of the leg; prop. = little belly from *pant-ex*, for *pantig-orra*; cf. Cat. *rentrell de la cama*, L. *venter cruris*, Gk. γαστρο-κνήμιον, Rh. *rantrigl* (*ventriculus*).

Papa Fr. E., from *papa*, whence It. Sp. *papà* used for the native *babbo* and *taita*. The same word is the It. Sp. Pg. *papa*, Fr. *pape*, E. *pope*. The L. *papa pappa* also = It. *pappa*, Wal. *pupē*, Sp. Pg. *papa*, O. Fr. *papin papette*, E. *pap*, L. It. *pappare* to eat pap = Sard. *papai* to eat (generally). It. *pappo* = bread, Sp. Pg. *papo* a morsel, also fowl's crop or craw (also *papera*), dewlap of oxen &c., Ven. Crem. *papola papa* fleshy cheeks, *papon papoto* fat, fleshy, Sp. *papudo* double-chinned, also It. *paffuto* = *papoto*, Sic. *baffù*, cf. Pie. Norm. *empafer* to fill. The notion of crop may be partly from L. *papula* pimple, swelling, which in Sp. = tumour on the neck, in It. = swelling.

Pape It. an interj. = L. *papæ*, Gk. παπαί; so Occ. *babai* = Gk. βαβαί, L. *babæ*.

Papero It. gosling, cf. Sp. *parpar* to quack or cackle; an onomatopœion. Diefenbach compares the N. Gk. παπία a duck. Cf. Sp. *paparo* a simpleton, clown.

Papier Fr. (E. *paper*) not directly from *papyrus* but from an adj. *papyrius*, so for *papiir*. The Sp. *papel* is from the sbst.

Pappagallo It., Sp. Pg. *papagayo*, Pr. *papagai*, O. Fr. *papegai papegaut*, E. *popinjay*, M. Gk. παπαγάς, N. Gk. παπάγαλλος. From *papa* priest and Fr. *geai*, E. *jay* (or *gallus*). The Ar. *babbaghá* is from the Rom., cf. Ar. *Boqrat* = Hippocrates. Cf. *parrocchetto*.

Pappalardo It., Fr. *papelard* a hypocrite; prop. one who affects to be abstemious, but is, secretly, fond of bacon (*pappe-lard*). Other It. expressions are *baciapile* (kiss-pillar), *stropiccione* (besom, as sliding about on his knees), *graffiasanti* (saint-clawer), *torcicollo* (neck-twister).

Pâque — *pasqua*.

Paquet paquete — *pacco*.

Par Fr. prep., O. Fr. also *per*; from L. *per*, It. O. Sp. O. Pg. Pr. *per*, Wal. *pre*. The O. Fr. *par* in *trop par dure* too too hard &c., is the Lat. *per* in *perdoctus*, cf. Ter. Andr. 3, 2, 6. *per ceastor scitus* = *perscitus*.

Par Fr. in the form *de par le roi* in the king's name = *part*, as it was also written in O. Fr.

Para — *por*.

Parafe (m.) Fr. a flourish with the pen in signatures &c.; from Gk. παράγραφος παραγραφή.

Paraggio It., Pr. *paratge*, Fr. *parage* birth, lineage; prop. equality of birth, from *par*, whence E. *disparage*.

Paragone It., Sp. *paragon parangon*, O. Fr. *parangon*, E. *para-*

gon prop. = comparison. It is from the Span. *para con:* e. g.
la criatura para con el criador, not from the Greek.

Parangon — *paragone*.

Parapet parapluie parasol — *parare*.

Parare It., Pr. *parar* to hold out, stretch forth, Sp. *parar* in
parar mientes animum advertere; also It. Fr. = E. *parry*, Sp.
to stop, leave off, prevent. From the L. *parare* to prepare
were derived the notions (1) of holding forth (prop. keeping
in readiness) (2) of holding off, keeping off, parrying (prop.
guarding, protecting, cf. *defendere*). From the notion of
guarding we get It. *para-petto*, whence Fr. E. *parapet;* from
that of warding off, It. *para-sole*, Fr. E. *parasol*, It. *paravento*
&c., Fr. *parapluie*. Hence also It. *riparare*, Sp. *reparar* (E.
repair) remedy, take care of, sbst. *riparo reparo*, E. *repair*
place of defence; It. *comperare comprare*, Wal. *compĕrǎ* to
buy; Sp. Pg. Pr. *emparar amparar* (cf. Sp. *embrollar ambrol-
lar*) to take seize, Fr. *s'emparer* to make oneself master of,
It. *imparare* (like *apprendere*) to learn; Fr. *se remparer* to in-
trench oneself, sbst. *rempart*, E. *rampart*; It. *sparare*, Sp. *dis-
parar* to discharge (agun). It. *parare* = also to make ready,
adorn, Fr. *parer* (E. *pare*), whence *parata*, *parade*.

Parbleu Fr., O. Fr. *parbieu*, for *par dieu* with a common disguis-
ing of the sacred name, cf. Sp. *par diobre (= dios)*, Fr. *morbleu*.

Parce — *ciò*.

Parchemin Fr., E. *parchment;* from *pergamena*, (*charta*), Gk.
πεϱγαμήνη, Pr. *parguamina* &c., O. Fr. *parcamin* with an
unusual change of the *g* into *c*, hence *parchemin*.

Parco It., Sp. Pg. *parque*, Pr. *parc pargue*, N. Pr. *pargou, par-
gado, pargagi*, Fr. *parc* (E. *park*) whence Fr. *parquet*, vb.
parquer. L. L. has *parcus parricus*, O. H. G. *pfarrich pferrich*,
G. *pferch*, A. S. *pearruc pearroc*, Gael. *pàirc*, W. *parc* and
parwg. The Rom. words are derived from the Celtic, and the
root is found in the Sk. *prich* conjungere, in the causative =
colligare. *Parc* = enclosure, cf. πόϱχος a fishing-net, πόϱϰης
a hoop, W. *perced* a bow-net.

Pardo Sp. Pg. dark-coloured, gray. From *pallidus paldus par-
dus;* cf. *escarpelo* from *scalpellum*, *surco* from *sulcus;* for the
transition of meaning, cf. O. H. G. *bleich* pallidus (O. E. *blake*)
with A. S. *blâc* pallidus, niger, *black*, Gk. πέλλος with πολιός.
From *pardo* comes *pardal* gray sandpiper, cf. Rh. *grischun*.

Parecchio It., Sp. *parejo*, Fr. *pareil* like, Wal. sbst. *pĕrĕache*
peer; dim. from *par*, L. L. *pariculus*. It. plur. *parecchi* =
several, prop. = several things of the same kind. Hence It.
vb. *apparecchiare*, Sp. *aparejar*, Pr. *aparelhar*, Fr. *appareiller*,
prop. = to pair (so still in Fr.), hence to combine, put together,
prepare, *apparel;* sbst. *apparecchio* &c.,

Pareil parejo — *parecchio.*

Parelle Fr. a plant, *rumex*, λάπαθον, Sp. *paradela;* from *pratum*, cf. Hor. *"herba lapathi prata amantis".*

Paresse — *pigrezza.*

Pargolo pargoletto for *parvolo parvoletto*, v. R. Gr. 1, 187.

Parias Sp., Pg. *pareas* (f. plur.) tribute paid by one prince or state to another; from L. *paria* equivalent, return, payment, cf. *par pari respondere* = *pariare* to pay, pay tribute.

Parier Fr. to bet, to wager, L. L. *pariare* to make like, prop. to set like against like, Pr. *pariar* = to divide, share equally, v. preced.

Parlar parlare parler — *parola.*

Parmi — *mezzo.*

Parven Pr., O. It. *parvente* evident, Pr. *parven*, *parvensa*, It. *parvenza* appearance; from *parere parens*, *v* inserted to distinguish it from *parens* a parent.

Paroisse — *parrocchia.*

Parola It., Sp. *palabra*, Pg. *palavra* (E. *palaver*), O. Pg. *paravoa*, Pr. O. It. O. Sp. *paraula*, Fr. *parole;* from *parabola* a parable, speech, word (so in early L. L.). It took the place of the L. *verbum* which, from religious scruples, was sparingly used (It. Sp. *verbo*, O. Sp. *vierbo*, Pr. *verbi*, Rh. *vierf)*; the Wal. *vorbě* (f. as O. It. *verba*), however = *parola*. Vb. It. *parlare*, Sp. Pr. *parlar*, Fr. *parler* (E. *parly*, *parliament*), O. Fr. *paroler*, L. L. *parabolare*, Fr. *parloir* in a nunnery = E. *parlour.*

Parpado Sp. eye-lid; a corruption of *palpebra*, Fr. *paupière* &c.

Parpaglione It., Pr. *parpalhò*, Lomb. *parpaj parpaja* butterfly; a corruption of *papilio*. Hence It. *sparpagliare*, Pr. *esparpalhar*, O. Fr. *esparpeiller*, Fr. *éparpiller*, Sp. *desparpajar* to flutter, scatter; so N. Pr. *esfarfalhà* from *farfalla* (q. v.) = *parpalhò*. Other names are: It. *farfalla*, Sard. *faghe farina*, *parabatola*, *calagasu*, Sp. *mariposa*, *alevilla*, Bresc. *barbel*, Pg. *borboleta*, Rh. *bulla*, Lorr. *boublé* &c.

Parque — *parco.*

Parrain Fr. godfather, Pr. *pairin*, Sp. *padrino* &c., L. L. *patrinus*. It would be more correctly written *parrin.*

Parrocchetto It., Sp. *periquito*, Fr. *perroquet*, E. *parroquet*, *parrot*. Prop. = priestling, from *parochus*, these birds being chiefly kept by ecclesiastics. The Sp. simple form *perico*, however, = Peterkin and parrot, is not from *parochus*, but is one of the many instances of names of men transferred to animals.

Parrocchia It., Sp. Pr. *parroquia*, Fr. *paroisse*, E. *parish;* L. L. *parochia* a corruption (the spelling from *parochus*) of παροικία *(parœcia* in Augustine, Fr. *paroisse)*, v. Duc. *parochia.*

Part Pr. prep. for Lat. ultra, trans; from *pars* in the sense of district, side.

Partigiana It., O. Val. *partesana*, Fr. *pertuisane*, E. *partisan;* Rabelais has *parthisane*, so *partuisane* borrowed, probably, its spelling from *pertuis pertuiser* to bore. The masc. *partisan* = the chief of a troop of light-armed (It. *partigiano*, E. *partisan*) and prob. gave the name to the weapon, cf. It. *gialda* from Pr. *gelda* infantry, It. *mugavero*, Sp. *gineta* lance from *ginete* horse-soldier, It. *rubalda* helmet from *rubaldo*.

Partire It., Sp. Pr. Fr. *partir* to depart, with and without the pronoun, orig. only with it (O. Fr. *se partir*); from *partiri*, *se partiri* to part.

Parvis Fr., O. E. *parvise* the fore-court or atrium of a church usually surrounded with cloisters, the cloister-garth. From *paradisus* (*para'is paravis parris* cf. *gravir*, *emblaver*, *pouvoir*, R. Gr. 1, 164), Neap. *paraviso*, It. *paradiso* = Gk. παράδεισος park. Many towns in England which had monasteries have a Paradise street. The Cloister-garth at Chichester is called the *Paradise*, at Chester the *Sprise*-garden. The same word is used for the area in front of any large public building, e. g. Westminster Hall; cf. Chauc. Cant. Tales (Prol.). "A Sergiant of law ware and wise, that often had been at the *Pervise*".

Pas Fr. as a complement of the negative; from *passus: je ne vois pas = non video passum* not a step.

Passa Sp., Pg. *passa* raisin; from *uva passa*.

Pasmo — *spasimo*.

Pasqua It., Sp. Pr. *pascua*, Fr. *pâque* Easter, Lat. *pascha* (wh. from Heb. *pesech* he crossed). The notion of feasting after a long fast connected itself with *pascua*, hence the *u; pasca* would have given *pâche*. Pr. O. Fr. *pascor* spring is formed like *nadalor* Christmas.

Pasquino It. the name of a statue at Rome, to which lampoons were affixed, hence Fr. *pasquin* buffoon, Sp. *pasquin*, It. *pasquillo* a lampoon.

Passamano It., Sp. *pasamano*, Fr. *passement* fringe, border, trimming. Sp. *pasamano* = also baluster, *porque pasamos por el la mano* (Covarr.), whence it was applied to any fringe. Al. from *passer* because of the motion of the hand in netting. The G. has *posament* (from the Fr.) lace, Swed. *pasman*, Hung. *paszma paszomán*, Pol. *pasaman*.

Passare It., Sp. *pasar*, Pg. Pr. *passar*, Fr. *passer*, Wal. *pĕsi*, E. *pass*. Often transitive and so better from *pandere* as freq. in sense of opening, passing through (cf. *pandere mœnia &c.* and *spassare = expandere*) than directly from *passus*, which gives *passeggiare*, Sp. *pasear*.

Passeggiare — *passare.*

Passement — *passamano.*

Pasta It. Sp. Pg. Pr., Fr. *pâte*, E. *paste;* from *pastus,* influenced by *pastillus,* Sp. *plasta* being formed after *plasma.* Hence It. *pastello,* Sp. Fr. *pastel* a crayon, Sp. *pastilla,* Fr. *pastille;* Fr. *appât* bait, pl. *appas* charms.

Pastoochia It. a tale; from *pasto, dar pasto* to allure with words.

Pastoja It. a shackle for cattle at pasture, L. L. *pastorium.* Hence It. *pasturale,* Fr. *pâturon,* E. *pastern* cf. *fetlock,* in G. *fessel;* vb. It. *impastoiare,* Fr. *empêtrer* for *empêturer* to fetter (E. *pester*), It. *pastoiare,* Fr. *dépêtrer* to unshackle.

Patan patrulla — *pata.*

Patata batata Sp. Pg., E. *potatoe* a word of American origin.

Pataud — *patta.*

Pâte — *pasta.*

Pateca Sp. pumpkin, water-melon; from Ar. *bì'tichah,* Pg. also *albudieca,* Cat. *albudeca.* Hence also Sp. Pg. *badea.*

Patin — *patta.*

Patio Sp. Pg., Cat. N. Pr. *pati* hall or court. According to Sousa an African word, *pathaion.*

Patois Fr.; cf. Rouchi *pati-pata* chattering, E. *patter;* an onomatopœion.

Patraña Sp., Pg. *patranha* a story; for *patarraña* from Cat. *patarra* wh. from *pata* a goose, cf. preced.

Patta Crem., N. Pr. *pata* a flap, Com. a foot, Sp. Cat. *pata,* Fr. *patte* a foot, paw, Sp. *patear* to treat; Sp. *pato pata,* Alb. *patë* a goose; Fr. *pataud* a turnspit (with broad feet); Sp. *patan* a clown; It. *pattino,* Fr. *patin* a skate, E. *patten.* Not, prob., from Gk. πάτος πατεῖν, but an onomatop. like G. *patschen.*

Pattino — *patta.*

Pattuglia It., Sp. *patrulla,* Fr. *patrouille,* E. *patrol;* vb. Sp. *patrullar patullar,* Fr. *patrouiller* to patrol. Also to stir any soft substance with hand or foot, also *patouiller* = E. *paddle, patouille* = *puddle, patrouille* a pot ladle. *R* is inserted, the root being *pat* to tread, cf. *patta:* cf. Rou. *patoquer patroquer patriquer patouger,* Champ. *patoiller platrouiller.*

Pâturon — *pastoia.*

Paumier paumoier O. Fr. to seize; from *palma* hand. Hence also Sp. *palmear,* Fr. *paumer,* L. L. *palmare* to slap with the hand *(paume).*

Paupière — *parpado.*

Pausare It., Sp. Pg. Pr. *pausar,* Fr. *pauser,* E. *pause;* from the late Lat. *pausare.* In trans. as well as intrans. sense we have It. *posare,* Sp. *posar* (sbst. *posada* resting-place, inn), Fr. *poser* (Prov. only *pausar*). Hence It. *riposare,* Sp. *reposar,*

Pg. *repousar*, Pr. *repausar*, Fr. *reposer*, E. *repose*. But Fr. *déposer, disposer, exposer, imposer, proposer* are from *deponere* &c., formed on the analogy of *pausar*, for Pr. has *dépausar* &c., the prop. Lat. form being only found where the simple verb is used in its Lat. sense, cf. It. *diporre*, Sp. *deponer* &c.; the Fr. and Pr. *pondre* is only used in the restricted sense of "laying eggs".

Pautonier — *paltone*.

Paver Fr., E. *pave;* from *pavire* with change of conj. as in *tousser*.

Pavese palvese It., Sp. *paves*, Fr. *parois* large shield, Wal. *pavézé*, Hung. *pais*, Boh. *paweza*. From *Pavia*, cf. *pistolesi* from *Pistoja*.

Pavillon — *padiglione*.

Pavois — *pavese*.

Pavot Fr. poppy. From *papaver*, the seeming reduplication being dropped and the term. changed, cf. *Trèves* from *Treviri;* cf. A. S. *papig, popig*, E. *poppy*, W. *pabi*. The Norm. *mahon* is the O. H. G. *mágo*, M. H. G. *máhen*, G. *mohn*.

Paxaro Sp., Pg. *passaro*, Wal. *pasére* bird; from *passer*, with *ar* for *er*, cf. *passer non passar* App. ad Probum, so *anser non ansar*, but Sp. *ansar: camera, non cammara*, Sp. *camara*.

Payen — *pagano*.

Payer — *pagare*.

Payla — *poéle* (1).

Pays paysan — *paese*.

Pazzo It. mad, furious, vb. *pazziare*. From O. H. G. *barzjan parzjan*, M. H. G. *barzen* to be furious, cf. *cucuzza* from *cucurbita, gazzo* = Sp. *garzo, pesca* from *persica, dosso* from *dorsum* &c. Hence It. *strapassare*, Sp. *estrapar*, Fr. *estrapasser, strapasser*, abst. *strapasso*.

Peage — *pedaggio*.

Peason O. Fr., Pr. *peazó* foundation, base; L. L. *pedatio* from *pedare* to support.

Pec O. Fr. fem. *peque pecque* (Molière), Pr. *pec pegua*, Pg. *peco*, B. *peca* stupid; from *pecus* which is so used even in Class. Latin.

Pecca It., Pr. *peca pec* fault, Sp. *peca*, Pg. *peco* speak; from *peccare*.

Pecchia — *ape*.

Pecchiero — *bicchiere*.

Pêche — *persica*.

Pechina Sp. a sort of mussel, from *pecten*.

Pecho pecha Sp., Pg. *peito peita* tax, contribution, vb. *pechar peitar* to pay tax; from *pactum*.

Pecilgar — *pellizcar*.

Pecora It. (f.) sheep, Wal. *pecure;* from *pecora,* orig. used as a collective, cf. E. *sheep.*

Pecores — *picorer.*

Peçonha — *pozione.*

Pedaggio It., Sp. *peage,* Fr. *péage* toll (paid by passengers); from *pes pedis.*

Pedante It. Sp. Pg., Fr. *pédant,* E. *pedant. Pedanti* = *quegli che avevano cura dei fanciulli insegnando loro e menandogli fuora* (Varchi); from παιδεύειν whence a L. L. vb. *pædare.*

Pedaso Sp. Pg. a piece; from *pittacium, pitacium* a piece of paper, cloth &c. Cf. also Pr. *pedas,* Occ. *petas,* Fr. *rapetasser* (to *patch).* V. *pezza.*

Pedone It., Sp. *peon,* Pr. *peon pezon,* Fr. *pion* foot-soldier, E. *pawn;* from a form *pedo (pes).* Hence Pr. *pezonier,* O. Fr. *peonier,* Fr. *pionnier,* E. *pioneer.* Fr. *piéton* requires a L. *pedito* (from *pedes,* L. L. *peditare).*

Pegar Sp. Pg. Pr. to cement, fasten, *empegar empeguntar* (comp. with *untar*) to pitch, *apegar* to adhere; from *picare.* Fr. *poisser empoisser* directly from *pix picis.* It. *impeciare* = Fr. *empoisser,* *empeser* (abst. *empois); impegolare* = Pr. *empegar; appicciare impicciare appiccare* to adhere, *impiccare* to hang up, *spiccare* to detach, not from *piccare,* cf. *appiccare* to take root — Sp. *pegar; pice* for *pec* (Lat. *plc*) was perhaps through the influence of the G. *pichen.*

Pego — *pelago.*

Peigne peine — *pettine.*

Peindre Fr. to paint; from *pingere,* It. *pignere,* but Sp. *pintar,* E. *paint.*

Pejo Pg. impediment, vb. *pejar, pejada* pregnant (cf. Sp. *embarazada);* from *pedica* with change of gender as in Fr. *piege;* for the *j* cf. Sp. *mege* from *med'cus.*

Pelago It., Sp. *pielago,* Pg. *peyo,* Pr. *peleg (peleagre)* sea, high sea, main, vb. Cat. *empelegar;* from *pelagus* which in L. L. and Romance involved the notion of deep, fathomless water (Pg. *pelago* well).

Pelare It., Sp. Pg. Pr. *pelar,* Fr. *peler* to pluck hair, *peel;* from *pilare.*

Pêle-mêle Fr. (E. *pell-mell);* the O. Fr. is *mêle-pêle, mêle* is clear enough but the second member, as usual in rhymed words of this kind (cf. *tire-lire, chari-vari* &c.) is difficult; is it O. Fr. *paesle* a pan, or *pelle* a shovel? Burg. *paule-maule* = earth thrown up.

Pelear Sp., Pg. *pelejar,* Pr. *peleiar* to fight, struggle, abst. *pelea* &c. From παλαίειν or from L. *palus* (fencing stick)?

Pèlerin — *pellegrino.*

Pelfro O. Fr. booty, *pelfer* to plunder; E. *pelf, pilfer.*

Pelisse — *pelliccia.*

Pelitre — *pilatro.*

Pella Sp. Pg. ball, mass; from *pila*, which is not found in the other Rom. languages. Sp. *pila*, Pg. *pilha*, Fr. *pile*, E. *pile* comes from *pila* a pillar.

Pella — *poêle.*

Pelle Fr. shovel, E. *peel*; from *pala*, It. Sp. Pr. *pala.* Hence It. *paletta &c., palette.*

Polleja Sp. harlot; from *pellis pellicula* in which sense it is also used, cf. *scortum. Pellex* would have given *pellega.*

Pellegrino It., Pr. *pelegrin pelerin*, Fr. *pèlerin, pilgrim;* from *peregrinus*, Sp. *peregrino.* From the Rom. come E. G. *pilgrim, pilger.*

Pelliccia It., Pg. *pellissa*, Fr. *pelisse*, E. *pilch*, O. H. G. *pelliz*, (G. *pelz;* from adj. *pelliceus pellicea.* Hence Pr. *sobrepelitz*, Fr. *surplis* for *surpelis*, E. *surplice.*

Polliscar pocilgar Sp., Pg. *bellizcar* to pinch; from *pellis*, cf. O. Fr. *pelicer* (from *pellis*, cf. *peliçon*) to pull.

Pelmazo Sp. slow, dull; usu. derived from πέλμα the sole of the foot, so, perhaps, orig. = heavy-treading, cf. Fr. *pataud* from *patte.*

Pelota pelote — *pillotta.*

Pelouse — *peluche.*

Peltro It., Sp. Pg. *peltre*, O. Fr. *peautre*, Du. *peauter*, E. *pewter.* Perhaps from Pr. *em-peltar* to stuff, graft, mix (tin with lead or quicksilver).

Peluca — *pilluccare.*

Peluche Fr. (f.) a stuff composed of linen and camel's hair, *plush;* from It. *peluccio, peluzzo (pilus).* Sp. is *pelusa* down on fruit, nap of cloth, O. Sp. *peluza*, Cat. *pelussa.* From same root is Fr. *pelouse*, Lim. *pelen.*

Penca Sp. Cat. prickly, sharp-pointed leaf, also lash; a Celtic word, W. *pinc* point, E. *pink.*

Penchor Fr. to hang, slope, Pr. *penjar pengar*, O. Sp. *pinjar;* from *pendicare (pendere).*

Pendeloque — *loque.*

Pendice It. slope, declivity; formed, on the analogy of *appendice*, from *pendere*, O. Fr. *pendant* a hill.

Pendon — *pennone.*

Pénil — *pettine.*

Penna It. peak of a mountain, Sp. *peña*, Pg. *penha* rock; from *pinna* a pinnacle, Pr. *pena*, Fr. *pignon*, It. *pignone;* Fr. *pinacle*, E. *pinnacle* from *pinnaculum.* The Celt. *pen* head, top, would have formed masc. derivatives.

Pennone It., Sp. *pendon*, Pr. *penò*, Fr. E. *pennon;* O. Sp. =

streamer. From *penna* feather; for Sp. *d* cf. *pendola* pen from *pennula;* so It. *pennoncello* = both streamer and plume.

Pensar pensare penser — *peso.*

Pente Fr. slope; for *pende* us *tente* for *tende;* from *pendere.* Hence *soupente.* Cf. It. *pentola,* E. *pent*-house.

Pentola It. a pot to hang over the fire; from *pendulus* (It. *penzolo*).

Penzolo — *pentola.*

Peña — *penna.*

Peon — *pedone.*

Pépie pepita — *pipita.*

Pepin Fr. a corn or grain, *pépinière* nursery-garden. Some derive it from *pepo* (O. Fr. *pepon,* It. *popone*) so = orig. a *pumpion* or cucumber seed (Sp. *pepino*). Cf. It. *pipita,* Sp. *pepita* seed, kernel, *pip. Pepo* is from the Gk. πέπων ripe.

Pequeño — *piccolo.*

Percer — *pertugiare.*

Perche Fr. a pole; L. *pertica,* Sp. Pg. *percha,* E. *perch.*

Perció — *ció.*

Perdice pernice It., Sp. Pr. *perdiz,* Fr. *perdrix,* E. *partridge;* from *perdix.*

Perdrix — *perdice.*

Peroxil — *petrosellino.*

Pereza — *pigrezza.*

Perfilar — *profilare.*

Pergamo It. a pulpit, stage; from *pergamum* a tower.

Periquito — *parrocchetto.*

Peritarsi It. to be ashamed. In Crem. Ven. Mil. *peritare perità* = to rate, tax, *perito* valuer. Perhaps from *pauritare* iterative of *paurire* (in *spaurire*), *au* being changed irregularly into *e,* so as to take the form of the O. L. *peritare.* But it may, better, be connected with the Sp. *apretarse* (v. *prieto*).

Perla It. Sp. Pr., Pg. *perala (perla),* Fr. *perle,* cf. O. H. G. *perala berala,* A. S. E. *pearl,* Nor. *perla,* L. L. *perulus perula, perla,* used instead of the L. *unio.* The trisyll. form seems the orig. one, cf. Ven. *perola,* L. L. *perula.* The derivations given are (1) *pirula* (from *pirum,* It. Sp. *pera*) cf. Sp. *perilla* ornament in the shape of a pear (2) *pilula* a globule (Ven. *pirola*) (3) *perna* mussel (v. Ducange), cf. Neap. Sic. *perna* = *perla,* It. *pernocchia* mother-of-pearl, but these may have conformed themselves to *perna,* (4) from G. *berala* (a corruption of *beryllus* or a dim. of *beere* a berry, cf. *baca*). This is Grimm's conjecture, and seems the most likely. The Wal. is *mergeritar.*

Pernice — *perdice.*

Perno It. Sp. Pg. hasp, bolt, *hinge*, Sp. *pernio* hinge, Fr. *perron* a flight of stairs; according to Menage from *perna*, but cf. Gk. περόνη.

Però It. Pr., Sp. O. Pg. *pero*, O. Fr. *poro pornec* for Lat. igitur, sed, autem, from *per hoc* and *pro hoc* the former used by Apuleius and others for propterea. Hence Sp. *empero*, Pr. *empero*; It. *perocchè*, L. L. *per hocque*.

Perol Sp. a pan, large kettle, Pr. *pairol*; from *patina*, whence *patin-ol patnol patrol* (cf. *engre* for *engue*), *pairol*.

Perola — *perla*.

Perpunte — *pourpoint*.

Perro Sp. dog (adj. = stubborn), Sic. *perru*. Diez gives no derivation, but connects it with the L. L. *petrunculus canis*. Is it from the Celtic? *Perro* is a common name for a dog in Wales.

Perron — *perno*.

Perroquet — *parrocchetto*.

Perruca perruque — *piluccare*.

Persa It. marjoram, N. Gr. πέρσα; from πράσον a leek.

Persica pesca It., Sp. *persigo prisco*, with Ar. art. *alpersico*, *alberchige* (Ar. *al-bersq*), Pg. *pecego*, *alperchi*, Pr. *presega*, Fr. *pêche*, E. *peach*, Wal. *pearsece*; It. *persico*, *pesco* (Sp. *melocoton*), Pg. *pecegueiro*, Pr. *pesseguier*, Fr. *pêcher*, Wal. *pearsec*; from *persicum*, *persicus*.

Persil — *petrosellino*.

Perso It., Pr. O. Fr. O. E. *pers* dark, of a colour between purple and black; L. L. *persus perseus "ad persei mali colorem accedens"* Ducange.

Pertugiare It., Pr. *pertusar*, Fr. *percer* (whence E. *pierce* and Sic. *pirciari*) = *pertuisier*; It. sbst. *pertugio*, Fr. *pertuis* a hole; from *pertundere pertusus (pertusiare pertusium)*.

Pertuis — *pertugiare*.

Pertuisane — *partigiana*.

Pesca — *persica*.

Pescuezo Sp., Pg. *pescoço* nape of the neck; from *post* (cf. *pestorejo*) and *cuezo* (v. *cocca*), so = hind-cask, cf. *testa*.

Peso It. Sp. Pg., Pr. *pens pes*, O. Fr. *puix*, Fr. *poids* (a form which points to *pondus*), E. *poise*, from *pensum*. Vb. It. *pesare*, Sp. Pg. Pr. *pesar*, Fr. *peser*, *poise*; Sp. *apesgar* to overload; also *pensare*, *pensar pessar* (Pr.) *penser* to think, from *pensare*, and with a different spelling, Fr. *panser* to attend upon, nurse, dress wounds &c., cf. L. *pensare sitim* to satiate thirst.

Pestaña — *pestare*.

Pestare It., Sp. *pistar*, Pr. *pestar*, also Sp. *pisar*, Pg. Pr. *pizar*, Fr. *piser*, Wal. *pisà* to stamp, tread, bray. The forms with *st* must be referred to L. *pistus* (It. *pesto*) for *pinsitus*, those with *s* to *pisare* (Varro). Hence It. *pesta*, Sp. *pista*, Fr. *piste* track, tread, whence It. *pistagna*, Sp. *pestaña*, Pg. *pestana* fringe (track or stripe on cloth), in Sp. Pg. also eyelash, cf. Cic. *fimbria* = end of locks of hair. Hence also It. *pestone*, Fr. E. *piston*.

Pestillo Sp., Cat. *pestell* bolt. Perhaps from *pes-it-illo* (cf. *cabr-it-illo*) for *pesillo* from *pessulus*, the form being varied so as to avoid confusion with *pesillo* a small weight, or so as to resemble *pistillum* a pestle.

Pestorejo Sp. nape; from *post (puest pest)* and *oreja* ear, cf. *pescuezo*.

Pesuña Sp. hoof; from *pedis ungula*.

Petaca Sp. portmanteau, wallet; from Mexican *petlacalli*.

Petardo It. Sp., Fr. E. *petard;* a coarse military word, from *peto, pet*, L. *peditum*. Hence Fr. *pétiller*.

Petate Sp. rush-mat; from Mexican *petlatl*.

Peteochie It., Sp. *petequias*, Fr. *pétéchies* (all plur.) fever-spots; a word introduced by physicians immediately from the Gk. πιττάκιον, not from L. *pittacium*.

Pétiller — *petardo*.

Petisoar — *pito*.

Petit — *pito*.

Peto Sp. breast-plate; from It. *petto*, L. *pectus*. From *pectorale* we have It. *pettorale*, Sp. *petral*, Fr. *poitral* (also = dewlap), E. *poitrel*, *petrel*.

Petrina — *poitrine*.

Pétrir Fr., Pr. *pestrir* to knead; from a form *pisturire (pistura, pinsere)*, cf. *cintrer* from *cinctura*, *accoutrer* from *ad-consutura*, It. *scaltrire* from *scalptura*.

Petrosellino petrosemolo prezzemolo It., Sp. *perexil*, Fr. *persil*, *parsley* (= A. S. *peterselige*, G. *petersilie*); from *petroselinum*.

Pettine It., Sp. *peine*, Pg. *pente*, Pr. *penche*, Fr. *peigne* comb; from *pecten;* vb. *pettinare* &c. Hence Fr. *pénil* (for *peignil*) groin, crines circa pudenda, Juv. *pecten*, It. *pettignone*, Sp. *empeigne*, Gk. κτείς.

Peu Fr. adv., in O. Fr. also an adj. *poies choses* &c.; from *paucus*, Pr. *pauc*, It. Sp. *poco*.

Peur Fr., O. Fr. *paour* fear; from *pavor*, It. *paura*.

Pévera It. also *petriola*, Mil. *pidria*, Romagn. *pidarja*, Com. *pledria*, Ven. *impiria* a wooden funnel; from *impletorium?*

Pezon — *picciuolo*.

Pezza pezzo It., Sp. *pieza*, Pg. *peça*, Pr. *peza pessa*, Fr. *pièce*, E. *piece*. L. L. *petium petia* = a piece of land. Diez derives it from πέζα a foot, edge, border (cf. *petiolus = pezzuolo*, v. *picciuolo*). The contraction from Sp. *pedazo*, would, he says, be too harsh. But another derivation which he mentions, that from the W. *peth*, Bret. *pez*, Gael. *peos* (whence a Lat. *pethia*, *petia*), seems more probable.

22*

Pezzente peziente It. beggar; from *petiens* for *petens*, cf. *caggiente* from *cadiens* for *cadens*, *veggente* for *videns*. Cf. Pg. *pedinte*.

Phiole Fr. a vial; from *phiala*, It. *fiala*, Pied. *fiola*.

Piaggia spiaggia It., Sp. Pr. *playa*, Pg. *praia*, Fr. *plage* shore. L. L. *plagia*, from *plaga* a region (It. *piaggia*).

Pialla It. a carpenter's plane, *piallare* to plane; for *planula planulare*, from *planus planare*, cf. *lulla* from *lunula*. *Pialla* also = adze, axe (for hewing), and this points to the O. G. *pial*, G. *beil*, E. *bill;* another form is *piola*.

Pianca Piedm. a plank for a bridge, Pr. *planca plancha*, Fr. *planche, plank*, whence Sp. *plancha* a plate of metal, Pg. *prancha* a board; from *planca* (Festus and Palladius). It. Sp. Pg. *palanca* a pole, lever, is from *palanga*, Pic. *pelangue*, Wal. *pélanc*.

Piara Sp. herd; from *pecuaria*.

Piare It., Sp. *piar* (Fr. *piailler*), to chirp; an onomatopœion.

Piastra It. plate of metal, Sp. &c. *piastra, piastre;* O. Fr. *plaistre* pavement, ceiling, Fr. *plâtre* stucco, *plaster;* It. *piastrone*, Pg. *piastrão*, Fr. E. *plastron;* It. *piastrello*. From *emplastrum* (ἔμπλαστρον) a surgical plaster, It. *empiastro*, Fr. *emplâtre*, Sp. *emplasto* = Gk. ἔμπλαστον. From *plastrum* (by rejection of the initial) was formed vb. *lastricare* to plaster, sbst. *lastrico astrico* (Mil. *astrich astregh*, Com. *astrach*), L. L. *astricus*, G. *estrich*. Hence also It. *lastra*, Sp. *lastra lastre* a slab of stone or metal, v. s. *lasto*, ph. also O. Fr. *astre aistre*, Fr. *âtre* hearth.

Piato It., Sp. *pleito*, Pg. *pleito preito*, Pr. *plait plag*, O. Fr. *plaid*, E. *plea*, law-suit, Rh. *pled* a word; It. *piatire piategyiare*, Sp. *pleitear*, Pg. *preitejar*, Pr. *plaideiar*, O. Fr. *plaidier, plaidoyer*. Fr. *plaider*, E. *plead*, Rh. *plidar*. From L. L. *placitum* which was used = a convention for the discussion of affairs of state *(placita habere)*, O. Pg. *placito, plazo prazo*, Sp. *plazo*.

Piatto It., Pg. Sp. *chato*, Pr. Fr. *plat* flat, It. sbst. *piatto*, Sp. *plato*, Fr. *plat, plate;* a root common to many languages and connected with Gk. πλατύς, O. H. G. *flaz*. Hence also Sp. Pg. *plata* silver, O. Fr. *plate*, E. *plate*, and *platina;* Sp. *chata* a flat-bottomed boat (It. *sciatta*, cf. Com. *sciatt* = Sp. *chato*).

Piazza It., Wal. *piatz*, Sp. Pg. Pr. *plaza plaça plassa*, Fr. E. *place;* vb. Fr. *placer*, E. *place:* from *platea* (πλατεῖα) a street, in Horace *platêa*, Goth. *platja*. It is first used by Lampridius = a court-yard (place).

Picaro — *picco*.

Piccino — *piccolo*.

Piccione It., Sp. *pichon*, Pr. *pijon*, Fr. E. *pigeon;* from *pipio*

(Lampridius), which is from *pipare pipire*, cf. Mil. *pipi* a little bird.

Picciuolo It. stalk, Wal. *picior* foot; from *petiolus* little foot, stalk; Sp. *pezon*, Ven. *picolo*, Mil. *picoll*, Piedm. *picol* = *pediculus*.

Picco It., Sp. Pg. *pico*, Pr. Fr. *pic*, *beak*, *peak* &c.; It. *picca*, Sp. Pg. *pica*, Fr. *pique pike*; It. *piccare*, Sp. Pg. Pr. *picar*, Fr. *piquer* to prick. From L. *picus* woodpecker, Sp. *pico*, Fr. *pic*; cf. W. *pig* a point, G. *picken*, *pickel*, E. *pick peck* &c. It. *picchio (piculus)* = woodpecker, blow, *picchiare* to knock; Fr. *picot* a pick-axe, *picoter* to pick with an axe; perhaps also Sp. *picaro*, It. *picciro* a sharper.

Piccolo It., Sp. *pequeño*, Pg. *pequeno* little, for which Pr. Cat. Fr. have *petit*. From the O. Rom. *pic* a point (v. *piccu*) so = minute (as It. *picco* is used = *punctum*, so *piccolo* = *punctulum*). The Wal. *pic* == drop, Alb. *picë*. Besides *piccolo* the It. has *picciolo* and *piccino (= pic-ciolo pic-cino* or *pit-ciolo pit-cino* from root of *petit)*; N. Pr. has *piccioun*, Lim. *pitsou*, fem. *pitsouno*.

Pichel — *bicchiere*.

Pichon — *piccione*.

Picorer Fr. to prowl in quest of plunder, prop. of cattle; from *pecus*, cf. Sp. *pecorea* marauding.

Pidocchio It., Sp. *piojo*, Pg. *piolho*, Pr. *peolh*, *pezolh*, Fr. *pou* (for *péou)* a louse; from *pediculus (peduculus)* L. L. *peduclus*. Hence It. *spidocchiare*, Sp. *despiojar*, Fr. *épouiller*.

Pièce — *pezza*.

Piedestallo It., Sp. *pedestal*, Fr. *piédestal*; formed with G. *stal*, v. *stallo*.

Piegaro It., Sp. Pr. *plegar*, Pg. *pregar*, Fr. *plier*, in comp. *ployer* (E. *ply, -ploy)*, Wal. *plecà* to fold; from *plicare*. Hence It. *impiegare*, Sp. *emplear*, Pg. *empleyar*, Fr. *employer*, E. *employ*, from *implicare*; It. *impiego*, Fr. *emploi*, E. *employ*; It. *spiegare*, Pr. *espleiar*, Fr. *déplier déployer* (E. *deploy)* from *explicare*, *de-explicare*, cf. *llegar*.

Piógo Fr. (m.) a snare; from *pedica*, It. *piedica*, Wal. *peadecé*, masc. Pg. *pejo*.

Pier *(pyer)* Fr. to tipple; from πιεῖν, cf. Sp. *empinar* from ἐμπίνειν, Fr. *trinquer* from G. *trinken*. Hence *piot* a draught of wine, vb. Norm. *pioter*.

Pierna Sp. leg, Pg. *perna;* from *perna* = the leg from the hip to the foot (Ennius), ham.

Pietanza It., Sp. Pr. *pitanza*, Fr. *pitance* (E. *pittance)* a monk's daily allowance. The It. form had once also the meaning of *pity*, and was altered from *pitanza* so as to conform to *pietà*, cf. O. Pg. *pitança* == charitableness. Prob. from O. Rom.

pile a morsel, small portion, through a verb *pitare* (Geno. *pittà* to pick).

Piéton — *pedone.*

Piètre It. poor, needy. For *piestre* from *pedestris?*

Pieu Fr. post. From *palus, pal, pcl, piel, pieu,* cf. in O. Fr. *cher (carus) chier, tres tries, tel tiel tieu.* As no instance of this process occurs in Modern Fr., Diez derives *pieu* from *piculus piclus,* so = It. *picchio.*

Pieve It. district, parish, Rh. *pleif,* It. *piovano,* Wal. *pleban* a parish-priest; from L. L. *plebs* parish church, *plebanus.*

Pieviale piviale It. mantle; for *piovale* = *plurialis.* Cf. *pimaccio* cushion = *piumaccio,* O. Pg. *chimaço* and *chumaço.*

Piesa — *pizza.*

Pifaro piffero piffre — *pipa.*

Pigeon — *piccione.*

Pigiare It. to press; a participial verb from *pinsere pinsus (pinsiare),* cf. *pertugiare* from *pertusus.*

Pigione It. house-rent; from *pensio,* Fr. *pension,* cf. *magione* from *mansio.*

Pigliare It., Sp. *pillar,* Pg. Pr. *pilhar,* Fr. *piller* to take, pill, *pillage;* from *pilare* in *expilarc, compilare.* The soft *l* is to distinguish it from It. *pillare,* Fr. *piler* to stamp, from *pila.*

Pignatta It. pot; from *pinea,* because the lid was shaped like a pine-cone. Hence Sp. *piñata.*

Pignon pignone — *penna.*

Pigolare — *pipa.*

Pigressa It., Sp. Pr. *pereza,* Pg. *preguiça,* Fr. *paresse* idleness; from *pigritia.*

Pihuela Sp. a fetter; with *piola* (cf. *vihuela viola*) from *pes pedis;* cf. *pi-ojo* from *pediculus.*

Pila — *pella.*

Pilatro It., Sp. Pg. Pr. *pelitre,* Fr. *pyrèthre,* E. *pellitory* a plant; from *pyrethrum* (πύρεθρον).

Pile — *pella.*

Piler pillar piller — *pigliare.*

Pillotta It., Sp. Pg. Pr. *pelota,* Fr. *pelote,* E. *pellet* (hence E. *pell*); from *pila,* L. L. *pilotellus* = Sp. *pelotilla.* Hence also Sp. Fr. *peloton,* E. *platoon.*

Pilori Fr., E. *pillory,* Pr. *espitlori,* Pg. *pelourinho.* Duc. from *pilier,* Grimm from M.H.G. *pfilaere.* The L.L. has *pilloricum, pellericum, pellorium, piliorium, spiliorium.*

Piloto It. Sp. Pg., also It. *pilota,* Fr. *pilote,* E. *pilot.* From the Du. *pijloot,* the origin of which is not clear.

Piluccare It. to stone grapes, Pr. *pelucar,* Pic. *pluquer,* Norm. Champ. *pluchotter;* Fr. *éplucher,* Rh. *spluccar* to pluck out. From Lat. *pilare* with suffix *uc* (R. Gr. 2, 333), not from

A. S. *pluccian*, E. *pluck*, which are from the Rom. Connected with *pilluccare* is Sard. *pilucca*, Lomb. *peluch*, Pied. *pluch*, Gen. *pellucco*, It. (corrupted) *perruca parruca*, Wal. *perocë*, Fr. *perruque*, E. *peruke (periwig)*, Occ. *pamparrugo*, Sp. *peluza* (cf. *machuca*, *almendruco* &c.).

Piment — *pimiento*.

Pimiento pimienta Sp., Pg. *pimento* (whence E. *pimento*) *pimenta* pepper, Pr. *pimenta* spice, Pr. *pimen*, O. Fr. *piment*, L. L. *pigmentum* a drink made of wine, honey, and spice, Fr. *piment* a medicine; from L. *pigmentum* a colouring material, hence juice of plants used for colouring, so anything aromatic.

Pimpa — *pipa*.

Pimpinella It., Sp. *pimpinela*, Fr. *pimprenelle*, E. *pimpernel*; from *bipinella* for *bipennula* (two-winged). The Cat. has *pampinella*, Pied. *pampinela* a mere corruption, for it has no connection with *pampinus*. In N. Pr. it is *fraissineto*, from *fraisse* = *fraxinus*.

Pimpollo Sp. sucker, sprout, Pg. *pimpolho*; for *pampinollo*, a dim. of *pampinus*, cf. sup. *pampinella* for *pimpinella*.

Pinaccia It., Sp. *pinaza*, Fr. *pinasse*, E. *pinnace*; from *pinus*.

Pincer pinchar pinso — *pizza*.

Pincione It., Sp. *pinzon pinchon*, Fr. *pinçon*, Cat. *pinsá* a finch. From W. *pink* (G. *finke*, E. *finch*) frolicksome, finch, cf. Fr. *geai* = gay and jay. The Bret. has *pint*, Bav. *pienk*, Slav. *pinka*, Hung. *pinty*; N. Pr. *quinson* for *pinson*, Pg. *pisco*.

Pino Pg. nail, point; *a pino* Sp. Pg. on tiptoe, cf. Sp. *empinarse* to stand erect (though this *pino* may be a different word, and derived from *pinus*, cf. *arbolarse*); from E. W. *pin*, Gael. *pinne*, O. N. *pinni*, G. *pinne*.

Pinque Fr. (f.), Sp. *pingue* (m.), *pinco*, Pg. *pinque* (m.), L. G. *pinke* (f.) a sort of ship, E. *pink*; from *pinus pinica*, *pinca*, cf. *pinaza* &c.

Pinta Sp. Pg. paint · spot, mark, from *pingere*; hence also a marked measure for liquids, Fr. *pinte*, E. *pint*, Wal. *pintë*, cf. *rubbio*.

Pintacilgo Sp., Pg. *pintasirgo* a goldfinch; from *pictus passerculus*.

Pinsa — *pizza*.

Pinson — *pincione*.

Pinata — *pignatta*.

Pioggia It., Sp. *lluvia*, Pg. *chuva*, Fr. *pluie*, Wal. *ploaie* rain; from *pluvia*. Hence Sp. *chubasco* squall, cf. O. Sp. *cheno* from *plenus*.

Pioletto It. (in Com. *piolet*) a little axe or bill; from the O. H. G. *bial pial*, G. *beil*, E. *bill*.

Piombare It. to sink perpendicular, to fall *plumb* down, *cadere* *a piombo;* Pr. *plombar,* Fr. *plonger* (with suffix *g* = *ic*, *plumbicare*, cf. *venger* from *vindicare*) a bye-form of *plomber,* cf. O. Fr. *clinger, enferger* by the side of *cliner, enferrer;* E. *plunge (plumb, plumb);* abst. Fr. *plongeon* a diver. Not derived from, though connected with, Bret. *plunia,* W. *plwng* = Sansk. *plavana* (Pictet), for the der. from *plumbicare* is supported by the Pic. *plonquer,* cf. Wall. *plone* = Fr. *plomb, plonki* = *plonger.*

Pion pionnier — *pedone.*

Ploppa ploppo It., Wal. *plop* (Alban. *plepi*), Wall. *plopp,* Pg. *chopo chonpo,* Sp. *popo chopo,* Cat. *clop,* Neap. *chiuppo.* From *pōpulus,* with a remarkable change of form to distinguish it from *pōpulus;* L. L. *ploppus,* Lomb. *pobbia,* Berr. *peuple* for *peuplier,* Jura *puble,* Lim. *piboul.*

Piorno Sp. Pg. Spanish broom; ph. for *picorno* from *pico* a point, cf. *pia* from *pica.*

Piot — *pier.*

Piota It. Dante Inf. 19, 120 = foot, sole, elsewhere = a grass-plot. From the Umbrian *plotus plautus,* cf. Festus: *plotus appellant Umbri pedibus planis......poeta quia Umber Sarsinas erat initio Plotus postea Plautus cœptus est dici.*

Piovano — *pieve.*

Pipa piva It., Sp. Pg. *pipa,* Pr. *pimpa,* Fr. *pipe pipeau,* Wal. *pipé,* E. *pipe;* from *pipare pipiare,* Fr. *piper* (= illicere aves pipilando, then = cheat, espec. at cards), whence also O. H. G. *pfifa,* G. *pfeife,* E. *fife,* G. *pfeifer* which became in It. *piffero,* Sp. *pifaro,* Fr. *piffre* and *fifre;* Rh. *fifa.* It. *pirolo,* Fr. *pivot* tap, E. *pivot* are connected. From *pipilare* is It. *pigolare* for *pirolare, g* for *v,* or, better, inserted in a form *piolare* for *pivolare.* From *pivare* we have also *piviere,* Fr. *pluvier,* E. *plover.*

Pipistrello It., also *ripistrello, rispistrello, vespistrello* a bat, from *vespertillus* for *vespertilio.*

Pipita It., Sp. *pepita,* Pg. *pevide pivide,* Pr. *pepida,* Fr. *pépie,* E. *pip* (in fowls); from *pituita (pevita pipita,* O. H. G. *phiphis).* Nearer the L. is the Mil. *puida purida.*

Pique — *picco.*

Pirouette Fr.; from a primitive *pive* (= It. *piva*) of *pivot* a peg, and *roue* a wheel.

Pis Fr. udder, O. Fr. breast, from *pectus,* Pr. *peitz,* Lomb. *pecc,* Lim. *piei* (f.).

Pisar piser piste — *pestare.*

Pisciare It., Wal. *pisà,* Pr. *pissar,* Fr. *pisser;* an onomatop. like the G. *zischen,* cf. Cat. *pixar,* N. Pr. *pichà,* Pic. *picher.*

Pistóla It. Sp., Fr. *pistole pistolet,* E. *pistol.* Orig. = a dagger (worn secretly, like the pistol), and, according to H. Stephanus, from *Pistoja, pistojese, pistolese, pistola.* Others derive it

from *pistillus*, It. *pestello* a pestle, with a change of form, cf.
Ven. *piston peston* a rifle, from It. *pestone* a large pestle. But
here the change of suffix is unusual, the form should be *pis-
tuola, ol* only following *i* as in *oriolo* &c. The *pistole* = a gold
coin is prob. the same word, cf. Claude Fauchet (1599): *ayant
les escus d'Espagne esté reduicts à une plus petite forme que les
escus de France, ont pris le nom de pistolets (little pocket pistols).*

Pitaud Fr. a clown; from *pedes-itis*, cf. *pietoa.*

Pito Sp. a small pointed bit of wood, O. Fr. *pite* a mite, Rou.
pete a trifle, Com. *pit* small; hence Sp. *pitorra* woodcock (from
its sharp bill), Wall. *petion* bee's sting, vb. Pr. *pitar* to bill,
Sp. *apitar* to instigate, O. Fr. *apiter* to pick with the fingers,
Pg. *petiscar* to nip; Mil. *pitin* small, Crem. *petern* trifle, Sard.
piticu small. From a root *pit* found in W. *pid* = point. Hence
O. It. *piletto petitto*, Pr. Cat. Fr. *petit*, N. Pr. *pitit*, Wall. *piti*
small, *petty*, dim. Pr. Cat. O. Fr. *petitet;* cf. *piccolo* from *pic.*
Petit is for *petet* by an euphonic change.

Pito Sp. a pipe, *pitar* to pipe; au ononatop., cf. *pita* a hen-call.

Pitocco It. a beggar, from πτωχός, perhaps influenced by *pit*
small, cf. Lomb. *piton* poor.

Pitorra — *pito.*

Piva — *pipa.*

Pivoine Fr., E. *peony;* from *pæonia* (παιωνία from Παιών), It.
Sp. *peonia.*

Pivolo — *pipa.*

Pivot — *pipa.*

Pizarra Sp. Pg., Cat. *pissarra* slate. Perhaps from *pieza* piece,
with suffix *arra*, cf. G. *schiefer* = prop. a fragment.

Pizca — *pizza.*

Pizza Ven. pricking, itching, Sard. *pizzu* beak, Rh. *pizza*, Mil.
pizz, Sic. *pizzu*, It. *pinzo* prick, Sp. *pinzas*, Fr. *pince*, It. *pin-
zette* pincers; also It. *pizzico*, Sp. *pizca* a mite, small particle;
Ven. *pizzare*, Wall. *pissi*, It. *pizzicare*, Wal. *pitzigà piscà*, Cat.
pessigar, N. Pr. *pessugà*, Sp. *pizcar* and *pinchar*, Fr. *pincer
épincer épinceler*, E. *pinch;* Pg. *piscar os olhos* to wink the
eyes. From Du. *pitsen*, G. *pfetzen*, itself from a root common
in Rom. *pit*, v. *pito*. Others derive *pinzare pinzo* &c. from *pictus,
pictiare, pinctus, pinctiare*. But *pingere* (Sk. *pinj* colorare) does
not mean orig. to pierce, embroider? in the phrase *acu pingere*
the sense of piercing belongs to *acus* not to *pingere.*

Pizzico — *pizza.*

Placard — *plaque.*

Place — *piazza.*

Plafond Fr. ceiling; from *plat fond* flat floor; hence Sp. *paston.*

Plage — *piaggia.*

Plaid — *piato.*

Plaindre Fr., O. E. *plain;* from *plangere,* Pr. *planher,* It. *piagnere,* Sp. *plañir.*

Plais plaissa Pr. hedge, O. Fr. *plaissier plessier* to hedge, Pr. partic. as sbst. *plaissat,* O. Fr. *plessie,* also Pr. *plaissaditz,* O. Fr. *pleisseis* a park, Fr. *Plessis;* from *plexus plexa* twisted, so *plais* = basket-work.

Plancho — *pianca.*

Plaque Fr. plate, vb. *plaquer,* sbst. *placard:* from Du. *plak* a flat piece of wood, a shaving, *plakken* to paste up, fasten, not from Gk. πλάξ, since the word is only found in Fr.

Plasta — *pasta.*

Plat plata — *piatto.*

Plâtre — *piastra.*

Playa — *piaggia.*

Plasa — *piazza.*

Plegar — *piegare.*

Plegaria Sp. public prayer; from *precarius.*

Pleige — *plevir.*

Pleita Sp. rush-matting; from *plectere.*

Pleito — *piato.*

Plessier — *plais.*

Plevir Pr. O. Fr. to pledge, Pr. *plieu,* Fr. *pleige* (= E. *pledge*), whence Ven. *plezo,* Sic. *preggiu; plevir* = *prœbere* (sc. fidem), cf. *temple* from *tempora, Planchais* = *Prancatius* for *Pancratius. Pleige* = *prœbium* a remedy, surety; Pr. *plevizo* = *prœbitio,* Fr. *plevine* warranty, E. *plevin, replevin.* W. refers to a G. source, Du. *pleghe* duty (G. *pflicht*), E. *plight.*

Plie Fr. a plaice == in meaning L. *platessa* (Ausonius), Sp. *platija,* Pg. *patruça,* E. *plaice. Plie* is for *plaie* from *plate* fem. of *plat* flat, and is altered in form to distinguish it from *plaie* = *plaga.*

Plier — *piegare.*

Plisser Fr. to fold; a participial verb, from *plicare plic'tus (plictiare).*

Plonger — *piombare.*

Ployer — *piegare.*

Plusieurs Fr., Pr. *plusor,* O. It. *plusori* a comparative for L. *plus (plures)* which was appropriated to form the Romance comparative; from *plus* was der. *plusior,* cf. Varro's *plusimus,* and L. L. *pluriores.*

Poche Fr. introduced from England; A. S. *pocca,* E. *poke.*

Pocima Sp. potion; from πότισμα.

Podar — *potare.*

Podestá It. m. a magistrate; Pr. *podestat poestat,* Sp. *potestad,* L. *potestas* all fem.

Podre Sp. pus, matter; from *puter,* = Pg. *podre.*

Poe O. Fr., Pr. *pauta*, Cat. *pota;* from Du. *poot* = G. *pfote* foot.

Poêle Fr. f. a pan, O. Fr. *paele paesle*, E. *peel pail;* from L. *patella*, It. *padella*, Sp. *padilla*. From Fr. *paele* come Sp. *payla* and Pg. *pella*.

Poêle Fr. m. a canopy, pall, O. Fr. *poesle;* from πέταλον, L. L. *petalum* a golden canopy hung over the Pope's head. *Pallium* would have given *paile*, Pr. *pali*. But v. Littré, p. 69, who makes *poêle* = *poile* = *paile*.

Poêle Fr. m. a heated room, a stove, O. Fr. *poisle*. L. L. has *pisele, pisalis*, which point to L. *pensilis, pēsile*, cf. the expressions *horreum pensile* (L.), *domus pensilis, camera pendens* (L. L.). A Rom. form *birle* for *pirle* is from *pisle*, as *varlet* from *vaslet*, L. L. *pirale*, O. H. G. *pheral*, not from πῦρ which could only have given *pirále*.

Poge — *poggia*.

Poggia It. rope at the end of a sailyard, Fr. *poge* (m.); from ποδίον (πούς). The *poggia* was on the right, as the *orza* was on the left. It is one of the numerous nautical words borrowed from the Greek, cf. *barca, sesto, golfo, artimone, falo*.

Poggio It., Pr. *pueg puoi*, O. Fr. *pui* a raised place (E. *pew pue*), Sp. Pg. *poyo* a stone bench near the door, O. Fr. *puiol;* from *podium* raised place; hence vb. It. *poggiare*, O. Pg. Pr. *poyar*, O. Fr. *puier* to mount; It. *appoggiare*, Sp. Pg. *apoyar*, Fr. *appuyer* to support, lean; abst. *appui*.

Poi It., Sp. *pues*, Pg. *poz*, Pr. *pois*, Fr. *puis*, from *post;* hence It. *dipoi dópo* (cf. *domani*), the latter a very old form for Wal. has *dúpe*, Pg. Pr. *depois*, Fr. *depuis*, L. L. *de post;* Sp. *despues*, Pr. *despuois*, Com. *despò*, Padu. *daspò* from *de ex post*. It. *poscia*, Pr. *poissas* is from *postea*.

Poids — *peso*.

Poignard — *pugnale*.

Poinçon — *punzar*.

Poindre Fr. to prick, also to spur a horse, whence sbst. *poindre* assault in battle, M. H. G. *poinder;* from *pungere*, Pr. *punher*, It. *pungere*, Sp. *pungir*.

Point — *punto*.

Poison — *pozione*.

Poisser — *pegar*.

Poisson Fr. fish; from *piscis*, Pr. *peis*, O. Fr. *pescion*, It. *pescione*.

Poitrine Fr., Pr. *peitrina* breast, from a form *pectorina*, Dauph. *peitwrina;* orig. = breast-piece, or girdle, cf. Sp. *petrina pretina* girdle. O. Fr. has *pis* = *peetus*. Hence O. Fr. *poictrinal petrinal*, E. *petronel* because worn in the girdle.

Poles — *poulier*.

Poledro *puledro* It., Sp. Pg. *potro*, Pr. *poudre*, O. Fr. *poutre* a colt; from L. L. *pulletrus poledrus;* Scaliger's *pulletra* for *pul-*

lastra in Varro, is a mere conjecture. *Puletro* may be from a
Gk. πωλίδριον for πωλίδιον, (πῶλος, cf. ἴππος, ἰππίδιον).
Sp. *potro* also = a wooden horse, cf. *equuleus* (G. *folter* from
poledrus), Fr. *poutre* a cross-beam to support another beam.

Poleggio puloggio It., Pr. *pulegi*, Sp. *poleo*, Pg. *poejo*, Fr. *pouliot* a plant, penny-royal; from *pulegium*.

Polichinelle — *pulcinella*.

Polilla Sp., Pg. *polilha* a moth; according to the Sp. etymologers
from *pulvis*, the *v* suppressed as in *fulo* from *fulvus*, *Gonzalo*
for *Gonzalvo*.

Polisson Fr. a blackguard, whence Sp. *polizon*; from *politio* one
who *polishes* the pavement, cf. *nourriçon* from *nutritio*. Roue.
polisso = a smoothing iron.

Polizza It., Sp. *poliza*, Fr. *police* bill, certificate, *policy* (of in-
surance &c.); a corruption of *polyptychum* a catalogue &c.,
usually in pl. *polyptycha* an account-book (πολύπτυχον), also
polecticum polecticum poletum, Fr. *pontié*.

Pollare It. to shoot, bud forth, whence *rampollare*; from *pullulare*.

Pollegar Pg., Sp. *pulgar*, Pr. *polgar*, O. Fr. *pochier* thumb; from
pollicaris (pollex).

Poltro It. lazy, dastardly, whence *poltrone*, Sp. *poltron*, Pg. *po-
trão*, Fr. *poltron*, E. *poltroon* all from the It., the prim. *poltro*
found only in Champ. *pleutre*. Connected with O.H.G. *polstar
bolstar*, E. *bolster*, cf. Fr. *lodier* (1) blanket (2) idler, and cf.
It. *boldrone boldra* a part of the bed furniture; the commen-
tators on Dante Inf. 24, 46 *(spoltre)* mention a sbst. *poltro*,
Mil. *polter*, Rom. *pultar* a bed. The dropping of the initial *s*
may be owing to the *lst* of the original, and the double initial
points to a G. source.

Pomo It. Sp., Fr. *pomme* apple; from *pomum*. Dim. It. *pomello*,
Fr. *pommeau*, E. *pommel*. Hence also E. *pomander* = *pomme
d'ambre*, and *pomatum* (made from apples), v. Wedgwood.

Ponce Fr., prop. *pierre ponce* pumice-stone; from *pumex*, It. *po-
mice*, Sp. *pomez*. Hence sbst. *poncis*, vb. *poncer*. Hence E.
pounce.

Ponceau Fr. purple, deep red; from *puniceus punicellus*, Pr. *pu-
nicenc*.

Pondre Pr. Fr., Cat. *pondrer* to lay eggs; from *ponere*, which,
in these three languages, is only found in this sense.

Ponente It., Sp. *poniente*, Pr. *ponent* west, prop. sun-setting,
ove il sol si pone; Wal. *apus* (partic. from *apune = apponere*),
Fr. *couchant*, cf. *levante*.

Pontare puntaro It. to press, insist on, resist; = Fr. *pointer*, to
point, cf. It. *pontar la lancia contra alcuno*.

Ponzoña — *pozione*.

Popar Sp. to caress, Pg. *poupar* to spare, save; from L. It. *palpare*.

x

Popone — *pépin*.

Poppa It., Pr. *popa*, O. Fr. *poupe* breast; from *pupa* a doll (cf. *coppa* from *cupa*), hence Rh. *popa*, Fr. *poupée* (E. *poppy*), G. *puppe*. Cf. It. *zita* from G. *zitze* a teat?

Por Sp. Pg. O. Fr., Fr. *pour* for L. *pro*, in Sp. Pg. also = *per*, so in early L. L. *non territus pro hoc sacrificio*. It is not found in It. but the Sard. has *po (= por)* prob. from the Sp., since *peri* is also used. O. Sp. O. Pg. *pora*, Sp. Pg. *para = pro ad*, Cat. *pera*, Prov. *per a*, O. Fr. *por a*.

Por puer O. Fr., Pr. *por pore* a particle = L. *porro* and used with certain verbs, such as *gitar, traire, volar* e. g. *por gitar* to throw away.

Porc-épic Fr. corrupted from *porc-espi*, Pr. *porc-espin* (O. E. *porpin* a hedgehog whence, by corruption, *porpentine* in Shakspere), It. *porco spino*, *porco spinoso*, Sp. *puerco espino*, E. *porcupine*. The Fr. connected it with *spica*.

Porcellana It., Sp. Pg. *porcellana*, Fr. *porcelaine*, E. *porcelain*. The word is of Italian origin; *porcellana =* (1) a shell-fish, *concha Veneris* (2) porcelain, which resembles the shell in transparency. *Porcellana* in sense (1) is derived from L. *porcus* in a secondary sense, cf. Fr. *pucelage* with the same meaning. V. Mahn, Untersuchungen, p. 13.

Porcellana — *portulaca*.

Porche Fr. (m.), Pr. *porge* porch; from *porticus*, It. *portico*.

Porendo poren O. Sp. O. Pg. = *por tanto* from *proinde*. Pg. *porem* is for *não porem*, as *pourtant* for *non pourtant*.

Porfia Sp. Pg. Cat. obstinacy, *porfiar* to dispute obstinately, O. Pg. *perfia*, O. Sp. *porfidia*, so from *perfidia*. Cf. *ἀπιστία* faithlessness and disobedience, and for the form cf. Sp. *hastio* from *fastidium*.

Poridad Sp., O. Pg. *puridade* = Sp. *puridad* secrecy, L. *puritas*.

Porra Sp. Pg. Cat. a club-headed stick; from *porrum* a leek, or from a B. root. Hence *porro* heavy, dull.

Portulaca It. Pr., Sp. *verdolaga* (through *verde*), Pg. *verdoaga verdoega beldroega*, a plant, *purslane*; from *portulaca*. From L. *porcilaca* (also *porcastrum*) comes It. *porcellana*, E. *purslane*; from *pulli pes*, Fr. *pourpier*.

Poruce — *appo*.

Posar poser — *pausare*.

Poscia — *poi*.

Posnée O. Fr. *posnée* haughtiness. For *poussonée* from *pousser?* or connected with W. *posned* (m.) = something round and swelling?

Possa poussa Pr. nipple; = bud, Fr. *pousse?*

Posta It. Sp. Pg., Fr. *poste*, E. *post*; from *positus*, because of the *relay* of horses.

Posticcio It., Sp. *postizo*, Fr. *postiche*, also *apposticcio*, *apostizo*, Pr. *apostitz* supposititious, counterfeit; L. *appositicius*.

Postierla — *poterne*.

Postilla It. Pg. Pr., Sp. *postila*, Fr. *apostille*, E. *postil* marginal note, comment; not from *positus* (wh. would have given *postella*), but from *post illa* (sc. *verba auctoris*).

Postilla Sp. scab; from *pustula*.

Postrar — *prostrare*.

Pot-pourri — *olla*.

Potage potaggio — *pote*.

Potare It., Sp. Pg. Pr. *podar*, O. Fr. *poder* to prune; from *putare* which is not found in Rom. in its figurative sense. Sp. *podon*, Pg. *podão* a hoe, O. Fr. *poun* from Sp. *poda* a pruning; Occ. *poudo* a pruning-knife.

Potasse Fr. from (1. *pott-asche* (also *kesselasche*), E. *potash*.

Pote Sp. Pg., Pr. Fr. *pot*; from Du. E. *pot*, cf. Pic. *potequin* = Du. *potekin*; W. *pot*, Gael. *poit*. The It. has no masc. form *potto*, but the fem. *potta* has the secondary meaning which is found also in the Irish *puite*, and in L. and It. *concha*, It. *raso*. Hence Fr. *potage*, E. *pottage*, It. *potaggio*, that which is prepared therein, cf. *formaggio* that made in a *forma*.

Poteau Fr., Pr. *postel* a post; from *postis*.

Potence Fr. a crutch, gallows; from L. L. *potentia* prop. = support.

Potere It., Sp. Pg. Pr. *poder*, O. Fr. *pooir* (*d* lost), Fr. *pouvoir* (*v* inserted to prevent the hiatus), Wal. *puteá* = L. *posse*, a new conjugation being formed as in *velle* &c., v. R. Gr. 2, 121. Sbst. It. *podere*, Sp. *poder*, Wal. *puteare* power, also = possession, estate (like G. *vermögen*), It. form.

Poterne Fr., E. *postern*; a corruption of O. Fr. *posterle*, Pr. *posterla*, It. *postierla*, from *posterula*.

Potro — *poledro*.

Pou — *pidocchio*.

Pouacre Fr. filthy; formed from interjection *pouah*, Burg. Norm. *polacre*, Pic. *polaque*, N. Pr. *pouldcre*.

Poudre Fr. (f.), E. *powder*, from *pulvis pulveris* (*pol're poldre*). Fr. *poussière* is for *pourrière* (cf. *besicle*), O. Fr. *porrière pouldrière*.

Poulain Fr. foal; from *pullus*, Pr. *polin*.

Poulier Fr. to hoist up, *poulie* (E. *pulley*, Sp. *poléa*, Pg. *polé*); from A. S. *pullian*, E. *pull*; but v. Wedg. s. v. *"pulley"*.

Pouliot — *poleggio*.

Pouls — *pulsar*.

Poupa — *upupa*.

Pour — *por*.

Pourpier — *portulaca*.

Pourpoint Fr., Pr. *perpouh*, Sp. *perpunte*, *pespunte*. Pg. *pesponto*:

L. L. *perpunctum*, so called because it was quilted. On *pour* for *per* cf. R. Gr. 2, 353.

Pousse poussif — *bolso*.

Pousser — *pulsare*.

Poussière — *poudre*.

Poussin Fr., Pr. *pouzin* a chicken; from *pullicenus* (Lampridius).

Poutre — *poledro*.

Poyo — *poggio*.

Pozione It., Sp. *pocion*, Pr. *poizó* drink, medicine, O. Sp. *pozon*, Fr. *poison*, E. *poison*: from *potio* a draught, a potion to work a charm or cure; vb. Pr. *poizonar*, Sp. *ponzoñar*, from *potionare*, whence Sp. sbst. *ponzoña*, Pg. *peçonha* poison. Cf. Sp. *yerba*, Pg. *erva* poisonous plant, poison, O. Fr. *enherber* to poison, and G. *gift* poison = prop. dose (δόσις).

Pozzo It., Wal. *putzu*, Sp. *pozo*, Pr. *potz*, Fr. *puits* (E. *pit*) well; from *puteus*. Hence vb. Pr. *pozar*, Fr. *puiser*, *épuiser*.

Pozzolana It. melted lava, so called because often found in the district of *Pozzuoli*.

Prace It. space between two furrows; from πρασία a garden-bed.

Prebenda prevenda It. Pr., Sp. *prebenda*, Fr. *prébende*, E. *prebend* daily supply for the monks &c. The Fr. *provende* (whence G. *pfründe*, E. *provender*), It. *profenda* has taken the *pror* from *providere*, cf. G. *proviant*.

Preboste — *prevoste*.

Prêcher Fr., E. *preach*, Pg. *pregar* &c., sbst. Fr. *prêche*, Pr. *prezic*; from *prædicare*.

Predella It. a foot-stool, Mil. *brella*; from O. H. G. *pret* = G. *brett* board.

Predella — *brida*.

Pregno It., Pg. *prenhe*, Pr. *prenh*, O. Fr. *prains*, from *prægnas*; vb. Pg. *prenhar*, Sp. part. *preñado*, Pg. *emprenhar*, Sp. *empreñar* &c.

Proguiça — *pigrezza*.

Preguntar Sp., Pg. *perguntar* to ask; from *percontari*.

Preindre O. Fr. to press, Pr. *premer*; from *premere*. Hence Fr. *épreindre* = *exprimere*, *empreindre* = *imprimere*, *depreindre* (O. Fr.) = *deprimere*. Cf. *imprenta*.

Prêle — *esprelle*.

Prendar — *nans*.

Prensar Sp., Cat. *prempsar* to press; from *pressare*.

Près presque — *presso*.

Presente It. Sp., Fr. *présent*, E. *present*; L. L. *præsentia* (900 A. D.), O. Fr. *presen* (1150 A. D.); from *præsentare* to present, offer.

Presso It., Pr. *pres*, Fr. *près* = L. *prope*; from *pressum*, cf. ἄγχι.

ἐγγύς. Hence It. *appresso*, O. Pg. *a pres*, Pr. *apres*, Fr. *après*; It. *pressoché*, Fr. *presque*.

Prestare It., Sp. *prestar*, Fr. *prêter* to lend; from *præstare* = to lend (Salvian, Venantius &c.).

Preste — *prete*.

Presto It. Sp. Pg., Pr. *prest*, Fr. *prêt*; from a late L. *præstus*. The Pg. has also *prestes* (indec.), cf. *lestes* and *lesto*.

Prêt — *presto*.

Prete It., Sp. O. Pg. *preste*, Fr. *prêtre*, O. Fr. Pr. *prestre*, *priest*, from *presbyter*; other forms are immediately from πρεσβύτερος, Pr. *preveire*, *preire*, Cat. *prebere*, O. Fr. *proveire pro-roire*, cf. Pr. *preveiral preveiral* from L. L. *presbyteralis presby-teratus*. It is remarkable that the It., though fond of the combination *st*, has lost the *s* in *prete*, Mil. *prevet pret*.

Prêtor — *prestare*.

Pretina — *poitrine*.

Pretto It. pure, unmixed (of wine &c.); for *puretto* from *purus*. But the *e* in *pretto* is open, and the contraction is unusual, hence Muratori derives it from O. H. G. *berht* = E. *bright*, where the meaning does not suit so well.

Proux — *pro*.

Preveiro — *prete*.

Provosto It., Sp. Pg. *preboste*, Fr. *prévot*, Wal. *preot*, *provost*; from *præpositus*. Hence also Sp. Pg. *prioste* syndic.

Pria It. adv. for *prio* from *prius*, the termination being prob. borrowed from *poscia*.

Priogo O. Sp., Pg. *prego* a nail, cf. A. S. *prica*, E. *prick*, Du. *prik*, W. *pric*.

Prieto Sp., Pg. *preto* pressed, thronged, miserable, mean, sordid (hence Sp. Pg. also = blackish), Pg. *perto* closely (It. *presso*), vb. *apretar*, *apertar* to compress, sbst. Sp. *presa* haste; *pretar* must be a freq. of *premo (premito)*.

Prigione It., Sp. *prision*, Pr. *preisô*, Fr. E. *prison*; from *prehensio prensio* seizure (so in Sp.). The It. and Sp. words have also the meaning of "prisoner".

Primavera — *ver*.

Primo Sp. Pg., E. *prime*, *la obra es prima* &c.; from *primus* for *primarius*, cf. Pr. *prim* (= E. *prim*) fine, pretty, *primbois* = fine, small wood for fagots, *prim preon* very deep, cf. Nævius: *prime probus*.

Primo Sp. Pg. *primo hermano* Sp. cousin, first cousin. Pr. *prim* = a near relative, *quart* a relative in the fourth degree.

Prince Fr., Pr. *prince primsi*; whence It. *prenze*, *prince*. From *princeps*; O. Fr. *princier* from *primicerius*.

Pringue Sp. grease, fat; from *pinguis*.

Printemps — *ver*.

Prioste — *prevosto.*

Prisco — *persica.*

Prision prison — *prigione.*

Pro It. Sp. Pg. Pr., O. Fr. *prou preu pro,* for which also It. *prode,* O. Sp. O. Pg. *prol,* Pr. *pron* profit; from L. *pro* used as a sbst. e. g. in It. *in pro o in contro.* For *proficiat* was written *pro faccia* for *prodest prod' è* (hence the *d*). Next, *prode* was used as an adj. *egli è prode = prodest* he is useful, brave, cf. M. H. G. *biderbe,* G. *frum* and L. L. *utilis* in both senses. The Pr. *pros* retains the *s* of declension as an integral part of the word, hence Fr. *preu.c,* Rh. *prus,* adv. Pr. *prosamen prousamen,* O. Fr. *prousement* though no adj. *proos, proosa* is found. From the O. Fr. *prou* comes sbst. *prouesse,* E. *prowess.* Some derive the adj. *pro pros* from *probus,* which is supported by the Pr. adv. *pro,* Fr. *prou = satis,* from *probe,* Cat. *prou: pro batre alcun = probe percutere aliquem.*

Proa - *prua.*

Proche Fr., Pr. *propi* near; from *propius* in *propiare, appropiare,* Wal. *apropià;* whence Fr. *approcher,* Pr. *apropchar,* O. It. *approcciare* approach. Cf. *reprocher.*

Proda — *prua.*

Profenda — *prebenda.*

Profilare It., Fr. *profiler* (borrowed), Sp. *perfilar* to draw profiles or outlines (Chauc. *purfile* = edge, border, E. *purfle, purl*), sbst. It. *profilo,* Fr. *profil* (E. *profile*), Sp. Lomb. *perfil.* From *filum* line, outline.

Profitto It., Pr. *proficg,* Cat. Fr. *profit,* E. *profit:* vb. *profittare, profeitar, profiter;* from sbst. *profectus.* Hence also (better than from *provectus*) Sp. Pg. *provecho proveito,* O. Pg. *profeito.*

Promener — *menare.*

Prône Fr. m. a sermon, *prôner* to preach; from *præconium (preone prone).*

Propaggine It., Pr. *probaina,* Sp. *provena,* Fr. *proviu* (for *provain* O. Fr.) a layer, shoot, vb. *provigner;* from *propago, propaginare,* whence also G. *pfropfen* (E. *prop*).

Propio It. Sp., Cat. *propi;* from *proprius,* Wal. *propiu,* Sp. Pg. *proprio,* Pr. *propri,* Fr. *propre* (E. *proper*).

Prosciutto — *suco.*

Prostrare It., Sp. *prostrar* (so Pg. Pr.), E. *prostrate;* from *prostratus (prosternere)* treated as though of the first conjugation.

Protocollo It. &c. From πρωτόκολλον the leaf prefixed and attached (πρῶτος κόλλα) to the Byzantine papyrus-rolls stating by whom, and under what "comes largitionum" each was published. Thence the name was transferred to the public records which, by edict of Justinian, were to be always accompanied by such a *protocol.*

Prou — *pro.*

Proue — *prua.*

Provano — *tezna.*

Provecolo provecho — *profitto.*

Provena — *propaggine.*

Provende — *prebenda.*

Provianda — *viande.*

Provigner provin — *propaggine.*

Prua It., Sp. Pg. Pr. *proa*, Fr. *proue* (E. *prow*); from *prora* with rare euphonic elision of the *r* for which *d* is substituted in the It. *proda*, the O. G. has *prol*. The It. *proda* in the sense of edge, is better from the G. *proth prort brort* than from *prora*.

Prude Fr. (E. sbst.) an adj. wanting in the sister-tongues and derived from the compound *prud' homme* for *preud' homme*, Pr. *prozom*, Sp. *prohombre*, It. *produomo* v. *pro*. Others derive it from *prudens*.

Prudere It., Pr. *prúzer*, Pg. Cat. *pruir* (for *prudir*) to itch; from *prurire*, cf. *produ* from *prora*.

Pruir — *prudere.*

Puce — *pulce.*

Pucelle — *pulcella.*

Puche Sp. pottage; from *puls pultis*, It. *polta*. Hence *puchero* a pot for cooking.

Pues, puis — *poi.*

Pugnale It., Sp. *puñal*, Fr. *poignard* a dagger; from *pugio pugionis*.

Pulser pults — *pozzo.*

Pular Pg. to hop, spring, bud, geminate; from *pullare* for *pullulare* to sprout.

Pulce It. f., Fr. *puce* f., Cat. *pussa*, Sp. Pg. *pulga*, Crem. *peulegh* flea; from *pulex* m.; vb. It. *spulciare*, Fr. *épucer*, Cat. *espussar*, Sp. Pg. Pr. *espulgar*, Vul. *esplugar*, Sp. = also *despiojar* (*pidocchio*).

Pulcella It., O. Sp. *puncella poncella*, O. Pg. Pr. *pucella*, Fr. *pucelle*, Rh. *purscella* maid, young girl, Pr. *pincel*, Fr. *puceau*, Rh. *purscel* youth. A dim. from *pullus* (in L. only of animals), dim. *pulicella* (A. D. 500), cf. O. Fr. *polle* a girl, *poulot* a little boy (still used in Berry and Normandy).

Pulcinella It., Fr. *polichinelle* a mask in the Neapolitan comedy; so called according to some, from *Puccio d'Aniello* of Acerra, the first to sustain the part; al. = little child, darling (prop. chickling [*pullo*]), thence transferred to the most popular stage-figure. Hence prob. E. *Punch*.

Pulga — *pulce.*

Pulsar Sp. Pg., Pr. *pulsar*, Fr. *pousser* (E. *push*); from *pulsare*, whence also Sp. Pg. *puxar* to thrust out, outbid; sbst. It.

polso, Fr. *pouls*, E. *pulse* from *pulsus*. The form *expulser* &c. is of more recent formation.

Punchar — *punzar*.

Punto It., Fr. *point*, Pr. *ponh* point used to strengthen a negative; from *punctum*; cf. *pas*, *rien*, *aucun* &c., R. Gr. 3, 395.

Punzar punchar Sp., Pg. *punçar*, It. *punzellare punzecchiare* to stick, E. *pounce*, a participial verb = *punctiare* from *punctus*. Sbst. It. *punzone*, Sp. *punzon*, Fr. *poinçon*, E. *punch*, G. *punzen*, *bunzen*; from *punctio*, which, becoming concrete, is made masculine, cf. *tosone*.

Pupitre Fr. from *pulpitum*, It. *pulpito*, *pulpit*.

Puput — *upupa*.

Puro It. particle used for solum and tamen; from *pure* = purely, merely.

Pusigno It. a meal after supper; from *post-cænium*.

Putput — *upupa*.

Putto It., Sp. Pg. *puto* lad, It. f. *putta* girl, harlot (Sp. *puta*, Fr. *pute*). A word from the spoken Lat., found in an epigram attributed to Virgil *"me perdidit iste putus"*, cf. Sk. *putra* = filius. *Putillus* in Plaut. becomes It. *putello*. From *putta* comes It. *puttana*, O. Sp. *putaña* harlot; instead of Fr. *putaine* we have *putain* (Pr. *putan*), from accusative *putam*, cf. *Eraïn* from *Eram*, *Bertain* from *Bertham*.

Putto It., O. Sp. *pudio*, Pr. O. Fr. *put* base, mean, disgusting; from *putidus*, as *netto* from *nitidus*.

Puzar — *pulsar*.

Puya pua Sp., Pg. *pua* prickle, shoot, layer; from *pugio-onis*, as *buba* from βουβών, cf. Sp. *mugron* in same sense, prop. = a dagger.

Puzzo puzza It. stink, vb. *puzzare*; from *putidus putius*, cf. *sozzo* from *sucidus*, *rancio* from *rancidus*.

Q.

Quà It., Sp. *acá*, Pg. *cá* from *eccu' hac*; cf. Pr. *sa sai*, Fr. *ça*, Lomb. *sciá* from *ecce hac*.

Quadro It. Sp. Pg. square, frame, picture, Pr. *cadre* frame, Pr. *caire* a square stone; from *quadrum*. Hence Fr. *carrière*, E. *quarry* (where square stones are cut), L. L. *quadraria*, to be dist. from *carrière* career; It. *quadrello*, Sp. *quadrillo*, Pr. *cairel*, Fr. *carreau* a small square, an arrow-head, bolt, E. *quarrel*; It. *squadra*, Sp. *esquadra*, Fr. *équerre*, E. *square*, It. Sp. also = a band of people, whence Fr. *escadre escouade*; It. *squadrone*, Sp. *esquadron*, Fr. *escadron*, E. *squadron*: all from *squadrare (ex-quadrare)* to square.

23*

Quaglia It., O. Sp. *coalla*, Pr. *calha*, Fr. *caille* (E. *callet* = Fr. *caillette*), Rh. *quaera*. E. *quail;* L. L. *quaquila*, au onomatop. connected with G. *quaken*, E. *quack*. The Cat. *guatlla*, Val. *gusala* is the G. *wahtala*. The Wal. is *prepelitzë*, *pitpëlacé*, Sard. *circuri*, Pied. *cerlach*.

Quagliare cagliare It., Sp. *cuajar*, Pg. *coalhar*, Fr. *cailler* to coagulate; from *coagulare*. From sbst. *coagulum* is Pg. *coalho*, It. *caglio* rennet, also *gaglio*, whence *galium* (Linnæus).

Qual — *cayo*.

Qualche It., O. Sp. *qualque*, Pr. *qualsque*, Fr. *quelque;* from *qualis quam* after the analogy of *quisquam*. Hence It. *qualcuno*, *qual-ched-uno*, Fr. *quelqu'un*.

Quan Sp., Pg. *quão*, Pr. *can* adv.; from *quam*.

Quandius Pr.; from *quamdiu*.

Quaresima It., Sp. *quaresma*, Fr. *carême* (m.), Wal. *përeásimi* Lent; from *quadragesima*, Gk. τεσσαραχοστή.

Quatto It., Pr. *quait*, Sp. *cacho gucho* crouching, *(s)quat;* Fr. *cache* hiding place; It. *quattare*, Fr.*cacher* to hide; Fr.*écacher*, O. Fr. *esquachier*, Pic. *écoachar*, Sp. *acachar aguchar* to *quash*, *squash*. *Quatto* = *coactus*, *quattare* = *coactare* (cf. *coagulare*, *cailler*, *flectere fléchir*). Another form from *coactus* is Fr. *catir* to press = O. Fr. Pic.*quatir*. From *cache cachet* seal, *cachette* hiding-place, *cachot* prison. Besides Pr. *cachar* we find *quichar*, N. Pr. *esquichá*, Rh. *squicciar*, cf. G. *quetschen*.

Quattrino It. a small coin = four danari.

Que — *che*.

Quebrantar — *crebantar*.

Quebrar — *crepare*.

Queo — *chaque*.

Queda Pg. fall = Sp. *caida* from *caer* (L. *cadere*), It. *caduta*.

Quedar quedo — *cheto*.

Queixo — *casso*.

Quelha — *calha*.

Quello It. as well as *colui* (prov. It. *quelui*), Sp. Pr. *aquel*, Pg. *aquelle*, from *eccu' ille;* Wal. *acel cel*, Pr. *aicel cel*, O. Fr. *icel cel* as well as *celui* from *ecce ille*, cf. *qui*.

Quelque — *qualche*.

Quemar Sp., Pg. *queimar* to burn. From *cremare*, cf. *quebrar*, *temblar*. It is unnecessary, with Larramendi, to derive it from the Basque.

Quenouille — *conocchia*.

Quercia querce (f.) It. an oak; from adj. *querceus*, cf. *faggio* from *fageus*.

Queso — *cascio*.

Questo It. and *costui* (prov. It. *questui*), Sp. Pg. *aqueste*, Cat. Pr.

aquest; from *eccu' iste;* so Wal. *acest cest,* Pr. *aicest cest,* O. Fr. *icest cest* and *cestui,* Fr. *cet,* from *ecce iste.*

Queue — *codu.*

Queux Fr. (f.) a whetstone; from *cos cotis,* Pr. *cot,* It. *cote.*

Queux O. Fr. (m.) a cook; from *coquus,* It. *cuoco.*

Quexar *(quejar)* Sp. to complain; from a freq. *questare* from *queri questus.* For *x* from *st,* v. R. Gr. 1, 225.

Qui — *che.*

Qui It., O. Fr. *iqui equi* and *enqui anqui,* Sp. Pr. *aqui;* from *eccu' hic;* also It. *ci,* Pr. *aici aissi,* Cat. *assi,* Fr. *ici ci,* Wal. *aici ici,* from *ecce hic.* Hence It. *qui-ci, li-ci.*

Quien Sp., Pg. *quem;* from L. *quem,* so *alguien, alguem* from *aliquem;* cf. for *quilibet,* Sp. *quien-quiera, quem-quer* (conj. of *querer* to be willing).

Quignon — *coin.*

Quilate — *carato.*

Quilla quille — *chiglia.*

Quimora — *chimera.*

Quin quinn Pr. interrogative pronoun, Wald. f. *quena;* from *quinam?* Wal. *cine.*

Quincaille — *clincaille.*

Quinci It. adv. of place, from *eccu' hincce,* cf. *quindi* from *eccu' inde, quivi* from *eccu' ibi* &c.

Quintana chintana It., Pr. *quintana,* O. Fr. *quintaine,* E. *quintain.*

Quiñon — *coin.*

Quitare quite quitte quitter — *cheto.*

Quivrer O. Fr. to wake, rouse; from E. *quiver* nimble, busy, A. S. *cvifertlike* restless, E. *quiver* (verb).

Quixada — *casso.*

Quixote — *coscia.*

Quizá quizas Sp., Pg. *quiça,* O. Pg. *quizais,* Sard. *chisà chisas,* Sic. *cusà* adv. for L. *fortasse;* from *qui sabe* (Sp. *quien sabe)* "who knows", in the Poem. d. Cid *qui sab.*

Quoi — *che.*

Quora — *ora* (2).

Quota It., Pr. *cota,* Fr. *cote* a contribution, *quota;* from *quotus,* Sp. Pg. *cota* also = an annotation, quotation. Hence It. *quotare,* Sp. Pg. *cotar acotar,* Fr. *coter* to quote; Sp. *cotejar,* Pg. *cotejar* to compare (bring together); Fr. *coterie* a body (prop. of contributors).

R.

Raban — *haubans.*

Rabano Sp., Pg. *rabāo* radish; from *raphanus,* It. *rafano.*

Rabarbaro It., Sp. Pg. *ruibarbo*, Fr. *rhubarbe*, E. *rhubarb*, a plant which is found growing wild on the banks of the Volga and in China; from *rha barbarum*, so called to distinguish it from *rha ponticum* (Pontus) a plant of the same kind known to the Romans.

Rabel — *ribeba*.

Rabesoo — *arabesco*.

Râble Fr. (m.), O. Fr. *roable*, Occ. *redable* an oven-rake; from *rutabulum*.

Rabo Sp. Pg. a tail, according to Diez, from *rapere* in allusion to the quick motion of an animal's tail, but better, with Mahn, from *rapum* a carrot, cf. G. *schwanzrübe* (tail-radish) = the thick part of the tail. Hence, perhaps, E. *rabbit*, cf. *bunny* from *bun* a tail, and cf. *raposo*.

Raboter Fr. to plane (Sp. *rabotear* to dock), whence *rabot* a plane; corresponds to Pr. *rebotar*, It. *ributtare* (v. *buttare*), to thrust back, *rebut*, Fr. *rabouter*; hence Fr. *raboteux* rough, refractory.

Rabrouer — *bravo*.

Raca racca Pr. a jade, mare, Fr. *recaille* rabble; prob. from Norse *racki*, E. *rack* hound (G. *rekel* clown), cf. *canaille* from *canis*.

Racchetta It. (corr. *lacchetta*), Sp. *raqueta*, Fr. *raquette*, E. *racket*; from a form *retichetta* from *rete*.

Race — *razza*.

Rachar rajar — *raggio*.

Rache Fr. (f.) sediment of tar; from a form *rasica* from *rasis* resin, cf. *ragia*, thus distinct from *rasche* rash scab, v. *rascar*.

Racher O. Fr., Wall. *rechi*, Pic. *raquer*, Pr. *racar*, Com. *racà* *recà* to spit; from O. N. *hràki* spittle, *hrækia* to spit, A. S. *hræcan* (wreak). Fr. *cracher* is of the same origin, Pr. *escracar* (abst. *crai*), Sic. *scaccare*, Rh. *scracchiar*.

Racine Fr., Pr. *razina* root; from a form *radicina* (radix), Wal. *rěděcině*.

Râcler — *rascare*.

Rada It. Sp., Fr. *rade* road (for ships); from O. N. *reide* preparation, equipment, Du. *reede*.

Rade — *raudo*.

Radeau Fr., Pr. *radelh* a raft; from *ratis*.

Radio O. Sp., Pg. *arredio* strayed; from a form *erraticus?*

Rado It. an altered form of *rarus*, v. R. Gr. 1, 248.

Radoter Fr. to talk nonsense, O. Fr. *redoter*; from Du. *doten*, E. *dote*, cf. W. *dotio*, Du. *dutten*, M. H. G. *totzen* to doze, be *toty*, G. *verdutzt* abashed.

Rafes rahes O. Sp., O. Pg. *refece* light, small, bad; from Ar. *rakhiç* easy, smooth, abst. *rokhç* cheapness.

Raffare It. in *arraffare*, Mil. *raffà*, Piedm. *rafè*, Rh. *raffar*,

O. Fr. *raffer*, Lorr. *raffua* to seize &c.; sbst. Piedm. *rafa* booty, Lorr. Ronchi *raffe*, It. *ruffaraffa* a scramble, Rom. *riffe raffa*, Rh. *riffa raffa*, Sp. *rifi-rafe* (E. *riff-raff*); It. *arraffiare* (for *arrafftare*), Fr. *rafler érafler*, sbst. It. *raffio* a hook, Fr. *rafle* in *faire rafle* to seize everything. From M. H. G. *reffen*, G. *raffen*, E. *raff* (from the Fr.); with *l* G. *raffel*, vb. O. N. *hrafla*, sbst. Du. Swed. *raffel*, E. *raffle*. Lorr. adj. *raffe* = sour (*raffen* = corripere), cf. O. H. G. *raffi*, E. *rough*, Com. *rap*, O. N. *hrappr*.

Raffio *rafler* — *raffare*.

Ragazzo It. boy, *ragazza* girl; according to Muratori, from ῥάκη rags, so = one who wears rags, a servant, boy, cf. *puer* = boy, servant (and cf. *fante*), or from *raca* homo nihili in St. Matt.

Raggio razzo It., Sp. Pg. *rayo*, Pr. *rai raig*, O. Fr. *rai*, Fr. *rayon*, E. *ray*, from *radius*; f. It. *razza* spoke, Wal. *razé*, Sp. Pg. Pr. *raya*, Fr. *raie* ray, stripe, streak; vb. It. *raggiare razzare* to beam, Pr. *rayar*, O. Fr. *raier roier* to beam, stream, Sp. *rayar*, Fr. *rayer* to stripe; from *radiare*. Sp. *rayar* = also to make strokes, lines, *rajar* to split, *raja* a splinter, Pg. *rachar raxar*, sbst. *raja racha*. The O. Fr. *raie* or *rée de miel*, Norm. *rève*, Fr. *rayon de miel* honeycomb, Pg. *raio de mel* point to O. S. *râta*, M. Du. *râte*, M. H. G. *râz*. Fr. *raie* = channel (for water), O. Fr. *roie*, Pr. *reya arrega*, is from *rigare*.

Ragia It., Rh. *rascha* resin; from an adj. *raseus rasea (rasis)*.

Ragoûter Fr. to provoke the appetite, hence *ragoût* (cf. *fricandeau* a dainty dish); from *re-ad-gustare*.

Raguer Fr. to rub, triturate; from N. *raka* to rub.

Raie — *raggio*.

Raifort Fr. horseradish; from *radix fortis*.

Railler — *rallar*.

Rain Fr. in *rain de bois*; from *rain* border, ridge.

Rainar — *hargner*.

Ralponce — *raperonzo*.

Raire Fr. to bellow (of a stag). On the analogy of *mugire*, *rugire* *vagire* was formed *ragire*, Fr. *raire*, It. *ragghiare*, cf. *mugire*, *muire*, *mugghiare*.

Raise O. Fr. *rèse* an expedition; from O. H. G. *reisa*, G. *reise*.

Raisin Fr., Pr. *razim* grape (E. *raisin*); from *racemus*, Sp. *racimo*, Pic. O. Fr. *rosin* (G. *rosine*).

Râler Fr. to rattle; from E. *rattle*, Du. *ratelen*, G. *rasseln*. Hence *râle*, E. *rail* (a bird) = Pr. *roufle*, E. *ruff*, from vb. *roufla* = *ronfler*, cf. Pic. *rousselet* from G. *rosseln*, cf. also Sp. *rouca*, G. *wiesenschnarcher*.

Ralingues Fr. (m. pl.) ropes to fasten the sail, bolt-ropes; from Du. *raa*, Swed. *ra* yard, and Du. *leik*, Swed. *lik* rope.

Rallar Sp. Cat., Pg. *ralar* to grate, plague, Fr. *railler*, E. *rail*,
rally; sbst. Sp. *rallo*, Pg. *ralo* grater. From a vb. *radiculare*
(radere).

Ralo Sp. Pg. thin. From *rarulus*, Plaut. *ralla vestis (l = ll* as in
novela, *apclar)*, or from *rarus* (R. Gr. 1, 217), the objection to
which is that the form *rale* is found in Lim. Rouchi, whereas
the change of *r* to *l* between vowels is unknown in Fr. The
form may, however, have been adopted from the Sp.

Ramadouer — *amadouer*.

Rambla Sp. Cat. sandy beach; from Ar. *raml* sand.

Rame — *risma*.

Rame It., Wal. *aramé*, Sp. *arambre alambre*, Pr. *aram*, Fr. *airain*
copper; from *æramen* (Festus), *aramentum* a copper vessel.
The Rh. is *tròm* a corruption of *iram cram*, like *uffónt* from
uffunt.

Rame Fr. (f.) oar has taken its form from It. Sp. Pr. *rama* a
bough, its meaning from *remus*, the proper Fr. form of which
(rein) was regarded as too slight an expression, cf. *rameau*
instead of *rain* from *ramus*. The Gael. *ramh* (m.) = bough
and oar, O. Ir. *rame* = *remi*. Rouch. is *rème* (f.), N. Pr. *remo*.

Rame ramette Fr. printer's form (Sp. *rama*, Wal. *rame*); from
the G. *rahm*.

Ramentevoir — *mentar*.

Ramequin Fr.; from G. *rahm* cream-cheese.

Ramerino It., Sp. *romero*, Cat. Pr. *romani*, Pg. *rosmaninho*, Fr.
ròmarin, E. *rosemary*; corruptions or adaptations of *ros ma-*
rinus.

Ramero — *ramingo*.

Ramfo It. (in Lomb. *ramf ranf)* cramp, from M. H. G. *rampf*,
G. *krampf*.

Ramingo It., Pr. *ramenc* == a young falcon that flies from bough
to bough *(ramus)*, so unsteady, Fr. *ramingue* wilful. *Ramingo*
= Sp. *ramero*, fem. *ramera* a prostitute.

Rammaricare — *amaricare*.

Rammentare — *mentar*.

Ramolaccio It. horseradish; by dissimilation for *ramoraccio*,
from *armoracia*, Columella *armoracium*.

Ramon Fr. a besom, *ramoner* to sweep a chimney; from *ramus*,
cf. Sp. *ramon* tops of branches, *ramonear* to lop.

Rampa It. claw, *rampo* hook, Pr. Sp. *rampa* cramp; vb. It. *ram-*
pare, O. Fr. *ramper* to clamber, Fr. to creep, part. Fr. E.
rampant (hér.), whence Fr. *rampe*, Sp. *rampa* mound. From
same root as *rappare* (q. v.), L. G. *rapen*, Bav. *rampfen* to
seize, claw, sbst. Lomb. *ramf ranf* cramp, cf. E. *cramp* in
both senses, G. *krampf*. Pr. drops the *m rapar* = *rampar*,
leò rapan = Sp. *leon rampante*. Hence It. *rampone* hook, vb.

rampognare to jeer, O. Fr. *ramposner ramponer* to scoff, E. *lampoon.*

Ran Pie. ram; from O. H. G. Du. E. *ram.*

Ranche Fr. f., E. *rung* of a ladder; from *ramex* bough, pole.

Rancho — *rang.*

Rancio — *arancio.*

Ranco It., Sp. *renco*, O. Fr. *ranc* hipshot, Ven. *ranco* distorted; vb. It. *rancare arrancare* to limp, *dirancare* distort, tear out, Sp. *arrancar* to wrest, force away, wrench (O. It. *arrancare*). From a German source; G. *rank*, Du. *wrongk* distortion, M. H. G. *renken* to wrench, Bav. *renken* to tear, A. S. *vrenc* deceit, Goth. *vraigus* crooked, E. *wring, wrong, wrench.* Thus *arrancar* is to be distinguished from Fr. *arracher* (q. v.), to with which the Sp. *arraigar* agrees in form but not in meaning. For Sp. *renco* we have also *rengo* conforming to, though not etymologically connected with, *derrengar* (q. v.).

Rançon Fr., O. Fr. *raançon*, E. *ransom*; from *redemtio.*

Rancore It., O. Sp. Pg. Pr. *rancor*, O. Fr. *rancaur*, Sp. *rencor*, E. *rancour*; from *rancor* (1) a rancid taste (Palladius) (2) rancour (Hieronymus and in L. L.); hence also Fr. *rancune*, It. O. Pg. *rancura* &c.

Rancune — *rancore.*

Randa Pr. extremity, Pr. It. *a randa* close upon, quite, urgently; also Sp. *randa*, Pg. *renda* point-lace, prop. the rim or border, cf. G. *kante*; from O. H. G. *rand = O. N. rönd* margo, extremitas, E. *round.* Hence O. Fr. *randir* to urge on; Pr. O. Fr. *randon* urgency, vehemence, haste, adv. *a randon* and *de randon*, Sp. *de randon, de rondon*, Pg. *de rondão*, E. *at random*, vb. *randonar randoner* to rush at.

Randello It. a stick, cudgel; from G. *rädel, reitel*, Com. *rat reglia.*

Rang Fr., Pr. *renc arrenc*, vb. Fr. *ranger arranger (range arrange)*, Pr. *rengar arrengar*; G. Du. Swed. *rang*, E. *rank*, W. *rhenge*, Bret. *renk*, Pied. *ren ran.* From the same root as *aringo* (q. v.), viz: O. H. G. *hring*, M. H. G. E. *ring*, so = prop. a collection of persons arranged in circular order, then, generally, a row, file, line, cf. O. H. G. *riga* (v. *riga*); from *ranger* Sp. *rancho* mess, *arrancharse* to form a mess, mess together.

Ranger Pg. to grumble, snarl, growl. Verbs of the 2nd Rom. conj. are, without exception, derived from the 2nd and 3rd of the Lat., so *ranger* must be referred to *ringere* rather than to Gk. ῥέγχειν ῥογχάζειν.

Rangifero It. Sp., Fr. *rangier*, Du. *reynger* rein-deer; from L. L. *rangifer*, which is a corruption of Finnish *raingo.* Fr. *renne* is from N. *hrein, rên*, E. *rein-deer*, G. *renn-thier.* The

A. S. has *hranas* (pl.), the O. E. *raine-deer, rane deer, rain deer*. V. Dasent in the "Times" of Nov. 15th 1862.

Rannicchiare — *niechiv.*

Ranocchia — *grenouille.*

Rapar Pr. — *rampa.*

Rapar Sp. — *rappare.*

Rapas Sp. Pg. boy, *rapuza* girl. Usually der. from *rapax*, and so to denote the *rapacity* of children, cf. *rapaceria* childishness, *rapagon* from *rapax*, as *perdigon* from *perdrix, raigon* from *radix.*

Râper — *raspare.*

Raperonzo raperonsolo ramponsolo It., Sic. *rapouzulu*, Romag. *rapouzal*, Sp. *reponche ruiponce*, Pg. *ruipoato*, Fr. *raipouce*, E. *rampion*, G. *rapunzel*; from *rapa* rape, with It. suffix.

Rapetasser — *pedazo.*

Rapière Fr. an old sword-blade (depreciative), E. *rapier;* for *râpière* from *râpe* rasp, so = a notched, useless blade?

Raposo Sp. Pg. f. *raposa* fox, for which we also find *zorra*, the L. *vulpes* only appearing in the fem. dim. *vulpeja*. From Sp. *rabo* tail, cf. *lobo lupino, cabra capruno.*

Rappa It. tuft, bunch; cf. M. H. G. M. Du. *rappe* stalk of grapes, = Piedm. *rap* (It. *grappolo*).

Rappare It. in *arrappare*, Sp. Pg. Pr. *rapar* to plunder (E. *rape*), Lorr. *rapouà* to devour. From L. G. Du. *rapen*, O. E. *raff, rap*, Swed. *rappa*, G. *raffen*. Of the same stock is the It. *rappa* a cleft in a horse's foot = Du. *rappe* scab, Ven. Lomb. *rapare rapà* to shrink, shrivel = Bav. *räpfen* to harden, to encrust.

Raquette — *racchetta.*

Rasare It., Sp. Pg. *rusar*, Fr. *raser* (E. *raze*) to shave. A freq. from *radere rasus.*

Rascare Sp. Pg. Pr. to scratch; Pr. *rasca*, O. Fr. *rasche*, E. *rash* (sbst.), for *rasicare* from *radere rasus*. Hence also It. *raschiare*, Cat. *rasclar*, O. Fr. *rascler*, Fr. *racler*, sbst. It. *raschia* = Pr. *rasca*, from a Lat. *rasiculare*. The Sp. Pg. *rasgar* to tear asunder, sbst. *rasgo* a sketch, flourish of the pen, is usually referred to *resecare*, though *rasguñar* to scratch and sketch is evidently from *rasicare.*

Raschiare — *rascar.*

Rascia — *raso.*

Rasente — *rez.*

Rasgar rasguñar — *rascar.*

Rasilla — *raso.*

Raso It. Sp., Fr. *ras* satin, Sp. *ras* a smooth place; from *rasus*. Hence Sp. *rasilla* a kind of serge. In the It. *rascia* serge (G.

rasch), some recognize *Rascia* (a Slavonic district, Dante Par. 19, 140) whence the stuff came, others *Arras* (but v. *Arazzo*). In an old It. poet we find: *vestiti di Doagio (Douai) edi Rascese.*

Raspare It., Sp. *raspar*, Fr. *râper* to rasp; from O. H. G. *raspôn* to scrape. Sbst. It. *raspo* a stalk of grapes, mango, Sp. Pr. *raspa* a stalk of grapes, beard of corn, rasp, Fr. *râpe* rasp; It. also *graspo*, cf. *gracimolo* for *racimolo*. Tabac *râpé* = E. *rappee.*

Rasse raise O. Fr., Pr. *rasa*, from O. N. *râs*, A. S. *ræs*, E. *race.*

Rassettare — *assettare.*

Rastro It. Sp. rake &c.; from *rastrum*, Sp. *rastro rastra*, Pg. *rasto* sledge, dray, truck; dim. It. *rastrello rastello*, Sp. *rastrillo rastillo*, Fr. *râteau* rake.

Rate Fr. (f.) milt; from Du. *rate* honeycomb, from its spongy cellular appearance, cf. *raggio.* Hence *dératé* brisk, gay = prop. without *spleen.* From the same root comes *raton* a cake.

Râteau — *rastro.*

Ratis ratin O. Fr. fern. Marcel. Empir.: *herbæ pteridis i. e. filiculæ quæ ratis gallice dicitur.* It is the W. *rhedyn*, Corn. *reden*, Bret. *raden.*

Rato Sp. moment; from *raptus.* The Cat. *estona* is from G. *stunde.*

Raton — *rate.*

Ratto It., Sp. Pg. *rato*, Fr. E. *rat* an animal unknown to the Romans. From O. H. G. *rato* (m.), A. S. *ræt*, L. G. *ratta*, Gael. *radan*, Bret. *raz.* From Sp. *rato* come *radear* to crawl, *radero* creeping, vile. The Ven. is *pantegan* (big-belly) from *pantex.*

Ratto It. quick; from *raptus.* Wall. *toratt* = It. *tutto ratto.*

Raudal — *raudo.*

Raudo Sp. rapid, O. Fr. Pic. *rade*; Sp. *raudal* a torrent; from *rapidus.*

Raus Pr., Bret. *raoz*, hence Pr. *rauzel*, Fr. *roseau*; from Goth. *raus*, whence O. H. G. *rôr*, G. *rohr*, cf. Rh. *ror.*

Rausa (rôruza) Pr., Lim. *roouso* sediment, crust of wine, Rom. *rosa* (with open *o*) a crust; cf. O. H. G. *rosa (roso?)* crusta, glacies.

Rausar rauxar rousar roixar O. Pg. to ravish, sbst. *rouçom.* From a L. *raptiare.*

Raüser — *rifusare.*

Raust Pr. rough; from *raucidus?* cf. G. *rauh* (1) asper (2) raucus.

Rautar Pr. subito auferre. From *raptare*, not found in the cognate tongues.

Ravauder Fr. to mend, repair; from *re-ad-validare.* *Ravauder* = also to tease, plague, *ravauderie* silly nonsense (botch-work).

Ravir Fr., E. *ravish;* from *rapere,* It. *rapire.* Hence also *raviu, ravine, ravage.*

Rayer rayo rayon — *raggio.*

Razione It., Sp. *racion,* E. Fr. *ration;* from *ratio* in L. L. = jus, right, due.

Razza It., Sp. Pg. Pr. *raza,* Fr. E. *race. Radicem* would have given It. *raccia;* so it is better to refer *razza* to the O. H. G. *reiza* line, cf. L.L. *linea sanguinis,* Fr. *ligne,* E. *line, lineage* &c. Cf. *tir* (Wall.) s. v. *tiere.*

Razzo — *arazzo.*

Re O. Fr. a pyre for burning malefactors, L. L. dim. *redulus* "*strues lignorum ardentium*". It is the L. *rete,* wh. appears also in the O. Fr. *reiz,* Sp. *red* net, grating, cage for prisoners, cf. O. Fr. *ardoir dedenz* un re.

Real Sp. Pg. a coin, Pg. pl. *reaes reis;* from *regalis,* whence also Sp. Pg. *real* Sp. a camp, Pg. king's tent (also *arraial*), and royal salutation.

Reame It., O. Sp. *reame realme,* Pr. *reyalme,* E. *realm,* Fr. *royaume;* from a form *regalimen (regalis),* cf. *ducheaume* O. Fr. for *duché,* which is the only other instance of such a formation. From *regimen* comes Fr. *régime,* Pr. *regisme.*

Rebaño Sp., Pg. *rebanho rabanho* flock, herd; from Ar. *ribba ribbi* a myriad, with Rom. suffix (rare), cf. *almir-ante, ammiraglio.*

Rebatar Sp. Pg. to carry off, assault; from *raptare,* v. Rom. Gr. 1, 281.

Rebbio It. tine of a fork, Sp. *rejo* spike. From an old form *ripil* of the G. *riffel* iron comb (cf. Du. *reppen,* E. *ripple* = G. *riffeln*)?

Rebeo — *ribeba.*

Rebentar reventar Sp. Pg. to burst; from *ventus.*

Rebondre O. Fr. Pr. to hide, bury, partic. *rebost,* O. Fr. *reboz,* from *reponere.* The Burg. has *rebôtre* = *remettre.*

Rebosar — *versare.*

Rebours rebrousser — *broza.*

Recado — *recaudar.*

Recamare recamer — *ricamare.*

Recare It. to bring; from O. H. G. *reichan,* G. *reichen,* E. *reach.*

Recato — *catar.*

Recaudar Sp., Pg. *recadar arrecadar* to collect taxes &c., O. Sp. O. Pg. *recabdar* to get, obtain, Sp. *recaudo* a tax-gathering, Sp. Pg. *recado* also = errand, message. *Captare* would give *recatar recautar, cautus recotar recoutar. Recaudar* (O. Pg. *recabedar,* sbst. *recabedo recabito*) is the It. *ricapitare* to effect, appoint, sbst. *ricapito* appointment, from *cupitare* to perfect (q. v.); cf. *caudillo, cadiello* from *capitellus.*

Recear — *zelo.*

Recensar — *rincer.*

Récere It. to spit; from *reicere* (Virg. Fest. &c.) for *rejicere*, but, probably, with some reference to the German, v. *racher.*

Rèche rèque Pic. sour, hence Fr. *rechin,* f. *rechigne,* Com. *reschign,* It. *arcigno* (from Fr.) sour, harsh, unfriendly, vb. Fr. *rechigner* to look sour, crabbed, to knit the brows, Com. *reschignàs,* Ven. *rancignare* (from the Fr.); O. Fr. *rechiguer rechiner,* Pr. *rechignar* = also to mutter, growl, Sp. Pg. *rechinar* to grate, creak, be reluctant. *Rèche,* for *resche resqne,* is from G. *resche rösche* harsh, rude, rough. It. *rincagnarsi* = Fr. *rechigner* owes its form to *cane,* cf. *stare in cagnesco.*

Rochef — *chef.*

Rechinar — *rèche.*

Réclf — *arrecife.*

Reciner — *dessinare.*

Recio Sp. strong, stout; from *rigidus,* though usually *g* only becomes *c* after a consonant, cf. *arcilla.* Hence *arrecirse* to be benumbed with cold.

Recodo — *cubito.*

Recol — *chelo.*

Recourre recousse — *scuotere.*

Recru Fr. (of wood) aftergrowth, *recrue* recruiting, vb. *recruter,* E. *recruit;* from Fr. *recroître.*

Recua Sp. Cat., Pg. *recova,* a drove of beasts; from Ar. *rakùba* a camel or other animal for riding upon.

Recudir — *cudir.*

Recular roouler — *rinculare.*

Redes — *redina.*

Redil Sp. Pg. sheep-fold; from *rete* net, Sp. *red* enclosure, cf. *re.*

Rédina It., Sp. (corr.) *rienda,* Pg. *redea,* Pr. *regna,* Fr. *rène,* O. Fr. *resgne,* E. *rein;* from *retinere;* Pr. *regna* = *reina* for *reina,* as *paire* = *patre.*

Redingote Fr.; from E. *riding-coat.*

Redo in It. *arredo,* Sp. *arreo,* Pg. *arreio,* Pr. *arrei,* O. Fr. *arroi,* E. *array;* It. *arredare,* Sp. *arrear,* Pg. *arreiar,* Pr. *aredar arrezar,* O. Fr. *arroier arréer,* E. *array;* also It. *corredo,* Pr. *conrei,* O. Fr. *conroi* equipment &c., Sp. *conroi,* Cat. *corren* benefit, favour, It. *corredare,* Pr. *conrear,* O. Fr. *conréer* to equip, adorn, Fr. *conroyer* to prepare leather (E. *curry*), clay, mortar &c. (sbst. *conroi*), Sp. *conrear;* also Pr. *desrei,* O. Fr. *desroi derroi,* Fr. *désarroi,* E. *disarray,* vb. Pr. *desreiar* &c. The simple *roi* is found in O. Fr. *mesure ne roi,* and in Sp. *arreo* (= *a réo*) successively, Pr. *darré* = Sp. *de arreo.* From a German source, Goth. *raidjan* to order, A. S. *ge-rædian,* M. H. G. *ge-reiten* to make *ready,* and more immediately connected, Du. *réden.* Others refer to the Celtic, Gael. *rèidh* smooth, ready, Bret. *reiz* rule, order = Fr. *roi*, as *feiz* = *foi*, *efreix* = *effroi*, *preix* = *proie*, all which, however, may be from the German.

Rodor Sp. circle, circular mat, O. Sp. prepos. *redor de* around, *ader-redor* for *arrededor*, Sp. *alrededor*, Pg. *as redor* &c. *Redor* is perhaps for *ruedor ruedol (rotulus)*, cf. *ruiseñor* from *lusciniolus*.

Redruña Sp. left hand; prop. the hand that "retreats" or "gives way" from *retro*, Sp. *redro*. The suff. *uño* is very rare (cf. *rid-uño*).

Rée — *raggio*.

Rofe It. thread; from Gk. ῥαφή, or, better, from O. G. *reif* string, cord, cf. Piedm. *tra*, Rh. *trau* from G. *draht* thread.

Refran Sp., Pg. *refrão* proverb, Pr. *refranh*, Fr. *refrain*, E. *refrain*. From *refrangere*, Pr. *refranher*, Fr. *refraindre*. So J. Grimm derives *fringutire* and *fringilla* from *frangere*, cf. O. N. *kleka* to break, *klaka* to sound, clink &c. For *refranher* the Pr. has also *refrinher* from *refringere*; the sbst. *refrim* clap, crack, owes its form to *fremitus*.

Refriega — *fregare*.

Refrogner — *frignare*.

Regain — *guaime*.

Regalare It., Sp. Pg. *regalar*, Fr. *régaler* to *regale*, make presents to; It. Sp. Pg. *regalo*, Fr. *régal* a present. The Sp. *regalar* means also to pamper, coax, O. Sp. to melt; this points to the L. *regelare* to thaw, melt as the origin of the Rom. word (not from *regalis*); cf. O. Sp. *plomo regalado* = molten lead, Papias *plumbum regelatum* = *liquefactum*; O. Fr. *regeler*, sbst. *regiel* = Sp. *regalo*.

Regañar Sp., Pg. Pr. *reganhar*, Pr. also *reganar* to show the teeth, snarl, growl, grumble. These words seems identical with the O. Fr. *recaner* = (1) to show the teeth (2) to bray, Berr. *réchaner*, *archaner* to neigh, *chagner* to snarl. From *cachinnare* to laugh with open mouth. The Fr. *ricaner (ri* for *re* perhaps from *ridere rire)* is only used for expressing the sneer of malice or the simper of idiotcy.

Regazo Sp. Pp. lap, skirt, *regazar* to tuck up the skirt; from Basque sbst. *galzarra* with the same meaning.

Regimber Fr. to kick; not from *rejamber (jambe, gamba)* for this would not account for the form *regiber* in O. Fr.; *m* is inserted before *b*, not rejected. Cf. E. *gib*.

Régime — *reame*.

Registro It. Sp., Pr. Fr. *registre* (E. *register*), Pg. *registo*, from L. L. *registrum* for *regestum* "liber in quem regeruntur commentarii quivis vel epistolæ summorum pontificum" Ducange.

Réglisse — *regolizia*.

Regocio — *gozo.*

Regoldar Sp. to belch; for *regolar* from *gola*, L. *gula.*

Regolizia legorizia It., Sp. *regalicia, regaliza*, Sp. Pg. *regaliz*, Pr. *regalicia regulecia, regalussia*, Fr. *réglisse*, E. *licorice*; from *liquiritia* (Vegetius), which is the Gk. γλυκύῤῥιζα.

Regretter Fr. to *regret*, Fr. E. sbst. *regret*. According to Mahn (who finds an O. Pr. *regradar regredar*) from *gratus*, It. *grado*, Pr. *grat*, O. Fr. *gret*, Fr. *gré*, cf. *grado;* It. *aggradare* &c. = to take with thanks, so *regradar* might = to long for, regret (to receive back willingly). Though this may be the true der., yet the form is, doubtless, partly owing to the Goth. *grêtan*, O. N. *grâta*, E. Prov. *greet* to weep (the L. *t* in such positions is usu. dropped in Pr., but cf. *agradar* as well as *agreiar*).

Rehen Sp., Pg. *refem arrefem* hostage; from Ar. *rahn, arrahn* pledge, hostage.

Rehusar — *rifusare.*

Reinette Fr. a sort of apple, *rennet;* from *reine reyina*, so = queen of apples.

Reja Sp., Pg. *relha* iron lattice-work; from *reticulum*, v. also *relha.*

Rejo — *rebbio.*

Relampago — *lampo.*

Relayer Fr. to change horses &c., sbst. *relais*, E. *relay.* From *religare*, cf. *frayer* from *fricare.* Al. from the E. *lay.*

Relha Pg. Pr., O. Fr. *reille*, Sp. *reja* ploughshare; from *regula?* O. Fr. *reilhe de fer* = regula ferrea.

Relinchar Sp., Pg. *rinchar* to neigh. *Hinnilitare* (Lucilius) would give Sp. *hinchar*, thence *re-hinchar red-inchar relinchar*, though such process is unusual. From *hinntiliare* for *hinnilitare*, come Pr. *endillar enilhar* (Cat. *renilyar*) *inhilar.*

Relox — *oriuolo.*

Reluquer — *luquer.*

Remate — *matar.*

Remedar arremedar Sp. Pg. to imitate; from *re-imitari.*

Remir Pg. to redeem; = Sp. *redimir*, L. *redimere.*

Remolacha Sp. beet-root; = It. *ramolaccio*, L. *armoracia* horse-radish, cf. *rabano.*

Remolcar remorquer — *remorchiare.*

Remorchiare It., Fr. *remorquer*, Sp. *remolcar* to tow; from *remulcum* a towing-rope.

Rempart — *parare.*

Remuer — *muer.*

Renard Fr. fox, O. Fr. *renardie* craftiness. From O. H. G. *Reginhart Reinhart* (counsellor) the name of the fox in the Fables; this in Fr. became an appellative and supplanted the O. Fr. *volpill* (= vulpecula), *goulpille, goulpil* (whence *goupillon*).

Rencilla — *reñir*.

Rencontre — *rimpetto*.

Renda — *randa*.

Rendere It., Sp. *rendir*, Pg. *render*, Pr. Fr. *rendre*, E. *render*, from *reddere;* sbst. It. *rendita*, Sp. Pr. *rendita*, Fr. *rente*, E. *rent*, from *redditum*, pl. *reddita*. Pott derives from *re-indere*, but this would not suit the sense well (cf. *rendre paisible = = placidum reddere*), and the *n* is a mere insertion for strengthening the form.

Rendija Sp. crack, chink, O. Sp. *rehendija;* a dim. from *fenda* split, Sp. also *hendrija* with metathesis of the *r*.

Rêne — *redina*.

Renfrogner — *frignare*.

Renge O. Fr. girdle, L. L. *rinca;* from O. H. G. *hringa (ring)* buckle, whence also Rh. *rincla* buckle.

Renifler — *niffa*.

Renou Pr. usury, prop. = sprout, short, Sp. *renuevo*, from *renovare*, cf. L. *fenus*, Gk. τόχος, O. *wucher*. Hence *renovier* usurer, Rh. *ranver*, Sp. *renovero*.

Renso It. fine flax; from *Rheims*, whence it was brought.

Rente — *rez*.

Reñir Sp., Pg. *renhir*, Cat. *renyir* to quarrel, Sp. *riña* quarrel, dim. *rencilla;* from L. *ringi*.

Renne — *rangifero*.

Reo It. guilty, also = bad, wicked, in which sense we have also It. *rio*, Wal. *rëu*. Sp. *reo*, Rh. *reus* are only used in the L. sense.

Repairer O. Fr., Pr. *repairar*, E. *repair*, sbst. O. Fr. Fr. *repaire* (in Fr. only = den, lair), E. *repair;* from *repatriare*, It. *ripatriare*.

Répit Fr., Pr. *respieit*, It. *rispitto* adjournment, *respite;* from *respectus* consideration, so = indulgence, forbearance. Vb. O. Fr. *respiter*, E. *respite* from *respectare*.

Repollo Sp., Pg. *repolho* cabbage, from *repullulare* to sprout. Sp. also = bud.

Reponche — *raperonzo*.

Représaille — *ripresaglia*.

Reprocher Fr., Pr. *repropchar*, sbst. *reproche repropche*, hence Sp. *reprochar*, *reproche*, E. *reproach*. As *approcher* from *appropiare*, so *reprocher* from *repropiare* to draw near, advance (trans.) throw back in one's teeth, cf. Pr. *reprochier reprovier* a proverb.

Reptar O. Sp. Sp. Pg. Pr., Sp. *retar*, O. Fr. *reter* to reproach, reprimand, to challenge. From *reputare* = reproach in L. L. cf. *si quis alteri reputaverit, quod scutum suum jactasset* L. Sal., cf. *appellare* used in the same way. The Rh. has *raridar*, *r* = L. *p, i : = n*.

Requin Fr. shark, a corruption of *requiem* which form is found in some dictionaries. The name was given by the Norman mariners, who regarded this dangerous fish with the greatest apprehension.

Res Sp., Pg. *rez* head of cattle; from Ar. *ràs* head, cf. *caput*, E. *head*.

Rescatar — *accattare*.

Réseau Fr. net-work, small net; from a L. *reticellum*: It. *reticella*.

Resemblar — *sembrare*.

Resma — *risma*.

Resollar — *sollar*.

Resquicio — *quicio*.

Ressembler — *sembrare*.

Ressort — *sortire*.

Resta It., Sp. *ristra*, Pg. *reste restia*, Pr. *rest* a string or trace of onions &c.; from *restis* a rope. Piedm. *rista* hemp corresponds to O. H. G. *rista* a bundle of flax.

Resta It., Sp. *ristre enristre* (m.), Pg. *reste riste ristre*, E. *rest* (of a lance &c.), whence Pr. *arestol*, O. Fr. *arestuel* handle of a lance; from *restare*, Roman *arrestare* to resist, so prop. = resistance, support.

Resta — *aresta*.

Restañar — *stancu*.

Restio It. (for *restivo*), Pr. *restiu*, Fr. *rétif*, E. *restive*; from *restare* to resist. Mil. is *restin*.

Restreindre — *étreindre*.

Retama Sp. Pg. broom (shrub); from Ar. *ratam*, *ratamah*.

Retar — *reptar*.

Rétif — *restiv*.

Retoño Sp. a shoot, sprout, *retoñar* to shoot, sprout anew. From *tumidus*, *retumiar (limpidus limpiar)*, *retoñar*, or from the Celtic, W. *twn* a projection.

Retro It. in Comp., Pr. *reire*, E. *rear*, O. Fr. *riere;* from *retro*, for which Sp. Pg. *atras*. Hence It. *dietro drieto*, Pr. *dereire derrier* (also adj.), Fr. *derrière* from *de retro;* It. *addietro*, Pr. *areire*, E. *arrear*, Fr. *arrière* from *ad retro;* Pr. *dereiran* = a form *deretranus*, Fr. *dernier* = *deretranarius*. The *r* is dropped in *dietro* for *diretro* as in O. Fr. *za en ayer* = Pr. *sa en areire*.

Retroenge retrowange O. Fr. also *rotruange, rotruenge, rotruhenge, rotuenge*, Pr. *retroencha, retroenza* a troubadour-song, ballad, dance-song; from *retroientia*, if an orig. Pr. *retroensa* (whence *retroencha*, Fr. *retroenche, retroenge*) may be supposed.

Reuper Pic. eructare = O. Sax. *ropizôn*, O. H. G. *rof-azôn*, G. *reup-sen*.

Refuser — *rifusare*.

Réussir — *escire*.

Revanche — *vengiare*.

Rêve Fr. dream, vb. *rêver* to dream, *rave*, in O. Fr. *resve resver*; the *s* however is not orig., since we have Pr. *reva*, cf. *esve* for *eve* (aqua). It is a prov. form for *rage (rabies)*, cf. *cage* and *caive; rabia raiva rêve*, E. *rave*. From *rêver* come Du. *reven, revelen*, M. H. G. *reben*; Fr. *rêvasser*, Burg. *ravasser*.

Revêche reves — *rivescio*.

Revel O. Fr. *(rivel)*, E. *revel revelry* = Pr. *revel* resistance, rebellion, from vb. *revellar*, O. Fr. *reveler*, L. *rebellare*, so = prop. incitement, rousing. The form *reviaus* is against the der. from *reveiller*.

Res Fr. abst. level, *rez-de-chaussée* ground-floor; from old part. *rés*, Pr. *ras*, L. *rasus*; also used as preposition in certain phrases, e. g. *rez terre* on a level with the ground, cf. *radere litus, rez à rez*, Pr. *ras e ras*, Pg. *rez e rez* close. Hence also Pr. part. pres. *rasen*, It. *rasente*. Cf. L. G. prep. *rôr* from *rôren* to stir, touch; Mil. *arent*, Neap. Pg. *rente*, from *hærens*; O. Sp. *pegante*, from *pegar* to cleave to; Pic. *tout serant*, from *serrer* to press.

Resar Sp. Pg., Cat. *resar* to recite, pray; from *recitare, rec'tare*.

Rezelar — *zelo*.

Resno Sp. an insect, a tick; from *ricinus*, It. *ricino*.

Rezza It. a sort of lace; from L. *rete*, pl. *retia*.

Rezzo — *aura*.

Rhume Fr. (f.) rheum, cold; from L. *rheuma* (ῥεῦμα), Pr. *rauma*, It. *rema*.

Ria Sp. Pg. Cat. mouth of a river; for *riba*, L. *ripa* bank, It. *riva* also limit, so = end of a river, cf. *arrivare* to reach the mouth of a river.

Ribaldo It. Sp. Pg., Pr. *ribaut*, Fr. *ribaud*, E. *ribald*; hence N. *ribballdi*, M. H. G. *ribballt*, It. (corr.) *rubaldo*. L. L. *ribaldus*, cf. Matthew Paris: *fures, exules, fugitivi, excommunicati, quos omnes ribaldos Francia vulgariter consuevit appellare*, = Gk. πανοῦργοι. The word *ribaldi* was also specially applied to the "enfans perdus" the "black guard" of an army, hence It. *rubalda* a sort of headpiece worn by such, Fr. *ribaudequin* a missile. The O. H. G. has a fem. *hriba (hripa)* prostitute, M. H. G. *ribe*, whence, with suffix *ald*, might be formed *ribaldo*; hence too Fr. *riber* to debauch a woman, perhaps also *ribler* to rove.

Ribeba It. a musical instrument, rebeck; from Ar. *rabâb*. Hence (corrupted) It. *ribeca*, Pg. *rabeca*, Cat. *rabaquet*, Fr. *rebec* (E.

rebeck), Pr. *rabey,* also Sp. *rabel,* Pg. *rabel arrabil,* O. Fr. *rebelle;* for change of *b* into *c,* cf. Sp. *jabeba jabeca* a Moorish flute.

Ribrezzo — *brezza.*

Ricamare It., Sp. Pg. *recamar,* whence Fr. *recamer* to embroider; sbst. It. *ricamo,* Sp. Pg. *recamo;* from Ar. *raqama* to weave a stripe in a piece of stuff, sbst. *raqm* striped embroidery.

Ricaner — *reguñar.*

Riccio It., Wal. *ariciu,* Sp. *erizo,* Pg. *ericio ouriço,* Pr. *erisson,* Fr. *hérisson (h* asp. but in O. Fr. *eriçon, ireçou* whence E. *urchin)* a hedgehog; from *erichus* (Varro). Hence vb. It. *arricciare,* Sp. *erizar,* Pg. *ouriçar,* Pr. *erissar,* Fr. *hérisser.*

Riccio It., Sp. *rizo* curled, frizzled, sbst. curl, Pg. *riço* shaggy stuff; vb. It. *arricciare,* Sp. *rizar,* Pg. *ouriçar eriçar riçar* to curl. From *riccio* &c., hedgehog, cf. L. L. *reburrus "hispidus, crispus",* and Ducange (h. v.): *habebat capillos crispos et rigidos atque sursum erectos et, ut ita dicam, rebursos.*

Ricco It., Sp. Pg. *rico,* Pr. *ric,* Fr. *riche (rich);* from O. H. G. *rihhi,* Goth. *reiks,* G. *reich.* Fr. *riche* seems to be a fem. of *ric* or *rique,* cf. *franc, blanc.*

Ricredersi It. to retract one's error, Pr. O. Fr. *se recreire* to retract, renounce, grow weary of a thing, L. L. *se recredere.* One who was vanquished in a judicial combat and forced to confess his wrong, was specially called *recreditus,* hence *recrezut recreu, recrezen recreant* (E. *recreant). Se recredere* or *credere* was a translation of the O. G. *sih galaubjan = recedere, deficere* of a friendly giving in or compliance, *galaubjan = credere* (G. *glauben,* E. *be-lieve).*

Riddare It. to dance, move in a circle, sbst. *ridda* a dance in a circle; from O. H. G. *ga-ridan,* M. H. G. *riden* to turn about, move in a circle.

Rider Fr. to wrinkle, *ride* wrinkle, curl, ripple, *rideau* curtain (from its folds); from *ga-ridan* to twist about, contort, whence G. adj. *reid* curled, twisted, v. *riddare,* or from A. S. *vridhan,* E. *writhe.*

Ridotto raddotto It., Sp. *reducto,* Fr. *redoute* (f.), E. *redoubt;* from *reductus.*

Riel Sp. a bar or ingot of uncoined metal; from *regula* a rod, *regellus.*

Rien Fr. used for L. *nihil,* from acc. *rem; je ne vois rien = non video rem, nihil video.* Pr. *ren re* = L. aliquid, quidquam, Cat. *res;* O. Pg. *has una rem, algun rem, algorrem;* Pr. *ganren = gran ren* much (Fr. *grand' chose),* N. Pr. *quauquarren (quelque chose),* O. Pr. *aldres (autre chose).*

Rienda — *redina.*

Riesgo — *risicare.*

Riffa It. (prop. *rifa* Com.), Sp. Pg. Cat. Sic. *rifa* scuffle, contest, raffle; vb. It. *ar-riffare* to play at dice, raffle, Sp. Cat. Pg. *rifar* to dispute, jangle, raffle, O. Fr. *riffer* to rifle, seize, Lorr. *riffer* to tease flax. From a German source, Bav. *riffen* (= G. *raufen* to pull, pluck), cf. O. Fr. *riffler* to tear, E. *rifle*, scuffle, Wall. *rifler* to run blindly about, Rouch. *rifeler* = *riffer*, abst. O. Fr. *riffle* a switch, stick (E. *rifle*), Norm. *rifle* blow, scab, perhaps also It. *riffilo* spish face, Pied. *riflador* file; from O. H. G. *riffil riffila* saw, G. *riffel* a flax-comb, riffler, vb. *riffeln*.

Rifiutare — *rifusare*.

Rifusare It., Pg. Pr. *refusar*, Sp. *rehusar*, Fr. *refuser*, E. *refuse*. From *recusare* with the *f* of *refutare*, It. *rifiutare*, Pr. *refudar* = respuere, rejicere (L. L.). We find in Pr. O. Fr. a second form without the *f* (cf. *preon* from *profundus*) *rehuzar reüsar*, *rehuser reüser rañser* to give way, get out of the way, *ruser* (espec. of wild animals) to turn or double so as to throw the dogs off the scent, whence Fr. *ruse* trick.

Riga It. line, row, *riga* rule, ruler, *rigoletto* circular dance, dance, G. *reigen;* from O. H. G. *riga* line, circumference, M. H. G. *rihe* = G. *reihe*.

Rigoglio — *orgoglio*.

Rigogolo rigoletto — *galbero*.

Rigole Fr. trench, O. Fr. *rigol*. From the Celtic: W. *rhig* incision, *rhigol* furrow, ditch, I. G. *rige* brook. It. *rigoro* may be corr. from *rivulus*.

Rigoletto — *riga*.

Rigoro — *rigole*.

Rigot Pr. curled hair, *rigotar* to curl, It. *rigottato* curled. From O. H. G. *riga* a row, circle.

Rima It. Sp. Pg. Pr., Fr. E. *rime;* vb. *rimare, rimar, rimer, rinne*. In Pr. also m. *rim*, Norm. E. *rym*. The Rom. word belongs rather to the O. H. G. *rim* numerus, O. Ir. *rim*, W. *rhif*, than to the L. *rhythmus*, which would give *rimmo* or *remmo*. Hence O. Sp. *adrimar*, Sp. Cat. *arrimar* to put in order, bring together, put one thing on another, stow (Fr. *arrimer*), cf. O. H. G. *rim* = row, Sp. *rima*, cf. also Fr. *enrimer* (Berry) to put in order, Sp. *rimero* things put in order over each other. N. Pr. *rimá* to approach = Sp. *arrimar*.

Rimbombare — *bomba*.

Rimpetto, di rimpetto, a rimpetto a qc. It. prep. for contra. From *petto (pectus)*, as *rincontra (re-in-contra)*, Fr. *rencontre*, from *contra*. For this use of *petto*, cf. Sp. *hacia, cara, frente;* cf. Dante Inf. 8, 115: *chiuser le porte nel petto al mio signor*, so It. *appetto*.

Rin O. Fr. (m.) well, Com. *rin* streamlet, Wall. *arène* canal; a

Celto-Germanic word, W. *rhin* (f.) canal, Goth. *rinnô* a stream, O. H. G. *rinnd*, G. *rinne.*

Rinceau Fr. foliage; for *rainceau* = It. *ramicello*, from *ramus.*

Rincer Fr.; for *rinser*, cf. Pic. *rinser*, E. *rinse*. It is the O. N. *hreinsa* to purify, G. *reinigen*. Distinct from Pr. *recensar*, Sp. *recentar*, Cat. *rentar* i. e. *recentiare*, *recentare* to renew, reform.

Rincon Sp., O. Sp. *rancon rencon*, Cat. *racó* a corner. Of the same origin as the Rom. *ranco renco*, so = something curved, Goth. *vraiqos* crooked.

Rincontra - *rimpetto.*

Rinculare It., Sp. Pr. *recular*, Pg. *recuar*, Fr. *reculer* to recoil; from *culus*, cf. G. *sich ärsen*, Du. *aerselen*. Hence Fr. adv. *à reculons* backwards, G. *ärschlings*, M. H. G. *erslingen.*

Rinfrignato — *frignare.*

Ringavagnare — *guadagnare.*

Ringhiera — *aringo.*

Ringla Sp., Cat. *rengla* line, row, Sp. *renglon*; from Fr. *rang*, or from *regula?*

Rintuzzare — *intuzzare.*

Riña — *reñir.*

Riñon — *rognone.*

Riolé O. Fr. striped; from G. *riege*, *reihe* a row, cf. It. *rigato* (from *riga*).

Riotta It., Pr. *riota*, O. Fr. *riote*, E. *riot*, vb. It. *riottare*, Fr. *rioter*, E. *riot* (distinct from Fr. *rioter* to titter); for *rivoter* from *riban* to rub, whence Du. *revot*, *ravot*. Cf. Sp. *refriega* quarrel, from *fricare.*

Riparo — *parare.*

Ripentaglio It. danger. Cf. O. Fr. *repentaille (repentir)* forfeit, penance-money.

Riper Fr. to scrape, *ripe* scraper; from prov. G. *rippen ribben* = G. *reiben* to rub, cf. Du. *ripf* (f.) scraper.

Ripido It. steep, from *ripa*; the term. *idus* is not found elsewhere in It., so, perhaps, the form was taken from *rapidus.*

Ripio Sp. Pg. small stone to fill up a crevice, *ripia* shingle, Pg. *ripa* board, lath. Sp. *ripiar* to plaster chinks in walls. The L. is *replum.*

Ripire It. to clamber; from *repere* with a change of conj., cf. *fuggire*. The Rh. has *rever* without change.

Ripresaglia rappresaglia It., Sp. *represalia*, Fr. *représaille*, E. *reprisal*; from *reprehendere reprehensus.*

Risicare It., Sp. *arriscar arriesgar*, Pg. *riscar*, *arriscar*, Fr. *risquer*, E. *risk*; abst. It. *risico*, *risco*, Sp. *riesgo*, Fr. *risque*, E. *risk*. Originally a nautical word, and = a dangerous rock, precipice, Sp. *risco* from *resecare*, cf. Sw. *skär* rock (scaur) from *skära* to shear, cf. *sheer* = precipitous; cf. N. Pr. *rezegá* to cut off, Mil. Com. *resega* saw and danger, vb. *resegà* to saw and to risk; hence also Pg. *risca* stripe (cutting), *riscar* to stripe.

Risma It., Sp. Pg. *resma*, Fr. *rame*, E. *ream* (of paper). The Gk. ἀριθμός became in It. *arismus* to correspond with *arismetica* (so L. L. Pr. O. Sp. Cat. O. E. *arsmetrik*), hence *rismo risma*, which latter, in Florence, also means a collection of people, a company.

Riso It., Pr. *ris*, Fr. *riz*, Wal. *ürez*, E. *rice*; from *oryza*. Sp. Pg. *arroz* is from Ar. *aruzz* or *ruzz* (al-ruzz, ar-ruzz).

Risque — *risicare*.

Rissoler Fr. to roast brown; from the Norse, Dan. *riste* = G. *rösten*, E. *roast*, Icel. Swed. *rist* = G. *röst*, hence dim. *rissoler* = G. *rösteln*. The H. G. *o* appears in It. *rosolare*.

Ristre — *resta*.

Ritorta It., Pr. *redorta*, O. Fr. *riorte reorte roorte rorte*, Norm. *rote* osier, withe, wicker; prop. = twisted, from *retorquere*, whence also Sp. *retorta*, Fr. *retorte*, E. *retort* a vessel of twisted form.

Ritroso It. stubborn; from *retrorsus* (= retroversus).

Ritto It. adj. right, as opp. left, prop. = straight hand (not crooked or maimed like the left hand), hence *marritto* comp. with *manus*. Hence It. *diritto dritto*, Sp. *derecho*, Pg. *direito*, Pr. *dreit*, Fr. *droit*, Wal. *drept*, L. *directus*; O. Fr. *endroit endreit* prep. for L. *versus*, Fr. sbst. *endroit* place, cf. *contrée*, G. *gegend*.

River Fr. to rivet a nail, whence Fr. *rivet* (sbst.), E. *rivet*; perhaps from Du. *rijven* or O. N. *rifa* to rake, clear away obstructions &c., O. H. G. *riban*, G. *reiben*, E. *rive*. N. Pr. *riblo* a rammer = O. H. G. *ribil (riban)* a pestle, *riblà* = river.

Rivescio rovescio It., Sp. Pg. *reves*, Fr. *revers*, *reverse*; from *reversus*, whence also Pg. adj. *revesso*, Fr. *revêche* harsh, untractable.

Riviera It., Sp. *ribera (vera)*, Pg. Pr. *ribeira*, Pg. also *beira*, O. Fr. *rivière* bank, shore, prop. parts about the bank or shore; from *riparia*. Influenced by *rivus* the meaning of "river" was added, Fr. *rivière* (E. *river*).

Riz — *riso*.

Rizo — *riccio*.

Rizzare It. to erect, from a L. *rectiare (rectus)*. From *directiare* we have It. *dirizzare drizzare*, O. Sp. *derezar*, Pg. Sp. *enderezar*, Pr. *dressar*, Fr. *dresser*, a-dresser, E. *dress*, *address*.

Roba It. O. Sp., O. Pg. *rouba*, Pr. *rauba*, Fr. *robe*, E. *robe*, Sp. *ropa*, Pg. *roupa* clothes, apparel, stuff, and in older sense booty, Rh. *rauba* estate; masc. Sp. *robo*, Pg. *roubo* robbery;

It. *rubare*, Sp. *robar*, Pg. *roubar*, Pr. *raubar*, O. Fr. *rober*, Fr. *dérober*, O. Sp. *robir*; from O. H. G. *roub* spolium, vb. Goth. *biraubôn*, O. H. G. *roubôn roupôn*, G. *rauben*, E. *rob*, cf. Gael. *robainn*, L. L. *raubare*. Hence O. Pg. *roubaz robaz roaz* thievish, formed like *rapax*. Wal. *robi* to take prisoner, from *rob* = Serv. *rob*, Alb. *robi ropi* prisoner, slave.

Robbio — *roggio*.

Robbo rob It., Sp. Fr. *rob*, Pg. *robe*, E. *rob*; from Ar. *rubb*.

Robin — *ruggine*.

Roble — *rovere*.

Robra Sp. a document to prove a sale; from *roborare*. Pg. *róbora (révora)*, L. L. *robora* = puberty; from *robur*.

Rocca roccia It., Sp. *roca*, Pg. Pr. *roca rocha*, Fr. *roche* rock (It. *rocca* also = bolt, lock), Cat. m. *roc* stone, Fr. *roc*; Pr. *rochier*, Fr. *rocher*; vb. O. Fr. *rocher* to stone; It. *diroccare dirocciare*, Sp. *derrocar*, Pr. *derrocar derocar*, Fr. *déroquer dérocher* to throw from a rock, throw down, Sp. *derrochar* to waste, throw away. O. Fr. *aroquer arocher* to dash to pieces. The word is found in Gael. *roc*, E. *rock*, Du. *rots*, Basque *arroca*, W. *rhwg* (a projection). Diez considers that it does not properly belong to any of these languages, and he derives it from a L. *rupea* or *rupica (rupes)*.

Rocca It., Sp. *rueca*, Pg. *roca* a distaff, from O. H. G. *rocco*, O. N. *rockr*. Hence *rocchetta*, E. *rocket*.

Rocchetto It., Sp. *roquete*, Fr. E. *rochet* (It. also *roccetto*), cf. Wal. *rochie* a woman's frock. L. L. *roccus* = O. H. G. *roc*, G. *rock*, A. S. *roc*, E. *frock*, O. N. *rockr*. Prop. = a garment with folds, cf. Pg. *enrocar*, It. *arrocchettare* to fold, from O. N. *hrucka*, Gael. *roc* fold, E. *ruck*, to *ruck*.

Rocchio It. a block of wood or stone; It. *ronchione*; from *rocca* a rock?

Rocco It., Sp. Pg. *roque*, Pr. Fr. *roc*, E. *rook* the castle in chess; from Pers. *rukh* (a camel with a tower for archers), which Forbes traces back to the Sanskrit *roka* a ship, that being the original form of the piece.

Roche rocher — *rocca*.

Rochet — *rocchetto*.

Rociada rocio — *ros* (1).

Rocin — *ros* (2).

Rodela rodilla — *rotella*.

Rôder Fr. to roam, prowl. The Pr. *rodar*, It. *rotare* to roll. For *rôder* is found *rouer*, Rou. *rouier*.

Rodilla — *rotella*.

Rodrigon Sp. vine-prop; from *ridica*, but with allusion to the proper name *Rodrigo*, cf. *rui-ponce* for *ri-ponce*.

Roffia — *ruffa*.

Roggio It., Sp. *roxo*, Pg. *rouxo*, Pr. *rog* (f. *roja*), Fr. *rouge*, also It. *robbio*, Sp. *rubeo*, Pg. *ruivo*, E. *ruby*, red; from *rubeus;* Fr. vb. *rougir*, Pr. *rogir.* Hence also *robbia*, Sp. *rubia* madder.

Rogna It., Sp. *roña*, Pg. Pr. *ronha*, Fr. *rogne*, Wal. *rĕia* (cf. *vie* with It. *vigna*, *sicriu* with *scrigno*) itch, mange; from *robigo robiginis* (Monage) a harsh, but possible, contraction *(robgn rogn).* Hence O. E. *ronyon.*

Rogner Fr. to cut, clip, O. Fr. *rooigner* to cut the hair, Pr. *re-donhar rezoynar*, Sp. (Murcia) *des-roñar.* From *rotundare*, whence Sp. *redondear*, cf. *Bergonha* from *Burgundia*, and cf. Sp. *cercenar*, v. *cercine.*

Rognie Pic. a trunk of a tree; from O. H. G. *rona* (f. *rono* m.), M. H. G. *rone* m., G. *rahne* f., a fallen trunk.

Rognone It., Sp. *riñon*, Pr. *renhô renhô*, Fr. *roignon* kidney, Wal. *rĕnunchiu;* from a form *renio (ren)*, cf. *vigliacco* from *vilis.* It. has also *arnione argnone*, cf. *arcigno* from Fr. *rechin.*

Rogo It. bramble, blackberry, Wal. *rug;* from *rubus (rovo rogo)* Sp. *rubo.*

Rogue Fr. adj. proud, haughty; borrowed from the Normans, O. N. *hròk-r* arrogant, E. *rogue* (Gael. *rôg*). Wall. has *aroguer* to address haughtily.

Roide Fr. stiff; from *rigidus*, It. *rigido.*

Roitelet Fr. a goldhammer (usu. a wren, G. *zaun-könig* hedgeking), from its golden crown or tuft; = *roi-et-el-et* with triple dim. suffix, cf. L. *regulus, regaliolus*, Gk. βασιλεύς, βασιλίσκος, τύραννος, It. *reattino*, Sp. *reyezuelo*, Pg. *are re*, also Norm. *ré-pepin*, Berr. *roi-bertaud*, Saintonge *roi-bédelet*, It. *re di siepe* (= *zaun-könig).*

Bojar — *rozar.*

Rolde rollo — *rotolo.*

Rôle — *rotolo.*

Roman — *romanzo.*

Romanzo It., Sp. *romance*, Pr. O. Fr. *romans*, Fr. *roman*, Rh. *romansch*, L. L. *romancium*, F. *romance* (language or composition); hence vb. Sp. *romanzar*, Pr. *romansar*, O. Fr. *romancier* to translate into Romance. From L. adv. *romanice: parler romans* = *loqui romanice.* O. Fr. *romans* took the form *romant* in the oblique cases, cf. *paisans paisant*, hence later nom. *romant roman*, adj. *romaut-ique*, *romantic.* Cf. O. Fr. *bretans* = *britannice*, Sp. *vascuence* = *Vasconice.*

Rombo It., Sp. *rumbo*, Pg. *rumbo rumo*, Fr. E. *rumb* (E. also spelt *rhumb*), point of the compass, line, course of a ship; vb. Fr. *arrumer* to trace the course of a ship on the chart; according to some from ῥυμός pole of a waggon, according to others from *rhombus.* But Fr. *arrumer*, Sp. *arrumar* = to stow, and must come from Du. *ruim* ship's-*room*. Cf. Norm. *arruner* to arrange, *déruner* to disarrange.

Rombo *frombo* It. a humming, buzzing, *romba fromba*, *rombola frombola* a sling, *rombolare frombolare* to sling; from *ῥόμβος* a top, *ῥομβεῖν* to whirl, sling. The *f* is onomatopoetical.

Rombo Pg., Sp. *romo*, Cat. *rom* adj. blunt, obtuse; from G. sbst. *rumpf*, Du. *romp* (E. *rump*) truncus. Pg. *rombo* sbst. = hole, cf. *buco*.

Romeo It. O. Sp., also *romero*, O. Fr. *romier*, E. *roamer* (vb. to *roam*) a pilgrim (prop. to *Rome*), cf. Dante, Vita Nuova: *chiamansi romei inquanto vanno a Roma*.

Romero — *romeo* and *ramerino*.

Romire It. to make a noise or bustle; from O. H. H. *hrômjan hruomjan* = G. *rühmen* to extol.

Romito It., Sic. *rimita* hermit; from *eremita*.

Ronca It. a sickle, javelin with a sickle-shaped point; from vb. *runcare* to mow. O. Fr. *ronsge* a spear.

Roncar Sp. Pg. Cat. to snore, snarl; from *rhoncare*, sbst. *rhonchus*.

Ronce Fr. (f.), Pr. *ronser* briar, thorn. From *rumex* a missile with barbed point (It. *ronciglio* hook, barb), cf. Fr. *chardon* = (1) thistle (2) spike. The Occ. is *roumec*. For the form, cf. Fr. *ponce*, Pr. *pomser* from *pumex*, Fr. *pouce*, Pr. *polzer* from *pollex*. From *rumex* also comes Pr. *ronsar* to sling, throw.

Roncear Sp., Cat. *roncejar* to loiter, behave sulkily, Sp. *roncero*, Pg. *ronceiro* slothful; perhaps of the same origin as the It. *ronzare* to hum.

Ronchione — *rocchio*.

Ronciglio — *ronce*.

Roncin — *rozza*.

Ronco Sp. O. Pg., Cat. *ronc* hoarse; for *roco* from *raucus* (Pg. *rouco*), taking the *n* of the verb *roncar* = L. *rhoncare* to snore.

Rondine *rondinella* It., Wal. *rêndunea*, Pg. *andorinha*, Pr. *ironda irondella*, Fr. *hirondelle* swallow; Wal. *rêndurea*, Pr. *randola*, N. Pr. *endriouleto andoureto dindouleto*, O. Fr. *aronde alondre arondelle*, Cat. *aureneta oreneta*, Val. *oroneta*. From *hirundo hirundinis*, Cat. *orin-eta* by loss of the *d*. Whence is the Sp. *golondrina* (*golondro* = hope, desire)? Ferrari recognises in it the Gk. *χελιδών*.

Rondon — *randa*.

Ronfler Fr., Pr. *ronflar*, Sic. *runfuliari*, Tusc. *ronfiare*, Ven. Lomb. *ronfare* to snore, snort; the root is seen in the O. H. G.

rof·azòn, O. S. *ropizòn* to belch, perhaps too in the Bret. *ruflà* to guzzle, Rh. *g-rufflar* to snort.

Ronger Fr. to gnaw, bite, champ. From *rumigare* to chew the cud, O. Fr. *ronger,* Sp. Pg. *rumiar ronzar,* Pr. *romiar,* It. *rugumare,* Mil. *rumegà,* Wal. *rumégà.*

Ronsar — *ronce.*

Ronsare It. to hum, buzz, sbst. *ronzone* a blue-bottle. From O. H. G. *rùnazòn,* M. H. G. *rùnzen.*

Ronsino — *rozza.*

Roña — *rogna.*

Roque — *rocco.*

Roquete — *rocchetto.*

Roquette — *ruca.*

Ros Pr. (m.) dew; the Pg. Sp. form from adj. *roscidus,* sbst. *rócio, rocio,* Sp. vb. *rociar* (cf. *limpidus limpiar*), Cat. *ruxar,* Pr. *arrosar,* Fr. *arroser* to bedew, besprinkle (E. *rose* of a watering-pot), whence Sp. Pg. *rociada,* Cat. *ruxada,* Pr. *rosada,* Fr. *rosée,* It. *rugiada* dew.

Rosa It. Sp. Pg. Pr., Fr. E. *rose.* From a form *ròsa* with long *o.* From *ròsa* come It. *ruosa,* Sp. *ruese,* Wal. *roasé.* We find a diphthongal form in Mil. *roeusa,* Piedm. *reusa,* Rh. *rósa.*

Rosée — *ros.*

Rospo It. toad; perhaps connected with *ruspo* rough, v. *escuerzo.*

Rosse — *rozza.*

Rossignuolo It., Sp. *ruiseñor,* O. Sp. *rosseñol roseñor, rouxinhol rouxinol,* Pr. Fr. *rossignol* nightingale, Pr. f. *rossinhola;* from *lusciniolus* from *luscinius luscinia.* Varro de ling. Lat. 5, 76 mentions only a dim. *lusciniola.* *L* was changed to *r* for euphony, to avoid such combinations as *lo losignuolo; ruscinia roscinia* are found as early as the 9th century. The Wal. uses *priveghitoare = pervigilatrix,* Alb. *bilbil* (= Pers. Turk. *bulbul, bùlbùl*).

Rosso It., Sp. *roxo,* Pg. *roxo,* Pr. *ros,* Fr. *roux,* Wal. *ros rosiu* red: from L. *russus* (rare).

Rosta It. (1) stoppage (Dante Inf. 13, 17 *rompieno ogni rosta*), Com. vb. *rostà* to hinder. (2) fan, tail, vb. *arrostare* to fan, to wag; from G. *rost* a flood-gate, the grate of a helmet, a fan. Wal. *rosteiu* grate, lattice = Serv. *rostilj.*

Rostire It. in *arrostire,* Cat. *rostir,* Fr. *rôtir,* Pr. *raustir* to roast; part. past as sbst. It. *arrostito,* Fr. *rôti* a roast; sbst. from the root Pr. *raust,* It. *arrosto.* It is the O. H. G. *róstjan* (Rom. *i* = O. H. G. *j*), sbst. *gi-rósti,* E. *roast,* also in Celtic, Gael. *róist,* W. *rhostio,* Bret. *rosta.*

Rostro Sp., Pg. *rosto* face, countenance, Wal. *rost* mouth. Lat. *rostrum* for *os* occurs in Plautus, Lucilius, Varro and Petronius; cf. A. S. *neb* os, E. *neb* rostrum, O. H. G. *snabul* rostrum, O. Fris. *snavel* os.

Rot Fr. Cat. belch; from *ructus*, It. *rutto*.

Rote O. Fr. E., Pr. *rota* a stringed instrument, crowd. From a G. form *(chrota*, M. H. G. *rotte)* of the Celtic *crot* (O. Ir.), *cruit* (Gael.), *crwth* (W.), the *chrotta Britanna* of Venantius Fort., E. *crowd, crowder*. It is named from the hollow frame; W. *crowth* = protuberance, belly, Gael. *cruit* a hump.

Rotella It., Sp. *rodela*, O. Fr. *roele* a round shield; It. *rotella*, Sp. *rodilla*, Pr. *rodela* knee-pan, knee; from *rotella* for *rotula*, cf. M. H. G. *knie-rade*.

Rôtir — *rostire*.

Rotolo rullo It., Sp. *rollo* rol, Pr. *rotle rolle*, Fr. *rôle*, E. *roll* (of paper &c.); from *rotulus;* vb. It. *rotolare ruzzolare*, Sp. *arrollar*, Pr. *rollar*, Fr. *rouler*, E. *roll*. Also Sp. *rolde* from *rotulus* as *Roldan* for *Rotlan*. Hence Fr. *contrôle* for *contre-rôle (counter-roll)*, check, stamp on money, *control*.

Rotta It., Sp. Pg. Pr. *rota*, O. Fr. *route*, E. *rout*, Fr. *déroute;* from *ruptus rupta*, whence also Pr. *rota*, O. Fr. *rote* = a troop, L. L. *rupta*, G. *rotte*, O. Fr. *arouter* to arrange; Fr. *route* road (E. *rote*) = via rupta, cf. O. Fr. *brisée* street, and *Mala-routa* (name of a place), Sp. Pg. *rota derrota* course, Fr. *routier, routine;* hence also Fr. *roture* = L. L. *ruptura* fresh land, a small farm, *roturier* one who held such a farm, a commoner, plebeian.

Roture — *rotta*.

Rouche — *ruche*.

Rouge — *roggio*.

Rouille — *ruggine*.

Rouir Fr. to ret or steep flax or hemp; from Du. *roten rotten*, G. *rösten*, E. *ret* (part. *rotten* = steeped).

Rouler — *rotolo*.

Roussin — *rozza*.

Route routine — *rotta*.

Rouvre — *rovere*.

Roux — *rosso*.

Rovajo It. north wind; of unknown origin. Menage gets it from *borearius (borealis)*, by corr. *robearius rovarius*.

Rovello rovella It. anger, *arrovellare* to enrage; from *rubellus*, cf. L. *ira rubens*.'

Rover O. Fr. to desire, request; from *rogare (roar rovar)* L. L. often = command. Not found in Pr., in It. *rogare* is only juristic, Sp. Pg. Cat. *rogar*, Wal. *rugă* = to beg (a favour), not like the Fr. to desire, order. So O. Fr. *enter-ver*, Pr. *entervar entre-var*, Wal. *intrebà*, from *interrogare*. Cf. *corvée*.

Rovere It., Sp. Pg. *robre roble*, Pr. *roure*, Fr. *rouvre* an oak ; from *robur roboris*.

Rovescio — *rivescio*.

Rovistare ruvistare It. to rummage; from *revisitare* (Menage).

Roxo — *roggio*.

Royaume — *reame*.

Rosar Sp. Pg. to weed out, stub up, nibble, fret, rub; a freq. from *rodere rosus*, so for *rosar*, or from an iter. *rositare*. From *rodicare* comes Pg. *rojar* to scrape, sweep the ground, trail, *rojão* a scraping on the fiddle.

Rossa It., Pr. *rossa*, Fr. *rosse* a jade, masc. Com. *roz*, Berg. *ros*. The It. form seems to exclude the der. from G. *ross*. A derivative is found in Pr. *rossi roci*, O. Fr. *roussin*, Sp. *rocin* and *rocinante*, Pg. *rossim*, and with inserted *n*, Pr. *ronci*, *roncin* O. Fr. (hence W. *rhwnsi*), Pic. *ronchin*, It. *ronzino* a nag, Lorr. Wall. *ronsin* a stallion, Fr. *roussin*. M. H. G. *runzit* = a poor, sorry horse.

Ru Fr., O. Fr. *rui* stream, channel; from *rivus* (cf. *tuile* from *tegula*), Ronchi *rieu*, Pr. *riu*, Sp. *rio*, It. *rivo*. *Ruisseau* = a form *rivicellus* for *rivulus*, It. *ruscello* (from the Fr.).

Rua — *ruga*.

Rubaldo — *ribaldo*.

Ruban Fr. ribbon. Not from *rubens*, for then we should have had *rubandier* not *rubanter;* prob. a compound with G. *band*, like *hauban*, *raban*, Du. *ring-band?* O. Fr. has also *riban*, E. *riband*, ribbon.

Rubbio It. a corn-measure; from *rubeus*, because the divisions were marked with red, cf. *pinta*.

Rubiglio — *ervo*.

Rubino It., Sp. *rubin rubi*, Pr. *robin*, Fr. *rubis*, E. *ruby;* from *rubeus*.

Rubio — *roggio*.

Ruca It. Pr., Sp. Pg. *oruga;* also It. *ruchetta*, Sp. *ruqueta*, Fr. *roquette*, E. *rocket* a plant; from L. *eruca*.

Ruche Fr. beehive (orig. made of bark, cf. Sp. *corcho* = cork and beehive), also hulk of a ship (also written *rouche*), O. Fr. *rusche rusque*, Pr. *rusca ruscha*, Piedm. Lomb. *rusca* bark, Dauph. *ruchi* tan, Com. *ruscà* to bark (a tree); a Celtic word, O. Ir. *rùsc*, Gael. *rùsg*, Bret. *rusk*, W. *rhisg* bark (E. *rusk*), Bret. *rusken* beehive.

Rúcio Sp., Pg. *ruço* greyish, light grey; from *russeus*.

Rue — *ruga*.

Rueca — *rocca*.

Ruer Fr. to throw, *se ruer* to throw oneself on, Du. *ruyen, ruer* (neut.) to kick. From *ruere*, like other verbs in *uere* (e. g. *argüer, minüer*) changed to the first conjugation.

Ruf — *ruffa*.

Ruffa It. a scramble, pulling; vb. *arruffare* to roughen, dishevel the hair, Com. *rufà-su* to frown, Pg. Cat. *arrufar* to curl, con-

tract, roughen, Sp. *arrufarse* to be cross, ill tempered (cf. It.
arricciarsi), Sp. *rufo* curly-haired (also red-haired), Pr. *ruf*
rough (Lim. *rufe*), Berr. *rufe rufle* morose. *Ar-ruffare* = G.
raufen (cf. *tuffare* = *taufen*), *rupfen* (cf. *zuffa zupfen*), cf. E.
ruff, *ruffle*, Du. *ruyffel* wrinkle, O. N. *rúfinn* rough, E. adj.
rough, O. E. *ruff*. In connection are Mil. *ruff*, Piedm. Com.
rufa, Romag. *rofia* scurf, dirt (cf. It. *roffia* thick mist), O. Fr.
roife rofée scurf, all = O. H. G. *hruf*, M. H. G. *ruf*, O. N.
hrufa rufa, Du. *rof* scurf, A. S. *hreofl* leprous. Hence It. *baruffa* fray, Com. *haruf* a tuft of hair, Pr. *barrufaut* fighter,
brawler, from O. H. G. *bi-roufan*, cf. *baroccio* for *biroccio*.
Sp. *arrufar* to incurvate, is from E. *roof*.

Ruffiano It., Sp. Pr. *rufian*, Fr. *ruffien* pimp, bully, E. *ruffian*;
it formerly meant not only "leno" but "amasius", hence
many have suspected a connexion with *rufo*, from the red
(blond) or curled hair (Sp. *rufo*) worn by such. Others connect it with *ruffa rufa* (scurf, dirt) as implying moral filth,
cf. Inf. 11: *ruffian baratti e simile lordura*.

Ruga O. It., Sp. Pg. *rua*, Pr. *ruda*, Fr. *rue* street, Alb. *ruga*;
from *ruga* a wrinkle, furrow, row. The Lat. meaning remains
in It. *ruga*, Sp. *arruga*, Pr. *ruga rua*. Al. from O. H. G. *riga*,
G. *reihe* a row.

Ruggine It. rust; from *ærugo*, Wal. *rugine*; Sp. *robin* from *rubigo*, *orin* from *ærugo*; Cat. *rovely*, Pr. *roilh roilha*, Fr. *rouille*
a dim. from *rubigo*.

Rugiada — *ros*.

Rugumare — *ronger*.

Ruido Sp. clamour; from *rugitus*, cf. *rut*.

Ruin Sp., Pg. *ruim roim* poor, pitiful, mean; from *ruina*.

Rulponzo — *raperonzo*.

Ruiseñor — *rossignuolo*.

Ruisseau — *ru*.

Rullo — *rotolo*.

Rumb — *rombo*.

Runer Fr. to whisper; from O. H. G. *rúnen*, G. *raunen*, O. E. *roun*,
cf. also O. Sp. *ad-runar* to guess, Goth. *runa* mystery (E. *runic*).

Ruscello — *ru*.

Ruse — *rifusare*.

Ruspare It. to scrape. From O. L. *ruspari* to examine (orig.,
prob., to scrape). .

Ruspo It. (1) new coin (2) rough. From O. H. G. *ruspan* to be
stiff, cf. *ruspil-hâr* rough-hair.

Russare It. to snore; perhaps from *ronchissare roncsare roxare*.
O. H. G. *ruzzôn* would have give It. *ruzzare*.

Ruste O. Fr. strong, violent, sbst. O. Fr. *rustié*, Pr. *rustat*; from
rusticus (cf. N. *rusti* a farmer), Fr. *rustre* a boor.

Rustre — *rusle.*

Rut Fr., E. *rut* (of deer); from *rugitus.*

Ruvido It. rough; from L. *ruidus* found in Plin. Hist. Nat. 18, 10 (23): *major pars Italiæ ruido utitur pilo* i. e. aspero et impolito, cf. *fluidus fluvido.*

Ruvistico rovistico It. privet; a corruption of *ligustrum* which was confounded with *ligusticum.*

Ruser Pr. to grunt (only in 3 sing. pres. ind. *rutz*); from L. *rudere.*

Ruzzolare — *rotolo.*

S.

Sabana Sp., Pr. *savena,* O. Fr. *savene* bed-covering, altar-covering, L. L. *sabanum savanum,* Goth. *sabans,* O. H. G. *saban* fine linen; from Gk. σάβανον a linen towel; hence Sic. *insavonare* to cover with a pall. The word is of Eastern origin (cf. *taffetas, camelot* &c.), Ar. *subaniya* a fine linen made at *Saban* near Bagdad.

Sabio — *saggio.*

Sable — *sciabla.*

Sable — *zibellino.*

Sabot — *ciabatta.*

Sabre — *sciabla.*

Sabueso — *segugio.*

Sacar Sp. Pg., O. Fr. *sachier,* Pic. *saquer* to draw, draw out, produce &c., (Fr. *saccade* jerk, pull), orig. to take, *sack;* L. L. *saccare,* from *saccus.*

Saccade — *sacar.*

Sacco It., Sp. Pg. *saco,* Fr. *sac,* E. *sack* (of a city); vb. It. *saccheggiare,* Sp. *saquear,* Fr. *saccager,* to *sack.* From L. *saccus;* cf. s. *sacar,* and cf. G. *plunder* = (1) baggage, pack, (2) plunder. Hence It. *saccomanno* = N. Pr. *sacaman,* Du. E. *sackman;* Sp. *sacomano* pillage.

Sacho Sp. Pg. hoe, vb. *sachar sallar;* from *sarculum, surculare,* It. *sarchiare* &c.

Saccomanno — *sacco.*

Sacre — *sagro.*

Sacudir — *cudir.*

Sade O. Fr. sweet; from *sapidus* savoury, cf. Pr. f. *sabeza* for *sabeda* = *sapida.* Hence Fr. *maussade* disagreeable, for *malsade.*

Sadio Pg. wholesome; prob. a corruption of *saudio* (from *saude* L. *salus*), cf. Pr. *salutatiu.*

Sáfara Pg. a stony waste, adj. *sáfaro* wild, intractable, Sp. *zahareño;* from Ar. *ça'hrá (sahara)* desert.

Safra *zafra* Pg. a large anvil; from Ar. *çachrah* a hard stone.

Safran — *zafferano.*

Safre Fr. greedy; from Goth. *safjan* to taste (for term. cf. *bafre, goinfre, goudiafre*), or = Du. *schaffer* (1) one who serves up eatables (2) a glutton, vb. *schaffen.*

Sage — *saggio.*

Sagerida — *satureia.*

Saggio It., Sp. Pg. *sabio*, Pr. *sabi satge*, Fr. E. *sage;* from *sapius* (cf. Petron. *nesapius*) *sabius savius*, O. Fr. *saire.* The Sic. has *varva sapia* beard-wise.

Saggio It., Sp. *ensayo*, Pr. *essay*, Fr. *essai*, E. *assay essay;* vb. It. *saggiare*, Sp. *ensayar*, Pr. *essaiar*, Fr. *essayer*, E. *assay.* From L. L. *exagium* (Sp. *ens = ex*) pensatio (cf. *examen* the tongue of a balance = *exagimen).*

Sagire It. to put one in possession, Pr. *sazir*, Fr. *saisir* to take possession of, E. *seize;* It. *sagina*, Pr. *sazina*, O. Fr. *saisine*, E. *sasine*, *seisin.* O. Fr. had also the It. signification, and so in Fr. *se saisir de.* Hence *dessaisir* Pr. *dessazir* to dispossess, disseisin. From O. H. G. *sazjan*, G. *setzen*, E. *set*, or, better for the sense, from *bi-sazjan, besetzen, beset* = occupy, so that the Fr. Pr. meaning would be the earlier. It. *sagire = sazjan as palagio = palazjum palatium.*

Sagro It., Sp. Pg. Fr. *sacre* a small hawk; a translation of the Gk. ἱέραξ, cf. G. *weihe*, O. H. G. *wiho* kite, prop. = sacer, cf. *turbot.* Al. from the Ar. *fakr.* Sagro, sacre, O. E. *saker* was also used for a kind of gun, cf. *moschetto.*

Sahir Pg. to depart, O. Pg. *salir;* from *salire*, Fr. *saillir.* The *l* was lost and *h* inserted to avoid the hiatus.

Sahumar Sp. to perfume; for *suhumar*, L. *suffumicare.*

Saie Fr. goldsmith's brush; from *seta* bristle.

Saime It., Sp. *sain*, Pr. *sagin sain*, Fr. *sain-doux* lard; from *sagina* Sp. *sainete* a dainty bit, also a farce. The form *-ime* and the gender (m.) are due to a L. *sagimen.*

Sain sainete — *saime.*

Sais Pr. (f. *saissa*) gray (of hair); perhaps the rare L. *cæsius* gray (of eyes), whence *ceis seis sais*, cf. *plais* for *pleis (plexum).*

Saisir — *sagire.*

Saison — *stagione.*

Saja It., Sp. Pr. *saya*, Fr. *saie*, m. It. *sajo*, Sp. *sayo* woollen over-coat, coat, also the stuff of which it was made, M. H. G. *sei*, O. Ir. *sai;* from *saga* (Ennius), usu. *sagum* a military cloak, according to Varro, of Gallic origin. *Sagulatus* (clad in the *sagulum*) became in Pr. *sallat*, vb. Pr. *sallar* to cover. From *saja* comes It. *sajetta*, Sp. *sayete*, Pg. *saieta saeta*, Fr. *sayette* serge, M. H. G. *seit.*

Sajar — *sarrafar.*

Sala It. Sp. Pg. Pr., Fr. *salle*, Wal. *salê* hall; from O. H. G. *sal* a house, dwelling.

Salade — *celata*.

Salassare It. to bleed, let blood; from *sangue lasciare*, cf. O. Pg. *sanguileirado*. Also It. *segnare* from Fr. *saigner*, Pr. *sanguar*, Sp. *sangrar*, L. *sanguinare*.

Salamoja — *moja*.

Salâvo It., Fr. *sale* dirty; the latter is from O. H. G. uninflected *salo* muddy, the former from the inflected *salawer*, gen. *salawes*. Hence Fr. vb. *salir*.

Salchicha — *salsa*.

Saldo — *soldo*.

Sale — *salavo*.

Salitre Sp. Pg. salpetre, Wal. *salitru*; from *sal nitrum*, It. *salnitro*.

Sallar — *sacho*.

Salle — *sala*.

Salma soma It., Sp. *salma xalma enxalma*, Fr. *somme* burden, Pr. *sauma* a she-ass; from late L. *sagma* (σάγμα), whence also O. H. G. *saum*. Isidore has: *sagma quæ corrupte vulgo salma dicitur*, cf. Sp. *esmeralda* from *smaragdus*. Hence It. *assomare* to load, Fr. *assommer* to cudgel; Fr. *sommelier* a butler, from loading or packing the casks of wine in the cellar, cf. It. *sometta* a little burden.

Salmastro It., Fr. *saumâtre* briny; from *salmacidus*, Pr. *samaciu*, O. Fr. *saumache*.

Salmuera — *moja*.

Salope Fr. slut, dirty wench; for *slope*, cf. E. *sloppy*.

Salpare — *sarpare*.

Salpêtre Fr., E. *saltpetre*; from *sal petræ*.

Salpicar Sp. Pg. Pr. to besprinkle; prop. with salt, cf. Fr. *saupoudrer; picar* = to prick.

Salsa It. Sp. Pr., Fr. *sauce* (for *sause*), E. *sauce*; from *salsus*. Hence It. *salsiccia*, Fr. *saucisse*, Sp. *salchicha*, L. L. *salsitia*, E. *sausage*.

Salsapariglia It., Sp. *zarzaparilla*, Fr. *salsepareille*, E. *sarsaparilla* a Peruvian plant; from Sp. *zarza* bramble and *Parillo* the name of the physician, who first used it.

Salvaggio selvaggio It., Sp. *salvage*, Pr. *salvatge*, Fr. *sauvage*, E. *savage*; from *silvaticus*, It. *selvatico salvatico*, Wal. *sêlbatic*. Hence sbst. It. *salvaggina*, Sp. *salvagina*, O. Fr. *salvagine* venison.

Salvano It. night-mare; from *silvanus*, so *selvatico* from *silvaticus*.

Sambue O. Fr. a housing, horse-cloth, used by ladies of rank, L. L. *sambuca*; = O. H. G. *samboh sambuoh sambuh* a sedan. It is, probably, the same word as the L. *sambuca* (1) a sort of harp (2) a military engine of similar shape, used for scaling walls.

Samedi Fr. saturday; contracted from *sabbati dies*, Pr. *dissaple*, It. *sábato*, Wal. *sĕmbĕtĕ* &c.

Sampogna zampogna It., Sp. *zampoña*, Pg. *sanfonha*, Pr. *sinphonia*, O. Fr. *symphonie chifonie*, Wal. *cimpoe* a musical instrument, shawm, bagpipe; from *symphonia*, cf. Venant. Fort.: *donec plena suo cecinit symphoniu flatu*.

Sanco — *zanca*.

Sancochar Sp. to parboil; from *semicoctus*.

Sandio Sp., Pg. *sandeu* foolish, simple, perhaps orig. = one full of wonder, who is always saying *sancte deus!* cf. *santiguarse* to bless oneself, also = to wonder, Wall. *doudieu* a hypocrite (doux dieu).

Sangle — *cinghia*.

Sanglier — *cinghiale*.

Sanglot — *singhiozzo*.

Sanna — *zanna*.

Sans — *senza*.

Sansonnet Fr. starling; prop. = little Samson.

Santiguar Sp. Pg. to make the sign of the cross; from *sanctificare*, cf. *amortiguar* from *mortificare*, *apaciguar* from *pacificare*, *averiguar* from *verificare (-iguar = -igrar = -ivigor* for *ifigar*, cf. *fragua = fabrica)*.

Santoreggia — *satureja*.

Saña Sp., Pg. *sanha* rage; from *insania*.

Sap O. Fr. Pr. fir, whence Fr. *sapin* fir, *sapine* fir-wood (L. *sappinus*). *Sap* belongs to a L. primitive form, v. *bubbone*.

Sape — *zappa*.

Sapére savére It., Pg. Sp. Pr. *saber*, Fr. *savoir;* from *sápere* with change of accent, following the analogy of other modal verbs *devére, potére, volére*. The L. *scire* is only found in the Sard. and Wal.

Sapo Sp. Pg. toad; from Gk. σήψ σηκός a poisonous snake, Lat. *seps?* The Basque word is *apoa zapoa*.

Sarabanda It. Pg., Sp. *zarabanda*, Fr. *sarabande*, a *saraband* (sort of dance); from the Pers. *serbend*, through the Spanish.

Sarcelle — *cercela*.

Sarcia — *sarte*.

Sardina It. Sp., Fr. E. *sardine* a fish; from L. *sarda, sardinia*, Gk. σαρδίνη, It. also *sardella*.

Sargento — *sergente*.

Sargia It., Sp. *sarga sirgo*, Pr. *serga*, Fr. *serge sarge*, E. *serge*, a woollen stuff with a mixture of linen and silk, L. L. *sarica;* from *sericus serica* silk, Basq. *ciricua*. Hence Sp. *xergon*, Pg. *xergão enxergão* a coarse stuff, straw-sack *(x = s* as in *ximio* from *simius)*, It. *sáryano* &c.

Sargotar Pr. to talk gibberish? for *sartagotar* (*sartago* a medley)? Burg. *sargoter*, however, = *cahoter*, cf. Sard. *sarrágu*.

Sarjar — *sarrafar*.

Sarna Sp. Pg. Cat. itch. Isidore: *impetigo est sicca scabies … hanc vulgus sarnam appellaut.* The B. is *sarra zarayarra*, cf. W. *sarn* plaster, *sarnaidh* crusty. Perhaps the Sp. Pg. *sarro* incrustation, sediment, belongs to the same root.

Sarpare salpare It., Wal. *sarpà*, Sp. Pg. *zarpar*, Fr. *sarper* to weigh anchor. From ἁρπάζειν, for *exharpagare*. Hence Sp. *zarpa* claw.

Sarracina Sp. a tumultuous contest. From B. *asserrecina*.

Sarrafar Pg. to scarify, make incisions; prob. a corruption of *scarificare*, Sp. *sarjar*, *sajar* (*scarfear scarcar*, L. *rc* = Sp. *rj*). B. has *sarciatu*.

Sarraja Sp., Pg. *serratha* a vegetable; *lactuca agrestis est, quam sarralium nominamus eo quod dorsum ejus in modum serra est.*

Sárria Sp. Pr. Cat. basket of rushes, net, O. Fr. *sarrie*, B. *sarrea*, also Sp. *sera*, Pg. *seira* panier. O. H. G. *sahar* = rush, L. L. *sarex* = *carex*, cf. ἄῤῥιχος a basket.

Sarriette — *satureja*.

Sarta Sp. string of beads; from *sertum*, *serta*.

Sarte sartie It. (plur.), O. Fr. *sarties*, Sp. *xarcia* *.xarcias* cordage, tackling; from L. Gk. ἐξάρτιον ship's tackle (ἐξάρτιον), which is from ἐξαρτίζειν to equip a ship; the f. from Gk. neut. pl.

Sarten Sp., Pg. *sartagem sartã*, Pr. *sartan*, cf. Sic. *sartauia* a frying-pan; from L. *sartago*.

Sas — *staccio*.

Sastre Sp. tailor; euphonic for *sartre* from *sartor*, It. *sartore*.

Satin — *seta*.

Satureja santoreggia It., Sp. *sagerida axedrea*, Pg. *saturagem segurelha cigurelha*, Pr. *sadreia*, Fr. *sarriette* a herb, savory; from *satureja*.

Sauce saucisse — *salsa*.

Saudade Pg. (quadrisyllabic) ardent longing, adj. *saudoso*. For *soledade* through a form *soidade*, and so would orig. denote absence from a desired object, cf. *disio*. But Marsh (on the English Language, Lect. III.) compares *saudade* with the Scandinavian *saknadr*, *saknad*, *saou*.

Sauge Fr., E. *sage*, from L. *salvia*, It. Sp. Pr. *salvia*, Wal. *salvie salie jale*.

Saule Fr. (m.) willow, for which Burg. Lorr. has *saysse*, Pr. *sauze sautz*, It. *salcio*, Wal. *salce*, Sp. *salce sauce sauz saz*, B. *saliga*, all from *salix salicis*, whence also Fr. *saussaie* = *salicetum*. The Fr. *saule*, however, is to be referred to O. H. G. *salaha*, *sàla*, cf. *gaule* from *valu*.

Saumâtre — *salmastro*.

Saumure — *moja.*

Saure — *sauro.*

Sauro soro It. *sorrel* (of a horse), Fr. *saure* yellowish brown (Pr. *saur sor* blond, yellow, red), O. Fr. *sorel* in *Agnes Sorel* i. e. Agnes the Blond, E. *sorel sorrel.* From L. G. adj. *soor,* E. *sear* dried up, vb. A. S. *searian,* O. H. G. *sôrên, saurên* to sear, Fr. *saurer* to smoke herrings (*hareng sauret* a dried, smoked, seared herring, or, according to Cotgrave, one that is smoked till it gets a *sorrel* hue, a *red* herring), cf. *coloraridus* (Pliny), *xerampelinus* (Juv.). Muhn derives *sauro* from the B. *zuria* white. The Pr. *eisaurar* = a L. *exaurare (aura),* Fr. *essorer,* whence It. *sorare* to let soar, to air, *s'essorer* to soar, Fr. sbst. *essor* flight; It. *sciorinare* to air.

Sauvage — *selvaggio.*

Saval Pr. bad, wicked, opp. *pros.* From *savus,* cf. *ibri-ai ver-ai* from *ebrius, verus.*

Savate — *ciabatta.*

Savoir — *sapere.*

Saya — *saja.*

Sayon Sp., Pg. *saião* executioner, officer of justice; from O. H. G. *sago* (G. *säger* = *sawyer*), L. L. *saio sagio.*

Saxon — *stagione.*

Sbaglio — *bagliore.*

Sbarro — *barra.*

Sbavigliare — *badare.*

Sberleffe — *balafre.*

Sbiadato — *biavo.*

Sbieco — *bieco.*

Sbiescio — *biuis.*

Sbigottire — *bigot.*

Sbirro — *birro.*

Sbrioco — *bricco.*

Sbrizzare — *sprazzare.*

Sbrocco — *brocco.*

Sbulimo — *bulimo.*

Scabino It. oftener *schiavino,* Sp. *esclavin,* Fr. *écherin* a sheriff. A German word: A. S. *scepeno,* O. H. G. *sceffeno sceffen,* G. *scheffen schöffe schöppe,* from *schaffen* to arrange, E. shape. The It. *scabino* was formed from L. L. *scabinus.*

Scacco It., Sp. *xaque,* Pg. *xaque,* Pr. *escac,* Fr. *échec,* E. *check* a figure (or move) at chess, *chess (jeu des échecs);* from Persian *shâh* king. Hence Fr. *échiquier,* E. *exchequer* a hall or court of justice, so called from its *checquered (échiqueté)* pavement or table-cover. O. Fr. *échec* = robber is the O. H. G. *schâch.*

Scaffale It. frame, stand; from M. H. G. *schafe,* Bav. *schafen,*

25*

Du. *schap.* Gen. *sraffo* = bedstead. Sic. Rh. *scaffa* = *scaffale.*
For G. *schaffot*, E. *scaffold*, v. *catafalco.*

Scaglia It., Fr. *écaille*, E. *scale*; vb. *scagliare*, *écailler*, *scale.*
From G. *schale*, vb. *schälen*, O. H. G. *scalja scaljan*, E. *shell*,
cf. Goth. *skalja* pot, tile. Hence also Fr. *écale* nut or egg-shell.

Scalabrone — *calabrone.*

Scalco It. cook; from Goth. *skalks*, O.H.G. *scalc* servant, found
also in *siniscalco*, *mariscalco.*

Scalfire It. to scratch, from *scalpere*, cf. *soffice* from *supplex.*
But whence *scalfitto* for *scalfito.* Is it from *scarificare*, *scarifi-*
cere, *scarfire scalfire scalfitto?* cf. Sard. *scraffiri.*

Scalmo scarmo It., Sp. *escalmo escalamo*, N. Pr. *escaume*, Fr.
échome (m.) row-lock; from *scalmus*, cf. *échameau* a raised
bank for vines from *scamellum.*

Scalogno It., Sp. *escalona*, Fr. *échalotte*, E. *shallot*; from *carpa*
Ascalonia the *Ascalon* leek.

Scalterire scaltrire to sharpen, polish, *scaltrito scaltro* (cf. *finito*,
adj. *fino*) sharp, cunning. *Scaltrire*, according to the Crusca,
is to shape from the rough, to make sharp, refine. It may be
from *scalpturire*, so *scaltro* is related to *scalpere*, as γλαφυρός
to γλάφειν. The *s* was thought to be *er*, hence *calterire* to
scratch, (caltrito = scaltrito in sense).

Scampare — *scappare.*

Scana — *zanna.*

Scancia — *escanciar.*

Scancio — *sguancio.*

Scandaglio It., Sp. *escandallo*, Pr. *escandalh* plummet, Alb. *scan-*
talë; vb. *scandagliare scandigliare* &c.; from *scandere*, cf. L. L.
scandília steps of a ladder; the plummet-line would be so
called, because marked at regular intervals. N. Pr. *escandalhi*
= to gauge.

Scandella It., Sp. Pg. Cat. *escandia* &c., a kind of wheat, L. L.
scandula. Prob. from *candidus*, cf. *wheat*, which is connected
with *white*, v. Bopp, Gloss. s. v. *sveta.*

Scappare It., Sp. Pg. Pr. *escapar*, Fr. *échapper*, E. *escape.* From
Rom. *cappa* mantle; *excappare* would = Gk. ἐκδύεσσαι.
Opp. *scappare* It. has *incappare.* It is to be distinguished from
It. *scampare*, O. Fr. *escamper* = *ex-campare (campus)* to quit
the field, Sp. *escampar* to clear away, Pr. Cat. to spread, cf.
espassar from *spatium.*

Scappino — *scarpa.*

Scarafaggio It., Sp. *escarabajo*, Pr. *escaraval* beetle; from *scara-*
baeus (scarabajus). It. *scarabone*, Pg. *escaravelho*, Pr. *escara-*
val, Fr. *escarbot* are from σκάραβος.

Scaraffare It. to snatch away; from M. H. G. *schrapfen*, Bav.
schrafen, Du. *schrapen* to scrape, cf. *escarbar.*

Scaramuccia schermuglo It., Sp. Pr. *escaramuza*, Fr. *escarmouche* a skirmish, whence G. *scharmützel*, E. *scaramouch*. From *schermire* to fight, O.H.G.*skerman;* the *-uccia* is merely terminational, cf. O. Fr. *escarm-ie*.

Scardo — *cardo*.

Scarlatto It., Sp. *escarlate*, Pr. *escarlat*, f. Fr. *écarlate*, E. *scarlet;* an Eastern word, not from *Galaticus* (as Heindorf and Marsh, Lect. on Eng. Lang.).

Scarpa It., Sp. *escarpa*, Fr. *escarpe*, E. *scarp* precipice, declivity; vb. Sp. *escarpar*, Fr. *escarper*, E. *scarp*. From O. N. *skarp*, O. H. G. *scarf*, G. *scharf*, E. *sharp*. It. *scarpa* shoe is so called because *pointed*, whence It. *scappino*, O. Fr. *escapin*, Sp. O. Fr. *escarpin* slipper, sock.

Scarpello — *escopro*.

Scarsella — *sciarpa*.

Scarso It., Pr. *escars escas*, Fr. *échars*, Sp. *escaso*, Du. *schaars*, E. *scarce*. From *excarpsus* for *excerptus* (root vowel used in comp. cf. R. Gr. 2, 344, *sus* for *tus*, cf. *nascoso*, *perso* &c.) reduced, contracted. In the sense of "slender" the It. also writes *scarzo*.

Scartare It., Fr. *écarter*, Sp. Pg. *descartar* to throw out cards, *discard;* from *carta* a card, L. *charta*. The O. Pr. has only *encartar* to register, from *carta*, Fr. *charte* a document, chart.

Scarzo — *scarso*.

Scatola It. a box, Rh. *scatla*, Wal. *scětulcě;* from G. *schachtel*.

Scegliere It. to choose. From *ex-eligere*, cf. for the doubling of the preposition *scilinguare*. *Ex-ligere* for *eligere* gives Sp.*esleir*, Pr. *eslire*, Fr. *élire*.

Scellino It., Sp. Pr. *escalin*, Fr. *escalin* a coin; from Goth. *skilliggs*, O.H.G.*skilling*, E.*shilling* (from *schild*, *shield*, cf. *scudo*).

Scemo It., O. It. *semo*, Pied. Pr. *sem* diminished, dwindled; vb. *scemare*, Piedm. *semé*, Pr. *semar* to diminish, O. Fr. *semer* to separate, Fr. *sechemer* to depart. L. L. has *semus simare scematio*. From *semis* half, cf. Sp. *xeme* a half-foot.

Scempio It. punishment; from *exemplum*.

Scendere It. to descend; from *descendere* (Sp. *descender* &c.), like *struggere* from *destruere*.

Scernere scernire It. to discern; from *excernere*, Pr. *cissernir* to select, part. *eissernit*, Pr. *eis = ex*.

Scerpare It. to tear to pieces; for *scerpere* from *discerpere*, with change of conjugation, v. R. Gr. 2, 117. Rh. *scarpar*, Com. *scarpà* from *dis-carpere*.

Scheggia It. a splinter, *scheggio* a precipice; from *schidia* (σχί-διον) used by Vitruvius in the former sense.

Scheletro It., Sp. *esqueleto*, Fr. *squelette* (m.), E. *skeleton;* from σκελετόν a dried body, a mummy.

Schenolre — *sguancio.*

Scherano — *schiera.*

Schermo It. fight, *skirmish;* vb. It. *schermire,* Sp. Pg. *esgrimir,* Pr. O. Fr. *escrimir;* from O. H. G. *skirm skerm* shield, vb. *skirman (skirmjan* is wanted for the Rom. forms), Bav. *schremen.* Hence It. *schermare,* Cat. *exgrimar,* Fr. *escrimer* to fence; sbst. It. *scherma scrima,* Sp. Pg. *esgrima,* Pr. *escrima,* Fr. *escrime.* One of the numerous words pertaining to the use of arms, which the Rom. nations received from their Gothic conquerors.

Schermuglo — *scaramuccia.*

Scherno It., Sp. *escarnio,* Pg. *escarnho,* Pr. *esquern,* O. Fr. *eschern* mockery, scorn; vb. It. *schernire,* Sp. Pg. *escarnir,* Pr. *esquernir escarnir,* O. Fr. *eschernir escharnir;* from O. H. G. *skĕrn,* vb. *skernòn* to mock, to scorn.

Scherzare It. to sport, sbst. *scherzo; f*rom O. H. G. *scherzen* to frolic, connected with O. H. G. *skerón* to be wanton.

Schiacciare It. to squash, crack, sbst. *schiaccia;* from O. H. G. *klackjan* to crack, *clack,* with intensive s, M. H. G. *zerklecken.* Quite distinct from Fr. *écacher (quatto).*

Schiaffo It. a box on the ear; from O. H. G. *schlappe,* E. *slap,* through a conjectural form *schlapfe.* N. Pr. has vb. *esclafà.*

Schiamazzare It. to cry out, sbst. *schiamazzo,* O. Fr. *esclamasse* (whence G. *schlamasse);* from *exclamare.*

Schiantare It. to crack, break, Pr. *esclatar,* Fr. *éclater;* sbst. It. *schianto,* Fr. *éclat* fragment, splinter, crack, hence Ven. *schiantizare* to lighten. The It. *n* is inserted, cf. *lontra = loutre; esclatar* is from O. H. G. *skleizen* for *sleizen* to break in pieces, *slice,* cf. O. Fr. *esclier = O. H. G. slizan.*

Schiatta It., Pr. *esclata,* O. Fr. *esclate* race, kind; from O. H. G. *slahta,* G. *ge-schlecht.*

Schlattire — *ghiattire.*

Schiavino — *scabino.*

Schiavo It., Sp. *esclavo,* Pg. *escravo,* Pr. *esclau,* Fr. *esclave* (for *éclou,* O. Fr. *esclo-s escla-s);* from G. *sclave* for *stare,* E. *slave,* prop. a *Slave* taken prisoner in battle; hence also It. *schiavina,* Sp. *esclaviua,* O. Fr. *esclaviue,* M. H. G. *slavine* a pilgrim's long robe.

Schidone — *spito.*

Schiena It., Ven. Piedm. Rom. Sard. *schina,* Sp. *esquena,* Pr. *esquena esquiua,* Fr. *échine* spine. From O. H. G. *skina* a pin, cf. Lat. *spina* thorn and spine; It. *schiniera,* Sp. *esquinela* greaves, from O. H. G. *skina skena* a tube, bone. Not from *spina,* for in the West *sp* does not pass into *sq.*

Schiera It., Pr. *esqueira,* O. Fr. *eschiere* a band; from O. H. G. *scara,* G. *schaar (share).* Vb. Pr. *escarir,* O. Fr. *escharir* to part, divide, L. L. *scarire* to fix, design, Pr. *escarida*, O. Fr. *escherie* lot. Pr. *escala*, O. Cat. *eschala*, O. Fr. *eschicle* are corruptions of *scara;* from *schiera* Ferrari gets *scheruno* a robber.

Schietto It. pure, smooth (Pr. *esclet*), Rh. *schliett* worthless; from Goth. *slaihts*, O. H. G. *sleht*, G. *schlicht schlecht*, E. *slight*. Neap. *schitto*, Rh. *schiett* == only, merely, Du. *slechts*, G. *schlechthin*, cf. It. *pure* from *purus*.

Schifo It., Sp. Pg. *esquife*, Fr. *esquif* a boat, *skiff;* vb. O. Fr. *esquiper* to fit out a ship (go on board), Fr. *équiper*, E. *equip*, Sp. *esquifar esquipar;* from O. H. G. *skif*, Goth. A. S. O. N. *skip scip*, E. *ship*. O. Fr. *eschipre eskipre* from A. S. *sciper*, E. *skipper*, G. *schiffer*.

Schimbescio — *sghembo*.

Schincio — *sguancio*.

Schiniera — *schiena*.

Schioppo It. corrupted *scoppio* a blow, crack, fire-arm, dim. *schioppetto scoppietto*, whence Sp. *escopeta*, Fr. *escopette* a carbine, blunderbuss, vb. *scoppiare*, L. L. *sclupare* to shoot. From the L. *stloppus* (or *sclopus*) (Persius), cf. *fist'lare = fischiare*. For *schioppo* also *stioppo*, cf. *stiaffo*, *stianto*, *stinco*.

Schippire It. to slip away, escape; for *sclippire* from M. H. G. *slipfen*, Du. *slippen*, A. S. *slipan*, E. *slip*, G. *schlüpfen*.

Schiuma It., Sp. Pg. Pr. *escuma*, Fr. *écume* foam, scum; from O. H. G. *scûm*, N. *skûm*, E. *scum*.

Schivare schifare It., Sp. Pg. Pr. *esquivar*, Fr. *esquiver*, O. Fr. also *eschiver* (E. *eschew*), Rh. *schivir* to shun; from O. H. G. *skiuhan*, G. *scheuen*. Adj. It. *schivo schifo*, Sp. *esquivo*, Pr. *esquiu*, O. Fr. *eschiu*, Rh. *schio = G. *scheu*, E. *shy*.

Schizzo It., whence, perhaps, Sp. *esquicio*, Fr. *esquisse*, sketch; from *schedium* (Apuleius) anything made extempore, Gk. σχέδιος, σχεδιάζειν to extemporize, make a sketch, It. *schizzare* &c. As *schizzo* for *schezzo*, so L. L. *schidu* for *scheda* (*scindera* and σχίδη being thought of).

Sciabla sciabola It., Ven. *sabala*, Sp, *sable*, Fr. E. *sabre*. From the Slavonic: Hung. *szablya*, Serv. *sablja*, Wal. *sabie* &c. (according to Frisch 2, 139 from L. Gr. ζαβός crooked).

Sciagura — *augurio*.

Scialacquare It. to squander; from *ex-adaquare* according to Menage, from It. *scialare* and *acqua* according to others.

Scialare It. to exhale; from *exhalare*, Sp. *exhalar*, It. also *asolare* to pant, Mil. *esalà*.

Sciame sciamo It., Sp. *enxambre*, Pg. *enxame*, Pr. *cissam*, Fr. *essaim* a swarm; from *examen*. Vb. Fr. *essemer*, L. *examinare*.

Sciamito It., Sp. *xamete*, Pr. O. Fr. *samit*, E. *samite*, G. *sammet;* from ἑξάμιτος ξάμιτος six-threaded.

Sciancato — *anca.*

Sciarpa ciarpa It., Sp. *charpa*, from Fr. *écharpe* girdle, whence
also Du. *scaerpe*, G. *schärpe*, E. *scarf*. O. Fr. also = a pilgrim's *scrip*, O. H. G. *scerbe*, L. G. *schrap*, E. *scrip scrap* (cf.
It. *ciarpa* = scraps, odds and ends). From *écharpe* probably
comes the dim. *escarcelle* (= *escarp-celle*) a pouch, whence Sp.
escarcela, It. *scarsella*.

Sciarra It. scuffle, fray, *sciarrare* to scatter, disperse; perhaps
from G. *zerran* to tear, whence *ciarrare*, and, with prosthetic
s, *sciarrare*.

Sciatta — *piatto.*

Sciatto It. rude, ugly; from *ex* and *aptus* (Menage), or from Sp.
chato flat, whence Rh. *sciatt* short and fat. V. *piatto.*

Scier Fr. to saw, *scie* a saw, It. *sega*; from *secare*, Pr. *segar* &c.,
O. Fr. *sier* and *soier*, cf. *plier* and *ployer* from *plicare*. Hence
Fr. E. *scion* a shoot or setting for *sicion* from *sectio*, cf. G.
schnittling and E. *cutting.*

Scilinguare It. to stutter; from *ex elinguare.*

Scimitarra It., Sp. *cimitarra*, Pg. also *samitarra*, Fr. *cimeterre*,
(m.) E. *scimitar*. According to Larramendi, from the B. *cime-
tarra*. Others derive it from the Pers. *shamshér*, or *shemshir.*

Sciocco It. dolt, foolish; from *exsuccus.*

Sciogliere sciorre *(sciolsi sciolto)* to loosen, also *disciogliere* &c.
to loosen, dissolve. (1) from *exsolvere* (2), or (1) and (2) from
dissolvere. *Asciogliere* to absolve is from *absolvere.*

Scioperare It. to cease from work, whence *sciopero scioperone*;
from *ex* and *operare.*

Sciorinare — *sauro.*

Scipare It. to waste; from *dissipare*, Sp. *disipar*, cf. *desver*, and
R. Gr. 1, 231. So *sciupare* from *dissupare.*

Scipido sciapido It. insipid; from *in-sipidus in-sapidus.*

Sciringa scilinga It., Sp. *siringa xeringa*, Pr. *siriuga*, Fr. *se-
ringue, syringe*; from *syrinx.*

Scirocco sciloocco sirocco It., Sp. *siroco xaloque*, Pg. *xaroco*, Pr.
Fr. *siroc, sirocco* South-East wind; from Ar. *schoruq* (*schary*
east).

Scivolare — *cigolare.*

Scodella — *écuelle.*

Scoglio It., Sp. *escollo*, Pg. *escolho*, Pr. *escueli*, Fr. *écueil* rock;
from *scopulus*. Pott, however, connects it with Σκύλλα (σκύλ-
λειν σκύλαξ) = tearer, destroyer (of ships), v. Kuhn's Zeitschrift 5, 255.

Scojattolo It., Sp. Pg. *esquilo*, Arag. *esquirol, escurol*, Fr. *écureuil*, E. *squirrel*; from *sciurus sciurulus*, L. L. *squiriolus*. The
combination *iu* being unusual, we find *scuirus* (whence *esquirol
escurol* squirrel) and *scurius* (whence *scoj-att-olo*, v. R. Gr. 2,

304); hence *sci* lost its soft sound. The more usual Sp. term is *ardilla*.

Scompigliare — *pigliare*.

Sconfiggere sconfissi sconfitto It. to strike, bruise, Pr. *esconfire esconfis esconfit*; from *ex-conficere*, but inflected as if from *ex-configere*.

Scoppiare — *coppia*.

Scoppio — *schioppo*.

Scorbuto It., Sp. Pg. *escorbuto*, Fr. *scorbut*, E. *scurvy*; from L. G. *schorbock*, Du. *scheurbuik* = G. *scharbock*, v. Frisch 2, 220.

Scorziare It., Sp. *escorzar*, O. Fr. *escorcer escoursser*, Wal. *horsi* to contract, to fold; from *curtus*, as *hansser* from *altus*. Sbst. It. *scorcio*, Sp. *escorzo* contraction, O. Fr. *escors escuers* fold, lap.

Scoreggia — *coreggia*.

Scorgere scorta — *corgere*.

Scornare It., O. Fr. *escorner*, E. *scorn*; prop. to show pride or insolence towards one, cornua sumere, from a form *ex-cornare*; sbst. *scorno*, *scorn*. There is, probably, a reference to the G., v. s. *scherno*.

Scorticare — *corteccia*.

Scorza It., Wal. *scoartzě*, Pr. *escorsa*, Fr. *écorce* bark; vb. It. *scorzare*, Pr. *escorsar*, Fr. *écorcer*. The sbst. is prob. derived from the vb. which is from *ex-corticare (cortex)*; for a form *ex-corticare*, v. *corteccia*.

Scorzone — *escuerzo*.

Scorzonera It., Sp. *escorzonera*, Fr. *scorsonère* viper's grass; 2 derivations are given: (1) *scorzone* a poisonous snake (v. *escuerzo*), = L. *serpentaria*, but this should give *scorzoniera*; (2) *scorza nera* = G. *schwarz-wurz*. The orig. form may have *scorzoniera*, by corruption *scorzonera*.

Scosso It. (only in Lomb. *scoss*) lap, bosom; from O. H. G. *scôz*, G. *schooss*. The Wall. has *hô* for *hôt*, Du. *shoot*.

Scotolare It. to swingle flax; from O. H. G. *scutilôn*, G. *schütteln*, cf. Wal. *scuturá* to shake, agitate. *Scotola* = *shuttle*.

Scotta It., Sp. Pg. *escota* sheet (naut.); from Swed. *skot*, G. *schote* (E. *sheet*), Du. *shoot*, from *schiessen, schieten*.

Scotta It. way; from *excocta*; also called *ricotta*. Com. *scocia* = *excocia* as *strecia* = *stricta* &c.

Scotto It., Sp. Pg. *escote*, Pr. *escot*, Fr. *écot*, L. L. *scotum* share, scot. It is the G. *schoss* (from *schiessen?*), O. Fris. *skot*, E. *scot* shot, O. Gael. *sgot*. The Fr. *écot* stump of a tree is the O. H. G. *scuz*, whence *scuzling*, G. *schössling*.

Scozzone — *cozzone*.

Scranna It. bench, stool; from O. H. G. *scranna*, G. *schranne*.

Scriocio scricciolo It. a wren; prob. an onomatop., cf. Illyr. zaritsch.

Scrocco It. parasite, spunger, Fr. *escroc* swindler, Mil. *scroch* rogue, Rh. *scroc* wight, vb. *scroccare* to spunge, Fr. *escroquer* to cheat. *Escroc* is identical with Du. *schrok* glutton, which, however, may be from the Fr. They are, perhaps, to be referred to the G. *schurke* rogue, O. H. G. *scurgo*, cf. It. *scorcone*.

Scudo scudiere — *écu*.

Souffla — *cuffia*.

Scuotere It., Pr. *escodre* (partic. *escos*), O. Fr. *escorre escourre* to shake off; from *excutere*. Sbst. It. *scossa*, Pr. *escossa*, Fr. *escusse* concussion, spring; from *excussa*. Hence It. *riscuotere*, Pr. *rescodre* (partic. *rescos*), Fr. *recourre* to recover, *rescue*, from *re-excutere*; sbst. It. *riscossa*, Pr. *rescossa*, Fr. *recousse*, E. *rescue*. Pr. *secodre*, O. Fr. *secorre secourre*, Fr. *seconer*, Sp. *sacudir*, Lomb. *secudi*, Rh. *saccuder* to shake, from *succutere* (It. *scuotere*); sbst. It. *secousse*.

Soure It. an axe; from *securis*, Wal. *sécüre*, Sp. *segur*.

Scuriada It., Fr. *écourgée* (for *escouriée*), Norm. *courgée*, E. *scourge*, Sp. *zurriago*; from *excoriata* sc. *scutica*, a thong made of leather.

Sdrajarsi It. to lay oneself at length; from Goth. *straujan* or O. H. G. *strewjan* sternere; *sd* == *st* as in *sdrucciolare*.

Sdrucciolo It. slippery, vb. *sdrucciolare* to slip, whence Sp. *esdruxulo* a word of two short final syllables; from O. H. G. *strûhhal* stumbling, G. *straucheln* to stumble.

Sdrucire — *cucire*.

Se Pr. in *anc-sé*, *de-sé*, *ja-ssé* == *anc sempre* &c.; also *en jasse per jasse*. Cherubini mentions a Mil. *passée* which he derives from *più assai*.

Seau — *secchia*.

Secchia It., Pg. Pr. *selha*, O. Fr. *seille*, also m. It. *secchio*, Pr. *selh* a pail; from *situla sit'la*, L. L. *sicla*, *siclus*. Hence Mil. *sidell*, Com. *sedell*, O. Fr. *séel*, Fr. *seau*, f. Mil. *sidella*, Com. *sedela*, L. *sitella*. Hence also the Ar. *al-satl assatl*, whence O. Sp. *celtre*, Sp. *acetre*.

Sèche — *seppia*.

Secouer secousse — *scuotere*.

Seda — *seta*.

Sódano It., Ven. *seleno*, Com. *selar*, Piedm. *seler*, Fr. *céleri*, E. *celery*; from σέλινον parsley = celery in late Greek, cf. Sp. *apio dulce*. *Parsley == petro-selinum*.

Sedia seggia It., Fr. *siége* (m.), seat, *siege*, It. *assedio asseggio* *siege*; vb. It. *assediare*, Sp. *asediar*, Fr. *assiéger* to besiege;

from *sedes* through a form *assedium assediare*, no such form as *sedia* being found.

Sega — *scier*.

Ségalo ségola It., Pr. *seguel*, Fr. *seigle* (m.), Wal. *sĕcăré*, B. *cekharea* rye; from *secale*, L. L. *sigala*, *sigilum*.

Segnare — *salassare*.

Sogno O. It., Pg. *sino*, O. Cat. *seny*, Pr. *senh*, Rh. *senn* a bell, O. Fr. (corr.) *seint saint;* from *signum* = bell in L. L., hence also B. *crinua*, cf. *tocsin*.

Sogo — *sevo*.

Segolo It. a hatchet; from *secula* a sickle.

Sogugio It. bloodhound, Mil. *saus savus*, Piedm. *sus*, L. L. *sigusius sinsius scusius*, Sp. *sabueso*, Pg. *sabujo* (from *sausius sabusius sabuiso sabueso*). Probably, like many other names of dogs, from the name of a place, *Segusium* or *Susa* in Piedmont. From *Segusius* for *Segusianus* came *Sensius* and *Segutius Segugio*.

Sogurelha — *satureja*.

Soiglo — *segale*.

Soignour — *signore*.

Soillo — *secchia*.

Soino Fr. E. a drag-net; for *saïne* from *sagena* L. It.

Soira — *sarria*.

Solon Fr. particle, O. Fr. *selone;* from *secundum*, with a reference to *longum*.

Som — *scemo*.

Soma som Coin., Mil. *semma* adv. = It. *ora*, e. g. *l'aot sem* = *l'altra volta;* from *semel*.

Somana semaino — *settimana*.

Somaquo Fr. (f.) a smack; from Du. *smak*, E. *smack*, cf. *senau* from Du. *snauw*, L. G. *snan*, E. *snow* (a small ship).

Semblant semblar sombler semejar — *sembrare*.

Sombraro sombiaro It., Sp. Pr. *semblar*, Fr. *sembler;* from *simulare similare*. Hence It. *sembiante*, Sp. *semblante*, Fr. *semblant;* It. *assembrare assembiare*, Sp. Pr. *asemblar*, Fr. *assembler*, E. *assemble*, L. *assimilare assimulare* (with a reference to *simul*); It. *rassembrare*, Pr. Sp. *resemblar*, Fr. *ressembler*, E. *resemble*. Hence also It. *simigliare somigliare*, Sp. *semejar*, Pr. *semelhar*.

Sómillant Fr. brisk, lively. From the Celtic, W. *sim* free, loose.

Semola It. Sp., Fr. *semoule*, E. dim. *semolina;* from *simila*.

Somonce — *semondre*.

Somondre Fr., Pr. *somondre semondre* to invite, summon, partic. *semons*, whence abst. *semonse*, *somonsa* (E. *summons*); from *summonere*, whence also, in the 1ˢᵗ conj. *sommer*, O. Fr. *semoner* (whence Fr. *semonneur*). The Fr. has also *semonce* a lecture, *semoncer* to lecture, reprimand. *Monere* in Rom. was treated as a verb of the 3rd conj., hence, a part. *monestus*, whence *amonestar*, v. Littré, p. 34.

Sena It., Sp. *sena sen*, Pg. *senne*, Fr. *sene*, E. *senna*; from Ar. *sand*.

Sencillo Sp. simple; a dim. from *simplex* = It. *semplicello*.

Senda Sp. Cat. path; from *semita*; It. *sentiero*, Sp. *sendero*, Pr. *semdier sendicira*, Fr. *sentier* from *semitarius*.

Sendos Sp., Pg. *senhos*, O. Pg. *selhos* the only distributive remaining in the Rom. languages in the orig. sense, L. *singuli singulos*, R. Gr. 3, 15. O. Sp. *señero* is from *singularius*.

Sénéchal senescal — *siniscalco*.

Senno It., O. Sp. Pr. O. Fr. Rh. *sen* understanding; from O. H. G. *sin*, G. *sinn*. Hence Sp. *senado*, Pr. *senat*, O. Fr. *sené* sensible, Fr. *for-cené* = It. *for-sennato* senseless.

Senopia — *sinople*.

Sensale It., Fr. *censal*, Pr. *cessal* broker; from *censualis* a collector, cf. Papias: *censuales sunt officiales qui censum per provincias exigunt.*

Sentare It. (Com.), Sp. Pg. Pr. *sentar* (Pr. only in part. *sentat*) to place, set, settle; a participial verb from *sedere sedens*, R. Gr. 2, 333. Hence It. *assentare*, Sp. Pg. *asentar*, O. Fr. *assenter*, Sp. sbst. *asiento* a seat &c.

Sentier sentiero — *senda*.

Sentinella It., Sp. *centinela*, Fr. *sentinelle*, E. *sentinel*, *sentry*. From It. *sentire* to hear, listen, cf. *scolta (scout)* from *scoltare*. But this would leave the middle syllable unaccounted for. Galvani derives it from *sentina* the well-room of a ship, where the *sentinator* was stationed to give notice of any leakage.

Senza It., O. It. also *sauza*, N. Pr. *senso*, O. Sp. *sines*, O. Pr. *senes seus ses*, O. Fr. *sens*, Fr. *sans*, also O. It. *sen*, Sp. *sin*, Pg. *sem*, Pr. *sen* preposition from L. *sine*, with epenthetic *s senes sens*, with euphonic *a senza* for *sensa*, as *manzo* for *manso*.

Sena — *insegna*.

Señor — *signore*.

Sépoulo — *spola*.

Seppia It., Sp. *xibia*, Fr. *séche* the cuttle-fish; from *sepia*.

Ser — *essere*.

Sera It. Pr., Wal. *seară*, Pr. m. *ser*, Fr. *soir* evening; Pr. vb. *aserar*, O. Fr. *aserier aserir enserir*, Wal. *inséra* vesperascere; from *serenus*, Sp. *sereno* evening dew, Pr. *seren*, Fr. *serein*, Neap. *serena*, also Pr. *serena* = It. *serenata*, Fr. *sérénade*, E. *serenade*. For the sense, cf. Gk. εὐφρόνη.

Sera — *sarria*.

Sérail — *serrare*.

Séran Fr. heckle, *sérancer* to heckle; from M. Du. *schrantsen* to tear, M. H. G. *schrenzen*, sbst. M. Du. *schrantse*, M. H. G.

schrantz. The regular form in Fr. would be *écrancer*, but cf.
M. H. G. *sranz* for *schrantz.*

Serba Sp. service-berry; for *suerba* from *sorbum*, It. *sorba.* For
ue from *o*, cf. *frente.*

Serge — *sargia.*

Sergente It. O. Sp., Sp. *sargento*, Fr. *sergent*, E. *sergeant*; from
serviens, cf. *pioggia* from *pluria*, cf. Pr. *sirven* (= *sergente*)
part. of *servir*, Piedm. *servient.*

Sergozzone — *gozzo.*

Serin Fr. a canary-bird; from σειρήν (= a singing bird in Hesychius).

Sermar — *esmar.*

Serment Fr. an oath; from *sacramentum*, O. Fr. *sairement*, Pr.
sagramen, L. prop. a soldier's oath of allegiance, a word
spread throughout the Roman provinces by the soldiery, v.
Pott, Kuhn's Zeitschrift 1, 348.

Sermollino It. wild thyme; from *serpyllum*, It. also *serpillo ser-
pollo*, Sp. Pr. *serpot*, Fr. *serpolet.*

Serorge O. Fr. brother-in-law; from *sororius.*

Serpe It. Pg. O. Fr., Sp. *sierpe*, Pr. Rh. *serp*, Wal. *şerpe* a serpent; a very old abbreviation of *serpens*, cf. W. *sarf*, Sk.
sarpa (nom. *sarpas*).

Serpe Fr., O. Fr. *sarpe* a bill, a pruning-hook; from *sarpere*,
Fest. *sarpere antiqui pro purgare dicebant*, L. L. *sarpa sarculum.* From *sarpa* in a passive sense, cf. *sarmentum* for *sarp-
mentum*, would come Sp. *serpa* a shoot, layer; *e* for *a* as in
alerce, lexos.

Serper — *sarpare.*

Serra O. It., Sp. *sierra*, Pg. Pr. *serra* a mountain chain or ridge;
prop. a saw, L. *serra*, cf. *serratus* serrated, *Montserrat.*

Serrare It., Sp. Pg. *cerrar*, Pr. *serrar*, Fr. *serrer* to fasten, to
press; abst. It. *serra* a throng, Fr. *serre* talon, grasp; It. *ser-
raglio*, O. Sp. *cerraje*, Pr. *serralh*, Fr. *sérail* prison, *seraglio*;
from *sera* a lock, bolt, L. L. *serra.* Sp. *c* is to distinguish the
word from *serrar* to saw.

Serrin Sp. (m.) saw-dust; from *serrago serraginis*, as *orin* from
ærugo.

Sertir Fr. to set a jewel; from *sertum*, L. L. *sertare* to festoon,
surround, enclose. N. Pr. is *sartir.*

Serventese — *sirvente.*

Serviette Fr. mapkin. *Servir une table* = to arrange the plates
&c., L. *ministrare*, *service* = E. *service* (of plate &c.), *ministerium*, It. *servito* course, Pr. *servit* service, whence *serriette* (for
servilette, cf. Sp. *servilleta*) not from *servir.* Hence *desservir* to
clear the table, *dessert*, E. *dessert.*

Serzir — *zurcir.*

Sescha cesca Pr. reed, sedge, Sp. *xisca* sugar-cane, B. *sesca*, L. L. *sisca*. From the Celtic: Ir., Gael. *seisg*, W. *hesg*, A. S. *sege secg*, E. *sedge*.

Seso Sp., Pg. *siso* understanding; from *sensus*.

Sesta seste It. compasses, It. O. Pg. *sesto* measurement, measure; vb. It. *sestare assestare* to measure, cut off, Sp. *asestar* to adjust a cannon, aim, level. From Gk. ξυστόν a mason's tool, a trowel, a level, or a square. From *sestare* come O. H. G. *seston* disponere, *sestunga* dispositio.

Sestiere It., Sp. *sextario*, Pr. *sestier*, Fr. *setier* a measure; from *sextarius*, O. H. G. *sehtari*; hence also It. *stajo* for *sestajo*, cf. Rh. *ster* for *sester*, Lorr. *steire*.

Seta It., Sp. Pr. *seda*, Fr. *soie*, L. L. *seta;* from the form *seda* is O. H. G. *sida* (as *pina* from *pena* for *poena*, *pris* from *pretium*), G. *seide*, Ir. *sioda*, W. *sidan*. From L. *seta* a bristle, a meaning still belonging to the Sp. and Fr., whence also It. *setone*, Fr. *seton*, E. *seton*. The full expression is found in L. L. *seta serica*. Hence It. *setino*, whence Pg. *setim*, Fr. E. *satin*.

Sétier — *sestiere*.

Séton — *seta*.

Soto Sp. hedge; from *septum*.

Settimana semmana It., Sp. Pg. *semana*, Pr. *setmana*, Fr. *semaine* week; from L. L. *septimana*, prop. = seventh, Wal. *sëptëmënë*, Ir. *sechtmaine*. The Cat. O. Pg. have, instead, *doma* from *hebdomas*, Sp. *hebdómada*.

Seuil — *suolo*.

Sève Fr. sap; from *sapa*, Pg. *seve* &c.

Sóveronde — *gronda*.

Sevo sego It. (*g* for *v* R. Gr. 1, 187), Sp. Pg. *sebo*, Pr. Wal. *seu*, Fr. *suif* (corr.), Norm. Rouchi *sieu* (E. *suet*) fat, suet; from *sebum sevum*.

Sevrer Fr. to wean; from *separare*, It. *severare*.

Sesso sezzajo sezzo It. = ultimo; from *secius*, cf. L. L. Gloss. *secius segnius*, found also in *da sezzo* opp. *da prima*.

Sfidare — *disfidare*.

Sgarrare — *garer*.

Sghembo It. oblique, crooked, Pied. *sgiubo;* from O. H. G. *slimb*, Bav. *schlimm schlemm* oblique. Sic. has *scalembru* for *sclembru sclembu*. Compounded with *blescio* (v. *biais*) we have *schimbescio schimbecio*.

Sghignare — *ghignare*.

Sgneppa It. woodcock; Com. *synep*, Wal. *sneap* (m.); from O. H. G. *snepfa snepfo*, G. *schnepfa*, E. snipe.

Sgombrare — *colmo*.

Sgomentare It. to frighten, be frightened; from *commentari* to meditate, *excommentari* to make one out of his senses.

Sgorbia — *gubia.*

Sgridare — *gridare.*

Sguancio It. crookedness, obliquity; from G. *schwank* flexible, Swed. sbst. *srank* crookedness, Du. *zwanken* to distort, hence perhaps *seancio* for *sguancio*, and, with inserted *i* = *l schiancio*, vb. *schiancire*. The Sic. *sguincia*, Neap. *sguinzo* awry (hence Sp. *esguince?*) is either a form of *synancio* or from G. *windisch, winsch* oblique, cf. E. *squint.* It. *schincio* = *sguinciu.*

Sguizzare — *guizzare.*

Sgurare It. (Lomb. *sgurà*), Sp. Cat. *escurar*, Fr. *écurer* to scour; not from G. *scheuern*, Du. *schuren*, E. *scour*, which are, prob., themselves from the L., but from *ex-curare.* Ven. and Pr. *curare* = to clean, Wal. *curat* = clean. .

Si It., Sp. *si*, O. Sp. *sin*, Pg. *sim*, Pr. Fr. *si*; from *sic* (*ita* was more commonly used as an affirmative). Sard. has *imo* or *emmo* from L. *immo.*

Si O. Fr. particle = until. In comp. *de si, dessi, desi que, tressi tressi que, entressi, enfressi.* The It. has *si* in the same sense, Inf. 29, 30: *non guardasti in là, si fu partito;* Cecc. Dec. 3, 9: *nè mai ristette, si fu in Firenze.* This may be a shortened form of *sin* (cf. *no* for *non*), and the word may have passed from Italy into France, or the Fr. word may be independent of the It., and may be derived from *signum* scopus.

Siorano Pg. pronoun for L. *quidam;* from *securus* in the sense of *certus.* Pr. has *seguran.*

Sido It. excessive cold, *assiderarsi* to be benumbed with cold; from *sidus* numbness, *siderari* to be benumbed, G. *erstarren.*

Sidro cidro It., Sp. *sidra*, Fr. *cidre* (E. *cider*), Wal. *eighcarin;* from *sicera* (σίκερα), by corruption *cicera*, whence *cidra* as Fr. *ladre* from *Lazarus.* The O. Sp. has *sizra.*

Sióge — *sedia.*

Sien Sp. (f.) temple (of the head); from *somnus* (v. *tempia*), whence *somn, suen, sien*, or from *segmen scgm segn sien* (cf. *des-den*) from *dignus*, and cf., according to Pott, *tempus* (from root τεμ) orig. = a division or part of the head (Forsch. 2, 54.).

Sien — *mien.*

Sierra — *serra.*

Siffler Fr. to whistle (O. Fr. also *sibler*); from *sifilare* an old form of *sibilare*, Pr. *siblar, siular*, also *chiflar*, Sp. *silbar* and *chiflar*, v. *cinfolo.*

Siglaton — *ciclaton.*

Sigle — *singlar.*

Signore It., Sp. *señor*, Pg. Pr. *senhor*, Fr. *seigneur;* from *senior*, like Gk. πρεσβύτερος and A. S. *ealdor*, E. *olderman. Senior* replaced the m. *dominus* whilst the f. *domina* remained. In

Pg., however, *senhor* was used f. as in L. *Senior* for *dominus*
is found in L. L., and is sometimes opposed to *vasallus*. The
oldest Fr. form is nom. *sendra*, contr. *sire*, acc. *seigneur*,
contr. *sieur*, whence nom. *messire*, acc. *monseigneur* and *monsieur*. For *sire* = *sendre* (prob. a North-French contraction)
cf. Picard. *térous* = *tiendrons*, *tére* = *tendre*. Of Fr. origin
are the Pr. *sire sira* (nom. and acc.), Sp. *ser sire*, It. *ser* and
sire (Pr. *sior*), E. *sir*, which replaced the A. S. *hearra*.

Silhouette Fr. a profile; so called from *M. de Silhouette* a finance-
minister under Louis XV., who was notorious for his parsimony. V. Sismondi Hist. des Français 29, 94.

Siller Fr. (intrans.) to run ahead (unv.), prop. to furrow the sea,
sillon a furrow, wake; from N. *sila* to cut, sever, with liquid
ll, as in *piller* from *pillare*. Cf. Mil. *sciloira*, Pied. *sloira* a
plough, v. *aratro*.

Siller Fr. to sew up a falcon's eyes; for *ciller*, from *cilium*.

Silo Sp., B. *siloa*, *ciloa* a granary, N. Pr. *silò*. Perhaps from L.
sirus, Gk. σειρός.

Sim — *si*.

Simigliare — *sembrare*.

Sin — *senza*.

Singélo Pg. single; from a dim. L. *singillus*, whence *singillarius*
('Tertullian').

Singhiozzo singozzo It., Sp. *collozo*, Pr. *singlot*, *sanglot*, Fr.
sanglot, Rh. *sanglut* a sob; vb. *singhiozzare*, *singhiottire*, *sollo-
zar*, *sanglotar*, *sangloter*; corrupted from *singultus*, *singultare*,
singultire.

Singlar Sp., Pg. *singrar*, Fr. *cingler* to sail (with a favourable
wind); from O. H. G. *ségelen*, O. N. *sigla*, G. *segeln* to sail,
with inserted *n* as in *singlaton*. Immediately from the G. are
O. Fr. *sigle*, G. *segel* a sail, vb. *sigler*.

Siniscalco sescalco It., Sp. Pr. *senescal*, Fr. *sénéchal*, E. *seneschal*
= prop. aged servant, from O. H. G. *sini-scalh*, L. L. *sini-
scalcus*, cf. *mariscalco*, *scalco*.

Sino and *insino* It. particle for L. tenus; prob. from *signum*, cf.
fino from *finis*.

Sinople Fr. green (in blazonry), whence Sp. *sinople*, and also
Pg. *sinople* a green jasper. But It. *senopia*, Pg. *sinopla*, E.
sinoper = red, red ochre, from L. *sinopis* red ochre, so called
from *Sinope* on the Black Sea. Cf. a MS. of 1400 (quoted in
Menestrier orig. des arm.): *sicut et in urbe Sinopoli rubicundum
invenitur et viride dictum sinoplum*.

Sione It. whirlwind; from σίφων a waterspout, Fr. *siphon*, L.
siphon.

Siquier siquiera siquiere Sp. adv. for L. saltim; from *si* and
quiera conjuctive from *querer*, so = *si velit*.

Sire — *signore.*

Sirgar Sp. Pg. Cat. to tow (naut.), sbst. *sirga* a tow-line; from a form *siricare* formed with suffix *ic* from σειράν.

Sirima It. the end of a strophe; from *syrma* (σύρμα) a train, Wal. *sërmë* a thread, Alb. *sirmë* silk.

Siroc — *scirocco.*

Siroppo solroppo It., Sp. *xarope*, Pg. *xarope*, *enxarope*, Fr. *sirop*, E. *syrup*, *sirop*, *shrub*; from Ar. *scharáb* drink, wine, coffee.

Sirvente Fr. (m.), O. Fr. *serventois*, Pr. *sirventés*, *sirventesc*, f. *sirventesca*, hence It. *sirventese*, a kind of song, eulogistic or satirical, opp. a love-song; from *serviens*, so lit. a servico-lay.

Sisa Sp. Pg. petty theft, pilfering, excise, vb. Sp. *sisar*, Pg. *scisar* to filch, cut away. Duc. makes it the same as Fr. *assise*, but, according to Diez, from Pr. *sensa* = L. *census*, as *siso* from *sensus*. *Scisar*, *sisar* may, however, be a freq. from *scindere*.

Sisclar oisclar Pr., *xisclar* Cat. to whistle; from *fistulare* (It. *fischiare*), with the *s* of *sibilare*.

Sitio Sp., Pr. *seti setje* place, site, vb. Sp. *sitiar asitiar*, Pr. *asetiar*, *asetjar* to besiege; perhaps from O. H. G. *sizan*, O. S. *sittian* (E. *sit*), cf. *bisittian* to besiege.

Sitot Pr. conj. for L. etsi; from *si tot (tout)* although, cf. It. *tuttochè*.

Sivels — *viaus.*

Sisel — *cincel.*

Slandra — *landra.*

Slinga *(schlinga)* Rh., Sp. *eslingua*, Pg. *eslinga*, Fr. *élingue* sling; vb. Pic. *élinguer* to sling (O. Fr. *tinder*); from O.H.G. *slinga*, (G. *schlinge*, E. *sling*.

Slitta It. sledge; from O.H.G. *slito*. Hence Com. *slitigà* to make smooth.

Smaccare — *macco.*

Smacco It. insult, vb. *smaccare* (to be distinguished from *smaccare*, from *macco*); from O. H. G. *smâhi*, G. *schmach* disgrace, vb. *smâhèn*, (G. *schmähen* to abuse, *smâhjan* to debase. The double *cc* is found also in *ricco* from *rihhi*, *taccola* from *táhha*.

Smagare O. It., O. Pg. *esmaiar* to be dispirited, dismayed, Pr. *esmaiar*, O. Fr. *esmaier esmoyer*, Berr. *émeyer* to dismay; also Sp. Pg. *desmayar*, E. *dismay*; sbst. It. *smago*, Pr. *esmai esmoi*, Sp. *desmayo*, E. *dismay*, swoon. The Fr. *émoi* anxiety, emotion, though usu. derived from *mouvoir*, is only another form of *esmai*. It is from the O. H. G. *magan* to be able *(may)* with the Rom. privative *es* = *des*, cf. O. H. G. *magèn* to be strong, *unmagèn* to faint. We seldom find the Rom. using the German word only in compounds, but cf. *tra-stullare* from O. H. G.

stullan. Some derive *smagare* from O. H. G. *smâhjan* to degrade, but this is found in *smaccare,* v. *smacco.*

Smalto It., Wal. *smaltz (jumaltz),* Sp. Pg. *esmalte,* Fr. *émail,* E. *enamel* (from the frequent combination *en émail, peindre en émail* &c.), L. L. *smaltum.* From O. H. G. *smelzan smalzjan smaltjan,* G. *schmelzen,* E. *smelt.* In the Fr. *émail, i* is inserted after *a (esmaill)* and the *t* dropt as in *gal* for *galt* from G. *wald.* •

Smalzo Ven. butter; from G. *schmalz* grease.

Smánia It. madness, *smaniare* to rage; from *mania,* Gk. μανία, It. also *mania.*

Smarrire — *marrir.*

Smeraldo It., Sp. Pg. f. *esmeralda,* Pr. *esmerauda,* Fr. *émeraude,* E. *emerald;* from *smaragdus* (σμάραγδος m. f.) Sansk. *marakata, g* changed to *l* as in *salma* from σάγμα, *Baldacco* from *Bagdad;* O. Sp. has also *esmeragde,* Pr. *maracde.*

Smerare It., Sp. Pr. *esmerar,* O. Fr. *esmerer* to clean; from *exmerare* as *spurare* from *ex-purare, syurare* from *ex-curare.*

Smeriglio It., Sp. *esmeril,* Fr. *émeri,* E. *emery;* from σμύρις σμίρις.

Smeriglione — *smerlo.*

Smerlo It., Pr. *esmirle* a sparrow hawk, merlin, Sp. Pg. *esmeril* a small piece of ordnance (cf. *falconete, moschetto* &c.); It. *smeriglione,* Sp. *esmerejon,* Pg. *esmerilhão,* Fr. *émérillon,* E. *merlin.* From *merla,* L. *merula* a blackbird? The O. H. G. has *smirl.*

Smilzo — *milza.*

Smorfia — *morfia.*

Smussare — *mozzo.*

Snello It., Pr. *isnel irnel,* O. Fr. *isnel ignel enel* nimble. From O. H. G. *snel,* G. *schnell,* though the *i* for *e (esnel)* is not easily accounted for.

So — *ciò.*

Soanar — *sosanar.*

Sobaco — *barcar.*

Sobajar — *sobar.*

Sobar Sp., Pg. *sovar* to knead, rub; from *subigere,* in usu. Rom. *subagere* (Sp. *sobajar*), contr. into *sobar* as *exporrigere* into *espurrir.*

Sobbissare — *abisso.*

Sobrino — *cugino.*

Sobriquet Fr. nickname, also written *sotbriquet,* so perhaps from *sot* and O. Fr. *briquet* = It. *bricchetto* a young ass; Piedm. *subrichet* = obstinate. The Pie. form is *surpiquet.* Others derive it from a form *supricus (supra).* But here the suffix *icus* instead of *aticus* is doubtful.

Soc Fr. plough-share, coulter, L. L. *socus*, L. Gk. ϲξόχος, Gael. *soc*, W. *swch* plough-share, snout; It. *zocco*, Pr. *soc*, f. Pr. Cat. *soca*, Fr. *souche* stock, stem. From the L. *soccus* (1) wooden shoe (2) support, stem, stock. *S* becomes *z* also in It. *zoccolo*, Sp. *zócalo*, *zoclo zucco*, Pr. *zors* a wooden shoe, Fr. *zocle*, *socle*.

Socarrar Sp. Cat. to singe; from B. *sucartu*, according to Larramendi, from *sua* fire and *carta* flame, but the *so* in the Sp. is prob. the preposition as in the synon. *sollamar*. For *socarra* = craft, cf. *soflama*.

Soda It. Sp. Pg. E., Fr. *soude;* from *solida*. The Sp. *sosa* (from *salsus*) = the plant from which it is made.

Sodo — *soldo.*

Sofà It. Pg., Fr. *sopha*, *sofa* (m.), E. *sofa;* from Ar. ϲoffah a bench.

Soffiare It., O. Sp. Pr. *suflar*, Fr. *souffler*, Sp. *soplar*, Pg. *soprar* to blow; from *sufflare*. Hence Fr. *soufflet* (1) bellows (2) box on the ear, cf. s. *buf*, and E. *blow*. The Pg. *assoviar* is connected.

Soffice It. weak, supple, yielding; from *supplex*, whence also Fr. *souple.* *F* for *p* is also found in *catafalco*, *caffo* and a few other words.

Soffratta O. It., Pr. *sofraita*, *sofracha*, O. Fr. *souffraite* defect, injury; O. It. *soffrettoso*, Pr. *sofraitos*, Fr. *souffreteux* poor, poorly; from *suffringere soffructus*, Pr. *sofranher*.

Soga It. (prov.) Sp. a cord, rope (in Dante = belt), Pg. Rh. *suga*, B. *soca*, Sp. also = a measure of length (L. Gk. σωχάϱιον, L. L. *soca soga*), vb. *soguear.* Diefenbach compares W. *syg* a chain, Bret. *sug* a towing-rope, Gael. *sugan.* In Sp. the word has the widest range.

Soglio — *suolo.*

Sogna O. It., Pr. *sonh*, Fr. *soin* care; vb. Fr. *soigner;* It. *bisogno*, Pr. *besonh besonha*, Fr. *besoin*, Rh. *basengs* need (Fr. *besogne* work, task), It. *bisognare*, Pr. *besonhar;* O. Fr. *essoigne*, *essoine* need, necessity, difficulty, excuse, *essoigner* to excuse oneself; O. Fr. *ensounier* to employ, *resoigner* to fear. In L. L. we find *sunnis sunnia sonia* in the sense of legal impediment (hence delaying about a thing, careful attention, care), in which Grimm recognises a Frank word = O. N. *syn*, vb. *synja*, L. L. *soniare* to take care of. Goth. has *sunja* truth, *sunjôn* to justify, O. S. *sunnea* excuse, necessity, hindrance, O. H. G. *sunne* = *essoigae* (L. L. *exonia exonium*) and *besoin*, which latter may be referred to an O. H. G. form (from another root) *bi-siunigi* scrupulositas, whence a sbst. *bi-siuni* may be inferred. Duc. derives from L. *somnium* and quotes a L. L. Gloss. *somnium* φϱοντίς, but this may be merely an adaptation of *sonium (soin)*, v. Pott, Kuhn's Zeitschrift 1, 340.

From *soigner* is O. Fr. *suignante* concubine, *soignentage* con-
cubinage.

Soñes soes Sp. dirty, mean. Not from *sub fæce*, which would
be too artificial, but, probably, from a form (used by the
Spaniard Prudentius) *suis* for *sus*, *z* for *s* which the Sp. is fond
of retaining, cf. *Dios*, *Carlos* &c.; for the accent on the last
syllable, cf. *juéz*. *Porcus* gives adj. *puerco*.

Soie — *seta*.

Soif Fr. thirst, O. Fr. (more correctly) *soi*, Pr. *set*; from *sitis*.
For *f* from *t* cf. *moeuf* from *modus*, *Maimbeuf* from *Magnobo-
dus*, and R. Gr. 1, 213.

Soin — *sogna*.

Soir — *sera*.

Solaper — *lapo*.

Solcio It. brine; from O. H. G. *sulza*, G. *sulze*. Pr. *solz soutz*
"carnes in aceto". *Solcio* is a rare instance of an It. m. from
an O. G. f. in *a*. A G. form *sulz* is also given.

Soldo It., Sp. *sueldo*, Pr. *sol*, Fr. *sol sou* a coin; from *solidus* a
coin formerly of gold, afterwards of silver, prop. of thick,
solid metal not of thin plate. Hence It. *soldo*, Sp. *sueldo*, Pr.
soul, Fr. *solde* (f., *solde* m. = balance) payment, pay; It. *sol-
dato*, Sp. *soldado*, Fr. *soldat*, Pr. *soudadier*, O. Fr. *soudoier*, E.
soldier, Lorr. Pic. Dauph. *soudard*, cf. It. *paga* = soldier. By
a change of the *o* into *a* we have It. adj. *saldo* also *sodo* (cf.
talpa topo), vb. *saldare* = Sp. *soldar*, Fr. *souder*, E. *solder*; but
It. *saldare*, Fr. *solder* to pay.

Sole — *suolo*.

Solfa It., Sp. Pg. Pr. gamut (in Sp. also = harmony); from
Guido's *ut re mi fa sol la* taken backwards, the *la* serving as
the article *(la solfa)*; hence vb. It. *solfeggiare* (whence Fr.
solfège), Sp. *solfear*, Fr. *solfier*; Sp. *solfeo*, *solfeador*, *solfista*.

Solfo solfo It., Sp. *azufre*, Pg. *enxofre*, Pr. *solfre*, *solpre*, Fr.
soufre; from *sulphur*.

Solive Fr. rafter, joist. Perhaps from the L. *solum*, Fr. *sol* (in
the sense of the floor of a house, It. *suolo*, Sp. *suelo*) and
O. Fr. *ive* = L. *equa*, cf. Fr. *poutre* = (1) mare (2) beam.
Isaac Vossius derives it from *sublica*, as O. Fr. *mendive* from
mendica, but the sense hardly suits; others again from *suble-
vare* through a sbst. *sublerium* = Sp. *solivio*, It. *sollievo* a
raising, support; but here we should expect *soulive*, cf. *sou-
lever*, *soulager*.

Sollar Sp. to blow, breathe; from *sufflare*.

Sollastre — *souil*.

Sollazzo It., Sp. *solas solaz*, Pr. *solatz*, O. Fr. *soulas*, E. *solace*;
from *solatium*; vb. *sollazzare*, *solazar*, *soulacier*, L. L. *solatiari*,
solatiare.

Solleticare It. to tickle; for *so-tellicare* from *sub-titillicare*, cf. Neap. *tellecare*. From *titillicare* we have also *dileticare* for *tileticare*.

Sollione It. dog-days; from *sub leone*, the sun being then in the sign of the Lion.

Sollo It. loose. For *soll'lo soltolo* a dim. of *solulus* as *mutolo* of *mutus* (cf. *assolto*). So *spalla* for *spat'la*.

Sollo Sp. a sea-pike, Pg. *solho*; from *suillus*.

Solloso — *singhiozzo*.

Soltar Sp. to loosen; for *solutar*, freq. from *solvo*.

Sombra Sp. Pg. Cat. shade. *Subumbrare = so-ombrar = sombrar* (Fr. *sombrer* to founder), whence the sbst. *sombra*, cf. Sp. *sombrage* = It. *ombraggio*. The Pr. form *sotz-ombrar* supports this derivation. The O. Sp. *solombra* shade, vb. Pr. Dauph. *solombrar* may be a mere corruption or may involve the article *so l'ombra*, cf. Lorr. *ailaurbe* = ombre, prop. *à l'ombre*. The Fr. E. adj. *sombre* (Du. *somber*) is the same word. Hence Sp. *sombrero* a hat.

Sommaco It., Sp. *zumaque*, Pg. *sumagre*, Pr. Fr. *sumac*, E. *sumach*; from Ar. *summâq*.

Somme sommelier — *salma*.

Sommeil Fr., Pr. *soneth* sleep; dim. from *somnus (somniculus)*, the dim. being used to distinguish between *som (somnus)* and *son (sonus)*. Hence *someilleux*, Pr. *somelhos*, It. *sonnachioso*, L. *somniculosus*.

Sommer — *semondre*.

Sommet son — *sommo*.

Sommo It., Sp. *somo*, Pr. *som*, O. Fr. *som son* summit; from *summum*, Fr. *son* bran (what is uppermost in the sieve), Sp. *soma* coarse flour. Hence O. Sp. prepositional *en somo*, O. Fr. *en som, en son* and *par som, par son*, e. g. *par son l'aube* = Pr. *sus l'alba, sus en l'alba*, It. *in sull' alba*. Hence Fr. *sommet* (for O. Fr. *som*), E. *summit*. Sp. Pg. Pr. *asomar*, O. Fr. *assommer* to bring up, or out, show, appear.

Somorgujo Sp. diver, vb. *somorgujar*; from *submergere*, with a rare suffix, cf. *gran-ujo, burb-uja*.

Sonda Sp. Pg., Fr. *sonde* sounding-line; vb. *sondar, sonder*, E. *sound*. As Sp. *sombra*, Fr. *sombre* from *sub umbra*, so *sondar* from *sub-undare*.

Sopa Sp. Pg. Pr., Fr. *soupe*, E. soup. From O. N. *saup*, O. H. G. *sauf* broth, O. N. *sup*, L. G. *soppe*, O. H. G. *suf*, E. *sop, sup*; vb. Sp. *sopar* to sop, Pr. *sopar*, Fr. *souper* to sup (eat supper), cf. Bav. *saufen* to eat sop. Of a different origin are the It. *zuppa*, Sp. Pg. *chupar* to sip, sup, Fr. *super*, cf. G. *zuppe zupfen supfen*.

Soplar — *soffiare*.

Sorare — *sauro.*

Sorbetto It., Sp. *sorbete,* Pg. *sorvete,* Fr. *sorbet,* E. *sherbet;* from Ar. *sharba, sharbat* a drink. Others derive it from *sorbere,* but derivatives in -*ett* from verbs are doubtful.

Sorce sorcio It., Sp. *soree,* Pr. *soritz,* Fr. *souris,* Wal. *soarece* mouse; from *sorex.*

Sorcier Fr. f. *sorcière,* E. *sorcerer sorceress,* sbst. O. Fr. *sorecrie,* E. *sorcery;* from *sort* lot, also = spell, enchantment. *Sorcier* is from *sortiarius,* It. *sortiere,* Sp. *sortero* from *sortarius.*

Sorgossone — *gozzo.*

Sorn Pr. gloomy, sullen, sbst. *sornura;* O. Fr. *sorne* twilight, Sp. *sorna* night; Fr. *sournois* malicious; It. *sornione, susornione* a dissembler, sneak, *susorniare* to grumble, mutter. From the Celtic, W. *sorn-aeh* growl, Corn. *sorren* to be angry, or from *Saturnus,* Pg. Com. *soturno,* Piedm. *saturno,* Sard. *saturnu,* Gen. *saturue,* Sp. Flor. *saturnino,* E. *saturnine.* Cf. *soul* from *satullus.*

Sornette Fr. trifle, nonsense; prob. from W. *sorn* trifle. An old Fr. vb. *sorner* is also given.

Sorra — *zavorra.*

Sortija Sp., Pg. *sortilha* ring. From *sorticula (sors)* so = prop. a magic ring. In a will dated 1258 we find: *que as suas sortelas das vertudes* (rings of magical virtue) *as gardem para as enfermas.* Cf. Pr. *sortilhier* a sorcerer.

Sortire It., Fr. *sortir (sorto, sors)* to go out, issue, spring, Cat. *surtir* to issue, spring, Pr. *sortir,* Sp. *surtir,* Pg. *surdir* to spring out or back, rebound; Fr. *ressortir (ressors)* to go out again, Sp. *resurtir* to spring back, Fr. *ressort* spring, elasticity. The most probable derivation is that from *surrectire* (cf. *sortir de son siège, de table* &c.), though participial verbs are usually of the 1st conj., but cf. *ammortire, quatir* (from *coactus*).

Sortire It., Fr. *sortir (sortiseo, sortis)* to get, obtain, It. also to draw lots, Sp. *surtir,* Com. *surti* to provide; from *sortiri;* It. *assortire,* Sp. *asortir,* Fr. *assortir,* E. *assort;* Fr. *ressortir* to be in the jurisdiction of, to appeal, *resort,* sbst. *ressort* appeal, jurisdiction, *resort,* It. *risorto,* cf. Duc. *ressortum quicquid intra sortes continetur seu jurisdictionis terminos.* The juristic meaning of the word is derived from that of the O. Fr. *resortir* to draw back, take refuge, *resort to,* sbst. *resort;* thence the sense of getting *(sortir),* recovering *(ressortir)* cf. *ricovrare* (1) to recover (2) to seek refuge at; *ricovrare ad un luogo* is like *les pairies ressortissent au parlement.*

Sosanar O. Sp. to mock, scorn, sbst. *sosaño,* O. Pg. *sosano* scorn; from *subsannare (sanna);* Pr. *soauar,* O. Fr. *sooner,* sbst. *soan, soaua.*

Sosegar (pres. *sosiego*), Pg. *socegar* to calm, be calm, sbst. *so-*

siego, socego, whence It. *sussiego*. For *sos-eguar*, from a L. *sub-æquare?* From *æquare* in O. Sp. we find *iguar eguar*, Pg. *igar*.

Soso Sp. (also *zonzo*) insipid; from *insulsus*, Pg. *insosso*.

Sostaro It. to still, calm, Pg. Pr. *sostar* to stop, restrain; from *substare*. Hence, perhaps, also Sp. Pg. *susto*, Sard. *assustu* fright, Com. *sust*, Ven. *susto*, Sic. *sustu* sorrow, trouble.

Sote — *zote.*

Soto Sp., Pg. *souto* a wood; from *saltus*, O. Pg. It. *salto.*

Sottecoo sottocchi It. adv. clandestinely; from *sott' occhio*, Ven. *sotochio.*

Sotto It., O. Pg. *soto*, Pr. *sotz*, Fr. *sous*, Wal. *subt*; from *subtus*, It. also *sottesso* (v. *esso*); Fr. *dessous* = It. *di sotto.* Hence It. *sottano* lowest, undermost, abst. *sottana*, Sp. *sotana*, Fr. *soutane* cassock.

Sou — *soldo.*

Souche — *soc.*

Souci Fr. care; from adj. *sollicitum*, with change of accent *sollicitum*, or from the vb. *se soucier*, N. Pr. *se soucidà*, from *se sollicitare.*

Soudain Fr., Pr. *sobtan* adj. and adv., E. *sudden*; from *subitaneus.*

Soude — *soda.*

Souder — *soldo.*

Soudre Fr. to solve, loose; from *solvere solv're*, as *poudre* from *pulvis pulveris.*

Soufler souflet — *soffiare.*

Soufre — *solfo.*

Souhait — *hait.*

Souil souille Fr. wallowing-place, Pr. *solh* dirt, *sulha* pig, *sulhou* porpoise, Fr. *souillon* slut, vb. Fr. *souiller*, E. *sully*, *soil*, Pr. *sulhar*, Ven. *sogiare*; It. *sugliardo*, perhaps also Sp. *sollastre* scullion. Pr. *sulha (sulhon)* is from *sucula*; Fr. *souil* from an adj. *suillus* swinish, and need not be referred to a German root, (Goth. *bi-sauljan*, or G. *sudeln.*

Soûl Fr. satiated, glutted; from *satullus*, O. Fr. *saoul*, Pr. *sadòl*, It. *satollo*, Rh. *saduls*, Wal. *setul.* Hence Prov. E. *sool* or *sowl.*

Soulager Fr. to relieve; not = Fr. *soulacier* from *solatium*, but = Sp. *soliviar* = *sub-leviare*, so for *souleger* which is found in O. Fr.

Soulier — *suolo.*

Soupçon Fr. (m.), O. Fr. *soupeçon* (f.) suspicion; from *suspicio*, Pr. *sospeisso.* O. Fr. vb. *suscher* from *suspicari.*

Soupe — *sopa.*

Soupente — *pente.*

Souple — *soffice.*

Souquenille — *guenille.*

Source — *sourdre.*

Sourdre Fr. to spring, rise; from *surgere*, Pr. *sorzer*, It. *sorgere*, Sp. *surgir*. From the old partic. *sors* comes the sbst. *source* for *sourse*, O. Fr. also *sorjon* (Fr. *surgeon* a sucker), *sordance*, It. *sorgente*, Sic. *surgiva*; so from *resordre resors* comes the sbst. *ressource*, E. *resource.*

Souris — *sorce.*

Sournois — *sorn.*

Sous soutane — *sotto.*

Souvent — *sovente.*

Sovatto soatto It. leather, strap; from *subactum* = tanned.

Sovente It., Pr. *soven*, *soen*, Fr. *souvent*; from *subinde*, with unusual change of *d* to *t*, perhaps on the analogy of *repente*, *frequente*, *immantinente.*

Soventre O. Fr. particle for L. *secundum*; from *sequente*, Pr. *seguentre*, Rh. *suenter.*

Soverchio It., O. Sp. *sobejo* (for *soberjo*), Pg. *sobejo* superabundant, excessive; from a L. *superculus*. Hence sbst. *soverchieria superchieria* abuse, over-reaching, whence Fr. *supercherie*, Sp. *superchería* fraud, deceit.

Sozzo — *sucido.*

Spaccare It. to split; from O. H. G. *spacha* log, Du. *spaecke* pole? The Sp. *espeque* prop, lever, seems connected.

Spacciare — *pacciare.*

Spada It., Sic. *spata*, Sp. Pg. Pr. *espada*, Fr. *épée*, Wal. *spate* sword; from *spatha* spatula, Gk. σπάθη. Found also in Alb. *spate*, B. *izpata*, and in W. *yspawd* shoulder, Ir. *spad*, E. *spade*, O. H. G. *spato*, G. *spaten*. In O. Sp. it is masc., also in Pr. *espas*, *ispieth*, but Cat. f. *la espi.*

Spago It., Hung. *sparga* twine, string. According to Ferrari, from *spartum* rush, Sp. *esparto* whence *sparticus sparcus spacus*. But we do not find Rom. masc. derivatives from forms in - *icus.*

Spaldo It., Ver. Ven. *spalto* balcony, plur. *spaldi* projecting gallery; prop. = battlement, opening, from G. *spalt* cleft, slit?

Spalla It., Sp. *espalda*, O. Sp. *espalla*, Pg. *espalda*, *espadoa*, Pr. *espatla*, Fr. *épaule*, O. Fr. *espalde* shoulder. From *spathula* dim. of *spatha* shoulder-blade of an animal, Wal. *spate* back, cf. Apicius: *spatula porcina*. The Sard. has instead L. *pala* (= Gk. σπάθη) used in Caelius Aurel. for a shoulder-blade. From *spatula* (not from *palus*) come It. *spalliera*, Sp. *espaldera*, Fr. E. *espalier.*

Spanna It. Rh., Wall. *aspagne*, masc. O. Fr. *espan*, Fr. *empan*

a span; vb. It. *spannare* (or from *pannus?*), Rh. *spaniar*. From
O. H. G. *spanna*, G. *spanne*, the m. forms from M. H. G. *span*,
E. *span*.

Spanu Sic. scarce; from Gk. σπανός.

Sparagnare sparmiare risparmiare It., Fr. *épargner*, Rh. *sparg-
nar*, Burg. *reparmer* to spare. From O. H. G. *sparôn sparén*,
E. *spare*, though the process is not clear, but cf. Lomb.
car-agn-are from O. H. G. *karôn* R. Gr. 1, 87, Fr. *lor-gn-er*
from *luren*.

Sparare — *parare*.

Sparaviere sparviere It., O. Sp. *esparvel*, Cat. *esparver*, Pr. *es-
parvier*, Fr. *épervier* sparrow-hawk, Fr. also sweep-not, Sp.
esparavel. From O. H. G. *sparwari* (G. *sperber* sparrow-hawk)
which is from Goth. *sparva*, E. *sparrow*, Rh. *spar*. Hence
also Rh. *sprer* vulture. Sp. is *gavilan*.

Sparpagliare — *parpaglione*.

Spasimo It., Sp. *espasmo*, Pr. *espasme*, Sp. Pg. also *pasmo*, E.
spasm; vb. It. *spasimare*, Com. *pasmà*, Sp. *espasmar pasmar*,
Pr. *esplasmar, espalmar, plasmar*, Fr. *pâmer;* from L. *spasmus*
(Pliny from σπασμός). The s was mistaken for *ex* and hence
dropt in some forms.

Spassarsi It. to amuse oneself, *spasso* recreation, whence G.
spassen to sport, sbst. *spass;* a freq. from *expandere expassus*.

Spavenio It. (for *sparvenio?*), *spavento*, Sp. *esparavan*, Fr. *épar-
vin* from O. Fr. *esparvain*, E. *spavin*. Menage derives it from
épervier, because the disease makes animals lift their feet like
hawks, an etym. confirmed by the Cat. form *esparavenc* = of
or belonging to a hawk, Val. *esparver*. The Sp. *esparavan*
also = a hawk.

Spaventare spantare It., Sp. Pg. *espantar*, Pr. *espaventar*, Fr.
épouvanter, Rouch. *épanter*, Wal. (with m for v) *speimeută* to
frighten, sbst. It. *spavento* &c.; from *expavere*, part. *expavens*.
In O. Fr. we find *espaventer, espauenter, espoenter, espoventer*
(v inserted), Rh. *spurentar*.

Spazzare It., Sp. *espaciar*, Pr. *espassar* to extend, spread, It.
spaziarsi, Sp. *espaciarse* to walk about; from *spatiari*.

Specchio speglio It., Sp. *espejo*, Pg. *espelho*, Pr. *espelh* mirror;
from *speculum*. The word is found in Fr. *espiègle* a trickish,
cunning fellow, Rou. *vilespièque*, from G. *Eulen-spiegel*, in Fr.
Ulespiègle. Hence vb. Sp. *espejar* to polish, clean, *despejar* to
clean away, remove.

Spedale — *oste* (2).

Spegnere It. to extinguish. From *expingere* to paint out, obli-
terate.

Spelta spelda It., Sp. *espelta*, Pr. *espeuta*, Fr. *épeautre* spelt; L.

spella (5th cent.) = O. H. G. *spelta, spelza spelzo*, A. S. Du.
E. *spelt*, G. *spelz*.

Speme spene It. (poet.) hope; an accusative form from *spem*.
This is better than to derive it, as others, from *spe* like *piene*
from *piè, mene* from *me, tene* from *te* &c., since *n* before a
vowel does not become *m* in It. though the reverse process
occurs, e. g. *fornire* for *formire, sono* from *sum*.

Spendere It. to spend, from *expendere*, Sp. *expender*, whence
also G. *spenden*, O. H. G. *spentôn*, E. *spend; spesa* expense
from *expensa*, L. L. *spensa*, whence G. *speise*, O. H. G. *spisa*,
Rh. *spisa; spendio* from *dispendium*. O. E. *spence* a store-room.

Sperone sprone It., O. Sp. *esporon*, Sp. *espolon*, Pg. *esporão*, Pr.
esperò, O. Fr. *esporon*, Fr. *éperon* spur; O. Sp. *espuera*, Sp.
espuela, Pg. *espora;* from O. H. G. *sporo*, acc. *sporon* (whence
the forms with *n*), E. *spur*. From the Rom. sbst. comes the
vb. It. *speronare spronare*, Sp. *espolear*, Pg. *esporear*, Pr. *espe-
ronar*, Fr. *éperonner*.

Spesa — *spendere*.

Spesso It., Sp. *espeso*, Pr. *espes*, Fr. *épais*, O. Fr. *épois espois*,
Alb. *spes* thick; from *spissus;* adv. It. *spesso*, Pr. *espes* often,
cf. Petron. *oscula spissa* frequent, Gk. πυκνόν, O. H. G.
diccho.

Spezie It., Sp. *especie*, Fr. *épice* (E. *spice*) drugs, spice; from
species = *spezie* in L. L., O. Fr. *espece*. Hence It. *speziale* an
apothecary.

Spiare It., Sp. Pr. *espiar*, Fr. *épier*, E. *spy*, Rh. *spiar;* from O.
H. G. *spehôn, =* G. *spähen*. Sbst. It. (m.) *spia*, Sp. *espia* (m.
f.), Pr. *espia* (f.), O. Fr. *espie* (f.), E. *spy*, also It. *spione*, Sp.
Fr. *espion;* from O. H. G. *speha* (f.) exploratio. The Du. has
spie.

Spiccare — *pegar*.

Spicchio — *spigolo*.

Spiedo — *spito*.

Spignere spingere It. to thrust out; from *expingere* on the analogy of *impingere*, cf. Pr. *espenher* and *empenher*.

Spigolo It. edge; from *spiculum* point, whence also *spicchio* head
of garlic, quarter of a pear &c., slice of orange &c., Ven. *spigolo*, Neap. *spicolo*, Ven. Ver. *spigo*, L. *spicus spicum*, cf. Rh.
spig mountain-peak. Rom. *spigul* = (1) *spigolo* (2) *spicchio*.

Spillo It. (corr. *squillo*), pin (E. *spill*). From *spinula*, as *orlo*
from *orula*, R. Gr. 2, 271; cf. *lulla* from *lunula, ella* from *enola*.
Hence also Fr. *épingle* (f.), N. Pr. *espinglo*, Neap. *spingola*
(from the Fr.), B. *ispilinga*, Champ. *éplingue*, *g* inserted to
separate the liquids in *épiule*. The Romag. has *spinell*. Cf.
Tac. Germ. 17: *tegmen omnibus sagum fibula aut, si desit, spina
consertum*.

Spinaoe It., Sp. *espinaca*, Pg. *espinafre*, Pr. *espinar*, Fr. *épinard*, Wal. *spenac*, E. *spinach;* from *spina*, tho It. from *spinaceus*, the Pg. from *spinifer.*

Spinetta It., Sp. *espineta*, Fr. *épinette*, E. *spinet* a stringed instrument; from *spina*, because struck with a pointed quill.

Spingare — *springare.*

Spirito It., Wal. *spirit*, Sp. *espiritu*, Pg. *espirito*, Cat. Pr. *esperit*, Fr. *esprit*, whence E. *spright* and *spirit*, O. Fr. *Espir.* The sanctity attaching to the word caused some anomalies, e. g. in the Sp. form with *u*, and the uncontracted Pr. form.

Spitamo It., Sp. *espita* span; from σπιθαμή.

Spito Neap., Sp. Pg. *espeto* spit, Fr. *épois* stag's horns; from O. H. G. *spiz*, Du. L. G. E. *spit.* We have also a synonymous form with *d:* It. *spiedo (spiedone*, corr. *schidone schidione*), Romag. *sped*, Gen. *spiddo*, Sard. *spidu*, Sp. *espedo espiedo.*

Spoglio spoglia It. (corr. *scoglio*, *scoglia*), O. Sp. *espojo* spoil; from *spolium*, L. L. *spolia.* For this Sp. has *despojo*, Fr. *dépouille*, Pr. *despueth*, *despuetha*, vb. *despojar*, *dépouiller*, *despolhar.*

Spola spuola It., Sp. *espolin* spool; from O. H. G. *spuolo* (G. *spule*, E. *spool*); Rh. *spul*, Limous. *espolo;* O. Fr. *espolet* spindle. The Fr. *époule* is for *espoule*, *époule*, Lorr. *ehpieule (ch = Fr. es).*

Sponda It., Pr. *esponda* margin, parapet; from L. *sponda*, the sense of which has not altogether disappeared from the Rom.

Sporto It. projection, balcony; from *sporgere*, L. *exporrigere.* But Menage derives *sportello* a little door from *porta.*

Sposo sposa It., Sp. *esposo esposa*, Pr. *espos esposa*, Fr. *époux épouse*, E. *spouse* orig. = betrothed like the L. *sponsus sponsa*, but afterwards = also consort (which is the only meaning in Fr. and E.); vb. It. *sposare*, O. Sp. Pr. *esposar*, Fr. *épouser* from L. *sponsare.*

Spranga It. bar, cross-beam, clasp; from O. H. G. *spanga* with inserted *r.*

Sprazzare sprizzare spruzzare It. to spirt, sprinkle = G. *spratzen spritzen sprützen.* So also *sbrizzare* to wet, Rh. *sbrinzlar*, cf. *sbrocco* for *sprocco.*

Sprecare It. to spill, squander; from A. S. *spree*, O. N. *sprek* a broken twig, cf. Sp. *derramar* from *ramo;* or from O. H. G. *sprehha*, M. H. G. *sprecke* spot, speck, A. S. *sprâncan*, G. *sprenkeln*, E. *sprinkle.*

Springare It. Dante Inf. 19, 120 (al. *spingare*) to sprawl, O. Fr. *espringuer* dance with leaps, Pic. to dance for joy; from O. H. G. *springan*, E. *spring.* O. Fr. *espringale* = (1) a dance (2) a machine for throwing missiles, a *springald*, It. *spingarda* a battering-ram, Sp. *espingarda* a small cannon.

Sprizzare — *sprazzare.*

Sprocco — *brocco.*

Spruzzare — *sprazzare.*

Spulciare — *pulce.*

Spuntone spontone It., Sp. *esponton,* Fr. *sponton,* E. *spontoon* a sort of pike; from It. *puntone (punto, punctum)* with strengthening *s.*

Squadra — *quadro.*

Squarciare It. to tear to pieces, prop. to quartor; from *ex-quartare* (It. *squartare,* Fr. *écarteler) ex-quartire.* Neap. *squartare* = squarciare.

Squelette — *scheletro.*

Squilla It., Lomb. Rb. *schella,* Sp. *esquila,* Pr. *esquella, esquelha,* O. Fr. *eschiele* bell; from O.H.G. *skilla, skella,* G. *schelle* bell, which come from vb. *skëllan* to ring, whence It. *squillare.* L. L. is *schilla.*

Squillo — *spillo.*

Squinanzia It., Sp. *esquinancia,* Fr. *esquinancie,* E. *squinancy, quinsy;* from κυνάγχη, L. *cynanche.*

Squittire It. to chirp, cry; cf. Bav. *quitschen.*

Stacca It., Sp. Pr. *estaca,* O. Fr. *estaque estache,* from A. S. *staca,* L. G. E. *stake.*

Staccare — *tacco.*

Staccio It., Neap. (more correctly) *setaccio,* Mil. *sedazz,* also Sp. *cedazo,* O. Fr. *saas,* Fr. *sas* sieve; L. L. *sedatium, sitaceum* for a L. *setacium* from *seta,* because made of hair. Wal. has *sete, sitize,* Norm. *set.*

Stadico statico It., Fr. *étage,* E. *hostage;* from *ostaticus, obsidaticus (obses).*

Staffa It. Rh. stirrup; from O. H. G. *staph, stapho* step, whence also L. L. *stapia.* Hence It. *staffetta,* Sp. *estafeta,* Fr. *estafette: cursor tabellarius, cui pedes in stapede perpetuo sunt* Ferrari; also *staffile* stirrup-leather, *staffilare* to scourge with a thong (Fr. *estafier* to bully), *staffilata* a blow, Fr. *estafilade* a slash, cut, vb. *estafilader.*

Staggio It., Pr. *estatge,* Fr. *étage* (E. *stage)* state, dwelling, story, floor &c.; from *stare status staticus* (Pr. f. *estatga* abode).

Staggire It. to sequester, seize, detain, *staggina* sequestrator. Like so many other legal words, of German origin; from *stdligòn* sistere, or from *stâtian (stâtian)* to fasten, hold.

Stagione It. season, Sp. *estacion,* Pg. *estacão* season, time; vb. It. *stagionare* to mature; from *statio,* cf. G. *stunde* moment from *stehn* stare. The Sp. Pr. *sazon,* Pg. *sazão,* Fr. *saison,* E. *season* (vb. *sazonar, assaisonner, sasonare, season)* can hardly come from *statio,* though we find *z = st* in Sp. *Zuñiga* for *Estuñiga.* Ducange derives them, with much probability,

from *satio* the nearest L. representative of "season", cf. the
expressions: *satio verna, æstiva, autumnalis* (Columella).

Stagno It., Sp. *estaño*, Pr. *estauh*, Fr. *étain* and *tain* (tin-foil *le
tain = l'étain*), E. *tin*. Not from *stannum* for the L. *nu*
passes into It. *gn* only before *i (grugnire* from *grunuire)*, but
from the O. L. *stagnum* found in *stagneus stagnatus*. Fr. vb.
étamer to tin from *étain* as *venimeux* from *venin (venom)*, cf.
abstemius from *abstineo*, according to some etymologers.

Stajo — *sestiere*.

Stallo It. O. Pg., O. Sp. *estalo*, Pr. O. Fr. *estal* place, abode,
Fr. *étal* stall *(étaler retail)*, *étau;* fem. It. *stalla*, Sp. *estula*,
O. Pg. *stala* stall, whence It. *stallone*, Fr. *étalon*, E. *stallion
= equus ad stallum*. From O. H. G. *stal* locus (G. *stelle*) stabulum, E. *stall*, vb. Du. *stallen* to expose for sale, G. *aus-
stellen*. From L. *stabulum* we have Pr. *estable*, Fr. *étable* (f.).
The Fr. *étau =* (1) stall, butcher's stall (so also *étal*, cf. *éta-
lier* a butcher) (2) a vice. In the latter sense *étau* might be
from *stal* in the sense of stand, trestle, frame, or from the
O. Flem. *stael* stock, Du. *steel*, but the Lorr. *citauque*, Bas.
estoka are evidently from the G. *(schraub-)stock =* vice, and
étau is probably an abbreviation.

Stambocco It. wild goat; from the O. H. G. *stainboc*, O. Fr. *bouc-
estain*, Rh. *stambuoçh*.

Stamigno It., Sp. *estameña*, Pg. Pr. *estamenha*, Fr. *étamine*, E.
stamin bolting-cloth, bunting, sieve; from adj. *stamineus* made
of thread.

Stampare It., Sp. Pg. *estampar*, Fr. *étamper* to stamp, punch;
from O. H. G. *stamphòn*, G. *stampfen*, E. *stamp*; Wal. *steamp*
sbst. from O. H. G. *stamph*.

Stancare It. to tire; Sp. Pg. Pr. *estancar*, Fr. *étancher*, E. stanch,
adj. Sp. *estauco*, Fr. *étanche*, E. *staunch* (water-tight), in Pg.
also *=* to weary. From *stagnare* to stop, hinder, whence to
tire; *gn* becoming *nc* as in sbst. Sp. Pg. *estanque*, Pr. *estanc*,
Fr. *étang* (instead of *étain)*, Bret. *staun* from *stagnum*, the
hardened form being used to distinguish the word from *stagnum* tin, though the soft *gn* is found in Sp. *retañar*, Val.
estanyar = estancar; Piedm. *stagn* has both senses. In Pr.
Cat. *tancar* to stop, Sp. *ataucarse* to constrain oneself, the *s*
is dropped as in Pg. *tanque* (E. *tauk*), for *estanque*, v. s. *stanga*.
Hence It. adj. *stanco* weary, Sp. *estanco*, Pg. *estanque* costive,
Pr. *estanc* still, stagnant, O. Fr. *estanc* dull, languid; It. may
be for *stancato*, but the rest must be from the sbst. *stagnum*
(v. R. Gr. 2, 267), since adjectives are not formed from verbs
except by means of suffixes. It. *mano stanca =* prop. the
feeble, hand (M. H. G. *tenc* left, Wal. *stunge*), cf. It. (Prov.)

mano storta the distorted hand, and cf. *senestrarsi un piede* to sprain the foot. V. s. *gauche.*

Stanga It. Rh. pole, bar, Fr. *etangues,* E. *tongs* (cf. *stanco*), properly = that which rests on two supports or bars, Fr. *stangue* anchor-stock (heraldic), Wal. *steange;* from O. H. G. *stanga,* G. *stange* a pole.

Stanza It., Sp. *estancia* abode, room, Pr. *estansa* position, Fr. *etance etançon* prop; from a form *stantia (stans stare).* The *stanza* of a song is supposed to be the store-room, where the poets' art is concentrated (Dante).

Starna It., Sp. Pg. *estarna* a sort of partridge; from (avis) *externa,* Fr. *perdrix grecque.* The O. H. G. *starn,* A. S. *stearn* is the name of another bird, the starling.

Stecco It. thorn, *stecca* staff, log, vb. *stecchire;* from O. H. G. *steccho* a prick, sting, Du. *stek,* E. *stick.* Cf. s. *etiquette.*

Stendardo It., Sp. *estandarte,* Pr. *estendart, estandart,* Fr. *etendard,* whence M. H. G. *stanthart,* E. *standard;* from *extendere,* It. *stendere le insegne.*

Stentare It. to be in want (E. *stint*), Rh. *stentar* to be weary, It. *stento* need, hardship; from *abstentare* for *abstinere,* to abstain, be hungry. Hence also It. *bistentare bistento,* Pr. (from *tentiare*) *bistensar, bistens,* O. Fr. *bestancier, bestans.*

Stesso istesso It. pronoun; from L. *iste ipse.*

Stia It. henroost; from O. H. G. *stiga,* G. *stiege* ladder, henroost.

Stimare It. from *æstimare,* L. L. *stimare.*

Stinco It., Mod. Ven. *schinco,* Mil. *schinca* shin-bone, shin; from O. H. G. *skinko* reed, pipe, M. H. G. *schinke* bone.

Stio, lino stio It. a sort of flax, sown in March; from *sativum* (Menage), like *staccio* from *setacium,* or, better, from *æstivum.*

Stivale It., O. Sp. *estibal,* O. Fr. *estival* a boot, whence O. H. G. *stiful,* M. H. G. *stirak,* G. *stiefel.* Properly a summer-boot, from *æstivale* (Ducange).

Stivare It., Sp. Pg. *estivar* to stow, pack, *estiva* ballast, cargo, *estivador* packer, *stevedore;* from *stipare.*

Stizzare — *tizzo.*

Stocco It., Sp. Pg. *estoque,* Pr. Fr. *estoc* = (1) E. *tuck* (weapon), (2) stock, Com. *stoch* a stick; from G. E. *stock,* Gael. *stoc.* The G. *stocken* is found in Pic. *etoquer.* For Fr. *etau = stock,* v. s. *stallo.*

Stoffa It., Sp. Pg. *estofa,* Fr. *etoffe,* masc. It. *stoffo,* Pg. *estofo* = E. *stuff;* vb. Sp. Pg. *estofar,* Fr. *etoffer, etouffer,* E. *stuff.* The vb. is synonymous with It. *stoppare,* Fr. *etouper,* E. *stop* (v. *stoppa*) and both alike are from L. *stuppa* tow, which in G. became *stupfa stuffa,* hence Sp. *estofa* = also quilted stuff, E. *stuff.* Sp. *estofar* to stew from O. H. G. *stuba, stove* is distinct from *estofar* to quilt *(stoffa)*. The Gael. *stubh* seems to be from the E., cf. *scabhal* from *scaffold*, *lobhte* = *loft*, *gibhte* = *gift*.

Stoja It., Sp. *estera* for *estuera* (as *frente* for *fruente*), Pg. *esteira* mat; from *storea*.

Stoppa It., Wal. *stupe*, Sp. *estopa*, Fr. *étoupe* tow; from *stuppa*. Hence It. *stoppino* match, Fr. *étoupin*, E. *toppin*, stopple, wad; It. vb. *stoppare*, O. Fr. *estopar*, E. *stop*, Fr. *étoupper* = L. L. *stuppare*.

Stoppia It., Pr. *estobla*, Fr. *étouble* = E. *stubble*, G. *stoppel*; the Fr. *éteule*, however, is the L. *stipula*, cf. O. Fr. *neule* from *nebula*.

Stordire It. to be deaf, to deafen, stupefy, O. Sp. *estordir atordir*, Sp. *aturdir*, Fr. *étourdir*, adj. *stordito*, *aturdido*, *étourdi*, stupid, heedless. Several derivations are given (1) from *turdus* a thrush, cf. Sp. *tener cabeza de tordo*, and Gk. proverb κωφότερος κίχλης, and cf. *ericiare* from *ericius* (2) W. *twrdd* noise, thunder, cf. *étonner* from *tonus* (3) E. *sturdy* (4) from *torpidus*, whence *extorpidire extordire*; as from *tepidus* comes *tiédir* to be lukewarm, so from *torpidus tourdir* to be numb.

Storione It., Sp. *esturion*, E. *sturgeon*, Fr. *étourgeon*; from O. H. G. *sturio*.

Stormo It., Rh. *sturm*, Pr. *estorn*, O. Fr. *estor* storm; It. vb. *stormire*, Pr. O. Fr. *estormir*; from G. *sturm*, E. *storm*, vb. *sturman* found also in W. *ystorm*, Bret. *stourm*, Gael. *stoirm*.

Storpiare — *stroppiare*.

Stoviglì stoviglie It. an earthen vessel; from O. H. G. *stouf* = O. N. *stoup*, A. S. *steáp*, E. *stoup*, dim. O. H. G. *stoufili*. Hence also O. Fr. *esteu*.

Stracoare It. to harass, weary (Pr. *estracar*), *stracco* for *straccato* exhausted; probably, from O. H. G. *strecchan* to *stretch* (on the ground).

Stracciare It., Rh. *stratschar*, Sp. *estrazar*, Pr. *estrassar* to tear to pieces; It. *straccio*, Sp. *estrazo estraza* rag. From *extractus extractiare*. Cf. *tracciare*.

Strada It., Sp. Pg. Pr. *estrada*, O. Fr. *estrée*, Pic. *étrée* street; from L. *strata* sc. *via*, cf. Virg. *strata viarum*, E. *street*. In Fr. a street was also called *chemin ferré*, Pr. *cami ferrat*, and sometimes simply *ferrée* (cf. *estrée*, *brisée*, *route*). Hence also It. *strato*, Sp. *estrado*, Pr. *estrá* for *estrat*; Fr. *estrade* (from the Sp.) raised platform, from *stratum*. Hence also Pr. *estradier*, O. Fr. *estraier* a rambler, *strayer (stray)*, cf. s. *estraguar*.

Strambo It. crooked, bandy-legged, Pied. *stranb* limping, Romag. *stramb* strange, odd, Wal. *stremb*, Alb. *stremp* oblique, false, Pr. *estramp* unrhymed (verse), *stramp*, hence It. *strambità* want of rhyme, perverseness, Mil. *strambà* to distort. From L. *strabus* squinting, cf. Sp. *estrambosidad* = It. *estrabismo*. Hence also Sp. *estrumbote*, It. *strambotto* burden of a song, prop. = that which transgresses ordinary rules, cf. Dante Inf. 7, 40 (of a man), Ven. *straboto* = blunder; adj. Sp. Pg. *estrambotico* strange, eccentric. F. Pasqualino has: *strammotta ridicula cantiuncula a strammu* (It. *strambo*) *ut innuatur deflexio a vera significatione in malam partem accepta*. But with *estrambote* cf. O. Fr. *estrabot estribot* (v. *estribo*) whence also a form *estrimbote*. It. *stramba* a rope of rushes is from a different root, cf. Bav. *strempfel* withy; the vb. *strambellare* is from *strampfeln* to struggle, cf. Rh. *stramblire* to shake.

Stranio strano It., Wal. *strein*, Sp. *estraño*, Pr. *estranh*, Fr. *étrange*, E. *strange*, hence It. *straniero*, Sp. *extrangero*, Pr. *estrangier*, E. *stranger*, Fr. *étranger*; from *extraneus*.

Strapasser strapazzare — *pazzo*.

Strappare It., sbst. *strappata*, Sp. *estrapada*, Fr. E. *estrapade*; from *strapfen* to draw, G. *straff* tight. V. *estraper*.

Strascinare — *trassinare*.

Strato — *strada*.

Stratto It. eccentric, extravagant; for *astratto* or *distratto* lost in thought.

Straziare It. to ill-treat, abuse, sbst. *strazio*; from *distractus*, *distractiare*.

Strebbiare — *trebbia*.

Strega It., Mil. *stria*, Pg. *estria(?)*, also It. *stregona*, Wal. *stregöe* witch, masc. It. *stregone*, Wal. *strigoiu*; vb. *stregare*; from L. *striga* night-bird, owl, also witch (Petronius and Apuleius), which is from *strix*.

Stregghia streglia It., Cat. *estrijol*, Fr. *étrille* curry-comb; vb. It. *strecchiare*, Sp. *estrillar*, Fr. *étriller* to curry; from *strigilis*.

Stribord Fr. (also *tribord*), whence Sp. *estribord*; from A.S. *steorbord*, E. *starboard* (G. *steuerbord*).

Strillo It. loud cry, vb. *strillare (trill?)*; from *stridulus*.

Stringa It., Sp. *estringa* string, vb. *stringare*. Not from *stringere*, which would give *strigna*, cf. *cigna* from *cingere*, but from the A. S. *string streng*, O. N. *strenger*, M. Du. *stringhe*, vb. *stringen strengen*, v. Grimm 2, 37, and cf. Pg. forms *estrinca estrinque*, Sp. *estrinque estrenque* rope.

Striscia It. stripe, strip, vb. *strisciare*. From the G. *strich*, though G. *ch* is not usually changed to It. *sci*; cf. *una striscia di paese* = G. *ein strich landes*.

Stronzare It. to cut, lop, from O. H. G. *strunzan*. Sbst. *stronzo stronzolo* dung, excrement, O. Fr. *estront*, Fr. *étron*, cf. G. *strunzen*, *strunzel* a piece, dirt, Du. *stront* dung.

Stroppiare storpiare It., Ven. *strupiare*, Mil. *struppià*, Rh. *strup-chiar*, Sp. Pg. *estropear*, Fr. *estropier* to maim, mutilate, abst. It. *stroppio* hindrance, check. Perhaps *storpiare* is the orig. form and comes from *extorpiare* for *extorpidare*.

Stróppolo It., Fr. *estrope*, *étrope* rope; from *struppus* (Gellius), Sp. *estrovo* from *stropus*. Cf. Du. *strop*, G. *strüppe*, E. *strap*.

Stroscio — *troscia*.

Strozza It. throat, *strozzare* to throttle; from O. H. G. *drozza* throat.

Struffo strufolo It. a heap of rags; perhaps from G. *strupf* anything torn, O. H. G. *stroufen* to pluck, tear.

Struggere It. to destroy; for *distruggere* = *destruere*. The *gg* stands for a euphonic inserted *j (destrujere)*, cf. L. L. *tragere* for *tracre* from *trahere*, cf. also O. Pg. *trager*, whence Pg. *trazer*, v. R. Gr. 1, 166.

Strusso It., Pr. *estrus* ostrich, from *struthio;* Sp. *av-estruz*, Fr. *au-truche* (f.) for *autrusse*, E. *o-strich*, from *avis struthio*, L. L. *strucio*.

Stucco It. E., Sp. *estuque*, Fr. *stuc;* from O. H. G. *stucchi* crusta.

Stufa It., Sp. Pg. *estufa*, Pr. *estuba*, Fr. *étuve* (E. *stew*) stove, vb. It. *stufare*, Sp. *estufar*, *estofar estovar*, Fr. *étuver* (E. *stew*); L. L. *stuba*, O. H. G. *stupa*, M. H. G. *stobe*, G. *stube*, Du. E. *stove*, A. S. *stofa*, Gael. *stobh* (from the E.).

Stuolo It., O. Sp. *estol* troop, retinue, crew, O. Cat. Pr. *estol* army, fleet, Wal. *stol* fleet; from στόλος, L. *stolus* (Cod. Theod.). The O. Fr. for classis was *estoire* (f.), whence M. H. G. *storje;* this answers to a L. L. *storium* (f. from neut.) which = *stolium* = στόλιον, cf. *navirie* = *navilie*. This is better than to take it from *estorer* (q. v.) = *instaurare*, for a derivative *instaurium* would not be regular.

Stutare — *tutare*.

Stuzzicare It. to drive on, impel, Mod. *stussà*, Rh. *stuschar;* from G. *stutzen* to thrust. Veneroni gives also *stozzare* to impress.

Sù — *suso*.

Subbia It. chisel; from *subula* awl.

Subbio It., Sp. *enxullo*, Fr. *ensouple* a weaver's beam; from *insubulum*.

Suo — *cucuzza*.

Succhiare It. to suck; from a L. *succulare*, from *sucus succus*, v. *suco*. *Succhiare* also = to bore, pierce, whence *succhio* a gimlet, prop. = a sucker.

Succiare sugare — *suco*.

Sucer — *suco*.

Súcido sozzo It., Sp. *sucio*, Pg. *sujo*, N. Pr. *sous* dirty; from *sucidus* moist, cf. *lana sucida. Sozzo* is from *sucius* as *sezzo* from *secius.*

Sucio — *sucido.*

Suco suoco sugo It., Sp. *suco, xugo*, Fr. Pr. *suc* juice; from *sucus;* hence It. *sugare*, O. Sp. *sugar* (cf. O. H. G. *sugan*), Pr. *sucar*, E. *suck;* It. *asciugare*, Sp. *enxugar*, Pr. *eisugar*, Fr. *essuyer*, Wal. *usucà uscà*, from *exsucare* to dry up, wipe off moisture; It. *asciutto*, Sp. *enxuto*, Pr. *eissug*, Berr. *essuy*, Rh. *schig* dry, Fr. abst. *essui*, from *exsuctus;* It. *prosciugare* from *per-exsucare;* It. *prosciutto, presciutto* (Pg. *presunto*) ham, from *per-exsuctus.* It. *succiare suzzare*, Fr. *sucer*, is from *suctiare (suctus)*, cf. Pr. *succiò*, Fr. *suction.*

Suore — *zucchero.*

Sud Fr., whence Sp. *sud*, Pg. *sul* (cf. Sp. *ardid*, Pg. *ardil*); from A. S. *sùdh*, E. *south.*

Suela — *suolo.*

Sueldo — *soldo.*

Suero Sp., Pg. *soro*, Sard. *soru* whey; from *serum*, the Pg. Sard. coming, probably, through a Fr. *soir*, for the change of an accented *e* to *o* before a single consonant is unexampled.

Súghero It. cork; for *sivero* from *suber*, the *v* being lost and *gh* inserted to avoid the hiatus, cf. *pavone paone pagone (paro)*. Ven. Cat. *suro* avoids the hiatus by a contraction.

Sugliardo — *souil.*

Sugna It. fat, grease; for *axungia* cart-grease, cf. Ven. *sonza (z = gi)*, Mil. *sonzgia.*

Suie Fr., Pr. *suia, sueia, suga*, Cat. *sutje* (m.) soot. Of these the original form *suga* may be referred to the A. S. *sòtig (sòtg)*, E. *sooty*, from abst. *sòt*, E. *soot*, whence also Gael. *sùith.*

Suif — *sevo.*

Suinter Fr. to sweat, ooze, abst. *suint suin;* from O. H. G. *suizan* (orig. *suitan*), E. *sweat*, with insertion of a nasal, v. R. Gr. 1, 332.

Suivre Fr. to follow; from *sequi*, Pr. *seguir* and *segre*, L. L. *sévere*, O. Fr. *sevre, sivre, suire, suivre*, E. *sue.*

Sujo — *sucido.*

Sumir — *sumsir.*

Sumsir sumpsir, somsir sompsir Pr. to sink, *somsimen* sinking, *somsis* abyss; a corruption of *submergere*, Pr. *somergir, g* after *r* becoming *s*, as in *esparser (spargere), terser (tergere);* so *sunrsir sunsir.* Sp. Pg. have *sumir, g* having vanished as in *espurrir (exporrigere), solar (subagere);* or is this from *sumere?* From *somsir* comes, probably, the Fr. *sancir* to founder; Pr. *samcimen* is found for *sumsimen.*

Suolo It., Pr. *sol*, sola, Sp. *suela*, Fr. E. *sole* (of the foot); It. *soglia, soglio*, Pr. *sulh, sol*, Fr. *seuil* threshold, Sp. *suela* floor;

It. *soglia*, Sp. *suela*, Pg. *solha*, Fr. E. *sole* (fish). The forms with the *l* pure are from *solum*, the others from *solea*. From adj. *solarius* we have It. *solajo*, *solare*, Pr. *solier*, *solar* floor, E. *sollar*, Sp. *solar* ground, Fr. *soulier* shoe.

Super — *sopa*.

Supercheria superoherie — *soverchio*.

Sur Fr. preposition; from *super*, Sp. Pg. Pr. *sobre*, O. It. *sor*: O. Fr. *sore*, *seure* from *supra*.

Sur Fr. sour; from O. H. G. A. S. O. N. *sûr*, W. *sur*, E. *sour*. Hence Rou. *suriele*, Wall. *sural*, Fr. *surelle*, E. *sorrel* = Du. *zuuring*.

Sûr Fr., O. Fr. *seür* (E. *sure*) *segur*; from *securus*, Pr. *segur*.

Surcot — *cotta*.

Sureau Fr. elder. *Sabucus* becomes in Sp. *sauco*, Wal. *sor*, Pr. *sauc*, B. *sauca*, O. Fr. Pic. *seü*; for names of trees the Fr. is fond of the term. *arius*, dim. *arellus*, hence from *seu* the form *sureau*. The O. Fr. *seür* is perhaps for *seür-eau* rejecting the dim. suffix.

Surgeon — *sourdre*.

Surgie Pr. surgery; for *srurgia* for *cirurgia*, *chirurgia*, hence O. Fr. *surgien*, E. *surgeon*, Du. *surgijn*.

Surplis — *pelliccia*.

Surtir — *sortire*.

Susina It. plum; perhaps because brought from *Susa* (Muratori).

Suso It., shortened *sù* (cf. *verso*, *ver*), Rh. *si*, Sp. O. Pg. *suso*, Pr. O. Fr. *sus*; from *susum* for *sursus*, contr. L. *sus* in *susque deque*. Hence Fr. *dessus*, O. Sp. *desù*.

Sussiego — *sosiego*.

Susto — *sostare*.

Suzerain Fr. prop. adj. *(seigneur s.)* a feudal word; from *sus* (= *susum*), on the analogy of *souverain*?

Suzzare — *suco*.

Svanire — *évanouir*.

Svellere svegliere It.; from *exvellere* for *evellere*.

Sverza — *verza*.

T.

Taba Sp. bone of the knee-pan; perhaps from Ar. *tabaq* a small bone between the vertebræ.

Tabacco It., Sp. *tabaco*, Fr. *tabac*, E. *tobacco*; an American word, prop. a tobacco-bowl.

Taballo — *ataballo*.

Tabarin Fr. a jack-pudding; the name of a mountebank of the 17th century (Roquefort).

Tabarro It., Sp. Pg. *tabardo*, Fr. F. *tabard*, M. H. G. *tapfart* short coat, coat-of-arms, W. *tabar*, L. Gr. ταμπάριον. Perhaps from *tap-es* a covering, It. *tappeto*, cf. Rom. *cap* and *cab* from *caput*, where also the *t* vanishes.

Tabique Sp. Pg. a partition-wall of lath and plaster; Sp. also *taxbique*, A. *taschbik* = twisting, plaiting, making lattice or net-work, the root being *schabaka* inseruit unam rem alteri, perplexuit, cancellatim struxit. V. Mahn, Untersuch. p. 71.

Tabouret — *tamburo*.

Tabust tabut O. Fr. Pr. outcry, disturbance, vb. *tabuster tabuter*, *tabustar tabussar*, *tustar turtar* to knock, disturb, It. *tambustare* to thrash; Pr. sbst. *tabtarta*, vb. *tabornar*. From *tabor tambor* (tambour, drum), whence also Pr. *talabust*, Fr. *tarabuster* to vex; L. L. *taburcium tuburlum* = *tabor*.

Tacaño — *taccagno*.

Taccagno It., Sp. *tacaño*, Fr. *taquin* niggardly; vb. It. *taccagnare*, Fr. *taquiner*, Lomb. *zaccagnà* to wrangle about trifles. From G. *zähe* tenacious, miserly, O. H. G. *zâhi*, cf. Lomb. *taaiaard* niggard. For *c* or *cc* from G. *h*, v. s. *gecchire*, *smacco*.

Taccia — *tacco*.

Tacco It. heel of a shoe (Sp. Pg. *taco* peg seems to be of different origin), Rh. *tac* spot, defect, Wall. *tac* plate, Rou. *tacy* a spot of land; f. It. *tacca* notch and spot, Pr. *taca*, O. Fr. Pic. *teque*, It. *tecca*, Fr. *tache*, It. *taccia*, Sp. Pg. *tacha* spot, Occ. *tacho* broad-headed nail; hence It. *taccone* patch, Sp. Pg. *tacon* heel of a shoe, *tachon* head of a nail, Rou. *tacon* = It. *taccone* and *taccia*; vb. Rh. *taccar* to notch, to cleave to, Ven. *tacare*, Lomb. *tacà* to fasten, Pr. *tacar*, Fr. *tacher* to spot, Pr. *techir*; It. *attaccare*, Sp. *atacar* = Fr. *attacher*, E. *attach* also = Fr. *attaquer* (the Picard form of *attacher*, v. Littré, Hist. d. la langue Fr., p. 13), E. *attack* (prop. to fasten on to, Gk. ἅπτεσθαί τινος); It. *staccare*, Fr. *détacher*, E. *detach*. The root is found in the Celtic as well as the German: Gael. *tac*, Corn. *tach*, E. *tack*, Du. *tack*, G. *zacke* point, tooth, vb. Du. *tacken*, E. *tack*, cf. O. N. *taca*, A. S. *tacan*, E. *take*. The original meaning seems to be "something fastening or fastened" then (2) patch (3) spot (4) stain, blemish. The It. meaning "notch" is to be immediately referred to *zacke*.

Taccola It. magpie, *taccolo* jest, *taccolare* to chatter; from O. H. G. *tâha* cornicula, or from a form *tâhala*, whence Germ. *dohle* jackdaw.

Tacha tache tacon — *tacco*.

Tâche Fr. (f.) task, job, vb. *tâcher* to try. For *tasche*, cf. E. *task*, Cat. Ven. *tasca*, Pr. *tasca tascha* rent, income; L. L. *tasca praestatio agraria*. Found also in Celtic: W. *tasg*, Gael.

taisg. As Fr. *tâche*, Pr. *tasc* from *taxus*, so *tâche*, *tasca* from *taxa* (L. L. for *taxatio*) = something demanded or exacted, cf. Rou. *tasque* = Fr. *taxe*.

Taféno It., Sp. *tábano*, Pr. O. Fr. *tavan*, Fr. *taon* (for *taan*), Wal. *teune* a gadfly; from *tabanus (tábanus* later *tabánus)*, cf. Papias: *asilus quem rustici tabanum vocant.*

Taffetà It., Sp. *tafetan*, Fr. *taffetas*, *taffeta;* from Persian *táftah.*

Tafur Pr. O. Fr. rogue, Sp. *tahur* gamester, cheat, Pg. *taful* also = debauchee, N. Pr. vb. *tafurá* to disturb, confuse. From Arab. *dahil* a cheat?

Tagaroto Sp. Pg. an Egyptian hawk; from the river *Tagarros* in Africa, on the banks of which it is chiefly found.

Taglia It., Sp. *taja*, *talla*, Pg. Pr. *talha*, Fr. *taille* cut, cutting, figure, *tally*, *tallage;* M. It. *taglio*, Sp. *tajo*, *talle*, Pr. *talh*, Fr. (only) *détail*, E. *detail*, *entail;* vb. *tagliare, tajar, talhar, tailler*, Wal. *telà* to cut; Pr. *talhador*, Sp. *tallador* (engraver), Fr. *tailleur*, E. *tailor* (for which It. has *sartone*, Sp. *sastre);* It. *tagliere*, Sp. *taller*, Pr. *talhador*, Fr. *tailloir*, Sp. *tajadero* chopping-block, trencher, plate, whence G. *teller;* and many other derivatives. From L. *talea*, cf. Nonius 4, 473: *taleas scissiones lignorum vel praesegmina Varro dicit de re rust. Lib. I, nam etiam nunc "rustica voce" intertaleare dicitur dividere vel exscindere ramum;* this verb is the Sp. *entretallar* to cut out, It. *frastagliare.*

Tai O. Fr. mud, vb. *entaiar;* from Du. *taai* sticky, clammy, O. H. G. *zâhi*, which was used as an epithet of lime, glue, or clay, G. *zähe*, Rh. *zais.* Sic. *taja* = mortar.

Taie Fr. pillow-case; from *theca* covering, O. Fr. (more correctly) *toie*, cf. *noyer* from *necare.* Cf. Rh. *teija* from *theca*, as *speija* from *spica.* The O. H. G. *ziechâ*, G. *zieche*, E. *tick* are also from *theca*, as *ziegal* from *tegula.*

Taie — *taita.*

Taille tailler — *taglia.*

Tain — *stagno.*

Tainar Pr. to loiter, delay, also trans. to delay, put off, impers. *me taina* = *il me tarde*, sbst. *taina.* Hence Pr. *atainar*, O. Fr. *atainer* to delay, also to dally, irritate, trifle (Bret. *atahinein);* sbst. *ataïna*, *ataïne*, Burg. *ataine*, Bret. *atahin* (m.). It is perhaps connected with Fr. *taquin, taquiner*, from G. *zähe* clammy, though no forms *tahin tahiner* are found.

Taisson — *tasso.*

Taita Sp. (in children's speech) father, Com. Neap. Pic. *tata*, Wal. *tate* father, Rh. *tat* grandfather, *tata* grandmother; hence O. Fr. Pic. Wall. *tayon* grandfather, Pic. Champ. *ratayon* great-grandfather. It is the L. *tata*, Gk. τάτα, Du. *teyte*, L. G. *taite tatte*, W. *tâd*, Ir. *daid*, E. *dad*, *daddy.* Fr.

taie is from *tata*, as *craie* from *creta*. Sp. *tato tata* = younger
brother, sister, Romag. *dad, dada*. The Goth. *atta,* Sw. *ätte,*
Gk. ἄττα, Alb. *at*, is also found in Rom.: Com. *atta* father,
Rh. *bis-at* great-grandfather, L. *atta* (Festus).

Taja tajar — *taglia.*

Tala Sp. Pg. Cat. felling of trees, vb. *talar* to fell trees, cf. Fr.
name *Boistallé.* Not identical with *tallar* to cut. It seems to
be an old Sp. word, B. *tala* "excidium sylvarum" (B. Gloss.),
cf. the names of Sp. places, *Tala-briga, Tala-mina, Tal-ori,
Tala-vera* &c., = E. term. *field, feld,* cf. Humboldt Urbew.
Hisp. p. 53. It may be the O. H. G. *zälön* diripere = L. L.
talare.

Taladro — *taraire.*

Talco It. Sp. Pg., Fr. E. *talc;* from Ar. *'talaq,* perhaps of Persian
origin.

Talega Sp., Pg. *talega,* Pr. *taleca* bag, sack; from θύλαχος?
Wal. *tileáge.*

Talento It., Sp. *talento talente talante,* Pr. *talen talan,* Fr. E.
talent. The O. Rom. meaning (It. *talento,* Sp. *talente talante,*
O. Fr. O. E. *talent,* Wall. *dalent*) was will, inclination, from
talentum (τάλαντον) balance, weight, inclination. A later
meaning was that of "talent", genius; perhaps derived from
the Parable of the Talents. Hence It. *attalentare,* Pr. *atalen-
tar,* O. Fr. *atalenter* to please, entice, charm.

Talevas O. Fr. a sort of shield; for *tavelas,* from It. *tavolaccio* a
wooden shield *(tabula).*

Talismano It., Sp. Fr. E. *talisman;* from Ar. *'tilsam* which is
from the Gk. τέλεσμα an incantation.

Tallo It. Sp., Pg. *talo,* Fr. *talle* (f.) shoot, sprout; from *thallus*
(θαλλός).

Tallone It., Sp. Pg. Fr. *talon* heel (E. *talon*); from *talus* ancle =
talaün in the Cass. Gloss., v. Duc. *talo.*

Tamarindo It. Sp., Fr. *tamarin,* E. *tamarind;* from Ar. *tamar
hindi* Indian date.

Tambo Pg. bridal bed; from *thalamus,* with *b* inserted, O. Pg.
tamo marriage-feast.

Tamburo It., Sp. Pg. *tambor atambor,* Pr. *tabor* (E. *tabor*), Fr.
E. *tambour,* M. H. G. *tambûr* and *tabûr* drum, Wal. *tambure*
lyre; dim. It. *tamburino* &c., Fr. *tabouret* (E. *tabret*) foot-stool;
from Pers. *'tambûr,* Ar. *'tombûr* lyre.

Tambussare — *tabust.*

Tamica — *tomiza.*

Tamigio It., Ven. *tamiso,* Sp. *tamiz,* Pr. Fr. *tamis* sieve; vb. It.
tamigiare, Fr. *tamiser* to sift. From the Du. *teems* sieve (cf.
O. H. G. *zemisa* bran).

Tampa tampon tampir — *tape.*

Tan Sp., Pg. *tão* adv. from *tantus*, R. Gr. 2, 447.

Tan Fr. E., vb. *tanner* to *tan*, Rou. *tener*, M. Du. *tanen*, *teynen*; hence Fr. *tanné*, E. *tawny*, It. *tané*, Sard. *tanou*, Du. *tancyt* (= O. Fr. part. *tancit*). From G. *tanne* fir, or from Bret. *tann* oak? The latter word is only found in one dialect of the Bret. and not elsewhere in Celtic. In L. L. we find "*aluta locus ubi pelles in calce pilantur et tanantur*".

Tana It. Rh. N. Pr. a den. For *sottana*, L. *subtana*, *subtanea*, as Com. *trana* from *sotterranea*, *subterranea*. Or is it formed from Fr. *tanière*, as a primitive word?

Tanaceto It., Sp. *athanasia*, Fr. *tanaisie*, E. *tansy*; from *athanasia* immortal.

Tanaglia It., Pr. *tenalha*, Fr. *tenaille* (O. Fr. *estenielle*) pincers, tongs; from *tenaculum*, pl. *tenacula* (Terentianus Maurus). The Sp. word is *tenaza* from *tenax*, pl. *tenacia*.

Tancar — *stancare.*

Tancer — *tencer.*

Tanche Fr., E. *tench*; L. It. *tinca.*

Tandis Fr. particle; from *tantos dies*, or from *tamdiu* cf. Pr. *tandius*, v. *quandius*.

Tanfo It. from O. H. G. *tamf*, G. *dampf*, cf. Champ. *tanfer* to pant = O. H. G. *tamfjan* to be stifled.

Tanghero — *tangoner.*

Tangoner Fr. to drive on, press; the L. L. *tanganare* to stick to, sbst. *tanganum*, cf. W. *tengyn* sticky, tenacious. Connected with it is the O. Fr. adj. *tangre* obstinate, = M. H. G. *zanger* sharp, obstinate, M. Du. *tangher* sharp, whence It. *tanghero*, Com. *tangan* gross, rude.

Tanière Fr. den, O. Fr. *taisniere*, *tesniere*; prob. contracted from *taissonnière*, and so orig. = badger's hole.

Tanque — *stancare.*

Tante Fr., O. Fr. *ante* (acc. *antain*), E. *aunt*, Pr. *amda*, L. *amita*, Lomb. *ameta*, Crem. *medda*, Rh. *onda*. The *t* is either merely euphonic as in *a-t-il*, *voilà-t-il*, *cafetier*, or is for *ta*, cf. in Wall. *c'est 's monfré* (*mon frère*) it is his brother, *s' matante* his aunt.

Taon — *tafano.*

Tape Fr. a tap, *tappu* Sic. a bung, hence Fr. *tapon*, *tampon*, E. *tompion* a stopple; Sp. *tapa*, Pg. *tampa* a lid; vb. Fr. *taper*, Sp. Pg. *tapar*, Flor. *tappare*, Com. *tapà*, Pr. *tampir* to stop up, cover; from Du. E. *tap*. We have another form in the It. *zaffo*, vb. *zaffare*, from O. H. G. *zapfo*, *zampillo* a jet of water. The Sp. *zampar* to hide is another form of *tapar* to cover.

Tape Fr. a tap (blow), vb. *taper*, *tapoter*; from L. G. *tappe* foot,

E. *tap.* A H. G. form of the same word is It. *zampa, ciampa* (cf. *zufolare, ciufolare*), foot, *zampare* to kick, *ciampare, inciampare* to stumble.

Tapia Sp., Pg. *taipa,* Sard. m. *tapia* a mud-wall, cf. Lomb. *tabia* a poor hut. Palafox's answer, when summoned to surrender Saragossa, was: *Guerra hasta la ultima tapia.* Prob. of Eastern origin, Turk. Ar. *'tābiah* rampart, bastion.

Tapino — *tapir.*

Tapir Fr. *(se tapir)* to squat, crouch, O. Fr. *s'atapir* to hide oneself, O. Fr. *tapin,* Pr. *tapi* hidden, disguised, *a tapi,* O. Fr. *en tapin* in disguise, espec. of pilgrims, hence O. Fr. *tapin* a pilgrim, *tapiner* to hide disguise, Fr. *en tapinois* by stealth, secretly, O. Fr. *en tapinage,* L. L. *tapinatio.* From a G. root widely found in Rom. (v. *tape* 1) *zapf* = a peg, wedge &c., Fr. *tapon* = bundle, Swed. *tapp; tapir* = to form into a bundle, huddle together, cf. Fr. *cacher.* Ducange derives from *talpa,* the influence of which is certainly seen in Champ. *taupin* secret. It. *tapino* poor, is prob. from ταπεινός; *talpino taupino* owe their forms to *talpa.*

Tapis tapiz — *tappeto.*

Tappeto It., Sp. Pg. *tapete tapiz,* Pr. *tapit,* Fr. *tapis* carpet; partly from *tapetum,* partly from *tapes tapetis.*

Taquin — *taccagno.*

Tara It. Sp. Pg. Pr., Fr. F. *tare;* from Ar. *'tir'h* or *'turra'h* thrown away, set aside.

Taradore — *taraire.*

Taragona — *targone.*

Taraire Fr. (m.), Fr. *tarière,* Sp. *taladro,* Pg. *trado,* Rh. *terader* auger, gimlet. From L. L. *taratrum* = τέρετρον. In It. *taradore* a vine-worm, the same word is seen with the suffix *tor,* though no verb *tarar* exists, cf. also Fr. *tar-aud* a borer, which presupposes such a verb. The word is also found in Celtic, W. *taradr,* Bret. *tarar, talar tarer terer* borer, Gael. *tora toradh,* cf. τόρος graver. From L. *terebellum* come It. *trivello,* Pr. *taravel,* Dauph. *taravella,* Pic. *térelle,* Pg. *travoella* borer, Sp. *teruvela* moth. For Sp. *taladro* for *taradro,* cf. L. *telebra* for *terebra* (v. App. ad Probum). To the same family belong Sp. *taraza,* Pg. *traça* moth, vb. *tarazar, traçar* to bite; perhaps = *teredo* with a change of suffix.

Tarántola tarantella It., whence Sp. *tarantula,* Fr. *tarentelle,* a *tarantula* (spider), so called because chiefly found in the neighbourhood of *Tarentum* (It. *Taranto*).

Taraud tarasa — *taraire.*

Tarason — *torso.*

Tarde Sp. Pg. (f.), Cat. *tarde tarda* evening, afternoon (from midday to night); from adv. *tarde* long, so late, cf. βραδύς long, slow, N. Gk. βράδυ evening.

Targa It., Sp. *tarja*, Pg. Pr. *tarja*, Fr. E. *targe*, Sp. also *darga adarga*, O. Cat. *darga*; vb. Pr. *se targar*, Fr. *se targuer* (to pride oneself, boast). From O. H. G. *zarga* defence, shield, whence A. S. *targe*, O. N. *targa* shield; the G. meaning "border, edge, brim" (cf. G. *zarge*) is still found in Sp. *atarjea* edge of a canal or sluice. The Sp. *adarga adaraga duraga* may be referred to the Ar. *addaraqah* leathern shield.

Targer O. Fr. to loiter, tarry, Pic. *atarger terger*. From *tardare* through a freq. form *tardicare*, as *juger* from *judicare*, cf. from *clinare clinicare*, from *pendere pendicare*. Rh. has with diff. suffix *tardinar*, and *tardivar*. O. Fr. *targer* is to Fr. *tarder* as O. Fr. *enferger* to *enferrer*.

Targone It., Sp. *taragona*, Fr. *targon*, E. *tarragon*, Wall. *dragronn*, Ar. *'tarkhùn;* from *draco*, in the sense of *dracunculus*, cf. Sp. *taragontéa* from *dragontea*. Hence also Pg. *estragão*, Fr. *estragon*.

Targuer — *targa.*

Tarida It. Sp. Pr. Cat. a ship, transport. Ar. *'taridah* a transport.

Tarier O. Fr. to vex, plague; from L. G. *targen*, Du. *tergen*, M. H. G. *zergen*, O. H. G. *zerjan*.

Tarière — *taraire.*

Tariffa It., Sp. Pg. *tarifa*, Fr. *tarif* (m.), *tariff;* from Ar. *ta'rif* publication ('*arafa* to know).

Tarima Sp. Pg. (also *tarimba*) trestle, bedstead, bench; from Ar. *'tarimah* bedstead.

Tarin Fr. siskin, Paris. *térin;* perhaps from Pic. *tère* = *tendre* (cf. *terons* = *tiendrons*), so prop. = the pretty, tender bird. So O. N. *lita* = (1) pretty (2) *tit.*

Tarir Fr. to dry, dry up; from O. H. G. *tharrjan*, *darrjan.*

Tarlo — *tarma.*

Tarma It. Sp., Rh. *tarna* moth, wood-tick; from *tarmes* (m.), with a change of declension L. L. *tarmus*, *tarnus*. It. *tarlo* is either a corruption of *tarmo*, or from a dim. *tarmulus.*

Tarracena — *arsenale.*

Tartagliare It., Ven. *tartagiare*, Rh. *tartagliar*, Sp. *tartajear*, Pg. *tartarcar* to stutter, Pr. *tartalhar;* Sp. *tartalear* a reel, be perplexed; adj. Sp. *tato*, Pg. *tátaro*, Sp. Pg. *tarta-mudo* stammerer; an onomatop., Du. *tateren* to stammer. Ar. has *tartara* titubare.

Tartana It. Sp. Pg., Fr. *tartane*, E. *tartan* (naut.) a boat with one mast; a derivative of *tarida*, q. v.

Tartaruga It. Pg., Sp. *tortuga*, Pr. *tortuga tartuga*, Fr. *tortue* a tortoise, L. L. *tortuca tartuca;* so called from its crooked feet *(tortus)*, cf. E. *tortoise* = Pr. *tortesa* crooked. Another name of the tortoise in It. is *botta scudaja* = G. *schildkröte*.

Tartufo — *truffe.*

Tas Sp. Fr., Pr. *tatz* a heap, vb. *tasser;* from A. S. *tass*, E. *tass* a heap of corn, which is the same word as Gael. *dais*, W.*dds*, E. *dais.*

Tasajo Sp., Pg. *tassalho* a piece of smoked flesh, hung-beef; from *taxèa* fat (Isidorus from Afranius)? or from *tessella?*

Tasca It. Pr., Fr. Provin. *tache, tasque, tasse*, Wall. *tah*, Wal. *tasce*, O. H. G. *tasca*, G. *tasche* purse. Perhaps = O. H. G. *zesche* a train, vb. *zaschen zeschen* to trail, drag = O. H. G. *zascòn*, so the purse would be that which trails or hangs from the neck or girdle. This is better than Grimm's der. from L. L. *taxaca texaca* a theft, so = receptacle of stolen goods, cf. the converse process in *sacco*, though in both cases the origin would be eventually the same, O. H. G. *zascòn* = to rob.

Tascar Sp. Pg. to dress or heckle hemp &c.; from O. H. G. *zascòn* to tear, Bav. *zaschen*, v. *tasca.*

Tasse — *tazza.*

Tassello It., Fr. *tasseau* a peg, clasp, bracket; O.Fr. *tassiel* also = a knob, knot, clasp (E. *tassel*); from *taxillus* a peg.

Tasso It., Pr. *tais taisò*, Fr. *taisson*, Sp. *texon* and with suffix *ug tasugo*, Pg. *teixugo*, L.L. *taxus, taxo* a badger; a word widely spread in Rom. (Wal. only has *ésure* = L. *esor* eater, E. has *brock, gray, badger*, Dan. *brok, gräfling*, Swed. *gräfsvin*); from O. H. G. *dahs*, O. L. G. *das*, G. *dachs*, where the *d* = *th*, cf. *tedesco* from *diutisc*, Pr. *ties*. The L. has *meles*, which appears in Neap. *mologna*, Fr. also *blaireau*, q. v.

Tastare It., O.Sp. Pr. *tastar*, Fr. *tâter* to feel, E. *taste*, G. *tasten*. A frequentative from *taxare*: *taxare pressius crebriusque est quam tangere* Gellius. Hence It. sbst. *tasto* handle of a lute, Sp. Pg. *traste*, Cat. *trast*, Andal. *tast.*

Tasugo — *tasso.*

Tâter — *tastare.*

Tato — *taita.*

Tato — *tartagliare.*

Táttera It. trumpery; cf. E. *tatters*, L. G. *tattern*, O. H. G. *zata* shaggy stuff.

Taudir O. Fr. to cover, Fr. *taudis* a hovel, Pic. *taudion;* prob. from a G. source, O. N. *tialld*, M. Du. *telde*, G. *zelt* tent, vb. O. N. *tiallda* to pitch tents.

Taüt — *ataud.*

Taveler Fr. to spot, speckle; from *table*, O. Fr. *tavele* a chess-board.

Tayon — *taita.*

Tazza It., Sp. Pg. *taza*, Pr. *tassa*, Fr. *tasse* a cup, Wal. *tas*, Serv. *tàs;* from Ar. *'tassah* a bason (from Pers. *tast* or *tasht*). Ar. *s* often = Rom. *z*, cf. Pg. *Zoleimão* from *Sulaimàn*.

Tè It., Sp. *té*, Fr. *thé*, E. *tea;* from the Chinese. Neap. *cha*, It. *ciù*.

Té até Pg., O. Pg. *atem* preposition; from *tenus ad-tenus*, O. Sp. *atánes*. The synonymous O. Sp. O. Pg. *fata ata* are from the Ar. *'hattd*.

Tea Sp. Pg. torch, *atear* to light; from *teda*.

Tecca — *taeeo*.

Tecchire It., *attecchire* to thrive, grow; from Goth. *theihan*, O. S. *thihan* = O. H. G. *dihan*, G. *gedeihen*. The Fr. is *tehir* (cf. *gecehire, gehir*) = (1) grow (2) make to grow. Cf. Piedm. *tec* thick, from O. H. G. *thik*, G. *diek*, E. *thiek*.

Techir — *taeco*.

Tecla Sp. Pg. Cat. Sard. key of a pianoforte &c.; from *tegula*. The late origin of the word is shown by its incorrect form (Sp. should be *teja*, Pg. *telha*).

Tegola tegolo It., Wal. *tegle*, Sp. *teja tejo*, Pg. *telha tijolo*, Pr. *teule* (m.), Fr. *tuile* (f.), whence *tuilier, tuilerie*, E. *tile;* It. *tegghia, teglia* lid; all from *tegula*, whence also Pg. *tigella* dish.

Tehir — *tecehire*.

Teiga teigula Pg. rush basket; from *theca*, or from *teges* (f.) matting?

Teigne — *tigna*.

Teiller Fr. to peel (hemp); from *tiliæ* (pl.) bast of the linden tree, O. Fr. *tille*, Rou. *tile;* It. *tiglio* the bark of hemp.

Teindre Fr. to dye, tinge; from *tingere*, It. *tignere*, Sp. *teñir*.

Teja telha — *tegola*.

Teler Fr. in *atteler* to harness, *dételer* to unyoke. Some have suspected a connection with L. *protelum, protelare*, which verb is not found in an uncompounded form (cf. s. *entamer*), but an O. Fr. *esteler* for *ateler* occurs, which points to the true etymon, the G. *stellen* to put, cf. Fr. *mettre*, Sp. *poner*, E. *put* used in same sense. *Atteler* and *dételer* are formed analogously to *attacher détacher*.

Tema Sp. obstinacy, prop. in defending a *theme, tematico* obstinate, Pg. *tema* theme, *teima* obstinacy; cf. It. *prova*.

Temblar — *tremolare*.

Témolo It. a grayling, Sp. *timalo;* from *thymlnus*, its flesh being supposed to smell like thyme.

Tempia It., Pr. *tempia*, Fr. *tempe* for O. Fr. *temple*, Wal. *temple*, E. *temple;* from pl. *tempora*, with common Rom. change of *r* into *l*. Sard. *trempa* = cheek. The Sp. is *sien* (q. v.), Pg. *fonte* (i. e. of pulsation), Cat. *pols*, Ven. *sono*, Sic. *sonnu* (somnus), cf. G. *schlaf* (prop. sleep), Parm. *dormidor*, Sard. *chizu* (= ciglio), Fr. *tin* (q. v.).

Tenaille — *tanaglia*.

Tencer O. Fr., Pr. *tensar* to strive, quarrel, Fr. *tancer* to scold, abuse, E. *taunt;* a participial verb from *tenere tentus*, so from a form *tentiare*, = to maintain assert, a meaning which the O. Fr. vb. also possessed. Hence O. Fr. *tenee*, *tençon*, Pr. *tensa tenson*, It. *tenza*, *tenzone*. For the compound O. Fr. *bestancier*, v. *stentare*.

Tenda It. Pg. Pr., Sp. *tienda*, Fr. *tente*, E. *tent*, Wal. *tinde;* from *tendere*, whence also Sp. *tendon*, Pg. *tendão*, Fr. E. *tendon*, but It. *tendine* as if from a L. *tendo tendinis*.

Tensa — *tencer*.

Tepe Sp. Pg. green sod, Piedm. Com. *tepa* moss, Bresc. *topa*.

Terchio — *terco*.

Terciopelo Sp. Pg. velvet; from *tercio* and *pelo*, so prop. = woven with three threads, *trilix*.

Terco Sp. obstinate, hard. From *tetricus*, It. *terchio?*

Terlis — *traliccio*.

Terne Fr. dull, wan, vb. *ternir* to *tarnish;* from O. H. G. *tarni* covered, *tarnjan* to cover, so darken, dull.

Tertre Fr. Pr. (m.), O. Fr. *teltre*, Wall. *tier* hill, hillock; from τέρθρον an end or point.

Terzuolo It., Sp. *torzuelo*, Pg. *treço*, Pr. *tersol tresol*, Fr. E. *tiercel*, E. *tassel*, Fr. *tiercelet*, E. *tercelet*, a male hawk, M. H. G. *terze*, *terzel;* from *tertius tertiolus*, because the third in the nest was supposed to be a male? For It. *terzeruolo* = a pistol, cf. *falconetto, moschetto, sagro*.

Teschio — *testa*.

Tesoira Piedm., O. Fr. *tezoire*, Pg. *tesoura*, Sp. *ti:era*, Pr. *tosoira* shears, scissors. Tho Pr. is the nearest the original, L. *tonsoria (ferramenta)* Palladius.

Tesserandolo — *tisserand*.

Tesson — *testa*.

Testa It. Sp. Pg. Pr., Fr. *tête* head; from L. *testa* a pot, cf. It. *coccia*, Sard. *conca*, G. *kopf* = in O. H. G. a cup, cf. R. Gr. 1, 54. The dim. *testula* gives It. *teschio* skull, as *fistula fischiare*. From *testum* come It. Sp. Pg. *testo*, Fr. *têt* potsherd = Fr. *tesson* for *teston*. Hence also It. *testiera*, Sp. *testera*, Fr. *tétière*, E. *tester*.

Testeso testè adv. for L. *nuper*. From *ante istum ipsum*, *antestesso*, cf. *fante* for *infante*, *bilico* for *ombilico*. As the It. had *giù* and *ginso*, *sù* and *suso*, in like manner was formed *testè* by the side of *testeso* (for *testesso*).

Testigo Sp. witness; from a form *testificus*, as *testiguar* from *testificare*, v. *santiguar*.

Tetta sitta seasolo oissa It., Wal. Alb. *tzitze*, Sp. Pr. *teta*, Fr. *tette*, *téton* teat; from the G.: A. S. *tite*, E. *teat*, G. *zitze*, cf. W. *titten*, Gk. τίτθη, with medial Cat. *dida* nurse, Sard. *dida ddedda* teat, W. *didi*, B. *dithia*, O. H. G. *deddi*.

Texon — *tasso.*

Tes Sp. (f.) smooth surface, bloom of the skin, Pg. *tez tes tex* outer fine skin or rind, vb. Sp. *atezar.* From *tersus* smooth, vb. *tersare.*

Theriaca theriaga Pg., *teriaca* Pr. It. Sp., Pr. It. Sp. *triaca*, Pg. *triaga* an antidote, confection; orig. antidote against the bite of poisonous animals, L. *theriaca* (Pliny, H. N.), Gk. θηριακή (sc. ἀντίδοτος Alex. Trall. θ. φάρμακα Galen), Ar. *tirydq.* Hence dim. L. L. *triaculum*, It. *triacla*, O. E. *triacle*, E. *treacle.* From the orig. meaning we get that of "confection", "electuary", and thence the E. *treacle* (It. *melassa*, Fr. *mélasse*, Sp. *melote*), which, being much used in electuaries, resembled them in appearance and consistence.

Ticchio It. freak, whim. From O. H. G. *ziki* kid, as *capriccio* from *capra?*

Tiède Fr. tepid; from *tepidus*, Pr. *tebe*, f. *tebeza*, Cat. *tebi*, Sp. *tibio.*

Tien — *mien.*

Tieroelet — *terzuolo.*

Tiere O. Fr., Pr. *tieira tieiro* row, troop; from O. H. G. *ziari* ornament, G. *zier*, A. S. E. *tier*; It. *tiera*, Brese. *tera.* The Wall. *tir* race (cf. *razza*) = *tière* as *pir* = *pierre.*

Tierno Sp., Pg. *terno* tender; from *tener*, Fr. *tendre.*

Tieso Sp., Pg. *teso* firm, hard; from *tensus*, It. *teso.*

Tifer O. Fr., Fr. *attifer*, Piedm. *tiflé*, O. E. *tife*, to deck, bedizen. From Du. *tippen* to cut the points of the hair, H. G. *zipfen;* cf. Com. *zifà via* to cut short off. Champ. *cifer chiffer* = *tifer.*

Tige Fr. f. stalk; from *tibia*, It. Sp. *tibia*, Wal. *tzeave* (Serv. *tzev*).

Tigella tijolo — *tegola.*

Tigna It., Sp. *tiña*, Pr. *teina*, Fr. *teigne* moth, scurf; from *tinea*, later *tinea*, v. R. Gr. 1, 145.

Tilde Sp., Pg. *til* m. a small line, dash or dot over a letter, Cat. *tilla;* from *titulus*, cf. *cabildo* from *capitulum*, and cf. Wal. *title* circumflex, Occ. *titule* dot over an *i.*

Tillac Fr. deck, whence Sp. *tillá*, Pg. *tilha;* from O. N. *thilia*, Sw. *tilja*, A. S. *thille*, O. H. G. *dili* floor = G. *diele*, E. *deal* a plank, cf. O. H. G. *thil* iina pars navis. The suffix *ac* may have been borrowed from L. L. *astracum*, G. *estrich* floor. But v. Grimm, s. v. *diele.*

Timalo — *temolo.*

Timbal timballo — *ataballo.*

Timbre O. Fr. a sort of kettle-drum; from *tympanum*, the *br* being borrowed perhaps from *cymbalum*. Fr. *timbre* = a clock-bell, a bell without a clapper, which, like a kettledrum, was struck from without; also = (1) a helm, from the resemblance in shape, Du. *timber*, Sp. *timbre*, (2) a coat-of-arms (3) a postage label (impressed with a figure or coat-of-arms).

Tin O. Fr., Pr. *tin ten* temple of the head. The Lim. *tim* is nearest the orig. L. *tempus*, L. L. *timpus*, *p* being dropped as in *tam* from *lampas*.

Tino Sp. Pg. skill, tact, also *atino*, vb. *atinar* to hit the mark. Perhaps from the prep. *tenus ad-tenus* (v. *te*), cf. O. H. G. *zil* = A. S. *til* = G. *ziel* a mark which coincides with the prep. *til*. From vb. *atinar* would come *atino*, whence *tino*.

Tio — *zio*.

Tique — *zecca*.

Tirare It., Sp. Pg. Pr. *tirar*, Fr. *tirer* to draw, abst. It. Sp. Pr. *tira*, Fr. *tire* pull, stretch; from Goth. *tairan*, O. H. G. *zeran*, E. *tear*. The Pr. vb. = also to be vexed, displeased, cf. It. *tiro* quarrel, O. Fr. *tire* trouble. Hence Pr. *tirassar*, O. Fr. *tiracer, tirasser*, Sp. *estirazar* to drag, to stretch. Hence also O. Fr. *attirer* whence E. *attire*, which it would be easier to refer to *tiere* row *(tier)*, were it not for the Pr. *atirar* which seems divergent from *aticirar*. Sbst. *attirail* = gear, apparatus, train, It. *attiraglio* are from *tirare*.

Tisana It. Sp., Fr. *tisane* ptisan (medical drink); from *ptisăna*, πτισάνη.

Tisnar tison — *tizzo*.

Tisserand Fr. weaver, whence It. *tesserandolo*; from *textor* with suffix *and* = O. H. G. *ing, inc*, cf. Fr. name *Teisser-enc*. O. Fr. has *tissier*.

Tixera — *tesoira*.

Tizzo It., Sp. *tizo*, also It. *tizzone*, Sp. Pr. *tizon*, Pg. *tição*, Fr. *tison* firebrand; from *titio*. Hence Sp. vb. *tiznar* to smut, blacken with soot &c., sbst. *tizne* soot; It. *attizzare*, Sp. *atizar*, Pr. *atizar atuzar*, Fr. *attiser* to stir, excite (E. *en-tice*), Wal. *atzitza*. It. *stizzo* brand, *stizza* anger, *stizzare stizzire* to excite, Rh. *stizzar* to extinguish.

Toalla — *tovaglia*.

Toba Sp. thistle-stalk; from *tupa* pipe, Pr. *touve*, cf. Fr. *tige* (1) pipe (2) stalk.

Toba — *tufa*.

Tobillo Sp. ankle; from *tuberculum* a bunch or swelling, or better immediately from *tuber*, for *tuberculum* would give *tobejo*.

Tocca It., Sp. *toca*, Pg. *touca*, Fr. *toque* cap, bonnet; from W. *toc*, vb. *tocio, tucio* to cut off, cf. G. *mütze* a cap, from *mutzen* to curtail, v. *almussa*. Hence also It. *tocco*, Rh. *tocc* a slice (of bread &c.), Sp. *tocon* a stump.

Toccare It., Sp. Pg. Pr. *tocar*, Fr. *toucher*, *toquer*, E. *touch*; from O. H. G. *zuchôn*, G. *zucken* to move, stir, draw, which meaning is found in the O. Fr. *se toucher de quelque chose* to disengage oneself from, escape from, and in Fr. *toucher de l'argent*, *ses appointements etc.* to receive money, one's salary etc., cf. L. *stringere* (1) to draw (2) to touch, *attingere* (1) touch (2) take, Goth. *têkan* touch, E. *take*. Wal. *tocá* = knock (at a door), cf. It. *toccare il liuto*, Fr. *toucher du piano*.

Tocha — *torciare*.

Tocho Sp. clownish, rude; cf. It. *tozzo* thick and short.

Tocino Sp. bacon, pickled pork. From *lucetum* or *tomacina?*

Tocon — *tocca*.

Tocsin Fr. E.; from O. Fr. *toquer* = *toucher* and *sein* or *seint* a bell, v. *segno*, = a Pr. *toca-senh*, Lim. *toco-sen*.

Todavia — *via*.

Toilette Fr. dressing-table-cover, dressing-table; from *toile*, L. *tela*.

Toise f. Fr. a measure; prop. the length of the outstretched arm, from *tendere tensus*. It. *tesa* stretching, cf. G. *klafter* fathom from *klaffen* to gape. Vb. O. Fr. *teser*, *toiser* to measure.

Toison — *tosone*.

Toivre O. Fr. cow, beast; from A. S. *tiber*, O. H. G. *zepar* a beast for sacrifice, whence G. *unge-ziefer* (an animal not fit for sacrifice) vermin, cf. Pg. *zevro zevra* an ox, cow, Sp. &c. *zebra*. So O. Fr. *Toivre* from L. *Tiber*.

Toldo tolda Sp. Pg. covering, awning, vb. *toldar* to cover with an awning. From L. *tholus* a dome, canopy, with Sp. *d* inserted.

Tôle Fr. (f.) iron-plate; from *tabula*, Prov. Fr. *taule*, cf. Pied. Com. *tola*, Mil. *tolla*, and cf. It. *fola* from *fabula*.

Tolo Pg. stupid, augm. *toleirão*. Not from G. *toll*, for H. G. *t* = L. G. *d* (E. *dull*) does not give a *t* in Sp., but perhaps shortened from Pg. *tolhido*, O. Pg. *tolido* maimed, numbed (v. *tullir*), cf. *manso* for *mansueto*.

Tomajo It. upper leather; N. Gk. τομάρι, Russ. *towar* leather.

Tomar Sp. Pg. to take, also to bear, which only in Cat. Of Goth. origin, cf. O.S. *tômian* to free, hence release, take away from, cf. Sp. *quito* free, *quitar* to take away.

Tomare — *tombolare*.

Tomate Sp. Pg., *tomatec*, *tomaco* Cat., Fr. *tomate*, E. *tomato* love-apple; from Mexican *tomatl*.

Tomba It. Pr., Sp. Pg. *tumba*, Fr. *tombe*, E. *tomb*; from L. *tumba* (Prudentius) = τύμβος with change of gender.

Tombacco It., Sp. *tumbaga*, Fr. E. *tombac* a metal, red brass, pinchbeck; from the Malay *tambága* copper, Pg. *tambaca*.

Tomber tombereau — *tombolare*.

Tombolare It., Sp. Pr. *tumbar*, Pg. Pr. *tombar*, O. Fr. *tumber tomber*, Fr. *tomber* to fall, *tumble*. It is the O. N. *tumba* to fall forwards, al. from *tumba* a heap, cf. Sp. *tropellar* from *tropel* a heap. Another form is found in It. *tomare*, Lorr. *teumei*, Champ. O. Fr. *tumer*, cf. O. H. G. *tůmôn*, G. *taumeln*, M. Du. *tumen*. From *tomber* comes Fr. *tombereau*, E. *tumbrel*, Burg. *tumereau*, a cart the body of which can be thrown up.

Tomiza Sp., Pg. *tamiça* a rope made of rushes; from *tomix*.

Tomo Sp. Pg. bulk, weight; from *tomus* = *volumen*.

Tomplina — *tonfano*.

Tona Pr., Fr. *tonne*, Wal. *toane*; Sp. *tonel*, Fr. *tonneau* cask, tun, also Fr. *tonnelle* arbour, tunnel-net, E. *tunnel* (because made with hoops like a cask). From O.H.G. O. N. *tunna*, G. *tonne*, E. *tun ton*, v. Grimm, 3, 457.

Tona Pg. thin rind or husk of trees or fruits. Prob. an indigenous word, cf. W. *tonn* (m.) husk, shell.

Tondino — *tondo*.

Tondo It. round, abst. disk, *tondino* hoop, plate (also in Sp.); from *rotundus*, by aphæresis. Hence *bis-tondo* roundish, where *bis* expresses the imperfection of the quality, Piedm. *bis-riond*.

Tondre O. Fr. Norm. (m.) tinder; from O.N. *tundr*, A. S. *tynder*, E. *tinder*, G. *zunder*. Hence also Pr. *tondres* rags.

Tónfano It. pool, whirlpool, = O. H. G. *tumphilo* gurges, M. H. G. *tümpfel*, G. *dümpfel*; N. Pr. *toumple*, Pr. *tomplina*.

Tonne — *tona*.

Tonnerre Fr. (m.), Pr. *tonedre*, E. *thunder*; from *tonitrus*, O. Sp. *tonidro*.

Tonte Fr. sheep-shearing; from *tondere*, cf. *pente*.

Tontine Fr. E. a species of life annuity, introduced into France, in 1653, by *Lorenzo Tonti* a Neapolitan.

Tonto Sp. Pg. foolish, stupid; from *attonitus* whence also Sp. *atontar* to stupify.

Topar tope — *toppo*.

Topin tupin Fr., Pr. *topi* a pot; from G. *topf*, Du. *dop*.

Topo It. rat, mouse; = Sp. *topo*, Cat. *taup* mole, from *talpa* (*talpus*).

Toppo It. block, Sp. *tope* top, end, O. Fr. *top* tuft; Fr. *toupet* tuft, *toupie*, Norm. *toupin* top, humming-top (pointed block, E. *top*); vb. Sp. *topar* to strike against, meet, It. *intoppare*. The word is widely spread: E. *top*, O. Fris. *top*, O. N. *toppr* tuft, O.H.G. *zopf*, Gael. W. *top* &c. To the same root belong Sp. *tupir*, Pg. *a-tupir*, *en-tupir* to press close, Piedm. *topon*, O. Fr. *toupon* stopple, cf. W. *top*, Du. *top* a heap, G. *stopfen* (E. *stop*).

Toque — *tocca*.

Toquer — *toccare.*

Torba It., Sp. *turba*, Fr. *tourbe* turf; from O. H. G. *zurf*, A. S. E. *turf*, O. N. *torf.*

Torca torcas, torche torcher — *torciare.*

Torchio torcolo It., Pr. *troll*, O. Fr. *treuil* press, Fr. windlass; from *torculum*, whence also Sp. *estrujar* = *extorculare extorclare.*

Torciare It. to twist, fasten, Sp. *atrozar* to fasten, truss (naut.), O. Fr. *torser* to pack up, Fr. *trousser*, Pr. *trossar*, whence O. Sp. *trossar*, Sp. *troxar* (cf. *puxar* = *pousser*), Pg. *trouxar*, E. *truss*; subst. Lomb. *torza torsa* truss of hay or straw, = L. L. *trossa*, Sp. *troza*, *torzal* a rope, Fr. *trousse*, Pr. *trossa*, Sp. *troxa*, Pg. *troxa*, E. *truss*; Pr. *trossel*, Fr. *trousseau*, O.Fr. *torseau*, whence It. *torsello*. From a vb. *tortiare (tortus)*; the G. *tross* is from *trossa*, as Du. *torsen* from *torser*. Hence also It. *torcia*, Ver. Ven. *torzo* torch (*tortum* twisted like a rope), O. It. *torticcio*, O. Fr. *tortis*, Pg. *torcida*. The Pr. *torcha*, Fr. *torche*, E. *torch*, O. Sp. *entorcha*, Sp. *antorcha*, Pg. *tocha*, vb. Fr. *torcher* to wipe (*torche* also = a wisp of straw), would come better from an old form *torca* (Pr. *torcar* = *torcher*), Sp. *ch* for *z*, cf. *panza pancho*. Sp. *torca* wisp, *tuerca* screw, *torcaz* ring-dove, are immediately from *torquere.*

Tordre Fr. to twist; from *torquere*, It. *torcere*, Pr. *torser*, so for *torc're torsdre*. Hence Fr. *bestordre* to distort, *bestors* crooked.

Toria Sp. layer, shoot. From *tório* (Columella) a sprout?

Toriga — *toura.*

Tormo Sp. a high insulated rock; for *torno*, from O. S. O. N. *turn (turris)*, Pr. *torn*, with a change of spelling, to distinguish it from *torno* a turn.

Torno It. Sp. Pg., Pr. *torn*, Fr. *tour* (m.), E. *turn*, whence It. *in-torno*, Pr. *entorn*, Fr. *au-tour*, *à l'entour* &c.; from *tornus* (τόρνος). Hence vb. It. *tornare*, Sp. Pg. Pr. *tornar*, Fr. *tourner* to turn, Wal. *turnă* to pour out (cf. Fr. *verser* = *versari*); from *tornare* (τορνεύειν) to turn in a lathe. The Rom. sense was probably known to the spoken Latin, as it appears in very early L. L. and in Wal., cf. also *retornare* = to return in Theophylact Simocatta (c. 600). The meaning of the L. word is expressed in It. by *torniare*, *tornire*. Hence It. Sp. Pg. *tornéo*, Pr. *tournei*, Fr. *tournoi*, E. *tourney*; vb. *torneare*, *tornear*, *torneiar*, *tournoyer*. O. Fr. *atorner* to prepare, adorn, subst. *atorn* "præparatio", Fr. *atour* adornment; E. *attorney.*

Toroson Sp., O. Sp. *torzon* gripes; from *torsio*, It. *torsione.*

Torrar Sp. Pg. Cat., Sp. also *turrar esturar* to toast; from *torrere*, *extorrere*, with a rare change of conjugation. The Rh. *torrer* is more correct.

Torsello — *torciare.*

Torso It., Pied. *trouss*, Sp. Pg. *trozo*, Pr. O. Fr. *tros* stump, trunk, piece, Pr. *tors* "pars"; vb. Sp. *trosar, destrosar* to break to pieces (unless from *destructus*). From *thyrsus* (θύρσος) sprout, O. H. G. *turso, torso*, G. *dorsch*, whence the meaning stalk, core, heart, Pr. *tros de caul*, Fr. *trou de chou*, O. Fr. *trox de pomme*, then, generally, anything broken off or severed, piece, fragment, in Sp. the only meaning. Besides the O. Fr. *tros* we find the provincial forms *trons, tronce, tronçon*, Pr. *tronsó*, vb. Sp. *tronzar*, O. Fr. *troncener* to shatter, E. *trounce*. Sp. has *tarazon*, Pg. *tração* for *trozon torzon*.

Torta It. Sp., Fr. *tourte*, Wal. *turte*, O. Fr. (corr.) *turte*, E. *tart*; from L. *torta* (twisted).

Torto It. Pg., Sp. *tuerto*, Pr. Fr. *tort*, L. L. *tortum* wrong; from *tortus*·twisted, perverted (cf. *wrong* from *wring*), so opp. to *directum, diritto, droit*. From adj. *tortilis* comes Fr. *entortiller*, Sp. *entortijar* to entangle.

Tortue tortuga — *tartaruga*.

Torvisco Sp., Pg. *trovisco* a plant found in the South of Europe. From L. *turbiscus* Isidorus: *quod de uno cespite ejus multa virgulta surgant quasi turba*.

Torzuelo — *terzuolo*.

Tosco It., Sp. *tósigo*, Pr. *tueissec*, O. Fr. *toxiche*, Wal. *toxice* poison; from *toxicum*. N. Pr. *tossec* also = toad.

Toso It. (prov.), Pr. *tos*, O. Fr. *tosel* boy, f. It. Pr. *tosa*, O. Fr. *tose* girl. From It. *torso* trunk, stem (cf. *garzone*), rather than from *tonsus* or *intonsus* as some derive it. The *r* is elided as in *dosso, giuso, ritroso, rovescio, pesca*.

Tosone It., Sp. *tuson*, Fr. *toison* fleece; from *tonsio* (a shearing) made concrete and masculine, except in Fr. which retains the Latin gender. In Berr., however, it is masculine.

Tosto It. O. Sp. O. Pg., Pr. *tost*, Fr. *tôt* adv. for statim, illico, It. also adj., Fr. also in *aussitôt, bientôt, plutôt, tantôt*. Usu. derived from *tostus*, cf. It. *caldo caldo*, O. Fr. *chalt pas*, G. *fusswarms*, E. *hot haste*; but Neap. Ven. *tosto* = fast, hard (prop. baked?), so Diez prefers to derive it from *tot-cito tot-citus* (cf. *amistà* = *amicitas, destare* = *de-excitare*). *Totus* is used to intensify expressions of haste, e. g. in It. *tutto in un tempo*, Fr. *tout à l'heure*.

Tôt — *tosto*.

Touaille — *tovaglia*.

Toucher — *toccare*.

Touer Fr. to tow, whence Sp. Pg. *atoar*; from E. *tow*. Hence sbst. *toue* a ferry-boat.

Touffe Fr., whence E. *tuff, tuft* (Pic. *touffette*), W. *twf*. A H. G. form for *touppe* = G. *zopf*, O. N. *toppr (top)*, = It. *zuffa*. Wal. Alb. *tufe* bush is perhaps the Gk. τύφη = ἀνθήλη.

Toupet toupie toupon — *toppo*.

Tour - - *torno*.

Toura Pg. a barren cow = L. *taura* (Festus, Varro, Columella). Hence Pr. adj. *tóriga turga* barren (of women). N. Pr. *turgea*, Pied. *turgia*, Norm. *torlière* (from *taurula*) = Pg. *toura*.

Tourbe - - *torba*.

Tourner tournois — *torno*.

Tourte — *torta*.

Toutefois — *via*.

Tovaglia It., Sp. *toalla*. Pg. Pr. *toalha*, Fr. *touaille*, E. *towel*; from O. H. G. *duahilla*, *twahilla*, M. H. G. *twehele*, which is from *duahan thwahan* to wash. Hence also O. Fr. *tooillier* to wash, rub.

Tozo Arag. short, dwarfish, *toza* stump, *tozar* to butt; from *tunsus* pounded.

Tozuelo Sp. nape of the neck, fat part of the neck. For *torzuelo*, from *torus* muscle, swelling.

Tra It. preposition; shortened from *intra* as *fra* from *infra*.

Trabacca — *tref*.

Trabajo — *travaglio*.

Traboccare — *buco*.

Trac Fr., E. *track*, Sp. *traque* a train of powder, Com. *trach* sound as of a blow, Fr. *traquer* to beat a wood, enclose game *(traquer un loup* to track), *détraquer* to remove, *traquet* trap, mill-clapper, Sp. *traquear* to crack, shake = It. *traccheggiare* to toy, Fr. *traquenard* an ambling pace, a dance, a trap, *tracas* bustle, vb. *tracasser*. In all these may be recognised the Du. *treck* stroke or O. H. G. *trach* (vb. M. H. G. *trechen*, pret. *trach*), cf. *détraquer* = Du. *vertrekken* to lead aside, whence G. *vertrackt* distracted.

Traça — *taraire*.

Tração — *torso*.

Tracas — *trac*.

Tracheggiare — *trac*.

Tracciare It., O. Fr. *tracier* to track, Sp. *trazar*, Fr. *tracer* to trace; sbst. It. *traccia* stroke, track, Sp. *traza*, Pr. *trassa*, Fr. E. *trace*. From *tractiare (tractus)*; hence also O. Fr. *trasser*, It. *trassare* (from Pr. *trassar?*).

Tracotanza — *coitare*.

Tradire It., Pg. Pr. Fr. *trahir* to be-tray; from *tradere*, cf. παραδιδόναι, Goth. *lêvjan*; sbst. It. *traditore*, Sp. Pg. Pr. *traidor*, Fr. *truitre*, E. *traitor*, L. *traditor*; Sp. *traicion*, Pg. *traição*, Pr. *trassiò*, Fr. *trahison*, E. *treason* (L. *traditio*, It. *tradizione)*.

Trado — *taraire*.

Tráffico It., Sp. *tráfico*, *tráfago*, Pg. *tráfego*, Pr. *trafeg*, *trafei*, Fr. *trafic*, E. *traffic*; vb. It. *trafficare*, Sp. *traficar*, *trafagar*,

Pg. *trafegueur*, Fr. *trafiquer*, E. to *traffic*. O. Pg. *trasfegar* to pour out, transfuse (v. *traxegar*) also = *trafegar* to traffic, and Cat. *tráfag* traffic, means also transfusion. If the words be identical, there is an unusual change of accent.

Tragar Sp. Pg. to swallow, Sard. *tragure*. From *trahere* (cf. Pr. *traire* to swallow), *trahicare tralgar tragar*, as from *volvere volvicare volcar*.

Trage Sp., Pg. *trajo* garb, dress; from Sp. *traer* to wear, L. *trahere*, L. L. *tragere*, cf. *struggere*.

Tragin — *traino*.

Tralla Sp. a roller; from *traha* a sledge.

Traino It., Sp. *tragin*, Pr. *trahi*, Fr. E. *train* (O. Fr. *traïn*), from *trahere*; vb. It. *trainare*, Pr. *trahinar*, Fr. *trainer*. The suffix *ino* is not added to verbs, so the It. and Sp. forms may have been borrowed from the Pr. Fr. *(trahim traïm)*. Cf. O. Fr. *ga-ïn* = It. *gua-ime*.

Tralce tralcio It.; from *tradux tradúcis* corrupted into *tranicis* (v. Duc. *tranex*), as *perdicis* into *pernice*; thence *trance tralce*, Lomb. *trosa*.

Trâle Fr., O. Fr. *trasle*; from O. H. G. *throscelâ*, A. S. *throsle*, E. *throstle*, O. N. *thröstr*, G. *drossel* (prov. *draschel*). It is called in Mil. *dress*, A. S. *thrisc*, E. *thrush*.

Traliccio It., Sp. *terliz*, Fr. *treillis*, O. Fr. *treslis* = G. *drillich*, E. *drill*; from *trilicium* and *trilix*.

Tramaglio It., Fr. *tramail*, Norm. *tremail* fishing-net (E. *trammel*), L. L. *tremaculum*, *tremaclem* (acc.), cf. Wall. *tramaie* basket-work. From *ter* or *tri* and *macula* (mesh) as *traliccio*, *treillis* from *tri-licium*.

Trambasciare — *ambasciata*.

Trambustare — *busto*.

Tramoggia It., Sic. *trimoja*, Pg. *tremonha*, Pr. *tremueia*, Fr. *trémie* mill-hopper; from *trimodius*, as containing 3 modii. But Diez prefers to derive it from *tremere*, for *trema-moggia*.

Tramontana It. (= North, North-wind, North-star) whence it has passed into Sp. Pr. Fr.; from *transmontanus* so = that which lies beyond the Alps.

Trampa — *trapa*.

Trampolo (usu. in plur.) It. stilts; from G. *trampeln*, E. *trample*, N. *trampa*, this from Goth. *trimpan*. Pr. *trampol* trampling is from the same origin.

Trance — *transito*.

Trancher — *trinciare*.

Tranguiare — *gozzo*.

Transe — *transito*.

Transito It. passage from life to death, decease, L. L. *transitus*, whence Sp. Pg. *trance* (an.), E. *trance*, danger, Fr. (f.) *transe*

fright. From *transitus*, whence also G. *transt*. Vb. O. Sp.
O. Fr. *transir* to depart, die, Fr. *transir* to chill or be chilled
with cold or fear, Sard. *transire* to stun, Sp. *transido* weary,
worn out, Pr. *transitz* semimortuus, in a *trance*.

Trape trapu Fr. thick, short, squat. From O. H. G. *taphar*
tapar gravis, G. *tapfer* valiant (E. *dapper*), cf. *taphari* a lump
and the vb. *tapfern* "maturare" = Fr. *traper* "egregie suc-
crescere". *Trape* is from *tapar* as *tremper* from *temperare*.

Trapiche Sp. Pg. a sugar-mill; from *trapetum*.

Trapo — *drappo*.

Trappa Pr., Fr. *trappe*, Sp. *trampa* trap, It. *trappola*, Rh. *trapla*;
vb. It. *attrappare*, Sp. *atrapar*, *atrampar*, Pr. *atrapar*, Fr.
atrapper to entrap; from O. H. G. *trapo* noose, E. *trap*, L. L.
trappa, cf. M. Du. *trappen* to trap.

Traquear traquet — *trac*.

Traquote — *trinchetto*.

Tras tra It. (in comp., for another *tra* v. s. v.), Sp. Pg. Pr. *tras*,
Fr. *très*, from *trans*. In Fr. it is only used as an adv. e. g.
très grand, *très cher*, It. *trasgrande trucaro*, cf. G. *übergross*,
E. *overgreat*, and cf. the comparative suffix, from the same
root (Sansk. *tri* transgredi), Sansk. -*tara*, Gk. -τερος. Hence
Sp. Pg. Pr. *detras*, L. L. *de trans* (Vulgate), and *atras*.

Trasegar Sp., Pg. *trasfegar*, Cat. *trafagar* to pour from one
vessel into another, to decant, turn upside down, sbst. *tra-
siego*, *trasfego*, *tráfag*. The derivation from *trans-æquare*
would not account for the *f* which is, probably, for *v*, *trans-
fegar* for *transvegar* = *trans-vicare* from *vicis*, so = to change,
turn, pour (cf. *verser*).

Trasfegar — *trasegar*.

Trasgo Sp. Pg. goblin, sprite; from *trasegar* so = one who turns
everything topsy turvy. For similar formations, cf. It. *lecco*
from *leccare*, *allievo*, *élève* from *allevare*, Fr. *juge* from *juger*,
It. *furbo* from *forbire*.

Trassare — *traceiare*.

Trassinare It. to track, to maltreat, *straseinare straseicare* to
trail, drag, sbst. *straseino* and *strascico*; probably from Pr.
traissa noose, *traee*, *trassa* track, *trace*, v. *traceiare*.

Traste — *tastare*.

Trasto Sp. Pg. old furniture; perhaps from *transtrum* a bench,
O. Fr. *traste* a beam.

Trastullo It. diversion, pastime, vb. *trastullare*; from O. H. G.
stulla a moment, hour, leisure-hour, cf. G. *stunde* (1) hour
(2) leisure-hour.

Travaglio It., Sp. *trabajo*, Pg. *trabalho*, Pr. *trabalh*, *trebalh*, Fr.
travail, E. *travail*, *travel* (cf. G. *arbeiten* in Bav. = to travel,
wander), It. *travagliare* &c. Diefenbach derives it from the

Celtic, Gael. *treabh* to plough, cf. G. *arbeiten* = to plough, till, but it may be better deduced from the Rom. vb. *travar* to hinder (*trabs*), the notion of annoyance, pain, labour, being derived from that of hindrance.

Travar Pg., Sp. *trabar* to join, seize, fetter, Pr. *travar*, Fr. *entraver* (sbst. *entraves*) to trammel, impede, Sp. *destrabar*, O. Fr. *destraver* to set free; from *trabs*, Pg. *trave* stocks, fetters.

Travieso Sp., Pg. *travesso* oblique, sbst. *traves* obliquity, bias, *atravesar* to lay athwart, cross; from *transversus*, Fr. *travers* &c.

Travoella — *taraire*.

Trasar — *tracciare*.

Traser — *esparcir*.

Trebbia It., Sp. *trillo*, Pg. *trilho* flail; vb. It. *trebbiare*, *tribbiare* to thresh, Pr. *trilhar*, O. Fr. *tribler* also = to crush, bruise; from *tribula tribulare*, whence compound It. *strebbiare stribbiare* to rub, polish. *Tribulare* was used by the ecclesiastical writers in a figurative sense = to torment, afflict, It. *tribolare*, Pr. *tribolar trebolar treblar* (also to trouble), O. Fr. *triboiller*, sbst. It. *tribolo* &c., Fr. E. *tribulation* &c.

Trebol — *trifoglio*.

Trébucher — *buco*.

Treccare It., Pr. *trichar*, Fr. *tricher*, O. Fr. *trecher* to cheat; sbst. Pr. *tric* trick. From Du. *trek*, E. *trick*, from vb. *trekken* to drag, M. H. G. *trecken* (pres. *triche*). The Fr. *triquer* is also from *trekken*.

Treccia It., Pr. *tressa*, Fr. *tresse*, O. Fr. *trece*, E. *tress*, Sp. *trenza*, Pg. *trança* tress, plait (of hair); vb. *trecciare* &c. to plait. From τρίχα threefold, trifariam, whence *trichea treccia* (as *braccio* from *brachium*); vb. *trecciare* = to plait in three. For the inserted *n* in Sp. Pg. cf. *manzana*, *ponzoña*. It. *trina*, Pr. *trena* (from *trinus*) = *treccia*.

Tref O. Fr., Pr. *trap* hut, tent; from *trabs* beam, pars pro toto, cf. Papias *tenda quæ "rustice" trabis dicitur*. In the sense of the L. word we have O. Fr. *tref*, Pr. *trau*. Hence O. Fr. *atraver* = *loger* (*loge* tent), Pr. *destrapar (destrabar)*, cf. *travar*. It. *trabacca* = *trabs*.

Trefe Sp. lean, thin, consumptive (also = spoilt, adulterated), Pg. *trefo trefego* cunning, crafty, hence Pr. *trefa* faithless, vb. *trefanar*, sbst. *trefart*. It is, perhaps, the Heb. *'teréfá*, which signifies that which has been torn by a wild beast, and, consequently, is unfit for food.

Trefego — *traffico*.

Trèfle — *trifoglio*.

Tréfonds Fr. ground, subsoil, bottom; from *terræ fundus*. The old spelling *tresfonds* is therefore wrong.

Tregenda It. a ghost-chorus, hence the saying "*andare in tregenda con le streghe*"; from *trecenta* = any large number.

Treggéa It., Pr. *dragea*, Fr. *dragée*, O. E. *dragge*, Sp. *dragea gragea*, Pg. *gragea, grangea* sweet-meat; from the Gk. τραγήματα sweet-meats, a word preserved in conventual houses.

Treggia It. noose, loop; from *trahea* pronounced *traja*, with change (rare in It.) of *a* to *e*.

Tregua It. Sp. Pr., Pg. *tregoa*, Fr. *trêve*, O. Fr. *trive*, L. L. *treuga*, E. *truce*. Prop. = surety, from O. H. G. *triwa, triuwa* fides, fœdus *(w = gu)*, G. *treue*, Goth. *triggva*, E. *true;* cf. O. Fr. vb. *s'atriver à qqun* fœdus inire cum aliquo.

Treille Fr., Pr. *trelha* vine-arbour, hence *treillis trellis* (cf. *traliccio);* from *trichíla* arbour (Virg. Copa).

Treillis — *treille* and *traliccio*.

Trembler — *tremulare.*

Trémie — *tramoggia.*

Tremolare It., Fr. *trembler*, E. *tremble*, Sp. *temblar*, W. *tremurà;* from *tremulus.*

Tremonha — *tramoggia.*

Trémousser Fr. to stir about actively, flutter; from *transmotiare (transmotus).* The particle denotes excess, as in *tressaillir.*

Tremper Fr., Pr. *trempar* to soak; for *temprer temprar*, from *temperare* to temper. O. Fr. *tremper une harpe* to sound, tune a harp = It. *temperare.*

Trencar — *trinciare.*

Tronza — *treccia.*

Trépano It. Sp., Fr. *trépan*, E. *trepan*, It. also *trápano;* from τρύπανον.

Trepar Sp. Pg. Cat. to climb; prop. to step, from G. *treppe* a step, stairs, M. H. G. *trappe*, Du. *trap*, O. N. *trappa* step, connected in origin with Pr. *trepar* (v. *treper*), cf. Occ. *escalo* steps, *escalà* to climb, L. *gradus*, Fr. *gravir.* Cat. Sp. *trepar* to bore through, *trepan*, is from the Gk. τρέπειν, Festus: *trepit* vertit.

Trepeiller trépigner — *treper.*

Treper triper O. Fr., Pr. *trepar* to hop, spring; Du. *trippen*, G. *trippeln*, E. *trip*, W. *tripio*, Bret. *tripa.* Hence Fr. *trépigner* to stamp, which, however, presupposes a noun *trépin* (v. *cligner*), O. Fr. *trepeiller* to run to and fro, flutter, *trepeil* unrest, Pr. *trepeiar* to sprawl.

Très — *tras.*

Trescare It., Pr. *trescar*, O. Fr. *trescher* to dance, Sp. Pg. *triscar* to caper, stamp, Mil. *trescà* to thresh; from Goth. *thriskan*, O. H. G. *drescan*, G. *dreschen*, E. *thresh.*

Trésor Fr., E. *treasure;* from *thesaurus*, It. Sp. *tesoro*, Pr. *thesaur*, O. Sp. also *tresoro*, Wald. *tresor.* The form with *r* is very

old, for it is found in the A. S. *tresor*, and O. H. G. *treso triso*
borrowed from the Rom. *Tresaur* is for *tensaur* (Plaut. *then-
saurus*, Bret. *tensaour*), as *frestra* for *fnestra fenestra*, *trotter*
from *flutare tolutare*.

Tresse — *treccia*.

Tréteau Fr., O. Fr. *trestel*, E. *trestle*; from Du. *drie-stal* three-
footed seat. For Fr. *t* = II. G. *d*, v. *tasso*.

Treuil — *torchio*.

Treva Pg. (usu. only in pl.) darkness; from *tenebræ*, Sp. *tinie-
blas* &c.

Trève — *tregua*.

Trevo — *trifoglio*.

Triaca triacla &c. — *theriaca*.

Tricare Neap., Lomb. *trigá*, Pr. *trigar* to stop, hinder, E. *trig*;
from *tricari* to make difficulties; sbst. Com. *trigon* loiterer =
L. *trico* shuffler (Lucilius), Fr. *trigaud*; Pr. *trigor* delay.
Hence It. *intricare intrigare*, Sp. *entricar*, *intrincar*, Pr. *entricar*, Fr. *intriguer*, E. *intrigue* = L. *intricare*; Sp. *estricar* = L.
extricare; It. *distrigare* to extricate, Gloss. Isid. *destrigare*
"consummare"; but Pr. *destrigar*, O. Fr. *détrier* = *trigur* to
impede, injure; hence Pr. sbst. *destric* (distinct from *destreit*)
disadvantage (opp. *enans* advantage). W. *trigo* a stay, loiter.

Tricher — *treccare*.

Tricoises Fr. pl. farrier's pincers; Du. *trek-ijzer (drag-iron)*
pincers. Cf. *treccare*.

Tricoter Fr. to knit, *tricot* knitting. A rare instance of the loss
of an initial *s* impure (cf. *palmer* for *épalmer*), *tricoter* being,
probably, from Du. *strik* loop, knot, *strikken* to join, knit,
cf. Fr. *étriquet* a fishing-net. Fr. *trique tricot* a cudgel, vb.
tricoter are, probably, from Du. *strijken* to strike, *strijker*,
striker; O. Fr. *estrique* = strickle, M. H. G. *striche*.

Trier Fr., Pr. Cat. *triar* to pick, cull, whence E. *try*, O. It.
triare; sbst. *trie*, *tria*. From *tritare* a freq. of *terere* to thrash,
Pr. *triar lo grá de la palha* to separate the corn from the straw,
cf. It. *tritare* = to triturate, sift, examine, Norm. *triller*, Rou.
trilier = *tritulare*. Piedm. *triè* has Fr. form and It. meaning.
Cf. *tria via* Pr. = *trita via*.

Trieu Pr. (m.) way, road; from *trivium*, so = O. Fr. *triege (g
from palatal *i*, cf. *neige)*.

Trifoglio It., Wal. *trifoiu*, Pr. *trefueil*, O. Fr. *trefeul*, E. *trefoil*,
with accent thrown back Sp. *trébol*, Pg. *trévo*, Fr. *trèfle*
clover; from *trifolium*, *trifolum* (cf. Sp. *acébo* = *aquifolium*,
Pg. *funcho* = *fœniculum*.)

Trifoire O. Fr. (f.) an artistic chasing or ornament in the shape
of a porch, L. L. *triforium (tri fores)*.

Trigar O. Pg. to impel, hasten (*os cavallos* &c.), sbst. *trigança* haste. Just the opposite of the Pr. *trigar* (v. *tricare*) to stop, hinder. Prob. of Goth. origin; *threihan* to press = A. S. *thringan* (E. *throng*), O. H. G. *dringan*, G. *dringen*.

Triglia It., Sp. *trilla* (Fr. *trigle?*) a surmullet; from τρίγλη.

Trigo Sp. Pg. wheat; from *triticum* with euphonic syncope of the middle syllable.

Trillare It., = G. *trillern* vibrare vocem, τερετίζειν, Sp. Cat. Pg. *trinar*, E. *trill*, Du. *trillen*.

Trillo — *trebbia.*

Trimer Pic. to move or work eagerly, Berr. to be tired out, N. Pr. *trimar* to go quickly. Chevallet recognises in it the Bret. *tremeni* = W. *tramwy* to run to and fro, cf. O. Sp. *trymar*, Bas. *trimatu* to be weary (from the Rom.).

Trinca Sp. Pg. union of three, a trinity; probably a corruption of *trinitas* altered from a reverential feeling, cf. R. Gr. 2, 462. Or is a form *trinicus (trinus)*, framed on the analogy of *unicus (unus)?*

Trincar trinchar — *trinciare.*

Trincare It., Fr. *trinquer* to drink, tipple, O. Fr. also *drinker*, sbst. *drinkerie*; from G. *trinken*, E. *drink*. Another expression borrowed from Teutonic drinkers is Sp. *carauz* (m.) an emptying of the glass, a drinking a bumper, whence Fr. *carousse* (f.), E. *carouse*, from the G. *gar aus* "quite (drained) out" (G. *garaus* = utmost ruin, end), cf. Rabelais: *boire carrous et alluz (= all aus)*. Cf. s. *brindisi*, and Covarruvias, s. v. *lanciscot;* others derive *carouse* from G. *krause* = E. *cruse*, a drinking-vessel. The It. *tedesco* (= German), Neap. *todisco*, is used to signify a toper.

Trinchetto It., Sp. *trinquete*, Cat. *triquet*, Fr. *trinquet*, E. *trinket*, Pg. *traquete* a fore-sail, fore-mast; Sp. *trinquetilla*, Fr. *trinquette* fore-stay sail; from Sp. *trinca (trinitas)*, because triangular, but Sp. *trincas*, It. *trinche* = ropes for lashing (connected with *tricoter?*).

Trinciare It., Sp. Pg. *trinchar*, Cat. *trinxar* to carve, Pr. *trencar* (Cat.), *trenchar* to cut off, *trench*, Pic. *trinquer*, O. Fr. *trenchier*, Fr. *trancher* to cut, decide *(tranchoir = trencher)*, Sic. *trincari* to quarry stone, Sp. *trincar* to chop, Pg. to bite off; sbst. It. *trincio*, Sard. *trincu* cut, Fr. *tranche* (f.) slice; Pr. *trenchet* edge, Sp. *trinchete, tranchete*, Fr. *tranchet*, Cat. *trinxet*, Sard. *trincettu trinchettu* knife; comp. Pr. *detrencar*, Fr. *detrancher*, *retrancher*, E. *retrench &c.* Of uncertain origin, perhaps from *internecare;* whence may come Pr. *entrencar, entrencar lo cim* to break off, destroy ='*culmum internecare*. Others derive from *interimere (interimicare).*

Trinquer — *trincare.*

Tripaille — *trippa.*

Trippa It., Sp. Pg. *tripa*, Fr. E. *tripe*. Of uncertain origin, though found in several languages, Du. *tripe*, W. *tripa* (pl.), Bret. *stripen*, B. *tripa*. Hence Fr. *tripaille* garbage, formed like *entrailles*.

Trique — *tricoter*.

Trissar trisar Pr. to grind, bruise; a participial verb *(tritiare)* from *tritus terere*, cf. *aussar* from *altus*. It. has only *tritare* not *trizzare*, but Sp. *triza* = a mite, particle.

Trivello — *taraire*.

Triza — *trissar*.

Tro Pr. particle for L. *tenus*, in full *entro*; from *intro*; so Com. *tro*, O. Sp. *entro*, v. s. *jusque*.

Trobar — *trovare*.

Trocar Sp. Pg., Fr. *troquer*, E. *truck*; abst. Sp. *trueco*, Pg. *troco*, Fr. *troc*. Either from Gk. τροπικός (L. *tropica* changes) *tropicare tropcar trocar*, or, better, from *vicis*, *traricare traucar trocar*.

Trooir O. Sp. to depart, die; from *traducere*.

Troféo It. Sp. Pg., Fr. *trophée*, E. *trophy*; from *tropæum* (τρόπαιον), with unusual change of the labial tenuis into the aspirate.

Troglio It. stutterer; from τραυλός.

Trogne Fr. f. a queer, ugly face, phiz, Pied. m. *trogno trugno*. Connected with the W. *trwyn* (m.), Corn. *tron* snout, and still more closely with O.N. *triona* f., Dan. *tryne*, cf. M.H.G. *triel* mouth, snout. The Du. *tronie* and L. G. *troonje* may be from the Fr. Perhaps the word is the same as the L. *truo truonis* a sea-bird, a cormorant, used by Cæcilius = a big-nosed man.

Trognon Fr. stump, stalk. For *tronc (truncus)* suppose an old Fr. form *tron*, obtained by a wrong division of *tronc-on (tronçon)*; hence would come *trognon*, as from *rein roignon*, cf. Sard. *trunca* = stalk of a cabbage.

Troja It., O. Sp. *troya*, Cat. *truja*, Fr. *truie* a sow. First in the Cassel Gloss. *Porcus Trojanus* = a Roman dish *quasi aliis inclusis animalibus gravidum* Macrob. Sat. 2, 9, with a reference to the Trojan horse, *"machina feta armis"*. Hence *porco di Troja*, and finally *troja* = a sow with young, cf. *bernia* = *panno d'Ibernia*. The Sp. word is not found in its proper sense, but = (1) a bawd (2) a sack filled with eatables; cf. Neap. *cavallo di Troja* = a glutton, Sard. *troju* = foul, dirty.

Trôler Fr. to cause to wander, lead astray, also to wander, stroll; E. *troll*, G. *trollen*, W. *trolio* to roll, roam, perhaps from a W. root *tro*, though the diphthong of the O.Fr. *trauler* (E. *trawl*), Occ. *s'entraulà*, seems to point to L. It. *travolare*.

Tromba It., Sp. Pg. *tromba*, Pr. *tromba trompa*, Fr. *trompe* (E. *trump*) trumpet; perhaps from *tuba* with inserted r, as in

tronar from *tonare*, and *m* as in *pimpa* from *pipa* (Diez). It
may, however, be an onomatop., though the Rh. *tiba* horn,
Wal. *tobe* drum, and the meaning of the It. *tromba* (tube) support the derivation from *tuba*. Hence It. *trombetta* &c., Wal.
trimbitze; vb. It. *trombare*, Pr. *trompar*, O.Fr. *tromper* to blow
the trumpet, Fr. *trompeter*. The word has another and distinct
set of meanings; It. *tromba* whirlwind, Fr. *trombe trompe* waterspout, Sp. *trompa trompo* whipping-top; from *turbo?* Sp. *trompar*, Fr. *tromper* to deceive, *se tromper* to err (prop. to lead in
a *circle*, lead astray), is probably connected with the latter
sense of *tromba*, cf. Sp. *trompar* to whip a top.

Trompe tromper — *tromba.*

Trompicar — *tropezar.*

Tron O. Fr. Pr. firmament, whence M. Du. *troon*. From W.
tron circle, bending, or from *torn (turn)*, cf. *tronar* for *tornar*.

Tronçon — *torso.*

Tronfio It. haughty; from Gk. τρυφή, whence also Wal. *trufie*,
vb. *trufi?*

Trono O. It., Sp. Pr. *tron*, Pg. *trom* thunder; vb. O. It. *tronare*,
Sp. O. Pg. Pr. *tronar*, Pg. *troar*, and *trorejar* for *troejar*; from
tonus tonare, with inserted *r*, cf. *tromba*; It. however has *tuono
tuonare.*

Tronzar — *torso.*

Tropa Sp. Pg., Fr. *troupe* (E. *troop*), hence It. *truppa*, Pr. *trop*
(herd); adj. It. *troppo*, adv. Pr. Fr.*trop*; L.L. *truppus*. Perhaps
from *turba turpa truppa* truppus, cf. *trouble* from *turbula*. The
W. *torv* is not nearer than the L., and the Gael. *drobh* is the
E. *drove*, = A. S. *draf* from *drifan* to drive. From *truppus*
comes Sp. Pg. Pr. *tropel*, Fr. *troupeau*, Sp. Pg. *atropellar tropellar* to trample, Pr. *atropelar*, O. Fr. *atropeler* to collect.
V. *tropezar.*

Tropezar Sp. Pg. to stumble, sbst. *tropiezo tropeço*; also Pg.
tropicar, Sp. *trompicar*. As *tropellar* from *tropel*, so *tropezar*
from the primitive *tropa*; O. Sp. has also *en-tropezar*, *en-
trompicar*. The suffix *ez* is strange, cf. *bostezar* (but the
present tense is not *bostiezo*, like *tropiezo*), *acezar.*

Troquer — *trocar.*

Tros trosar — *torso.*

Troscia It. channel, gutter, *stroscio* noise of falling water, *stros-
ciare* to fall (of water); from Goth. *ga-drausjan* to flow down,
fall, G. *dreuschen*, L. G. *drusen.*

Trosqu'à — *jusque.*

Trota It., Sp. *trucha*, Pg. *truita*, Pr. *trocha*, Fr. *truite*, E. trout;
from L. L. *tructa* (Gk. τρώχτης).

Trottare It., Sp. Pr. *trotar*, Fr. *trotter*, E. Gael. *trot*, W. *trotio*,
sbst. *trotto*, *trote*, *trot*. From *tolutare (ire tolutim)*, *tlutare*, *tro-*

tare (cf. *chapitre* from *capitulum*, and cf. also *trotier* O. Fr.
= *tolutarius*).

Trou Fr., Pr. *trauc*, Cat. *trau* hole, *trouer*, *troucar* to bore.
Perhaps = Pr. *trabucar* (*buco* It. = hole) prop. to fall, from
buc trunk, whence for the sake of distinction, a second form
traucar.

Trou de chou — *torso*.

Trouble Fr. (m.) E., vb. *troubler*, *tourbler*; from *turbula*.

Troupe — *tropa*.

Trousse — *torciare*.

Trouver — *trovare*.

Trovare It., Pr. Cat. *trobar*, Fr. *trouver* to find, Rh. *truvar* to
find a verdict, O. Fr. *trouver une loi*. In Wal. the word is
altogether wanting, in Sp. and Pg., which substitute *hallar*,
achar, it is found only in the sense of to "versify", *trova*
verse, though *trobar* is found = *trovare* in O. Sp. Sard. has
instead *crobare* = It. *accoppiare* and *incontrare*. The orig.
sense is to fetch, seek, so It. *truovami an ago* = fetch me a
needle, Tasso: *Goffredo trova* fetch Godfrey, cf. It. *ritrovare*
to search thoroughly, Rou. *retrouve* = *recherche*. The connexion is easy. The word is derived from *turbare* to turn
topsy-turvy (in searching for, ἀνατρέπειν τῇ ζητήσει), cf. It.
frugare, *rovistare*, and cf. *trouble* from *turbula*, *tropa* &c. from
turba. This der. is confirmed by the O. Pg. *trovar* = *turbare*,
Neap. *struvare* = *disturbare*, *controvare* = *conturbare*.

Trovejar — *trono*.

Troxa torsa — *torciare*.

Troso — *torso*.

Truan Pr. (f. *truanda*), Fr. *truand*, Sp. *truhan*, Pg. *truão* vagrant,
beggar (Sp. buffoon), E. *truant*; vb. Pr. *truhandar*, Fr. *truander*,
Sp. *truhanear*. From the Celtic: W. Corn. Bret. *tru* wretched
= O. Ir. *trôg*, v. Dief. Celt. 1, 150. The *f* of the O. Sp. Pr.
trufan would seem to be borrowed from *truffa trufa* trick, the
t of the L.L. *trutannus* from the O. H. G. *truhting* companion.

Trucco It. a game with balls (E. *trucks*, Sp. *trucos*), Sp. *truco*,
Pr. Pied. *true* thrust, push, Com. a stamping, N. Pr. *truco* f.
a bruising, crushing; vb. Pied. *truchè*, Com. N. Pr. *trucà*, Rh.
trukiar to stamp, press, thrust, Ven. *s-trucare* to squeeze out.
The root is seen in the G. *druck drucken*, A.S. *thryccan*, O. N.
thryckia to thrust, press.

Trucheman — *dragomanno*.

Truffa It., Sp. Pg. Pr. *trufa*, Fr. *truffe*, B. *trufa* jest, fib; vb.
truffare, *trufar*, *truffer* to jeer; It. *truffaldino*. Probably the
same word as the following *truffe*, *truffle*, cf. O. Fr. *trufle* =
truffle and *trifle*, Mil. *tartuffol* = (1) truffle (2) dotard, Neap.
taratufolo simpleton = It. *tartufolo*.

Truffe Fr. (f.), Com. *trufol*, Gen. *trifola*, E. *truffle* = Sp. *turma;* Cat., with inserted *m*, *trumfo trumfa* a tubercle, potato; from L. *tuber* with transposition of *r*, and change of *b* into *f*, *truffe*, *trumfo* (also Sp. = tumour), *turma*. The fem. form may have arisen from the plur. *tubera*. The It. *tartufo* (= *tartrufo*), Mil. *tartuffol*, Ven. *tartufola*, Pied. *tartifla*, Rh. *tartufel*, Occ. *tartifle*, Fr. (Berr.) *tartufle (Tartuffe)*, are from *terræ tuber*, cf. Sp. *turmas de tierra*. Other dialects have the form without *r*, Genev. *tufelle*, Occ. *tufeda*, Sp. *co-tufa*, cf. Sic. *cata-tuffulu;* Ven. *tufoloto* = a short fat man, a lump. These are, probably, from *tar-tufo*, dropping the first syllable. From *tartufola*, by dissimilation, the G. *kartoffel*, Prov. G. *tartoffel* = N. Pr. *trufa*.

Truhan — *truan*.

Truie — *troja*.

Truiller O. Fr. to enchant, bewitch; from O. N. *trölla*, subst. *tröll*, M. H. G. *trolle*, E. *droll*.

Truite — *trota*.

Trujal Sp. oil-mill; from *torcular*.

Trujaman — *dragomanno*.

Trumbo — *truffe*.

Trumeau Fr. leg of beef, pier, O. Fr. shin-bone (of men); hence *trumelière* (1) greaves (2) window-shaft or pier, space between two winds. From G. *trumm* end, piece *(thrum)*, Bav. kegel-*trümmer* (pl.) beams running between two windows.

Truogo truogolo It., Wal. *troc* trough; from O. H. G. *trôg*, E. *trough*. We find also O. Fr. *troc*, Norm. *treu tros* kneading-trough.

Trusar truisar trussar Pr., Lomb. *trusà trussà*, E. *thrust;* Pr. *atruissar atriusar;* from L. *trusare*, *trusitare*.

Tudel Sp. Pr., Pied. Com. *tuel*, Fr. *tuyau* tube, pipe. It is the O. N. *tùda*, Dan. *tùd*, Du. *tuit*, G. (Prov.) *zaute*.

Tuer — *tutare*.

Tueroa — *torciare*.

Tuero Sp. log of wood, Pg. *toro* trunk, Lomb. *toeur (tör)* a block; from *torus* muscle, swelling, cf. Sp. *muñon* = (1) muscle (2) stump. Hence Sp. *atorarse* to remain fixed (like a block).

Tuffare It. to dip, immerse; from O. H. G. *taufan*, G. *taufen*, cf. *rubare* from *roubôn*.

Tufo tuffo It., Sp. *tufo* vapour, N. Pr. *toufe* choking vapour, adj. Lorr. *toffe* suffocating; Fr. *étouffer* to suffocate. From τῦφος vapour, also arrogance, pride (L. *typhus* Arnob.) = Sp. *tufo*, pl. *tufos* hair-locks, Pg. *tufos*, vb. *tufar* to puff out, *atufar* to vex, harass, *tufão* whirlwind = Gk. τυφών. Cf. also Sp. *tufar*, Lomb. *toffà*, Rh. *toffar tuffar* to smell, stink.

Tufo It. Pg., Fr. *tuf*, Sp. *toba* a stone; from *tophus*.

Tuile — *tegola*.

Tulipano It., Wal. *tulipan*, Sp. *tulipa tulipan*, Fr. *tulipe*, E. *tulip;* from Pers. Turk. *dulband* (whence It. *turbante turban*) a turban, from the resemblance in shape. The Pers.Turk. name for tulip is *lala.*

Tullirse Sp., Cat. *tulirse* to be maimed, crippled = Pg. *tolherse de membros*, from *tollere*, O. Sp. *toller.*

Tumba — *tomba.*

Tumbar — *tombolare.*

Tumer - *tombolare.*

Tuorlo torlo It. yelk of an egg; from *torulus* muscle, fleshy, nutritive part; Pied. *torlo* a tumour, boil.

Tuper — *toppo.*

Turar turare — *atturare.*

Turcasso — *turquois.*

Turchese It., Pr. Sp. *turquesa*, Fr. E. *turquoise*, It. also *turchina;* the "Turkish" stone.

Turcimanno — *dragomanno.*

Turco O.Sp. contemptuous, uncircumcised; from *Turco* a Turk. Cf. Sic. *turcu*, Piedm. *turch* stiff, unbending &c.

Turlupin Fr. a punster; name of a buffoon, temp. Louis XIII. (Menage).

Turma — *truffe.*

Turquois O. Fr. quiver, M. H. G. *tarkis*, hence, on the analogy of *carcasso*, the It. *turcasso*. From Pers. *tarkash.*

Turrar — *torrar.*

Tutare It. to appease, *attutare*, *stutare* to quench, extinguish, Pr. *tudar*, *atuzar*, *estuzar*, Lang. *tuda*, Fr. *tuer* (cf. *tuer la chandelle*, *le feu* &c.). Not from Goth. *dauthjan*, O.H.G. *totan* (E. *doubt*, *death*), which would give Pr. *daudar* or *taudar*, Fr. *touer*, but prob. from *tutari* to defend, ward off, render harmless, extinguish, L. *tutari famem* = It. *attutare la fame.*

Tuttavia — *via.*

Tuyau — *tudel.*

U.

Ubbia It. superstitious dread, foreboding. Perhaps (1) from *obviam* an omen at starting (ἐνόδιον), or (2) from *uh* and *via* begone! away! (abominantis), or (3) = Pr. *avia* ill-luck.

Ubino — *hobin.*

Uccello It. (poet. *augello*), Pr. *augel*, Fr. *oiseau*, L. L. *aucellus* bird; from *aucella aucilla* (Apicius, Apuleius) with change of gender; Sp. dim. *avecella* = L. *avicella*. Hence It. *uccellare* to fowl, go fowling, M. H. G. *rogelen*, O. Fr. *oiseler* to hop like a bird.

Uffo It., Sp. Pg. *ufo* in *a uffo*, *a ufo* in vain, to no purpose, whence Sp. Pg. *ufano* idle, vain, Pr. *ufana, ufanaria, ufanese* idleness, vanity &c. The O. H. G. sbst. *ubbâ* or *uppâ* was similarly used, *in uppôn* = in vain. Cf. Goth. *ufjô* superfluous, and for the G. *p*, cf. Com. *a up*. Others derive it *a uffo* from *ex uffo* = *ex ufficio* "gratis".

Uggia It. shade (in bad sense), figur. dislike, aversion, foreboding, *aduggiare* to shade harmfully, injure. Perhaps from *obviam*, cf. O. Sp. *uviar* to meet, happen, or, better, from *odium* with change of gender, as in *noja* from the same word (*u = o*, as in *uscio = ostium*), cf. *essere in uggia, venire in uggia ad alcuno* = L. *in odio esse, odio venire alicui*. Hence *uggia* would mean (1) hateful, pernicious (to plants) shade, evil foreboding, foreboding.

Ugola — *huette*.

Uguanno It., O. Sp. *hogaño*, O. Pg. *ogano*, Pr. *ogan*, O. Fr. *ouan*, Rh. *uòn*, adv. for L. *horno*; from *hoc anno*. It. *unguanno*, Pr. *ongan* may be "*hunc annum*". Cf. *antaño*.

Uncir Sp., O. Sp. *juncir* to yoke oxen; from *jungere*, cf. *ercer* from *erigere*.

Uña Sp., Pg. *unha* nail, claw; from *ungula*, It. *unghia*.

Uomo It., Wal. *om*; Sp. *hombre* (from *hom'nem* as *fembra* from *fem'na*), Pg. *homem (homin-)*, Pr. O. Fr. *hom*, acc. *home*, whence Fr. *homme*. From the O. Fr. nom. *hom* or *om* comes *on* = E. *one*, G. *man*; for a similar distinction between the pron. and the sbst. cf. O. Fr. *ma* (E. *me* in *methinks* &c.) and *man*, Du. *man* and *men*, Dan. *mand* and *man*. Hence It. *omaggio*, Sp. *homenage*, Pr. *homenatge*, Fr. *hommage*, E. *homage* = *hominaticum*, where *homo* has the L. L. sense of "servant".

Uopo It., Wal. *op*, O. Sp. *huevos*, Pr. *obs*, O. Fr. *oes*; from *opus*. In the Fr. *oes* the *p* has vanished, and *o* become *oe* = *ue*, cf. *oevre uevre, boefs buefs*.

Uosa It., O. Sp. *huesa*, O. Pg. *osa*, O. Fr. *hose*, W. *hos*, L. L. *hosa osu*; Fr. *houseau*; It. *usatto* boot; from O. H. G. *hosa* "*caliga*", G. E. *hose*.

Upa aupa Sp., Cat. *upa* up! rise up! vb. Sp. *upar* to rise up. Goth. *iup, iupa âvos*), O. Sax. *up, ûp, upa*, E. *up*, A. S. vb. *uppian*, O. N. *yppa* to raise.

Upiglio It. garlic; from *ulpicum, ulpiculum*.

Upupa It. *hoopoe*, Mil. *buba*, Romag. *poppa*, Pied. *popo*, Pg. *poupa*, also It. *bubbola*, Sp. *abubilla*; also Pr. *upa*, Fr. *huppe* (the asp. from the G. wied-*hopf*, cf. E. *hoopoe*), which latter came to mean a tuft or crest (such as the hoopoe's). These names are derived from the bird's note, as are also Gk. *ἔποψ*, Sp. *pulput*, Fr. *puput*, G. (prov.) *wutwut*, E. *peewit*.

Uracano It., Sp. *huracan*, Pg. *furacão*, Fr. *ouragan*, E. *hurrí-cane;* a Caribbean word.

Urca Sp. Pg. a sort of ship; from L. *orca* a jar, vessel, cf. *urca* = L. *orca* = a grampus.

Urce Sp. Pg. heather; from *erice.*

Uria — *augurio.*

Urlare It., Wal. *urlà*, Fr. *hurler* (*h* asp.), O. Fr. also *huler uler* perhaps through confusion with G. *heulen* (E. *howl*), Pg. *huívar* (cf. *couve* from *caulis*); from *ululare* as *zirlare* from *zinzilulare.* The Sard. is *urulare*, Pr. *udolar.* From *huler* comes Fr. *hulotte* owl. Rou. *cahuler* = *cat-huler* to cry like a cat. In the It. *chiurlare* the first syllable is difficult.

Urraca Sp. Pg. magpie. From the B. *urraca* magpie, which is from *urra* a nut. *Urraca* was also used in Sp. (O. Sp. *Hur-raca, Orraca*) as a female name, orig. a nickname "Chatter-box". *Urraca*, an unintelligible word to Spanish ears, was transformed into *Marica* (little Mary), which has the same meaning, cf. *magpie* == *magot (Margaret) -pie.*

Urtare It., Pr. *urtar*, Fr. *heurter* (for the O.Fr. *hurter*) to thrust; abst. It. *urto*, Fr. *heurt* thrust, knock; comp. O. Fr. *dehurter*, N. Pr. *dourdà* (so *derbá* from *deherber*), Norm. *dourder.* The word is found in M. H. G. *hurten hurt*, Du. *hurten horten hurt hort*, E. *hurt, hurtle*, but is not found in the older Teutonic dialects, whither it was probably introduced from the language of the French tournaments. The origin is Celtic: W. *hwrdh* (1) push (2) goat (L. L. in England *hurdus hurdardus*), cf. G. *bocken* to push, butt, from *bock* a goat, Fr. (Bourgogne) *boquai*, L. *arietare.*

Usatto — *uosa.*

Usbergo osbergo It., Pr. *ausberc*, O.Fr. *halberc hauberc* (*h* asp.), E. *hauberk*, Fr. *haubert;* from O. H. G. *halsberc*, A. S. *heals-beorg*, O. N. *hálsbiörg* (f.) = that which protects *(bergen)* the neck *(hals)*, M. H. G. also *halsveste*, cf. G. *koller* jerkin (from *collare* a collar). The Fr. has lost the *s* between two con-sonants, cf. *hals halterel haterel* (E. *halter*) for *halsterel.* The O. It. has a fem. *sberga* for *usberga.*

Usoio It., Wal. *uṣe*, O. Sp. *uzo*, Pr. *uis us*, O. Fr. *huis*, from *ostium;* It. *usciere*, O. Sp. *uxier*, Fr. *huissier* porter, E. *usher*, from *ostiarius.*

Usoire — *escire.*

Usignuolo — *rosignuolo.*

Usted Sp., pl. *ustedes* personal pronoun of the 2nd person, contr. from *vuestra merced*, cf. It. *vossignoria*, G. *euer gnaden*, E. *your honour.* So *usencia* from *vuestra reverencia*, *useñoria* from *vuestra señoria;* some forms reserve the *v*, Cat. *vosté* and Sp. *vosasté*, Cat. *vosencia vosenyoria.*

Utello It. oil-flask; a dim. of L. *uter.*

Uviar ubiar, hubiar huyar O. Sp. to help, meet; from *obviare* (the *h* being erroneous) in late L. = to help; *uviar* is older than *obviar*, It. *orriare* to hinder. Hence *ant-uviar* to prevent, sbst. *antuvio.*

V.

Vacarme Fr. (m.) tumult, outcry; from the M. Du. interj. *wacharme* alas wretch! by dissimilation, for *gacarme*, v. *vague.*

Vacío Sp., Pg. *vasio* empty, vb. *vaciar, vasiar;* from *vacivus.*

Vaglio It. sieve; from *vallus* (Varr.) a dim. of *vannus.* The Mod. has more correctly *vallo, ll* becoming liquid only before *e* or *i.* Vb. *vagliare,* Lomb. *vantà — vannitare.*

Vago It. (1) unsteady (2) lustful, desirous (3) seducing, charming, as sbst. a lover. Orig. = an inconstant lover, L. *vagus.*

Vague Fr. (f.) wave, vb. *vaguer* to surge; from O. H. G. *wâc,* Goth. *vêgs,* M. Du. *waghe,* E. *wave,* G. *woge; vague* is by dissimilation for *gague.* From the Fr. come O. Pg. *ragua,* Pg. *vaga.* Fr. *vaguer* to roam is from *vagari.*

Váguido Sp., Pg. *vágado váguedo* giddiness; adj. Sp. *vaguido* giddy. From Goth. *vagjan,* O. H. G. *wegjan,* A. S. *vagian,* E. *wave,* G. *wogen,* whence sbst. O. H. G. *wagida wegida.* Thus *vaguido* is for *gaguido* (v. *vague*), and from the same root as the preceding word.

Vaho — *bafo.*

Vainiglia It., Sp. *vainilla* and *vainica,* Pg. *bainilha baunilha,* Fr. *vanille,* E. *vanilla* an American plant; dim. from Sp. *vaina* husk, pod (L. *vagina*).

Vaisseau — *vascello.*

Vaiven Sp., Pg. *vaivem* fluctuation, inconstancy; from *va viene* or *va y viene* "come and go", 'move to and fro'.

Vajo It. a kind of fur, Pr. *vair,* whence *vairador* furrier; from *varius.*

Vajuolo vajuole (f. pl.) It., Sp. *viruela, viruelas,* Fr. *vérole* pox, L. L. *variola;* from *varius.*

Valanga — *avalange.*

Valet valetto — *vassallo.*

Valigia It., Sp. *balija,* Fr. *valise* (whence G. *felleisen*). Perhaps from *vidulus,* whence (as from *capillus capillitium,* cf. *grandizia, grandigia, contigia* from *comtus*) might come *vidul-itia, velligia* (as *strillo* from *stridulus*), *valligia, valigia.*

Valise — *valigia.*

Vampo vampa It. flame, heat, vb. *avvampare;* from *vapor* with loss of *r* as in *sarto, pepe, cece;* hence also *vampore,* Wald.

vanpor. Without *m* we have *vapa*, Alb. *vape*, Wal. *vepae;* Sp. *hampa* (for *fampa*) brag, boast, cf. It. *menar vampo* to boast; Burg. *vambée* cloud of smoke.

Vanello vanneau — *vanno.*

Vanno It. (usu. in plur.), whence Fr. pl. *vanneaux;* from *vannus.* The lapwing is called in It. *vanello*, Fr. *vanneau*, Mil. *vanell* (cf. E. *lap-wing*), in It. also *pavoncella.*

Vantagio — *anzi.*

Vantail — *rentaglio.*

Vantare It., Pr. *vantar*, Fr. *vanter*, E. *vaunt;* sbst. It. *vanto*, E. *vaunt;* from *vanitare* (Augustine), *vanus.*

Varare It., Sp. Pg. Pr. *varar*, O. Fr. *varer* to launch a ship; from *vara* a cross-beam, slanting beam (stocks), Sp. = a rod, pole. Pg. *varar* also = (1) to draw a ship to land (2) to be stranded, which meaning also belongs to the Sp. *varar*, whence *desvarar* to get a ship afloat.

Varangue Fr. f. the first timbers, floor-timber, of a ship, hence Sp. *varenga*, from Swed. *vränger* (pl.) the ribs of a vessel.

Varcare valcare vallicare It. to step across, pass, Rh. *vargar* to
• pass, out-run, sbst. It. *varco* passage. Wedg. derives it from the E. *balk*, Sw. *balka* to pass over in ploughing &c. (whence *balk* = the separation between one division and another, a beam, Fr. *bauche*, *ébaucher*). But Diez from *varicare* to stride (cf. *prævalicare*), move on, pass, cf. L. *passus* step, prop. = the *expansion* of the legs. Cf. L. L. *varicat* "ambulat", Gloss. Isid.

Varech Fr., Pr. *varec* wrack (sea-weed), Fr. also = wreck. From E. *wrack*, *wreck*, A. S. *vräc.*

Varenga — *varangue.*

Varlope Fr. f. plane; from Du.L.G. *weerloop* (from *wider-laufen* to run back?). Hence Sp. Pg. *garlopa*, Lim. *garlopo.*

Varon — *barone.*

Varvassore — *vassallo.*

Vas Pr. prepos., corr. from *ves vers* = L. *versus*, *devas*, *davas* from *de versus.* From *davas* comes the Pr. particle *daus das dous deus (devas).*

Vasa vase — *gazon.*

Vasca It. tub, also *basca.* Prob. from *vasica (vas)*, though other derivations are given, Celtic *basgawd*, G. *waschen*, B. *uasca* (a pail).

Vascello It., Sp. *baxel*, Pg. *baixel* ship, Pr. *vaissel*, Fr. *vaisseau*, E. *vessel*, Wall. *vahai* coffin; from *vascellum (vas vasculum).* For *vessel* = a cup &c., the Sp. has *vasillo*, *baxillo*, It. *vasello.*

Vassallo It. Pg., Sp. *vasallo*, Fr. E. *vassal*, L. L. *vassallus.* The oldest L. L. was *vassus*, a form unknown to the Rom., which took the fuller *vassal.* This in O. Fr. = (1) vir (2) pugnator;

vassalage = prowess, cf. *barnage* from *baro*. From the W. *gwds* young man, servant, cf. O. H. G. *degan* (1) young man (2) champion, hero (3) servant. The Rom. *vassal* (no suffix *all* being known) is from the W. adj. *gwas-awl* "serving". The word is very old, for the later form would have been *guassus guassal*, cf. *verne* from *gwernen*. Hence O. Fr. *vaslet varlet* a boy, Fr. *valet*, It. *valetto*. An inferior vassal, or under-tenant was called Fr. *vavasseur vasseur*, Pr. *vasvassor*, *valvassor*, L. L. *vavassor*, *vavassorius*, O. Fr. f. *vavassore*, whence It. *varvassore*, *barbassore*, O. Val. *vervesor*, probably from *vassus vassorum*. V. Pott, Forschung. 2, 347.

Vástago Sp. a shoot; of uncertain derivation. Some refer it to βλάστος βλαστικός.

Vaudeville Fr. a popular song, ballad; from *Vau-de-vire* in Normandy, where the *vaudeville* was first introduced about the end of the 14ᵗʰ century by Olivier *Basselin*.

Vautour — *avoltore*.

Vautrer (&c.) Fr. to wallow; in O. Pr. *veautrer*, *voutrer*, *voitrer*, *voltrer* = It. *voltolare* from *volvere*.

Vaya — *baja* (2).

Veado Pg. stag; from *venatus*, Sp. *venado*, Wal. *vunat*.

Veau Fr., O. Fr. *veel* (E. *veal*); from *vitellus*; hence Fr. *vélin*, E. *vellum*, Fr. *véler* to calve.

Veaus viaus viax O. Fr. particle for L. *saltem*; from L. *vel* (= etiam) with an adverbial *s* added. It is found in comp. with *si*, O. Fr. *sivels*, Pr. *sivals sivaus* (for *vels*, as *vas* for *ves*, *vers*). Cf. s. *veruno*.

Vec — *ecco*.

Vecchio veglio It., Wal. *veachiu*, Sp. *viejo*, Pg. *velho*, Pr. *vielh*, Fr. *vieil vieux* old; from *vetulus vetlus veclus*, which latter is found in an ancient grammarian "*vetulus non veclus*".

Vece It. sbst., adv. Sp. Pg. *vez*, Pr. *vetz*, Fr. *fois*, N. Pr. *fes*; from L. *vicem*, cf. Hor. *plus vice simplici* = *plus d'une fois*. Hence O. Sp. O. Pg. Pr. *vegada*, Rh. *gada*, *g* for *z* as in Sp. Pr. *perdigon*, Pg. *perdigão* from *perdiz perditz*.

Vedetta It. watch, scout, Fr. *vedette*, E. *vedet*, *vedette*. Not from *videre*, for the suffix *ett* is rarely, if ever, added to verbs, but, perhaps, a corruption of It. *veletta* (v. *veglia*).

Vedija Sp. lock of wool, entangled hair, cf. Rh. *vadeglia*, Com. *vedeglia* lock, flock; hence Sp. *guedeja* (*gu* = *v*) lock of hair, mane of a lion, Pg. *guedelha gadelha* long hair, velvet. Perhaps by dissimilation for *velilla* or *vellilla*, = *vellicula*, from *vellus*.

Vedro O. Pg. old; from *vetus veteris*, cf. It. *Castel-vetro*, Sp. *Mur-viedro*.

Vega Sp. Cat. Sard., Pg. *veiga* open plain. From the Basque,

either from *bera* deep soil, or from *be-guea* without cavities,
i. e. flat (Larramendi).

Veggia It. cart-load; from *vehes*, later *reges vejes* (v. Ducange),
changed to the 1ˢᵗ declension. For the *g* or *j*, cf. *struggere*.

Veglia It., Sp. *vela*, Pg. *vigia*, Pr. *velha*, Fr. *veille* watch; vb.
vegliare &c., Sp. *veleta* weather-cock, It. *veletta* sentinel; from
vigilia, *vigiliare*.

Velaire viere O. Fr. (m.), Pr. *veiaire*, O. Sp. *vejaire* judgment,
view, also sight, countenance. L.L. *vicarius* = judge, whence
a abst. *vicarium* judgment, hence *reiaire* (cf. an old form *vigaire*
Honnorat) (1) judgment (2) sight (3) (from abstract to concrete, as G. *gesicht*, E. *sight*) countenance. Wall. has *vir* =
viere, as *plr* = *pierre*.

Velllaquerie — *vigliacco*.

Veille veiller — *reglia*.

Veit viet vieg Pr. veretrum; from *vectis* = veretrum in L. L.
For Pr. *vieg* cf. from *lectus* Pr. *liet*, *lieg*, Fr. *lit*.

Vela — *veglia*.

Velar Sp. Pg. to marry, prop. to veil, hence the bride was
called *velada* (husband = *velado*), cf. L. *nubere*, Goth. *liugan*
(Grimm).

Veletta — *veglia*.

Velhaco — *vigliacco*.

Velleità It., Sp. *veleidad*, Fr. *velléité*, E. *velleity;* a scholastic
word, derived from *velle*.

Velours Fr. (m.) *velvet.* The *r* is an insertion, cf. Nicot *veloux*
velous, Matt. Paris *villuse* from *villosus*. The It. is *velluto*, Sp.
veludo, O. Fr. *vellu-eau*, from *villutus* (E. *velvet*); hence Fr. vb.
velouter (ou from *villosus).*

Veltro It., Pr. *veltre*, O. Fr. *viautre* greyhound (hence O. E.
fewterer hound-keeper), Corn. *giulter;* O. Fr. *viautrer* to hunt.
From L. *vertragus* (Martial.: *non sibi sed domino venatur vertragus acer).* A Celtic word, cf. Ælian.: αἱ δὲ ποδώκεις κύνες
αἱ κελτικαὶ καλοῦνται οὐέρτραγοι κύνες φωνῇ τῇ κελτικῇ; from
Ir. *traig* a foot; with intensive *ver*, v. Dief. Orig. Europ.
p. 330.

Venaison Fr., Pr. *venaisò*, E. *venison;* from *venatio* (concrete for
abstract).

Vencejo Sp. string; from a dim. *vinciculum* of *vinculum*.

Venda — *benda*.

Vendange Fr., Pr. *vendanha*, Bret. *bendem*, *vintage;* from *vindemia*.

Vendaval Sp. Pg., v. *vent d'amont*.

Vendredi — *venerdi*.

Venerdi It., Fr. *vendredi*, Pr. Cat. *divendres* Friday, from *Veneris dies*, *dies Veneris;* Sp. *viernes*, Pr. *venres*, from *Veneris*,

Wal. *vineri*, Ven. *benere*, Romag. *venar*. Pg. has *sexta feira*.
Sard. *chenábura*, *chenáura*, *cenabara* is, probably, from *cæna
pura*, Friday being a fast day.

Vengar venger — *rengiare*.

Vengiare It., Sp. *vengar*, Pg. *vingar*, Pr. *vengar*, Fr. *venger* to
revenge; from *vindicare* (Wal. *rindecà* to heal i. e. save, vin-
dicate). Comp. Pr. *revenjar*, O. Fr. *revenger*, E. *revenge*, Fr.
revancher, abst. *revanche*, cf. O. Fr. *nache* = *nage*.

Vent d'amont Fr. East-wind, land-breeze, *vent d'aval* West-
wind, sea-breeze, the E. being the higher ground. Hence
Sp. *rendaval* = South-West-wind.

Venta Sp. a road-side inn, O. E. *vent*, also = sale, It. *vendita*;
O. Fr. *vente* = *market*, cf. Sp. *fonda* = inn, L. L. *funda* =
market-place.

Ventaglio It., Sp. *ventalle* fan, Pr. *ventalh*, Fr. *ventail* vent, *vantail* folding door, *éventail* fan, It. *ventaglia* &c., E. *ventail* (of
a helmet), from *ventus*, cf. *ventana*.

Ventaja — *anzi*.

Ventana Sp. window; orig. = vent, air-hole, from *ventus*, cf.
O. N. *vind-auga*, E. *wind-ow*, Dan. *vindue*, and for the suffix,
cf. *solana* from *sol*. The Pg. word is *janella*, from *janua?* Sp.
finiestra, *hiniestra* are obsolete.

Ventavolo It. North-wind; a corruption of *ventus aquilus?*

Ver Pr. O. Fr. spring; Sp. *verano*, Pg. *verão* late spring; comp.
Pr. *primver*, It. Sp. Pr. *primavera*, Wal. *primevare*, O. Fr. *pri-
mevere*, Basque *primadera* spring, orig. (as still in Sp.) early
spring; for this Fr. has *printemps*, Pied. *prima*, Occ. *primo* (f.).
Ven. has *verta*, Dauph. *pipa*, v. *piva*.

Vera — *riviera*.

Verano — *ver*.

Verdolaga — *portulaca*.

Verdugo Sp. (1) young shoot (2) dagger, tuck (also a gaoler
"qui vergis credit"), It. *verduco*; from *verde*, *viridis*. The latter
meaning also belongs to the O. Fr. *verdun* (Marot, Rabelais),
but this is from *Verdun* where such weapons were made.
Amadis is called *le chevalier de la verte epée*; is this "*verte*"
connected? Besides rod or shoot, *verdugo* in Pg. also = a
plait or fold, hence Sp. *verdugado*, Pg. *verdugada averdugada*
a hooped petticoat, *farthingale*.

Vereda Sp. Pg. a path; *per quam veredi vadunt* Ducange, cf.
vréder.

Vergel verger — *rerziere*.

Verglas Fr. (m.) glassy ice; from *verre* (m.) and *glace* (f.).

Vergogna It., Pg. Pr. *vergonha*, Fr. *vergogne*, Sp. *vergüenza*,
O. Sp. *vergüeña* shame; from *verecundia*, cf. *Bourgogne* from
Burgundia, *d* becoming *z* in the Sp.

Véricle Fr. a paste jewel; from a L. *vitriculum*, dim. of *vitrum* glass, pl. *vitricula*.

Vericueto Sp. a rough road; from B. *biregueta* which = *bidegue-ta* an impassable spot, v. Larramendi.

Verjus Fr. sour grapes, E. *verjuice;* from *vert jus* = green juice.

Vermeil vermejo — *vermiglio*.

Vermena It. shoot; from *verbena* twig, orig. sacred twig.

Vermiglio It., Sp. *bermejo*, Pg. *vermelho*, Pr. Fr. *vermeil*, E. der. *vermilion; L. L. vermiculus;* from *vermiculus* insect, cf. *carmesino*, and v. Marsh, Lectures on the Engl. language, and Mahn, Untersuch. p. 62.

Verne Fr., provin. *vergne*, O. Fr. *berne*, Pr. *verna vern*, N. Pr. *vernho averno* &c., Pied. *verna* alder. From *arbor verna* or, better, from W. *gwern* (f.) (1) a marsh (2) = *coed gwern* alders, sing. *gwernen*, so Bret. *gwern*, Ir. *fearn*.

Vernice It., Sp. *berniz barniz*, Pr. *vernitz*, Fr. *vernis*, E. *varnish*, W. *bernais*, G. *firnis;* vb. It. *verniciare*, Sp. *barnizar*, Pr. *vernissar*, Fr. *vernisser*, E. *varnish*, also It. *vernicare*, Pr. *bernicar*, and Fr. *vernir*. This last is the orig. form, and might come from G. *bernjan* for *brenjan* to make gliston, but G. initial *b* is not thus weakened. L. Gk. βερνίκη would be formed from *vernice*. *Vernir* is probably *vitrinire* to glaze (cf. *vitrinus* for *vitreus* in Pr. *vetrin*) = It. *vitriare*, Sp. *vedriar*, Sard. *imbidri-are*(Menage). Eastlake, however, says (Materials for a history of oil-painting, p. 220) that *varnish* must be a lineal descendant of Gk. βερονίκη, as referring either to the golden hair of the Egyptian princess, or to the city *Berenice*, where the amber-coloured nitre was found. *Veronica* was patron Goddess of painters.

Verole — *vajuolo*.

Véron Fr. a small speckled fish, minnow, Com. *vairm;* from *varius*.

Verone It. an open gallery, balcony. Perhaps from *vir*, on the analogy of ἀνδρών &c.

Verrat Fr. boar; from *verres*, O. Fr. *ver*, *ferrat* (for *verrat*). Differently formed are Rou. *verrou*, *verau*, *verrot*, Norm. *vérard*, Sp. *verraco*, Pg. *varrão*.

Verricello — *verrina*.

Verrina It., Sic. *virruggiu* bore, gimlet, Rou. *vérin* screw, Fr. *vrille* (for *verille*) gimlet; hence It. *verricello* reel, Fr. *vrille* also = the screw-like tendril of the vine. Perhaps from *veru*, *verrina* from *veruina* (Plautus). *Verrina* is in Sard. *berrina barrina*, Cat. *barrina*, Sp. *barrena (?);* Pg. *verruma* perhaps belongs to the Ar. *bairam* or *barimah*.

Verrou verrouil Fr., Pr. *verrolh* a bolt; from *veruculum (veru)*.

Pr. *ferroth*, Pg. *ferrolho*, Sp. *herrajo*, Wall. *féron* are either from *ferrum*, or, at least, have borrowed its initial letter.

Versare It., Pr. *versar*, Fr. *verser*, Wal. *versà* to pour; from *rer-sare*, cf. Wal. *turnà*. The same word occurs in O. Sp. *bosar*, Sp. *rebosar* = L. *vorsare*, *revorsare*.

Veruno It. pronoun = *nullus*; O. It. also *vernullo*, L. L. *verullus verhullus;* Prov. It. *vergotta rergott* aliquid. *Veruno* is from *vel unus*, and with particle of negation = L. *ne unus quidem* or It. *nè pure uno*. The change of *l* to *r* between vowels is unusual in It., but may have arisen from the analogy of *vel-nullus*, *vel-gulta*. Cf. O. Fr. *vels un* (v. *veaus*) and Wal. *vre-un*.

Verve Fr. (f.) rapture, spirit. Is it from a L. *verva* = ram's head (found in an inscription), cf. *capriccio* from *caper?* But the O. Fr. has the sense of throw, cast, swing, cf. *verve poétique*, and this points to the Du. *werp* = *worp* jactus, cf. *élan* from *lancer*.

Verveux — *bertorello*.

Versa Lomb. Pg., Sp. *berza*, Wal. *vearze*, It. *verzotto* cabbage; hence Sp. *bercero* greengrocer; from L. *viridia* (pl.) garden produce. Menage makes It. *berza* shin the same word, prop. cabbage-stalk, cf. Fr. *tige*, It. *gambo*. It. has also *sverza* (1) cabbage (2) splinter.

Versiere It., Sp. *vergel*, Pr. *vergier*, Fr. *verger* garden; from *viridiarium* or *viridarium* (Pr. also *verdier*). E. *verger* is from Fr. *verge* a rod *(virga)*.

Vesce Fr. vetch; for *vece*, from *vicia*, It. *veccia*, E. *vetch*.

Veta Sp., Pg. *beta* vein in wood, stripe, ribbon (Pr. *veta*); from *vitta*.

Vétille Fr. trifle, Pied. *vetilia*, vb. *rétiller*, *vetilié;* perhaps from *vitilia* basket-work, cf. *gerræ* = (1) wickerwork, *vitilia* (2) trifles, nonsense, *vétilles*, v. Festus.

Vetrice It. osier; for *vetice*, from *vitex*.

Vetta It. (1) top, head, point (2) rod; from *vitta* head fillet worn by the priests, so = top &c., cf. *apex*.

Veuf — *vide*.

Veule Fr. weak, O. Fr. vain, idle, empty, frequently in the combination *veulz et vains;* perhaps from L. *vola* = hollow of the hand, because (1) hollow = empty, or (2) for *van-vole* (*ventvole* Thom. de Canterbury, p. 26) = *vana vola*, afterwards altered to *vain et vole*.

Vezo vezzo vizo — *vizio*.

Vi — *iri*.

Via It. particle, *una via* = once, *due via tre* twice three; from *via*, cf. Nor. *gang*, Du. *reis*. *Via* was hardened into *fia*, O. Fr. *fie*, hence It. *fiata*, O. Fr. *fiede*, *fiée*, *foiée*, Wall. *feie*. Comp.

It. *tuttavia*, Sp. *todavia*, O. Fr. *toutesvoies*, Fr. *toutefois*. For Fr. *fois* v. *vece*.

Via, su via It., Sp. *via*, Pr. O. Cat. *via sus* interjection, come! from *via* away!

Viaggio It., Sp. *viage*, Pr. *viatge*, Fr. E. *voyage*, Wal. *viadi*; vb. *viaggiare* &c.; from *viaticum*.

Viande O. Fr., Pr. *vianda*, E. *viand* meat, Fr. *riande* flesh-meat (O. Fr. *carn*), cf. use of the E. *meat*; from *vivenda*. From the Fr. come It. *rivanda*, *provianda* (E. *provender*).

Vias O. Fr., Pr. *viatz* (*vivatz*) adv. for L. *cito*; from *vivacius* (cf. *ocius*, *citius*), Gl. Cass. *vivaziu*. N. Pr. has *vivacer*, *viacer*.

Viautre — *veltro*.

Vicenda It. turn, change; from *vice*, *vece*, the verbal termination *enda* (*leggenda* &c.) being added to a sbst.

Vidame Fr. (a feudal word) from *vice dominus*, whence G. *viz-thum*.

Vide Fr., O. Fr. Cat. *vuid*, Pic. *wide*, Pr. *ruei*, *voig*, Wall. *vud*, Rh. *vid*, E. *void* empty, from *riduus*, with a transposition of the first *u*; vb. *vider*, O. Fr. *vuidier*, Pr. *vuiar voidar*, E. *void*, Cat. *vuydar*, from *viduare*; comp. *dévider* to wind off, O. Fr. *desvuidier*. The diphthong will not permit the der. from O. H. G. *wit*, E. *wide*. Another form of *riduus vidua* is found in *veuf veuve*, Pr. *veuva*, *vezoa*, Sp. *viuda*, Pg. *viuva*, It. *vedova*, Wal. *veduve*, E. *widow*.

Vidimer Fr. to attest a document; from *vidimus* "we have seen it".

Vie via It. adv. used with comparatives; from *via*, *vie più duro* = (many) times harder. This is better than to derive it, with Diez, from *vis* or from L. adv. *vive*.

Vieillard viejo — *vecchio*.

Vielle — *viola*.

Vierge Fr. virgin, irregular for *verge* to distinguish it from *verge* = *virga*, O. Fr. usu. *virge* = *vierge*, *verge* = *virga*. O. Fr. had also *virgine* = Pr. *vergena* the Virgin Mary.

Viernes — *venerdi*.

Vieux — *vecchio*.

Vies — *biasciu*.

Viga Sp. Pg. a beam, Pr. Cat. *biga*. Is it prop. the pole of a chariot, L. *biga* chariot?

Vigia — *veglia*.

Vigliacco It., Sp. *bellaco*, Pg. *velhaco* mean, bad, Fr. *veillaquerie*; from *vilis* (R. Gr. 2, 253), or an appellative from *Valachus* Walachian.

Vigliare It. to sweep away the chaff, hence sort, pick; from *verriculare* for *vergliare* (*i* for *e* to distinguish it from *vegliare*). Hence sbst. *viglio*.

Vignette Fr. orig. the marginal decoration of a book; prop. = little vine, vine-branches being represented in such illustrations.

Vignoble Fr. (m.) vineyard, for *vignole* = It. *vignuola?* or from *vini opulens* (not Rom., only in It. *opulente*), cf. *serpe serpens?*

Viguier Fr. Pr. judge, district-magistrate, Sp. *reguer;* from *vicarius* prop. deputy.

Vihuela — *viola.*

Vilain — *villa.*

Vilebrequin Fr. wimble, drill; from L. G. *winboreken*, cf. G. *windelbohrer*, M. Du. *wimpel-kin*, E. *wimble.* It corresponds to Sp. *berbequi*, Pg. *berbeguim*, Pic. *biberquin &c.*

Villa It. country-house, Sp. *villa* market-town, borough, Fr. *ville* town, city. In the L. Sal. we find *villa* in the sense of "hamlet", "village", in O. Fr. Pr. = L. or Sp. Hence It. *villano*, Sp. *villano*, Pr. *vilá*, O. Fr. *vilain* husbandman, whence, in a moral sense, mean, wretched, ugly, villanous, which was the chief meaning in Pr., the only one in Fr. and E. *(villain)*, the Fr. preserving the old spelling with a single *l* from associating the word with *vil (vilis).*

Villancico Sp. a hymn with music sung on festivals, such as Christmas and Corpus Christi; prop. a country song, from *villano* (cf. Pg. *villancete*, Sp. *villanesca*).

Vilordo — *lordo.*

Viluppo It. confusion, entanglement; vb. O. Sp. Pr. *volopar*, O. Fr. *voleper;* It. *inviluppare*, Pr. *envolopar enveloper*, N. Pr. *agouloupá*, Fr. *envelopper*, E. *envelope;* Pr. *revolopir* to throw around. The etym. is doubtful. Is it from *volup*, so that *vilupparsi* would be = to coax or cocker oneself, keep oneself warm, wrap oneself up? The forms with *lp* for *lop lup* must be contractions (e. g. O. Val. *envolpar*, Romag. *agulpé*, Ven. *imbolponare*).

Vinchio It. withe, osier; from *vinculum*, hence *avvinchiaré*, cf. *vinculatus* (Cæl. Aurel.).

Vincido It. soft from moisture; for *viscido* from *viscidus*, *pane vincido* = moist, viscous bread; Sard. *bischidu.* Wal. *veasted* (from *viscidus*) = withered.

Vinco It. osier. As *vinchio* from *vinculum*, so *vinco* from a supposed primitive *vincum.*

Viola It. Sp. Pg., Pr. *viula viola*, Fr. *viole*, E. *viol*, Wal. *vioare;* hence *violino*, *violone*, *violin &c.* The Pr. forms, with the accent on the first, must be the oldest. The L. L. is *vitula*, which can only come from *ritulari* to skip like a calf (cf. G. *kälbern*), to make merry; the violin was the usual instrument of merrymakers, hence called *vitula jocosa* (Ducange). Skipping, dancing, and playing music are mutually connected (cf. *giga*, *carole*), hence *vitula* from *vitulari*, as *leva lever* from *levare*. From *vitula* we have by transposition *viutla* (as *reuza* from *ridua*, *leune* from *tenuis*), whence *riula viola* (as *rolar* from *rot'lare*), hence It. *viola*, Sp. *vihuela* (*h* to avoid the hiatus), Fr. *viole*, O. Fr. *vielle*, *viele vitella*, M. H. G. *vigele*. If the O. H. G. *fidula* found in Otfried, M. H. G. *fiedel*, E. *fiddle* be the same word, as is probable (for *f* = *v*, cf. *ferrat*, *fidelli* for *rerrat*, *videlli*), we have in the O. G. an earlier instance of *vitula* than can be found in the L. L.

Viorne Fr. = L. *viburnum*, It. *viburno*.

Vipistrello — *pipistrello*.

Vira Sp. Pg. Pr., O. Fr. *vire* arrow, bolt, Bret. *bir;* Sp. *virote*, It. *veretta*, *rerettone* spear, shaft. *Vira* cannot come regularly from *věru*, though *veretta* may be thence-derived. Perhaps it is from *vipera*, Sp. *vibora*, in a Neap. chronicle: *et parme che al cor me jonga una vira* = *vipera*.

Virar Sp. Pg. Pr., O. Fr. *virer*, Pied. *vrě* to wind, twist, Rou. *virler* to roll, Sp. also *birar* to tack; abst. Pr. *viró* circle, circumference, only used adverbially or prepositionally, e. g. *en-viró*, Fr. *en-viron;* vb. *environar*, *environner*, F. *environ*, It. *invironare*. Not from *gyrare*, for *gi* does not become *vi*, but perhaps a word handed down from the "lingua rustica". L. *viria* = bracelet, ring for the arm, O. Fr. *vire*, Romag. *rira*, Com. Ven. Rh. *vera*, It. *viera* ring, also from a L. *viriola*, Sp. *virola birola*, O. Fr. *virole* ferrule. Plin. Hist. Nat. 33, 12 has: *viriolae Celticae dicuntur*, *viriae Celtibericae*. Humboldt refers to the Iberian, whence the word passed to the Celts, cf. Basque *biruncatu* to twist, turn, but this is L. *verruncare;* the proper name *Viriatus* (clasp-wearer) is of the same origin.

Virole — *virar*.

Viruela — *vajuolo*.

Vis Fr. screw (f.), Pr. *vitz*, O. Fr. *vis* winding stairs; from *vitis* = tendril of a vine, then = anything of a similar spiral form, cf. It. *vite* tendril, screw, O. Fr. *viz*, Pied. *vis* or *vi* screw.

Visciola It., Wal. *visine* (M. Gk. βίσινον), Fr. *guigne* (O. Fr. *guisne*), Sp. *guinda*, Basque (Navarre) *gaile* a kind of cherry, O. H. G. *wihsela*, G. *weichsel*, a word which is also found in Slavonic, cf. Schmeller 4, 17.

Viscus — *vizio*.

Vislumbre Sp. faint, dim light; for *bis-lumbre* (v. *bis*).

Viso O. It., Pr. O. Fr. *vis* with substantive verb and dat. of the person: *fu viso a me* = *visum fuit mihi*. Comp. It. *arviso*, Pr. Fr. *avis* in the same sense, and as abst. = E. *advice*, Sp. *aviso* information, vb. *avvisare* &c. From *avviso* with a change of preposition (as e. g. in *entice* from *attiser*) we have E. *invoice* (letter of advice).

Vispo — *visto.*

Visto It., O. Fr. *viste*, Fr. *vite*, Pr. *vist*, Gasc. *biste* adj. and adv. brisk, quick &c., in O. Fr., but not in N. Fr., of persons. The It. *visto* is the orig. form, and is for *avristo* for *avveduto* circumspect, hence alert, ready, quick, cf. It. *all' erta* on the watch, with Fr. *alerte*, E. *alert.* In Piedm. adv. expressions *vist non vist* and *vist e pris* = in a moment, *vist* is evidently a participle.

Vite — *visto.*

Vitecoq O. Fr. Norm. snipe; from A. S. *vudcoc*, E. *woodcock.*

Vitriuolo It., Sp. *vitriolo*, Pr. Fr. E. *vitriol*; from *vitrum*, because of its vitreous nature.

Vivac — *bivouac.*

Vivole It. (pl.), Sp. *abivas adivas*, Fr. *avires*, L. L. *virolæ* glands (of horses), hence a disease therein, E. *vives*, G. *feifel.* The der. is unknown.

Vizio It. fault, vice, also desire, lust, in another form *rezzo* vicious habit, habit, also delight, caressing (Rh. *rezs*); *viziato* spoilt, also sly, cunning; *vezzoso* charming; *avvezzare inrezzare*, Wal. *invetzà* to accustom, use; *disrezzare, desvetzà* to disuse. Sp. *vicio* = vice, lust, like the It. and, besides, = luxuriant growth of plants; *vezo* habit; *ricioso* (1) vicious (2) luxuriant; *vezar arezar* to accustom, *desvezar, malvezar.* Pg. *vicio vice, viço* luxuriant growth, *victoso* vicious, *viçoso* luxuriant (hence *Villa viçosa* i. e. in a luxuriant country); *vezo* custom, *vezar avezar* = Sp. The Pr. *vici* = vice, cunning (Cat. pleasure), *vetz* habit; *viziat veziat vezat* cunning; *vezar, avezar* = Sp., *envezar* to lust, and so O. Fr. *voisié, envoisier.* All from *vitium* = (1) bad habit, and, thence, habit generally (2) lust, cf. Fr. *vice.* O. Fr. *viseus voiseus* sagax = It. *vezzoso* with the sense of *viziato*, the O. Fr. abst. *voisdie* is perhaps a der. from adj. *voisié*, = a Pr. *vezadia* contr. *vesdia, voisdie.*

Vizzo guizzo It. weak, flaccid; from *vietus* treated like rudis &c., v. *fuio.*

Vœu Fr. (m.), E. *vow*; from *votum*, Pr. *vot*, vb. *vouer*, Pr. *vodar*; *dévouer*, L. *devotare*, E. *devote.*

Vogare It., Sp. *bogar*, Pg. Pr. *vogar*, Fr. *voguer* to sail, row; abst. It. Pg. *voga*, Sp. *boga*, Fr. *vogue* (1) rowing, course of a ship (2) E. *vogue.* For *gogare* (cf. *vague*) from an O. H. G. *wogòn*, G. *wogen* = O. H. G. *wagen*, M. H. G. *wagen*, G. *bewegen* to set in motion, *in wago wesan* = être en vogue.

Voire voir O. Fr. Pic. adv.; from L. *vere.*

Voisdie — *vizio.*

Voison O. Fr., Lorr. *veho*, Wall. *wiha* polecat, L. L. *veso*. From A. S. *vesle*, E. *weasel*, M. H. G. *wisel.* Hence, perhaps, Norm. *veson* a lewd woman.

Voiture Fr. carriage; from *vectura*, It. *vettura.*

Volcar Sp. to upset, overthrow, Cat. *bolcar*, *embolicar* to entangle, Limous. *boulcà* to pour out; for *volvicar* from *volvere.* Pg. *emborcar* for *embolcar?*

Vole — *veule.*

Voler — *embler.*

Volere It., Pr. *voler*, Fr. *vouloir*, Wal. *vreà*, Sp. only in comp. e. g. *si-vuel-qual* for *quilibet;* from *velle*, but conjugated as from a root *vol*, cf. L. L. *roleam* for *velim*, *volerem* for *vellem.* Wal. *vreà*, subst. *vreare* = *vlere vrere* by contr. from *volere*, cf. Lomb. *voré.* Hence It. *voglia*, vb. *invogliare* to bring one to one's will, to *inveigle.*

Volgere It. (also *volvere*) owes its *g* to a supposed analogy to verbs conjugated in the same form: *volgere volsi volto*, *ergere ersi erto* &c.

Volpilh Pr. cowardly; from *vulpecula.* Hence vb. O. Fr. *goupiller* to treat cowardly.

Volta It. Pr., Fr. *volte voûte*, Wal. *bolte*, Sp. *boveda* (Pg. *abobeda* from a Pr. form *vouta*), E. *vault;* from *volvere volutus*, Rom. *voltus* (It. Pr.), hence vb. *voltare*, Sp. *voltear* &c., cf. s. *bulto.*

Vore — *orlo.*

Voto It. empty, vb. *votare.* *Voto* is probably *volto* hollowed out, cf. Neap. *vota* — *volta*, *votare* — *voltare*, Ven. *luna roda* the waning moon with It. *la luna volta* the moon wanes. The Ven. *vodo*, Pied. *void*, Lomb. *voeuid*, Sard. *boidu*, *boitu* (vb. *s-buidai*) must be referred to the O. Fr. *vuid* (E. *void*), Fr. *vide.*

Vouer — *voeu.*

Vouloir — *volere.*

Voûte — *volta.*

Voyer Fr. road-surveyor; from *viarius*, in O. Fr. = *vicarius*, v. Ducange.

Voyer Fr. in *convoyer* to convoy, *envoyer* to send, subst. *convoi*, *envoi (convoy, envoy);* from *conviare*, *inviare.* It. *convojare* is from the Fr.

Vrai Fr., O. Fr. Pr. *verai* true; not from *verax* but from *veracus*, cf. from *ebrius ebriacus*, Pr. *ybriai*, *Cambrai* from *Cameracum*, *Douai* from *Duacum.*

Vréder Fr. to run to and fro; from *veredus*, cf. Sp. *vereda.*

Vrille — *verrina.*

W.

Waggon Fr. from the E. *waggon*, A. S. *vâcen* = G. *wagen*.
Warlouque — *berlusco*.
Welke O. Fr. = A. S. *veolc*, E. *welk*, M. Du. *welk*.
Werbler werbloier O. Fr.; from G. *wirbeln*, E. *warble*.
Wigre O. Fr. spear; from O. N. *vigr*, A. S. *vigar*, *vigur*.
Wilecome O. Fr., vb. *welcumier;* a word introd. in the 12th cent.
from the A. S. *vilecume*, *vilcumian*, E. *welcome*; the "loving
cup" was also called *vilcom*, Hung. *billikom*, It. *bellicone* (Redi),
Fr. *vidrecome*.

X.

Xaloque — *scirocco*.
Xamete — *sciamito*.
Xaque — *scacco*.
Xaqueca Sp. Pg. head-ache; from Ar. *shaqiqah*, one side of
the head.
Xara Sp. Pg. (1) wild rose (2) dart, arrow, adj. Sp. *xaro;* cf.
Ar. *sha'râ* rough, bristly, bushes, shrubs.
Xarcia — *sarte*.
Xarifo Sp. fine, showy, well-dressed; from Ar. *sharif* noble,
cf. the Turk. *hatti sherif* noble hand writing = royal decree.
Xarope — *siroppo*.
Xato xata Sp. calf; from Ar. *sha't* shoot, twig, scion?
Xauro — *augurio*.
Xefe — *chef*.
Xeme — *scemo*.
Xerga — *gergo*.
Xergon — *sargia*.
Xeringa — *sciringa*.
Xibia — *seppia*.
Xicara Sp. chocolate cup, hence Pg. *chicara*, It. *chicchera;* from
the Mexican *xicalli*, v. Mahn, p. 18.
Xisca — *sescha*.
Xugo — *suco*.

Y.

Y — *ivi*.
Ya — *già*.
Yantar O. Sp., Pg. *jantar*, Rh. *ientar* to breakfast; from L. *jen-
tare*, L. L. *jantare*.
Yedgo — *eppio*.

Yegua — *cavallo*.

Yelmo — *elmo*.

Yermo — *ermo*.

Yerno Sp. son-in-law; from *gener*, Pg. *genro*, Fr. *gendre*.

Yerto Sp. rough, stiff; from *hirtus*, Pg. *hirto*, It. *irto*. O. Fr. *en-herdir* to bristle up.

Yesca — *esca*.

Yeuse — *elce*.

Ypréau Fr. a sort of elm; from *Yprés* where it abounds.

Yunque — *incude*.

Z.

Zabullir Sp. to plunge, dive; from *sub-bullire* to bubble.

Záooaro záoohero It. a lump of excrement (on sheep &c.); from O.H.G. *zahar*, M.H.G. *zaher* (G. *zähre* tear) drop, dropping, cf. Gk. δάχρυ. Ven. is *zacola*. From *pillola* we have *pillacchera* with same meaning.

Zaffata zaffo — *tape* and *ceffo*.

Zafferano It., Sp. *azafran*, Fr. *safran*, Wal. *sofrán*, E. *saffron;* from Ar. *za'farán*.

Zafo Sp., Pg. *safo* free, vb. *zafar, safar* to free, clear, adorn; from Ar. *sahd* to peel, shave, trim.

Zaga Sp. O. Pg. load on the back of a carriage, back part of a thing, O.Sp. *zaga* (Sp. *azaga*) behind; Sp. *rezaga* rear. From Ar. *sdqah* rear, or from Basque *atzaga* end (*atzea* hinder part).

Zagaia azagaia Sp. Pg., O. Fr. *arcigaye, archegaye*, It. *zagaglia* point of a spear, Moorish javelin. From Ar. *al-khdziq*.

Zagal Sp. Pg. shepherd, stout youth, swain. From *sagum*, or from Ar. *zugal* bold?

Zahareño — *safara*.

Zahorra — *zavorra*.

Zahurda Sp. hogstye; from B. *sar* to enter and *urdea* swine (Larramendi).

Zaino It. Sp. Pg. brown, chestnut-colour; from the Ar.

Zaino It., Sp. *zaina* a shepherd's pouch; from O.H.G. *zain* pipe, or *zaind* basket.

Zalagarda Sp. ambuscade; from O. G. *zdld* ruin and *warta* ambush.

Zalea Sp. sheepskin with the wool on; from B. *osa ulea* all wool, v. Larram.

Zamarro Sp. sheepskin, *zamarra, chamarra*, Sard. *acciamarra* coat made of sheepskin, It. *zimarra*, hence Fr. *chamarrer* to trim with fur; properly house-coat, from B. *echamarra* (Larramendi).

Zambo Sp. bandy-legged; from *scambus*.

Zambra Sp. Moorish festival; Ar. *zamr* song, or *sâmirah* company.

Zampa zampar zampillo — *tape*.

Zampogna zampoña — *sampogna*.

Zana It. basket; from O. H. G. *zeinâ*.

Zanahoria Sp., Pg. *cenoura* carrot; from the B. where it = yellow root, Cat. *safranaria*.

Zanca It. Sp., Pg. *sanco* shank, long bone, stalk, Sp. *zanco*, Lomb. *zanch*, Ven. *zanca* stilt, Pr. *sanca* cothurnus, Sard. *zancone* shin. Also Pg. *chanca* long foot, Sp. *chanco chanclo* patten, clog. From A. S. *scanca*, E. *shank* = an O. H. G. *scancho*.

Zanco It. left; for *stanco* wearied, left, as *zambecco* for *stambecco*.

Zanefa — *cenefa*.

Zangano Sp., Pg. *zangão* drone, idler. It is the It. *zingano* gipsy.

Zanna It. tusk, hook; from O. H. G. *zand, zan*, G. *zahn* a tooth. Another form *sanna* is found, the *s* of which is probably due to L. *sanna*.

Zanni It., E. *zany* the clown in a comedy; a provincial form of *Gianni* for *Giovanni*, v. Menage.

Zanzara — *zenzara*.

Zapata — *ciabatta*.

Zappa It. Rh., Sp. *zapa* spade, Fr. *sape sap;* vb. *zappare* &c. to sap. From σκαπάνη, σκάπτειν, *sc* becoming *z* as in *zolla* from *skolla?*

Zaque Sp. wine-bottle; from B. *zaguia, zaquia*, from *zato-quia* leathern bottle, Larram.

Zara — *azzardo*.

Zaragüelles Sp. (m. plur.) a kind of breeches or drawers, L. L. pl. *saraballa, sarabella, sarabara* "fluxa et sinuosa vestimenta" Ugatio, L. Gr. σαράβαρα, Ar. *sirwâl*, whence Pg. *ceroulas*.

Zaranda Sp., Pg. *cirandа* sieve, screen; from Ar. *sarada* "contexuit".

Zarcillo Sp., O. Sp. *cercillo* ear-ring; from *circellus* (Apicius), B. *circillua*.

Zarco Sp. Pg. light-blue, Sic. *zarcu* pale; from Ar. *zaraq* subst., *azraq* adj. blue.

Zarpa zarpar — *sarpare*.

Zarria Sp. dirt, mud; from B. *zarria, charria* hog.

Zarza Sp. thorn, thorn-bush, bramble (whence *zarzaparilla*, v. *salsapariglia*); from B. *zartzia*, from *sartu* to penetrate and *cia* point, whence also *zarzaidea* raspberry-bush (*idea* companion or *aidea* connexion).

Zata — *zatta.*

Zato Sp. morsel of bread; from B. *zatoa* morsel.

Zatta sattera It., Sp. *zata, zatara* raft; of unknown origin.

Zavorra It., Wal. *saburę*, Sp. *zahorra, sorra* ballast; from *saburra.*

Zassa sassera long curly hair, from O. H. G. *zatd*, G. *zolte* shaggy hair.

Zeba It., Sp. *chibo chivo* kid; the root is found also in the O. H. G. *zibbe* lamb, Alb. *tzgiep, tsjap*, Wal. *tzap* he-goat = Lomb. *zaver.*

Zebelina — *zibellino.*

Zebro It., Sp. Pg. E. *zebra*, Fr. *zèbre;* a South African word.

Zecca It., Rh. *zece, zecla*, Fr. *tique*, E. *tick* (insect); from Du. *leke*, M. H. G. *zèche*, G. *zecke.*

Zecca It. mint, Sp. *zeca seca;* hence *zecchino* a gold coin; from Ar. *sikkah* a stamp or die, mint.

Zediglia It., Sp. *cedilla*, Fr. *cédille*, a *cedilla* used to show that a *c* has the sound of *z* (formerly written *cz*, e. g. *canczon* = *cançon, czo* = *ço); a dim. of *zeta.*

Zelo It. Sp. Pg., Pg. also *cio* for *cilo*, Fr. *zèle*, E. *zeal;* from *zelus* (ζῆλος). Hence It. *zeloso*, Sp. *zeloso*, Pg. *cios*, E. *zealous;* also with a palatal initial (as in *giuggiola* from *zizyphum*, *gengiovo* from *zinziber*), It. *geloso*, Pr. *gelos*, Fr. *jaloux*, i. *jealous*, sbst. *gelosia* &c. *jealousy*, also = a Venetian blind, Sp. *celosia.* Comp. Sp. vb. *rezelar*, Pg. *recear*, sbst. *rezelo, receo.*

Zendale sendale It., Sp. Pg. Pr. O. Fr. *cendal*, M. H. G. *zendal*, *zindal*, G. *zindel*, also It. *zendado*, Pr. *sendat*, M. H. G. *zendat* a sort of taffeta, chiefly used in France for banners, Sp. also a fine linen stuff; usu. derived from *sindon.*

Zensara sansara It., Wal. *tzenzariu*, Sp. *zenzalo*, O. Fr. *cincelle* gnat, mosquito, so O. H. G. *zinzila zenzala* gnat, cf. Alb. *zinziras* cricket; an onomatop., cf. L. *zinzitulare* to chirp; cf. M. H. G. *getse* gnat from *gal* song. Hence Pg. vb. *zinir zunir* to hum (of insects).

Zensovero, sensero and *gengiovo* It., Sp. *gengibre agengibre*, Pr. *gingebre*, Fr. *gingembre*, E. *ginger*, Wal. *ghimberiu*, M. Du. *ghinchere* (G. *ingwer*); from L. *zingiberi* (ζιγγίβερι), *zinziber* an Oriental word. Ar. *zanjabil.* From *g* = *z*, cf. *zelo.*

Zeppa It. wedge, *zeppare* to cram full; *zeppo* crammed. From O. H. G. *zapfo*, M. H. G. *zepfe*, G. *zapfen* peg, whence also *zaffo.*

Zero It. Sp. Pg. E., Fr. *zéro;* from Ar. *çifron, çifr*, v. s. *cifra* in which the *c* = Ar. *ç* (ﺹ). Mil. has *nulla.*

Zeste Fr. (m.) the *zest* of a nut; from *schistus* (σχιστός), cf. *fis* (Com.) from *fissus*. For *z* = *sch*, cf. *cédule* from *schedula*.

Zevro — *loivre*.

Zezzo — *sezzo*.

Zezzolo — *tetta*.

Zibellino It., Pr. *sebeli*, *sembeli*, Sp. Pg. f. *cebellina*, *zebellina*, Fr. *zibeline*, L. L. *sabellinus*, *sabellum*, O. Fr. E. *sable*, G. *zobel*; a Slavonic word, Russ. *sobol*, Serv. *samur*, Wal. *samur*. Ar. *sammur*.

Zibetto It., Fr. *civette*, E. *civet*; an Oriental word, M. Gk. ζαπέτιον, v. Pott, Lassen's Zeitschrift 4, 17. Sp. is *gato de algalia*.

Zibibbo It. a Syrian raisin; from Ar. *zabib*.

Zigrino — *chagrin*.

Zimarra — *zamarro*.

Zimbello It., Sp. *cimbel*, Pr. O. Fr. *cembel* decoy-bird, decoying; vb. It. *zimbellare*, O. It. *cimbellare*, Pr. *cembelar*, O. Fr. *cembeler (encembeler)* to decoy. *Cymbalum*, dim. *cymbellum*, was the bell which summoned the monks to their meals. O. Fr. Pr. *cembel* also = a meeting of players at a game, espec. a tournament, hence vb. *cembeler*, O. Sp. *cempellar* to tilt, joust.

Zio It., Sp. Pg. *tio* uncle, It. *zia*, Sp. Pg. Pr. *tia* (Pr. *sia*) aunt; from late L. *thius thia* (θειός, θεία).

Zipolo It. peg in the cock of a vessel; from G. *zipfel* tip, cf. Du. E. *tip*.

Zirbo It. caul, L. L. *cirbus;* from Ar. *tarb*.

Zirigaña Sp. adulation; from B. *zurigaiu*, *churigaña* (whitewashed).

Zirlare It., Sp. *chirlar*, *chirriar*, Pg. *chirlar chilrar* to chirp; from L. *zinzilulare*, contr. *zilulare*.

Zito It. boy, *zita* girl, also *citto citta*, *zitello zitella*, *cittolo cittola;* of the same origin as *zitta* teat; cf. Pied. *teta*, L. *mamilla* in both senses.

Zitta — *tetta*.

Zitto It., f. *zitta*, Sp. *chito chiton*, Fr. *chut*, Wal. *citu* an interjection, hush! an onomatop., like the L. *st*. To *chut* belongs Fr. *chuchoter* to whisper, *chucheter* to twitter, N. Pr. *chitá* to whisper.

Zoccolo — *soc*.

Zoira — *zorra*.

Zolla It. Rh. clod; from O. H. G. *scolla*, G. *scholle*, v. *zanca*.

Zompo — *zoppo*.

Zonza — *soso*.

Zoppo It., Sp. *zopo zompo*, Wald. *zop*, Rh. *zopps* lame, maimed, cf. O. Fr. *chope* log, stump; vb. Fr. *chopper* to knock against (O. Fr. *sopper*), It. *zoppiare* to halt, Cat. *ensopegar* to stumble;

from G. *schupfen* to push, Du. *schoppen*, cf. also Du. *sompe* lame, *sompen* to halt.

Zorra Sp. Pg., O. Sp. *zurra* fox, hence Pg. *zorro*, B. *zurra* cunning. Prob. from vb. *zurrar* to shave off the hair, because the fox loses his hair in summer (Covarruvias), cf. ἀλωπεκία baldness, from ἀλώπηξ. *Zorra* would thus be a nickname of the fox, as it is also = a harlot, cf. *scortum*. Perhaps the Pr. *zoira* "vetus canis" is connected.

Zorsal Sp. Pg. a thrush; from Ar. *zorzúr*, or from B. *zozorra*.

Zote Sp. Pg., Fr. *sot*, Piedm. *sot*, E. *sot*; according to some, from the Semitic, Rabbin. *shôteh* fool. But Pictet refers it to the Ir. *suthan* blockhead, rogue, *sotaire* fop, and these he traces to the Sanskrit.

Zotico It. boorish, rude; from *exoticus*, according to Menage, but It. *z = x* is not elsewhere found.

Zozobrar Sp. to be weather-beaten, founder (of a ship); from *so* under and *sobre* over, so = to be turned upside-down.

Zucca — *cucuzza*.

Zucchero It., Sp. Pg. *azúcar*, Pr. Fr. *sucre*, Wal. *zehar*, O. H. G. *zucura*, G. *zucker*, E. *sugar*; from Ar. *sukkár as-sukkar* (whence, immediately, the Sp.), this from the Pers. *shakar*, Sansk. शर्करा, Gk. σάκχαρ, σάκχαρον, L. *saccharum*. Sugar was cultivated by the Arabs in Egypt, Crete and Syria and also in Sicily and Spain. From Egypt it was imported to Venice, from Spain to France.

Zuffa It. scramble, row; from G. *zupfen* to pluck, as *ruffa* from *rupfen*; Swiss *zuffe* = bundle.

Zufolo — *ciufolo*.

Zumaque — *sommaco*.

Zumaya *sumacaya* Sp. an owl; from B. *zumba-caya* able to mock; or from Sp. *zumba-cayo* mocking-daw.

Zumbar Sp. to sound, hum; an onomatop.

Zumo Sp. juice, sap; from ζωμός sauce.

Zupia Sp. sour wine, refuse; from B. *zupea zurpea* sediment.

Zuppa — *sopa*.

Zura *zuro zurana zurita zorita* dove, stock-dove.

Zurcir Sp., Pg. *cirzir*, *serzir*, Cat. *surgir* to baste, stitch, patch; from *surcire*.

Zurdo Sp. left, left-handed; orig. awkward, from *surdus* deaf, Sp. *no ser zurdo* = to be clever.

Zurlo It. also *zurro* lust, heat; connected with L. *surire* (Apuleius).

Zurrar Sp., Pg. *surrar* to curry, tan, drub. Orig. = to shave, so, perhaps, a contraction of *surradere*.

Zurriaga Sp. thong, whip; from B. *zurriaga*, cf. *scuriada* (cf. *z* from *sc* in *zambo* &c.).

Zurrir surriar Sp. to hum, buzz; an onomatop., L. *susurrare*.

Zurron Sp., Pg. *surrão* a shepherd's wallet, leathern scrip; from Ar. *çurrah* a purse. Cat. has *sarró*, B. *zorroa*.

Zutano citano Sp. = L. quidam. According to Mahn, from G. *so-than* for *so-yethan (so-done)* from *thun* to make; *sothun* is found in Prov. Germ., and in Dan. *saadan*, Swed. *sådan*, Du. *zoodanig*.

ENGLISH VOCABULARY.

Note. English words, which are identical in form with Romance words, are not inserted here.

A.

Abandon	— bando.
Abet	— beter.
Abyss	— abisso.
Accost	— costa.
Accontre	— encire.
Achieve	— acabar.
Acquaint	— conto.
Admiral	— almirante.
Adjust	— guista.
Advantage	— ansl.
Adventure	— avventura.
Advice	— viso.
Adze	— accia.
Aglet	— aguglia.
Agree	— grado.
Aim	— esmar.
Alas	— lasso.
Alembic	— lambicco.
Alert	— erto.
Allegiance	— lige.
Alligator	— lacerta.
Allow	- allodio, allouer.
Alloy	— lega.
Almond	— mandorla.
Alms	— limosina.
Ambassador	— ambasciata.
Amber	— ambra.
Amble	— ambiare.
Ambry	— armoire.
Ambush	— bosco.
Amenable	— ammainare.
Amuse	— muso.
Ancestor	— ancêtres.
Anchovy	— acciuga.
Ancient	— insegna.
Andiron	— landier.
Anguish	— angoscia.
Anneal	— niello.
Annoy	— noja.
Anthem	— antienne.
Antic	— antique.
Appanage	— appaner.
Apparel	— parecchio.
Approach	— proche.
Apricot	— albercocco.
Apron	— nappa.
Arbalest	— arbalète.
Arbour	— albergo.
Arch	— aragon.
Arraign	— desrener.
Arras	— arazzo.
Array	— redo.
Arrear	— retro.
Arris	— arista.
Artisan	— artigiano.
Ash	— ascua.
Assart	— essart.
Assay	— saggio.
Astonish	— étonner.
Atheling	— adelenc.
Attach	— tacco.
Attack	— tacco.
Attire	— tirer.
Attorney	— torno.
Auburn	— balbran.
Aumbry	— armoire.
Aunt	— tante.
Aunter	— avventura.
Avow	— voen.
Azure	— azzurro.

B.

Babble	— babil.
Babe &c.	— babbeo, bava.
Baboon	— babbuino.
Bachelor	— baccalare.
Badger	— blairean.
Baffle	— beffa.|
Bait	— beter.
Balk	— balco.
Ball	— balla, ballare.

Balloon, ballad	— balla, ballare.	Bleach	bianco.
Ballast	— lasto.	Bleak	— bianco.
Balluster, banis-		Blemish	— blême.
ter	— balaustro.	Blink	— bianco.
Banner	— banda.	Blow	— buf.
Barbican	— barbacane.	Blue	— biavo.
Bargain	— bargagno.	Board	— borda.
Barge	— barca.	Boat	— batto.
Baratry	— baratto.	Roast	— bozza.
Barnacles	— bornio.	Bold	— baldo.
Barouche	— biroccio.	Bolster	— poltro.
Barrel	— barra.	Bolt	— blutor.
Barrister	— barra.	Bombazine	bambagio.
Barter	— baratto.	Booty	— bottino.
Barren	— bréhaigne.	Borage	— borraggine.
Basil	— bis.	Borel	— bourreau.
Basin	— bacino.	Bottomry	— bomerie.
Bastard	— basto.	Bowel	— bndello.
Baste	— basta.	Brace	— bressin.
Bat	— bastone.	Brag	— brague.
Bat (-horse)	— basto.	Braid	— brete.
Bate	— battere.	Brase	— bragia.
Batter	— battere.	Brasier	— bragia.
Battery	— battere.	Brass	— bragia.
Battle	— battere.	Brawn	— brandone.
Bawdekin	— baldaccbino.	Brazil	— brasile.
Bawdrick	— bandré.	Breach	— brèche.
Bawson	— balza.	Break	— brisez.
Bay (sbst.)	— baja.	Breech	— braga.
Bay (adj.)	— bajo.	Breeze	— briser, brezza.
Bay (at bay)	— bada.	Brew	— bras.
Bay (vb.)	— bada.	Brick	— briser.
Bayonet	— baïonnette.	Bride	— bru.
Beadle	— bidello.	Bridle	— brida.
Beak	— becco.	Brim	— berme.
Beaker	— biccbiere.	Broach	— brocco.
Beat	— battre.	Brocade	— brocco.
Beaver	— bevero.	Broccoli	— brocco.
Become	— avenant.	Brock	— brocco.
Bedel	— bidello.	Brocket	— brocco.
Bedizen	— badigeon.	Broil	— broglio, bruciare.
Beefeater	— buf.	Brooch	— brocco.
Beer	— birra.	Broth	— brodo.
Beestings	— beter.	Brotbel	— borda.
Believe	— ricredersi.	Brown	— bruno.
Belfry	— battifredo.	Brown (study)	— broncio.
Bench	— banco.	Brolder	— bordo.
Beverage	— breuvage.	Browse	— broza.
Bezant	— bisante.	Bruise	— briser.
Bezel	— bis.	Brush	— broza.
Bias	— biais.	Buck	— bouc.
Bier	— bara.	Buck, buck-	
Bitch	— biche.	asbes &c.	— bucato.
Blade	— biado.	Bucket	— bac.
Blank	— bianco.	Buckle	— boudo.
Blaze	— blasone.	Buckram	— bucherame.
Blazon	— blasone.	Budget	— bolgia.

Buffet	— buf.	Carriage	— carriera.
Buffoon	— buf.	Carrion	— carogna.
Bulge	— bulto.	Carvel	— caravello.
Bulk	— bulto.	Case	— cassa.
Bull	— bolla.	Cash	— cassa.
Bullet	— bolla.	Cassock	— casacca.
Bullion	— bolla.	Cat	— gatto.
Bulwark	— boulevard.	Catch	— cacciare.
Buu	— bugna.	Cater	— accattare.
Bundle	— benda.	Caterpillar	— cbeuille.
Bunion	— bugna.	Cattle	— accattare.
Bunt	— bugna.	Caudle	— bolla.
Buoy	— boja.	Causeway	·· calzada.
Burden	— bordone.	Cavalcade	— cavallo.
Burgeon	— bourgeon.	Cavalier	— cavallo.
Burgh	— borgo.	Cavalry	— cavallo.
Burine	— burino.	Celery	— sedano.
Burn	— bruno.	Cemetery	— cimeterio.
Burnish	— bruno.	Centre (vb.)	— centinare.
Buskin	— borzacchino.	Centrie	— cimeterio.
Buss	— busso.	Chafe	— cbauffer.
Buss	·· bus.	Challenge	— cbalouge.
Bustard	— ottarda.	Chamberlain	— camarlingo.
Butcher	— bouc.	Chap	— cbaupir.
Butt	— bozza.	Chapel, chaplet	— cappa.
		Chapman	— cbaupir.

C.

		Chapter	— capitolo.
Cabbage	— cabus.	Chattels	— accattare.
Cabin	— capanna.	Check	— scacco.
Cabinet	— capanna.	Cheer	— cara.
Caitiff	— cattivo.	Chemist	— alchimia.
Cajole	— gabbia.	Chequer	— scacco.
Caliver, calliper	— calibro.	Cherry	— ciriegia.
Cambric	— Cambrai	Chess	— scacco.
Camlet	— cambellotto.	Chief	— cbef.
Camous	— camuso.	Chimney	— camiuata.
Camphor	— canfora.	Chisel	— cincel.
Canoe	— cane.	Chivalry	— cavallo.
Cant	— canto.	Choose	— choisir.
Canteen	— canto.	Chopine	— cbapa.
Cantle	— canto.	Chough	— cboc.
Canton	— canto.	Chub	— cbabot.
Canvas	— canape.	Cider	— sidro.
Cape	— cappa.	Cipher	— cifra.
Caper	— cappero.	Civet	— zibetto.
Caper	— cabrer.	Claim	— cbiamare.
Capstan	— cabestan.	Clarion	clairon.
Captain	— capitano.	Clash	— chiasso.
Caraway	— carvi.	Clear	— chiaro.
Carbine	— carabina.	Climb	— grimper.
Careen	— crena.	Clock	— clocbe.
Career	— carriera.	Clod	— crotte.
Carmine	— carmesino.	Close	— chiudere.
Carnival	— carnevale.	Clove	— cbiodo.
Carob	— carrobo.	Cluck	— cbiocciare.
Carouse	— trincare.	Coach	— cocchio.
		Coast	— costa.

Coat	— cotta.	Cream	— crema.
Cochineal	— cocciniglia.	Cress	— crescione.
Cock	— cocca.	Cricket	-- criquet.
Cock	— coq.	Crimson	— carmesino.
Cockade	— coq.	Cripple	— groppo.
Cockchafer	— hanneton.	Crock	— cruche.
Cockle	coqnelicot.	Crop	— groppo.
Cockney	— cuccagna.	Crosier	— croccia.
Cod	— cosse.	Crotchet	— croccia.
Coffee	— caffe.	Crowd	— rote.
Coffer	— cofano.	Crupper	— groppo.
Coffin	— cofano.	Cruse, cruskin	— crisuelo.
Cog	— cocca.	Crutch	— croccia.
Coil	— cogliere.	Cuckoo, cuckold	— cuceo.
Colander	— couler.	Cue	— coda.
Cole	— cavolo.	Cullis	— couler.
Combe	-- combo.	Culverin	— conlouvre.
Comfort	— confortare.	Cumber	— colmo.
Commodore (Pg.		Cup	— coppa.
capitão mor)	— capitano.	Cupola	— coppa.
Companion	— compagno.	Cure, curate &c.	— cura.
Comrade	— camerata.	Curfew	— couvre-feu.
Conduit	— docciare.	Curlew	— corlieu.
Coney	— coniglio.	Currant	— Corinthe.
Constable	— contestabile.	Curry	— redo.
Contraband	— bando.	Curtail	-- tagliare.
Contrive	— trovare.	Curtain	— cortina.
Control	— rotolo.	Curvet	— corvetta.
Coop	— coppa.	Cushion	— coltrice.
Cope	— cappa.	Custom	— costuma.
Copper	— cuivre.		
Copperas	— copparosa.		
Cordwain	— cordovano.	**D.**	
Cornelian	— corniola.		
Corporal	— caporale.	Daffodil	— asphodèle.
Coat	— coûter.	Dagger	— daga.
Cosy	— cheto.	Dais	— tas.
Cotton	— cotone.	Damage	— dommage.
Count	— contare.	Damask	— damasco.
Count (sbst.)	— conte.	Damsel, dan	— donno.
Counterpane	— coltrice.	Damson	— damasco.
Country	— contrada.	Dandelion	— dent-de-lion.
Courser	— coso.	Dandle, dandy	— dondolare.
Covenant	— convine.	Dapper	— trape.
Covent	— convine.	Darling	— dorelot.
Coverlet	— couvre-lit.	Darraign, dar-	
Covet	— cupido.	reine	-- desrener.
Covin	— convine.	Date	— dattero.
Coward	— codardo.	Daub	— addobbare.
Coy	— cheto.	Daunt	— ducndo.
Crag	— cran.	Dean	— doyen.
Crane	— grone.	Debauch	— bauche.
Cranny	— cran, carne.	Debt	— dette.
Crape	— crêpe.	Decant	— canto.
Crash	— écraser.	Decay	— cadere.
Crawfish	— écrevisse.	Decoy	—
Crawl	— grouiller.	Defalcate	— falcare.
		Defray	— frais.

Delay	— délai, dileguare.	Emerods	hémorroïdes.
Deliver	liverare.	Emery	smeriglio.
Demean	— ammainare.	Employ	— piegare.
Demesne	— domaine.	Enamel	smalto.
Demure	— mûr.	Encroach	- croccia.
Denizen	— eus.	Endeavour	— devoir.
Deploy	— piegare.	Endow	— douer.
Despatch	— dépêcher.	Enhance	— anzi.
Despite	— dépit.	Ensign	— insegna.
Detach	— tacco.	Entail	— taglia.
Detail	— taglia.	Entice	— tizzo.
Deuce (at play)	— deux.	Entire	— intero.
Device, devise	— divisu.	Ennre	— augurio.
Diaper	— diaspro.	Equerry	— scudo.
Die	— dado.	Equip	— schifo.
Diet	— dieta.	Ermine	— armellino.
Disaster	— astro.	Errant	erre.
Discard	— scartare.	Escape	— scappare.
Dismay	— smagare.	Escheat	— cadere.
Distrain,distress	— détresse.	Eschew	— schivare.
District	— détresse.	Escort	— corgere.
Ditty	— dechado.	Escutcheon	— scudo.
Dock	— docciare.	Esil	— aisll.
Dolt	— doudo.	Esquire	— scudo.
Dosol	— donillo.	Essay	— saggio.
Dote, dotard	— radoter.	Essoin	— sogna.
Douse	— docciare.	Exchequer	— scacco.
Dower, dowager	— douer.	Ewe	— ouaille.
Down	— duna.	Ewer	— eau.
Drab	— drap.	Eyre	— erro.
Draff	— dragne.		
Dregs	— dragne.		
Drill	— tralicclo.	**F.**	
Drink	— trincare.	Fail	— fallire.
Droll	— drôle.	Fairy	— fata.
Dross	— dragne.	Fallow	— falbo.
Drove	— tropa.	Faldstool	— faldistorio.
Drug	— droga.	Falter	— faltare.
Drugget	— droguet.	Fancy	— fantasie.
Dub	— addobbare.	Fardel	— fardo.
Duke, duchy &c.	— duca.	Farm	— ferme.
Dungeon	— duna.	Farrier	— ferro.
		Farthing	— ferlino.
E.		Farthingalo	— verdugo.
		Fash	— fastio.
Eager	— aigre.	Fashion	— façon.
Eagle	— aigle.	Faulchion	— falcone.
Easo	— agio.	Fault	— falta.
Ebb	— ébe.	Fawn	— faon.
Eglantine	— aiglent.	Fay	— fata.
Electuary	— lattovaro.	Feat, feature	— fattizio.
Ell	— alna.	Feo	— feo.
Embarrass	— barra.	Feeble	— fievole.
Embassy	— ambasciata.	Felt	— feltro.
Embrocation	— brocca.	Fennel	— finocchio.
Embroider	— bordo.	Ferret	— furon.
Emerald	— smeraldo.	Fers	— fierce.

Fescue	— festuca.	Furbish	forbire.
Feud	– faide.	Furmety	frumentée.
Feudal	fio.	Fustian	- fustagna.
Fowterer	veltro.		
Fiddle	— viola.		**G.**
Fief	— fio.		
Field	— tala.	Gabion	— gabbia.
Fife	— pipa.	Gain	-- guadagnare.
Filigree	- grano.	Gaiter	— guêtro.
Fillet	— ül.	Galingal	- galanga.
Filter	— feltro.	Galley	— galla.
Finch	— finco.	Gallimawfrey	— gallimafréc.
Fine (sbst.)	— finanza.	Gallon	— jalc.
Fine (adj.)	— fino.	Galloon	— gala.,
Fitchet	— fissau.	Galosh	— galoscia.
Flag	— flacco.	Gambison	— gambais.
Flail	— fléan.	Gamble, gambol	-- gamba.
Flap	— fiappo.	Gammon	— gamba.
Fleam	fiama.	Gander, gannet	— ganta.
Fleet	— flotta.	Gangreno	— cangrana.
Fletcher	— freccia.	Gaol	— gabbia.
Flitch	- flèche.	Garble	··· garbillo.
Flock	fiocco.	Garden	— giardino.
Flounce	·· froncir.	Gargle, gargoil	· gargatta.
Flour	— fleur.	Garland	- ghirlanda.
Flute	·· flauto.	Garment	-- guarnire.
Fodder	— fodero.	Garner	— grenier.
Foil	— folle.	Garnet	— grana.
Foin	·· faint.	Garnish	—· guarnire.
Fold	— falda.	Garret	— guarire.
Fool	-- folle.	Garrison	— guarnire.
Forage	— fodero.	Garter	— jarra.
Foreign	— fuora.	Gaudy	goda.
Forfeit	— forfare.	Gauge	— janger.
Foumart	— faina.	Gauntree	— cantiere.
Founder	— fundo.	Ganze	— gaza.
Foundry	— fondere.	Gavel	— gabella.
Frail	— frêle.	Gay	— gajo.
Fray	— fregare, frayeur.	Gazette	— gazzetta.
Freak	— fregare.	Gibbet	— ginbbetto.
Freebooter	— filibuster.	Gilly - flower	— girofano.
Freeze	—	Gimmals	— jumeau.
Fresh	— fresco.	Ginger	— zenzovero.'
Frieze	·· fregio.	Gipser	·- gibier.
Fret	-- frette.	Gizzard	— gésier.
Friar	— fraire.	Glare, glass	— glaire.
Frigate	— fregata.	Glean	— glaner.
Fright	— frayeur.	Glove	— lua.
Fringe	— frangia.	Goal	— gaule.
Frippery	— friper.	Goblin	— gobelin.
Frock	— rocchetto.	Gooseberry	— grosella.
Fuel	— fuoco.	Gore	— gheronc.
Fumitory	— fummosterno.	Gormandize	— gourmand.
Fund	— fondo.	Gout	— gotta.
Funnel	— fonil.	Gown	— gonna.
Fur	— fodero.	Graff, graft	— greffe.
Furbelow	— falbalà.	Grain	— grana.

Gramary	— grimojre.
Grant	— creanter.
Grate	— grada.
Grease	— gras.
Greet	— gridare.
Grill	— grada, bruciare.
Gripe	— griffer.
Groan	— grugnire.
Groat	— grosso.
Grocer	— grosso.
Grogram	— grosgrain.
Group	— groppo.
Grouse	— grigio.
Grudge	— gruger.
Gruel	— gruau.
Grumble	— grommeler.
Grunt	— grugnire.
Gudgeon	— goujon.
Guerdon	— guiderdone.
Guild	— goldra.
Gulf	— golfo.
Gull	— giallo.
Gurgeons	— gruger.
Gusset	— guscio.
Gutter	— gotta.

H.

Habergeon	— nsbergo.
Hack	— acciare.
Hack, hackney	— baca.
Halbert	— alabarda.
Hale, haul	— halar.
Halm	— chaume.
Halter	— nsbergo.
Hammock	— amaca.
Hamper	— anappo.
Harass	— barer.
Harbinger	— albergo.
Harbour	— albergo.
Hardy	— ardire.
Harlequin	— arlecchino.
Harlot	— arlotto.
Harness	— arneso.
Harold	— araldo.
Harp, harpoon	— arpa.
Harridan	— baridello.
Harry	— barer.
Hasb	— acciare.
Haste	— hâte.
Hatch	— acciare.
Hate	— baïr.
Hauberk	— usbergo.
Haunch	— anca.
Haunt	— banter.
Have	— haver.
Haven	— havre.

Hawser	— alzare.
Hazard	— azzardo.
Hearse	— berse.
Hedge	— bale.
Heinous	— baïr.
Helm, holmet	— elmo.
Henchman	— anca.
Herald	— araldo.
Hermit	— ermo.
Heron	— aghirone.
Herring	— aringa.
Hiccough	— hoquet.
Hideous	— bide.
Hilt	— elsa.
Hoarding	— bordo, bagordo.
Hobby, hobble	— bobino.
Hoist	— issare.
Hook	— hoc.
Hornet	— frelon.
Hose	— nosa.
Host	— hneber, oste.
Hostage	— ostaggio.
Housing	— bonsse.
Howl	— urlare.
Hulver	— houx.
Hurly-burly	— cbarivari.
Hurdle	— horde, bagordo.
Hurricane	— uracano.
Hurt, hurtlo	— nrtare.
Hutch	— bnebe.

I.

Imbrue	— breuvage.
Imp	— ente.
Impair	— empirer, piro.
Impeach	— ompêcher.
Indite	— dec.
Infantry	— fante.
Ingot	— lingot.
Ink	— inchiostro.
Inveigle	— volerc.
Invoice	— viso.
Issue	— uscire.

J.

Jabber	— jabot.
Jack, jacket	— giaca.
Jail	— gabbia.
Jar	— giara.
Jargon	— gergo.
Javelin	— giavelotto.
Jaw	— joue.
Jay	— gajo.
Jealous	— zelo.
Jelly	— geler.

Jennet	— ginete.	Lick	— loccare.
Jeopardy	— jeu parti.	Liege	— lige.
Jerfalcon	-- girfalco.	Limb	— lembo.
Jessamine	— gesmino.	Limbo	— lembo.
Jet	— gettare. ↖	Limehound	— limier.
Jewel	— godere.	Limn	-- enluminer.
Jig	— giga.	Lineage	— linea.
Jolet	-- giste.	Linnet	— linot.
Jolly	-- ginlivo.	Lintel	— linde.
Jostle	— giusta.	Liquorice	— regolizia.
Journey	— giorno.	List	— lista.
Joust	— ginsta.	Lists	— liccia.
Juggle	— giocolaro.	Litter	— lettiera.
Julep	— giulebbe.	Livery	— liverare.
Junket	— giuncata.	Lizard	— lacerta.

	Loadstone, load-
K.	star — locman.
	Loaf, loafer — gaglioffo.
Kerchief — couvre-chef.	Lodge — loggia.
Kerseymere — casimiro.	Loin — longe.
Kettle — cazza.	Lorimer — loiro.
Kickshaw — quelque chose.	Lot — lotto.
Kitchen — cucina.	Lout — lordo.
Knife — canif.	Lovage — levistico.
	Losenge -- insinga.
	Lumber — lombard.
L.	Lurch — lurcio.
	Lure - logoro.
Label — lambeau.	Lute -- linto.
Lace — laccio.	Lutestring -- lustrino.
Lack — lacca.	
Lackey — lacayo.	
Lacquer — lacca.	**M.**
Lake — lacca.	
Lampoon — rampa.	Mace — macco, mazza.
Lamprey -- lampreda.	Mackarel — maquereau.
Laniard, lanner — laniero.	Mad — matto.
Lap, lappet — lambeau.	Mail — maglia.
Lapis lazuli -- azzurro.	Maim — magagna.
Latch -- laccio.	Maintain — mantenere.
Latten — ottone.	Malapert — aperto.
Launch — lancia.	Mall — maglio.
Laundry --- lavanderia.	Mallard — malart.
Lavender -- lavanda.	Malmsey — malvasia.
Law - lague.	Manage -- manoar.
Lay - lai.	Mandarin — mandaro.
League — lega.	Mandrake — mandragora.
Lease — lasciare.	Mangle — mangano.
Leash — laisse.	Mangold — manigoldo.
Leaven — levain.	Mannekin — mannequin.
Lecher &c. — loccare.	Manner — maniero.
Leden — ladino.	Manor -- mas.
Lees — lia.	Mansion -- magione.
Leisure — loisir.	Mantle — manto.
Lemon — limone.	Manure — manœuvre.
Level — libella.	Mar — marrir.
Lover, levy — levare.	March, marquis — marca.
Leveret — lièvre.	Marchpane — marsapane.

Market	— marché.	Moult	— muer.
Marjoram	— mujarana.	Mount	— avalange.
Marl	— marne.	Mourn	— morne.
Marl, marline	— merlin.	Much	— mucho.
Marmelade	— membrillo.	Muff, muffle	— muffarc.
Maroon	— elmarrao.	Mullion	— mezzo.
Marsh	— mare.	Mummery	— momerie.
Marshal	- mariscaleo.	Mur	— mormo.
Marten, martlet	— martora.	Murder	— meurtre.
Marvel	... maraviglia.	Muscle	— moule.
Mask	— maschera.	Muse	— muso.
Mason	— maçon.	Mushroom	— mousse.
Mass	— messa.	Musket	— moschetto.
Mastiff	— magione.	Muslin	— mussolo.
Mate (check-		Mustard	— mostarda.
mate)	— malto.	Muster	— mostrare.
Matriculate	— marguillier.	Mutiny	— meute.
Mattrass	— materasso.	Mutton	— montouc.
Mangre	— grado.	Muzzle	— muso.
Maund	— manne.	Mystery	— mestiero.
Meagre	— maigre.		
Mead	— mes.	**N.**	
Meddle, medley	— mischiare.		
Medlar	— mespilo.	Nag	— haca.
Megrim	— magrana.	Necromancy	— negromante, gri-
Menial	— magione.	Nias	— nido. [moire.
Mention	— mentare.	Nico	— nescio.
Merchant	— marché.	Nightmare	— cauchemar.
Mercy	— mercé.	Nowel, newel	— noyau.
Mere	— maro.	Nuisance	— nuire, nuocere.
Mesh	— maschera.	Nutmeg	— mugue.
Mess	— mets.		
Messuage	- magione.	**O.**	
Mew, mews	-- muer.		
Mew (bird)	— mouette.	Onion	— oignon.
Mien	— mine.	Ointment	— oindre.
Mile	— miglio.	Orleal	— ordalie.
Milt	— milza.	Ordure	— ordo.
Minion	— mignon.	Oriole	— loriot.
Minish	— minuzzare.	Osproy	— orfraie.
Minstrel	— mestiero.	Oss	— oscr.
Minnet, minute	— minuzzaro.	Ostler	— oste.
Mirror	— miroir.	Ostrich	— struzzo.
Mischance	— méchauce.	Otter	— loutra.
Mischief	— menoscabo.	Ounce	— lonza.
Miscreant	— rieredersi.	Oust	— òter.
Mitten	— mezzo.	Owl	— urlarc.
Mizen	— mezzo.		
Moat	— motta.	**P.**	
Mock	— moquer.		
Mohair	— moire.	Pace	— passo.
Moist	— moneio.	Paddle	— pattuglia.
Molo	· mulot.	Pall	— poéle.
Moor	— amarrar.	Paint	— peindre.
Morocco	— marrochiuo.	Palaver	— parola.
Morsel	— morcean.	Palfrey	— palafreno.
Mote	— motta.	Pall	— palio.

Pallet	— paglia.	Pioneer	— pedone.'
Palsy, palasye	— paralysie.	Pip	— pipita.
Pane, panel	— pan	Piston	— pestare.
Pannier	— paniere.	Pit	— pozzo.
Pansy	— pensée.	Pitcher	— bicchiere.
Pantry	— pain, pane.	Pittance	— pietanza.
Parade	— parare.	Plaice	— plie.
Paramount	— avalange.	Plantain	— llanten.
Parchment	— parchemin.	Plaster	— piastra.
Pare	— parare.	Platoon	— pillotta.
Parish	— parrocchia.	Plea, plead,	— piato.
Parley, parlia-		Please	— plaisir.
ment	— parola.	Pledge	— plevir.
Parlour	— parola.	Plover	— pipa.
Parrot	— parrocchetta.	Plough	— aratro.
Parry	— parare.	Pluck	— piluccare.
Parsley	— petrosellino.	Plunder	— sacco.
Parsnep	— pastinaca.	Plunge	— piombare.
Partisan	— partigiana.	Plush	— peluche.
Partridge	— perdice.	Ply	— piegare.
Pastern	— pastoja.	Pocket	— poche.
Patrol	— pattuglia.	Poise	— peso.
Paunch	— pancia.	Poke	— poche.
Pavilion	— padiglione.	Policy (docu-	
Pawn	— pan.	ment)	— polizza.
Pawn	— pedone.	Poltroon	— poltro.
Pay	— pagare.	Pomander, po-	
Peach	— persica.	matum	— pomo.
Pearl	— perla.	Pompion	— pepone.
Peasant	— paese.	Popinjay	— pappagallo.
Pedestal	— piedestallo.	Poppy	— pavot.
Peel	— poêle.	Porcupine	— porcépic.
Peewit	— upupa.	Porpoise	— marsouin.
Pellet, pelt	— pillotta.	Portcullis	— couler.
Pell-mell	— pêle-mêle.	Postern	— poterne.
Pelice, pilch	— pelliccia.	Posy	— pensée.
Pencil	— pinceau.	Potatoe	— patata.
Penthouse	— ponte.	Poultry	— poule.
Peony	— pivoine.	Pounce	— punzar.
People	— peuple.	Pounce	— ponce.
Perform	— fornire.	Pound	— pan.
Periwig	— piluccare.	Powder	— pondre.
Pester	— pastoja.	Power	— pouvoir.
Petrel	— petto.	Praise	— pregio.
Petronel	— petto.	Pray	— pregare.
Petty	— pito.	Preach	— prêcher.
Pew	— poggio.	Prentice	— apprendre.
Pewter	— peltro.	Press (- money,	
Pick	— becco.	-gang)	— presto.
Pierce	— pertugiare.	Priest	— prete.
Pilgrim	— pellegrino.	Prim, prime	— primo.
Pill, pillage	— pigliare.	Print	— imprenta.
Pillory	— pilori.	Profile	— profilare.
Pin	— spillo.	Provender	— prebenda.
Pinch	— pizza.	Provost	— prevosto.
Pinnace	— pinaccia.	Prow	— prua.
Pinnacle	— penna.	Prowess	— pro.

Prowl	— prole.		Ransom	— rançon.
Proxy (procura-			Rape	— rappare.
cy)	— procurare.		Rappee	— raspare.
Prude	— pro.		Rascal	— raca.
Pucker	— pocbe.		Rase, raze	— rasare.
Pudding	— bonder.		Rasb	— rascar.
Puddle	— pattnglia.		Rattle	— râler.
Puisne	— pnis - né.		Rave, ravel	— rêve.
Pule	— piauler.		Ray	— raggio.
Pull, pulley	— poulior.		Raze	— rasare.
Pummel	— pomo.		Ready	— redo.
Pump	— bomba.		Realm	— reame.
Pumpkin	— popone.		Ream	— risma.
Punch	— punzar.		Rear	— retro.
Puuch	— pulcinella.		Rebuff	— buf.
Puny	— puis - né.		Rebuke	— buqner.
Purchase	— cacciare.		Rebut	— raboter.
Purfle	— profilare.		Recreant	— ricredersi.
Purl	— profilare.		Recruit	— recru.
Purloin	— pourloigner.		Redoubt	— ridotto.
Purse	— borsa.		Reef	— arrecife.
Purslain	— portulaca.		Refrain	— refreindre(refrin
Pursue	— poursuivre.		Rein	— redina. [gere).
Purvey	— pourvoir.		Reindeer	— rangifero.
Push	— pulsar.		Release	— lasciare.
Putty	— potée (pot).		Rellsb	— leccare.
			Remember	— membrare.
			Rennet	— reinette.
Q.			Rent	— rendere.
Quail	— quaglia.		Repair	— repairor.
Quaint	— conto.		Replevin	— plevir.
Quarantine	— quarentaine.		Reply	— plegare.
Quarrel	— querelle.		Reprisal	— ripresaglia.
Quarrel	— quadro.		Reproach	— reprocher.
Quarry	— quadro.		Reprove	— provare.
Quay	— cayo.		Requite	— cheto.
Queer	— guercio.		Rescuc	— scuotere.
Quibble	— quolibet.		Respite	— répit.
Quince	— cotogna.		Restive	— restio.
Quinsy	— squinanzia.		Restrain	— restreindre(strin-
Quire	— cabier.		Ret	— ronir. [gere).
Quit,quite, quit-			Retail	— stallo.
tanco	— cheto.		Retrieve	— trovare.
Quiver	— couire.		Rhubarb	— rabarbaro.
			Riband, ribbon	— ruban.
R.			Rice	— riso.
			Rickets	— rachitis.
Race	— razza, rasso.		Rifle	— riffa.
Racket	racchetta.		Ring	— aringo.
Rafflo, raff	raffaro.		Rinse	— rincer.
Rail (vb.)	— râler.		Risk	— risicare.
Rally	— rallier.		Rivet	— river.
Rampart	— parare.		Roam	— romeo.
Rampion	— raperonzo.		Roast	— rostire.
Random	— randon.		Rob	— roba.
Rank, rango	— rang.		Rochet	— rucchetto.
Ransack	— sacco.		Rocket	— rocca, rnca.

Roll	— rotolo.	Soar	— sauro.
Ronyon	— rogna.	Search	— cercare.
Rook	— freux.	Season	— stagione.
Rose	— ros, rosa.	Second (sbst.)	— minuto.
Rosemary	— ramarino.	Sedge	— sescha.
Rot	— ronir.	Seo (sbst.)	— siége.
Rote	— rota.	Seisin, seize	— sagire.
Rowel	— rota.	Semolina	— semola.
Ruby	— rubino.	Seneschal	— siniscalco.
Ruff, ruffle	— ruffare.	Sepoy	— cipaye.
Rule	— regola.	Seraglio	— serrare.
Rusk	— ruche.	Sergeant	— sirvonte.
		Sever	— séparer.
		Sexton	— sacristain.
	S.	Shagreen	— chagrin.
		Shallop	— chaloupe.
Sable	— zibellino.	Shallot	— scalogno.
Saffron	— zafferano.	Shammy	— camozza.
Sage	— saggio.	Shank	— zanca.
Sago	— sauge.	Share	— schiera.
Salet	— celata.	Shawl	— chále.
Samite	— sciamito.	Shawm	— chalumeau.
Sap	— séve.	Sheet	— scotta.
Sarcenet	— sargia.	Shell	— scaglia.
Sarsaparilla	— salsapariglia.	Sherbet	— sorbetto.
Sash	— cassa.	Shilling	— scellino.
Saunter	— Sainte Terre.	Ship	— schifo.
Sausage	— salsa.	Shock	— ciocco.
Savage	— salvaggio.	Shop	— échoppe.
Save	— salvo.	Shore	— écore.
Saw	— scier.	Shy	— schivare.
Scaffold	— catafalco.	Sill	— suolo.
Scald	— scaldaja.	Simnel	— semola.
Scale	— scaglia.	Sir	— signore.
Scamp, scamper	— campo.	Sirup	— siroppo.
Scantling	— échantillon.	Skate	— échasse.
Scaramouch	— scaramuccia.	Sketch	— schizzo.
Scarce	— scarso.	Skiff	— schifo.
Scarf	— sciarpa.	Skipper	— schifo.
Scarlet	— scarlatto.	Skirmish	— schermo.
Scion	— scier.	Skirret	— chirivia.
Scimitar	— scimitarra.	Slander	— landra.
Scorn	— scherno.	Slap	— schiaffo.
Scot	— scotto.	Slave	— schiavo.
Scour	— sgurare.	Slight	— schietto.
Scourge	— scuriada.	Sling	— slinga.
Scout	— ascoltare.	Sloop	— chaloupe.
Scrap	— sciarpa.	Sluice	— esclusa.
Scrape	— scaraffare, escra-	Slut	— salavo.
Scratch	— grattare. [per.	Smelt	— smalto.
Screen	— écran.	Sniff	— niffa.
Screw	— écrou.	Snipe	— sgueppa.
Scrip	— sciarpa.	Snuffle	— niffa.
Scullery	— écuelle.	Soar	— sauro.
Scullion	— écuelle.	Noll	— sonil.
Scum	— schiuma.	Sojourn	— giorno.
Scurf, scurvy	— scorbuto.	Solace	— sollazzo.
Scuttle	— écoutille.		

Solder	— soldo.		Stuff	— stoffa.
Soldier	— soldo.		Sturgeon	— storione.
Sole	— suolo.		Suck	— suco.
Soot	— suie.		Sudden	— sondain.
Sorrel	— sur.		Suet	— sevo.
Sot	— zote.		Sugar	— zucchero.
Sound	— sonda.		Suit	— suite.
Sour	— sur.		Sully	— souil.
Souse	— salsa.		Summerset	— sobresault.
Span	— spanna.		Summon	— semondre.
Spare	— sparagnare.		Sumpter	— salma.
Sparrow	— csprohon, spara-		Surfeit	— surfait.
	[riore.		Surge	— sourdre.
Sparrow-grass,			Surgeon	— surgia.
sperage	— asparago, as-		Surplice	— pelliccia.
	perge.			
Spavin	— spavenio.		**T.**	
Spell	— épeler.			
Spice	— spezie.		Tabour, tabret	— tamburo.
Spill	— spillo.		Tack, take	— tacco.
Spinach	— spinace.		Tailor	— taglia.
Spite	— dépit.		Tallage, tally	— taglia.
Sprout	— brote.		Tambour, tam-	
Spur	— sperone.		bourine	— tamburo.
Spy	— spiare.		Tammy	— tamigio.
Squad, squadron	— quadro.		Tampion	— tape.
Square	— quadro.		Tank	— stancare.
Squire	— scudo.		Tansy	— tanaceto.
Squirrel	— scojattolo.		Tap	— tape.
Stallion	— stallo.		Target &c.	— targa.
Stanch	— stancare.		Tarnish	— ternir.
Standard	— stendardo.		Tart	— torta.
Stannary	— stagno.		Task	— tâche.
Staple	— étape.		Tassel	— tassello.
Starboard	— stribord.		Taste	— tastare.
Starling	— starna.		Taunt	— toncer.
Starve	— negare.		Tawny	— tan.
Stencil	— étincelle.		Tea	— tè.
Stew	— stufa.		Tear	— tirer.
Stickle	— charpie.		Touch	— tauche.
Stint	— stentare.		Tent	— tenda.
Stirrup	— estribo.		Tester	— tosta.
Stop	— toppo.		Tetter	— dartre.
Store	— estorer.		Thick	— tecchire.
Stoup	— stovigli.		Thrall	— drille.
Stout	— estout.		Throssel, thrush	— tréle.
Stove	— stufa.		Thunder	— tonnerre.
Stover	— estovoir.		Tick	-- taie, zecca.
Strait	— estrac, étroit.		Tier	— tière.
Strange	— stranio.		Tile	-- tegola.
Strap	— strappolo.		Timbrel	— atabalio.
Stray	— estrayer.		Tin	— stagno.
Street	— strada.		Tinsel	— étincelle.
Stretch	— straccare.		Tinder	— tondre.
Strive	— estribo.		Tobacco	— tabacco.
Strop	- stroppolo.		Toilette	toile, tela.
Stubble	- stoppia.		Tompion	— tape.

Top	— toppo.
Tortoise	— tartaruga.
Touracy, tourna- ment	— torno.
Tow (vb.)	— toner.
Tow (sbst.)	— stoppa.
Towel	— tovaglia.
Town	— duna.
Track	— trac.
Trail	— traille.
Traitor	— tradirc.
Trammel	— tramaglio.
Trance	— transito.
Travail, travel	— travaglio.
Trawl	— tröler.
Treachery	— tradire.
Treacle	— theriaca.
Treason	— tradire.
Treasure	— trésor.
Treat, treaty	— trattare.
Trefoil	- - trifoglio.
Trellis	— trcillo.
Trouch	-- treucar.
Tress	— treccia.
Trestle	- - trétcau.
Tribulation	— trebbia.
Trick	— treccare.
Troll	— tröler.
Troop	— tropa.
Trough	— truogo.
Truce	— tregua.
Truck	— trocar.
Truss	— torciare.
Try	— trier.
Tuck	— stocco.
Tuff, tuft	— touffe, toppo.
Tulip	— tulipano.
Tumble, tumbrel	— tombolare.
Tun	— tona.
Tunn	— tona.
Turban	— tulipano.
Turn	— torno.
Turtle	— tartaruga.
Turtle (-dove)	— tourterelle.

U.

Umber, umbrage	— ombre, ombrage.
Umpire	— non pair.
Uncle	— oncle.
Urchin	— riccio.
Usher	— uscio.

V.

Valance	— avalange.
Van	— anzi.

Van	—vanno.
Vantage	— anzi.
Varnish	— vernice.
Vault	— volta.
Vaunt	— vantare.
Veal	— veau.
Vellum	— vcau.
Velvet	— velours.
Venison	— venaison.
Vouture	— avventura.
Verdigris	— vert - de - gris.
Vial	— phiole.
Village, villain	— villa.
Vinegar	— vinaigre.
Viol, violin	— viola.
Viper	— givre.
Visor	— visière.
Void	— vide.
Volley	— volée.
Vouch, vow	— vocu.

W.

Wad	— ovata.
Wado	— guado.
Wafer	— gaufre.
Wage, wager	— gaggio.
Waif	— gaif.
Wait	— guatare.
Walk	— gualcare.
Walnut	— gauge.
War	— guerra.
Ward, ware	— guardare.
Warn	— guarnire.
Warrant	— guarento.
Warren	— garenno.
Wasp	— guêpe.
Waste	— guastare.
Wastel	— gâteau.
Watch	— guatare.
Wave	— vague.
Waymenting (Chauc.)	— gaimenter.
Weak	— gaucho.
Welcome	— wilecome.
Welsh	— gauge.
Wend	— gandir.
Werewolf	— loup - garou.
Wicket	— guichot.
Wide, widow	— vide.
Wile	— guile.
Wimble	— vilebrequin.
Wimple	— guimple.
Wind, windlass	— ghindare.
Window	— ventana.
Wizard	— guiscart.
Woad	— guado.

Woo	— guai.	Yelp	— glapir.
Woodcock	— vitecoq.	Yew	— iva.
Wren	— guaragno.	Yule	— giulivo.
Writhe	— rider.		
Wrong	— torto.		

Y.

		Zany	— sanni.
		Zeal	— zelo.
Yelk	— moyeu.	Zero	— cifra.
Yellow	— giallo.		

Z.

www.ingramcontent.com/pod-product-compliance
Lightning Source LLC
Chambersburg PA
CBHW032020110726
47901CB00004B/1142